VOLUME II.

CONTAINING THE FOLLOWING COMPLETE STORIES:

Aldobrand, the Bandit Baron of Rheinstein.
The Legend of Godesburg.
The Spectre Knight ; or, the Brothers of Heimburg.
The Moat Tower ; or, the Witch of the Rhine.
The Black Sentinel ; or, the Shepherd Lord of the Castle.
The Spectre Hand of Ehrolstein.
The Prince's Envoy ; or, the Siege of Ehrenbreitstein.
Rheineck ; or, Rudolf the Red Heart.
Rudesheim ; or, the Legend of the Red Butt.
The Sapphire Ring : a Legend of Speilberg.
The Tyrant Duke ; or, the Pearl of the Danube.
Heben : The Legend of the Nun's Tower.
The Legend of the Drachenfels.
The Mystic Veil.
Hugo Androski ; or, the Secret of the Holy Cave.
The Fate of Count Voslau : a Legend of the 10th Century.
The Captive Prince : a Story of Durrenstein.
Clara the Beautiful ; or, the Fate of the Felicians.
The Mining Student : a Legend of Schemnitz.
The Damsels of Werfenstein ; or, the Fiend of the Whirlpool.

"BOYS OF ENGLAND" OFFICE,

173. FLEET STREET.

"HOLD, FATHER! OR YOU WILL LOSE FOR EVER THE PROOF YOU SEEK."

THE BARONS OF OLD
OR THE ROBBERS OF THE RHINE

[No. 1.]

MORDREDA,
THE
WHITE WOLF.

A Legend of the Tower of Bayen.

A T the upper end of Cologne rises the Gothic tower of Bayen, a stately, picturesque structure, dating from the 14th century.

From its position projecting into the river, it serves to stave off the ice shocks from the city below in winter.

Like most of the castellated edifices that crown the banks of the Rhine, this tower is said to owe its existence to the

"'DO NOT DESPISE ME, MOTHER,' CRIED THE GOBLIN SPRITE."

incidents detailed in the following legend :—

Many years back there lived on the borders of a forest in Bavaria, an old wizard, named Hela.

His precise age no one knew, but as the oldest of the inhabitants of the district in which he dwelt had known him from their youth, and as their dead and gone ancestors had spoken of him as an equally familiar object in the days of their boyhood, and as in all that time he had not altered in the least, or grown a whit more feeble, though his hair and beard were long, and white as snow, it was supposed he had existed for centuries, and that he had discovered the art of prolonging life to an indefinite period.

He lived in a solitary hut at the extreme verge of the forest, where he performed his dark arts, and worked his spells unmolested.

The old man had an only child—a daughter—Mordreda, a maiden of surpassing loveliness, and as wicked as she was beautiful.

But, with all her charms, no one had ever asked her hand in marriage.

There was a fiendish expression in her dark gleaming eyes that chilled as well as fascinated ; and the youths she encountered, though they could not help admiring, feared rather than loved her.

There was, besides, the same mystery attached to her as to her father.

Year after year fled by, and she never seemed to have grown older, but to be as young and fresh as though time had lost its power to touch her.

But if her father owed his continued health and strength to the dark arts he had studied, his daughter had preserved her youth and beauty by means as horrible as they were revolting.

Proud of her unparalleled loveliness, she had searched in her sire's books of magic, and there she read that the flesh of young children, eaten raw, was an infallible preservative of youth. To this horrible expedient she resorted, and with perfect success, although she often experienced great difficulty in the accomplishment of her terrible schemes.

She would prowl stealthily about the cottages of the peasants until a child appeared, and then lure the unsuspecting innocent away with caresses and kind words until she reached some lonely spot, where, having first strangled her victim, she made her loathsome repast upon its body, burying the remains for a future meal.

This went on for years, and still her guilt was undiscovered, and still she continued fair and blooming as a summer flower.

The number of children thus mysteriously destroyed spread a complete panic far and wide, for she often had to travel long distances to secure her prey.

But no one thought of suspecting the beautiful Mordreda of such unnatural practices ; while she herself, from indulging in cannibalism as a necessity, became at last addicted to it from choice.

Her appetite became so thoroughly depraved that she cared for no other food.

It was whilst she was away on one of her predatory rambles she encountered the powerful Baron Grimbold. The knight was returning from the chase, and at the first sight of the beautiful Mordreda, his heart was hopelessly ensnared.

He was a rough stern border bandit—though a baron, who knew not only how to hold his own, but also how to appropriate the property of others who were not strong enough to oppose him.

But before Mordreda his rough spirit yielded.

" Save thee, fair maiden !" he exclaimed as his eyes lighted on her, "whither goest thou, if I may be so bold ?"

" I have lost my way, sir knight," returned Mordreda, with a modest affectation of timidity, "but I would fain return home."

" 'Tis well I have met thee, then," continued Grimbold, " for the day is waning, and thou look'st fatigued with thy wandering. If, therefore, thou wilt deign to accept the shelter of my castle's roof to-night, to-morrow I will conduct thee safely to thy journey's end."

Mordreda, who was as ambitious as cruel, and who probably foresaw how this would end, placed herself gratefully under the protection of the stalwart baron, who, setting her before him on his steed, carried her away as joyously as he would have done the most priceless treasure.

A costly banquet was served when they reached the castle, and Grimbold grew more and more in love the longer he gazed upon her flashing eyes and raven locks. He pledged her in the wine cup, and swore by his sword that she was the fairest angel the earth had ever known. Mordreda smiled upon her enamoured host, and as they parted for the night she said, with a sweet blush :—

"You will be sure to take me home to-morrow ?"

The baron promised faithfully that he would, according to his word, but that promise, like many others he had made, was never kept, nor did the morrow that saw Mordreda depart from the castle ever come until she rode forth as the wife of its owner. Thus far her ambition was satisfied. She was now a baroness. Her table groaned under the choicest viands, the richest wine flowed in her cups.

But all the dainties could not banish from her recollection the food to which she had so long been accustomed.

Her cravings for human flesh were terrible, and besides she feared for the loss of her beauty, should she neglect the means of perpetuating it.

She therefore commenced her old practices.

Two of the children of the baron's chief huntsman disappeared suddenly at different times, and several others in the neighbourhood. Still without the slightest suspicion attaching itself to the destroyer of the innocents. At length time drew on when the baroness herself was to become a mother.

A lovely boy was born, heir to the title and estates of the staunch Grimbold, who adored his wife after his own rough fashion, and gave a sumptuous banquet in honour of the happy event.

And was the fair Mordreda—the young mother—equally rejoiced at the innocent treasure Heaven had given her? Not a whit.

Horrible to state, instead of the love a parent should have felt as she gazed upon her firstborn, the only sentiment it kindled in her breast was the revolting unnatural desire to destroy it that she might gorge herself with its tender flesh.

Little did the baron dream as he stood by the cradle of the infant smiling down upon its sleeping form from his bronzed bearded face the fate its unnatural mother had decreed it.

What human means could not avert, Heaven in its just indignation accomplished.

It was night. The castle was hushed in silence, when Mordreda rose from her bed, leaving her husband buried in profound repose, and with noiseless step proceeded to the chamber were the nurse, who had charge of the infant, slept. She had taken care previously to administer to the woman a powerful narcotic, and she slumbered soundly.

Gliding in like some wandering ghost, with pale, stern, rigid features, and eyes that dashed with lurid ravenous light, she placed the lamp on the floor and hastily took the babe from the arms of its lethargic guardian.

Then, seizing the light again, she hurried away to a distant lonely part of the castle, and prepared to execute the horrible task.

"I must preserve my beauty," she muttered, hoarsely, "though I sacrifice my own child !"

She was about to unwrap the embroidered cloak in which the infant was covered when a deep stern, but withal melodious voice exclaimed—

"Hold, wretch! What wouldst thou do ?"

She paused and turned in the direction of the sound, and beheld, standing at a short distance, enveloped in a clear, soft luminous mist that rendered him perfectly distinct, a venerable form, robed in white and with a crown upon his head, whose face and aspect wore an expression of the deepest benignity, mingled with pity and indignation.

"Who art thou that inquirest into my actions ?" she said with insolent boldness.

"I am Odin !" was the stern reply, "and I demand again, what art thou about to do?"

"That concerns not thee !" she answered

"Impious, daring infidel !" returned the deity, severely, "thou wouldst shed innocent blood, thou wouldst strangle thy sleeping child that thou mayest feed upon its flesh."

"Is it not my own, part of myself ?" was the audacious rejoinder.

An angry light gleamed from the wild eyes of Odin as he exclaimed, vehemently, "Yes! What thou holdest there close to thy treacherous bosom is thine own, part of thyself! See what it is !"

Mordreda, struck by the emphasis with which these words were pronounced, uncovered the sleeping infant.

But instantly she uttered a cry of dismay ; instead of the lovely features of her child, she gazed upon the hideous lineaments of a grinning goblin.

"This is not my child !" she screamed ; "it is a vile changeling."

"It is the only child thou shalt ever have," returned the deity ; "a fiend thyself, what shouldst thou give birth to but a fiend?"

At these words the goblin imp she carried uttered a hoarse sarcastic laugh, and, turning his eyes with an expression of derisive mockery upon Mordreda croaked out—

"You can't strangle me, I'm too tough; and you couldn't eat me, I'm too hot. I should scorch you to a cinder. Ho! ho!"

With a terrified shudder the scared baroness threw the monster from her, who fell with a slap on the bare floor with the utmost complacency, and then went through a series of goblin evolutions, either to stretch his limbs or warm himself, or for the amusement of his noble parent.

Mordreda, in the meantime, looked on with a kind of stony and bewildered horror.

"Is this to be my punishment?" she asked at length, "to have this gibbering ape ever at my side?"

The goblin sprite at these words, who was spinning like a teetotum on the point of his peaked forefinger, with his heels in the air, turned a brisk somersault, and came down at Mordreda's feet.

"Don't despise me, mother," he said, looking up in her face with a roguish look in his cunning eyes, "I'm not very handsome, but it's better to have a son like me than none at all!"

She would have turned away, but the imp caught her by her dress, and restrained her.

A humorous but diabolical grin overspread his features as he added—

"You'll find me a good friend after all; and if you treat me well, we shall go on very well together. We shall soon understand one another!"

The little demon chuckled immensely at this, and even Mordreda felt that between this spirit of evil and herself there was one bond of union at least—the bond of sympathy.

His presence oppressed her less than that of the venerable white-haired being who stood quietly gazing on her with his mild but now stern eyes.

Mordreda writhed under their fixed reproof, and she cried at length, passionately—

"I know my punishment, leave me! your presence tortures me!"

"No," replied Odin, "you only know a part!"

Mordreda flashed her black eyes with fearful apprehension upon the benignant speaker, who continued—

"Your punishment is to become the beast you most resemble!"

As he spoke the deity touched her with his sceptre.

In an instant wild barking howls announced that the transformation was completed.

A large white she wolf and cub stood in the places lately occupied by Mordreda and her goblin son.

"Remain thus," said the venerable figure, "to shun the day and bay the moon at night—to be a curse and terror to humanity, with all the power of resembling what you have been and what you are for ever."

With these words the deity vanished; the lamp had become extinguished, and as the moonlight streamed in at the window, Mordreda stood in the centre of the chamber, gnashing her fierce, wolfish fangs with her impish cub gambolling around her.

She uttered one long wild wail of despair, which in her present character was a prolonged terrible howl, and then her instinct prompted her to seek to leave the castle that could no longer be a home to her.

With the skulking, cautious step of the animal into which she was changed she left the apartment followed by her offspring.

But too late; the baron had awoke and missed his wife from his side.

Presently he heard the wolf's howl, and springing from the bed, and seizing his sword, hurried from his bedchamber.

The sturdy hunter knew the sound well, and he hastened forward along the stone passages, shouting—

"Mordreda, where art thou?"

Suddenly a white wolf came bounding along right before him.

There was no retreat, and the brave Grimbold stood on his defence.

"By Odin," he cried, "thou gaunt intruder, thou hast rushed into the jaws of the enemy."

He made a blow at the brute, but in the dim, uncertain moonlight that flickered through the loopholes over his head, he missed his mark.

In an instant the desperate animal had sprung upon him, and fastened her fangs in his throat.

There was a brief but fierce struggle, a gurgling sound was heard, and the baron, lay a corpse upon the stone floor.

In the meantime the domestics, aroused by the shouts of their master and the howling of the wolf, had hurried from their beds, only, alas! in time to see Mordreda, the white wolf, glaring at them, opening her bloodstained jaws threateningly, with her cub yelping at her side as she stood over the dead body of her husband.

But they knew her not, and with loud cries of terror and dismay they fled away, leaving the road open for the mother and son to quit the castle, and fly for safety to the covert of the forest.

 * * * * *

Since the moment she left him, the old wizard Hela had heard no tidings of his daughter, but the power he possessed informed him that she still lived.

One cold winter's night, when the snow was on the ground, as he sat over his fire he heard a scratching as if from the paws of an animal at his door.

He started from his seat with an exclamation, and at once threw it open.

There upon the threshold without stood a gaunt, famished white wolf, with her cub by her side.

The animal, instead of springing upon the old man, crept in and crouched at his feet.

After a pause of wonder, Hela murmured—

"Yes, yes; it is—it is my child!" And then he cried, suddenly, "Mordreda!"

The animal thus addressed uttered a low whine, and licked his feet and hands.

This act confirmed the wizard in his opinion, and he remained for some moments gazing silently at his transformed daughter, whose bones, from famine, nearly pierced her skin.

"Some enchanter has transformed her to this shape!" he exclaimed at length; "but if I have any art or skill, she shall be restored to her own!"

The wizard at once, by a powerful incantation, conjured to his assistance a fiend from the iceclad regions of St. Gotthardt.

The demon appeared glistening with frost, his eyes sparkling like rubies.

"I have flown hither on the wings of the northern blast in answer to thy summons," he said, "What wouldst thou?"

"I would have thy aid, great Morok!"

answered the wizard, pointing to the white wolf that lay with her tongue out, panting and prostrate upon the floor, "this is my child, reduced by some potent spell to her present state; canst thou help her?"

The fiend replied—

"The hand that worked this change upon your daughter is the hand of Odin, who is more powerful than I am. I can thwart, but not overrule his decree."

"Canst thou not restore her to her former shape and beauty?"

"I can, but not entirely, and then only upon certain conditions," answered Morok.

"She cannot answer thee," returned Hela, "but in her name I accept them whatever they may be. What are they?"

"First, your child must at the end of every month become a wolf for the space of twelve hours, during which time she must sacrifice a child to me. If she fail in this, or if in her transformed state she fall beneath the hand of man, I claim her body and soul. If, on the contrary, she pays the tribute I demand, and passes the allotted term scathless, she will be herself again till another month transpires, when for a like season she will be as she is now, a wolf. But though these transitions continue for centuries, so long as she fulfils the terms of my contract, her youth and beauty will remain in all their perfection. Are you content?"

At these words the wolf sprang up, and crouched gratefully at the fiend's feet, and the cub rolling over playfully, attracted the wizard's attention for the first time.

"But what is this?" he inquired, doubtfully, before answering Morok's question.

"No matter," the latter answered; "but since you wish to know, that wolf's cub stands in the place of your daughter's child; at the same time he is one of us. Now do you consent to my terms?"

"I do!" exclaimed Hela.

The white wolf gave a howl of joy, and Morok, placing his icy hands upon the heads of both animals, cried—

"By the withering powers of hell,
Thus I crush this potent spell!
Prove I do not boast in vain,
Take your former shapes again!"

That instant the charm was dissolved, and Mordreda started to her feet in all her former youth and loveliness, as did also her goblin son in all his impish ugliness and deformity.

"Do not forget the compact!" said

Morok, solemnly, as he floated upwards on the cold night blast.

The Baroness Grimbold thus restored to her former shape, returned home, to the surprise of the domestics, who thought her dead.

Then she heard the news—no news to her—that her husband had been slain by a wolf.

Mordreda still resided at the castle, but always became absent as the end of each month came round.

At the same time also there was always a child missing in the neighbourhood, till from the traces of the ferocious animal, that were perceptible when the snow was on the ground, the warning of the scared villagers became a terrible proverb—

"BEWARE OF THE WHITE WOLF!"

    ◈   ◈   ◈   ◈   ◈

An atmosphere of gloom seemed to hang over the old castle as though a curse rested on it.

Without assigning any reason the domestics left one by one, till at last the baroness found herself alone in the deserted building.

Gradually it fell to decay.

Still its mistress in her young, bright beauty remained unchanged.

At length, however, one day, she also disappeared, and the silence of death reigned within its crumbling walls.

    ◈   ◈   ◈   ◈   ◈

On the banks of one of the many tributary streams that pour their contents into the Rhine, and almost at its conflux with that river, stood the castle of Oswald, Count of Brisac.

The count, a handsome, generous-hearted man, had lost his wife a few years after his marriage, but not until she had borne him four sons, whom she left behind as pledges of her affection.

The bereaved husband, who doted on his children, devoted himself assiduously to their bringing up, and spared no labour in instructing them as they grew in such knowledge as in those early times he was able to impart, and they were capable of receiving.

Of these Conrad was the eldest, Franz the second, Leopold the third, and Wilhelm the younger.

The count watched his children with delight, as they grew up into handsome, sturdy boys.

About four years after the death of his lady there suddenly came a report that his territories were infested by an enormous white she wolf and cub.

Many children had been carried off by these prowling monsters whose depredations filled the peasants in the neighbourhood with consternation and dismay.

The animals had been seen by many, so it was affirmed, but no one had dared attack the savage brutes, whose ravages continued unchecked.

The count, on hearing this, summoned Casper, his chief huntsman, and inquired of him the facts of the case.

"It is true, my lord," replied Caspar, "I have seen the animal myself, and never did I behold one more formidable in appearance."

"Were you within reach of the monster?" asked the count.

"I was," returned the huntsman, "I came suddenly upon the dam and cub in an avenue in the forest. I had not my crossbow with me at the time, but I cast my spear at her, and could have sworn I pierced her side, for, as your highness knows, I do not often miss my mark."

"True, good Caspar," interposed his lord, "but what led you to think you had struck the wolf?"

"From the fact that I could not find my spear again, and from a trail of blood which followed the retreating footsteps of the animal."

"Then you did put it to flight?"

"Yes, my lord, and followed in chase, feeling confident that I should overtake it, and perhaps—though I might have had a sharp struggle with the brute—finish it with my hunting knife. Just, however, as I fancied myself close upon it, it went crashing through the thicket with a hideous howl, and I saw it no more."

"Strange!" ejaculated the count after a thoughtful pause.

"It was, my lord, very strange!" admitted the huntsman, "but," he lowered his voice, "if I may speak my thoughts—"

"Undoubtedly, Caspar."

"Then, your highness, I believe this terrible animal to be no wolf at all, but a fiend!"

In those dark times superstition was rife amongst all classes, and the good Count Oswald, though not very credulous, was not entirely exempt from its influence.

"It may be as you say, Caspar," he said in an impressed tone; "let us consult the good Father Anselm, and hear his opinion."

The father was a venerable monk, who lived in the count's household as his chaplain and minister.

A pious, kind-hearted man, who loved his lord and his family.

"Truly," replied Anselm, who had frequently heard of the ravages of the terrible white wolf, "it is well-known that the spirits of evil have power to assume strange shapes and forms, and that they are permitted, for some reason which we cannot fathom, to roam about on the earth to the great terror and dismay of the sons of men. It may be that this fierce animal is such."

"And yet on the other hand," suggested the count, "a white wolf is not an impossibility in nature, for I myself once killed one with my own hand."

"I have also," said the huntsman, "but they are rare in Germany."

"At least," answered Father Anselm, "let us pray that, whether animal or fiend, we may be speedily delivered from so great a scourge, which has already rendered so many homes childless."

"It is very terrible, indeed!" exclaimed the kind-hearted noble, "but we must use every possible means to hunt down the monster. I will lead the chase myself."

The count's sons who were present at the above conversation were filled with indignation against the prowling brute that stole away and devoured little children.

Their young blood was fired within them, and they unanimously volunteered to accompany their father in the hunting expedition.

The count smiled and patted their curly heads.

"You are brave boys," he said, "but you are yet too young for such a fierce encounter."

"Oh, but I should like to fight with this cruel beast!" exclaimed Conrad, the eldest, a lad of ten years old.

"So should I, dearly!" added his brothers Franz and Leopold.

"I'd kill the wicked wolf and cut off his head," lisped pretty little fair haired Wilhelm, the youngest.

"Well, well, we must see what can be done," said their father. "You had better, Caspar, summon the stoutest hearted of my dependants, and we will scour the forest in search of this terrible pest."

Caspar eagerly undertook this commission, and a time was fixed for the grand hunt.

It was arranged to take place on the first day of the month of December.

The weather was intensely cold, and the ground glittered with frozen snow, whilst the rivers and streams were solid as ice could make them.

It was on the last night of November, the count's sons happened to be in the courtyard of the castle.

They had been amusing themselves in the clear moonlight with making an enormous white wolf of snow, which, having fashioned to their satisfaction, they attacked vehemently, and showered their blows upon the effigy as heartily as though it had been the original.

"There! there!" cried Wilhelm, triumphantly, as he delivered a blow from the stick his small hands grasped, "I've knocked off his head! I said I should!"

His brothers laughed and cheered lustily, as that portion of the snow animal yielded to the child's prowess, and fell with a dull crunch from the body on to the ground.

But before another blow could be struck a sound reached their ears from without the castle wall that made them pause.

It was a prolonged howl.

"Did you hear that?" asked Conrad.

"Yes! yes!" returned his brother, eagerly.

"It is the howl of a wolf, I am certain," said Conrad, his face flushing with excitement.

"Oh! wouldn't it be a great feat if we could kill it?" exclaimed Leopold and Franz.

"There are four of us!" cried brave little Will. I think four strong boys, as we are, ought to be a match for one wolf!"

A desperately rash idea fired the youths.

"We will try and kill this wolf!" said Conrad, determinately; "but Willie, dear, you musn't come out!"

"Oh! but I want to," cried Wilhelm. "I want to cut off his head!"

"Wait a moment," Conrad exclaimed, "whilst I run for some weapons."

The youth hurried to the armoury, and presently returned with three spears, and a light, sharp arrow to amuse his brother.

Having distributed these, he mounted to the turret, and looked forth.

Nothing was visible.

"Do you see the wolf? Is it a white one?" asked his brothers, eagerly.

"There is no wolf at all!" he answered, in a tone of disappointment.

The boys received this intelligence ruefully, and Conrad descended from the turret.

"And so there is nothing to be seen?" said Leopold and Franz, with much chagrin.

"Nothing!" was the dejected reply.

"But it was certainly the howl of a wolf that we heard."

"Yes."

"Perhaps something has startled the beast, and put it to flight."

"Perhaps so."

This was, of course, merely surmise, and was incorrect.

The beast was neither startled, nor had it taken flight, but was close at hand, crouching in the shadow of the wall, with her cub by her side.

A fierce, gaunt, hungry, white she-wolf.

Presently Conrad said—

"Suppose we go forth with our spears, and try and find the brute? If we could kill it, our father would be proud, and we

CONRAD HURLED HIS SPEAR AT THE WOLF.

should be looked upon as brave boys by the whole country."

To this proposition the brothers eagerly assented.

It did not strike them to ask their father's permission.

In their eager love of enterprise all they thought of was the triumph of slaying the wolf. The idea that the wolf might kill them never entered their minds.

It was arranged that the three elder ones should reconnoitre in the immediate vicinity of the castle, and that if they found no traces of the animal, they were to return for their young brother, Wilhelm.

They accordingly unfastened the wicket

door in the massive gate, and stepped forth.

They proceeded cautiously, grasping their spears, but still saw nothing of the animal they sought.

"The beast has certainly taken flight," remarked Conrad.

At this moment a shrill scream from Wilhelm filled them with horror.

"It is our brother's voice!" they cried.

It was too true.

The little fellow, unable to restrain his curiosity, had stolen from the gate, and been instantly seized by the prowling monster.

The next moment, the white wolf

dashed past them, dragging along in her hungry, foaming jaws the body of their unhappy brother, at whose hands, distended in an agony of fear, the cub snapped greedily, as it ran by the side of its fierce mother.

For an instant the boys remained rooted to the spot, appalled at this fearful catastrophe.

Suddenly Conrad started from his terrified stupor, and cried—

"Let us follow at once! If we remain to call for help, the wolf will be beyond pursuit! We must pursue the brute ourselves, and rescue our poor brother!"

With a cry of enthusiasm the brave trio started off.

The wolf, encumbered by the weight of the prey she dragged along, had slackened her pace, and the boys soon came in sight of her.

"There she is!" shouted Conrad. "Quick! we may save our dear Wilhelm yet!"

Redoubling their speed, they rapidly gained upon the retreating animal, which, hearing steps behind, turned with an angry growl at bay.

Conrad hurled his spear, and it struck the wolf in the right shoulder.

THE TOWER OF BAYEN.

On receiving the wound she uttered a sharp cry of pain, and, turning round, fled with precipitation, still, however, dragging the poor victim she had seized with her.

She was soon out of sight ; but, nothing daunted, the courageous lads continued their pursuit, guided by the blood spots that left their traces in the snow.

At length, after journeying some distance, the blood spots suddenly disappeared.

"She has reached her lair!" Conrad exclaimed, "there must be some cavern near at hand."

They looked on all sides carefully, and with intense anxiety, but no cave met their view.

The moonlight faded, and the morning gradually stole over nature's wintry face.

Chilled, wearied, and heartbroken at the loss of their brother; they wept bitter tears, and felt their search was hopeless.

Suddenly a howl of anguish startled them.

It was the howl of a wolf, and at a short distance from where they stood they beheld a narrow opening in the rocks.

"The monster is in there!" they cried simultaneously, "let us enter."

At the same moment the shouts of the huntsman, and the count, their father, who having missed them had come out in search, were heard.

The party came galloping rapidly forward.

"Our brother Wilhelm! our poor brother!" cried the boys, distractedly, "the wolf has seized him!"

"Good Heaven in its mercy spare the child!" murmured the count, as, directed by his sons, he approached the mouth of the den.

A cry was heard within that made him pause. It was not the cry of a child, or the howl of a wounded wolf, but the wail of a woman in evident pain.

Lighting a torch the count and his followers entered, when a most unexpected sight met their gaze.

No wolf or wolf's cub was to be seen, but instead, stretched upon the rocky floor of the cave, lay a lovely female form, insensible from the loss of blood, which flowed from a wound *in the right shoulder*.

Her head was supported by a dwarfish, stunted, wizen-faced, nondescript individual, who sat glaring at the visitors from out his cunning round eyes with the utmost coolness.

All the information this personage condescended to give of himself was that he was the page of the lady he was attending, who had been attacked and wounded by robbers, and whom he had borne to the shelter of the cavern.

"Who is your mistress?" asked the count, as he gazed pityingly at the pale features of the lovely sufferer.

"The Lady Mordreda," replied the page.

But the most appalling sight had yet to come.

For in a corner of the den was discovered the dead body of the hapless Wilhelm, torn and mangled, evidently by the keen fangs of some carnivorous animal.

The agonised father uttered a cry of horror.

"How came this body here?" he cried, wildly.

"It was carried hither by the white wolf," sobbed the brothers.

But the withered up page knew nothing of this.

He had seen no wolf, he affirmed.

A litter was formed, and the count, having bound up the white shoulder of the wounded lady, she was placed upon it and conveyed to the castle, together with the mangled remains of poor little Will.

But the ravenous brute whose cruel fangs had destroyed him had evidently escaped.

❖   ❖   ❖   ❖   ❖

The lady Mordreda remained beneath the hospitable roof of the Count of Brisac until she was healed of her wounds.

It then became palpable to every one that, whilst the count was healing his lovely patient, she was wounding him: in other words, that he was deeply in love with her, little dreaming how much she was implicated in the deplorable fate of his child.

Finding that he could not be happy without her, he resolved to marry her, and stated his intentions to his spiritual adviser, Father Anselm.

To his surprise, and not a little to his indignation, the good old man protested against the match.

"Wed her not, my lord!" he said, earnestly; "I would not willingly harbour unjust suspicions against any living soul, but I mistrust that woman. She hath an evil eye, and surely as thou weddest her harm will follow. Therefore be warned!"

The count was displeased.

Though kindly natured, he was hot tempered, and he exclaimed, irritably,—

"Pshaw! good Anselm, thou art in thy dotage. Whatever be the danger that may accrue from this marriage it will not light on thy shaven crown; therefore be content. Let the evil, whatever it be, fall upon me and mine."

"A terrible responsibility!" murmured the old man.

True to his resolution, the count proposed to the fair Mordreda, and was accepted.

The nuptials were solemnised with great rejoicings, and the count seemed perfectly happy with his second wife.

To the little, old-fashioned, ugly, dwarfish page, however, he could never reconcile himself.

Oolf, as he was called, was almost constantly in attendance on his mistress, until the count became jealous of the intrusive pigmy and suggested his dismissal.

But the countess, proud and confident in her charms, was very self-willed and arbitrary; she would not hear of it, and peremptorily insisted on his remaining.

The count, who loved her, yielded reluctantly, and the nondescript page still waited on his mistress as usual.

It was impossible to conceive anything

more hideously grotesque than this strange being.

Stunted in his youth, with crooked body and shrivelled limbs, and a head inordinately large in proportion to the rest of his person, and almost destitute of hair, save a tuft that stuck upright in the centre of his skull ; with round, red, cunning-looking, piggish eyes ; and a mouth which, when extended in one of his diabolical grins, reached from ear to ear, and disclosed a set of jagged, discoloured fangs ; and, added to this, a complexion yellow and dried up as that of a mummy, he presented, with the stature of a child, the aspect of a shrivelled old man ; whilst in strength and incessant agility he outrivalled the most mischievous monkey that ever existed.

Mischief seemed to be his delight, his native element, and one freak followed another with such rapidity that he contrived to keep everybody about him in a state of perpetual turmoil.

He would yoke three of the count's hounds together, and tying a pine torch to each of their tails, and setting them in a blaze, send them flying madly through the castle chambers yelping with terror and pain as the resinous material attacked their sides and back, to the imminent danger of causing a disastrous conflagration.

Sometimes he would clamber up to the castle top, and whilst the domestics were gathered round the roaring kitchen fire he would come clattering down the spacious chimney into the midst of the burning embers, where he would sit with his usual diabolical grin on his features, picking out dainty bits of glowing charcoal, which he devoured with evident relish. One of his favourite gambols was to post himself at the top of the stairs as the servants were carrying up the various dishes into the dining-hall. As soon as he saw one ascending, he waited until the man was about midway, and then, curling himself up into a ball, he would launch himself from the top, rolling over and over with great velocity, and knocking the luckless domestic's legs from under him, who invariably fell, dish and all, with a prodigious clatter, and, oftener than not to the bottom of the stairs, with very serious injury to himself.

The consequence of these malicious freaks was that everybody hated Oolf, from the count down to the lowest menial in the castle.

The count's sons, who were brave and spirited, as they were good and kindly natured, resisted his mischievous practical jokes, and on more than one or two occasions, if it had been possible for this impish individual's neck to have been dislocated the youths would have accomplished it for him.

But there seemed to be a spell that attached itself to him to keep him from harm.

The servants of the household did not scruple to express their firm belief that Oolf was a fiend in human form, and certainly his appearance, and his infernal habits and malice, fully warranted such a supposition.

The good Father Anselm studiously avoided him, and he avoided Father Anselm.

If ever they chanced to meet, the holy man crossed himself devoutly and murmured a prayer that sent the unholy Oolf flying as if for his life.

The only being who delighted in the goblin page was his mistress Mordreda, and she protected him on all occasions, and even encouraged him in all his wicked and malicious practices.

There was also one remarkable peculiarity in the habits of the countess.

This was that on the last day in every month she would leave the castle for twelve hours, taking her page invariably with her.

No one, not even her husband, knew her motive for so doing ; no one knew whither she went.

But during the period of this absence the white she-wolf was sure to make her dreaded appearance, and some unfortunate child was sure to fall a victim to its fangs.

Conrad, who was now growing up to manhood, was more capable of reflecting, and as he observed the strangeness of his mother-in-law's behaviour, the wild flashings of her eyes, and the incoherent ravings she would give utterance to at certain times ; and added to this, too, the demoniac attendant, whom she seemed to love far more than her husband, his own father, who had no power over her at all, he began to think there was something terribly unholy and unnatural in her.

He had not forgotten his young brother, or the night when he had tracked the white wolf to the cavern, and found there, instead, the senseless form of the beautiful woman whom his father, in his infatuation, had married.

But since the wolf had not left the cave where did it go to?

The youth pondered over these facts deeply.

The wound too he had given the wolf was in the right shoulder.

Mordreda's wound was also in the right shoulder. The more Conrad meditated the more perplexed he became.

He was inclined to believe his mother-in-law was an enchantress, but more than this—although he could not reasonably account for such a mysterious transmigration, he became possessed with a kind of vague suspicion that Mordreda and the white she-wolf were one.

Soon after this an event occurred that in a great measure confirmed his suspicions.

His brother Leopold sickened and died.

On the night after his death Conrad and Franz had retired to rest, and were speaking as they lay in bed of the loved companion they had lost, when suddenly the howl of a wolf resounded, not outside the walls, but in the very corridor of the castle.

A cold chill ran through their veins as the unearthly yell broke the silence of the solemn hour.

"It is the white wolf's howl!" murmured Franz to his brother.

"There are no wolves here," returned Conrad, meaningly.

"I am sure that was the cry of one," persisted his brother.

"So am I," replied Conrad, solemnly, "as sure as I am that the voice that just now sounded in our ears was the voice of Mordreda."

"Our father's wife!" exclaimed Franz, in aghast surprise.

"Yes, our father's wife!" echoed Conrad. "Nay, I dare say more to thee, my brother," he continued: "I believe that it was she who destroyed our dear little Wilhelm."

"Good Heaven! Can it be possible?"

"I fear so—but hark again!"

Once more the melancholy howl reached the ears of the brothers.

Conrad sprang from the bed and kindled the lamp.

"I am resolved to penetrate this horrible mystery, if possible!" he exclaimed.

"I am with you heart and soul, my brother!" cried Franz, following him.

"What do you suspect that sound portends?"

"I hardly know," returned Conrad, with a half-suppressed shudder; "but," he continued, lowering his voice almost to a whisper, "thou knowest the body of our dear Leopold lies in the empty chamber in the eastern wing of the castle?"

"Yes."

"The sound seems to come from thence," Conrad continued, "and if the strange horror I feel now as I speak does not deceive me, I would swear that we shall find in that chamber of death either a white she-wolf or our father's wife!"

"What could she want there, and at this hour?" asked Franz.

"That I dare not answer," returned Conrad, "but I feel certain she is there for no good purpose. Come, let us see, and end the doubts that are more horrible even than certainties."

Taking their swords in their hands they left their room, and proceeded silently along the lonely passages until they reached the eastern wing.

A few seconds brought them, by a sudden turn, within sight of the apartment they sought.

Why did they pause suddenly, and recoil with a nameless horror?

At the door they beheld—not a wolf, but Mordreda on her hands and knees in the attitude of one, gnashing her teeth with hungry eagerness, and howling piteously, as if for entrance.

The door was locked, and she evidently could barely restrain her impatience until it could be opened.

The brothers clutched each other's hands and stood riveted to the spot.

Just then Oolf, the goblin page, advanced with the key of the room, which he had been to fetch.

"It's here! it's here!" he cried, with a fiendish grin on his horribly cadaverous face.

"Quick! quick! open the door, or I shall tear it down!" exclaimed Mordreda, with desperate eagerness, "I am ravenous—starving!"

As soon as the key turned in the lock, and the door swung open on its hinges, the fair cannibal sprang in with all the avidity of the animal whose nature she bore.

Her unsightly attendant followed.

"Shall we go forward?" murmured Franz.

"Yes, and at once," replied Conrad, "ere the sacred clay of our dear brother be polluted by these fiends."

They advanced hastily but noiselessly to the door and looked in.

The demon page had removed the coffin-lid, and Mordreda had laid her hand upon the breast of the unconscious dead, and stood with fierce gloating eyes and closely-set teeth gazing rapturously upon the solemn spectacle.

Then she bent her head down, when Conrad, unable longer to endure his horror, burst into the room, sword in hand, followed closely by Franz.

"WRETCH! fiend!" shouted Conrad: "what horrible act do you contemplate? I demand to know in the name of Heaven!"

At this solemn adjuration Mordreda uttered a wild shriek of terror, whilst Oolf rolled himself up in a ball at her feet and remained trembling, with his teeth chattering like those of an ape.

But the former quickly recovered herself, and, though the bitter light of thwarted appetite gleamed in her eyes she effectually restrained any outburst of passion, as she said, in a tone of assumed surprise, but with dignity—

"I do not understand what you mean, Conrad, by these epithets. You must be mad. What have I done to deserve them?"

"What you have done?" replied the youth, sternly, "Heaven and your own conscience can alone tell; what you were about to do, you and the fiend you serve are the best judges, monster!"

"No more, sirrah!" cried the incensed beauty, darting a fiendish glance of hate towards her reproacher as she spoke. "If, out of love for the departed, I choose to come in the silence of night to gaze upon him in his peaceful slumber, what is it to thee? Begone, and do not intrude upon my meditations!"

Conrad's love and indignation were kindled into a fierce flame by these words.

"I will not begone!" he shouted, the crimson blood flushing up into his spirited, handsome face, "I throw off all allegiance to thee, vile woman, though thou art my father's wife, and I order thee hence!"

"Dost thou dispute my bidding?" cried Mordreda, fiercely, "Oolf, thy sword to drive these insulting villains hence!"

"I defy him and thee!" continued Conrad, hoarse with rage. "Thou art no woman, but an unnatural monster; as for that grinning ape at your feet, let him not attempt to draw upon me. I scorn him as I scorn the powers of hell; and for thyself, if thou darest again to desecrate the lifeless form before us with but a touch of thine accursed fingers, I'll rend thee piecemeal as I would wert thou the white she-wolf thou so closely resemblest!"

As these words poured out in wild excitement from the frenzied lips of the young nobleman, Mordreda uttered a piercing cry and fled precipitately from the chamber.

From that moment neither Conrad nor Franz ever left their brother's remains till they saw them deposited in the ancestral vault.

Conrad detailed these circumstances to Father Anselm, who fully agreed with him in his opinion, and took upon himself the task of pointing out to the count the character of the woman to whom he had allied himself.

But Count Oswald, charmed with the dazzling beauty of his fair bride, would not listen to aught against her.

But Conrad, although Mordreda knew it not, watched her unceasingly.

He had determined to discover the mystery that took her away from home at the end of every month, and some remarks he had heard her make to her favourite page had given him the clue he sought.

He had heard her say to Oolf—

"We shall not have to wander far for our next meal."

"No," Oolf replied, licking his lips; "only to the tomb in the park. Ho, ho! how I long to be there! How delicious it will be to think that I, who have played with him so often, shall at last pick his bones! He! he! he!"

"We have only two nights more to wait," returned Mordreda, gloatingly; "and oh! how I wish they were over. I can scarcely endure the delay."

"You'd like to eat me if you could—wouldn't you?" grinned the frightful little dwarf.

"You, my dear Oolf? No, no! I should never wish that," she replied, affectionately.

"I think you'd find me rather too tough," chuckled the goblin, mirthfully.

This conversation, which evidently pointed at a deed of horror at which Conrad shuddered, he revealed to Franz and Father Anselm, and by the advice of the latter, on the last day of the month the trio presented themselves before the count, when Conrad commenced the recital of his suspicions.

His father grew highly incensed at his son's audacity.

" I will not hear these accusations," he cried.

" But you shall hear me, father !" exclaimed the young man, sternly. " For Heaven's sake, for your own sake, for our sakes, who love you, cast aside this mad infatuation and listen to the truth. Father, you have married a fiend, a ghoul, who satiates her accursed appetite on human flesh ! "

The count uttered a cry of horror, and started from his seat.

Father Anselm strove to calm him, and at length succeeded in inducing him to listen.

At the termination of his son's terrible recital he was much moved.

" Send for the countess," he said ; " give her at least the opportunity of justifying herself."

" The countess has left the castle with the hideous abortion who waits upon her, and will not return for twelve hours," replied Conrad. " You forget, father, this is the last day of the month."

This was always a sore point with the count, who had often demanded an explanation from Mordreda, and been as often insolently refused.

He paused thoughtfully for some moments, and then said, with determination,—

" I will watch to-night. We will go together, and if I find the horrible suspicions you have hinted at true, I swear solemnly, much as I have loved my wife, she shall die by my hand ! "

" So shall the spell be broken and the curse be removed !" exclaimed Father Anselm, solemnly.

❖ ❖ ❖ ❖ ❖

It was a bright moonlight night, and the frozen snow glittered in the rays of the luminary like myriads of diamonds.

It was near midnight when Conrad came to tell his father they were ready to start.

He had watched Mordreda and the page to the sepulchre, and so timed his actions that they might come upon the guilty despoilers in the midst of their unholy work.

The party consisted of the count and his two sons and Father Anselm.

All but the latter were armed with their crossbows, and he, not fighting with carnal weapons, carried with him only a prayerful spirit.

Silently they approached the tomb where reposed the ashes of their ancestors.

In the moonlight it looked like a fair marble edifice, too white and pure to contain corruption.

As they drew near, the soft snow on which they trod causing no sound, they perceived that the iron door of the tomb was open, proving that strange feet were within.

Placing themselves behind a tree they watched. Presently, to their horror, they beheld Mordreda and the page come forth, dragging eagerly the coffin containing the body of Franz.

The count could scarcely forbear shrieking with horror.

" Hold ! hold, father !" entreated Conrad, " or you will lose for ever the proof you seek."

This argument silenced him, and they remained looking on in silence.

Oolf was not idle, but went to work with a large hammer he carried, crashing in the lid of the coffin.

In a short time it was demolished, and then with a hideous howl like that of a wolf, Mordreda and her parasite commenced their filthy and repulsive meal.

With eager voracity they tore the flesh with their teeth from off the bones, until the gazers could endure the sickening sight no longer.

Besides, they had seen enough.

Without a word the Count Oswald and Conrad drew up their crossbows, and placed a bolt in each.

" Are you ready ?" asked the former, under his breath.

" Yes, father !"

" Now, then !"

A sharp twang was heard, and then a wild howl of agony.

" Forward !" cried the count, fiercely.

They hurried to the spot, and found— neither Mordreda nor the page, but the gaunt white she-wolf and her cub, both writhing in the agonies of death.

" Wretch ! accursed fiend ! " cried Oswald of Brisac, " thus ends your vile life, and thus is severed the fatal tie that has bound me to thee."

With a final howl of anguish the animals lay motionless, when, at that moment, old

Hela the wizard staggered forward, and, falling on his knees, embraced his transformed child.

"You shall not die, Mordreda!" he cried. "It is not yet too late. Tell me," he whispered fondly, "do you still live?"

A faint moan was the only answer.

But that seemed to cheer the questioner.

"It is not too late! Morok, Morok!" he shouted, "great fiend! I summon thee: haste hither, I implore thee."

In an instant a rushing, mighty wind rolled across the plain, and in a few seconds the fiend Morok came, borne upon the blast, and stood before them, glittering in his frozen crown and gemmed with icicles.

"Save my child, I entreat you," cried the old wizard, becoming suddenly feeble.

"I cannot! she has broken her compact."

The dying wolf moved as if she would have spoken if she could.

But speech was denied her, and she could only glance towards the coffin expressively.

The fiend comprehended her glance, and said in reply to her—

"True! but that is not a child. Our compact was a child."

"Nevertheless, thou canst spare her, good Morok!" pleaded Hela, trembling as though stricken with ague or the palsy; spare her, if only for a time, that she may be revenged upon her destroyers."

"Yes, I can do that!" answered the fiend, with a grim smile.

"And thou wilt?"

"Yes."

The ice demon waved his crystal sceptre, and then stood in a listening attitude.

Gradually there fell upon the ears of the count and his sons a distant pattering sound of many feet.

"Hark!" exclaimed Morok, looking towards the white wolf. "Your friends are hurrying to your aid. Rouse thee!"

Mordreda struggled to rise, and splashed with her fore paws in the blood that had flowed from her.

But her strength seemed to increase, and she uttered a wild barking cry of exultation as the sounds grew louder.

"What mean they?" asked Conrad of his father.

At this moment a confusion of sounds equally wild was borne upon the night wind.

The count recognised them in a moment.

"It is the cry of wolves," he exclaimed: "we must save ourselves. Quick, to the castle, ere it be too late!"

The party hurried away.

The castle, being near at hand, was soon reached, and the gates closed.

The chief huntsman met them in the courtyard.

"A pack of wolves are sweeping down across the plain," exclaimed the count hastily; "but here we are safe."

As he spoke, loud howls rent the air, so that his voice was scarcely heard.

Caspar hastily ascended to the turret and looked forth, and, having done so, uttered an exclamation of dismay.

"My lord, my lord!" he cried, "we are beset by wolves on every side; their name is legion."

The count and his sons hurried up to the turret, where a strange and startling sight awaited them.

On every side, far as the eye could reach, there appeared nothing but a dense mass of wolves, led on by the white she-wolf and her cub.

They surrounded the walls, and it was evident from the manner in which they arranged themselves in order for their fellows to mount over their bodies, that the bulwarks would soon be scaled.

"Save yourself, my lord!" shouted the huntsman, loudly, "no power could stand against such a host of these brutes. To the castle, quick!"

They hurried to the interior and closed the doors. The entire troop passed over the walls and filled every square inch of the courtyard.

The doors began to crack with the pressure.

"They will be in upon us in a few moments," said the huntsman, ominously, "and then——"

Here a wild howl stopped the speaker.

"Let us ascend to the upper tower," cried the count, "it is our only hope."

They rapidly ascended to the highest point, and as they reached the top, a violent crash and howling announced that the door had given way.

The river ran beneath the turret on which they stood.

"Let us leap for our lives!" cried Conrad, "the wolves may lose the scent, and we may still escape."

"'Tis in vain, the river is frozen, and

we should be dashed to pieces," returned the count.

"No, no," shouted Franz, joyfully, "it moves, it moves, the ice has broken up."

"In answer to my prayers," murmured Father Anselm, "this is a good omen, that Heaven is on our side ; fear not, let us leap into the stream below, and trust to Heaven to deliver us."

As they approached the edge of the turret, the howls of the ascending wolves rang in their ears.

Without a moment's hesitation, they sprang forward, and fell splashing into the waters beneath.

For an instant the icy cold chilled and benumbed them, then they struck out, and in a few seconds they had all clambered up on to the large floating blocks of ice that came sweeping past.

Conrad and Franz were together.

"Courage, my brother!" exclaimed Conrad, hopefully, "we shall yet escape."

"Alas!" returned Franz, "look."

He pointed as he spoke, to the wolves who were leaping down in crowds into the water, and swimming after them.

Foremost in the chase were the white wolf and her cub.

Soon these two savage foes reached the block of ice on which the brothers knelt.

The latter had no weapons, and as they essayed to keep off the intruders with their hands the wolves snapped at them with their teeth.

Then placing their forepaws on the edge of the ice, the fierce animals quickly dragged themselves up, and the pursuers and the pursued were side by side together, whirling and crashing along.

But it was no longer the white wolf and her cub to which they were so near, but Mordreda and Oolf in their original shapes.

Each was armed with a long-bladed dagger.

"Now where is your triumph?" cried the former, her fierce dark eyes flashing fire, "Strike, Oolf!" she exclaimed.

The daggers flashed in the air, when suddenly the form of the god Odin was seen hovering over their heads in a luminous cloud, whilst on a block of ice close at hand appeared the good Anselm on his knees, with the Count of Brisac and Caspar the huntsman.

At the sight of the majestic Odin, Mordreda and Oolf were stricken powerless.

The daggers fell from their hands, and Morok, the ice fiend, appeared at their sides.

"Come," he said, "your time has expired."

Seizing them in his arms he dragged them away shrieking until he faded in the distance.

Then followed a wondrous change.

The wolves vanished—the night passed—and as the bright morning dawned, the blocks of ice were arrested in their passage up the Rhine by a projecting bank.

Here the count and his sons landed, with Caspar and Father Anselm, who blessed the spot, and it was here that the nobleman afterwards built the Tower of Bayen as a token of his gratitude to Heaven, and to commemorate the great deliverance of himself and children from the snares of MORDREDA, THE WHITE WOLF.

END OF MORDREDA, THE WHITE WOLF.

The second complete Story is entitled,

"THE LEGEND OF THE SEVEN VIRGINS."

THE BARONS OF OLD
OR THE ROBBERS OF THE RHINE

[No. 2.]

THE LEGEND
OF THE
ROCKS OF THE SEVEN VIRGINS.

THE traveller journeying up the Rhine from Cologne to Mayence, after sweeping along the rapid current of the Lurleyburg, and perchance listening to its wonderful echoes, passes a group of seven small rocks, known as the "Rocks of the Seven Virgins."

Hardly have they faded in the distance

"HER TREACHEROUS HUSBAND HURLED HER FROM THE BATTLEMENTS."

when he comes upon the picturesque tower of Oberwesel, standing in solitary loveliness on the right bank of the river, amidst the ruins of what was once a town of note, celebrated for its churches, religious institutions, steeples, bells, and richly-decorated altars, of which at the present time few vestiges remain.

But it is not here we must linger, but rather pass on to the spot where stand the time-worn relics of past grandeur with which is connected the history of the "Seven Beautiful Countesses of Schönberg," whose fate forms the subject of the above legend.

Towering above the ruined city of Oberwesel is a large and craggy rock, surmounted with the remains of the noble castle of Schönberg, the domain of an ancient family that sprang from the far distant past, but whose lineal descent may be traced from the days of Charlemagne, the great Emperor of the West.

It is of the former remote period, when almost every mail-clad baron was a robber as well as a warrior, and when "might over right," was the law of existence, we have to speak.

The castle of Schönberg, with its massive towers and noble battlements, stood proudly forth, rearing its head in almost impregnable security.

The shadow of the rock on which it rested darkened the waters of the giant river that washed its base, and whose waters were a barrier on the one side, whilst on the other, steep and precipitous rocks rendered its approach by any insidious foe difficult and dangerous.

In this stronghold dwelt the Count Ottar of Schönberg, a man of powerful frame and strong, unbridled passions.

In his banquet hall the shouts of revelry and the songs of his boon companions, as they assembled after a day spent in the chase, or in some marauding expedition, might have been heard long after midnight, sending their echoes across the bosom of the silent Rhine, and making the quiet hour of repose hideous with their boisterous and ungodly mirth.

But though Count Ottar was, as times went, considered a powerful noble, there were others as powerful and as reckless.

Amongst those was one who looked upon the majestic heights of Schönberg (which in English means "Beautiful Hill") and its fine old castle with a greedy eye.

This one was Leolf, the Baron of the Black Plume, so called from the colour of the feather he wore in his iron helmet.

The chieftain had a castle and territorial possessions, inland, but he looked upon all these with a soured and discontented spirit, and coveted some more imposing habitation, whose walls should look down on the majestic Rhine.

Of all the castles that stood upon the banks of the noble river, none so much appealed to his fancy or so greatly excited his desire for possession, as that of Schönberg.

Accordingly calling together his vassals and serfs, he laid siege to this envied fortress.

This took place at a most inopportune season—just as the Count Ottar was about to celebrate his wedding with the beautiful Rhoda, the orphan daughter of a deceased baron, to whom he had acted as guardian, and whom he was now about to wed in order to secure the prospect of an heir to succeed to his title and domains.

There was little love in the count's nature, and he married as a mere matter of course.

As for the fair orphan herself, she had little choice in the matter.

Immured, as she had been almost from childhood, in the secluded heights of Schönberg, her heart had no opportunity of following her imagination; and if she sometimes sighed as the minstrel sang the triumphs of some brave and handsome knight, her thoughts went no further.

All she ever saw of the opposite sex were her guardian and his mail-clad companions, and of these, he seemed to her to be the least objectionable.

When the marriage was proposed by Count Ottar she offered no objection.

If she did not love him, she loved none other, and she prepared to receive him as her future lord and master.

The wedding day was fixed and great preparations were making for the forthcoming nuptials, when one morning, a few days before the marriage was to take place, the warder of the castle was surprised, as the mist rolled away from the rocky steeps of Schönberg, to see the plain beneath bristling with pikes and spear heads.

The intentions of the assembled multitude were evidently hostile, but all doubt on this point was speedily set at rest by the appearance of a herald who rode forth, and, winding his horn, demanded parley with the Count Ottar.

The count, who had been revelling late on the overnight, and draining deep draughts of Rhenish wine to the health of his future bride, had not left his couch.

But, on being informed of the summons by the warder, he sprang from his bed, and throwing a bear-skin mantle over the shirt of chain mail in which he had slept, and seizing a spear, went, thus accoutred, at once upon the battlements.

The Count Ottar was a sufficiently bold man; but, whether his nerves were unstrung by the previous night's excesses, and he lacked his usual *hardiesse*, or some sudden qualm seized him, his dark cheek paled slightly as he gazed upon the formidable host with which which his rocky domain was beleagured.

He, however, quickly recovered himself in the fresh morning air, and, advancing to the turrets, haughtily demanded the reason of the assembly.

The herald then declared—

"The powerful deity, Odin, having appeared to my liege master, the Baron Leolf of the Black Plume, and promised him the Castle of Schönberg, as a reward for his piety and valour, I am here on his behalf to demand whether you are ready, in accordance with the divine will, to exchange your possessions for his.

"If so, open your gates, and the deed of transfer can be arranged without delay or quarrel. If not, I am empowered by the Baron Leolf to declare that he will never withdraw his troops till he has ransacked your castle from cellar to roof with fire and sword, and planted your head upon its battlements!"

At this daring proposition, Count Ottar was fairly thunderstruck.

But its very audacity roused all the natural courage and chivalry of his disposition, and enabled him to reply.

"Tell your aspiring master," he shouted, "that his statement is a base lie! I, like himself, am a worshipper of Odin, and the great deity teacheth not his children to war against each other. Bid the Baron of the Black Plume content himself with his own possessions, with which I desire not to interfere, and let him not meddle with mine, which descend to me by right of ancestry. The castle in which I dwell I will not part with for any other, but defend to my last breath, therefore let your master depart, lest harm come to him; and whereas he threatens rapine and slaughter on all within its walls, let him beware, lest the fire and sword he so vauntingly decrees us, turn upon himself, and lest his head not mine, transfixed by this spear, shall be held forth as an example to all braggarts who boast of deeds they are unable to accomplish."

The Count Ottar having shaken the spear he held defiantly, was about to retire, when the Baron Leolf, conspicuous by his gigantic stature and the sable effigy in his helmet, rode forward.

"Count Ottar of Schönberg, stay and hear me," he cried in a clear voice that rang out distinctly in the morning air; "is it your intention imperiously to resist the decreed will of Odin?"

"I do not believe it to be his will," returned the count; "it is your own rapacious covetousness and unbridled audacity that suggest the decree, not Odin, and to you I have but one answer, scorn and defiance!"

Having uttered these words in a tone answerable to their purport, he hurled his iron gauntlet towards the baron, and turning contemptuously away, strode from the battlements.

War being now declared, both sides prepared for attack and resistance.

The count, taken as he was unawares, had only the servants and retainers within the walls to assist him in giving battle to the foe.

But they were all true men, and he accordingly armed and placed them in the most advantageous positions, where, protected by the projecting buttresses, they could gall the besiegers with their arrows with impunity.

From the giant copper in the baronia kitchen was supplied a continual stream of boiling water, which, dashed from the battlements upon the foe beneath had a terrible and potent effect.

The day declined, and darkness put an end to the first day's struggle.

At early dawn howeve on the following morning, while the light was yet dim and grey, the attack was recommenced.

Had not the castle stood where it did, on an eminence, it could not long have resisted the overpowering numbers of the besiegers.

But by dint of great energy and untiring watchfulness on the part of Count Ottar, the second day passed, and the enemy was still kept at bay.

That night the thought entered the mind of the count that he would send a message to a neighbouring chieftain, Ulrich of Rhinwold, for men and succour.

His domains lay on the left bank of the Rhine, and a message could easily be sent to him across the river.

But who was to take it?

The number of fighting men in the castle was so small that none could be spared.

In this emergency the beautiful Rhoda volunteered her services, and undertook to cross the Rhine, and convey her future lord's missive to his friend Ulrich.

The swarthy face of the count beamed with admiration at the courage of his fair betrothed, and he accepted her offer without hesitation.

Disguised as a page, her long fair hair gathered up into a knot behind, Rhoda entered a boat and reached the opposite bank in safety.

The next day dawned, but she returned not.

During the night the besiegers had not been idle.

They had cut down quantities of timber, and, dragging the large trunks and branches up the rock, had piled them against the castle walls.

In a short time the crackling of the wood and the smoke announced that these had been set on fire.

The danger now became more and more imminent; the massive masonry grew intensely hot, and began to give signs of crumbling.

But still no signs of Rhoda's return.

In a fever of anxiety, Count Ottar descended by a narrow flight of stone steps that led to the water's edge, and looked out anxiously across the broad bosom of the Rhine.

At length a boat came in sight.

It was Rhoda returning.

She had fulfilled her mission, but, unfortunately, Ulrich of Rhinwold was from home on a border expedition, and had all his followers with him.

Count Ottar received this unwelcome intelligence with a fierce oath, and poor Rhoda, who had performed the service so boldly and faithfully, drooped her head sorrowfully and passed on into the castle.

The loud shouts of the besiegers reached the count's ears, and as night was now drawing on, the red glare of the burning timber that was gradually carbonising the heated walls, fell ominously upon his sight.

Ottar of Schönberg was a reckless, godless man, who, instead of uttering a prayer to Heaven in his extremity, seemed in his desperation rather intent upon claiming the attention of the powers of darkness.

He still lingered after Rhoda's disappearance, at the bottom of the steps, looking moodily at the dark waters that rolled in gloomy silence before him.

At length, as a fresh burst of triumph from the enemy reached him, be broke forth desperately—

"Is there no power above or below that may be invoked to drive this accursed Leolf hence?"

Hardly had this impious inquiry passed his lips when a vivid flash of lightning lit up the broad bosom of the mighty river followed by an awful peal of hoarse thunder.

The count started.

These elemental portents seemed so much like an answer to his question.

Before he had time to recover from the shock, a terrible form rose from the bosom of the dark stream, and slowly glided to the bank.

As he approached, the water upon which he moved glowed with phosphorescent flashes of green and crimson flame.

His appearance was ludicrous in the extreme, being half flesh, half fish.

His body was of a pale, ghastly bluish tint, over which hung a drapery of slimy weeds, revealing, between the folds, the glittering scales with which his amphibious person was covered.

His face was that of a monster with fiery eyes, and a mouth full of shark-like teeth, whilst in place of hands and feet, long webbed claws protruded from the extremities of his limbs.

From his head, on which glittered a twisted wreath of river snakes, descended long, dripping weed-like locks, and he grasped a sceptre at the end of which hung suspended, as though it lived there, some horrible aquatic reptile like a lizard.

This terrible being having reached the bank, fixed his glaring eyes upon the Count Ottar, who, with his hand grasping the hilt of his sword, stood riveted to the spot in the profoundest horror.

The monster was the first to speak.

"Thou hast summoned me, mortal, from my river depths. Thou needest help?"

"Yes!" faltered the count, to whom the word "help" had restored the power of speech, "canst thou assist me?"

"I can, upon certain conditions," was the reply.

"Before making terms with thee, dread being," went on the count, "I must first know to whom I speak."

"I am Rhinblatzz, the Demon of the Rhine!" answered the figure.

"And you can drive away the foes that now swarm around my castle, and extinguish the flames that threaten to consume it?" asked Ottar, eagerly.

"I can," returned the demon, "but I must have something in return."

"What would you have?" the count inquired.

"You are about to wed the Lady Rhoda," said the monster.

"I am."

"Do so. Lead her to the altar—let the marriage rites be pronounced. Attend the wedding banquet, and in due course, conduct your wife to the bridal chamber, but no more! she must be your bride only in name. You will lead her from the window on to yonder terrace."

The demon pointed to a turret that projected far out over the river.

"And then, without a word of warning or farewell, you will snatch her up in your arms, and pure and spotless, as you bore her in her blushing loveliness from the altar, you will hurl her into the dark waters beneath. I shall be waiting to receive her.

The count recoiled with horror.

Reckless as he was, and little as he loved his beautiful ward, he still shrank from so horrible a compact.

"Is there no other way of ensuring my own safety but by sacrificing my bride?" he asked, tremulously.

"None," returned the demon, but I can promise thee that thou shalt rejoin her in death! Come, decide quickly! Do you consent?"

The count hesitated an instant, but just then a louder shout than he had yet heard from his foes, and a flash of more than ordinary brightness, told that the work of destruction was approaching a climax.

This resolved him.

" Yes, yes, I consent, dread being ! " he cried.

" 'Tis enough ! " answered the monster, as, stretching out one of his scaly arms that seemed to extend at pleasure to any length, he encircled the count's body as in the fold of a serpent, and drew him to the brink of the river with resistless force. Then, taking from his scaly belt a parchment and an iron pen, he plunged the sharp point of the latter into the count's wrist.

For an instant, Ottar felt as though every drop of blood in his body had frozen into ice.

But this passed off, and the water demon said, imperatively—

" Sign this ! "

Without pausing even to read the infernal document, the count signed his name in his own blood.

" 'Tis well ! " exclaimed Rhinblatzz. " I am now your slave ; command me ! "

" Disperse my foes, and destroy Leolf of the Black Plume," cried Count Otta.

" Your wish shall be obeyed ! " answered the demon, as with another flash of lightning and a terrible clap of thunder, he disappeared into the river's depths.

Again the enemy's shouts reached the ears of the almost bewildered Ottar, and at the same moment, Karl, the warder, came hurrying down the steps.

" All is lost, my lord," he cried ; " the gates have given way."

A loud, unearthly mocking laugh answered this piece of information, and then a violent crash of thundering weight was heard.

" Follow me ! " shouted the count, as he flew up the step, sword in hand, and hurried towards the gates.

There the cause of the crash was perceptible.

Part of the stone arch had fallen,

Leolf of the Black Plume, who had headed the assault, and his principal retainers, were lying crushed to atoms beneath the ponderous mass.

A violent hurricane of wind had blown the blazing trunks down on to the enemy, causing great destruction.

Then followed a fearful storm of mingled wind and rain, that extinguished the flames, and cooled the heated walls of the castle, whilst it scattered those of the assailants who remained alive in wild terror.

When the morning dawned, not one was to be seen.

" Rheinblatzz has kept his word ! " exclaimed the count, joyfully, and he quaffed a cup of Rhenish to the demon, forgetting the fearful price at which he had secured his protection.

    o   o   o   o   o

And now the wedding day had arrived. The castle was thronged with guests, and all was ready for the ceremony.

The fair Rhoda, in her white bridal attire, looked like some fair statue cut in marble.

There was no joy in her face but neither was there sorrow.

Some few of those who gazed upon her fancied she was not happy—that her young heart owned some other love.

But it was not so.

Hers was only the listlessness of indifference.

On the brow of the count sat a thoughtfulness almost approaching gloom, but he banished it by repeated draughts of wine, and at the altar he smiled lovingly upon his young bride.

A grand banquet followed, and during the repast, no laugh was more joyous than that of Count Ottar of Schönberg.

The feast was ended.

The song and dance followed, and so the evening wore away, until the guests, wearied with their carousals, had sought their chambers, and silence reigned throughout the old castle.

The bell tolled the hour of midnight as the Count Ottar, flushed with wine, remembered the terrible task he had to perform.

" Come, my fair bride," he said, in a

voice which his deep potations, if not remorse, rendered thick and hoarse, "let me lead you to your nuptial couch."

With a slight, and—to the count—an imperceptible shudder, the hapless young bride placed her white hand in that of her husband, and suffered herself to be led away.

The moon was shining brightly as they entered the nuptial chamber.

Again she shivered as the grotesque shadows fell athwart the floor.

But no caress, no word of soothing endearment, came from her husband's lips to cheer her.

He went to the window and looking out, said—

"What a lovely night, Rhoda! Shall we walk forth ere we retire to rest, and watch the moonbeams as they play upon the silver waters?"

"As you will, my lord," was the obedient reply.

Count Ottar opened the window, and together the murderer and his victim stepped out upon the terrace.

Slowly he led the unsuspecting girl to the turret-edge.

Her eye looked upon the silvery Rhine as it lay bathed in the moonlight, and with an involuntary emotion of delight, she exclaimed—

"Oh, how beautiful! How heavenly!"

These were her last words, for her treacherous husband, seizing her suddenly in his arms, hurled her from the battlements.

One wild shriek of terror broke from her lips, as her white dress went fluttering down, and the next moment she was enfolded in the deep waters, with her bridal garment for her shroud.

She did not sink at once, but floated slowly along upon the surface as though the waters were loth to engulf so fair a victim.

The count, with pallid, stern features, and compressed lips, watched her as she glided away, until at length a gigantic arm rose from the depths, and encircling the hapless Rhoda, dragged her down, and she was seen no more.

⁰   ⁰   ⁰   ⁰   ⁰

In these dark times of which we write, a life, however pure and beautiful, was not accounted the precious thing it is at the present day.

There was some suprise expressed at the mysterious disappearence of the beautiful countess, but as no one—*not even her husband*—could give any satisfactory explanation, the event soon died away into oblivion.

All that remained to perpetuate the sad event was a small rock which soon after rose from the bosom of the Rhine at the very spot where its waters closed over the " Virgin Countess."

The count married a second wife, who died within a year of their union, leaving behind her a son and heir.

Ottar little heeded his lady's decease, but devoted himself to the bringing up of his son, who with such an instructor, could at the age of twenty-one, hunt, and drink, and swear with the best—or worst, rather—of his time.

But life, however long, will come to an end, and the time drew near when the Count Ottar must prepare to take leave of every earthly thing.

It was a fearfully stormy night as the old nobleman lay in his bed dying.

His son, Enric, stood by his couch, endeavouring to soothe his father's las moments.

But in vain.

The nearer the fatal time approached, the more vehement was the count's agony of mind.

" Lost, lost, lost !" were the only words he uttered.

His son, ignorant of the fatal compact his sire had made, could only imagine these ejaculations were prompted by delirium.

But suddenly a violent clap of thunder shook the old castle to its foundations, and the dying count uttered a piercing shriek as the terrible form of the Rhine Demon appeared before him.

The fiend fixed his eyes upon his victim with a mocking smile, as he said—

"Your time has expired. You must come with me."

The conscience-stricken nobleman groaned piteously.

"I promised you you should rejoin your wife in death," the demon continued. "I am here to conduct you to her. Come, she awaits you."

"No, no; not yet, not yet!" raved the terrified Ottar. "I live still; you cannot claim me yet. Avaunt, fiend! torment me not; there will be time enough after I am dead."

"Time exists for thee no longer, count," sternly replied the demon. "I am the angel of death, sent to summon thee; therefore, prepare thyself."

"Oh, I cannot, I cannot!" groaned the wretched man. "So laden as my soul is with guilt, how can I prepare? Oh, is there no respite? no way of escape from your fiendish power?"

"Yes, there is still one way," returned the demon.

RUPERT HELD ALOFT AN IVORY CRUCIFIX.

"Oh, name it, name it!" entreated the dying sinner.

"Your son, Enric, can deliver you."

"How—how? Tell me quickly, for my breath fails me."

"By promising to sacrifice his virgin bride as you did."

"He will promise," eagerly burst out the count. "You will, Enric; you will save your poor unhappy parent, will you not?"

He stretched out his hands in an agony of entreaty to the young man, who, in silent horror, had stood gazing upon the terrible form of the Rhine Demon, and listening to his conversation with his father.

The words he had heard, though fraught with horror, were still mysterious, and he said, in a tone of awe—

"What mean you, my father? Save you from what?"

Gasping for breath, and supported in his son's arms, the guilty Ottar made his confession, and then once more piteously besought his son to save him.

In the horror of the moment, young Enric vowed to accede to his request.

"I will save you, my father, though, in so doing, I must sacrifice a wife, and peril my own soul!" he exclaimed.

Another violent clap of thunder rolled as the demon drew the youth towards him, and having dipped the pen in his blood, made him sign the compact.

This done, the fiend vanished.

The count, thus left undisturbed, was allowed to die quietly in his bed, and was buried peacefully in the sepulchre of the Schönbergs.

Whilst his bones were mouldering there, time was going on, until at length Enric of Schönberg sought the daughter of a neighbouring chieftain in marriage.

The night before the nuptials, however, the Rhine Demon appeared to Enric, and reminded him of his promise.

The young man, who had almost for

CASTLE OF SCHONBERG.

gotten the circumstance, indignantly denied the compact.

But the demon was not to be outbraved, and produced the blood-signed deed.

"You will either keep your word with me or rue it bitterly," he said. "My terms are binding. I must have either your virgin bride or yourself!"

Enric, being strongly infected with the family selfishness, not wishing to lose himself, determined, as his father had done before him, to sacrifice his bride.

And for the second time was the shriek heard from the old turret at midnight.

For the second time did a white bridal dress flutter in the moonlight as the newly-wedded wife, hurled to destruction by her husband, floated down the Rhine waters, until at the same spot as before the demon grasp dragged her to destruction, and an exulting voice shouted—

"Two!"

Then silently arose another rock by the side of the former, as though to show the atrocious deed was neither unmarked nor forgotten.

As the Count Ottar had done, so did the Count Enric.

Having murdered one wife, he married another, who died, leaving issue one son.

And then, in the progress of time, the once youthful Enric drew near his end, when precisely the same incident as we have previously related took place.

The demon appeared, the guilty victim pleaded.

The son consented to release his parent, and signed the fatal compact.

This continued until seven Counts of Schönberg had successively come into the world, lived, died, and been buried.

During this term seven rocks had risen from out the depths of the Rhine, showing how fatally the demands of the rapacious water fiend had been satisfied.

The eighth, who had given the same promise to his father on his death bed as hedesir pcessors had done, and, like them signed the compact with the Rhine Demon in his own blood, was now living.

Count Rupert of Schönberg, though a true branch of the family tree, was of a nobler type than his ancestors.

Brave, handsome, and chivalrous, he was at the same time generous, unselfish, and possessed of a heart that could melt at a tale of sorrow and love truly and sincerely.

Besides this, he had listened to the words of the holy St. Goar, a devoted Christian missionary, who, in defiance of the wrath of Odin and the persecutions of his followers, had preached the Cross along the banks of the Rhine till he reached Schönberg.

Here it was he first met the Count Rupert.

The words of the venerable pilgrim went to the heart of the young noble.

As he unfolded before him the wondrous tidings of the Cross, Rupert felt the mists of error in which he had been hitherto enveloped clear away from his benighted mind like morning vapours before the rising sun.

The dark, idolatrous and blood-stained worship of the heathen was renounced for the pure, mild, and loving doctrines of Christianity.

Count Rupert of Schönberg became a sincere convert.

And not he alone.

The beautiful Gunilda, daughter of a renowned chief, known as Bertram of the Silver Belt, to whom he had given his heart, also embraced the Christian religion, that she might worship the same divinity as her adored Rupert.

The young count and his beautiful betrothed loved each other with all the warmth of tender, ardent natures.

The time fixed for their marriage rapidly drew near.

Once more the old castle was alive with busy preparation.

In the calm satisfaction which Count Rupert felt in contemplating his prospects of happiness with his young bride, and in the light of revelation, which had banished from his mind all its past superstitions, it is not surprising that the demon's compact should, if it had not utterly faded from his memory, at least have been regarded by him as a visionary dream.

He was therefore not a little startled when, two nights before the day appointed for his marriage, the haunting fiend, with his hideous aspect and his dripping locks, appeared to remind him of his promise.

The young Christian count, his first surprise over, listened to the warning calmly.

He felt he could claim protection from a higher power.

But the insatiable demon showed him the compact he had signed, and exclaimed with his usual sarcasm—

" Either your wife, or yourself ! "

The Count Rupert snatched a crucifix from the table and held it up before him, when, with a frightful howl of rage, the demon disappeared.

The young nobleman was much perplexed what course to pursue.

The idea of sacrificing his beloved Gunilda, as his ancestors had done their wives, was so abhorrent to his nature that he could not bear to think of it.

Then the thought crossed him that it would be wiser perhaps and safer not to marry.

And yet what reason could he give to his young betrothed ?

The one, the only reason, involved the recital of a tale of so much horror that he shuddered at the prospect of relating it.

At length he resolved to communicate his doubts to the good St. Goar.

The holy man heard his young convert patiently to the end, and then appeared to relapse into thought.

" What do you think of this, father ? " asked the count after a pause.

The good old pilgrim knelt silently down, and prayed fervently for several minutes before answering, and then taking Rupert's hand in his, he said, in a solemn and earnest tone—

" Most assuredly, my son, it is a grievous and a heinous sin to make a compact with the fiend, and though you did this thoughtlessly and in your ignorance, it may not be lightly passed over."

" But surely, father, that compact can have no power over me now ?" exclaimed Rupert, inquiringly.

" Not over your soul, most assuredly," returned the old man : " for the cross I preach has power to absolve from all sin. Your soul is safe."

" If it be so," answered the count, " then what have I to fear, even though my body should suffer ?"

" The body, no less than the soul, is in the hands of its Creator," said the old pilgrim, solemnly ; " and though, as a conquence of our sins, it is necessary that death should for a time have power over the former, it is only that it may be purified from its earthly dross, and fitted to dwell in those heavenly regions into which nothing that defileth can in any wise enter."

Rupert was silent for a moment, and then he said—

" Father, with this compact—fatal as it has been to seven innocent women—

hanging over my head, ought I to marry Gunilda ?"

" I see no reason to hinder your union with your betrothed," replied the good old man. " Marriage is a holy bond, sanctioned by Heaven itself. You both love each other, and your bride will not make the eighth victim."

" No, father," exclaimed Rupert, vehemently. " I would rather a thousand times perish myself."

" Then marry, my son," said the pilgrim saint. " And, whether in life or death, Heaven will bless your union."

This being resolved upon, the preparations continued, and at the appointed day and hour the wedding guests assembled, and the good father St. Goar married the noble couple according to the rites of the Christian church.

The usual banquet and festivities followed, and at midnight the lovely Gunilda was conducted by her husband, his fostering arm thrown tenderly around her, to the bridal chamber.

No shuddering, shrinking terror crossed her mind as they entered the stately old room, into which, as it had often done before, the curious moonbeams peeped.

Gunilda loved and trusted her husband, and with him she felt she was safe.

Rupert did not, as his predecessors had done, invite his newly-made bride to walk out upon the turret, to gaze upon the moonlit Rhine.   But he said instead—

" My dearest, best beloved, let us kneel together, and thank Heaven for the happiness we enjoy—for the bliss of feeling that we are united in bonds that one hand alone can sever."

The young wife imprinted a loving kiss upon her husband's lips, and together they knelt reverently whilst Rupert implored a blessing upon their union.

The prayer finished, the count led Gunilda to the window, and, pointing out upon the turret, he said—

" My own love, for the last seven generations the wives of the Counts of Schönberg have perished on their wedding nights."

"So I have heard," she replied, in a low tone, drawing closer to her husband.

"I am the last descendant of our family, and you are my bride; have you no fear?"

"None, dearest!" answered Gunilda, confidently; "so sure am I you would not harm me."

"Harm you!" cried the count embracing her fervently: "not for ten thousand worlds."

There was a moment's hesitation, and then he said—

"I have shrunk hitherto from narrating the terrible causes of these sacrifices, but I feel that I ought no longer to keep you in ignorance, therefore, with your permission, I will at once tell you the secret.'

"Let me hear,' dearest!" murmured Gunilda.

The count seated himself on the window dais, and drawing his wife to his side detailed to her the entire history of the fatal compact, from the time it had been first entered into by his ancestor, Ottar of Schönberg.

It was a terrible narration.

But Gunilda heard it calmly, and when it was finished, she said with a smile, as she threw her arms around her husband—

"The number is complete; there will be no more victims."

Hardly had she spoken these words when a violent blast of wind shook the door of the chamber, and—without the usual accompaniments of thunder and lightning—the Demon of the Rhine appeared before them.

His countenance was bitterly malignant as he glared at the count, and he exclaimed in a voice of thunder—

"Why am I kept waiting? Why hast thou not kept thy compact?"

"It is an unholy compact which ought never to have been made, and which it would be an additional sin to keep," returned Rupert, boldly.

"Wilt thou not keep it? Dost thou think to cheat me of my lawful prey?" shouted the demon, hoarsely, as he darted fiery flashes from his eyes.

"There is no compact between us," replied the count, firmly. "The spell that bound me to thee is disolved—the compact rendered null and void. The grace of Heaven has set me free. Avaunt, fiend! by this holy symbol, I defy thee!"

Encircling his beautiful bride with his arm, he held aloft an ivory crucifix.

At the sight of the cross, the discomfited demon recoiled in evident terror.

"You have escaped me!" he said, in a tone of mingled bitterness and fear. "I cannot resist that tremendous sign. But I have still some power left; though I cannot destroy your souls, I can still inflict vengeance on your bodies."

"On *my* body if you will—not my wife's," interposed Count Rupert. "You have no power over her."

"Ha, ha!" laughed the fiend, hideously. "Man and wife are one, consequently I have power over *her*, as well as yourself, as you shall feel."

"What would you do, monster?" cried the count, anxiously.

"Bid the last enemy place his icy hand upon your hearts, and still their throbbings for ever," answered the demon.

"You mean that our mortal nature must pay the penalty of sin?" remarked Rupert calmly.

"I do!" raved the fiend, in a paroxysm of impotent fury. "Already the hand of death is on you both!"

As he spoke, he waved his wand, and a ghastly skeleton bearing a dart appeared.

The hideous messenger pierced with his weapon first the count and then his wife.

An icy chill ran through their veins.

"And now, demon," cried Rupert, faintly, though composedly, "in the Great Name I trust, I command thee hence! Leave us to die in peace."

Again the young nobleman held forth the crucifix, at the sight of which the Rhine Fiend, uttering a tremendous yell, vanished, together with his grim attendant.

A dizzy faintness seized upon the count and countess, and unable longer to support themselves, they sank down together on the ground.

At the same moment, a light of more than earthly brightness filled the chamber, and melodious sounds of seraphic sweetness seemed to float around.

The door opened, and the holy pilgrim entered.

"Father," murmured Rupert, "you have come in time to bless us ere we die."

The saint raised his hands, and pronounced upon them a most solemn benediction.

As he finished, with a smile of ineffable peace upon their tranquil features, the Count and Countess of Schönberg drew their last breath.

"They die in righteousness, and they are blessed for ever," murmured the old man.

Then, as he spoke, the bodies of the dead appeared to undergo a change.

Gradually they became more and more spiritual and transparent.

At the same time, the interior of the castle, its timbers, garnishings and draperies, its floors, staircases and furniture, seemed to moulder into dust, and then melt into thin air, until, of the once proud Castle of Schönberg nothing remained but the giant skeleton of its stone walls.

Over this the shadowy form of its late master and mistress hovered for a time, and then slowly rising in the air, floated away, until they paused over the seven rocks.

Again the melodious sounds were heard, as seven bright forms, clothed in robes of aerial lightness, rose from out the deep waters, and joining their kindred spirits in the air, winged their upward flight far beyond the reach of mortal eyes.

The old pilgrim stood on the ruined turret in rapt silence, listening to the sweet music, and watching until the angelic forms faded from his view.

Then he sighed deeply, but instantly checking even this slight semblance of a murmuring spirit, he exclaimed—

"They are happy, why should I sigh? If it be the will of Heaven that I tarry a little longer upon earth, why should I regret? Heaven's will be done! I shall go to them, but they will not return to me."

The sweet sounds ceased to vibrate on the good man's ear, but he went on his way rejoicing.

Years and years have rolled by since then, but the ruins of the proud old Castle of Schönberg exist to this day, and the seven rocks still mark the legendary spot where the "Seven Virgins" met their untimely fate beneath the flowing waters of the Rhine.

THE
RED ROBBER OF HEIDELBERG.

 N the haunted Neckar, in the circle of the Lower Rhine, stands the ancient town of Heidelberg, over which frowns the castle, backed by a huge mountain clothed in sombre verdure. For ages it had stood there, a wonder of architecture and a tower of strength, but now a ruin, blighted by the hand of Heaven, though resistant to those of man.

It was a noble structure, with its splendid arch, huge tower, ramparts and fosse, its hanging terraces and massive walls—at once a palace, a prison, and a fortress.

It was the palace of the Electors of the Palatinate, and here was a capacious tun, which held no less than eight hundred hogsheads, and was generally kept full of the best Rhenish wine.

For it was a custom that every person should drink therefrom who ever visited the Elector's court, and such a dose was prescribed sometimes by the prince that his guests found locomotion a matter a impossibility till they had slept off the fumes of the liquor.

In those days, when to get gloriously drunk was looked upon as the height of enjoyment, and when might was considered right, and he who was strongest made war upon the weaker with impunity, even those highest in power, and who should have meted out justice to rich and poor alike, were generally the most oppressive and bloodthirsty.

The princes were generally little better, and often worse than robbers.

With impregnable fortresses, and hosts of armed serfs or retainers, they made their own will law, and set at defiance peasant, burgher, and monarch.

It was during these feudal times that the Elector Palatine, a cruel, bloodthirsty tyrant, issued an order that the people should provide him with as much grain as could fill his granaries free of all charge, and vowed that if the same was not stored by a certain day, he would hang from the tower of his castle a score of the richest burghers.

There were none who dared dispute his will, even if they felt disposed, but this is doubtful, since a cruel prince is sure to be surrounded by unprincipled and merciless followers.

At this time there was a great dearth of corn, and the people heard the demand of the tyrant in the same frame of mind as they would their death-sentence.

In vain the most influential men of the Palatine assured him of the impossibility of complying with his request.

In vain they represented that many were on the brink of starvation.

In vain they complained of the oppression that was heaped upon them, and besought him to be merciful.

Foaming with rage, the tyrant struck with his mailed hand one of the suppliants to the ground, and bade his followers drive the others from the castle with blows.

Bleeding and sorrowful, the little band of pleaders returned to tell the story of their treatment, and the ill success of their mission, and a wail of sorrow was heard on all sides.

In vain the people strained every nerve to obtain the corn, but they could not provide a tithe of the quantity demanded; and as the day arrived on which the demand was to be complied with, despair was on every face, terror in every heart.

Who should go and tell the Elector that his demand was impossible of compliance, and beseech his mercy.

None cared for the office, for each feared for his life.

But the tyrant must be met ere he swooped down upon them with his armed men, and the worthy Fritz Runheim, an aged and respected burgher, volunteered for the dreaded duty.

Each anxious for his own safety, none lifted their voice against it, but his own son Frederick, a noble-looking youth, of twenty, the pride of his father, and the solace of his declining years.

"You shall not go to the tyrant," he said. "If there is none other will kneel at his feet and implore his mercy, be that my task."

"No, my son," replied Fritz. "The Elector will neither respect youth or beauty; but my grey hairs may soften his heart. Besides, my years can be but few now, and if I fall, I am but as a withered oak, of little use in this world."

"It must not be," said Frederick. "The tyrant's heart cannot be softened by age no more than youth. I am strong, you are weak; I may, at least, be able to strike à blow in defence of my life, and perhaps rid the world of a wretch whose deeds disgrace his manhood, and shame humanity."

And the young man loosened his dagger in his sheath, and turned to depart on his his errand.

"Stay!" cried Fritz; I command you."

The young man paused. Obedience was his parent's due, and this he always showed him.

"Remain here, and comfort and cheer, if you can, our suffering friends. Be mine the task to meet the oppressor."

"Father, I implore you, stay!" cried the youth, seizing his hand, and pressing it to his heart.

"Son, I command you to stay while I go. Age has more discernment than youth. The passions are hot when the heart is young, and a hasty word or angry look may blast our hopes. I will have my will. Say no more, but remember that obedience in all things to a father is the right of every son."

The young man dropped the hand he held, and bowed his head in submission.

"If I cannot save, I will avenge you, father!" he exclaimed. "Go, and Heaven shield you! Your blessing, father, ere you depart."

Frederick sank on his knee, and the old man, laying both hands upon his head, blessed him.

Then, as the youth rose, he clasped him to his heart.

"If we meet no more on earth, we shall meet above, where tyranny and oppression are unknown."

And releasing his son from his arms, he waved his hands to the people, and strode with a firm step towards the castle.

The hearts beat with mingled hope and fear, and the eyes were dim with tears, that watched him as with an unfaltering step he proceeded on his way.

The feelings of Frederick were almost overpowering.

Fain would he have sped after his father, but that he knew would anger the parent he had loved so well. And muttering an inward prayer for his safety, he followed him with his eyes till he was lost to view.

When he stood before the castle, old Fritz looked up at its frowning battlements, and for the first time his heart throbbed with fear.

The sombre look of those solid walls struck a chill to his bosom, and something seemed to whisper to him that he would never pass from them alive. Yet he did not shrink from the task he had undertaken.

"I have lived more years than thousands of my fellow-men," he muttered to himself; "and therefore why should I fear to die now, if it be Heaven's will? Down, faint heart—if I perish, I do so in a good cause, and he who dies nobly dies well."

He approached the entrance to the castle, and demanded of the men-at-arms who guarded it to be taken before the Elector

Guarded on either side, they led him

into the fortress, and as he passed in, he felt that he had looked his last upon the world.

In the great hall the tyrant sat surrounded by his armed attendants.

There was a frown upon his brow, as, with a slow and faltering step, the old man approached and fell on his knees before him.

"My lord," he said, looking up into the angry face of the prince, "I come, an humble suppliant, from the citizens to ask that mercy at your hands which even the most callous heart could not refuse to the unoffending."

"Guard well your words, old man," cried the Elector, "and bethink you in whose presence you kneel."

"My lord," said Fritz, "in vain has been every effort on the part of the people to obtain for you the grain you have demanded at their hands. They implore you to consider that their poverty, and the great scarcity that exists, utterly prevent them, willing as they are, performing a task that is impossible."

As Fritz spoke, the frown on the tyrant's brow darkened.

He rose from his seat with flashing eyes and furious mien.

"What!" he thundered. "Do they refuse to obey me?"

"No, my lord," returned Fritz, meekly. "Gladly would they do so were it in their power."

"And what puts it out of their power?" cried the Elector.

Fritz was silent.

"Speak!" cried the tyrant.

Fritz rose to his feet.

"My lord, pardon me—yourself," said the old man.

"Knave!" thundered the other. "What mean you?"

And he laid his hand upon the hilt of his sword, and half drew it from its scabbard.

The old man looked round upon the faces of the retainers, and saw that all were scowling upon him; not one look of pity did he mark in that armed assemblage.

He turned his eyes upon the angry face of the enraged noble, and drawing himself up to his full height, Fritz replied, in a firm yet respectful voice—

"My lord," he said, "I am an old man, but I remember now the advice given to me by my mother threescore years ago; that was, never to utter a lie even though the truth may send me——"

"To perdition with your mother. Answer my question, and quickly," cried the noble.

"I will, my lord, and truthfully," said Fritz. "You have oppressed the people, drained them to the dregs, to support you in state, and a host of men to fight your battles, and plunder your weaker neighbours; you have torn from them the wages of their toil, robbed them of the rewards of the sweat of their brow; you have ground them to the dust by oppression and tyranny, and now——"

"Hold, varlet," cried the furious prince, "or I'll tear your lying tongue from your throat, and fling it in your face."

And he struck the aged man upon the lips with his mailed hand, cutting them with the blow.

For a moment Fritz staggered beneath the shock, then wiping his bleeding mouth with his hand, he fixed his eyes upon those of the tyrant.

"Coward!" he exclaimed.

There was not a quiver in the voice that spoke the word—loud and distinct it rang through that vaulted chamber.

It fell upon the ears of the Elector like a thunderbolt, causing him to recoil a pace, and startled the men-at-arms like the clarion's blast, and caused each to rush forward and point his spear towards the bosom of the aged citizen.

"Coward!" fairly gasped the astounded noble, his face blanching white with passion, and with clenched hand on his sword.

"Yes, coward!" cried Fritz.

This Story will be concluded in our next. Also, our next No. will contain
"THE BLACK SPECTRE OF STOLTZENFELS."

"'BARON OF STOLTZENFELS, THY HOUR HAS COME!' THUNDERED THE BLACK SPECTRE."

THE BARONS of OLD
OR THE ROBBERS OF THE RHINE

[3rd. Story Continued and Concluded.]

THE RED ROBBER
OF
HEIDELBERG.

"BY the soul of my father, I will endure no more," roared the Elector, drawing his sword from its scabbard, and making every plate in his mail ring like a death knell. "Hoary-headed villain, my sword's point shall sever your insolent heart in twain!"

"Strike, coward," cried Fritz, present-

"'HOLD, VARLET!' CRIED THE FURIOUS PRINCE."

ing his breast to the stroke. "This heart never quailed before the steel of an honourable man, and it will not shrink from that of a villain and a murderer!"

The upraised hand of the noble dropped to his side, and the point of the steel presented at the heart of Fritz, clanged upon the stone floor of the hall.

That noble look, that undaunted mien cowed the soul of the tyrant.

For a moment he stood glaring at the defiant burgher, and leaning on his sword.

Then he spoke in a cold, measured, merciless tone.

"Old man, within this court I hold the power of life and death, and there is none to hold forth a hand to baulk my will. I would strike you dead with my own hand where you stand, but that would be an honour too great for so insolent a caitiff. Your punishment shall be more worthy your offence, and one that shall teach all those of your kind a warning how they dare speak to their prince and master."

Old Fritz curled his cut lips in scorn.

"The tongue that can wag so glibly shall be cut from your mouth, and with it tied around your neck, you shall be exposed on the battlements of the castle, an example and a warning to your fellows. Lead him hence, and let the trumpet summon the populace to witness the execution of their prince's mandate."

He waved his hand, and the soldiers surrounded the horrified Fritz.

"Ha! your cheek pales," said the Elector, in a taunting tone. "Methought, I could humble that defiant mien, and cow that bold heart of thine, old man."

"Never!" cried Fritz. "It is not fear for myself that whitens my cheek, but abhorrence for the monster whose merciless heart shall yet stand more appalled than ever will that of his captive. Prince, I fear you not; I scorn your power, and laugh at your cruelty. I can bear torture and death as a man, and praying that those I leave behind will yet avenge me!"

"Away with him," cried the prince, "and on the ramparts tear out his lying tongue before the gaping crowd!"

The rude men-at-arms seized the old burgher, and roughly dragged him from the hall, leaving the Elector to pace the stone floor, foaming with rage, and clanging his mailed heels on the stones till they awoke the echoes of the gloomy pile.

Nor did he pause in his walk till the clarion's piercing blast sounded far and wide, and summoned the citizens before the castle to witness as merciless a deed as ever was perpetrated at the will of a tyrant.

The soldiers bore the unresisting old man to the ramparts amid jeers and taunts.

Fritz knew that all appeal for mercy to that heartless band would be unavailing.

It was a fearful doom, and the good old man felt he could welcome death a thousand times rather than endure the torture, and it was a hard struggle for him to seek to appear calm when the slightest show of fear would but add to the taunts which assailed him on all sides.

On hearing the summons, the anxious citizens began to hope that Fritz had succeeded in his mission, and that the Elector was about to proclaim from his court his determination to forego the demand he had made.

But Frederick felt no such hope. A deep cloud had fallen upon the brow of the young man.

It was with a fluttering heart, then, that he made his way towards the castle with his fellow-citizens.

As they mounted the ascent a gloom fell upon them all, for, surrounded by armed men, they saw the old burgher on the ramparts, his arms pinioned behind his back, and his grey head uncovered.

The battlements were lined with the rude soldiery, and the entrance guarded by double the usual number of spearmen.

Having arrived sufficiently near, a herald appeared upon the walls, and, while a deathlike silence reigned, he called out, in a loud voice,—

"Citizens of Heidelberg, our noble lord, the Elector Palatine, having made demands of you which you have refused to comply with, and having been insulted in his own palace by one of your people, he summons you before the walls of his castle that you may witness the punishment he has awarded to one who presumes to set him at defiance, in order, by this example, that you may learn how dangerous it is to disobey his commands, or approach his presence with murmurings and discontent. It is, therefore, the will of our prince that the tongue be cut from the mouth of Fritz Runheim, and that his body be pierced with spears and thrown from the ramparts into the moat."

There was a deathlike silence for some moments, then from every bosom broke forth a shriek.

Frederick clasped his hand to his brow and staggered like a drunken man.

"Holy Virgin!" he gasped, "do I hear aright?" One glance at the pallid faces around him, one look at his grey-headed father, and he doubted no longer.

Placing his hand upon his dagger, he sprang several steps before the others, and, in a voice that rolled like thunder towards the ramparts, he cried,—

"Villains! you dare not do this deed! Prince, you dare not blacken your name with infamy by such a crime. Your honour, your manhood, chivalry, all will be blasted if you raise but a finger to injure that weak, defenceless old man."

At this moment the Elector appeared on the walls, and motioned to the soldiers.

"Mercy, prince!—mercy!" shrieked Frederick, sinking on his knees on the earth, and extending his clasped hands appealingly.

But the Elector motioned again to the soldiers, who, seizing the old man, bent back his head while one forced the point of a dagger between his lips.

"Fiends!—devils!" shrieked the young man, springing to his feet. "Are you men that you stand gaping appalled? Is there no arm to strike the tyrant dead? Follow me! None stir?—then I go alone, to save or avenge my father!"

He sprang forward, uttered a shriek of horror, and stood still, with his hands clasped to his heart, his eyes fixed upon the ramparts, where stood a soldier, holding upon the point of his lance the tongue he had cut from the mouth of the aged Fritz.

"Behold the tongue that insulted our prince and master!" cried the herald, "and tremble lest you meet a like fate!"

"Too late to save, but not too late to avenge!" cried the horrified youth, as he again sprang forward.

With his bared dagger in his hands and fury gleaming from his eyes, Frederick reached the entrance to the castle.

The attention of the guards being riveted upon the horrid spectacle above, they did not observe his approach till he was amongst them.

They now threw their spears forward to bar his passage, but he beat them down, and fled past them into the fortress.

In a short time he had reached the ramparts, and striking right and left with his dagger he neared the bleeding form of his fainting father and that of the fierce Elector. But ere he could reach them a line of steel surrounded him, and twenty spears pointed at his breast.

"Father, father," he cried, as he struck madly at the glittering points, and sought to carve his way to the old man's side, "this hellish deed shall not go unavenged. Prince, fiend, devil, thy bloody work shall turn the hands and hearts of all Germany against my father's murderer!"

The fierce face of the Elector was calm, and triumphant as he leaned on his sword, and fixed his eyes on the maddened youth.

"The cub is worthy his sire," he sneered, "he has come to see his father die ere he surrenders his own worthless life. Curb his impatience by finishing the execution at once."

And he laughed a brutal laugh as he motioned to the executioners to proceed with their horrible work.

Furious, maddened, desperate, the young man strove to cut his way to his father's side.

In vain.

His dagger was dashed from his hand, his arms were seized, and held to his side, spears were pointed at his head and body, and he was powerless to move hand or foot.

Fain would he have closed his eyes to shut out the sight that followed, but he could not, and he sank on his knees as he saw his father's body pierced by a dozen spears, and fall at the feet of the tyrant.

Another shriek of horror from the crowd, another brutal laugh from the prince, and Frederick, with the strength of a giant, sprang to his feet, flung off the hands that held him, and leaped towards the tyrant.

But the soldiers flung themselves before the prince, and barred his way, and brought to a sudden stop by the spear points, he stepped in the blood of his father, and fell across his body.

Rising to his knees, he looked into the upturned face of his parent, and burst into tears.

The Elector and the rude soldiers looked on with indifference.

A minute he knelt beside the dead, and then, tearing his cloak from his shoulders, he steeped it in the pool of blood at his feet, and, holding the ensanguined garment in his hand, arose.

"Father, I could not save, but I will avenge you," he cried. "Prince, this deed of thine shall bring you more misery than ever I feel now. In cold blood you have murdered a good and honourable man. His blood cries out for vengeance, and it shall be answered. Here, over the dead body of my murdered father, by this ensanguined garment, I swear that while one thread clings to the other I will cling to one hope—revenge for the foul deed. If for a moment I falter, this shall remind me of my oath. Father, rest in peace; tyrant, beware of the man who wears the bloody mantle. Night and day, sleeping or waking, the avenger will be on your track. Tremble, tyrant, tremble!"

"Cut him down!" cried the Elector, himself springing forward as he spoke.

But waving the garment above his head,

with a bound he cleared the spears thrown before him, dashed along the ramparts down the staircase, through the hall, and out of the castle.

A flight of arrows were sent after him, but none struck him, and dashing through the crowd of horrified burghers, he sped on, and was lost to sight in the woods.

Terror-stricken, the people fled to their homes; and, the corpse of old Fritz hurled from the battlements into the moat, the Elector retired from the ramparts, furious at the escape of the youth, and vowing to be revenged upon the populace if he were not given up into his hands.

Parties of mounted spearmen were dispatched in all directions in search of Frederick, but no trace of him could be found.

The citizens were accused of harbouring and concealing him, which they denied, and truthfully, for none knew whither the youth had fled, and the Elector, furious at being unable to vent his wrath on the head of the man who threatened and defied him, did so upon the innocent burghers, and gave leave to his followers to rob and pillage and destroy to their heart's content.

The poor suffering people were unable or unwilling to defend their property; but the wrongs under which they laboured made many of them reckless, and all more or less disposed to disobey the will of the tyrant prince.

Having for a time satisfied his rage, things were allowed to go on quietly at Heidelberg, and the Elector, with half his men-at-arms, left his palace, and was absent several months.

It was thought by the citizens that he had gone on a warlike expedition against a neighbouring castle, but this was found to be erroneous when he returned, bringing in his train a lovely princess, whom he had espoused at Mayence, and whom he loved as desperately and dearly as even his cruel nature could hate.

For a time all was gaiety and feasting at his palace, and the warrior prince gave himself up entirely to the charms of love, and the populace begun to hope that the influence of his wife would turn the Elector from a cruel tyrant to a generous and merciful prince.

Nor did his passion for the lady moderate in the least—her every wish was law to him; so fiercely did he love her that had she bade him leap from the battlements of his own castle, he would have done it unhesitatingly to please her.

So powerful were the passions of this man, that in love or hate they carried him to the utmost bounds; and he either loved to madness, or was cruel to the uttermost.

A year passed, and the cry of an infant son was heard in one of the chambers of the castle, and the stern face of the prince was wreathed in smiles, and his heart filled with gladness.

Yet another year of peace and prosperity to the burghers of Heidelberg passed down the current of time, and the scene in the castle was one of unusual splendour.

The banqueting hall was filled with knights and nobles, and the great tun brimmed over with the best and choicest of wine, for it was the birthday of the infant prince, and well and nobly did the Elector resolve to keep it.

About this time the country around became startled and alarmed at the appearance of a gang of robbers, commanded by a man attired from head to heel in bright red.

His face was disguised by a colouring of red, and even the scabbard of his sword and dagger, and the quiver for his arrows were of a blood-red.

Hitherto he had molested none of the citizens, but had encountered small parties connected with the palace; and many of the good things intended for the castle were, after more or less fighting, surrendered into the keeping of this mysterious freebooter.

On the day before the banquet, a train of nobles was stopped within a short distance of their host's stronghold, their attendants routed, their steeds and arms taken from them, and they sent on their way on foot.

The prince was furious when this last circumstance came to his ears, and the subject being again mentioned at the banquet, he swore that he would burn down every tree and vine, and invade every cave for miles around, but he would capture and destroy the Red Robber and his band.

The words had scarcely passed his lips when a loud peal of defiant laughter issued from the further end of the hall; and as the nobles sprang to their feet with their hands upon their swords, they perceived in the doorway the tall form of a man, clothed from head to heel in blood-red.

For a moment astonishment seemed to paralyse the limbs of the prince and his guests; and then, bounding from his place, he drew his sword from the scabbard with an oath, and sprang along the hall.

There was a flash of light as five hundred blades were unsheathed at once; but at that moment every light in the hall was extinguished, and a shower of arrows rattled on the mail of the alarmed guests.

Then followed a loud defiant peal of laughter, and all was still.

There was a shout for the guards, cries, and maledictions, and the men-at-arms, from every part of the castle, came running to the hall.

But the Red Robber was gone, and nothing remained to show that he and his band had been within the precincts of the Elector's palace but a few wounded nobles and a quantity of arrows, with their shafts dyed a blood-red.

The prince was furious, his guests desperate, and his followers crestfallen.

The soldiers having had permission to drink as much from the tun as they could imbibe, were either drunk, or had kept no guard; and while all were engaged in enjoying themselves, and doing honour to the heir of the Elector, the daring band had penetrated into the castle, and in the confusion beat a safe retreat.

The confusion having somewhat subsided, and the guards being properly posted throughout the castle, the prince sought his wife's apartment, and found her kneeling in the centre of the room, wringing her hands and sobbing hysterically.

On seeing her husband she sprang into his arms and wept upon his bosom.

"What means this grief, sweet wife?" he asked, as he threw his arms around her, and stroked her raven tresses with his hands, "Your lord is safe and unharmed."

"Oh, my lord, my lord," she sobbed.

"Calm yourself," he whispered, "What brings these tears to your eyes on such a joyful day?"

"Joyful!" she sobbed; "oh, say wretched—wretched day."

"Wherefore? You have heard of the Red Robber penetrating into the castle and your fears are too great. I will hunt the knave to his kennel, and destroy him and his band ere a month has passed."

"It is not that which wrings my heart with anguish, my lord. My child—our son."

The arm of the prince dropped from his wife's waist, and he stood as though changed to stone.

"Our son? Speak! What of him?"

"Is gone!"

"Gone! Whither gone?"

And the prince staggered back and clutched at the wall for support.

"Gone, my lord, gone! Heaven only knows where; but my heart, my sorrowing heart, tells me he is dead.'

"No, no!" almost shrieked the prince, "from dungeon to tower the castle shall be searched. I will find him if, stone by stone, I tear the mighty fabric down with my own hands. Gone! lost to us. Oh, Holy Mother! spare my heart this terrible . pang!"

And, for the first time in his life, the heart of that proud, merciless man was crushed and seared, the haughty head was bowed, the strong limbs trembled, the flashing eye lost its fire!

Throughout that vast pile there was not a man more humbled, not a heart more crushed.

The prisoner in the lowest dungeon, momentarily expecting death, felt not the pangs experienced at that moment by the Lord of Heidelberg.

The banquet was brought to a sudden and painful close.

Mirth was turned to sorrow, and a gloom fell upon the castle.

Not a nook of the immense building but was searched.

Nobles and retainers mounted in haste, and scoured woods, plains, and rivers' banks.

Through the city they went, searching every quarter, but no tiding of the missing child could be gleaned from far or near.

Never had such a blow fallen upon the proud possessor of that stately castle.

The guests departed to their homes; the gay trains filed along the banks of the river, and the last who had come to pay homage to the Elector, and revel with him in his happiness, had left him in despair.

But his cup of bitterness was not yet full. The shock which the loss of her child had given the heart of the princess had undermined her health, and day by day she sank, till death closed her eyes in peace, and laid her soul at rest.

Robbed of his gentle partner, the whole fury of his soul burst forth again with redoubled violence.

The bad passions which had slumbered for a time were roused to unmerciful fury, and woe to the poor wretch who fell beneath his displeasure.

A word—a look consigned a man to a dungeon, and the noble who presumed to upbraid or thwart his will, found him in arms against him.

Despite all his endeavours, he was unable to capture the Red Robber, whose band daily grew larger, and whose boldness gathered strength as his followers gathered in numbers.

From base to summit the mountain had been scoured.

Not a rock, or brake, or cavern that

could be traced, on the banks of the Rhine, but the armed followers of the Elector penetrated.

But as they returned to the castle in scattered bands, carrying with them the spoils of some worthy burgher, or the stocks of the peasant, they were surrounded by a vast band, and the Red Robber wrested from them their booty, and carried it none knew whither.

In an age of superstition, such as that when these events transpired, it is not surprising that the depredations of this strange personage should strike terror to the souls of the rude soldiery, and timid citizens, and that they should come to believe that he was none other than the evil one himself.

This suspicion gained ground, till at length he became dreaded and feared alike by prince, people, and the soldiers.

It was a noticeable fact, however, that he never levied mail on the burghers, but confined his raids to the nobles, while upon the Elector he was most severe.

To guard against him every post was doubled, and the prince, who before had defied the strongest noble in the land, began to fear this mysterious robber.

Time went on, and year by year the tyrant became more oppressive and more cruel, till at length twenty years had passed over his head since the death of his dearly-loved wife, and the loss of his innocent babe.

The tyrant, incensed by the inability of the citizens to comply with a demand he had made upon them, and resolved to punish what had been no fault of theirs, had swept down upon the defenceless people with all the followers he could withdraw from the castle, and terribly had he made his rage felt.

With slight resistance he had robbed them of their corn and cattle, and worldly goods.

And as the moon rose over the mountain-top, and silvered the waters of the river, he returned at the head of his band, bearing with him the spoil of many a home.

His anger appeased by his cruel work, and worn out with the exertions of the day, he retired to his couch at an earlier hour than usual.

The sentinels were set for the night on tower and rampart, in passage and hall.

And the tired raiders flung themselves on their pallets to rest their wearied limbs, or sleep off the fumes of the wine they had stolen, and silence fell upon the castle.

The measured tramp of the drowsy guards alone broke the stillness, or the murmuring waters of the river, as it flowed on in the moonlight.

Then from yawning chasm, vine-trellised rock, and wooded mountain, issued armed men.

They swarmed down the mountain's side—they climbed up the river's bank, till a huge band had assembled at the base of the castle.

The drowsy sentinels marked not their approach till close to the castle walls, and then the alarm was sounded on the ramparts.

At the first notification of their presence being discovered, a tall form sprang to the head of the band.

He was robed from head to heels in blood-red.

His face was of the same colour as his dress, and in his hand he held his bared, gleaming sword.

By his side was a youth, noble in form and handsome in feature, armed, like himself, only with sword and dagger.

"The tyrant's minions sleep not," said the Red Robber; "and surprise is impossible. If there be one man who fears to assault that castle and avenge the wrongs of the oppressed people, let him turn back."

No one stirred.

"There is not one," said the youth, "whose heart is craven—not one who would not willingly die could he bury his steel in the tyrant's heart, and wash out, in the oppressor's blood, the infamy of his reign. May mine be the hand to do it, is the prayer of Fritz Runheim."

And the young man shook his glittering blade with vehemence as he spoke.

"Noble boy," said the robber, "you, at least, will not disgrace your father."

"Never, father," said the lad. "Men call you robber; but I, father, deny that you are one. Your hand never took the goods of another that were justly his own. If you have warred, it has been against the oppressor, and not the oppressed. I know not why you chose the course you have taken, but, be it what it may, I had rather be the son of the Red Robber of Heidelberg than heir of that proud tyrant who calls that vast castle his, and stoops to rob and oppress the poorest of his fellow men."

"Brave boy," said the robber, "my teaching has not been in vain. Would—but there is no time for words. Archers to the front!—spearmen, stand ready! The moment for action has come!"

As he spoke the ramparts swarmed with men, the light of torches flashed along the battlements, and the trumpet's brazen tongue sounded in the air, while the clang of arms awoke the echoes far and near.

At the word of command a flight of arrows sped through the moonlight, rattled upon the stonework and breastplates of the defenders, and laid many bleeding on the battlements.

Down behind the ramparts sank the soldiers, and a flight of arrows from behind the masonry showered upon the assailants, throwing them for the moment into confusion.

While yet their ranks were decimated the doors of the castle were thrown open, and a swarm of men poured out, headed by the prince.

His gleaming sword flashed in the moonlight—his thundering tone of command rang loud and clear through the din.

" Spearmen to the charge !" shouted the Red Robber, flinging himself at their head. " Behold the tyrant, and do your work well."

" Father," cried the young man, " suffer me to command here. My indignant heart pants to imbrue my sword in the oppressor's blood. Be mine to rid the world of a monster, and, should I fall, be it thine to avenge me."

" Go, then," cried the robber, " and let this steel your heart and nerve your hand —*that man* murdered my father."

" Then I will slay him, or he shall slay me," cried the youth. " Forward to the charge !"

He threw himself in front of the spearmen and dashed forward.

A smile lit up the face of the Red Robber —a smile that few could read, so strange, so unnatural was it in expression.

" He will avenge me," he muttered, " and I will avenge him ! Oh, tyrant, my revenge is not yet complete !"

As the spearmen charged, the archers sent flights of arrows hurtling through the air ; but those behind the ramparts received little injury, while the band below suffered greatly.

The crash of arms as the two bodies met was terrific, and many a man lay writhing in death, and was trampled under foot, as after the first shock the soldiers fell back, and the robbers charged them impetuously.

" Death to the tyrant !" roared the young robber, as he pressed the retreating foe.

" Down with the robbers !" cried the prince.

But as he spoke, he still retreated, fighting bravely as he fell back.

The archers followed the spearmen, led on by the Red Robber, who made no effort to reach the side of his son, but seemed more anxious that he should face the tyrant than himself, despite the fact that he had ever panted to imbrue his sword in the blood of the cruel Elector.

" On, on ; charge—charge !" cried the youth. " The tyrant fears our strength, and well he may, for we are the avengers of innocent blood !"

And in his eagerness to cross swords with the prince, he dashed forward impetuously as the soldiers once more gained the shelter of the castle.

So rapid was his movement, that he stood alone beneath the entrance with his foes.

Before his followers could reach him, a terrific flight of arrows met them, and they were driven back, leaving the youth a prisoner in the hands of the soldiers.

In vain the robbers endeavoured to follow—flight after flight of arrows and bolt fell among them, and they saw that the defenders were too powerful, and that their hope to obtain an entrance by surprise having failed, they could not effect their long wished-for purpose, and that, while sheltered by those impregnable walls, the tyrant was safe.

The Red Robber withdrew his men to a safe distance, and in moody silence watched the massive pile, in which that brave youth was now a prisoner.

In that wild band his will was supreme law.

None dared dispute it—none would have attempted to do so.

Turning to his followers, he spoke—

" In yonder fortress my son is a prisoner, at the mercy of a tyrant. Our united strength is powerless against those walls. Where all *must* fail, one may succeed. I go to save that boy or avenge him. Murmur not, it is my will. If by sunrise I come not back, return to your haunts, and await the hour to avenge me."

He waved his hand and strode towards the fortress—none presuming, unbidden, to follow him.

Arriving before the walls, he sounded a blast upon his bugle, and the Elector himself leaned forward to hear his words.

The Red Robber could not mistake that face, as the moonlight fell upon it.

It was one he had cause to remember till death !

" My lord," he cried, in a loud tone, " my dress will tell you that it is the Red Robber, whom you have been so anxious to capture, who now speaks. You hold my son a prisoner. Swear upon your honour that he shall go unarmed wheresoever he listeth, and I surrender myself into your hands to do with me whatever you will."

"I swear!" said the prince, a gleam of devilish joy flashing in his eye.

"On your honour as a noble?"

"By all the saints! by all I hold sacred! by my honour!"

"Enough. I am alone. I surrender myself your prisoner."

In a few minutes the dreaded Red Robber passed into the castle and surrounded by armed men, was ushered into the hall, where sat the prince ready to receive him, and where, with iron manacles upon his limbs, stood the proud youth who called him father.

With an indignant look, the robber fixed his eyes upon the triumphant face of the prince.

"My lord," he said, pointing to the youth, "is this a prince's honour?"

"I sit not here to answer the questions of a robber, but to punish him," returned the tyrant.

"Your plighted word?—your oath?"

"I spurn it as I spurn thee," cried the prince, rising. "Think you I would parley with a villain? I made the promise to free the son that I might destroy the father. I have long waited for this time to come."

"HE RESTED, BY A LAST EFFORT, ON ONE KNEE, AND PULLED THE STRING."

"And so have I, liar and tyrant!" cried the Red Robber.

The prince laid his hand upon his sword, and half drew it from its scabbard.

"If I had been disposed to be merciful, those words have changed me," he said. "Robber, on the battlements of my castle at sunrise, I will hang you both side by side."

"And you will murder my son even as you murdered my father in cold blood twenty years ago?"

The prince started

"Villain, who are you"? he asked.

"One who swore never to rest night or day till he had crushed your heart and blighted your peace for ever! Look upon me, tyrant! The Red Robber of Heidelberg is the son of that old man whose tongue you cut out and whose body you slew because he dared speak the truth to a monster. I am he who steeped my mantle in his blood, and from that day since have robed myself in red that I might never forget my oath of vengeance. I am Frederick Runheim, the avenger!"

A loud, scornful laugh broke from the lips of the prince.

"The words you have uttered then do I fling in your teeth, villain and liar! The oath you have sworn you have broken! I live! you die! I triumph, you fall, and *I* am the avenger."

The robber laughed and curled his lips scornfully.

"You witnessed the fate of your father," said the prince, after a pause. "The scene wrung your heart, and you shall now behold the fate of your son, and while you swear fresh oaths of vengeance I will hang you by his side to show how vain is the boasting of fools, and how great is the power of their masters!"

With a smile on his face the prince strode away, and the soldiers bearing off the two robbers in different directions, prevented their speaking a word to each other.

Bright and glorious rose the orb of day, lighting up the mountain tops and fringing the bedewed leaves of the forest with gold.

On the very spot on which old Fritz had met his death stood the prince, surrounded by a large body of his followers

Above them towered a rude wooden structure intended for a gallows on which the Red Robber and his son were to die!

Never did the tyrant look so pleased and so fiendish as when, with his arms still manacled, but with his head erect the young robber was placed beneath the scaffold, and the rope put round his neck.

VIEW OF THE CASTLE OF HEIDELBERG.

And as he stood thus, the Red Robber was brought upon the ramparts.

He had been deprived of his sword and dagger, but his limbs were free, though precaution had been taken to render him harmless by having him surrounded completely by armed men.

As he confronted the prince, he fixed his eye upon him, and in a deep voice said,—

"My lord, I appeal to you for the last time to spare that youth, to keep your oath, lest Heaven should punish you for breaking it."

"I have said he shall die in your sight, and nothing can change my will," replied the count.

"Father, plead not for me," said the youth. "I am prepared to die; but, with my dying breath, I curse the tyrant, and call down Heaven's vengeance on his guilty head."

"Those words are his last," cried the prince. "Let his body dangle in the air, and his father revel in his misery."

The next moment the youth was raised from his feet, and the prince and the robber gazed upon the struggling form, convulsed by agony, strangled by the will of a tyrant.

Gradually the struggles ceased, the limbs became rigid, and the young robber was dead.

The prince turned with a look of triumph to the Red Robber.

"Have you no threats to make, no vengeance to swear, against your lord before you share the fate of your son?" he said, in a sneering tone. "Or is the father's heart more callous than that of the son?"

"Aye, my lord, a thousand times more callous; the son's heart wept tears of blood for the father, the *father's* heart triumphs in the death of the son. But, oh, my lord, is he dead?—really dead?"

"He has spoken his last word, breathed his last breath; nor earth nor hell can bring back the life again."

"Then, tyrant," cried the Red Robber, drawing himself up to his full height, "you shall learn the triumph is not thine, but *mine*. Thou shalt feel the pangs that I have felt, and confess that the oath of vengeance I swore over my father's body on this very spot has been most religiously kept. Look upon that hanging corpse, strangled to death by your will—gaze upon that convulsed and blackened face—look upon that noble form, and curse the hour that gave you being, Lord of Heidelberg. Behold your bloody work, and sink appalled, for your merciless hand has strangled—*your own son!*"

The sword dropped from the hand of the Elector, and he stood as if suddenly stricken into stone, glaring wildly upon the speaker.

"Prince," continued the robber, "you have broken your oath. *I* have kept mine. On the night of the banquet I bore that child from your castle. I reared him to a robber's life, and taught him to hate the man who slew my father. To spare his life I offered you my own; but your merciless soul panted for blood, and in that of your own son have you imbrued your hands. Tyrant, my work is done; my father is avenged, and you are punished!"

And the robber pointed with extended hand to the swinging body of the youthful prince.

"Holy Virgin!" gasped the prince, sinking on his knees, and clasping his hands. *My son! my son!*"

Thine! robber, perjurer, murderer—*thine!*" cried the robber. "Whose is the triumph now? Vengeance is mine, and thou, proud prince, art accursed for ever and ever!"

Then, with a sudden bound, he sprang from the soldiers who guarded him, and leaped over the ramparts into the moat.

"Life for life!" shrieked the prince, springing to his feet. "Shoot him—slay him! he shall not escape me!"

The soldiers fixed their arrows to their bows as the bold robber scrambled up the side of the ditch.

He had reached the dry earth when a shower of arrows sped towards him.

One only struck him—between the shoulders; but it was a fatal wound, and the Red Robber knew that he had received his death-blow.

Foaming, mad with rage and despair, the Elector leaned over the battlements, and glared upon the dying man in whose fate even then he could triumph.

The dying man dragged himself along by his hands till he reached a spot on which a bow lay, dropped there by one of his wounded archers in their retreat, and fixing an arrow that had been shot at him from the battlements thereto, he rested by an effort on one knee, and pulled the string.

True to its aim it went.

Its barbed point penetrated the right eye of the tyrant.

As the Elector fell back dead behind the masonry, the form of Frederick Runheim sank on the earth gasping—

"Father, thou art avenged!"

His eyes closed, his limbs stiffened out, and death had claimed the Red Robber of Heidelberg!

THE BLACK SPECTRE
OF
STOLTZENFELS.

THE lordly ruin of Stoltzenfels (proud castle) stands upon a high rock upon the right bank of the Rhine, proceeding from Cologne, and only a few miles from the noted city of Coblentz.

The castle is totally dismantled, but the outlines of several high towers are still distinguishable.

The view from the rock, commanding a bend of the river, is picturesque in the highest degree.

The Rhine here expands, and becomes broad and placid as a lake.

This place was often the scene of duels, and a favourite resort of duellists, in that age when it was considered necessary to uphold honour at the point of the sword, or force falsehood down the throat of the libeller with a bullet.

In the beginning of the fifteenth century, Archbishop Werner was lord of Stoltzenfels Castle.

We must explain that in the middle ages, the titles of bishop and archbishop, and abbot, &c., were not necessarily ecclesiastical.

Thus it was that Archbishop Werner also held the titles of Lord of Branbach and Margrave of Lahnstein, and certainly had little in his character consonant with a sacred title.

In his early youth he had been distinguished for vices and excesses, and, later, for what was then deemed even more unholy, the practice and study of magic arts.

He was not the direct heir to the barony of Stoltzenfels—the son of the last lord still lived—but a dispute had arisen with regard to the legitimacy, and Werner, his second cousin and next claimant, had brought such incontestable proofs of the illegality of the late baron's marriage that the young Sir Berthold was forthwith disinherited, and cast on the world totally without resources.

What could he do?

He took the desperate course usual in those rough-and-ready ages; he turned robber.

In the forest adjoining what he considered his rightful estate he assembled a band of lawless followers, and lived, gipsy-wise, on the proceeds of marauding expeditions.

He soon became so formidable that the archbishop found it necessary to come to terms with him and allow him a stipulated sum, in order that he and his dependents and friends should be allowed to pass through Berthold's forest domains unmolested.

But what was worse to Berthold than even the loss of the estate and title, and the disgrace of illegitimacy was that Werner had obtained the hand, if not the love, of Erilda of Marksburg, the heiress of a family related to that of Stoltzenfels, and a whilom sweetheart of Sir Berthold.

Her marriage with Werner was entirely an affair of policy and family interest; her own heart had no part in it.

She loved Berthold, and at the time when he was the acknowledged heir, her parents approved the match, but as soon as Werner's claim was acknowledged, they reversed their decision and ruled that she should marry the new lord, Archbishop Werner.

As the authority which parents at that time exercised over their children was absolute, she could not refuse to abide by their decision.

So, having bidden farewell to the only man she had ever loved, she was compelled to school her heart to endure a union with one whom she both disliked and dreaded.

At that time she had never seen Werner, and the accounts she had heard of him were far from prepossessing.

He was many years older than herself, and it was said that ever since a violent fever, which had brought him to the brink of the grave, his aspect had been one of chronic ill-health and premature age.

His temper was said to be haughty and imperious, and his nature destitute of any soft or humane feelings.

At the time when this marriage was arranged, Werner was travelling in the East, whence he returned only a week or two before the time arranged for the ceremony.

He visited the castle of the Baron of Marksburg, and there Erilda first saw him. She fully shared the astonishment which inspired all at his appearance.

Instead of being, as she had expected, a man prematurely aged and feeble, the archbishop presented a particularly youthful and vigorous appearance.

He was known to be middle-aged, or past ; he looked like a young man in the prime of life.

All his ailments had so completely vanished in that voyage to the East, that even his friends scarcely recognised him as the same man.

Despite all this, Erilda was not favourably impressed with him. There was something sinister and sardonic in his aspect, and even his youthfulness was not prepossessing ; it seemed something unnatural, weird, and indescribably repellant.

The returned baron was attended by a certain Oriental named Hassan, a man of advanced age and reverend aspect, but as swarthy of hue as a Persian or Indian.

"It is to this learned man," Werner explained, " that I owe my restoration to health and youthfulness. His skill is

CASTLE OF STOLTZENFELS.

wonderful, greater than can be found among our most learned practitioners. For this reason I have appointed him my private physician."

The marriage took place with great pomp and festivity, and Erilda was taken to be mistress of the castle of Stoltzenfels.

Wealth and luxury surrounded her, but in her innermost heart she was far from happy.

She felt that she could never love Werner, even if the remembrance of Berthold had been quite obliterated.

Her lord's demeanour, though at first sufficiently kind, soon changed to indifference and coolness.

The festivities attending the marriage

over, he was no longer the devoted bridegroom, but neglecting his wife, he devoted himself with renewed ardour to his magic studies, and would remain for many days shut up with Hassan in his sanctum in the highest towers of the castle.

To that mystic region, which was filled by all the appliances of alchemy, and other abstruse studies, Erilda seldom or never penetrated ; indeed her husband forbade her presence.

Nor did he ever communicate to her the purpose of his studies, further than that their main object was that chimera of mediæval students, the Philosopher's Stone— the mighty talisman which, when found, would turn everything it touched to gold, and enable the fortunate possessor to rule the whole world.

Hassan was said to have gone far towards discovering it, and this was the reason his services were so much valued by his patron.

These occupations on the part of the archbishop caused comments by no means favourable—indeed he was generally called Werner the Wizard, and Hassan was complimented with the credit of being the Evil One in person.

Hearing these rumours, certain ecclesiastical dignitaries (to whom, as a titular archbishop, Werner was subject) remonstrated with him, but the wealthy and powerful baron could afford to make light of their exhortations, and would not change his course of life.

After a few months had passed in this way, a strange and fatal event occurred.

Hassan the physician was found one morning dead in his room.

From external evidence, it would appear that he had in the dark struck his head against a cabinet or closet in one corner of the apartment, and had been killed instantaneously by the shock.

Beyond this, the room itself was so filled with potent drugs and medicaments, that the searchers thought these alone sufficient to poison anyone by the noxious atmosphere they created.

However, the vital spark was undoubtedly extinct in Hassan, and, not being a Christian, he was privately buried in some unconsecrated ground near the castle.

The only person who seemed to take his death to heart was Werner.

He now shut himself up in his study more persistently than ever, seldom seeing the baroness or anyone else.

A little after this a son was born to the Baroness Erilda, and was hailed with delight as the first heir to the new dynasty.

But, though made so much of by friends and dependents, it did not appear as if the child's advent gave much pleasure to his parents.

The baron, abstracted in his mystic studies, and a prey to consuming regrets, scarcely noticed his young heir, while the mother seemed to have for him less than a mother's affection.

There was one person who was still less gratified with the advent of the new comer.

This was young Sir Berthold, the outlaw, who, when he became acquainted with it, was quite taken aback with the news.

"Farewell to all hopes of inheritance," he said. "This child will cut off the faint chance I had of succeeding after the archbishop's death, while he will prove a bond to endear Erilda to her lord, and so completely alienate her from me, that she will quite forget my existence. And I, fool that I am, cherish this hopeless affection in secret as ardently as ever."

He gave a sigh as he came to this stage of his reflections, while proceeding alone through the forest to join his outlawed companions.

It was dusk, and he now found himself approaching a spot which had already obtained an evil name—the grove where a plain stone obelisk marked the unconsecrated tomb of Hassan the physician.

The knight crossed himself, and looked, not without some fear, at this unhallowed spot.

Suddenly he was startled by perceiving a shadowy and gigantic figure standing close to the obelisk.

It seemed to bear a fearful and exaggerated resemblance to him who was sleeping below.

Yes, there were the swarthy complexion, the piercing eyes, the gleaming teeth, and the oriental garb of the Baron of Stoltzenfels' former companion.

"Go not, Berthold of Stoltzenfels," said the spectre, "until you have stopped and listened to me. I have that to say which concerns you much."

"Who and what are you?" asked Berthold.

"The spirit of one departed!" was the reply, "condemned to haunt the place until its purposes are accomplished. I know your desires; you would prove your legitimacy—inherit the barony of Stoltzenfels, and wed Erilda of Marksburg."

"Thou hast guessed my very thought, mysterious being," responded the young Ritter, in amazement.

"And each of these wishes shall be gratified," responded the apparition, "if you will attend to my words."

"Fiend, tempt me not; such offers can only mean to draw me into a compact with the spirits of evil."

"Mistake not; I am not the fiend—I have no design upon your soul, but I would use you for my own purposes, while at the same time, assisting you. Listen, and I will unfold a dark narrative explaining all."

The outlawed knight, who was personally courageous, and not more superstitious than many of that age, felt so strong a curiosity, that he was not awed by the aspect of the being that addressed him.

There were several paces between him

and the Black Spectre, and he even dared to approach it nearer, but forbidding him by a gesture, the spirit leant its phantom hand upon the obelisk, and fixing its eyes upon the knight with a sort of fascination that detained him, it related this narrative in a solemn and unearthly voice—

"In the city of Mossoul, in Asia Minor, for years lived Hassan the Sage, a man who studied so deeply the lore of the Arabians, Persians, and Hindoos, as to have reached a pitch of knowledge known not in the so-called civilised but really barbarous nations of Christendom."

"Blaspheme not the name of Christianity," interrupted the young knight, "nor say aught against the Fatherland, or thou and I shall not agree."

"Bigoted and narrow-minded mortal— but I will not quarrel with thee.

"This Hassan, that I spoke of, had gained much reputation in Asia for his skill, at the time when a certain German lord, who had travelled in Italy and Greece, passed through those Eastern regions. This Lord Werner of Stoltzenfels, that I allude to, was also a practiser and a student of mystic arts, and attracted, as he said, by the fame of Hassan's skill, he came to visit him.

"This Werner was not more than middle-aged, but enfeebled by a recent serious illness, and reduced to the feeblest state, he looked as if his years would not be many. His first purpose was, therefore, to see if the skill of Hassan could restore his health ; his next to seek his aid in discovering two mighty influences — the philosopher's stone, and a still more priceless boon—the elixir of life."

"And what may that be ?" asked the young chief of robbers, curiously.

"What? Why, the most potent medicine that can be conceived—a magic draught, which will restore the most debilitated frame, bring back youth to those sinking into decrepit age, and prolongs man's life to hundreds of years."

"By the saints, a most useful and wonderful nostrum," cried the knight; "and did Archbishop Werner obtain this mighty potion ?"

"Hassan," proceeded the spectre, "had by years of study, discovered the secret of preparing the elixir, but it was a secret too precious to trust to others. All the wealth of the Lord Werner could not buy it from him, yet he agreed in all other things to assist him, and prescribed for him at different times a few drops of this magic distillation."

"And with what effect ?"

"With the effect you yourself perchance have witnessed.

"Werner was from that time not only restored to health and vigour, but his aspect became youthful as it had been twenty years before. He came home, therefore, confident of pleasing his youthful bride, who, in common with all others, was amazed at his change of appearance."

"Speak no more of that," said Berthold, a cloud passing over his brow; "it wounds me to speak of Erilda, or of her husband."

"But I must speak of them, for your sake and mine. The Baron Werner had induced the Arabian physician to enter his service and accompany him to Germany, in order to assist him in his magic studies. With his aid, he hoped soon to discover the philosopher's stone, if not also to obtain the secret of the elixir.

"For many months, Hassan served his patron faithfully, devoting all his time and skill to his service.

"But a few weeks since his death took place.

"The cause of that death seemed plain, but deceitful appearances only concealed a crime."

"What crime ?" asked Sir Berthold, his attention much aroused.

The phantom voice, which sounded terrible in that gloomy place, and at that lonely hour, replied—

"Hassan was murdered by Archbishop Werner."

"Murdered ! Great Heaven ! is it possible ? Evil as he is, I could not have dreamed him capable of that, and yet, after all, the murder of an——"

"I know what thou wouldst say, sir knight—that the murder of an infidel by a Christian is scarcely a crime at all. But life is life, and murder is murder, and the life of Hassan was more valuable than thou mayst suppose ; and know, besides, that Werner is no Christian."

"No Christian ? But he can scarcely be one, or he would not meddle with magic, and the devilish arts of pagan idolaters. But wherefore did he commit this dastardly crime ?"

"He murdered Hassan for the sake of the elixir of life."

"Proceed," said Berthold.

"Thus it came about.

"Though Hassan assisted all his other researches, he still kept his secret of this preparation, but, from time to time, he gave the baron a few drops from the phial that he carried about his person. This not only kept Werner in health, but enabled him to preserve his wondrous youthfulness of appearance.

" At last this persistent refusal of Hassan to part with his great secret, led to a quarrel between him and his patron, and the former even refused to part with the customary modicum of the elixir. The consequence was, that Werner felt his health decline, and the next few days he suffered both in mind and body, but he would not make terms with the physician, who being proud also, was determined to curb the haughty spirit of his lord.

" But the latter had evolved a dastardly scheme, which he put promptly into execution.

" Hassan was sleeping calmly in his small chamber in the higher tower. He had locked as usual the door, and his precious elixir was still securely concealed about his person. Midnight had long passed, and a small lamp threw its faint radiance over the apartment. Werner, who had possessed himself of a false key, stealthily entered.

" He looked on the sleeping man—the man so aged, yet so vigorous in the possession of the secret of health and long life. That secret was perhaps concealed about his person in the form of a recipe—at any rate the phial was there. The baron resolved to obtain it.

" He first felt under the pillow, gently raising Hassan's head, but not waking him. The elixir was not there. Then he noticed that the old man's right hand was clasped closely to his breast. Further investigation proved that he held there a small phial concealed in that part of his robe. A wild feeling of exultation possessed the baron ; the great talisman was within his reach.

" First gently, next exerting all his strength, he endeavoured to take it from the old man's grasp. In so doing he awoke Hassan, who saw at once his object. A desperate struggle took place. The aged physician was far the stronger of the two, and would have conquered, but Werner had brought a weapon with him, and his victim was entirely unarmed.

" Cautious and calculating even at that moment of excitement, Werner took care not to use the blade of the dagger, but the hilt.

" Watching his opportunity, he gave the old man a fearful blow on the temple with that part of the weapon.

" Hassan, with a low groan, fell forward—dead.

" In the madness of his eagerness to compass his own ends, the baron felt neither remorse nor horror at his crime.

" He proceeded to search the body for the elixir.

" He obtained it with difficulty even then, for the grasp of the dead almost defied his efforts, but all his seeking failed to discover any writing or recipe relating to the concoction of the potion.

" But in that tiny bottle he knew there was enough of the precious fluid to ensure him health and long life.

" With maddening joy he placed it in the breast of his doublet, and having laid the body of the old man in such a position that his death would seem to have resulted from striking his head against the furniture, he eagerly took out the magic phial."

" Which, it seems, with all its power," remarked Berthold, " was not able to ensure its possessor from a violent death."

" The elixir of life," responded the phantom, " can cure all diseases, but it cannot guard against the treachery and brute force of man.

" But for that treacherous blow I might have lived ages upon the earth."

" And what did the archbishop after this ?"

" He held aloft the clear, colourless liquid to the light.

" ' Now,' he exclaimed, ' for restored health, youth and long life as lord paramount of Stoltzenfels.'

" But just as he was raising it to his lips the castle clock, in its deep, solemn tones, struck the hour of two.

" In his present excited state the least sound would disturb the guilty man.

" A shock went through him.

" His hand trembled violently, and despite his efforts to save it, the precious phial fell to the floor, broken to pieces, and its priceless contents spilt."

" How great a disappointment," exclaimed Berthold.

" Aye, I tell thee knight, that the loss was greater than the loss of untold sums in gold, for it involved that which all the gold in creation cannot purchase.

" The baron was frantic with disappointment at seeing that priceless fluid trickling through the cracks of the floor.

" In vain he sought to gather it up, and, as a last effort, he fairly threw himself on the floor, and with his tongue licked up the few tiny drops that still remained."

" And next—— ?" asked Berthold.

" He sprang to his feet, wonderfully reinvigorated, exultant and hopeful, and proceeded to search the room.

" But finding nothing to reward his researches he left the chamber of death, locked it behind him, and returned to his own.

" Such is the crime that rests upon the soul of the baron of Stoltzenfels.

"He gave me this tomb, but, though my body repose in it, my spirit will not rest till he is punished.

"Already retribution follows him.

"From that night he has not known a happy moment.

"I, the Black Spectre, the ghost of the murdered Hassan, haunt his dreams, and oft appear to him in his waking moments.

"The drops of the elixir which he had last swallowed had benefited him for a time, but their effect is now wearing off, and age and disease will return to him.

"But all this does not fill the measure of my revenge, and to complete it I need your assistance."

"In what way can I give it?" asked the knight, in a perplexed tone.

"Werner," replied the phantom, "is proud of his magic skill, and no punishment can be fitter than that which makes him the dupe of some charlatan. His desires are to obtain the secret of the elixir, and to discover the philosopher's stone.

"He will listen to any one who offers to assist him in this. Find me out, therefore, two men shrewd at deception. Let them assume the guise of physicians, enter his service, and pretend to assist him in his magic studies."

"In truth, I may be of use to you there, Meinherr Phantom," responded the young captain; "Hans Berger and Klaus Landstein are the very two rogues that would delight in such a scheme."

"The one was formerly a quack doctor, and the other an expert street juggler. They are now consummate robbers, but will doubtless consent to the enterprise, if well rewarded."

"They shall be amply rewarded," replied the phantom; "but they will be under my guidance, and if you will listen, I will give you instructions how to prompt them to their part."

Young Berthold listened attentively, but afterwards said—

"But in all this I see not how my own ends are forwarded one jot."

"You shall become Lord of Stoltzenfels," replied the shadowy Hassan, "after the death of Werner."

Berthold started, and sought to penetrate those shadowy features.

"Aye, but supposing that he discovers this elixir and lives for ever? Moreover, remember he has a son now."

"He will never discover the elixir," replied the phantom. "The secret perished with Hassan, whose disembodied shade is forbidden to reveal it. He shall perish. As to Eborhard, his child, he is under a spell, a curse from his very birth. His life will be short, his death disastrous."

"Poor Erilda!" murmured Berthold.

"She is to be congratulated rather than pitied," answered the spectre, "for losing a child which would be to her but a source of misery and woe. When my vengeance is completed, she shall be thine, and thou be recognised as the rightful Lord of Stoltzenfels."

"That does not follow," remonstrated Berthold, doubtfully; "my claim has, alas! been utterly set aside."

"Mistrusting knight! know that the story of thy illegitimacy was forged by the baron, who holds, concealed, the proofs of thy legitimate birth."

"Is it possible? Forger and murderer, as well as sorcerer, this archbishop deserves to be destroyed and exterminated as a noxious worm! But how know I, O mysterious shadow, that thy tale is true, and thou deceivest me not?"

"By all that I believed when on earth, I swear to its truth!" exclaimed Hassan, solemnly.

"And in all this I am not asked to league myself with evil spirits?"

"Never; thy soul is safe! Assist me faithfully, and I will promise to overthrow thy enemy, establish thy legitimacy, and give thee Erilda of Marksburg."

"Our compact, then, is concluded," said the young knight. "I swear fidelity for my part of it."

Thereupon he kissed the cross-shaped hilt of his sword.

Immediately afterwards the phantom melted away into dusk, and naught was seen but the white tomb surrounded by dark foliage—naught heard but the wailing of the evening breeze.

Sir Berthold, much impressed by this mysterious interview, took his way thoughtfully to the rendezvous of his robber companions, arrived there, and was welcomed cordially by them as usual.

Presently he called aside Hans Berger and Klaus, and had a long private conference with them.

Archbishop Werner sat alone in his magic sanctum.

It was a chamber of moderate extent, but so filled with books, mathematical instruments, and the other paraphernalia of abstruse studies, that its natural form and aspect were scarcely distinguishable.

The completion of this Story will be found on pages 61 *to* 64 *of our next Number, which will contain also the complete story of*
"*THE BARON'S REVENGE.*"

With this Number is Presented a SPLENDID COLOURED PICTURE.

THE BARONS OF OLD OR THE ROBBERS OF THE RHINE

[No. 5.]

THE BARON'S REVENGE.

ON the right bank of the Rhine is situated the Chateau of Argenfels, celebrated as the cradle of the family of Von der Leyen, and is near the village of Honningen.

Not far from Argenfels, many centuries

"THE YOUTH FONDLY PRESSED HIS LIPS TO HERS."

ago, the towers of a stately castle reared their embattled heads, and the following legend is recorded of it :—

It was while might was right, and the feudal lords respected neither the people, nor the laws, that the owner of this pile, having made prisoner a kinsman of a neighbouring noble, and the baron incensed by what he considered an insulting demand for his release, marched down upon the unsuspicious noble with all his force.

The baron well knew that, though Count Thurga possessed but a small fortress and an insignificant band of retainers, he was a bold man, and that he would not surrender while it was possible to hold out.

So he resolved upon a piece of treachery to obtain admittance into the count's castle.

The youth whom the baron had imprisoned was a great favourite with Count Thurga, for he was bold and intrepid, and possessed a handsome face and noble form.

Still he always looked upon him as a servitor, and none would have been more surprised and dismayed than would the count himself to have learned that the brave young Hermann had won the love of his only daughter, the fair-haired Lorenze.

Had but a shade of suspicion that such was the case ever crossed the mind of the brave count, Hermann would have been expelled the castle, even if no worse fate had befallen him ; and the liberty of the young lady greatly abridged.

But the count dreamed nothing of this ; and when he heard that his brave young kinsman, on being assailed by several of the baron's followers, had slain three of them with his sword before he was overpowered, and that for this the baron had consigned him to one of his dungeons, the count needed no persuasion from his daughter to haughtily demand his release in terms that were anything but complimentary to the noble who held him in his power.

In order to enable himself and followers to gain access to the count's castle, and, with fire, sword, and pillage avenge the affront, the baron had the youth mounted in the centre of the cavalcade, and sent a messenger forward to inform the count that he himself would surrender Hermann into his hands, and express his regret for the harshness he had shown towards him.

From the tower the count and his daughter observed the distant cavalcade, and while commenting upon it, the messenger arrived before the castle.

The count went down to meet him, leaving Lorenze still looking at the band as it came along the valley, with their arms and accoutrements flashing in the sunlight.

"Oh, if my father had but such a band of retainers !" she thought. "No wonder that the baron can make his power felt on every side, and that his name is a terror for miles around. Comes he in peace or war ? I'll e'en descend, and learn what his messenger has to say. Pray the saints his words be good, for, powerful as his master is, my father will defy him, and, with such terrible odds, we should suffer much."

And, thus muttering, Lorenze descended to the courtyard, where now stood the count in converse with the messenger.

"How say you ?" said the count ; "your lord regrets his conduct to my kinsman and to prove the sincerity of his sorrow, he himself conducts the youth back to my castle ?"

"It is even so, Count Thurga."

"Then it shall be a generous welcome I will extend to him," said the count. "Lorenze, the baron himself brings back Hermann, and comes to pledge his friendship in a draught of Rhenish, and, by St. Goar, he shall have a welcome worthy of him."

The girl's eyes sparkled with delight when she heard that in the train of the baron rode her lover.

But she dared not give vent to her feelings in words, lest she should excite her father's suspicions as to the relationship between herself and the brave Hermann.

"Go thou within, good fellow," said the count, "and make free with my winecasks."

And he beckoned a retainer to take charge of the messenger's horse.

"Nay," said the man, "I'll bear back to my lord baron how gladly you will meet him ; for, until I return, he knows not the welcome you will extend towards him."

"Be it as you will," said the count.

The man leaped into his saddle, and was about to set spurs to his horse, and dash from the courtyard, when a loud shout startled them all.

And up the incline to the castle they saw a horseman spurring madly towards the bridge, and behind him, at some little distance, several others in hot pursuit.

"What means this ?" cried the count, a suspicion of the treachery flashing across his mind.

"'Tis Hermann! I know his white plume ! He rides for life !" cried Lorenze, clinging to her father's arm. "See—he waves his hand, as if warning us of danger."

The count seized the bridle of the messenger.

But the man, drawing his short sword, plunged his spurs deep into his horse's flanks, and the animal, rearing up, would have trampled the count beneath his hoofs had he not let go his hold and sprung back.

As he did so, the messenger urged his steed across the courtyard, and crossed the moat at a bound.

Scarce had he done so when the foremost horseman rode up, his sword flashing in the sunlight, his horse flecked with foam.

Ere the messenger could turn his steed Hermann was abreast of him.

His sword flashed round his head, and cleft through helmet and brain.

The messenger of the baron rolled out of the saddle, and a riderless horse went galloping down the incline.

Without pausing to look behind him, Hermann spurred over the bridge.

And pulling up so suddenly that his steed fairly sank upon its haunches, he thundered out—

"Up bridge!—down portcullis! To arms! to arms! Treachery! treachery!"

Men flew to obey the order, given in well-known tones.

There was a rattling of chains.

The bridge was raised, the portcullis lowered, and the pursuers drew rein before the yawning fosse, chafing with rage and disappointment.

With his hand upon his sword, the count looked questioningly at Hermann.

"My lord," said the youth, extricating his foot from the stirrup, and springing to the ground, "but that I succeeded in escaping from my guards, three hundred armed foes had gained entrance to your castle. The man whom this blade has laid in the dust was sent to you by the treacherous baron, to open a path for his band with fair words, to be followed by foul deeds."

"How, then, the baron comes not in peace?"

"No. He comes, he says, to chastise your insolence, and give yourself and followers to the sword, and your castle to pillage. To give an appearance of friendship to his visit, he took me from my dungeon, returned me my sword, and mounted me by his side, but, resolved to warn you of your danger or perish in the attempt, I succeeded in escaping just in time."

"The saints be praised," cried Lorenze, clasping her hands together. "And you are safe, Hermann, you are safe."

"Yes, fair lady, though somewhat weakened by confinement in the baron's dark dungeon and bad fare, yet I am strong enough to strike a blow in defence of those I love, and hurl defiance in the teeth of the powerful robber baron who seeks our destruction."

"No time for words or fair speeches now. My daughter, to your chamber; Hermann, to your post.

"Ho, there! Man the ramparts!—guard the bridge! I'll don my harness, and show this bold baron that Count Thurga despises treachery, and has yet to learn what it is to yield to a foe."

So saying the count turned and strode hastily into the castle, followed by Hermann and his daughter. Lorenze took this opportunity to press the hand of the youth, and, looking up in his face, whispered—

"Oh! the hours of agony I have endured in your absence! My heart has throbbed with pain while my face has worn a smile."

"Dear Lorenze," sighed the youth, "would that your father knew our love—would that I dared reveal it to him."

"No, no," she said, "for that would be to make him your foe, and lose you for ever!"

The youth heaved a deep sigh, then, snatching her hand to his lips, he kissed it, and said, hurriedly—

"Fly to your chamber. Hark to those shouts. The assailants are preparing to storm the castle. Should they succeed, which the saints forbid, and the eyes of the cruel baron rest upon that lovely face, I tremble for what might follow. Hie thee to thy chamber, and there pray for Heaven's aid for the weak against the strong."

"And for thee, dear Hermann, and for thee," she whispered.

And, wringing his hand, she sprang from his side.

The count was soon equipped in his armour and ready for the fray.

From point to point he went visiting the men at their quarters, exhorting them to bear themselves bravely, and speaking words of cheer, and then he mounted the ramparts, and surveyed the scene below.

Five times the number of his own followers were drawn up below.

Along their ranks rode the furious baron, followed by his standard-bearer, giving orders for the assault.

Having done this, he called upon the count to surrender.

The reply he received was a flight of darts and arrows hurled among his men.

The baron rode back, and his followers, retreating some distance down the incline, dismounted, and leaving their horses, with the baron at their head, once more ascended the hill.

Those on the battlements sent showers of arrows and stones among them, but, falling on their armour, they did little damage.

Approaching almost to the ditch, the line of assailants suddenly opened, and those behind rushed forward through them, bearing with them long pine-stems, which they pushed across the ditch, while their companions kept up an incessant fire of arrows at those on the walls.

These stems, placed crosswise, formed a rude bridge, and on to this a number of the baron's retainers immediately swarmed, and reared others against the walls.

One after another they were thrown down, and those who guarded at the entrance being called from their post to aid in repelling the attack on the walls, the few that remained to guard the bridge decided to lower it, and, by giving admittance to the invaders, secure their own safety.

To the surprise of both assailants and defenders, the bridge was seen to fall, and the count and Hermann hurried from the ramparts as the baron and his followers swarmed over it. Resistance was now useless.

The few who offered opposition to the baron were cut down and driven back into the castle.

In the great hall the two nobles met, the count deserted by all save Hermann and half-a-dozen of his followers.

"Surrender!" said the baron, haughtily eyeing the defiant count.

"Not while I can wield a sword," replied Thurga. "Your life or mine, tyrant."

And he aimed a blow at his adversary.

It was caught upon the shield of the baron, and a dozen swords flashed around the head of the brave Thurga.

Hermann sprang before him.

But his weapon was beaten from his hand, and together with the count he was hurled to the earth.

The sword of the baron was at the throat of the count, and those of his followers raised to strike the prostrate Hermann, when, with a loud cry, Lorenze sprang before the would-be murderers, and sinking upon her knees, held her clasped hands up appealingly to the victorious noble.

"Hold! hold!" she cried. "Spare them! spare them!"

The swords of the baron and his followers were stayed in their descent, and the former gazed long and earnestly upon the fair girl at his feet.

The contracted brow was raised.

The rage that gleamed in his eyes changed to a look of admiration, and bending forward, he caught Lorenze by the arm, and raised her to her feet.

"Lady," he said, "would you ransom the lives of your father and his followers? Would you save his castle from pillage and destruction? You have the power to do so, but you must decide at once,"

"Oh, speak! speak!" cried Lorenze.

"You are fair and noble; your beauty charms me. Give me your love, and if your father consents to bestow your hand upon me, he changes a powerful foe into a friend, and gains in exchange an ally whose strength is acknowledged on all sides, and whose power and wealth are greater than those of half the princes of the land."

Lorenze shrank back.

She turned her eyes upon those of Hermann, and was silent.

"Rise, count," continued the baron.

"Stand back," he added to his followers. "That ignoble posture ill befits brave men."

"His retainers drew back, and the count and Hermann arose.

"Men of deeds are seldom men of words," the baron went on; "therefore mine are few and to the purpose. Count, your life and possessions are mine by right of conquest. Give me your daughter in marriage in lieu thereof, and at the same time gain power for yourself and a husband worthy of your child."

The count hesitated a moment.

Her heart, for all he knew to the contrary, was free, and if he gave Lorenze to the baron, he would wed her to a man able to defend her, and at the same time obtain for her a position as high as ever he could hope for her to fill.

Certainly, the means which the baron had adopted to obtain possession of his castle were not very honourable ones.

But then honour was a commodity in which these robber barons were sadly deficient, and wealth and bravery had more weight in the minds of these feudal lords than aught else.

The count had much to gain, and nothing to lose, by the bargain, except the companionship of his daughter, and so he decided quickly how to act.

"My lord baron," he said, "I am willing that my daughter shall become your wife."

Lorenze clasped her hands and looked appealingly at her father.

The count either did not or would not notice the mute appeal.

Hermann placed his hand to his heart to still its wild beatings. These words had pained it more deeply than could the sword's point of the now happy baron.

He darted a look at Lorenze, their eyes met, and each read the agony of the other's soul therein.

But neither spoke.

Each knew it was useless to seek to change either the count's promise or the baron's will.

They could only wait and hope that chance or fate would throw the means in their way to prevent the hateful alliance.

The baron extended his hand to the count.

"Then, in return," he said, "I give you the hand of friendship, and henceforth your foes are my foes, and all the means in my power shall be freely at your disposal. We shall sheath the sword, and broach the wine-cup, and instead of making your castle resound with the clang of war, its walls shall echo to the sounds of revelry. Lady, your hand."

One agonised look at her father and Hermann, one deep-drawn sigh, and Lorenze placed her trembling hand in that of the baron, and suffered him to raise it to his lips.

A shudder passed through her frame as he did so, and an icy coldness fell upon her heart.

The followers of the count and the retainers of the baron now mingled fraternally together, and hands were clasped in friendship that but a few minutes before were raised in enmity.

Hermann stole sadly away, and communed with his own thoughts in silence and solitude.

The count led the way to the banqueting hall, and the baron followed him, holding the hand of Lorenze, who felt like a dove in the claws of a vulture.

The tables were spread, and the choicest wines were broached, and victor and vanquished drank to each other and swore eternal friendship.

The baron was all smiles and good humour, but in vain he tried all his arts to bring the smile to the lips of Lorenze, or the light of pleasure to her eyes.

Bending over her as she sat between them, the baron addressed Thurga saying—

"Count, a lover is ever impatient; are you content that I espouse your lovely daughter within the month which to me will seem an age?"

"Be it as you wish," said the father.

"How says the lovely Lorenze?" asked the baron, addressing the trembling girl.

"I shall be equally as well prepared to surrender my hand, baron, in a month as in a year."

"My halls, fair lady, will need some care bestowed upon them to make them worthy the reception of one so lovely as yourself.

"And now, sweet Lorenze, one smile to gladden my heart—one look to treasure in my soul till the day I return to bear you to the altar."

One hand clasped hers, the other, thrown around her waist, pressing her to his heart.

How could she smile when her heart was sad; how look tenderly into those piercing eyes when her own were filled with indignation?

But she remembered how powerful he was—how necessary it was to her parent's safety and her own happiness to dissemble, and she forced a smile to her lips.

Then, when he released her trembling form, she sped away from the hall and sought her own chamber. And long into the night sat the baron, the count, and their retainers quaffing deep draughts of Rhenish wine, swearing eternal friendship and making the walls of the castle resound with laughter, song, and jest.

Nor was it till the sun was high in the heavens that the baron and his retainers mounted their steeds and took their way once moor towards their own halls to prepare for the expected bride.

While yet the count and his newly-made friend kept high revel in the banqueting hall and Lorenze wept in her chamber, a sad and miserable youth approached her lattice, and tapped upon the panes.

"Lorenze," he cried.

She opened her lattice.

"Hermann, dear Hermann," she cried. "Alas, we are very wretched."

"Will you submit to this sacrifice, Lorenze?—will you, indeed, become this proud baron's bride?"

"Is it Hermann who asks me this," she said, "when I wear a dagger at my girdle, and would sooner become the bride of death, than rest in the arms of the man I hate?"

"You have raised a mountain from my heart by your words, dear Lorenze!" cried the lover. "But how to escape this terrible fate? There is but one way—only one."

"Speak it, Hermann, and I will bless you!" she cried, eagerly.

"Fly with me."

"Whither?"

"Anywhere, but first to the priest. I already possess your love; give me the right to protect you—give me the name of husband, and we can defy the worst."

"You are master of my heart—you shall be master of my actions. Hermann, advise, I will follow—command, and I will obey."

"Then come; the pleasures of the wine-cup they will not leave to mark our flight. This night we will away, and kneel before the shrine of the chapel in the rock. The good father will join our hands, as Heaven has joined our hearts, and united in wedlock, who dare sever the holy bond?"

"Be it so. I will descend to the courtyard. The guards are all withdrawn. Meet me there, and bear me wheresoever thou wilt, for I am thine, only thine, Hermann, my beloved!"

The youth then fondly pressed his lips to hers, and turning from the lattice, made his way to the courtyard.

The anxious lover paced rapidly up and down the courtyard until Lorenze appeared.

Then, taking her hand in silence, he led her quickly across the bridge.

She turned and looked up at the red sandstone walls, and for a moment she hesitated.

But it was for a moment only, and then, grasping the arm of her lover, they sped quickly away in the darkness.

Half-an-hour's walk brought them to a little chapel, built between the opening of some rocks.

The lights on the altar streamed through the little windows, and a priest knelt before the shrine in prayer.

Waiting until the holy man arose from his knees, the lovers approached him, told him all, and implored him to unite them, and rob the baron of his victim.

The priest consented, and side by side before the altar stood Lorenze and Hermann, and the good priest made them man and wife.

As he pronounced the benediction, a figure that had followed them from the castle, and unseen remained a witness of their nuptials, stole silently from the chapel.

"Here, beneath these walls, good priest, I pray you give us sanctuary until I can find a home for my bride, or reveal our marriage to her father."

"That will I," said the priest. "The true son of the Church must ever hold out his hand to the oppressed. Through yonder door convey your bride, and there rest in peace till you shall see fit to bear her hence."

And, pointing out the way, he turned again to the altar and his devotions.

When the baron rode away from the castle of Count Thurga, he was in a perfect good humour with himself and all the world.

The emotions of love filled his heart, and the fumes of the wine filled his head.

He was just in that state which so long as things went on to his own fancy, rendered him one of the best fellows in the world; but the moment anything occurred to mar that happiness, he would become a devil incarnate.

He had not ridden far from the castle, when a man approached him, and drawing his attention, intimated a desire to speak to him.

A mortal so contented as himself at that moment could not refuse to listen to even the humblest of his train, and he bade the fellow speak out.

"My lord baron," said the man, "last night while I guarded the horses, two persons left the castle. I followed them to the chapel in the rocks, and saw them married by the priest. I thought it might concern you, my lord, as they were none other than your late prisoner, and the daughter of Count Thurga."

The baron pulled his horse up so suddenly that the animal had some difficulty in keeping his feet, and its rider in keeping the saddle.

"What!" thundered the baron. "Knave, I'll cleave you to the waist, if you utter such a lie to me."

"My head be the forfeit if I lie," said the man. "Turn but you horse's head towards the chapel, and see if I speak not the truth."

"That tongue of thine shall never speak again, if thou hast told me that which is false; and if true, by St. Goar, I'll have such a revenge that all the world shall tremble when they hear of it. The smooth-faced Hermann wed my affianced bride, and that on the very night in which we plighted our troth! Woe to them all if I have been befooled! And woe to thee, fellow, if thou hast deceived me!"

The veins in his face swelled with passion, and a look of such fury flashed from his eyes, that the informant backed his horse quickly, lest, in his ungovernable anger, the baron should strike him from his saddle.

Followed by his whole troop, the baron galloped off in the direction of the chapel among the rocks.

Arriving before it, he flung himself from

his steed, and bidding his informant follow him, thrust open the unfastened door and strode into the sacred edifice.

Before the little shrine three forms were kneeling. They were those of the priest, Hermann, and Lorenze.

The clang of mailed feet sounding on the stone floor of the chapel caused the trio to raise their bowed heads, and turn their eyes towards the intruders.

With a cry of surprise, Hermann rose to his feet, and with a shriek of despair Lorenze sprang from her knees and clung to her lover for protection.

Slowly the priest rose and turned, but not a muscle of his impassive face moved as he fixed his eyes upon the furious baron.

Grasping the hilt of his sword with a fierceness that made its metal scabbard ring against his mailed leg, he thundered out—

"What brings the daughter of Count Thurga here in the company of that man? Speak! I have the right to know, and, by Heaven! I will be answered!"

Lorenze clung the closer to her lover, and Hermann's hand grasped the dagger at his girdle.

"Peace, my son," said the priest, in a meek tone. "The voice is raised only in praise or prayer within these sacred walls."

"Speak!" again thundered the baron.

"I will answer you," said Hermann, boldly. "This fair lady owes obedience to none but me—her husband."

"Ah!" cried the baron, springing a step forward, and drawing his sword. "Then the knave lied not, and yon white-faced priest has dared to join your hands in marriage, and rob me of my bride."

"Hold thy desperate hand," cried the priest. "Remember where you stand. By the rites of the Church have I joined these two, and by the laws of that Church I forbid any man to part."

"Hark you, priest," cried the baron. "I acknowledge no law but my own, and scorn all power but might of arms. Ho! there."

In a few moments fifty armed men stood within the walls of the sacred building.

"Beware, man of blood and sin, beware!" cried the priest, "lest the thunderbolts of the Church be hurled upon thy head, and the wrath of Heaven annihilate thee and thy band."

"On the mountain, in the valley, and on the waters I have defied death and destruction a hundred times; think you I shall tremble at the words of a priest? No;

my own will is the law I obey. Seize them both."

"Hold!" cried the priest. "They have fled hither for sanctuary, and woe to him who violates it."

"They shall find sanctuary within the walls of my fortress. If there be any bold enough to tear them therefrom, let them try. I come to claim my bride and my prisoner. Back, priest; you are too contemptible for my sword."

He hurled the priest aside, and seized the arm of Lorenze.

Quick as a flash of lightning leaped the dagger of Hermann from its sheath.

But it was struck from his hand ere it could be raised for the blow, and his arms were pinioned to his side by the followers of the baron.

One wild, prolonged, piercing cry broke from the lips of Lorenze, and she fainted on the arm of the baron.

"Be warned, be warned, ere it is too late!" cried the priest, placing himself before the furious noble.

But again he was hurled back, and, raising the drooping form of Lorenze in his arms, the baron carried her from the chapel, and placed her before him on his steed.

In vain were the frantic struggles of Hermann.

He was secured to the girth of one of the followers' horses, and the baron gave the order to march.

At a good pace the cavalcade set forth on their journey, and the agonised youth was at times fairly dragged along over the uneven ground.

Long and deathlike was the swoon of Lorenze, and when at length she opened her eyes, the walls of the baron's stronghold were frowning down upon her.

It would be in vain to attempt to picture the agony of those two young hearts, joined to be separated almost immediately.

It was late in the day when the last of the baron's retainers entered the castle, and the almost lifeless form of the trembling Lorenze was carried to an apartment, and Hermann was borne to a dungeon, and left in darkness and in solitude to ruminate upon what had transpired and what was in store for them.

No wonder that the heart of the brave youth sank within him, that he flung himself upon the stone floor and laid his throbbing brow against the damp walls, and beat his breast with his clenched hands.

No wonder that when the baron had departed, the door closed upon her, and a guard set outside, Lorenze sank on her knees beside the couch. and prayed and wept as if her heart would break.

Throughout that long, weary night sleep visited not the eyes of the lovers ; its soft influence was denied them both.

On the following morning the baron entered the chamber of Lorenze.

He found her kneeling on the floor, and her face buried on the couch.

There was a smile on his face as he approached her, but it was the smile of a fiend gloating over his victim.

His hand rested upon her shoulder ere she was aware of his presence but, as if electrified by the touch she sprang to her feet, and, with flashing eyes, confronted him.

"Sweet lady," he said, trying to take her hand, "you receive your lover somewhat coldly."

"My lord baron." cried Lorenze, struggling to speak calmly, "I am the wife of another."

A black frown gathered on the baron's brow.

"Aye," he said, bitterly, "you have placed a barrier between us, but you forget that I can remove it. While you remain the wife of another you cannot be mine, but to secure my own happiness, I will make you a widow, and leave your hand free."

"Monster, you dare not!" shrieked Lorenze.

THE CHATEAU OF ARGENFELS.

"Lady, you know not my power or my nature. For your sake I spared your father and your lover. The reward of my clemency was your hand. I fulfilled my part of the agreement, and you shall fulfil yours."

"My lord," cried Lorenze, sinking on her knees, "in mercy spare me. Fear for the safety of those I love led me to dissemble. I could not be your wife. I cannot love you."

"But you shall," said the baron.

"Impossible. Were my husband dead, I never could consent to become yours, and without my consent you could never make me your wife."

"Then I will gain your consent to our union."

"Never! Nothing you can ever do or say can change my firm resolves."

"We shall see," said the baron. "What words may be powerless to obtain, deeds shall gain. Follow me."

She shrank back, but the baron seized her arm, and drew her through the doorway along a stone passage, down several flights of steps, till the growing darkness told her she was approaching the dungeons.

A signal from the count brought to his side two men, bearing lighted torches.

"Lead the way," he said, motioning them to precede him.

"Oh ! what would you do ? Whither would you take me ?" gasped the trembling bride.

"To your husband," he said, coldly.

With his hand clasping her arm, he led her on, till at length they paused before the door of Hermann's prison.

The torch-bearers stood back, and the baron striking the door with his foot, drove it open, and revealed the dungeon, flooded with the light of a wood fire in its centre ; the brave Hermann bound hand and foot lying on the cold earth, and several rude men around the fire heating therein slender bars of iron.

The terror that seized upon the heart of Lorenze rendered her powerless to move or speak, and encircling her waist with his arm, the baron lifted her into the dungeon.

"Lorenze ! Lorenze !" cried Hermann, struggling in vain to rise.

"My husband !" shrieked the girl, making an effort to reach his side.

The baron, however, held her back, and pointing to the fire, said, in a whisper—

"Fair lady, I have brought you here that I might win that consent you refuse to give in a more cheerful part of my castle. See those irons heated in the fire, and think of the torture they can inflict upon the flesh of him you call your husband."

"Mercy, mercy !" cried Lorenze.

"It is *you* who can grant it to him, not I. His life is forfeited. He must die. Swear to consent to become my bride so soon as he is no more, and his death shall have no pangs."

"No, no ; I cannot, dare not," sobbed Lorenze. "Spare him, and I will pray for you."

The baron laughed a loud, brutal laugh.

"Lorenze," cried Hermann, "plead not to him. I am prepared for the worst, and can die as a brave man should die. But oh ! with my dying breath, I implore you never to wed with the wretch who would win a woman's love at such a price. Spurn and defy him as I do, and pray to the saints to avenge us on his guilty head ! "

"I will—I do," cried Lorenze. "Fiend —for man you are not—do your worst. I defy, scorn, abhor you ! "

"Haughty girl," thundered the baron, grinding his teeth with rage ; "I will yet bring you to my feet. You shall sue for the love I have offered. Men, do your work, and let this defiant woman see how fearful is the power she scorns—how terrible is the torture her own hand inflicts upon the man she has made the rival of the proudest baron of the Rhine."

"Man, devil ! " shrieked Lorenze, struggling desperately to free herself from the hold of the baron ; "as you hope for salvation, have mercy—have mercy ! "

The baron held her firm, and motioned to the men.

Two of them flung themselves upon the recumbent body of Hermann. With a pair of pincers another took a thin bar of heated iron from the fire, and approached the prisoner.

With a shriek that seemed to come from a bursting heart, Lorenze sank upon her knees, and covered her face with her hands to shut out the horrible sight.

But a cry of pain from the lips of Hermann caused her to take them from before her eyes, and then she filled the dungeon with her cries as she saw the heated iron forced through the lips of her husband, and bent over till it secured them together, and rendered it impossible for him to part them without tearing the flesh asunder.

One more effort she made to reach his side, and then, flinging her arms wildly above her head, she fell forward on her face on the floor of the dungeon insensible.

When Lorenze again recovered sensibility, she was lying on the couch in the chamber to which the baron had borne her on the day of her capture.

She felt ill and weak, and looking around, she perceived the baron standing near the window, gazing out upon the scene beyond.

With eyes of loathing, she watched him as he stood there, quite unconscious of her recovery, and felt, had she the strength, how she would avenge the terrible cruelties he had shown to her husband.

Turning suddenly, he perceived her awake and conscious, and hastily approaching her, attempted to take her hand.

She withdrew it shudderingly.

"Approach me not," she cried, "unless it be to kill me."

"Kill you, fair lady ? " he said. "Men do not slay the thing they love. Nay, give me your hand—that hand that so soon will be mine. The barrier is breaking down ; three days' misery and fasting have done their work, and soon there will be no obstacle to our union."

Three days, then, she had lain insensible, and Hermann still lived through the torture—lived in agony of body and mind in his dark, loathsome dungeon.

By an effort she rose from her couch.

"My husband ! " she said. "Wretch, why do you not slay him ? "

"Give but the word, and his misery shall be ended. Consent to be mine, and the dagger's point shall sever a life that is ten thousand times worse than death."

" Oh, fiend, what do you ask ? "

" That which I am resolved to obtain."

" It can never be. Man, man, your heart must be harder than the stones of your castle."

" Yet it can, and does, love you."

" Love ? Fiend, speak to me no more. Away ; and leave me to die, as you have left him."

And she turned from him in disgust and loathing.

" Entreaties prevail not," he said. " Then other means must be tried. I would spare your heart a pang, fair lady, but you will it otherwise. There is food and wine ; they will give you strength ; you will need it. In an hour, I will come again to bear you to your husband."

He left the apartment, and as he did so, she saw a couple of guards posted at her chamber door.

Not even from that apartment could she dare hope to escape.

True to his word, at the expiration of the time named, the baron returned, and bade her follow him.

She complied, for she knew that resistance was useless ; and by the same route as they had gone before, they arrived at the dungeon of Hermann.

Commanding one of his retainers to give him a torch, and another to open the prison door, he led Lorenze within the terrible apartment, and held the light high above his head, so as to throw its rays over the dungeon.

In one corner lay the unfortunate Hermann, and as he turned his gaze upon the intruders, Lorenze saw with horror the fearful change that had come over him.

His face was pale ; his eyes glassy and sunken ; his hair was fast turning grey.

There was the cruel iron clenched through his lips, the terrible wound where the heated wire had passed through the flesh and the half-consumed beard and moustache.

Beside him stood a vessel containing water, and a loaf of black bread, neither of which he could taste, but placed there to enhance his sufferings.

The thongs had been removed from his legs, but a chain secured to either wrist allowed him to move his hands as high as his head or as low as his knees.

He rose to his feet, and slowly approached the visitors ; but when he held out his manacled hands, as if he would embrace his wife, the baron spurned him back with his foot.

Faint with hunger, thirst, and pain,

Hermann recoiled, and fell of a heap on the floor of his dungeon.

" Fiend ! " cried Lorenze.

" Rail on, lady, for there are none here to heed it. I have brought you to your husband's prison, that you might judge for yourself how terrible is the doom to which you have consigned him."

" O, monster ?" she cried, as he held her firmly to his side. " I would give my life to shield him from a single pang."

" And yet refuse your love to save him from this torture," sneered the baron.

" Monster ! In mercy slay him and end his misery."

" Give but the signal, Lorenze, and he dies," said the baron.

" I cannot."

" Then he lives till exhausted nature gives out—lives within this dungeon, with food and drink by his side, which he cannot enjoy—lives with the pangs of hunger gnawing at his vitals, and thirst driving him to madness—lives with that iron preventing him uttering a single word, to prolong his life, or ease his sufferings ! "

" Oh, Heaven ! strike the monster dead with thy lightnings ! " cried Lorenze. " Hermann, my beloved, I am powerless to aid you, and my heart is breaking."

" It is false ! you can aid him, you can release him from his torture. Consent to be mine in a week, a month, and that moment ends his agony."

" Oh, fearful alternative ! " cried Lorenze. " Is there none other—none ? "

" None," replied the baron.

" I cannot accept it," she cried. " And yet to see him suffer thus—to know that I —but no, no ; I cannot—cannot consent."

" And yet you love him ? " said the baron.

" I do, I do."

" And refuse to end his sufferings—refuse to stay the torture ? "

" What—what shall I do ? " cried Lorenze, wringing her hands in agony.

The baron drew her closer to his bosom.

Hermann again staggered towards them.

By the light of the torch she read that appealing look in his eyes, and, tearing herself from the arms of the baron, she shrieked,—

" I will not—will not be thine ! "

Hermann joined his hands together as if in joy at her words, and Lorenze clasped him in her arms.

" Hermann ! Hermann ! " she cried, " Heaven will avenge us ! "

The baron tore her from him, and Hermann, springing back a pace, raised his heavy chain above his head ; but, with a loud, scornful laugh, the villain flung himself upon him, and hurled him violently to the earth.

Seizing the horrified Lorenze in his arms, he bore her from the dungeon, and bade the attendants secure the door.

Paralysed with fear and horror, the baron bore the half-fainting girl to her chamber, and, as he left her, said—

"To-morrow you shall see him again, and mark how his agony increases with time. Nay, ask not me for mercy; pity I have none. You can spare him; the means are in your power, and from you alone can an end come to his tortures."

But for that appealing look from Hermann, the resolution of Lorenze would have failed her, and, to put an end to the miseries of her husband, she would have consented to wed his murderer; but that look decided her, and she resolved never to espouse the wretch who held her in his power.

The next day she was compelled again to visit the dungeon.

The agonies of the doomed man were greater than the day before.

The fearful pangs of thirst had driven him to madness, and he beat his head against his prison walls, and would have dashed out the brains of the baron with his chain, had he not been prevented by the attendants.

Still Lorenze remained firm in her refusal.

The fifth day she was again dragged to the dungeon.

The chain which secured the hands of the ill-fated prisoner had been shortened, and wearied with the paroxysms, he lay panting and gasping on the floor of his dungeon, unconscious of all around him.

"Death will soon put an end to his sufferings, and rob you, vile wretch, of your triumph," said Lorenze.

"He will yet linger for days," said the baron, "and a few drops of water forced between his ironed lips will prolong his sufferings."

Lorenze glared at the inhuman monster with a look that spoke more forcibly than words could have done her horror and her abhorrence, and with a smile, the baron left her to herself.

That night was dark and cloudy—a mist rested on the waters of the Rhine, and had Lorenze been awake and gazing from her prison window, she could not have seen the armed bands marshalling in silence within arrow-shot of the castle walls.

When the baron and his retainers had departed from the chapel among the rocks, the good priest, who had joined the hands of Hermann and Lorenze together, made his way to the castle of Count Thurga.

Here, to the father, he revealed all that had transpired, and upon the impulse of the moment, the count would have gathered his retainers and pursued the baron.

But the priest warned him not to do so, lest he shared the fate of his daughter and her husband, and counselled the count to seek the aid of other nobles whom the baron had oppressed, and with their united forces, besiege the stronghold of their mutual enemy.

This advice the count adopted, and set forth upon his mission.

It was not, however till the evening of the sixth day after the capture, that their bands could be mustered beneath the walls of the baron's stronghold.

But now the united forces of those who had been prevailed upon to aid in the rescue of Lorenze, and the punishment of the baron, exceeded in number those of the cruel noble three to one.

Slowly and silently through the mist they drew near to the castle, and had planted their rude ladders against the walls, ere a single note of alarm had been given, or the faintest outline of their forces been seen from tower or battlement.

The count was the first to ascend, and had gained a footing upon the walls ere danger was observed by those on guard.

Then the alarm was sounded.

Lights flashed from every window, the sounds of preparation were heard, but the invaders leaped over the walls, and fell upon the guard, cutting them down, and driving them before them into the castle.

So sudden and unexpected had been the attack, and so desperate the assault, that before the baron had donned his armour and was prepared to lead on his men to the conflict, the greater number of his followers had been slain, and the assailants were masters of the ramparts, and swarming through the passages and halls of the buildings, seeking the baron with loud cries and threats of vengeance.

A hundred torches were kindled, and their red glare lit up every portion of the building, and showed the surprised baron how desperate was his fortune.

The lion saw that he was brought to bay, but he determined to fight to the last, and bite while he died.

Hurrying then to the apartment where Lorenze was a prisoner, he sprang upon the terrified girl, and, seizing her in his arms, he bore her up the steps of the tower.

"Never shall they tear you from me,"

he cried. "Stifle those screams; you but waste your breath. Ha! they scent their prey; but they come to their death!"

As he spoke, several men, headed by the count, bounded up the stairs of the tower.

"Surrender!" cried the count. "Baron, your castle is in our hands."

"Count Thurga," cried the baron, "if you held my castle, I hold your daughter. Follow me, and she dies!"

Up he went, and, guided by the light of the torches, the count and his retainers followed.

Out upon the highest battlement plunged the baron, and, waving his sword, he shouted—

"Here I make my stand. The first who places his foot upon these stones, I plunge my sword into her heart, and fling her body from the tower. Another step, and she dies. I swear it by the blood of St. Goar!"

Ere the words were fairly out of his mouth, a stone, hurled from a sling, struck the baron on the head, and releasing his hold of Lorenze, he staggered back.

Before he could recover himself, the count had sprung before him, and, grasping his daughter with one hand, with the other he plunged his sword into the body of the baron.

A dozen weapons were raised to smite the villain, and Lorenze fainted in the arms of her father as their glittering blades descended to his heart.

When she recovered consciousness, which she did in a few minutes, she was lying upon the count's breast, and as she looked up in his face, she perceived a body swinging above her from the stone-work of the tower.

The stalwart form, the glittering mail, the emblazoned armour, told her at a glance that it was her persecutor, the baron, whose dead body the indignant and outraged nobles had consigned to such an ignominious doom.

"Fear not, my child," cried the count. "You are safe."

With a cry she sprang from his arms.

"Hermann, my husband!" she cried. "Father, follow me! Oh, that it may not be too late!"

Without waiting for a reply, she sprang away down the steps of the tower, and after her hurried the count and several others.

"This way! this way!" she shrieked. "Hermann—husband, I come to save you!"

By the light of the torches, borne by those who followed, she sped on.

Nor did she pause till she stood before the dungeon door.

"He is there—there!" she shrieked. "Beat down the door! Hermann—dear Hermann! save him! save him!"

Eager hands withdrew the bolts, and flung open the door.

Eager feet sprang into the noisome cell.

With a wild cry, Lorenze sprang forward, and stooping, clasped her arms about the body of her lover lying on the floor of the dungeon.

With a strength that seemed surprising, she raised him up, and looked into his face, and a cry of horror broke from everyone present.

"Hermann! Hermann!" she exclaimed; "it is I, your wife! You are saved! you are saved!"

The glassy eyes brightened for a moment as they looked into hers.

The manacled hands were slightly raised, and then the head of Hermann dropped upon her bosom with a leaden weight.

The truth flashed upon her in a moment, and slowly Lorenze sank to the earth, still enfolding in her arms the dead body of her husband.

Rescue had come too late.

He had lived to see his wife torn from the power of their persecutors, and then death had rescued him from all further suffering.

They took the dead body from her arms, and drew it from her sight, and the count, bending over his daughter, raised her up, and clasped her to his bosom.

For a moment she looked up into the sorrowing eyes turned down upon her own, and then with a loud, wild, maniacal laugh, she tore herself away, and fled from the dungeon.

Away, laughing and shrieking, through the passages she ran.

Chamber after chamber was passed.

Flying she knew not, cared not whither —distancing all her pursuers!

And passing from the castle, she gained the banks of the river, and plunged into the woods.

Long and fruitless was the search that was made for her by her father and his friends.

But she was never discovered, though night after night her wild cries and maniacal laughter resounded along the shores of the Rhine, in the vicinity of the castle.

END OF THE BARON'S REVENGE.

[4th. Story, Continued from page 48.]

THE BLACK SPECTRE OF STOLTZENFELS.

IT was morning, and the baron, ere he commenced his day's studies, sat for awhile buried in reflection.

He then looked around him despondently.

Care had deeply lined his face; streaks of grey were seen in his hair; a general air of weariness and mental suffering had overspread his countenance.

"One short month," he murmured; "and the effect of the elixir is almost totally gone; all my efforts have failed to discover the secret of distilling even one tiny drop of that precious fluid.

"I feel that in a short time I shall be more debilitated and prematurely aged than I was even after the fever, and then my torture of mind, and this remorse—

"'YOU SHALL BECOME LORD OF STOLTZENFELS,' SAID THE SPECTRE."

this continued memory of that dastardly, and, alas! useless murder.

"Great Heaven! what shall I do?"

At this moment an attendant knocked at the door. The baron rose and admitted him.

"My lord, two venerable men, having the guise of learned doctors, are below, and desire an interview."

"Karl, you know that I never receive strangers; why did you admit them?"

"So please your honour, they said they were so certain that if you knew their errand, you would not only admit but welcome them."

Werner hesitated.

"It is well. I will see them," he said, and followed his attendant to a lower chamber.

The baron's visitors were indeed two men of venerable aspect.

One, the eldest, had a grey beard of patriarchal dimensions, and wore large spectacles.

The second, somewhat younger, had a most acute and penetrating countenance.

Both were dressed in the sombre robes of the learned faculty.

"We have sought you, my lord," began the elder, "struck by the rumours of your skill in magic studies. I beg to announce myself as Doctor Antonio Canucci, of the University of Padua."

"And your companion?"

"Professor Diedrich Kranach, of Leyden. We have travelled much in various parts of Europe, and have lately come from the East."

"And how think you to assist me?" asked the baron.

"In seeking the two great principles which form the object of your life and ours. Professor Kranach does not claim yet to have discovered, but he confidently believes he is on the track of discovering the philosopher's stone; while I need only say that I was formerly the assistant of one of the greatest practitioners in the world."

"You allude to the sage Hassan of Mossoul?"

An involuntary shudder passed through Werner's frame at these words.

But anxious hope predominated over fear—he eagerly questioned the pretended physicians. Their replies were such that he could not but believe in them.

Ultimately, he promised them a large payment to take up their abode at the castle, and give him the constant benefit of their services.

But first he led them to his study, and tested in various ways their medical knowledge, with satisfactory results.

Hans and Klaus had played their parts well, prompted by Berthold, from the instructions he had received from the Black Spectre; and, aided by their natural shrewdness and the real knowledge they possessed, the two robbers contrived to impose upon the proud and learned Archbishop Werner, and made him confidently believe he was fortunate in securing their services.

From that time Werner was scarcely ever absent from his sanctum, and always in companionship with the learned doctors Canucci and Kranach.

None others knew what mysterious rites were performed in that magic chamber, but strange rumours were abroad of spirits seen and ghostly noises heard, unearthly music, and poisonous vapours.

Above all, the Black Spectre greatly troubled the Castle and domains of Stoltzenfels.

At dead of night it was seen on the battlements, in the courtyard, or traversing noiselessly the long corridors.

None ever dared to approach the room in which Hassan had died, and all avoided the mausoleum in the grove, where his ghost was said to be constantly visible.

All this was thought to proceed from the ungodly studies of the Baron of Stoltzenfels and his minions, and again the Ecclesiastical Council remonstrated with him, and threatened to deprive him of his title of archbishop if he continued these forbidden pursuits.

But Werner answered more defiantly than before.

He cared not for the clerical title; let them take it and welcome, if they could, but he held it as a right, and would not give up one tittle of his power and independence at any council's bidding.

Archbishop Werner was accordingly excommunicated, but he seemed to regard this terrible punishment very lightly.

All this time he was, as he fondly believed, arriving nearer and nearer to the goal of his hopes, the possession of the philosopher's stone and the elixir of life.

His chemical experiments were incessant. He spared no toil, or time, or expense in them, and always had the zealous co-operation of the two mock doctors.

But in all this the archbishop did like the dog in the fable, that lost his food in grasping at that belonging to his image in the water.

In his researches for the stone which would turn all to gold, Werner's real fortune was being rapidly expended and, in trying to find the giver of health and long life, Werner's own health was being rapidly undermined. His youthful aspect had quite left him; his hair had become grey, his form bowed; a whole cycle seemed to have passed over his head since his marriage.

And now came round the anniversary of the birth of Count Eborhard, Werner's infant heir. Some rejoicings were made at the castle that day, and the baron, throwing off for once his distracted habits, took pleasure in the congratulations and festivities that prevailed. The baroness, too, seemed proud and happy, at least, more so than ordinarily. For it is useless to disguise that her life since her marriage had been an unhappy one; Werner's frequent seclusion and abstraction, alternating with displays of violent and exacting temper, made her sigh for her old home, and frequently think how much happier would have been her fate if allied to Sir Berthold. Added to this, the baroness was pious, and felt much concerned at the spiritual danger which she deemed that her husband incurred by his magic studies.

Her child was little consolation to her, always ailing, and with something weird and unearthly about him, such as to suggest more the idea of some goblin changeling than of a mortal child. Truly the young heir of the Stoltzenfels seemed to have been born with a curse upon him.

But of late he had improved wonderfully, and his parents could not but feel some joy and hope on the auspicious occasion when he had reached his first birthday.

They were sitting on the battlements of the castle, enjoying the calm summer weather. The child was playing beside its aged nurse, the baron and baroness were engaged in conversation, and several friends and visitors were gathered at a distance ; and suddenly, at the other end of the battlements, the only portion then in shade, there loomed the awful and dreaded figure of the Black Spectre. Gigantic and distorted as it was, its form and lineaments presented a recognisable likeness to the murdered Hussan. The eyes, strangely luminous, were fixed on the baron, the teeth gleamed, and an expression of mocking triumph lit up the phantom countenance.

Werner sat for a moment, as if paralysed, gazing in terror at this awful apparition, invisible to all others, and presaging, as he feared, some evil impending. He was not wrong. The next moment, with a rapid motion, the phantom stretched forth its hand, secured the child—the attention of the nurse being for the moment otherwise engaged—and hurled it over the battlements.

An infant cry arose on the air, mingled, at least in the agonised baron's ear, with a peal of fiendish laughter, and these words seemed to be whispered to him—

"This is one portion of my revenge !"

The next moment the Black Spectre had vanished, and, alas ! the heir of the Stoltzenfels had disappeared also.

All was confusion and distress. The baron, springing from his seat, rushed distracted to the fatal spot. Erilda, with a heartrending shriek, did the same, and the nurse was full of bewailings and self-reproaches. The seneschal, pale and agitated, came rushing up with the dread intelligence that they had found the mangled remains of the infant, dashed to pieces on the stony courtyard below.

Fearful was the anguish of the unhappy Werner. Not all his magic skill could conjure back one spark of life into that tiny corpse—the only hope of his house, snatched away by a fearful destiny of retribution. We will not dwell upon the scene. Suffice it that the child was buried with all honours, and Werner went back, after a time, to his magic studies, more wretched and despondent than he had ever been before.

But still his dominant hope—the hope of attaining one, if not both, of the talismans so long striven for—supported him, and in this he was encouraged by the two pretended doctors. His belief in these visionary pursuits grew almost to a mania. The most singular rites, the wildest vagaries, were indulged in by him and his assistants. They induced him to spend large sums in the forwarding of the great enterprise, whereby they contrived to enrich themselves at his expense.

At length one day, after a series of these experiments, Dr. Antonio Canucci announced—

"We have nearly reached our goal. I have consulted the stars, and they tell me that seven days from this will be a propitious time."

The baron reflected ; strangely enough, this date would be the second anniversary of the murder of Hassan.

But though this looked ill-omened, he felt a great hope that he would, after all, baffle the spectre, and attain the coveted prize.

"When once the elixir is discovered," he said, " I will leave this place, and travel again in foreign lands, renewing the period of youth, and health, and joy, which I once knew.

"It is a good sign that the Black Spectre has not haunted me of late."

Thus sanguine, he worked on with his assistants in the completion of the elixir.

At length the eventful day arrived. Behold Werner seated at his furnace-fire, surrounded by the ingredients of his magic compound, a pair of delicate scales and other chemical apparatus. Beside him his assistants, in the background, watching and taking part.

"Two more grains of the red powder," murmured the Doctor Antonio, " and I am much mistaken if the combination be not complete now."

They watched the effect with breathless interest. The red powder, stirred up in the decoction, produced for a moment a rich flame of the same colour ; this subsided, and he then poured out a portion of the fluid in a silver measure.

"It must be passed through the furnace once more," continued Antonio, " to purify and extract the rarer essence."

He and Kranach proceeded to perform this closing process. The night was far advanced, and soon the horologe struck the midnight hour.

"The new day has arrived," cried Werner, " the day that is to give me the power of renewed youth and long life. See ! the elixir flashes in silvery sparkles, the pure essence comes forth in liquid drops; the phial will soon be full, and then——"

"It is filled now," said Canucci, drawing off some of the liquid, "drink, my lord—but stay, let me first test the effect of the potion;" and raising one of the tiny silver measures to his lips, he swallowed a few drops. His face at once lit up with an expression of radiant delight.

"O ye gods! heavenly! I feel a new life tingling through my veins. I feel the freshness, the delight, the unbounded health and spirits of a child. Let us all rejoice; the elixir of life is found!"

"Give me the phial," cried the baron, stretching forward eagerly.

Canucci gave it to his hands; he seized it greedily, placed it to his lips, and, without taking breath, drained the contents to the last drop.

Then he looked around, a fearful indescribably oppressive feeling had suddenly come over him, his head felt dizzy, strange noises were sounding in his ears—the room seemed to spin round and round like a wheel, and the light of the lamp to dance like some erratic meteor.

He saw the faces of his two assistants lit up with a mocking smile, as they glared upon him; and worst of all, he saw, at the other end of the apartment, the horrible form of the Black Spectre.

No mortal countenance ever wore such an expression of fiendish triumph, no mortal lungs gave forth such a peal of sardonic fiendish laughter.

"Werner of Stoltzenfels," exclaimed the phantom, "thy hour has at last come—my subtle vengeance is completed. Thou art caught in thy own net, thou hast fallen a victim to thy own credulity. What thou hast swallowed is not the elixir of life—but the elixir of death—the very deadliest of known poisons."

The words went like iron to the soul of the wretched Werner; he knew that they were true—that all hope was over for him; a cold perspiration suffused his trembling and sinking frame, rapidly being overcome by the effects of the draught.

"Mercy! mercy!" he gasped, faintly.

"No mercy for thee!" thundered the phantom. "This day two years ago thou didst commit a dastardly murder for the sake of the elixir, the secret of which on mortal man shall ever know. My spirit has been condemned to walk the earth till its retribution is complete. I have haunted your nightly couch, appeared to you during your daily studies. I have taken away your son, the son born under the shadow

of crime. I have disclosed to Berthold the ground by which you have kept him from his rightful inheritance; and I have invited these two knaves, robbers of his band, to make you their dupes. Ere six months have fled thy wife shall be the bride of Berthold, the acknowledged Lord of Stoltzenfels, whilst thy body reposes in the cold tomb, and thy soul——"

A shriek of anguish cleft the ashy lips of the expiring baron. He half lifted himself from his chair, as if to implore or to defy his supernatural enemy, but the words died away into a gurgling murmur, the poison had worked its rapid deadly effect—he sank back—a corpse.

   *   *   *   *

In six months, as the spectre had foretold, Erilda was the bride of Berthold.

Her love for her late lord could not naturally have been of so intense a nature as to lead anyone to marvel that she did not take his death greatly to heart.

On the morning after the memorable night the two mock doctors were undiscoverable.

They had fled, taking with them everything of value they could possess themselves of.

It is scarcely necessary to explain to the reader that the expert easily appeared to taste the poison without really doing so.

The Archbishop Werner was found in his study with the phial in his hand, and it was conjectured that he had either poisoned himself or been poisoned by his assistants.

On searching his body the document was found which incontestably proved Berthold's legitimate birth and Werner's fraud.

Some difficulty was found in obtaining the ecclesiastical sanction to bury the magic-working and infidel baron in consecrated ground; but this was at length accomplished.

Berthold was acknowledged and congratulated by all, and now that fortune turned in his favour, soon found friends.

Having discharged his robber band, he gave them each a good sum on condition of leaving his domains for ever.

The estate was much impoverished, but Erilda, who, after a period of retirement at her father's home, was induced to give her hand to her former lover, by this time inherited a fortune in her own right.

Joy and prosperity again reigned at the castle, which ceased to be associated with *diablerie* and magic rites, and from that time the Black Spectre never more haunted the castle or estate of Stoltzenfels.

END OF THE BLACK SPECTRE OF STOLTZENFELS.

Our Next Number will contain Two Stories "THE SPECTRE OF RHEINFELS."

"THE BARON UTTERED A PIERCING CRY, AND FELL BACKWARDS INTO THE RHINE."

THE BARONS OF OLD OR THE ROBBERS OF THE RHINE

THE
SPECTRE OF RHEINFELS.

ON the heights of an angle of the yellow Rhine, the square towers of Rheinfels reared their massive heads.

This magnificent ruin is an extensive structure, and in a cleft of the rock, near which the town of Goarhausen now stands, the great apostle of the Rhine,

"THE BARON GLARED UPON THE APPROACHING SPECTRE."

St. Goar, took up his residence, and it was from here that the King of the Franks summoned him to Treves, where the Hermit of Rheinfels commanded a glittering sunbeam to hold his cloak, which it did in obedience to his order.

With the name of this saint Rheinfels will ever be associated ; but our business now is not with St. Goar, but with those less pious and more worldly than the hermit.

Long before the searing hand of time had crumbled the massive masonry of Rheinfels, there dwelt in the castle a cruel, proud baron whose very name was a terror to those who, by land or water, found it necessary in pursuit of either business or pleasure to come within the vicinity of his stronghold.

Setting alike the laws of God and man at defiance, it can be no wonder that his followers were equally cruel, merciless, and unprincipled as himself, and when he made descents from his mountain eyrie, which he often did, robbery, murder, and sometimes worse followed in his train.

He levied black mail upon all ; the horseman, the pedestrian, the boat upon the river—all had to comply with the demands of the master of Rheinfels, and the slightest resistance was punished with a severity that disgraced even the dark ages.

The last rays of the setting sun glinted upon the towers of Rheinfels, throwing the river's bank into shadow and fringing the distant horizon with a blood-red hue.

The waters of the Rhine rolled peacefully between their narrow banks, and a silence, almost painful, reigned upon the scene.

On the ramparts, gazing intently through the gathering gloom out upon the distant waters, stood two men.

One was of a tall, commanding stature, with a face that would have been handsome had not a deep scar, crossing it from the left ear to the chin, marred its beauty.

The other was scarce half the height of his companion ; but with a frame closely knit, and with muscles that proclaimed prodigious strength.

His features were harsh, cruel, and forbidding.

His front top teeth extended over his lower lip, and were pointed like fangs, and he had a villainous squint in his left eye.

His hair was thick, wiry, and matted, and his body, bare to the waist, showed every muscle and sinew of the powerful dwarf.

His bearing was bold almost to defiance, and his voice more like the roar of a lion than the tones of a human being.

"My eyes are more piercing than yours, my lord baron," he said, taking his hand from his forehead, and turning his gaze upon the face of the taller man.

"Can they see the boat, Gulf?" said the noble.

"I have strained mine in vain. I can see nothing upon the river."

"I see a sail dancing upon the waters, and could almost swear there's a pretty face beneath it."

"Ha, I see it now," returned the baron. "By St. Goar, but that sail sets my heart trembling, for it bears a bird to my rocky nest that an emperor would covet, and half the nobles of Germany envy."

"Ho, ho," laughed the dwarf, "an you get her to sing in your cage I'm mistaken."

"What mean you, rascal?" asked the baron, with some anxiety in his tones.

"That the proud Baron of Rheinfels may swoop down like a hawk upon his prey, but his prey will never love the hand that destroys her—never!"

"Be less bold in speech," said the baron. "Remember, here my will is law."

"Ho! ho!" laughed the dwarf, showing his fangs and rolling his eyes. "Who disputes the will of my lord the baron? Show me the caitiff, and this right hand——"

He paused, and shook his huge clenched fist in the air.

The baron looked upon his follower with a glance of pride and satisfaction.

"None will dare dispute it," said the noble, "save, perhaps, she who now comes so unsuspiciously to her future home! And if she do, what matter? I can tame her proud spirit, or break her stubborn heart!"

And setting his teeth together, he turned and walked hurriedly along the ramparts.

"Aye," muttered the dwarf ; "the devil could not do it better. Once the wolf has the lamb in his claws, she'll find it better for her to smile than frown. If she do the first, she may rule in Rheinfels, but if she try the last, there'll be work for the dwarf. Ho! ho!"

And shaking his shaggy beard, he followed like a hound the footsteps of his master along the ramparts.

Suddenly the noble paused and looked out on the stream.

The instant he became motionless his follower came to a dead stop.

"By St. Goar!" cried the baron, straining his eyes through the gathering darkness ; "but there seem three sails upon the river instead of one."

"I see them plainly, close together, and the tide is bringing them swiftly hither.

"Ho! ho! There will be other plunder than my lord looked for."

"There has been little enough of late," returned the noble. "It would seem that all fear to approach Rheinfels."

"And well they may," returned the dwarf, "unless they come in bands, armed and ready to fight for their lives and possessions, for it's little the master of this castle leaves them."

The baron looked upon the horizon from which the last ray of sun had glided, and then down again upon the dark river.

"The moon will not rise in time to aid us," he said.

"Well, perhaps it is better. They must not escape us in the darkness. Follow me!"

"To the death!" said the dwarf.

The baron hurried from the ramparts, followed by the dwarf, who, at the prospect of strife or plunder, became terribly fiendish in his expression.

Descending to the great hall, the baron summoned his followers.

By the light of half-a-dozen pine torches, the wild followers of the feudal baron gathered around him.

The red glare fell upon a band of men armed with sword, dagger and spear.

Some wore iron corslets.

Others were naked about the shoulders, but all fierce and desperate, as they waited for their lord to speak.

Standing in their midst, his form drawn to its full height, his plume falling over his brow, and his huge two-edged sword in his hand, he spoke—

"Our unwilling guest is on her way to the castle of Rheinfels, and if my eyes deceive me not, there are those with her who will bare blades to bar her passage to my halls.

"Three boats will shortly be beneath my castle walls. One contains the treasure which is mine alone, and woe to him whose rude hand assails her! The rest I leave to you. Into the boats, and conceal yourselves in the water-passage till the plash of their oars proclaim them beneath the shadow of my towers. Then, like hawks, sweep down upon the prey."

A shout awoke the echoes of the gloomy pile.

"Remember, not a hand must rudely clasp the girl who is among them. With the rest let them go their way in peace if they will, after you have plundered them,

but if they resist, a bare blade and the waters of the Rhine! Now away!"

The men hurried from the hall, and the dwarf, springing from his master's side, returned in a moment, bearing in one hand an embossed shield and in the other a heavy mace.

The shield he presented to the baron, the mace he flung across his own shoulder, as though it had been but a thin switch, and then, falling back, waited for the noble to precede him.

The baron looked down upon his follower, and, with a smile that distorted his scarred face, said—

"By St. Goar, but you had better remain behind, or my dove will think the Lurley hath sent one of her fiends to welcome her. Thy misshapen carcase will affright her."

"Ho! ho!" laughed the dwarf, "I'll do your bidding, master. "She'll make my acquaintance, anon, as did the fair Hellegunda, when, wearied of her love, you gave her into the keeping of your faithful Gulf."

"Peace!" cried the baron.

"Ho! ho! the shriek she gave when this hand clasped her slender wrist. Never did demon of wood or water utter such a one. I hear it at night when sleeping on my pallet, and start up to see——"

"What!" intercepted the baron, quickly.

"Her ghost pointing at me with her delicate hand, and looking at me with those lustreless eyes."

The baron grasped the shoulder of the dwarf.

"Gulf, do you lie?" he asked.

"No," returned Gulf. "In the tower, on the ramparts, in the halls, have I seen her night after night. The red blood trickling down her white bosom, that look of agony on her face which she wore when my dagger gleamed before her eyes.

"Do I lie? Would I did!"

"A dream, a fancy!" cried the baron. "And yet," he added, speaking to himself, "does not the Lurley sing on the rocks? and the wood fiends and cave fiends infest the river banks and forest? What though they do ; shall I, the lord of Rheinfels, tremble? Never! I defy them all!"

"And I," said Gulf. "But let me go with you, my lord. My hand may ward a steel from your heart, who knows?"

"Come, then, for the boats are fast approaching."

And, with his bared sword in his hand, he strode from the hall, followed by Gulf.

Torches fixed in the clefts of the stonework threw a ghostly glare over the vast apartment and, from the deep shadow which their rays failed to penetrate, stole forth a tall, graceful figure, robed from head to foot in white flowing garments.

Her face was as pale as the robe she wore, and long tresses of flaxen hair fell across her shoulders and down her back.

On her breast, just over the region of the heart, was a blood-red stain.

She glided on so softly that not a footfall could be heard on the stone floor.

She reached the centre of the hall, paused, and looked around.

Then a smile, faint and unearthly, passed over her marble face.

For a moment she stood gazing in the direction whence the two men had gone, and then, gliding across the hall, she took a flaming torch from its nook, and sprang quickly towards the stairs leading to the ramparts.

Meantime, beneath an arch built under the bank of the river, three boats filled with armed men lay concealed.

In one of them sat the baron and the dwarf.

The former, with his bared sword lying across his knee, was listening intently for the splash that should announce the close vicinity of their prey.

A deathlike silence reigned among the men, as, with the action of the waters, the little vessels rose and fell in their dark hiding-place.

Soon a sound reached their ears.

It was the fall of paddles in the stream.

The baron adjusted his shield to his arm, and arose, and Gulf, grasping his heavy mace, placed himself by his side.

Nearer and nearer came the sound, till right opposite the towers of the castle the wanderers had made their way.

Then the deep tones of the noble gave the command to issue from the archway, and the next moment the three boats were gliding out upon the stream.

It was too dark to see their prey, but the sound of the paddles told their whereabouts, and guided the desperadoes.

"Be ready," cried the baron.

There was a murmur of assent.

"Hold," thundered the baron, in a tone of command, "for such is the will of the Baron of Rheinfels!"

His boat struck the foremost vessel of the three as he spoke, and a shriek from a woman's lips rang out over the stream.

"Ha," cried the baron; "that voice is sweeter than the Lurley song."

And, stretching forth his hand, he seized the arm of a shrieking and terrified girl, and with a sudden jerk, lifted her to his side.

Consternation for a moment seized upon the occupants of the surprised boats, but the next they sprang to their feet, their arms in their hands, prepared to defend themselves and their charge.

As they did so, a light appeared on the ramparts of the castle, and, to the astonished and terrified gaze of all, a tall, ghostly form was seen, waving above her head a lighted pine torch.

Its rays, falling upon her white face and form, showed upon her bosom a red stain over her heart, and, as she stood there, waving the fiery beacon, as a warning of danger to the travellers, the count and the dwarf recognised features they had both seen before, lit up with smiles, and overcast with misery.

The count grasped fiercely the arm he held, and leaned for support upon his sword, while over his face a cold sweat broke out, and his limbs fairly trembled.

The effect upon the dwarf was even greater.

His mace fell from his grasp into the water, and he covered his face with his hands, and sank down upon his knees, crying—

"Hellegunda! It is the spirit of Hellegunda!"

Upon the men in the other boats the effect was startling and appalling.

Their upraised arms dropped to their sides, and the boats were suffered to drift from each other, while, in superstitious awe, they beheld and trembled at the supposed apparition on the walls of that frowning fortress.

Then through the deathlike silence pealed a frightful shriek—long, loud, and piercing.

The torch dropped from the hand, and the figure was hid in darkness.

Two cries echoed that of the spectre.

One broke from the lips of the girl in the boat, the other from those of the dwarf.

These cries, and the increasing weight upon his hand, awoke the count to his position, and the fact that his captive, overcome by her terror, had fainted.

He also saw that the boats had parted, and that his own had drifted close to the arch.

"To the castle! to the castle!" he cried. "Forego your plunder! Leave them to go their way!"

The men accustomed to obey the slightest command, and terrified by their superstitious fears, commenced paddling for the arch with might and main, leaving the boats and travellers they had come to rob further unmolested.

"Is it gone? is it gone?" gasped Gulp, taking his hands from his eyes.

Assuring himself that the apparition was no longer to be seen, he rose from his knees.

The boat reached the arch, and was gliding beneath it, when a voice called out—

"Robber! villain! yield your captive!"

It came from a boat close beside their own.

"Whoe'er you be," cried the count, "seek safety in flight, and thank the Baron of Rheinfels he suffers you to depart with so small a loss."

"Coward, restore her to my arms, or—"

"Away, and live," interrupted the count. "Follow, and you die!"

"Giela, Giela," cried a voice, "speak, my child, speak!"

A loud laugh from the count was the only answer to this, as, followed by his boats, he sped up the archway.

Voices came to the ears of himself and his followers, but they were more distant, and it was evident that the friends of the fainting girl had passed the archway, and, in the darkness, were giving pursuit to those they imagined were still upon the stream. Then the sounds died out entirely, and, lifting the girl in his arms, he bade Gulf procure a light, and show the way into the castle.

The dwarf sprang from the boat, followed by the baron, who, waiting not for the light, made his way through the darkness up an incline, closely followed by several of his retainers.

The light of a pine torch at length flashed upon the scene, and through a narrow passage, and up a flight of stone steps, and under a low doorway, the robber noble bore his insensible burden.

Not till he had reached the great hall did he release his hold, and then, laying her back in his own chair of state, he looked into her face.

Into the hall the dwarf alone had followed him; his retainers had gone to their quarters, alarmed at what they had seen, and annoyed that their expedition had been so profitless.

"Beautiful Giela," said the count, taking one of her nerveless hands in his.

Then becoming aware that the dwarf stood beside him, he turned quickly, and, in a loud tone cried—

"Begone."

Gulf knit his brow at the haughty tone, and sullenly withdrew.

Sinking on one knee, the count pressed her hand between his own, and strove to arouse her to consciousness.

But so deep was her swoon, it seemed as though life had fled.

Anxiously he gazed into that pale, youthful face, so calm, so lovely.

She was indeed a beautiful girl; and as she reclined there before him, with her raven tresses, escaped from their fastenings, floating over shoulders white as alabaster, he felt that he would risk even life itself to gain from those motionless features one single smile.

For some time he watched in vain, but at length Giela showed signs of recovery.

She opened her eyes and stared about her in bewilderment, but at length, as she perceived the baron kneeling before her, she realised the whole truth of her position, and sprang wildly to her feet.

"Father—Alphonso," she cried, clasping her hands. "Holy Mother, where—where are they?"

"It matters not, fair Giela," said the baron. "They no doubt are quite safe, and you are with one who loves you, in the Castle of Rheinfels."

The girl clasped her hand to her forehead, and tottered back.

"A prisoner in the hated stronghold of the robber baron?" she cried. "Holy Mother, protect and shield me."

"Calm yourself, Giela," said the noble, "You have nothing to fear from me. Rough as I am, you can make me tender as a woman. If I have torn you from your friends, it is because I, the proudest baron in Germany, love you—a burgomaster's daughter."

"Love me!" she said, still recoiling.

"Aye, fair Giela, and with a passion which no common kind can feel. I, who can bring the proudest to my feet, here kneel to you, Giela; I love you."

He tried to take her hand, but she tore it from him, and sprang across the hall.

The baron rose with a terrible frown upon his brow.

"Giela," he said, and his voice was terrible in its calmness, "I have stooped to sue, and I now rise to command. The Lord of Rheinfels never yet possessed a wish that he did not gratify. I have marked your beauty, and vowed that your love should charm my heart, and your presence grace my castle."

"My lord, my lord, I implore you," cried Giela.

"You know my power and my pride; I have humbled the one, and am prepared to show the other. I offer you the proudest position a woman of your sphere could ever hope to attain; do you accept it?"

"Oh, mercy, my lord ; you know not what you ask," she sobbed.

" 'Tis you who know not what you decline, girl. A hand that is the envy of many ; a position a princess could occupy with pride. Do you spurn these ? I have both the power and the will to enforce what I beg ; to command for what I have sued."

"Alphonso, Alphonso, my betrothed, where are you in this hour of my misery ?" she moaned.

"Your answer," he cried. "Will you be mine ?"

"Willingly, never," she cried, drawing herself up proudly. "Though but a commoner's daughter, I spurn with loathing the love of one who, though noble by birth, is a base and heartless man."

The scarred face of the baron glowed purple with rage.

He sprang forward, and seized her wrist in a grasp that pressed it like a vice, and caused her to cry out with pain.

"Girl," he hissed through his clenched teeth, " think not your haughty tones and insulting words will soften the heart of the master of this proud fortress. No ; they but steel it against you. You are my captive, and you shall become my slave. Within these walls there are none to dispute my word—without, they are all powerless. You shall be mine, and when I am tired of your love I'll spurn you from me, as you would now spurn me."

"Your acts are those of a villain, and your words those of a coward. You are strong and I am weak, but I fear you not, proud baron. High and powerful as you are, there is yet one higher and more powerful than yourself, and He will protect me !"

"Fool," cried the baron. "There is none can shield you ; you are mine, and neither man nor fiend can save you."

He drew her towards him, but with a loud cry Giela sank upon her knees.

"Holy Virgin, save me, save me !" she shrieked aloud.

A loud, brutal laugh broke from the lips of the baron.

It was echoed by another sound, one that thrilled his very blood with awe, and caused him to release his hold of Giela and start back.

It was a wild, unearthly shriek, such an one as they had heard pealed out on the ramparts that night.

As the baron glared in the direction whence it came, his face paled, his lips quivered, and his limbs trembled ; for with one hand pointing to the blood-stain on her bosom, and the other held warningly above her head, the spectral form of Hellegunda glided down the centre of the hall towards them.

The ghastly glare of the pine torches fell upon a face expressionless as marble, and the baron, by a violent effort, laid his hand to his side in search of his sword.

It was not there.

He had left it in the boat, and he was unarmed save with his dagger.

Quickly his trembling hand sought the handle of the weapon, and as he bared its glittering blade, that unearthly shriek again rang through the hall ; and in his superstitious terror, he suffered the weapon to fall with a clang upon the stone floor.

Rivetted to the spot by his fears, the baron glared upon the approaching spectre, as with noiseless glide she came towards him.

Close to the side of Giela she came, and then, lowering her upraised hand, she extended it towards the baron.

Her lips moved not, yet from between came these words—

"Woe to Rheinfels ! Woe to its robber master ! His days are numbered—his fate is recorded, and his grave is ready Tremble, Baron of Rheinfels, the word is spoken—thou art doomed !"

" 'Tis false !" he cried, in a husky, choking voice.

But as he spoke his eyes rolled wildly, he swayed like a drunken man, and then fell to the floor insensible.

The superstitious belief, in those times inherent alike in the bosom of peer or peasant, had so affected the bold, bad baron, that, despite every effort, overcome by fear and terror, he had really fainted

His swoon was not of long duration ; but when he recovered and sprang bewildered to his feet, the great hall was in utter darkness, and he was alone.

"Ho, there !" he cried in a still tremulous voice. "Gulf ! Guards ! Ho, there, ho !"

There was a rush of feet, a clang of weapons, and Gulf, the dwarf, sprang into the hall, bearing a lighted torch in his hand, and followed by several armed men.

The light of the single torch revealed the baron, white and trembling, standing in the centre of the hall, his eyes rolling wildly around the dark shadows like one in a dream.

The dwarf sprang to his side.

"My lord baron," he cried, "what is your bidding ?"

The voice of his faithful attendant seemed to arouse him, and, laying his hand upon the dwarf's shoulder, he said in a husky whisper—

"She has been here, and torn my prey from my grasp."

"Who, my lord?"

"Hellegunda."

Gulf paled. "Then woe to Rheinfels," he said.

"Peace!" cried the baron; "echo not the words she uttered."

Then, rousing himself, he cried aloud—

"Light the torches! Lights! give us lights! Search the castle; guard well its approaches! My prize must not escape me. By St. Goar, if the shadow elude my grasp, the substance shall be mine. Away, and do my bidding!"

The dwarf had kindled the torches and illuminated the great hall, and now he turned to follow the soldiers who hurried on their task.

"Stay, stay!" cried the baron, grasping Gulf's shoulder. "Leave me not alone. I fear not the living, though they come in armies; but the dead strike terror to my soul."

He sank into his chair of state and wiped the perspiration from his brow with his hand.

The dwarf crouched down at his feet and looked up into his master's face.

"And did she proclaim woe to thee?" asked Gulf, rolling his eyes around the hall as if expecting to see the dreaded vision.

"Aye, did she!" said the baron, "and her words have struck more terror to my soul than could the united forces of all Germany, arrayed against me. Oh, Gulf, that you had stayed your hand on that fatal night."

"I am but your slave, sworn to obey you," said the dwarf. "It was your command that the deed should be done, and my duty to execute it."

"Had you hesitated to perform, I had, perhaps, been merciful."

"Had you hesitated to command, I had never done it. Would I had not."

"Aye, would you had not," cried the baron, springing up, "then this curse had not fallen. But away with such childish fears. I am strong and powerful, and will defy the worst. Give me wine to fire my soul, and rouse my stagnant blood to action. Lurley, ghost, or demon, I will defy them all."

And he paced the hall furiously, while Gulf obtained for him a cup of wine.

Raising the vessel to his lips, in one deep draught he imbibed its whole contents; and then, flinging the cup from him, across the stone floor, he cried—

"I have been a woman, now I am a man. Give me my sword and dagger. For the first time, my heart has known fear—'tis the last. Spite of all, Giela shall be mine, and woe to those who step between us."

A laugh of derision seemed to come through the walls of the apartment.

The dwarf clutched at the chair and sank into it, and the count fired with the wine and rage, sprang towards the spot from whence the sound proceeded.

But nothing but the hard stones met his sight, and he returned to the side of his follower.

"Fool, do you still tremble?" he said, shaking the dwarf roughly. "Arouse yourself, as I have done. We are but the dupes of our fears; the victims of trickery or treachery. Or, if a curse has, indeed, fallen upon Rheinfels and its master, I will fight against it to the last gasp. Boldly I have lived, and bravely I will die!"

And drawing himself up to his full height, he looked once more the brave, defiant man he had ever been.

The captain of the guard now entered the hall, bearing in his hand his master's sword.

"Everywhere, my lord baron, have we searched, but in vain; no trace can we find of the girl, and it is impossible she could have escaped from the castle, as the sentinels are all at their posts, every entrance is guarded, and every loophole within view. She must have been spirited away by the Nixies."

The baron foamed with rage, and paced the hall like an angry tiger.

Pausing, at length, before the dwarf, he brought his hand down heavily upon his shoulder, crying—

"I have sworn the girl shall not escape me, and I have found a way to bring her again to my feet, if she still be alive and hidden within these walls."

"How, my lord?" asked the dwarf.

"She loves. To-night, with her father and her betrothed, she would have landed at St. Goar, and even to-morrow's sun would have seen them wedded, had not I swooped down upon them, and torn her from his arms. Hers is a nature that would sacrifice all for the man she loves. To-morrow I will make a descent upon the town, secure her lover, bring him hither, and doom him to a torturing death, from which there shall be but one escape."

"And that, my lord baron?"

"The transfer of her love to me. If she love him as I believe she does, she will destroy herself to save him; and if this bring her not to my feet, I will kill him in revenge for her scorn. Tell the captain to double the guards in passage, rampart, and tower; and you, faithful Gulf, throw your pallet outside my chamber door, and guard well your lord from ill."

He took a pine torch from the wall, and strode proudly from the hall.

Gulf followed him with his eyes till he had disappeared, and then went forth upon his mission.

The guards were doubled, and Gulf stretched himself outside the chamber door of the baron.

Silence reigned throughout the castle and the silvery moon, now risen, lighted up the walls of Rheinfels, and sparkled on the waters of the Rhine, as they rolled on past the towering battlements of many a robber baron, whose stronghold frowned down from the rocky heights on its banks.

Morning came, and with the sun rose the baron, unrefreshed by his troubled slumbers.

Angry with himself for suffering himself to be so moved by the apparition, and furious at the girl having eluded his grasp, he was in no humour to forego the resolve of the night before ; and the morning meal having been consumed, and the captain's report of the night containing nothing agreeable to him, he issued an order for half his band to assemble in the courtyard.

In a short time the courtyard resounded with the tramp of armed men and the hoofs of horses.

Before the entrance to the castle stood the dwarf, holding the white charger of

THE CASTLE OF RHEINFELS.

the baron, and close behind him was his esquire, mounted on a brown steed, clad in mail, and bearing his master's shield and lance.

The captain marshalled the men into order, and sat immovable as a statue at their head, awaiting the coming of the baron.

They had not to wait long.

Attired in a coat of mail, his long plume dancing in the morning breeze, and his huge sword girded to his side, the baron approached his charger.

The dwarf held the stirrup, and, with a spring, the baron was in the saddle ; then, stooping over the saddle bow, he whispered to the dwarf—

" Gulf, there will be work for you to-night, if Giela kneels not at my feet. See that your torture irons be in readiness, and your blade keen."

The dwarf bent his head, and the baron, striking his spurs into his charger's flanks, dashed along the courtyard, followed by his esquire.

In a moment the whole troop was in motion.

At that moment the loud piercing scream, which had startled him the night before, was heard.

The baron turned in his saddle and looked up at the battlements, expecting to see the apparition, but only the form of the guards met his gaze, as they tramped back and forth in the sunlight.

The baron set his teeth hard, plunged his spurs once more into the side of the charger, and rode swiftly on, followed at a good pace by his retainers.

Down upon the town, like a hawk upon its prey, swept the robber band, nor drew they rein till the very centre of the town was reached.

The inhabitants swarmed out of their houses, and looks of consternation passed between them, for well they knew that the lord of Rheinfels did not come thus, unless he meant mischief.

Issuing an order to the captain, the baron drew up in front of a small chapel, and his officer, taking with him several of the men, entered one of the dwellings with a couple, leaving the others on guard outside.

Soon he returned, bringing with him an aged man, whose blanched face and trembling limbs bespoke his fear.

Leading him up to the baron, the soldiers fell back, and the old man sank upon his knees beside the charger.

"What would my lord baron," he said, in a trembling tone, "with his servant?"

"Hark ye, old man," said the baron, frowning as he spoke; "I seek the truth, and it may save you and your townspeople a good deal if you speak it quickly. Three boats arrived at St. Goar last night, an hour ere the moon had risen."

"True, my lord baron."

"Their freight was——"

"An aged burgomaster, a young vine-grower, and several of his friends and servants, with a goodly quantity of merchandise."

"Where are they now?"

"The people are distributed about the town, and the merchandise is within the chapel behind you."

"And the young vinegrower?"

"Is there also, my lord."

"Good," said the baron. "And the aged burgomaster also?"

"No, my lord, he has gone."

"Whither?"

"To seek the emperor."

"He!—what!—wherefore should he seek the emperor?"

The old man was silent.

"Speak!" thundered the baron.

And his hand rested on his sword.

"To ask his aid in rescuing from your hands his daughter, who was to be wedded last night in this chapel."

A loud, derisive laugh broke from the baron.

"Fool!" he cried, "does he think the emperor has power sufficient to wrest her from those walls, or from the iron hand of the baron of Rheinfels? Enough—go your ways. For your information I spare you and yours from molestation at the hands of my followers. You love your townsmen and have influence with them. Warn them, then, to yield whatever I may ask, with a good grace. My castle is somewhat empty, and my coffers, too, and they must be replenished, old man—must be, either willingly or unwillingly. Do you hear that?"

"My lord baron, pardon me, the town is very poor," pleaded the old man.

"That is false. I know better; therefore, let your fellows see to it that we return laden. If they refuse to give, we take, and pay back in hard blows, remember."

And the baron significantly tapped the hilt of his sword.

The old man arose, bowed, and beat a hurried retreat, and was soon advising his neighbours to give up whatever was demanded of them, a piece of advice which he was not slow to give, seeing that he himself was exempt from plunder.

Sending his men off in different directions to levy contributions upon the inhabitants, and retaining about two score by his side, the baron demanded admittance into the chapel.

This demand was answered by an aged priest, who flinging open the little door, confronted him.

"What seeks the Baron of Rheinfels," asked the priest, "that he comes in war-like array to this sacred spot?"

"That which he has the power to take, holy father," replied the baron. "Stand aside, that my men may enter."

"If you come to worship, my voice shall bless you, but if you come to rob or war——"

"Out of my path!" thundered the baron, "or my sword shall cleave a passage through your body, old driveller."

And the baron drew his sword and raised it for the blow.

The old priest grasped the crucifix at his girdle, and held it up before the baron.

"Man of blood and crime," he cried, in a calm voice, "behold this sacred symbol, and tremble for your sins! Back to your fortress—back in peace, or beware the vengeance of Heaven!"

"Back, thou fool! Preach to dotards and drivellers, but not to me. Out of my path! No! Then my sword against thy symbol, presumptuous priest!"

With his sword the baron struck the crucifix from the hand of the priest.

Again his heavy weapon was raised to deal him a blow on the head, when the descending blade was caught upon steel, and, dashing the priest aside, a youth sprang before him and confronted the angry noble.

"Coward and robber," cried the youth, brandishing his sword before the surprised and discomfited baron. "Ignoble wretch, whose hand is raised to assail the innocence of youth, and the grey hairs of the aged, where have you placed her?—where have you taken my Giela?"

"Where thou shalt see her in my arms, insolent boy—where thou shalt gaze upon her and die!"

"Restore her to me, or I'll have your coward heart from out its base casket!"

"Never—she is mine! Think of her no more!" said the baron. "Seize him and convey him to the castle!"

"Back!" cried the youth. "Back! if there be one spark of chivalry in your base souls. Baron Rheinfels, if your courage is equal to your cruelty, send back your followers, and man to man, blade to blade, I challenge you to combat"

"Does the lion fight with the dog?" cried the baron. "Can a noble accept the challenge of a hind?"

"Baron Rheinfels, your craven heart quakes before the blade of an honest man. Coward, will this then rouse your courage?"

The youth's sword flashed through the air; the blade severed the fastenings of the baron's helmet, which fell from his head, exposing a face livid with passion.

Ere the brave youth could again raise his weapon, a blow from behind laid him senseless on the ground.

A dozen spears were thrust forward to pierce his body, when the priest sprang across it, and, holding up the crucifix he had regained, he shouted—

"Back! or the curse of our church be upon your body and soul for ever and ever!"

The men recoiled before the malediction, and the baron, pointing to the recumbent youth with his sword, exclaimed—

"Hold your hand! Strike not at his body. I will strike at his soul. Alive, he will minister to my revenge—dead, he is but so much carrion—worthless. Raise him up and bear him to the castle; there I will return the blow he gave me."

The retainers advanced to obey, but the inhabitants, smarting under the mail which was being levied upon them, and emboldened by the presence of the priest, and the courage of the youth, sprang forward to oppose them.

Nothing could have suited the angry baron better.

Taking the helmet from the hands of his esquire, he put it on his head, and calling upon his men to follow him, he charged upon the people.

The townsmen met the shock bravely, but ill-armed as they were, they were soon driven back, and cries, groans and the clash of steel, told how desperate was the contest.

The huge sword of the robber baron flashed from side to side, falling heavily on the unprotected heads of his foes, and beneath its stroke fell youth and age.

A shout arose above the din, and the men who had been dispatched upon their errand of plunder, now hurried to the aid of their chief.

Seeing this, the townspeople lost heart, wavered and fled, many of them only to fall by the lances and spears of the advancing soldiers.

In a few minutes all that remained were the robbers and the wounded, and the aged priest bestriding the insensible form of the brave youth and holding the crucifix high above his head.

"The dogs have shown their teeth," said the baron, "and bitterly shall they repent it. Stand back, old man, or I'll trample you beneath my horse's hoofs."

And he drove his horse against the priest.

To save himself from falling, the old man seized the bridle.

Enraged, the baron rose in the stirrups and drove his sword into the priest's body.

A cry of pain escaped the poor old man, and he fell back over the body of the now recovering youth.

Still grasping the crucifix in his hand, he struggled upon his elbow, and holding the cross towards the baron, he cried—

"Woe to Rheinfels! Woe to thee, base-souled noble! With my dying breath I curse thee and thy house for ever! I die, but the saints will avenge me, and on thy head hurl a terrible and speedy doom!"

And, laying the crucifix on his lips, he kissed it and fell back dead!

Bold, bad man that he was, the Baron of Rheinfels shrank beneath these words, and felt a regret at what he had done.

It was but for a moment, however.

Recovering his usual mein, he bade his followers secure the youth and plunder the chapel, and then, with the brave young vinegrower bound hand and foot and flung across the saddle-bow of one of the retainers, he led the way back to the castle.

In the courtyard the dwarf stood ready to hold his master's bridle.

His eyes glistened when he saw the spoil they had secured, and that the baron was uninjured, for he felt for him that affection which could only exist between two such natures.

Dismounting, the baron pointed to the bound youth, whom two of the retainers were lifting from the horse.

"Be he your charge," he said, "and see you guard him well. He has the heart of a lion, though he wears the face of a lamb. The roughest fare, the darkest dungeon, be his portion till I decide his fate."

"He is wounded in the head," said the dwarf.

"'Tis nothing, and has not robbed him of his strength or courage ; so look to him well, or beware my anger."

"My life be forfeit if I fail," said the dwarf.

The baron entered the castle, and the dwarf surrendering the steed to an attendant, walked up to the prisoner, who calmly and defiantly glared upon his captors.

"Unbind his feet, and lead him this way," said Gulf.

The youth uttered not a word, but suffered his feet to be unbound, and guarded on either side and in the rear, followed the dwarf across the courtyard into the castle, down a flight of steps till he paused before the door of a dungeon.

In a cleft of the wall of the passage was stuck a pine torch, whose flame revealed the horrors of the place, as Gulf flung open the door of his prison.

"This is to be your dwelling so long as my lord shall please," said the dwarf. "Enter."

The youth hesitated, and well he might.

From its interior came a damp and noisome smell, and the heart of the youth sickened as he gazed into its gloomy precincts.

"Unbind my arms," he said. "What! do six strong men fear an unarmed and wounded man ?"

"No," said the dwarf ; "for with this hand alone could I crush the life out of your body."

The youth gazed upon that sinewy frame, and brave as he was, felt how help-less he would be in the hands of that powerful dwarf.

Gulf unfastened the lashings from his arms, and suffered them to fall to the floor of the passage.

The moment his arms were free the yonth made a spring to escape, but the hand of the dwarf seized his shoulder, and hurled him back against the wall as though he had been an infant.

The next moment the retainers thrust him into the dungeon, the door was closed upon him, and he, who had that day hoped to clasp a lovely bride in his arms, was a wretched prisoner in a dungeon of Rheinfels.

As the heavy bolts shot into their sockets with a grating sound, all his calmness, even hope itself deserted him, and he flung himself down upon the hard floor, and gave himself up to despair.

Excited at what had transpired, and gratified at having in his power the means which he believed would bring to his arms the lovely Giela—for, since it was impossible that she could have left the castle, he knew she was hidden some-where within the walls—the count divested himself of his armour, and took his seat in the banqueting hall.

Here were assembled all but those who kept guard, and pleased with himself, the baron drank deeply, allowing the same license to his followers ; nor did he rise till the deep draughts of Rhenish wine which he had quaffed had fired his im-petuous blood, and made his eyes sparkle with a fiendish gleam.

Then, beckoning to the dwarf, he strode from the banqueting hall to the great hall where he had borne Giela the night before.

The sun had long sunk behind the mountains, and the full moon was peeping over the towers of the castle, and throwing a thin streak of silver upon the bosom of the Rhine.

The pine torches glowed and crackled in the clefts of the wall, and lit up the hall till not a shadow fell upon its stone floor.

As the baron flung himself into his chair of state, his eye lighted upon something at his feet, and stooping, he raised it from the floor.

It was a silken braid—one that he had seen wound in the tresses of Giela, as she knelt at his feet.

His eye blazed up, and a smile crossed his face.

"She has been here," he said, "Her hiding place cannot be far off. I have the power to call the dove from her nest, and make her flutter on my bosom. Entreaties nor threats prevail, but torture can and will. Go, dwarf, heat the irons till they grow red and bright, and then bring the captive hither. His shrieks of agony shall summon her more quickly to his side than ever did the soft notes of lover's lute call maiden to her wooer's arms."

And, twisting the silken braid around his hand, the baron sank back in his chair, with a grim smile of satisfaction lighting up every feature of his scarred face.

The dwarf hurried from the hall to per-form his bidding.

"Now," cried the baron aloud, "she is mine, and spirit nor fiend will not keep her from me."

A loud, shrieking peal of laughter caused him to spring to his feet, and glare around him.

"She here?" he cried. "But she shall not baulk me of my prey. If I suffer myself to be foiled to-night, may the curse of the priest, and the spectre's warning, be fulfilled this very hour!"

He drew his sword, and shook the glittering blade, while a look of defiance gleamed from his eyes, and he stood prepared to meet whatever might confront him.

Another peal of laughter rang out from the further end of the hall, and then silence reigned in the apartment.

Desperate with rage and wine, the baron awaited the presence of his captive—the youth he resolved to torture, that he might bring the concealed Giela to his feet.

With his eyes rolling wildly, and his bearded face filled with rage and dismay, Gulf bounded into the hall, and fell upon his knees at the feet of the baron.

"My lord!" he cried, "the prisoner has escaped, though no bolt is drawn from his dungeon door."

"Escaped!" thundered the baron, seizing the dwarf by the throat. "Liar! traitor!"

And foaming with rage, he flung the dwarf from him, and struck him in the face with his hand.

The dwarf clenched his fists, and ground his teeth, then dropping his hands to his sides, he bowed his shaggy head before his furious master.

"Liar! traitor!" said Gulf. "My lord baron, if I be a liar or traitor, let this heart be a sheath for your sword.

And the dwarf laid his hand upon his breast, and advanced a step towards the baron.

The baron raised his sword, but lowering its point on the instant, he said—

"No! Every man in Germany may turn against me, but not you, dwarf—not you!"

The dwarf fell upon his knees and clasped the legs of the noble.

"Never, master—never!" he cried looking up in the baron's face. "My life for yours a thousand times, could I give it. Gulf the dwarf a traitor to his lord! Bid him fling himself from the topmost tower upon the jagged rocks, or hurl his body on thy foemen's steel, but brand me not a traitor, for no more faithful slave ever crouched at the feet of his lord and master!"

"Rise, Gulf, and forgive me!" cried the baron. "This is *her* work, but though she summon all the fiends to oppose me, my captives shall not escape! Sound the alarm! Rouse the men to arms! Man tower and battlement! Scour passage and dungeon! Neither man nor fiend shall thwart the will of the Baron of Rheinfels!"

Again that strange wild laugh appeared to come from the side of the hall, and springing to the spot, the enraged baron plunged his sword forward with a desperate lunge, exclaiming—

"Down to thy grave, accursed spirit; I defy thy powers."

His sword's point struck the thick wall, and the blade was shivered to the hilt.

Another peal of laughter, and the baron, goaded almost to madness, fled from the hall, calling aloud upon his retainers, and followed by the dwarf.

While the baron was raging through the passages, calling upon his men to search every spot, three persons stood upon the ramparts, within the deep shadow thrown by the towers.

One, robed in flowing white garments, with a red stain upon the bosom, looked spectral and unearthly in the dim light.

"Fly," she said, "and heed not me. Within the castle are many nooks known only to myself, and the belief that I fell beneath the dagger of the dwarf causes them to look upon me as a being of the other world.

"I have unlocked your dungeon door, but, if it close upon you again, I may be powerless to save you.

"This vine will bear your weight. Descend by it to the rocks; then speed to the river, where you will find a boat upon the bank. Away, lest you share the fate of Hellegunda! Away, ere it is too late!"

"Come, Alphonso—come!" pleaded Giela; "hark to the tramp of armed men and the clash of steel. Save me, Alphonso—save me!"

The youth pressed the hand of Hellegunda, grasped the waist of Giela, and seizing the bine of a huge vine which was secured to the masonry, he threw himself over the ramparts with his burden.

Down—down he went till he reached the rocks below.

Then he was seen from the battlements.

A cry was raised, and the baron sprang upon the ramparts.

One look upon the moonlit rocks beneath, and he turned with a thundering voice, saying—

"To the rocks—to the river, or they will escape! Quick! quick! He who brings them back shall not go unrewarded!"

Then turning again, he saw the vine by which they had descended.

"Ha, ha!" he laughed. "By this I'll reach their side! Fiend or woman, I shall foil you yet!"

Grasping it with both hands, he threw himself over the ramparts, and Hellegunda sprang from the shadow of the walls, a dagger gleaming in her hands.

"Hold, Baron Rheinfels!" she cried, bending over the ramparts; "or your life-blood dyes the rocks yonder!"

The baron looked up.

"Woman or spirit, I defy you!" he cried.

And, suffering the vine to slip through his hands, he decended so quickly that he avoided the blow aimed at his breast, and reached the rocks in safety.

The woman thrust the dagger beneath her robe, and drawing herself up, grasped the vine.

"Never shall another share the fate of Hellegunda!" she cried. "If they cannot escape, I will save them from his persecution!"

In a few moments she reached the rocks, and looking up, saw the figure of the dwarf descending by the way she had come.

Seizing the vine she gave it so violent a shock that Gulf released his hold, and fell heavily at her feet.

The next moment she had sped down the rocks in pursuit of the baron, guided not only by the moonlight, but by the numberless torches that now began to flash from the battlements.

The fugitives had reached the banks of the stream, when a loud terrified cry broke from the lips of Giela, and the baron stood before them.

At their feet rode a small boat, beside them stood the angry baron, behind them reared the walls of his fortress swarming with his armed retainers.

All this the brave Alphonso took in at a glance, and flinging himself upon the count, he strove to hurl him back and gain the boat.

But the loss of blood caused by his wound had so weakened his frame that he was thrown to the earth, and the baron with a shout of joy stretched forth his hands to seize the trembling Giela.

Ere he could grasp the maiden, a flash of light descended before his eyes, and he staggered back, followed by the white robed figure of Hellegunda, and the blood streaming from a wound in his breast.

Back to the edge of the bank he tottered—again there was a flash of light in his eyes, and again the dagger of the woman he had wronged pierced his bosom.

Grasping the hand that held the weapon, he uttered one piercing cry, and fell backwards into the river, carrying with him Hellegunda.

As she sank beneath the surface, she waved her disengaged hand to the fugitives, as though warning them to fly, and springing into the boat, they saw the dwarf hurrying to the bank, while the torches revealed the forms of men descending from the ramparts by the same means as they themselves had escaped.

To cast the boat loose was the work of a moment, and as it floated out into the stream, the dwarf sprang to the bank.

"Master—master!" he shrieked, "I will save you, or perish with you!"

The next moment he sprang from the bank into the river, and with loud shouts several of the retainers hurried down the rocks.

As the dwarf rose to the surface, so also, right before him rose the spectral figure of Hellegunda, the moonlight playing full upon her white marble features and lighting them up with a ghastly hue.

A scream, such as a strong man might utter when finding himself in the paws of a tiger, broke from the lips of the dwarf, and he turned to flee to the shore, but again the hand of Hellegunda was raised, still grasping the dagger.

It flashed in the moonlight—there was a shriek that was echoed back from the rocks, and the dwarf sank like a stone into the bosom of the Rhine.

"Woe to Rheinfels—woe to Rheinfels!" cried the voice of Hellegunda, and then slowly the marble face sank beneath the moonlit waters, and on their surface alone was seen the boat containing the lovers drifting quickly down the silvery tide.

Not one of those rude men, who now swarmed upon its banks, offered to molest or follow the fugitives. Awe-bound they stood glaring upon the spot where the white form had disappeared, and terrified by the words she had uttered ere the waters had closed over it for ever.

The lovers escaped, and were wedded in the little chapel at St. Goar.

The bodies of the Lord of Rheinfels and his faithful follower were found, but that of Hellegunda was never discovered, but there are those who yet assert that, when the moon shines brightly on the waters of the Rhine, a spectral form rises from out them, opposite the ruins of the castle, and that its voice is heard in the stillness of the night, crying.—"Woe to Rheinfels!"

THE END OF THE SPECTRE OF RHEINFELS.

THE BANDIT'S BRIDE.

AMONG the many castles and ruins which stud the Rhine banks, and beneath which flow its rich waters, teeming with riches in the way of trout and salmon, while the shores are glorious from vines and other produce, no one has more singular legends in connection with its walls than that of Rodenstein.

Its history would fill volumes, but one legend will suffice.

The Barons of Rodenstein were usually regarded as a wild and savage race, never pausing at any deed which enabled them to win power or wealth, while their dungeons were popularly believed to have contained more victims that was usual, even with men whose honour was a name, whose virtue was a pretence, and whose chivalry was of the character which entirely ignores the rights of *meum* and *tuum*.

It was with surprise therefore that the people who dwelt around and about the castle discovered at last that they owned a lord satisfied with his lawful possessions, and happy in the society of a beautiful wife and child.

But it is often stated, with some show of authority, that people are never satisfied.

The Baron Roger, who was so gentle, so true to his own self and subjects, was soon made a jest of as effeminate, and many were found to sneer and jeer at him who ought to have known better.

True it was that the robbers of the neighbourhood took heart of grace under this mild rule and commenced to extend their depredations. But if Roger of Rodenstein was a mild and beneficent ruler, he was a brave man.

Summoning his vassals and men-at-arms to his assistance, he made a rapid incursion into the forest, and not only severely punished the robbers, but for the time being quite despersed their gangs.

After this he was immensely popular, and lived for a short time in peace.

But he was blinded by his own placid nature, and not believing in certain hints which reached him of danger, one day found himself surprised by the Black Band of Sigismund de Hetzell, and his castle captured and pillaged.

Not satisfied with this retaliation, during the assault the brave baron was slain with his wife, and their babe, the only one left, hurled by the savage robbers over the battlements.

Then, and then only, the robbers retired.

Rodenstein soon found a new master in the person of Randolph, cousin to the late lord, who appeared at the end of four months to claim his succession.

He was a young man of sombre character and repulsive mien.

Immediately on taking possession he gave a grand festival, to which were invited many who six months before would not have been allowed to enter within the castle gates.

Among the guests were the monk Ambrose, the head of a neighbouring monastery, several of his most jovial crew, certain wild soldiers, and no less a personage than Sigismund of Hetzell, the robber chief of the forest.

The presence of this man in the towers of the knight murdered by his own gang gave rise to many remarks, which, however, were spoken under the breath of all.

One thing, however, was certain.

He was by far the most jovial of the crew and out did even the monk in his merry tales. As to the drinking on this occasion, no one ventured to count up the number of wine flasks, which, according to the facetious saying of King Eustache, yielded up the spirit on this occasion.

The wild orgies lasted about four days, when a sudden summons compelled the priest and his party to leave, upon which the robber chief offered to escort him on his way.

As the good priest had to pass through the well-known haunts of the bandit the offer was one too good to be refused.

As the ride was a long one, and only one halt in an old town was possible, they started early in the evening.

The night was fair when they started, and the party, who had supped ere they departed, were merry in the extreme.

One of the monks was a jovial storyteller, and amused his friends and the robbers by his singular stories of adventure.

They reached the town, which they had to pass through, about eight, and truly a dismal and wretched place it was, that part of it which they crossed being a collection of narrow lanes and miserable huts, with a poisonous atmosphere reeking over a lazy and filthy stream.

The monk in a low voice pointed out such spots as Hole of the Accursed, Jews' Street, Cutthroat Cross, Rogue's Alley, and such like localities.

Wretched huts were crammed with a vicious population, spending their wretched evenings in the lowest debauchery.

Hastening out of this Heaven-forsaken place, the whole party again made for the wood, the garrulous monk leading the way.

Suddenly, as they entered upon a road between two rows of tall trees, he gave a cry, and before any one could assist him, he was pitched over his horse's head into the middle of the road.

"Heaven have mercy upon me," he said, "a light, a light!"

A torch was soon procured, and several waving in the air, it was found that the mule he rode had stumbled over the body of a woman, a dark and swarthy Bohemian, whom they all at once saw had been murdered—doubtless by some of the uncanny inhabitants of the vile districts they had just passed through.

But lying unconscious and yet alive beside the corpse was a child, fair and lovely, and at a glance easily distinguishable from the dusky daughter of an evil race.

"The wretch has stolen a Christian child to rear it to the imps of darkness," said the priest, lifting the babe in his arms. "It lives; Heaven has sent us this way to save it. Here, Clopect," addressing a portly serving-man who had a sumpter mule with a large basket on each side him, "put the child amongst your provender. And now forward for there is a storm."

"Aye," and a heavy one," grunted the robber chief with a laugh, "an' you haste not you will be wet to the skin."

The fat and jovial monks, who knew more of good cheer than of rough weather, shuddered, nor were they at all reassured by the fierce and vivid flashes of lightning which began to play in the heavens.

All pressed forward, while none spoke save Clopect, who under his teeth swore at the increased load placed upon his sumpter mule.

But uselessly, as he dare not disobey his master.

And still the lightning flashed and the wind howled through the trees as they advanced.

Soon heavy rain drops began to fall, and still further urged the party forward.

Suddenly they came upon a thick mass of trees, so close together as apparently to be impenetrable.

But here the robber chief interposed his authority.

"Follow me—one by one. It is of no use being in a hurry, as I must go slowly."

As he spoke, he passed between two tall upright trees and disappeared.

The rest following his example, found themselves in a narrow path where only one rider could pass.

At the end of half an hour, they reached an open space, on the other side of which was a large cavern, within which the whole party were able to take shelter from the storm, now becoming fearful in its intensity.

But the hollow in the mountain side was vast, and when lit up by torches and fires, for which there was ample material, was no bad resting-place out of the terrible combat of the elements, which increased in fury and violence every moment.

"'Tis seldom visited," said the robber chief, dryly, "except by some personal friends of mine, who, in case of accident, leave certain provisions and creature comforts behind."

After which exordium none were surprised to have wine, bread, and pasties placed before them in great abundance, by some stern-looking men who appeared as if by magic, from recesses in the rocks.

The babe, which was apparently over a year old, and a girl, was placed on a bed of straw, where, to the surprise of all, it was presently tended and fed by a handsome boy of six, whom the robber chief patted affectionately on the head.

"Few who knew the history of this spot," continued the robber chief, "would venture here. They would prefer the open wood with all its dangers."

"But why?"

"'Tis said that at certain times the demons come here and hold festival, and their comrades are all the dead felons that have suffered on gibbets, all the Jews and other miscreants who have died within the year. Know you not that here once stood a strong and massive castle, inhabited once upon a time by the Baron of Irnandre, whose mother sold him to Satan at his birth? He adored the father of evil, and committed most awful crimes out of love for his false diety. This cavern has re-echoed with the shrieks of unhappy maidens, of babes stolen for unholy purposes, of priests condemned to die of starvation, and to deny Heaven."

Every priest crossed himself with holy horror, while some looked as if they too would have preferred the terrors of the forest

"At last his crimes having excited the heavenly wrath, the castle and all within it were destroyed during a fearful thunderstorm, such as we never witness. But the evil did not cease here. The disembodied spirits, the ghostly apparitions of the wicked were so terrible as to drive all people away from the neighbourhood. One of the few who escaped, and who knew where the treasures were concealed, after wasting all his substance in rioting, and feeling his end approaching, begged and prayed the then bishop to exorcise the multitude of the dead and send their souls to peace. But on hearing that before making this demand he had spent all his money," grimly observed the bandit, "the bishop refused, and hence we know not when we may again be visited by these ghostly horrors."

Silence followed.

The fact was all were getting weary and sleepy.

"THE CLOTH WAS RAISED, AND DISCLOSED THE EMPEROR SURROUNDED BY A BRILLIANT COURT."

It was nearly morning, and despite the thunder and lightning, the wind and the rain, the feeling had not once ceased.

In half an hour all slept, nor woke until late the next day, when a splendid sky, a bright and cheery sun greeted them pleasantly and drove away the horrible nightmare of the previous day.

Here the robber and his guests parted.

Sigismund de Hetzel had never assaulted the church, and more, whatever his secret motive, held it in high esteem.

The babe was taken away with great difficulty from the boy, who, however, was promised that he should see it whenever he liked.

The canon who had taken the babe was a man of rank and prestige, so that though he was superior of a monastery, he had a house outside the city of Cambray, where he resided with a large retinue and household, governed by a pious niece who at once took charge of the babe, which the priest refused to send to a poorhouse, slightly to the scandal of that censorious age.

He was rewarded, for when the girl reached seventeen years of age and he was a bishop, she was the prop and joy of his house.

But in the meantime, many events had occurred.

The completion of this Story will be found on pages 93 to 96 of our next Number,
which will contain also the complete story of
"*THE PHANTOM BELL.*"

With this Number is Presented a SPLENDID COLOURED PICTURE.

THE BARONS OF OLD OR THE ROBBERS OF THE RHINE

THE PHANTOM BELL.

ON the right bank of the Rhine is situated the old and picturesque village of Welmich.

Above this village rises a high steep mountain of lava, and upon this huge volcanic mound towers one of the most perfect castles on the Rhine.

This feudal fortress is perhaps one of

"'IS FALKENSTEIN BUT A COWARD?' SAID THE DARK STRANGER."

the most difficult of access of any of those numerous strongholds built by the barons of old, the way to it being almost perpendicular, and its position on the summit of the steep mount rendering it almost impregnable to assault.

This noble ruin is the Castle of Thurnberg, commonly called the "Mouse."

It is asserted that the reason of its gaining this appellation was that in the twelfth century, the borough which occupied the site of this fortress was often molested by a strong castle called the "Cat," and that to put an end to a state of things that were becoming unbearable, the owner of this borough razed it to the ground and built a castle much larger and stronger than the neighbouring one, declaring that from that time forth the "Mouse" should devour the "Cat."

So the "Mouse" became the general term applied to this stupendous castle, and the mountain on whose high summit it stands is doubtless the only one that ever brought forth a mouse of such noble proportions.

The round tower, though partially dismantled, is of great height.

On all sides the walls are immense, but the windows are shattered and the roofs have fallen.

It contains many subterranean passages and caves now wholly or partially filled up.

The round tower is an immense pit, which descends far below the level of the river, and is a spot filled with awe to the rude peasantry.

Among the ignorant denizens of that part of the country the tower abounds with spectres, and lurid flames, which, though hidden by the light of day, play around the summit of the tower after nightfall, while from it shrieks and groans are believed to issue as from lost souls in agony and despair.

Few castles on the yellow river possess a greater charm for the traveller or terrors for the ignorant peasantry, and few indeed whose legends are so many or so terrible, and from among them we select the following :—

Baron Falkenstein was a bold, bad man, who refused to believe in the existence of a God, and who set alike both human and divine laws at defiance.

The honest trader, the marauding baron, the priest and the peasant he robbed alike with impunity, and, if the humour was on him, did not hesitate to murder as well as steal.

Sec c in his mountain fastness, and in the strength and bravery of his vassals, he laughed to scorn all the powers that from time to time were brought against him.

Time only rendered him more implacable and cold-blooded, and so increased his crimes and his cruelties that it began to be believed that Falkenstein either was in league with the devil or was the very devil himself, and brave men, eager to rise against such a tyrannical monster, hesitated and trembled to oppose him.

The nature of Falkenstein was not likely to permit him to forget a real or fancied injury.

Ere the walls of his fortress had frowned from the heights of the lava mountain, his property had often been assailed by the bold lords of Die Katze, and now that his strength was greater than theirs he set about avenging himself for the injuries he had in times gone by received at their hands.

Falkenstein having decided upon a plan of action was not long in putting it into execution.

To the surprise and terror of the Count Edrec he perceived the forces of the Lord of the "Mouse" drawn up one fine morning before the frowning walls of the "Cat," and soon after received the summons of Falkenstein to surrender his fortress and himself into his hands.

Count Edrec was a brave man, and though he was quite certain that the "Cat" was no match for the "Mouse," and that it was only a work of time for Falkenstein to reduce his stronghold and put its defenders to the sword, he buckled on his armour and resolved to sell his life and possessions dearly.

So closely had Falkenstein invested the castle during the hours of darkness that Count Edrec found not only every means of escape closed but all hope of sending for succour entirely cut off.

This rendered Count Edrec somewhat anxious for the safety of his daughter, a lovely virgin of eighteen, who was installed within the castle.

However there was no help for it.

The count must either surrender or fight to the last.

The latter course he chose, as he had little faith in the honour or mercy of Falkenstein.

The fight was fierce and sanguinary, but the claws of the "Cat" were soon rendered powerless to inflict further harm, and the assailants swarmed on the battlements and through the halls, leaving a red track of blood in their paths, and howling their cries of victory.

It was not till many a stalwart vassal of Falkenstein had fallen beneath the double-edged sword of the gallant Count Edrec, that the brave knight fell, covered with wounds, across the threshold of the apartment where his daughter Imragina listened in horror to the clash of arms, and prayed for her parent's safety.

As she flung herself across the body of her dying sire, the bold, bad Baron Falkenstein paused before her, and as he leaned upon his gory sword, gazed enchanted upon the angel face and lovely form of the beauteous daughter of Count Edrec.

"'Twere sin indeed to slay one so lovely," he muttered. "The eagle shall bear this dove to his mountain eyrie, and teach her there how to owe obedience to the Lord Falkenstein."

Even while these thoughts flashed through the mind of the baron the brave Count Edrec's soul took its flight, and his lively daughter swooned upon his pulseless bosom. Falkenstein threw down his shield upon the stone floor, and placing his reeking sword beside it, raised the insensible Imragina in his arms.

"By the yellow sands of the mighty Rhine, thou art a prize worthy an emperor," he muttered, as he looked into the white face of the scarcely breathing girl.

"An I had known the count possessed a child of such rare beauty the sword of Falkenstein had not rested so long in its scabbard. No matter, my ancient foe lies powerless to ever wield steel more; and the 'Mouse' has not only conquered the 'Cat,' but possessed himself of its kitten, and he'll hold her more securely than ever cat held mouse yet."

He spurned the dead body of Edrec with his foot, and strode across the hall with his still senseless burthen.

His followers flocked around him.

"Spare none, but those who will swear allegiance to the Baron Falkenstein," he said, "all else put to the sword, and then bear what treasures are within these walls to my castle. Ho, there, Osric! follow me with my sword and shield."

The youth he addressed bounded forward, secured the sword and shield of Falkenstein, and silently followed him from the castle.

That night Imragina sobbed and wrung her hands in the castle of Thurnberg, and the only answer to her cries and lamentations, was the heavy footfall of the sentinel in the stone passages without.

She was a prisoner in the castle of the "Mouse"—a captive of the cruel and merciless Falkenstein.

And what was to be her fate?

This question she asked herself several times, and it was answered at length.

The fastenings of her prison were removed, and the Baron Falkenstein entered the apartment.

Flushed with wine and victory, his eyes sparkled with a fiendish light.

He approached Imragina, who retreated as he advanced, to the further end of the apartment.

"Wherefore do you fly me?" he asked. "Times were when the 'Cat' sprang at the 'Mouse;' now it trembles before it. Nay, be not so coy. Though you are my captive, Falkenstein admires beauty too much to destroy it. Give me thy hand."

"Hence! touch me not, my lord. The blood of my father stains your soul, and the heart of his child abhors his murderer!"

"Nay, lady, this hand is guiltless of the count's death, though my heart panted to bury my sword to its hilt in his bosom. We have long been foes, and Falkenstein but availed himself of the opportunity to avenge many a blow dealt at him by the sire you owned. Men who live by the sword must expect to fall by the sword, and in making captive of thyself I but follow the law which guides men of my stamp, and if I put you not to death, it is only your beauty that fights so bravely for you, and places at your feet the Baron Falkenstein, who never bent knee before."

And the baron sunk on one knee before her, and seized her hand.

Imragina strove to tear her hand away.

But the grasp on her fingers tightened till she fain would have screamed with pain.

By an effort she suppressed the cry, and fixed an indignant look upon the upturned face of the baron.

"Would I had the strength to wield my father's sword!" she cried, boldly. "This hand should pierce your heart."

"Your eyes have done that," he said, "and now that, added to your beauty, I see you possess a soul as undaunted as my own, my love burns with a fiercer flame, and I would make thee Baroness Falkenstein, though all the world stood arrayed against me."

He sprang to his feet and flinging his arm round her waist, drew her quickly to his bosom.

With a strength which in one so frail and lovely seemed almost superhuman, Imragina thrust him from her, and with clenched hand stood confronting the surprised and angry baron.

"I Baroness Falkenstein!" she cried,

"I thy wife! By the soul of my father, I had rather be the bride of Satan than thine. I may be thy captive, proud baron, but not all the powers on earth can make me thy wife."

Terrible was the look that beamed in the eyes of Falkenstein.

Fearful was the expression of his rage-convulsed face.

His fingers closed like a vice on the hilt of his sword.

His teeth grated together, and he stamped upon the stone floor, in maddening rage.

"By the blood and bones of my ancestors," he thundered, "my own will alone shall bring you to my arms. I who could strike you dead at my feet, spare, honour, love you, and you defy me—me, Baron of Falkenstein!"

And, with a clang, he drew his sword, and half raised the glittering blade.

"Strike!" cried Imragina, presenting her bosom to the blow. "Strike! God will avenge me!"

A loud scornful laugh broke from the baron's lips.

"Let women and cowards prate of unseen powers. I despise and defy them. The only law I obey is my own will, and to that will I will bend thee, proud Imragina, though every baron in Germany buckled on his mail in your defence. Here, within my castle, on this volcanic rock, I defy all who would dare assail me, and here you shall bend and acknowledge me thy husband and thy lord, ere to-morrow's sinking sun shall redden the yellow waters of the Rhine."

He turned, strode to the door, paused with his hand upon it, and fixed his eagle glance upon Imragina.

The girl, pale, but defiant, stood in the centre of the apartment, the torch burning in a cleft of the wall throwing a red glare on her face.

"I have spoken," he said, "and that which Falkenstein resolves must and shall be. No words—I'll hear them not. Be ready, then, when I shall come hither again. There is no escape for you. Willing or not, to-morrow you become the bride of the baron of Falkenstein."

He fixed a look of undying resolve upon her, and then flinging open the door, sprang over the threshold into the passage beyond, and closed it behind him with a loud clang.

For several moments Imragina stood glaring upon the door through which he had passed, and then, aroused by the footfall of the sentry without, she started, shook her clenched hands in the air and shrieked aloud—

"Baron Falkenstein, you lie! By the power above I would rather die a thousand deaths, which fiends alone could invent, than become thy bride!"

She strode furiously across the floor, her majestic figure drawn proudly up, her eyes flashing, her hands clenched, and her whole form trembling with passion.

"I am but a woman," she cried, pausing beneath the window, and looking up at it. "My puny strength hurled against these massive walls would be but as a summer wave breaking upon a rock-bound shore. If I cannot escape these walls, I can die within them—perish at the feet of him whom I am powerless to destroy."

She continued to wander her prison up and down, till casting her eyes up, she perceived through the window a bright star twinkling in the blue sky beyond.

For some time she stood watching it, and as she looked a feeling of hope took possession of her soul.

She fell upon her knees.

Every trace of passion vanished, and an expression of the greatest humility took possession of her features.

Clasping her hands, she extended them towards the star.

"Save me," she cried, "from this unbeliever—from this merciless knight—restore me to freedom, and I vow to devote the remainder of my life to the church."

She still continued kneeling, her wan, meek, blue eyes fixed upon the bright star, when a draught of cold air played upon her neck and shoulders, the ringing of a musical bell sounded in her ears, and turning her head, she beheld the door of her prison standing wide open.

Springing up, she approached the door, and looked into the passage beyond.

Beside the open door stood the sentinel, leaning upon his spear, with his eyes fixed on the ground.

All was silent save the ringing of the bell, the tones of which came from the base of the mountain, and floated up through loophole and doorway, and filled the castle with its musical sound.

The sentry moved not, spoke not, but stood as though suddenly turned to stone.

Imragina stretched forth her hand and touched him.

As well might she have touched the stones of which the castle was formed—they were alike immoveable.

She spoke to him.

He replied not either by look, word, or gesture.

She took the torch from the cleft in the wall, and held it so that its rays fell full upon his face.

Not a muscle moved.

Could he be dead!

No; the brightness was still in his eyes, the hue of health upon his cheek, the flesh warm, but animation was utterly suspended, and every faculty for the time slumbered.

What could it mean?

The tones of the bell, swelling up louder and louder, alone replied to the question she had asked herself aloud.

Taking the spear from the unresisting hand of the sentry, and holding the torch high above her head with the other, Imragina passed along the passage.

At the end of this passage another door stood open, and beside it a sentry, as motionless as if turned to stone.

Through this door she passed, descended a narrow stairway, at the bottom of which was yet another open door and an immoveable sentinel, and found herself in the large banqueting hall of the castle.

At the table at the further end of the hall sat the Baron Falkenstein, with several knights and his officers, and on either side of the tables, which ran lengthways down the hall, sat down some hundred and twenty retainers.

Torches blazed from the walls, and lit up the scene.

A deathlike silence reigned throughout the hall.

Not a sound reached the ears of Imragina, save the ringing of the bell.

Falkenstein sat with a goblet of wine in his hand, which he had raised half-way to his lips.

The knights and retainers each remained in the attitude in which they were when the strange spell fell upon them.

For a few moments Imragina paused in wonder and dismay, then as if warned by the tones of the bell, she moved slowly along the hall.

Between the rows of men she strode, but not a head was raised, not a word was spoken.

She paused before the table at which Falkenstein sat, but not a motion did he make, not an eyelid quivered.

He, like all the rest, was utterly dead to her presence.

Again she moved on.

Not an eye followed her, not a hand was raised to stay her—not a voice broke the terrible silence.

A door at the far end of the hall stood open; she passed through it.

A flight of steps lay beyond.

She descended these, and found herself in a low vaulted passage.

By the light of the torch she carried she continued her way, and from its gradual decline she was not slow to perceive that she was in one of those subterranean passages beneath the castle.

Still the tones of the bell rang in her ears, and guided and lured her on by its sound.

For some time she continued to walk on, till at last a gust of cold air extinguished her torch, and she was in utter darkness.

For a moment she paused, but looking up she perceived the stars glimmering, and discovered that she had reached the mouth of the subterranean passage.

She sprang forward with a cry of joy, turned and looked back.

High above were the walls and towers of the castle; the faint light of the crescent moon falling upon its masonry, and bathing mountain and stronghold in a soft, white, spectral light.

Turning she gazed down upon the priory at the base of the mountain, in the steeple of which was a silver bell, presented years and years before by Winfred, Bishop of Mayence, and which was imbued with supernatural powers.

It was the tones of this bell that had floated into the castle, and now rung out over mountain and valley.

Beyond the priory lay the Rhine, crowded with mountains, on which frowned many a robber's stronghold, and above all rode the young moon and the bright stars in the clear night-sky.

The first thought of Imragina was unbounded thankfulness for her escape from the castle above her; the next the vow she had made when on her knees she gazed through her prison window at the star in the sky.

Her deliverance she felt sure had been brought about by that vow, and though now that she once more breathed the pure free air of heaven, and felt herself, to a certain extent, beyond the power of Falkenstein, she did not feel quite so reconciled to a life within the cloisters, still she had no intention of violating the promise she had made.

And as if to keep her well in mind of that promise the bell rung louder and louder.

Supporting her footsteps down the steep path by the aid of the sentinel's spear, she slowly moved towards the priory of Welmich, from which now arose the voices of the choristers, and their hymns of praise mingled with the sound of the bell.

The excitement under which Imragina had been labouring now somewhat abated, and she thought calmly over all that had transpired, and shed bitter tears for her father's fate.

Then came the recollection of a circumstance to her mind, which made her regret the hasty vow she had taken.

It was that the son of a neighbouring baron, a brave, handsome, intrepid youth of twenty, had, some short time before, defended her from a small band of wood robbers, and had won her heart by his noble bearing and chivalrous conduct; but the youth's father being at enmity with Count Edrec, she had not dared avow her passion to her parent.

But for this affection, now that her father was no more, she could have entered the priory without a single pang at parting with the world.

But the die was cast—the vow was registered—and however painful, it must be fulfilled.

And so she hurried her footsteps, and sped on down the mountain, and stood before the portals of the priory.

The prioress received her with open arms, and the sisterhood embraced and welcomed her affectionately; and, as the portals of the sacred edifice swung to behind her, the silver bell ceased to ring, and the spell that had fallen upon every soul in the castle was removed, and every open door silently closed.

Falkenstein uttered the half-spoken word that had died upon his lips, and raised the goblet to them.

The knights continued their jest, the retainers their conversation.

The sentries in passage and staircase continued their walk, and none knew that sense and power had been taken away from them by the tones of the bell, even for a single moment.

The man who guarded the door of the chamber in which Imragina had been confined, suddenly perceived that his spear was gone, and looked round in wonder and dismay, firmly believing that some spirit of the mountain had deprived him of it, and half feared to glance along the dim passage, lest his eyes should encounter some denizen of the other world.

When relieved of his post, he kept his own counsel, lest the circumstance should reach the ears of Falkenstein, whom he knew feared neither man nor fiend himself.

The night passed away, and the sunlight streamed into the windows of turret and hall, glinted along the pavements, and sparkled on the armour of knight and vassal, and upon the arms that hung upon the walls.

Baron Falkenstein, being himself an unbeliever in a divine power, was quite prepared to dispense with any priestly rite, but he felt that he must submit to some ceremony to force Imragina to become his wife.

Having made up his mind that she should espouse him whether she liked or not, Falkenstein despatched a messenger to the priory, and commanded the prior to appear before him forthwith, promising to bestow a guerdon on him if he came willingly, and threatening to descend on the sacred edifice if he did not.

Having chosen the youth Osric as his messenger, and despatched him on the errand down the mountain, Falkenstein visited the prison of Imragina to prepare her for her fate.

To his surprise the chamber was empty.

Falkenstein looked up at the window, down at the floor, round at the walls, and finally out of the doorway, and then springing forward with the howl of a tiger, he seized the sentry and flung him into the apartment, nearly breaking his back against the wall, and sent his spear flying out of his hand across the room.

"Where is she?" thundered Falkenstein, drawing his sword and holding its point close to the bewildered and terrified man's throat. "Speak, or by the blood of my ancestors I will bury my sword in your heart, and fling your carcase down the mountain!"

"My lord, my lord!" shrieked the man, retreating before the angry baron.

"Speak, speak!" cried Falkenstein, "whither has she flown—where has she gone—who has aided her to escape from hence?"

"My lord, I knew not that your prisoner was not here," replied the man. "I swear the door has not been opened since I have stood sentry before it. I swear it on the cross."

"Bah!" cried the baron. "Tell me when she fled and whither she is hidden, or your mangled corpse shall lie at the base of the mountain for the birds and beasts to feed on."

"My lord," pleaded the man, "I am not the only one who has been sentry here since last night, and if I had been it were impossible I could open the door, since you alone possess the key."

The baron started and lowered the point of his sword.

What the man had spoken was true.

He had possessed the key, and there was not a duplicate one in the castle, or, indeed, in existence.

Falkenstein grew more and more surprised.

He himself had secured the door on the previous night, and had unfastened it now.

He examined the window carefully.

It was too high to be reached, and even if reached it was too small to afford egress or ingress to any person.

The walls were solid on all sides ; the flooring was the same.

Indeed, there was but one way of leaving the chamber, and that was by the door, and that he himself had locked, and retained the key on his own person.

The more the baron wondered the more confused and bewildered he became, and then, utterly unable to divine by what means Imragina had escaped from the room, he turned furiously upon the sentinel, and demanded that he should explain what he himself was powerless to understand.

Of course this was impossible, and foaming with rage, and smarting with disappointment, Falkenstein struck the man a heavy blow on the cheek with the flat of his sword, and sprang from the apartment to order every portion of the castle to be searched from the top of the highest tower to the bottom of the lowest dungeon.

In this search he himself assisted, foaming and chafing, and vowing revenge.

Not a spot but had been visited, yet still no trace of Imragina, and Falkenstein sat down to wonder and think how she could have eluded him, when not a door had been opened, not a sentry had been passed, and all access to or from the castle had been cut off by the drawbridge being up and the portcullis down, and a good look out kept from watch tower and rampart.

Osric returned in due time from his errand, bearing with him the spear of the sentinel, which he had found close to the portals of the priory, and also the astounding information that Imragina, daughter of Count Edrec, had the night before entered the priory, determined never more to look upon the outer world.

He furthermore brought in reply from the prior that, as the baron could but require his presence for one object, and that object being defeated by the escape of Imragina from his power, he should not come, and he advised the baron to mend his ways, and pray for the salvation of his soul.

Falkenstein listened with feelings of mingled surprise and rage, and when Osric had done, he sprang to his feet and thundered out—

"Summon every man in the castle, knight and vassal, to appear before me here, armed and harnessed. Give me that spear, Osric, and, by the blood of my ancestors, he who stands before me without his spear, I bury

this weapon in his heart, for it is he who has proved a traitor and aided my captive to escape. Away, and do my bidding."

Osric sped from the hall, and Falkenstein paced the hall with quick and furious step.

"I will tear her from her refuge," he hissed through his clenched teeth. "Let fools and believers tremble to invade the sanctuary, I am none of these, and would as mercilessly slay priest and nun at the altar as I would wet my sword in the blood of my foe. The church shall be no refuge for her, though to tear her from it I have to hurl every stone of the edifice into the waters of the Rhine."

In obedience to his command, every man in the castle, knight and vassal, assembled in the hall, till not one remained on tower or rampart.

They ranged themselves around, each clad in his mail, each bearing his arms, each eager to learn the cause of the summons.

Sternly Falkenstein walked along their ranks, eyeing every man minutely ; then, suddenly drawing himself back a pace, he poised the spear he held in his hand, and with all his powerful strength, buried its sharp point in the body of the only man who appeared in that hall bereft of the weapon.

It was the ill-fated sentry of the night before.

Uttering a loud shriek, the man fell dead at the feet of Falkenstein, who, placing his foot on the neck of the still quivering corpse, looked around upon the surprised throng, and with a fiendish gleam of triumph in his eye, cried—

"This is the traitor who assisted my captive to escape ! This spear, borne by him last night, was found at the very portals of the place in which she has taken refuge, and with it have I stilled his traitor heart !"

He tore the weapon from the wound, and held it up to the gaze of all.

"By the blood that stains it, I swear, so shall perish every traitor to Baron Falkenstein !" he cried, hoarsely. "And now, bear hence the body, and hurl it into the pit of the round tower ; and then, knights and vassals, prepare to follow me to the Priory of Welmich, where I go to demand my captive at the hands of these priests, or float its altars in the blood of its defenders !"

He waved his hand.

Four of the retainers stepped forward and raised the bleeding body, which they bore silently from the hall.

The knights and men-at-arms filed slowly

out of the large apartment, and Osric alone remained with his master.

"Osric," said Falkenstein, after a long pause, "how could the caitiff, whom I've laid dead at my feet but now, have aided Imragina to leave the castle? There are no duplicate keys, the portcullis has not been raised nor the drawbridge lowered, and all egress was cut off by the subterranean passages, for no hand but my own could have opened the way through them. You have a clear head, Osric; think for me, and tell me how this has all been done."

Osric shook his head.

"My lord," he said, "it can only have been done by a miracle."

Falkenstein frowned.

"A miracle, and by whom performed?" he asked, pettishly.

"By God, the saints, or those deputed by them."

"Out on you, for a drivelling fool," thundered Falkenstein. "I am not the man to be frightened by the terrors or powers of one whose existence I deny. Go, bring me my armour, for the sun shall not set to night ere I possess my bride or yon priory lies a heap of smoking ruins."

Osric turned upon his heel; for well he knew it was useless to seek to argue with, or convince the baron.

He shortly returned with the baron's mail, assisted to place the armour upon

THE CASTLE OF THURNBERG.

him, and then stood back in silence, bearing his lance and shield.

"And you, Osric," said Falkenstein, fixing his eyes upon the youth, while a contemptuous smile curled his lips. "You, who bid so fair to become a brave knight, and carve by feat of arms a name upon the scroll of history, can tremble at this priest-craft and the unseen power they profess to worship. Thus knaves make fools their dupes. Away with all such fancies and terrors; I defy all the powers these sons of the church will pretend they can raise against me, and he who trembles at their words or deeds is unworthy to be a follower of the Baron Falkenstein."

And he strode from the hall, followed by Osric.

The notes of the bugle horn rallied his men around him, the portcullis was raised, the drawbridge lowered, and placing himself at the head of his force, Falkenstein went forth from his stronghold, and led the way down the mountain.

The sunlight sparkled on his armour, the mountain breeze fanned his fevered cheek, and toyed with the graceful plume in his helmet.

The birds carolled overhead, the torrent roared beneath them, and the priory lay basking in the sunlight, with silence reigning supreme throughout its cloisters.

The completion of this Story will be found on pages 103 to 106 of our next Number.

[Continued from Page 80.]

THE BANDIT'S BRIDE.

FROM the memorable night in the cavern, the boy who had been so kind to the babe, and whose name was Harold Hertzell, had been a pupil of the good bishop, who wished to separate him wholly from his bad surroundings.

No difficulty was made on the part of the bandit chief, and at twenty-three the quondam young robber was a young soldier of fortune, in the service of the Emperor of Germany.

He and the girl Lina had been at first educated together, and had remained friends.

It will not surprise the reader, therefore, to know that they were secretly affianced. Lina, about whom the good people generally knew nothing, as a protégé of the bishop, was considered deserving of recognition, and mixed in very good society.

She was patronised by burghers and their wives, and had penetrated into very wealthy families in Cambray.

Here she met with many suitors, the more as the bishop mentioned a certain sum which he should give her on her marriage.

This was the state of affairs when Harold Hertzell, fearful of rivalry, divulged his state of feelings to his patron the bishop.

The priest, much amazed, and yet not angry, asked some days to consider; and as Harold was going to the emperor's headquarters shortly, decided to give him an answer on his return.

That evening, when the good bishop had eaten his evening meal, and was in that state of beatitude which a good conscience allows a man to possess after eating, a stranger was announced. He was a pilgrim from the Holy Land, and was at once admitted.

He was to all appearance an aged man, his cowl not concealing the long, straggling white hair, nor the haggard, wan and wrinkled face. He bowed low with profound humility.

"What can I do for you?" asked the bishop.

"You have a girl in your household named Lina," he asked; "send for her to hear the last words of a dying man; hasten, or it will be too late."

Astonished as he was, the bishop still obeyed, and the girl was summoned. She came in, looking so bright, beautiful, and happy, that it was painful to see the change on her face as she met the sinister eyes of the pilgrim fixed upon her.

"Lady," he said, bowing low, "you have a mark—a kind of star on your right side; you have a mole on the back of your neck?"

"I have," she faltered.

"Have you, reverend sir, any jewel found on her neck when a babe—a bauble?"

The astonished bishop opened a secret drawer of his table and brought out a string of wooden beads with a small silver cross.

"Merciful Heavens, I thank you," cried the pilgrim, falling on his knees to the girl. "Baroness of Rodenstein, Countess and Suzeraine of Cambray, Hereditary Canoness of Zalfell, let me be the first to acknowledge your rank and state. Accept my homage, and my congratulations."

To describe the astonishment and amazement of the bishop and his adopted child would require the junction of pen and pencil.

"Strange, weird man, who and what are you?" said the former, recovering himself.

"The Baron of Rodenstein, the usurper of his brother's rights," said the pilgrim, throwing off his sacred robes, and standing before them in a heavy suit of rusty armour. "Never since the fatal night on which my brother was slain, not by my hand, but by my orders, and my niece given over to the mercy of a gipsy woman, who was murdered for the money which I gave her, have I known peace. I tried, as you know, revel and wassail in vain. Thrown nearly upon a supposed deathbed, I tried a pilgrimage to the Holy Land, and found no rest. At last I came home to lay my weary bones in my native earth, and heard from Sigismund Hertzell, the robber chief, that my niece lived. I hastened here to make restitution. Child, do you forgive me? Priest, will you give me absolution?"

Lina, Baroness Rodenstein, Countess of Cambray, and Canoness, was too bewildered to speak.

The bishop himself was quite off his equanimity. After a moment's reflection, however, he requested the stricken man to accept his hospitality.

In the morning they would speak.

"As you will, holy sir. But all I can accept is a cup of water and a crust of bread—with a hard bed. Give me this, and I will render thanks."

The bishop's orders were given, and the pilgrim led away to a cell.

Long was the conference between the good priest and his ward, whose mind was dazzled beyond measure at the prospect before her.

To her the position was an unreality until her guardian explained it to her.

Poor Lina may be forgiven if, when she learned that she stood on a level with every dame at the emperor's court, save and except the imperial family, her heart beat a little wildly, and her whole soul was intoxicated with vanity and joy.

Little thought, we grieve to say, was given to her own true love.

Morning brought other thoughts. The pilgrim was at the last gasp. He had, however, signed a parchment confessing all, and proving Lina all she now claimed to be.

Then, with the forgiveness of his niece and the forgiveness of the church, he died.

Marvellous was the change in the bishop's house. In those days Roman Catholic prelates lived in a very mundane style, so that the burgher gallants who had persecuted the pretty girl with their attentions, were succeeded by young noblemen and soldiers who approached the lovely baroness with respect and deference.

Her estates and monied possessions were large, and her rank and influence great.

So particularly thought Sir Montacute of Cologne, a young knight of high rank and degree, but of reckless and dissipated character, who, though he had recklessly made away with the greater part of his fortune, still had mortgaged estates which the money, in the coffers of a certain merchant of Cologne, belonging to Lina would pay off, and make him wealthy once more.

In addition to this he was a relative of the bishop.

In those days courtships were quickly carried on, and three weeks after the young and obscured damsel emerged from the chrysalis state into that of a full grown butterfly of fashion, Lina found herself called upon to decide in her own mind between the lord of many an acre and a favourite of the emperor, and a poor soldier of fortune, with the taint of brigand birth upon his name.

The knight Montacute was handsome, frivolous, gay and heartless, but he was a man of his time, with every accomplishment then known, especially the power of playing and singing, as well as reading the lays of the troubadour. In soft nonsense he was unequalled.

It is not therefore surprising that Lina was placed in a difficult position.

It is true that Harold was the friend of her youth, the companion of her studies, and finally her accepted and affianced husband. But then vanity, and the new sense of rank and dignity whispered that it was the gipsy and nameless girl who had plighted herself, and not the high and mighty baroness.

Suffice that one evening, after dinner, Lina made Sir Montacute happy by promising to be his wife, after which she retired to her bower, where she was already waited on by a number of damsels and attendants, who vied with each other in their efforts to please the new and high-born heiress.

One of them was playing the zittar to her mistress, while another sang; the young girl whose fate had so suddenly changed, was, however, silent and sad, when suddenly the curtains which veiled a window, open to the evening breeze, parted, and Harold stood before her.

It is difficult to say which looked most amazed—the youth or the damsel. For a moment both were silent, when, Lina, recollecting her changed position, assumed a grave and chilling air, and spoke.

"To what do we owe this intrusion?" she said.

"Then it is true," he gasped; "my gentle Lina is a proud and haughty dame, who scorns to know her old friends!"

"Nothing of the kind," replied the girl, with a pleasant smile—"and to prove it, I forgive the rude entrance. Maidens, leave us for a space, while I explain all that has happened to Master Harold."

He stood in silence, transfixed and still, as the maidens defiled to the right and left, like a chorus on the stage.

"And this," he said, as soon as they were alone, "is the end of my dream. I have fought; I have done deeds of valour and heroism; I am on the high road to the emperor's favour, and all to win the bride who swore to be true to me, and now fortune favours her, and I am cast on one side, for a noble cutthroat, a vile voluptuary, a man of nature so base, he would slit the weazand of his father for gold."

"Of whom speak you?" cried Lina, with a faint blush of shame.

"Of Sir Montacute of Cologne, whose name is Tostoï the assassin. And you are as good as wedded to this man. Woman in heart, a deceiver ever—I could never have believed it. But the time will come when you will repent your connection with this titled ruffian."

"As well wed him as the untitled robber," replied Lina flippantly, but only from lip-temper.

"It is well. I deserve the reproach. I should have been wiser in the past. Farewell. I shall look to Sir Montacute for this insult. Let him beware."

And turning away he leaped from the window just as a handmaid entered. She heard these last words, ere she summoned her mistress to a meeting with her holy guardian the bishop.

Meanwhile Harold, who had returned from his expedition, full of hope and joy, having been promised promotion by the emperor, sped on his way. He had not changed his dress, and wore his travelling dress with sword and dag and feathered toque. He strode along with angry steps, his soul bursting with pent-up fury. There was nothing he could not have done, to wreak vengeance on his rival, and to humiliate her who had coldly betrayed him.

He entered one of the long and intricate streets of the town, on his way to the hostelrie, and was within a dozen yards of the house, when he heard the clang of swords.

A moment more, and under the light of a wretched old oil lamp, he saw a man of a tall, commanding mien, defending himself against three men-at-arms, one of whom was clearly an officer of rank. With a ringing cry, he drew his sword, and dashed to the rescue.

As he called out, the officer turned, and the attacked, taking advantage of the moment, ran him through the body. Harold dashed up at the same moment, but the remaining ruffians fled.

"Are you hurt sir?" said Harold, noticing that the other leaned heavily on his sword.

"I am," replied the stranger, in a commanding tone, "and but for you had been dead. Give me your arm—my residence is at hand. The sooner I reach it the better, as doubtless those who hounded these villains on have others at their service."

The youth readily obeyed, and helped the other to walk, which he did slowly to a house, which stood in the street in perfect darkness. Leaning against the door, he pressed some secret spring, and it opened.

Moving along a dimly lighted passage, the stranger cast open a door which led into a room, the faded finery of which spoke of former grandeur. From a couch, a lady of haughty and commanding mien, of middle age, but very beautiful, rose and advanced hurriedly.

She spoke in a language unknown to Harold, and was answered in the same.

Her eyes flashed with indignation, and turning to Harold, she thanked him warmly.

"Accept this ring," she said, "from her who was, and help Heaven, will be again, Maud, Queen of England. This is my husband, the Earl of Kent. But what say you, young man?—our further residence is, we see," she added in a sarcastic tone, "displeasing to your emperor. We must escape this very night."

"I can guide you in safety wherever you may wish to go," replied Harold, amazed at the rank of the nobleman he had saved; "This ring I will keep while I have breath to breathe."

The youth mentioned here, that in the scuffle he had lost his feathered cap, and requested that one might be procured him, which was done.

No further time was wasted. The wounds of the earl were dressed, horses procured, and, with a slender retinue, the wandering queen, so soon once more to be reinstated, started on her way.

It would have been impossible to have found a better guide than Harold, and it was the third day ere he left them, after the earl had extorted his history from him.

It was ten days ere he re-entered the town, and made his way to where he had left his slender luggage. After a halt of one night for repose, he determined to rejoin the camp of the emperor, and there devote himself henceforth to his new profession.

Just, however, as he ordered his horse, a number of officers burst into his room, and arrested him on a charge of murder. No name was mentioned.

He was thrust into a hideous cell, where he was detained without any explanation of the charge, and only when he was a shadow of his former self, from the vile atmosphere of his den, and the horrid food, was he taken forth.

To his amazement, he was at once arraigned in the public court, crowded not only with judges and other legal functionaries, but by all who could obtain admission.

His surprise was all the greater when on entering the dock, he found, separated from him only by a bar, the beautiful though false Lina, Baroness Rodenstein.

She was supported by two nuns.

Then for the first time, Harold Hertzell heard the charge against him.

He and Lina were accused of jointly conspiring to compass the death of Sir Montacute of Cologne, and further, Harold Hertzell was accused of himself inflicting the death wound upon the young knight.

The first part was proved by the evidence of the eavesdropping waiting maid; the second accusation was supported by the cap of the accused being found upon the spot where the body of the knight was discovered.

Besides, the two attendant ruffians swore to him as having attacked their master without provocation, and then escaped.

Now Harold knew that the Earl of Kent had been set upon by Sir Montacute, who had been killed while attempting the foul assassination.

But where was his evidence?

All he could do was to deny the whole story from beginning to end.

An unknown person had been killed on the night he had lost his cap, by a gentleman to whose assistance he had come.

This was all he could say, upon his honour.

Lina knew nothing whatever of the matter.

Sir Montacute was her affianced husband, and what motive could she have to slay him?

The court might have been influenced by this appeal, but that a powerful noble was present, who by her death would become heir.

After a short deliberation, therefore, the two were condemned to death, their heads to be severed from their bodies, and their bodies to be burned.

Despite their vigorous protests they were sent to prison, their execution being deferred for the formal approval of the emperor.

The once lovers exchanged looks, as they were led away.

Harold was reproachful, Lina imploring, but not a minute was allowed them.

Both lay soon in separate cells, and for weeks and weeks chewed the bitter cud of despair.

Then Harold was led from his prison cell, and thrust into a litter with black curtains, and hurried off at a rapid pace under the guidance of a large escort. A day elapsed ere they stopped, and then again he was placed in a stone cell.

At noon he was visited by a monk and also a barber with some fresh clothes.

This personage trimmed his hair and beard, and made him appear a little less like a savage than before, after which he again entered a litter with the monk, who spoke not one word.

Presently he was told to alight, and was dragged along a dark passage until he found himself in a small narrow passage, on one side of which was a large black cloth.

This was suddenly raised, and disclosed the emperor surrounded by a brilliant court.

"Advance," said the wily potentate, who for state reasons had wished the death of the Earl of Kent.

"Advance, Sir Harold of Benhaven in England, and knight of the Holy Cross in Germany, to secure the reward you merit for saving the life of a dear cousin, now monarch of the British Isles."

Shivering with excitement and doubt, the ex-bandit approached the throne.

"Ah—the signet ring of my cousin Maud," said the emperor, glancing at his finger, "why showed you not that before?"

Harold stammered something which had no particular meaning, and then boldly blurted out something about Lina.

"Said we not so?" cried the emperor, addressing the burly baron who should have been the successor to Rodenstein; "your son must seek another bride.

"His first boon we cannot refuse—unless indeed the lady is of a different opinion."

But Lina was not, and, even when the emperor called forth the good bishop and ordered the marriage to take place at once, was dutifully obedient.

This wedding, however, changed the title of the young adventurer, for by an imperial decree he was made Baron Rodenstein, and lived many years to enjoy his title.

There was much rejoicing among all classes—especially from one circumstance—during his life, the whole district under his sway was wholly free from any disturbance from the Robbers of the Rhine.

END OF THE BANDIT'S BRIDE.

THE BROTHERS;

OR,

THE FRATRICIDAL DUEL.

THE celebrated pilgrimage of Born-hofen is situated on the right bank of the Rhine, about two miles south of the confluence of the Rhine and Lahn, and nearly a mile south of Boppard.

Above this pilgrimage rise the ruins of the castles of Sternberg and Leibenstein, commonly called "The Brothers," which gave rise to the following legend :

These grey square towers, long since fallen into decay, were formerly the residence of a branch of the noble family of Bayer of Boppard.

At the period when this story opens, the aged Knight of Leibenstein had just sunk to his last sleep, and willed to his two sons, Conrad, the elder, and Henrich, the younger, the castles.

BORNHOFEN AND THE RUINS OF "THE BROTHERS."

Conrad had Leibenstein, and the care of his father's ward, the beautiful Hildegard Brömser, a lady just budding into womanhood, very rich and very affable, but an orphan.

To Henrich he gave the castle of Sternberg.

Perhaps no two men ever possessed more violent tempers or suffered their passions to urge them to greater lengths than did these two brothers.

Into every scene of vice and debauchery they plunged.

Intemperance and gambling were of daily and nightly occurrence, and the walls of their castles echoed and re-echoed with noisy mirth, oaths, and execrations.

Both turned their eyes with love upon

the beautiful Hildegard and then fixed them on each other with undying hatred.

Hildegard, disgusted at the rude scenes continually enacted in the halls of Conrad, confined herself almost entirely to her chamber, and never joined her guardian or his friends if possible to avoid doing so. She was very wretched, for, though her fortune was a large one, she was absolutely alone.

If she fled, whither could she go?—only to the castle of Sternberg ; and it would be leaving one distasteful spot for another equally as bad.

So she sat day after day by her lattice, looking out upon a scene from which she would only too gladly flee if she had any one to flee to.

Conrad, anxious to possess her fortune, determined to obtain her hand, if possible ; and, seeking her one day when she was gazing from her window, he took her hand and drew her to a seat beside him.

"Hildegard," he said, in tones more soft than she had ever heard him speak before, "why is it that you absent yourself so studiously from the company of myself and friends ?"

She strove to withdraw her fingers from his grasp, but he retained them with a gentle pressure, and drew her still nearer to him.

"Because," she replied, looking sorrowfully into his face, "I can find no pleasure in listening to the songs of half-drunken men."

"Half-drunken men!" he returned. ' Are they not knights and gentlemen who sit at my board ?"

"By birth they are so, but in manners they are rude. I sit and tremble when I hear their oaths. I start in terror when sometimes the clash of steel resounds beneath me. Gambling and rude pleasures are their usual pursuits, and though such doings may afford you gratification, they are to me distasteful in the extreme."

"Your presence, fair Hildegard, might subdue our rough natures," said Conrad.

"Or bring insult upon myself," she replied.

"By Heavens! the tongue that uttered a word to pain you, or the hand that rudely touched but the hem of your robe, I would sever with my dagger!" cried Conrad, a fierce look flashing from his eyes and his white teeth set hard together.

"Thus I might be the cause of blood being spilt," she said. "But you press my hand too hard ; I beg you release it."

"Not yet, fair Hildegard. Suffer me to imprison it within mine own, and hear what I would say to you."

The pressure was slightly relaxed.

Yet he still kept her taper fingers captive.

She made no reply, and he went on,—

"Hildegard, you have arrived at woman's estate. Nineteen summers have passed over that fair brow, and time has hourly traced more beauties on that face."

She turned her head away as the gleam of those dark eyes pierced her own.

"Suffer me to go, Conrad, I beg of you," she cried.

"Not yet. I have come to speak, and speak I will. You are a child no longer, and have none to consult beside yourself. Hildegard, I love you !"

"My lord !" she exclaimed, tearing her hand away with a sudden jerk.

Her cheeks became deathly in their pallor.

A coldness stole over her.

Her limbs slightly trembled.

"Yes, Hildegard," he said, in more impassioned tones. "I love you. We have grown up together for years ; we have sat at the same board, enjoyed the same sports. We have seen each other daily—know each other well, I am tired of a single life—you of solitude. Hildegard, will you become dearer still to me — will you be the wife of Conrad of Leibenstein ?"

He seized her hand and fell upon his knees before her.

His flashing eyes sought her own.

She strove to withdraw her hand.

She averted her face from his gaze.

"Speak !" he cried, in a voice husky with excitement. "Hildegard, will you be mine ?"

She slowly turned her face towards him and looked down into his upturned eyes.

Her lips trembled and her voice sank almost to a tremulous whisper as she replied,—

"Conrad, I—I cannot."

"What !" he cried, springing to his feet, the blood flushing his face and neck, his eyes gleaming savagely, and his broad chest rising and falling with hardly suppressed passion. "Cannot! said you *cannot* ?"

"Such was my reply."

"You will not be my wife?—you love me not?"

"I cannot—dare not," she replied.

"And wherefore not?" he asked. "My birth is as proud as your own, my——"

"My lord," she interrupted, "I should never suffer birth or fortune to weigh with me in such a case. Your father was a parent to me, and I shall ever love and honour his memory. His sons have been my friends. I respect you, but can never become more to you than I have ever been."

"Is this your answer?" he said.

"It is."

"Will you give me hope?"

"I cannot."

"You love another!" he cried fiercely.

"I do not."

"'Tis false!" he exclaimed passionately, flinging her hand from him. "It is false! you love my brother Henrich."

She smiled faintly and shook her head.

"Henrich can never be more to me than a brother," she said, "nor I dearer to him than a sister."

"He has poisoned your mind against me," he exclaimed. "He loves you, and would tear you from my arms by lies and deceit."

"You wrong him, Conrad."

"Do not deny it," he cried, fiercely. "Do not think to deceive me. I know his hatred for me—it is as bitter and deadly as mine for him, but he shall never possess you. I would strike him dead at the altar, and with my dagger's blade bare his traitor's heart to the gaze of his would-be bride."

And he partly unsheathed the weapon in his girdle with a hand that shook with passion.

Hildegard retreated several paces in fear.

"Will you reconsider your decision?" he asked after a moment's pause.

"Conrad, I have decided! Hildegard Brömser can never become the bride of the Knight of Leibenstein."

"Then, by all the fiends in hell! she shall never become the wife of Henrich of Sternberg!" he thundered, driving back the half-bared blade into its mounted sheath. "Hildegard, you might have tamed my fiery nature, and turned a man into an angel. You have chosen to make him a devil."

"Conrad, are you a man?" she said, sorrowfully.

"I have loved you long, loved you dearly," he went on, "and have loved in vain. I will sue no more. You refuse me your hand: woe to him who has the temerity to seek it!—he dies!"

He cast a fearful look upon her, and strode from the chamber, closing the heavy door behind him with a force that made the grey wall of the castle ring again.

Hildegard, faint and pale, tottered to a and sank heavily into it.

Clasping her hands together, she bowed her head upon her palpitating bosom, and burst into tears.

"Oh," she cried, "that ever I should be compelled to embitter the enmity of these two unnatural brothers; but I cannot, dare not, will not, give my hand where my heart would sicken and wither, and plunge myself into a misery ten thousand times deeper than that which I have endured since the good old Knight of Leibenstein, broken in health and blighted in peace by the unnatural conduct of these children, who should have softened his downward journey, died a broken-hearted man and left me to the care of his son."

And then, as the memory of the good old knight came upon her heart, she sobbed louder and deeper, and was wretched in the extreme.

To the banqueting hall strode the haughty Conrad, his eyes flashing, his bosom heaving, with passion.

Sullenly he took his seat among his assembled guests, young knights of desperate courage and ready for anything, whether it were to throw the dice, empty the bumper, stop the peaceful traveller, or quarrel and fight among themselves.

The wine went round, and deep and frequent were the draughts imbibed by Conrad, and, as he drank, his passion rose, till at length he sprang up, and raising a goblet above his head, he shouted,—

"Drain to the dregs: A bitter malediction fall on Henrich of Sternberg!"

Every cup was raised and emptied, and then, as if relieved by what he had said, Conrad flung the goblet to the floor and sank back in his seat.

But long after did those assembled continue to drink, till at length they became overpowered by the fumes of the wine and sank upon the table or floor, and snored in drunken sleep.

The hatred which Henrich bore his brother was only equal to that which Conrad bore for him.

His love too was as warm and fierce for Hildegard.

He knew his brother's passion for his late parent's ward, and the demon jealousy raged in his heart, and prompted him to acts that a knight and a man of honour should never stoop to commit.

Among his brother's followers were those whom he made creatures of his own, and by bribes and presents induced them to become spies on Conrad and Hildegard.

Every word, act, and look were reported to him, and with every fresh account his anger and jealousy burned with a fiercer fire.

He was pacing the courtyard of his castle in moody thought when one of these men sought audience with him, and leading the way to a chamber he closed the door behind them, and turned to confront the spy.

"Well, Hans," he said, fixing his eyes upon the man's face; "well, how fares the lovely Hildegard?"

"But ill, my lord. Daily her cheeks grow pale and her eyes dim."

"The bird pines in my brother's cage," muttered Henrich. "She was wont to be blithe and gay; the smile was ever on her lips and the light in her eyes. Be it my task to rekindle the dying flame. What of my brother?"

"His hatred against you, my lord, increases with time," replied Hans.

"And mine towards him," bitterly said Henrich. "Are Hildegard and he much together?"

"She avoids him all in her power," said Hans.

"Ah, I am glad to hear you say that fellow."

"In vain he seeks to induce her to leave the seclusion of her chamber, and mingle with his guests, and, save when she mounts her steed for a gallop over the country, she keeps within her own chamber, and sits silent and melancholy by her lattice."

"Is it so? Then the Knight of Leibenstein finds little favour in her eyes."

"Very little, my lord. She detests him."

"Good," smiled Henrich. "And how does my brother bear her coldness?"

"He chafes like an angry lion, and vents his spleen on all about him."

Henrich laughed aloud.

"Your news is good, Hans, and there is gold for thee," he said, placing a coin in the hand of the spy.

"The anger of your brother towards yourself, my lord, grows deeper and louder. But a few nights since he drained a goblet to your confusion."

"He did?"

"Yes, my lord, and his guests followed his example to a man."

"So!" said Henrich, his face flushing with passion, "he is not only himself my enemy, but seeks to make his friends also."

"Such is his design," said Hans.

"Watch him well, and keep your ears open that no word he utters may escape thee. Keep a wary look also upon Hildegard, and report faithfully to me."

"I will, my lord; you can trust me."

"I think I can."

"You can, indeed."

Henrich looked into the man's eyes as if he would read his thoughts.

The scrutiny appeared to satisfy him.

He placed his hand on Hans' shoulder and sank his voice to a whisper,—

"You wear a keen blade," he said.

Hans nodded.

"And can use it well?"

"It has pierced a hole in many a carcass, my lord," he said.

"And you love gold," remarked Henrich. The eyes of Hans sparkled.

"Wouldst earn thy pouch full?" said Henrich, still looking into the fellow's eyes.

"Aye, my lord, if you will but show me the way," replied the other.

"Your dagger's point will do that," replied Henrich. "I hate the Knight of Leibenstein. Come to me with the news that he is dead, and I will fill thy pouch with golden pieces till it overflows. But if your tongue wags one word of what I say, your reward shall be a lingering death in my deepest dungeon.

"My lord," said Hans, "I would earn your gold, but——"

"What?" interrupted the knight.

"The risk is too great. Fifty swords would avenge him. Yet, my lord, I see a way by which your desires may be accomplished."

"Speak it," said Henrich.

"The country is infested by robbers. I am known to the chief of one daring band. If you will agree to pay well for the deed, I can induce them, at the first opportunity, to waylay the Knight of Leibenstein, and earn your gold."

"That would take suspicion from myself," mused Henrich; "for our hatred of each other is notorious, and suspicion would, doubtless, rest upon me. Be it so, good Hans. I can trust you to see to this?"

"You can, my lord."

"Enough. Come soon, and say that Conrad of Leibenstein is no more."

Hans bowed himself from the apartment, and Henrich paced the floor with a smile on his face and murder in his heart.

Suddenly he paused.

Then sprang to the door.

"Hans! Hans!" he called.

The fellow returned.

"Say at what hour does the fair Hildegard roam from the castle?"

"One hour before sunset."

"With how many attendants?"

"But two or three, my lord; often with none at all."

"You can depart. Remember, silence and despatch."

"I will remember."

Hans was gone and Henrich continued his walk.

"And so," he muttered, "my brother finds little favour in the eyes of the lovely

The completion of this Story will be found on pages 107 to 112 of our next Number.

THE BARONS OF OLD
OR THE ROBBERS OF THE RHINE

THE LOVERS
OF
FALKENBURG.

FALKENBURG, more commonly known as Reichenstein, is situated on the left bank of the Rhine, and in that portion of the stream which can with truth be called the castellated river.

The castle is perched upon the summit of a rocky height, and below is the celebrated feudal fortress of Rheinstein.

Most of these strongholds of knightly highwaymen were condemned as robber nests, and fell before the strong arm of the law in 1282.

There are few of these feudal residences

"THE KNIGHT POINTED OUT THE CUSHION WHERE SHE WÅS TO KNEEL."

that have not one or more legends attached to them, and the following is recorded under the head of the Lovers of Falkenburg.

It was a beautiful morning.

The warm sun, riding in a cloudless sky, poured down its golden beams upon the earth.

The Rhine lay like a golden flood, and the banks, hills, and mountains were reflected in the old river and its tributaries.

It was just the morning to draw forth the sportsman to the woods and mountains, and lure him on in the exhilarating chase till he had plunged into the gloomy interstices of the forests, where the verdure was so thick and dense that even the powerful rays of the summer's sun could not penetrate it.

The sound of the horn, the cry of the huntsman, and the roar of the wild boar, would now and then be heard.

The flapping of the wings of the feathered tribe as, startled from their leafy coverts, they flew screeching away over the tree tops, ever and anon awoke the echoes of the wilds.

Beyond this silence reigned in the forest, where many a wild boar lay concealed.

Sir Otho of Falkenburg having no other occupation on that particular morning, and being a young man of an excitable temperament and industrious habits, had attired himself for the hunt, and with some twenty of his followers, had departed from his stronghold and entered the woods.

A brave man was Otho of Falkenburg, and though poor alike in wealth and power compared to the neighbouring barons, he was rich in courage, as many a scar left on the body of his foes could plainly testify.

The knight of Falkenburg was also a very handsome man, and possessed a pleasing manner that was anything but distasteful to the fair sex, and not a few of the nobles of the Rheingau would have been proud to make Sir Otho their son-in-law, but for one thing.

And that was, Sir Otho was poor when compared with the owners of those robber strongholds that frowned upon the rushing waters of the Rhine.

So Sir Otho was a bachelor.

He had seen eight and twenty years pass on their way to eternity, without having encountered the lady whom he felt at all inclined to make his wife, or the noble who would be willing to bestow upon him his daughter in marriage.

As love did not occupy any of his time, the chase did, and none could be more passionately fond of it than Sir Otho of Falkenburg.

Sir Otho and his attendants were not long in starting a huge boar, and giving chase.

In the excitement of the chase, Sir Otho and his companions became separated; till at length the knight, perspiring at every pore, found himself alone in a portion of the forest so dense and so dark that he could not see half a dozen yards on either side.

Wearied by his exertions, he sat down on the ground and wiped the perspiration from his face.

Unslinging the horn at his side, he was about to raise it to his lips, and sound a blast to recall his followers to his side, when a sound smote his ears that caused him to pause, holding the instrument within a few inches of his mouth and listening intently.

Then he dropped the horn, grasped his spear, and sprang quickly to his feet, as the deep tones of a wild boar rang out but a short distance from the spot on which he stood.

But this was not that which had before startled him.

The sound he had heard, or fancied he had heard, was of a very different kind to that uttered by an enraged animal.

It was the tones of a woman crying for aid.

A moment he paused, and then he heard a crashing among the branches to his right, another roar, and another cry in the plaintive tones of a female.

Now the knight of Falkenburg was as gallant as he was brave.

Grasping his spear firmly, he sprang in the direction of the sounds.

Plunging through the thick undergrowth, he sprang out into an open space or kind of avenue formed by the forest giants; just in time to be hurled back into the bush, by a terrified and bleeding steed that was galloping madly past the spot at that moment.

The knight scrambled up with no other injuries than a few scratches on his face and hands, and grasping his spear once more, looked around.

The horse had buried itself in the forest, and was now nowhere to be seen, but on turning his gaze in the opposite direction, he perceived a man spring from behind a tree, sink quickly upon one knee and plant the end of his spear firmly in the earth.

Ere he could move, speak or think, a loud roar shook the forest, and with a crash and a bound, a huge boar sprang from the opposite direction and bore down with maddened fury upon the huntsman.

The sight of the animal and the man's

danger instantly caused the knight to dash forward to his aid.

But ere he had taken half a dozen steps the tusks of the boar had gored the breast of the man, and the hunter lay dying on the earth.

As he rolled over and the furious animal gored at him with his terrible tusks, a wild scream of terror rang through the woods.

"A woman's voice, by St. Goar!" cried the knight, taking no further heed of the boar, which seemed intent upon its prey, and bounding through the brushwood in the direction of the sound.

His heart beat violently as he came in sight of a young girl, clinging for support to the lower branch of a tree.

Her face was pallid from terror, and her limbs trembled with horror at the sight on which she gazed.

Despite her fear and agony, Sir Otho thought his eyes had never encountered a face so beautiful and a form so matchless.

Her dress betokened her of high rank, and it was evident that she had not come there on foot.

This was not a time for ceremony or knightly greeting, so springing to her side, Sir Otho flung his arm around her trembling form, and in his rich, mellow tones, cried, "Fair lady, how can the knight of Falkenburg serve one so lovely as yourself?"

Her eyes turned from the savage brute and its victim to the flushed face of Sir Otho, with an appealing glance.

"Sir knight," she replied, hurriedly, "my steed, wounded by the boar, has thrown me from its back, and galloped madly away, and my attendants are I know not where, save he who lies there before us. Oh, sir knight, the fearful beast will destroy us."

And she clung to him in her terror.

"Nay, tremble not thus, fair lady," he cried, "the knight of Falkenburg must lay dead at your feet ere the brute can assail your sweet self. 'Tis a huge animal, but my spear's point has pierced the brain of many a one as powerful."

At this moment the boar looked up with a terrible roar, as of triumph at its victory.

"This way," cried Otho. "Behind those trees you will be in greater safety. Ah, you cannot walk. Your fall has injured you. Then these arms shall place you in safety before this hand avenges your own fears and yon brave fellow's death."

As he spoke, Sir Otho lifted the lovely form in his arms, and bore her quickly through the dense foliage till he had placed her on a spot where the trees grew so closely together that their trunks almost touched each other.

"Here, lady, you will be free from all danger," he said. "These massive trunks will form a barricade through which nothing can pass. Rest here till I lay the head of yonder boar at your feet."

And he turned to go.

The girl seized his arm.

"No, no, sir knight," she cried. "Risk not your life, I implore you."

And she clung to him almost frantically.

The knight of Falkenburg looked into the pleading eyes and now flushed face, and a strange thrill passed through his heart.

It was a feeling he had never before experienced, and one for which he could scarcely account.

Fain would he have gone to attack the brute, which continued to walk round and round its victim, lacerating him with its tusks, and yet something seemed to hold him back.

It was not fear.

That was a stranger to the breast of Otho of Falkenburg. It was something that he himself could not explain, but which that impassioned glance he fixed upon the face of his trembling companion but too plainly revealed. It was love.

Though but the growth of a few moments, still it was love, and a love for which the knight of Falkenburg would have willingly laid down his life.

"Stay, stay!" she cried. "Do not leave me. Oh, if you, too, should be slain?"

Then she checked herself suddenly, and cast her eyes to the earth as her face became suffused with a deep blush.

But another loud roar from the boar caused her to look up, and cling yet more desperately to Otho.

Then came a loud crash as the brushwood was trampled beneath the furious hoofs of the enraged animal.

"Unhand me, lady!—unhand me!" cried the knight, tearing himself free, and throwing his spear forward.

A wild scream of terror broke from the girl.

The fierce brute was tearing down upon them. Not a moment too soon had the knight prepared to meet the assault.

With its head lowered, its tail erect, and its fearful tusks covered with gore, on dashed the maddened beast towards the spot on which the knight and the lady stood.

Firmly Otho planted his feet on the grass-covered earth. Desperate was the strength with which he grasped his spear.

The girl clasped her hands together, and leaned for support against a tree.

Her eyes were fixed upon the boar; her

lips muttered a prayer for the safety of Sir Otho.

Then came the shock.

The knight was forced to his knees by the fury of the charge.

A wild scream of terror broke from the lady.

A cry of joy burst from the lips of the knight.

A fearful roar of agony issued from the throat of the boar.

A moment it reared up on his hind legs, and then rolled over on the earth dead— the point of the spear fixed through its eye into the brain.

Slowly the knight rose, and turned towards the girl.

One trembling look she gave at the dead brute at their feet.

One thankful glance she fixed upon Otho —then, holding out her arms towards him, sank half-fainting on his breast.

The knight encircled her form with his arms, and held her to his bosom.

The triumph of the hunter was forgotten in the wild torrent of emotion that now raged in his breast.

Nor did the lady seek to withdraw herself from an embrace that was so fervent on the part of one to whom she had been known for so short a time.

She had never learned to disguise her real feelings. Respect and gratitude had sprung into her heart for the young knight— if indeed no stronger passion had yet found entrance, and this she showed but too plainly in the pressure of the hand—in the glance of the lovely blue eyes.

"You have saved me from a frightful doom," she said. "But oh, had you perished?"

"I had done so in a noble cause, fair lady," he said, "and where is there a brave man who would hesitate to sacrifice his own life for one so fair and beautiful as yourself?"

"And yet we are strangers," she said, "though I have long known the brave knight Sir Otho of Falkenburg, by report."

"May we never be strangers more, fair lady," he said, gallantly.

"No," she replied, "that must never be— you have saved my life, and that must make me respect you for ever."

"I feel that we can never forget each other," he said, looking into her eyes.

"Never," she replied quickly. "Who can forget their preserver?" And she looked shudderingly down at the dead boar.

"I promised to lay its head at your feet," he said, drawing his short sword. "But," he added, quickly, "I had forgotten your poor follower. There is no danger now. Remain here. I will see if there be any hope for the poor fellow.

He sprang from her side, and made his way to where the victim of the boar lay.

He bent over the maimed wretch.

He was quite dead.

Otho returned to the lady.

In answer to her inquiring glance he merely shook his head.

"Poor Fritz," she said, "he was a faithful follower of my father. Sir Conrad will regret his fate sorely."

"Sir Conrad!" said Otho, starting back, "What! Sir Conrad of Rheinstein?"

"Yes—my father," she replied.

"Then you are——?"

"Evelinda," she replied, "the only child of the knight of Rheinstein."

"Then am I a thousand times more happy in having been of service to you," said Otho. "The owner of the neighbouring castle to my own is a brave and gallant knight, whom I respect and honour, though jealousies have somewhat at times made us enemies, and deprived me of the chance of ever having before beheld his lovely daughter."

"I have but just returned to his castle after an absence of many years."

"No wonder then we have never met before."

"I have but a short time left the convent where he placed me when but a child."

"Happy, indeed, am I to have served him with my poor, weak arm. But I forget you are hurt by your fall?"

"It is nothing. My ankle is a little injured," she said.

But a twinge of pain passed across her face that assured the knight she suffered much.

"A score of my followers are in the woods," he said. "I will summon them. They shall form a litter and bear you home."

"You will accompany me, and receive the thanks of my father?" she said quickly and anxiously.

"I would not leave you till I saw you safe in your father's arms," he replied. "Would I could ever remain by your side."

The look he gave her as he spoke once more summoned the warm blood to her cheeks. She did not reply.

But a sigh broke from her lips, and her gaze sought the earth.

Unslinging his horn, he placed it to his lips, and blew a loud blast.

This summons was answered from three distinct points, and none of them very far distant.

The knight paused for a few moments, and then blew another blast, and returned the horn to his side.

"My followers will soon be here, lady," he said, "and we will convey you to the castle."

A grateful look was her reply.

In a short time the knight and the lady were surrounded by the attendants of Otho.

Their short swords were soon busy in lopping branches from the trees, and a litter was quickly formed for Evelinda.

Another was constructed to carry the dead boar and its victim.

All being in readiness, Evelinda was placed tenderly on the green boughs, and with the knight holding her hand and walking by her side, the cavalcade set out for the castle of Rheinstein.

The way was long, and the path rough and toilsome, but however tedious it may have been to the knight's retainers, the journey was a very pleasant one to Otho and Evelinda.

In fact the time passed away so quickly that they did not observe its flight, and it was with surprise, if not with sorrow, they came in view of the towers of her father's castle.

Scarcely had they done so when they perceived a cavalcade approaching.

CASTLE OF FALKENBURG.

"It is my father," said Evelinda; "alarmed at my long absence he hás come forth in search of me."

Such was the idea of Otho, but on a nearer approach, the knight who rode at the head of the party proved to be Sir Warbeck, the lord of Ehrenfels.

This noble was an ill-tempered, ill-looking man of fifty.

Few respected, but all feared him, for he was one of the wealthiest and most powerful barons of the Rhine.

He was one who had always allowed his evil passions full scope, and there was scarce a vice in which he did not indulge.

The effects of this indulgence had left their marks plainly on his countenance, and stamped in indelible signs the debauchee and the ruffian.

The knight of Rheinstein had no very great respect for him, but found it to his interest to cultivate his friendship, much to the disgust of Evelinda.

He was a constant visitor of Rheinstein since the arrival of Evelinda, and forced his attentions upon her to a degree that was painful and annoying.

No wonder, then, she felt anything but pleased at seeing him at the head of her father's retainers in search of her.

The two parties met and came to a pause.

Otho saluted the knight with ease and grace, but found his salutation not returned, and a look of savage annoyance on the face of Sir Warbeck.

"I have come forth in search of you," said Sir Warbeck, addressing himself to Evelinda. "Your father's fears for your safety, and your long absence, rendered me extremely anxious. Your horse, wounded, returned to the castle some time since."

"Thanks to this good knight I am safe," said Evelinda. "But for him I fear I should not have again seen my father."

Sir Warbeck turned frowningly to Otho.

"Where is your attendant?" he said, not deigning a word to the young noble.

"Dead," she replied. "He is lying on yonder litter. A cruel boar deprived him of life, and but for the knight of Falkenburg I had shared his fate."

The frown grew more dark on the brow of Sir Warbeck.

"I will relieve the knight of any further trouble," he said. "Ho, there! convey this lady and her attendant to the castle."

This was addressed to his followers.

The men came forward to obey the order.

"Pardon me, sir knight," said Otho, as a flush of passion rose to his face. "Having brought her so far, we will convey her thither ourselves."

Sir Warbeck bit his lips with rage.

Evelinda looked smilingly upon her preserver.

Warbeck observed the glance exchanged between them, and his eyes flashed fiercely.

"Sir knight," he cried, "when the lord of Ehrenfels gives an order he intends it to be obeyed. Men, take the litter."

"No," said Evelinda. "Those who have brought me thus far shall convey me the rest of the journey. You forget, Sir Warbeck, that the men you presume to command are my father's followers, not your own."

"What!" cried the angry noble, "would you tell these hinds not to obey me?"

"I tell them to obey me," she replied, haughtily. "Return to the castle, and tell my father that Sir Otho of Falkenburg, having saved his daughter's life, is now bringing her to his presence."

The followers of Rheinstein immediately turned to depart.

"Hold!" cried Sir Warbeck, fiercely. "I command you to stay."

"And I command you to go," said Evelinda, "unless," she added, turning to Otho, "you tire of your task and would have it otherwise."

"No, lady," replied Otho; "I could never tire of being with one so lovely as yourself."

The words were plainly uttered, and fell on the ears of the knight of Ehrenfels with a force that drove him almost to madness.

His hand grasped the hilt of his sword.

"Sir knight," he said, in a hissing tone, "have a care in what terms you address this lady. Be careful that you presume not too much upon the service you have rendered her."

"Sir Warbeck," returned Otho, calmly, "I am not the man to presume upon any service, nor the one to stand by and see a lady insulted and annoyed; nor, indeed, to submit to insults or annoyance myself."

"You are too bold in speech," cried Warbeck. "You forget that you address the knight of Ehrenfels."

"Not so," replied Otho. "It is the lord of Ehrenfels who forgets that he speaks to a knight and a gentleman who wears a sword, and is prepared to draw it if occasion requires."

And he tapped the hilt of his weapon significantly.

More ungovernable grew the rage of Sir Warbeck.

"Do you threaten me?" he cried. "Me!—who could raze your castle to the ground, and sweep you from the banks of the Rhine."

Otho smiled scornfully.

"My lord," said Otho, "I do not threaten. I leave threats to you, and reserve deeds for myself."

"You shall suffer for this; you shall answer for this boldness."

"When called upon to do so, I shall not fail to be ready. Now, my lord, we will proceed on our journey, lest your anger render you despicable in the eyes of this lady."

"Not a step further shall you advance," cried Warbeck, half drawing his sword.

"Dare you bar my passage!" thundered Otho.

And his bright sword leaped from its scabbard.

"Hold!" cried Evelinda. "Sir Warbeck, for my sake, I implore you to suffer me to proceed as is my wish—Sir Otho, you are too brave, too generous not to return your sword to its scabbard, if I implore you to do so."

"Fair lady," said Otho, thrusting the weapon back, "did you command it, I would bury it in my own heart."

Warbeck ground his teeth, and bending his head, replied—

The conclusion of this Story will be found on pages 123 *to* 128 *of No.* 8.

[Continued from page 88.]

THE PHANTOM BELL.

Before the sacred edifice Falkenstein halted his followers, and attended only by Osric advanced to the portals.

The good prior and his brethren saw the baron and his followers advancing in martial array, and were not slow in divining the cause of their coming.

They were but few in number and powerless to oppose the haughty baron, but they possessed a power which not all the barons of the Rhine could have defied—their silver bell, blessed and anointed by Bishop Winfred and endowed with a power greater than that ever possessed by man.

They therefore, threw open their portals and came forth to meet Falkenstein.

No sooner did the baron perceive the door open than he took a step forward.

The aged prior held aloft the crucifix, and bade him stand in a tone so haughty that even Falkenstein started back.

"Desecrate not the floor of this holy building with thy polluted feet," he cried, "lest the indignant hand of Heaven strike the atheist dead upon the threshold."

"Dare you speak thus to me, drivelling dotard?" thundered the baron.

"What seeks the unbeliever Falkenstein at the house of God?" said the prior.

"That which he will bear hence if he wash your altar in the blood of its priests, and give to the sword every woman within its walls. I come hither for my captive, the fair Imragina, daughter of Count Edrec, and I go not hence without her."

"Away!" cried the prior, "or shall I show thee, presumptuous noble, how powerless thou art to harm the children of the Lord?"

"Defied! I, Baron Falkenstein, defied by a drivelling priest! By my knighthood, but your craven blood smokes on the rock at my feet. Ho, there! down with them! Smite! Smite!"

The Baron Falkenstein, foaming with rage, clasped the hilt of his sword, and drew it from its scabbard.

Another moment it was raised to deal the threatened blow.

His followers poised their javelins and levelled their glistening points at the bosoms of the priests, who calmly kept their ground within the porch of the priory.

But as the baron, knight, and vassal, prepared to strike the blow, the tones of the silver bell rung loud and clear from the steeple, and with the first stroke every hand became nerveless, every faculty was deadened; every man in the baron's train became, as it were, on the instant changed to stone.

The prior raised the crucifix he carried above the head of the baron, and held it there.

The sword of Falkenstein fell from his grasp, and the spell which bound him was removed.

Still, though the sense of seeing, hearing, and understanding was restored to him, he was powerless to move hand or foot.

"Baron Falkenstein, man of blood and sin, where is your power now to tear from the bosom of the church the virgin who reclines upon it, and in its embrace seeks that peace the world cannot give? Where is your power to annihilate the brethren of this sacred house? Gone! That power you spurn—that heaven you deny shows you now, puny man, how contemptible is your strength—how vain are your boasts— how worthless your threats! As well might you, Baron Falkenstein, seek to hurl back the advancing tide with your hand as tear from the bosom of the church the sister Imragina; for that bell, gifted with supernatural power and blessed by St. Winfred, hath but to sound one note, and not all the forces of the Barons of the Rhine could raise a hand to do violence to the church and its children."

The baron glared at the priest and at his men, who stood like statues, each with his weapon ready to deal a blow, yet powerless to raise or lower them a single inch.

"What demon's aid have you obtained to thus paralyse the faculties of myself and followers? What mighty spells have you conjured up, that you can thus, in one moment, destroy the power of the bravest band that ever noble led upon the banks of the Rhine?"

"We seek not the aid of demons," said the prior. "Faith and humility are the only weapons we use. You see the power possessed by yon bell—a power that never can be destroyed so long as it *shall hang where the true faith is adored.* Go, then, rash man, back to your mountain nest and leave us in peace."

"I must, I will," said Falkenstein. "Remove the spell from my people, and I will retire to my castle, even without her whom I had sworn to re-possess."

The prior raised the crucifix and the bell ceased to ring.

Every weapon fell from the hand that grasped it, every sense was restored to that armour-clad band.

"Secure your weapons," said Falkenstein, "and without a blow follow me back to the castle. I came to fight with men, but am opposed to supernatural powers. Here we are powerless so long as yon bell hangs in the spire of this priory."

He raised his sword from the earth, and his followers securing their own weapons, he placed himself at their head and pointed up the mountain.

"Priest," he said, "yonder bell is the first foe that ever conquered the Baron Falkenstein. My soul cannot brook defeat, and I will conquer yet! Aye, I will conquer yet."

"Beware! be warned," said the prior, "your strength but comes from man, ours from Heaven. Smile in derision, Baron Falkenstein, but, bad, bold man, the hour may yet come when you shall acknowledge that power you now deny, and ask its mercies when too late."

"Enough, babbler," roared the baron, "hence to your prayers, and leave me to my revenge, which may be tardy, but which shall be sure; follow, follow!"

He turned and hurried up the steep sides of the mountain, never once casting a glance behind at the prior and his brethren holding aloft the sacred symbols of their faith.

Once more like an angry lion the baron paced the halls of his castle, vowing a bitter revenge on the prior and his fellows, yet feeling assured that it was beyond his power, or indeed any human power to gratify it while that bell remained in the steeple of the holy building.

How could it be removed; no human hand, he felt certain could do that, and in vexation and rage, he beat his mailed breast with his clenched hand, and ground his heavy heel into the stone flooring.

"By the blood of my ancestors," he cried aloud, "I would give my very soul to him who would place that bell at my feet, though it were the black fiend himself."

Scarce had he uttered these words than a knight, clad in sable armour, stood before him, as if he had risen through the stones at his feet.

Falkenstein started back.

The sable knight advanced a step, laid his hand upon the shoulder of the baron, and in a low sepulchral voice exclaimed—

"It is a compact. The silver bell of Welmich I will place at the feet of the Baron Falkenstein, and from that moment his soul is mine."

"Thine!" cried Falkenstein, "Who, sir knight, are you?"

The knight raised his visor. Falkenstein shrank back.

"The arch-fiend himself," said the dark stranger. "Is it a compact or is Falkenstein but a coward and a boaster after all."

"No, by my knighthood," cried Falkenstein, "and he who would impute fear or cowardice to me, man or devil, should feel my sword's point."

As he spoke he drew his sword and thrust it at the sable knight, shivering its well-tempered blade to atoms on the black breastplate.

"My armour is invulnerable, baron," said the demon, "But grieve not for your sword. I will temper you a blade within the ever-burning fires of these mountains that shall as far surpass your own as that shattered steel surpassed the blades of your followers. Now, is it a compact?—the bell thine, your soul mine."

"It is!" cried Falkenstein.

"Your hand," said the fiend.

Falkenstein extended his hand; the demon grasped it.

Falkenstein felt a strange sensation in his hand. He raised it before his eyes, and saw a large black spot in the centre of his palm, as if burnt there by fire.

"This mark," he said, looking questioningly at the demon.

"Is the seal to our compact—the seal of ——!"

As Falkenstein suffered his extended hand to fall to his side the demon disappeared.

The black spot on his hand annoyed him, and he waited impatiently for the demon to return with the coveted bell.

It was not, however, till midnight, and when Falkenstein sat alone in his own bedchamber, that the black knight appeared before him, bearing in his arms the phantom bell.

Falkenstein gazed upon the silver bell with unfeigned delight, and inwardly muttered a vow that never more should it hang in the belfry of a house of prayer.

"I have performed my part, baron," said the fiend, "and your soul being mine, you must of course obey me in all things."

"This was not in the compact," said the baron.

"Indeed," said the fiend. "Then if you refuse to become the slave of my will on earth, I must at once convey you to that region where none dare dispute my authority."

"Stay, I will do your will on earth. Speak it—what are your commands?"

"That you will bring hither all your captives and, alive, hurl their bodies into the deep pit of the round tower of your castle, unshriven, there to die ; and for this I give you life so long as the bell shall remain silent."

"Then shall I live long to enjoy my bride," he cried ; "for until that bell is suspended to that where the true faith is adored, it will never ring more!"

"Till your own hand shall hang the bell on such a support, you shall live ; and the only demand I make is, that your captives and foes shall, unshriven, be hurled into the depths of the round tower pit."

"Enough!" said Falkenstein ; "though a fiend, you are a generous master."

"Then farewell, till the hour of your doom!" cried the demon.

"Farewell," cried Falkenstein.

But ere the word was uttered, the demon vanished, leaving on the spot where he had stood a magnificent sword and beside it the coveted bell.

For some moments the baron examined and admired the instruments of music and of death ; then raising his sword above his head, he cried.

"To-morrow, Imragina is mine! And to-morrow, fiend, every priest and nun of the priory of Welmich will I consign to thee, unshriven."

On the following day, at an early hour, Falkenstein and his retainers once more bent their steps down the mountain.

The good old prior smiled as he saw them again draw up before the sacred edifice.

"Cruel and infatuated man," he cried, as he confronted the baron, "were not the proofs of the power we possess here of sufficient force yesterday, that you must again descend upon the priory this morning?"

"Peace, driveller!" cried Falkenstein ; "know that your power is broken, and Baron Falkenstein has come to bear away his bride, and avenge his previous defeat upon every soul, save her, who has been sheltered within these walls."

As he spoke he seized the prior by the throat and hurled him among his followers.

The prior raised his crucifix, and then turned deadly pale and trembled violently, at the same time looking with surprise and horror at the terrified brethren.

"The bell! the bell!" he gasped.

Falkenstein laughed derisively.

"Know, priest, that your bell will ring no more in your steeple ; that the supernatural power on which you relied is destroyed, and that Falkenstein can no longer be defied or defeated."

Then turning to his vassals he cried—

"Smite all who dare to oppose you. Now, priest, lead me to the fair Imragina, or dread the vengeance of the Lord of the 'Mouse.'"

"Beware! beware the curse of the church."

"Silence, and obey!" cried Falkenstein, striking him on the lips with his mailed hand ; then, turning, he entered the priory, followed by nearly all his vassals.

The brethren fled in terror before the armed host, and the women were seized and torn from their apartments by the brutal band.

Imragina, unable to escape, stood at last confronting the triumphant baron.

"So, my fair captive," he cried, "we meet again, never more to part till death. That lovely form will better grace a castle than a convent, and I will take good care that you never escape me again, so long as I have life and power."

He seized her arm, and drew her forcibly towards the door.

"My lord baron," she cried, "you may force me to your castle, but shall never force me to become your wife!"

"Ha, ha!" he laughed ; "fair lady, we shall see. You have no longer a friend in the phantom bell."

"I have a friend in heaven," she cried, "and He will save me from you."

"Away with them to the castle!" cried Falkenstein, "and set fire to this hive, which has so long annoyed the sight of the Lord of the 'Mouse'."

An hour later, and red flames were leaping round the walls of the priory, and in the great hall of the "Mouse" sat the Baron Falkenstein surrounded by his knights and vassals, and confronted by Imragina, the priests, and the captive nuns.

"Spite of your faith," sneered the baron, addressing the aged prior, "my captive is again in my power, the priory will soon be a heap of ruins, and every being who resided within its walls but a short time since, save the daughter of Count Edrec, whom I reserve to cheer my solitary hours, will be buried, mangled and shapeless, far below the bed of the Rhine."

"Man of blood and sin," said the prior, "since, by some mysterious power, you have deprived us of our bell, and the powers that bell possessed, we can but bow to the will of heaven and accept our fate without a murmur at its decrees. But ere our eyes are closed in death I do implore thee repent, lest that bell be the instrument to destroy you."

"I will take care it never shall!" cried Falkenstein; "like thine, its tongue shall be hushed to human ear. Away with them to the round tower—youth and age, priest and virgin, to the pit with them—to the pit! Let not one escape, but reserve till the last, and for my hand, this presumptuous prior. Osric, bring after me the silver bell you will find in my chamber. Imragina, your hand. Fair lady, you shall witness the power and the vengeance of your future lord."

The retainers of the baron drove the priests and nuns out of the hall before them, and pale with terror Imragina suffered herself to be led along by the baron, who, with a gleam of fiendish joy, led her to the edge of the round tower pit.

One by one the holy brother and sisterhood were precipitated into the fearful abyss, till the prior alone remained, his hands upon his bosom, his eyes turned meekly towards heaven.

Now his turn had come, and, Osric having brought the bell to the spot, the baron caused it to be hung round the neck of the holy man, and then, grasping him by the shoulder, he said—

"Thus shalt thou thyself destroy for ever the power of the bell in which you trusted. Deep down into the bowels of the earth shalt thou carry it."

Falkenstein forced him back to the edge of the pit as he spoke.

"Now, prior, see if the bell can save thee and thy fellows. Ha! ha! ha!"

He thrust him over the edge.

As the prior shot swiftly down the chasm, his voice rolled up loud and clear.

"Baron Falkenstein, the bell will ring thy doom. Thy own hand has hung it where the true faith is adored!"

With a howl of rage Falkenstein retreated back from the edge of the pit, and glared wildly upon his followers.

"Fill up the pit!" he cried, "that no sound may come from its depth. Hurl rocks and and stones into the chasm! Fill, fill, ere that fatal bell can sound!"

Every hand commenced hurling pieces of rock and stones into the pit, till some sixty feet had been filled in, and the terrified look on the face of Falkenstein, had given place to a smile of triumph.

Then he stretched forth his hand to grasp that of Imragina.

"My revenge is now complete," he said. "Now for love and pleasure! Now thou art indeed mine!"

He grasped her hand, but released it on the moment, for from the depths of the pit arose the musical tones of that silvery bell.

At the same instant a figure, clad in sable mail, sprang from the pit, and laying his hand upon the shoulder of Falkenstein, cried in a voice of thunder—

"And thou art mine! Falkenstein, the bell has rung—thy hour has come!"

The next moment flames and sulphurous smoke darted from out of the pit, and through the centre of these the horrified spectators saw the sable-clad knight bear the blanched and trembling Baron Falkenstein.

Another moment, and smoke and flames had disappeared, and so also had the bold, bad baron and the knight of the sable mail.

But from the pit rang the tones of the bell.

The knights and vassals, as soon as they recovered from the terrible shock they had received, sped from the castle, leaving Imragina kneeling and praying alone at the round tower.

And while she prayed, a youthful knight, with a small band of retainers, entered the castle, and found her on her knees beside the terrible pit.

It was the youth to whom she had given her love, and who, hearing of the fate of her father, had resolved to tear her from the captivity of Falkenstein, or die, and had arrived at the castle only to find it deserted by all but her.

Long was the struggle between love and duty that Imragina underwent; but finally, at the personal intercession of her lover, who journeyed to Rome for that purpose, the Pope absolved her from her vow, and she became a happy wife.

And from that time forth the bell was heard to ring under the tower on the anniversary of the death of Falkenstein, and groans and shrieks issued from the bowels of the mountain: and there are not a few who positively assert they may still be plainly heard by placing the ear to the earth at the foot of the round tower of the Castle of the "Mouse."

END OF THE PHANTOM BELL.

[Continued from page 96.]

THE BROTHERS.

HOW his proud heart must chafe—with what joy that knowledge comes to mine. Every pang he feels is a gleam of sunshine to my own. I will seek Hildegard. I may find more favour in her eyes. I love her as fiercely as I hate him. Oh, that he could see her in my arms. How I would glory in my triumph!"

For several evenings, about an hour before sunset, the Knight of Sternberg rode in the vicinity of his brother's castle, and returned after dark to his own in no very enviable frame of mind. Hildegard had remained in seclusion.

At the expiration of about a week, as he sat on his horse looking in the direction of Liebenstein, he perceived a single rider issue from it, and come in the direction whence he stood.

His heart beat rapidly as he recognised the form of Hildegard.

On she came at a gallop, never dreaming whom she was about to encounter, till sticking his spurs into his horse's flanks, the Knight of Sternberg urged him to her side, and his voice rang in the ears of the lovely girl.

She drew rein quickly.

"Henrich!" she said, giving him her hand.

"Yes, fair Hildegard, it is Henrich, who has sought you in vain for several days. I could not come to the castle, since, you know, the bad blood between myself and its owner."

"It is sad, very sad," she said, "that two brothers should be at war. It is unnatural that those who should be bound by the strongest ties of affection should be thus estranged."

"We can never be friends more, Hildegard," said Henrich. "But let us not speak of that, but talk on a theme nearer to my heart."

She made no reply.

"Let me assist you to dismount," he said. "I have much to say to you."

"Nay," she replied. "Say what you have to say, Henrich, where you sit."

"Hildegard," he began, "there has been a void in my heart since my father's death drove me from the castle of Leibenstein and your presence, and left you to the care of my brother. Night and day have I pined to hear your sweet voice, and see your sweet smile."

"Pardon me, Henrich," she said, hurriedly; "the sun is sinking fast. I must return to the castle."

"No, no!" he cried; "not yet. I have sought you long; do not flee me now. I will be brief in what I have to say. Hildegard, I have sought you to tell you how devoted I am to you—that you alone can lift the veil from my spirits—that you alone can render me happy."

"Henrich," she said in a pained tone, "I implore you speak not to me thus, but suffer me to depart."

He placed his hand on her bridle.

"Not yet, Hildegard. You must hear me."

"I cannot."

"I implore you," he said. "Hildegard, I love you. I would make you mine."

"In mercy let me go," she pleaded.

But he threw one arm around her waist and drew her to him. "Hildegard," he said in hurried, husky tones, "I will be your very slave; your every word shall be to me a command. I will make your life the envy of the world. Your happiness shall be my only thought—my every desire. Oh! turn not from me. Speak! In mercy say you will be mine!"

She freed herself from his grasp, and turned her flashing eyes upon his face.

"Henrich," she said, in a voice she struggled to make firm, "it can never be. What do you ask?—that I should become the bride of one whose natural affections are dead—of him whose hand and voice are now raised against his brother—whose bad, unnatural passions bowed his father's grey head with sorrow, and embittered his last moments! Speak not to me of love. I cannot be thine."

"Hildegard, I implore you to be merciful," he pleaded.

"I cannot listen to you. It is impossible. Ere you speak of love, teach your heart to study friendship. Love can never dwell where brotherly affection is unknown!"

"Be mine, and I will go to my brother

and take him by the hand. What has made us the enemies we are? Yourself."

"I?" she said, starting and looking at him reproachfully.

"You," he replied. "We both loved you, we both pined for the one heart, and jealousy—deep, bitter jealousy, took possession of us. You have made us foes; you can make us friends."

She shook her head.

"Hildegard, I have never sued to mortal before. See me humble myself before you. Give me but a look, a word, to bid me hope; command what you will, only say you will be my bride."

"I have said it is impossible. Henrich, it can never be, never—never."

"Do you love my brother?" he asked, hissingly.

"I do not."

"He loves you?"

She was silent.

"He would make you his wife?"

Still she answered not.

He laid his hand upon her horse's neck, and looked into her eyes.

"Hildegard," he said, in a deep, husky voice, "your beauty charmed the souls of myself and Conrad. For a smile from you we would have flown at each other's throat.

"The love we both coveted has turned brotherly love to devilish hatred.

"This refusal of yours but embitters the strife. He woos you, but he shall never wed you.

"He will try all his arts to lead you to the altar, but never shall he stand there by your side.

"Go back to his castle, and tell him how low I stooped to sue for your love, and how you gloried in the pangs your refusal inflicts."

He struck her horse a sharp blow on the neck, and, rearing up, the animal started off with its rider.

Hildegard turned a sorrowful look behind her, and, in the gathering twilight, saw a face convulsed with passion and a form trembling with rage.

In a minute he was lost to her view, and, shortly after, with her eyes filled with tears, and her heart overflowing with sorrow, she passed into the castle, and hurried to her chamber.

Henrich sat gnawing his lip with vexation, watching her graceful form as it faded gradually from his sight, and then he turned his horse's head towards his own castle, muttering in bitter tones, as he urged the animal to its greatest speed—

"But for him, but for Conrad, she might be mine. He is the block in my path. My curses on him! But my vengeance will fall soon, and then will she listen to my vows? Can I hope to win her to my arms? 'Tis the only chance, the last and only one."

He turned in the saddle, and shook his clenched hand in the direction of the Castle of Leibenstein, and muttered a deep and bitter malediction against its owner.

Then, turning, he urged his horse on at redoubled speed, and gained the walls of Sternberg.

About a week after this incident occurred, Conrad, attired for the chase, attended by a couple of followers, went forth to hunt.

Led on by the excitement of the chase, he wandered far from his castle, and the sun was sinking behind the mountains before the grey square towers of Leibenstein came in view.

As the last rays of the sinking orb threw their gleams across the horizon, from the cover of a stunted clump of trees, the forms of half-a-dozen men, rudely attired and rudely armed, issued forth into the path the Knight of Leibenstein and his two followers were pursuing.

Conrad, all unsuspicious of danger, came on in moody silence, while his followers, bending beneath the weight or the profits of the day's sport, conversed together in subdued tones.

Suddenly, and without a moment's warning, they were surrounded, and around their heads flashed the gleam of half-a-dozen weapons.

Not a moment did Conrad hesitate.

His hand grasped the hilt of his sword.

In less than a moment its blade had leaped from its scabbard, and his back was planted against the gnarled trunk of a dwarfed tree.

Dropping their burdens to the earth, his followers bared their blades, and, turning each his back against that of his friend, confronted the strangers.

As sudden as had been the surprise, as speedy was the preparation for defence.

"How now, varlets," cried Conrad; "what means this? What is it you seek with us?"

"The life of the Knight of Leibenstein!" cried a tall, powerful fellow, who evidently was the chief of the band of ruffians.

"An' you take it, it will cost you dear," shouted Conrad, "Stand firm, men, and show these villains that the men of Leibenstein wear a strong blade, and know well how to use it."

"Down with them!" thundered the

robber chief. "This to thy heart, Knight of Leibenstein. 'Tis the Wolf of the Woods who strikes the blow."

"Ah, ah!" cried Conrad, as he parried the stroke of the robber, whose name had spread terror to the souls of many in those parts. "Wolf, I'll draw thy fangs, and then cut out thy villain heart."

Loud was the clash of steel on the evening-air, as Conrad and his two brave followers parried the blows aimed at them by the robbers

With his back to the tree, Conrad kept three of the ruffians at bay, while the remaining three attacked his two followers.

His mail turned aside many a fatal blow, but he could do no more than defend himself, and perspiring at every pore, he battled on, growing weaker every moment.

His followers, shoulder to shoulder, fought desperately, and soon two of the robbers fell beneath their blades.

Seeing this, one of those attacking the knight went to the aid of the remaining assailant, leaving the knight only two to contend with.

One of these was soon rolling on the earth, cloven through the skull by the sword of the knight, and he stood confronted alone by the Wolf of the Woods.

Desperately they fought, till at length, by a well-aimed stroke, Conrad sent the weapon of his adversary flying from his hand, and ere the Wolf could draw his dagger from his belt, the point of the knight's sword was at his throat; at the same moment, the two remaining robbers fell beneath the blade of the followers, who turned to the assistance of their master.

The Wolf, finding himself alone, and at the mercy of those whom he had attacked, fell upon his knees, and held up his hands appealingly.

"Mercy, Knight of Leibenstein!" he cried.

"Dog!" thundered Conrad. "Wherefore sought you my life?"

"Plight me your knightly word to spare my life, which I know is justly forfeit to your sword, and I will reveal to you the name of him who employed me in this work."

"Ah, then, 'tis another, and not thyself, who seeks the death of Conrad of Leibenstein? Speak his name quickly, or you die!"

"Your word to spare my life, or I am silent," said the Wolf.

"You have it. Now, quick, or my sword's point shall stop your tongue for ever."

"Know, then, Knight of Leibenstein, that 'tis your own brother," said Wolf.

"Henrich?"

"The Knight of Sternberg."

"He has employed you in this work. He has sought the aid of robbers to encompass what his own coward hand and craven heart feared to seek for himself," said Conrad, bitterly.

"Through one of your own followers," said Wolf, "he has bought our services for the deed."

"Varlet, you lie!" thundered Conrad. "That my brother seeks my life I well believe; but that one of my followers should aid him in the despicable work is false as hell!"

"It is true! I swear it. Hans is but a spy of the Knight of Sternberg, and he it was who, in his name, bought our aid for your destruction."

"Swear it."

"I do."

"Upon the hilt of this sword, swear it, or with its point I pierce your villain heart."

The robber laid his hand upon the cross hilt of the knight's sword and took the required oath.

"Enough," said the knight. "Remove his dagger from his girdle; bind fast his arms, and bring him to the castle."

The two followers quickly obeyed the order, and Wolf stood bound and powerless before his would-be victim.

Darkness by this time had closed over the earth, and the lights gleaming from the windows of the castle alone pointed out the direction in which its grey massive towers reared their heads to the sky.

Guided by these lights, they pursued their way with their captive, the knight walking on in moody silence, chafing with indignation and dreaming of revenge.

Arriving at his castle, Conrad instantly summoned all his followers into his presence, and placing Wolf in their midst, bade him point out the man whom he had asserted had induced him to undertake his destruction.

Not a moment did Wolf hesitate.

He strode up to Hans, and placed his hand upon his shoulder.

If doubt had remained on the knight's mind of his complicity, that doubt vanished in an instant.

The face of Hans turned deathly pale.

His limbs shook as if palsied, and he turned to flee.

But ere he had taken a step the hand of Conrad seized him by the throat.

The point of the knight's sword touched his heart.

Hans fell upon his knees and clasped his hands.

"Spare me, spare me!" he cried. "I will confess all—everything; but spare me, my lord. Oh, spare me!"

Conrad spurned the craven wretch with his foot and sent him sprawling on the floor.

"Dog!" he thundered, "I will spare you but for an hour. Make your peace with Heaven, for by that Heaven I swear that in one hour you shall die."

In vain were his appeals for mercy.

The knight was furious and inexorable, and Hans was dragged away shrieking piteously.

Conrad's was not a nature to pity or forgive, and turning to Wolf he said,—

"I plighted my word to spare your life, but not to grant you liberty. In a dungeon of my castle your days shall be passed. The light of Heaven you shall never see again. Away with him."

The followers laid hands upon the robber.

"Knight of Leibenstein," cried Wolf, "I sued for my life, and you now condemn me to worse than death. Grant me one more prayer. Bid your followers sheath their swords in my bosom, but in mercy condemn me not to a dungeon."

"I have said," returned Conrad, fiercely. "He that raises his hand against the Knight of Leibenstein shall find no mercy in his heart. To the dungeons with him!"

Wolf was borne from his presence, and the angry knight sought the chamber of Hildegard.

In pain and in silence she listened to his recital of the attack on his life by the myrmidons of Henrich, and turned a cold ear to his pleadings for her love.

Still more infuriated by her treatment of his suit, he again descended to the great hall, and gave the order for the immediate execution of the spy.

Then, as was his wont when angry, he drank deeply, and, the wine adding fire to the flames of rage which filled his breast, he commanded that the head of Hans should be severed from his body, enclosed in a box, and sent to his brother Henrich, with the following message :—

"Your friend has failed. If you have the courage to try with your own hand to take the life you seek, I will hunt alone, two days hence, in the glen at the back of my castle. If you come not, you are a coward as well as a villain."

On the following day a small box was placed before Henrich.

It had been left at the castle, and the messenger had departed as soon as he had resigned its custody into the hands of one of the followers of the Knight of Sternberg.

With his own hands Henrich opened the box, and started back with a look of horror on his face.

There within it lay the head of a human being—the glassy eyes wide open, and a look of agony on the convulsed features.

Upon the forehead was a slip of parchment, on which were traced a few lines in rude characters.

For a few moments Henrich glared upon the frightful object before him, and then he stretched forth his hand and took the parchment.

"It is the head of Hans," he muttered, "and this is the writing of Conrad!"

He perused the lines, and crumpled the parchment in his hand.

"So," he muttered, "the attempt has failed, and I have been betrayed. Fool! why did I trust other hands than my own to rid me of my hated brother, and my hated rival!"

He flung the parchment to his feet, and crushed it beneath his heel.

Then Henrich hastily closed the lid of the box to shut out from his sight the horrible look of those glassy eyes, that seemed to glare upon him.

"Coward and villain," muttered Henrich; "those are the titles he addresses to me. Enough, Conrad, I will make you confess that your brother is no coward. You hunt alone, behind your castle. You shall find sport enough and work enough, for, by the mouldering remains of our dead father, one of us shall never see the morrow's sun. I will meet you there, foot to foot, and blade to blade."

He summoned an attendant, and bade him carry the box to the banks of the Rhine, and throw it into the river, and then he raised the parchment from the floor, and perused it again.

"To-morrow," he said, "there will be but one suitor for the hand of Hildegard, but one heir to the castles of Sternberg and Leibenstein!"

Bright and glorious rose the sun over mountain tops, flinging its rays of golden beauty upon the grey walls of the castle, and flooding with burnished gold the waters of the Rhine.

Alone, from out his castle strode the noble form of the knight of Leibenstein.

Attired for the hunt, and armed only with sword and dagger, he strode on with unfaltering steps, and head erect, but with a face convulsed with passion, an eye flashing with rage, and a heart throbbing with revenge.

He reached the deep glen that lay behind his castle, and then he paused and looked around.

The sunlight flooded its verdant sides, the birds carolled merrily, all nature seemed rejoicing, but the heart of that bold, bad man found no charm in the beauties around him—it was filled with desperate and unnatural passions.

"Not here," he said. "I knew the coward feared to seek the life he covets, and rid himself of a rival by his own hand. I hated him before, I spurn and despise him now. He will not come—his craven heart fails him!"

"Liar! he is here!" cried a loud voice behind him.

With his hand upon his sword. Conrad sprung round and stood face to face with his brother.

For some few moments these two men glared upon each other. All the wicked passions of their degraded hearts gleaming from their flashing eyes—hatred, deep bitter, lasting hatred, plainly stamped on every feature.

"Aye, you have come," said Conrad, at length. "Come to your doom."

"No words," cried Henrich, "but let deeds speak for you. My sword speaks for me and Hildegard."

"This makes her mine," cried Conrad, drawing his sword.

"Or mine," exclaimed Henrich, unsheathing his weapon.

The next moment their blades crossed with a clash, and brother stood opposed to brother.

For a moment the glorious sunlight glinted on their steels, and then the burnished orb of day buried its bright disc behind a cloud, as though it would not witness a scene so terrible, so unnatural. Long and loud the clang of steel rang out upon the balmy air and echoed through the glen, startling the feathered songsters from their leafy coverts, and sending them fleeting to the mountains.

Firm, desperate, panting, they fought on—a brother's sword crossing a brother's steel—a brother's hand seeking a brother's life.

It was a desperate fight, those two evenly matched men, each possessing strength and skill—each filled with hatred—each panting for the other's blood.

From many a wound the life stream oozed, but still they fought on, till at length by a desperate blow, both blades were shivered to their hilts, and they paused for breath.

But not to meditate upon the fearful crime in which they were engaged.

No better thought stole upon their hearts —no spark of brotherly love influenced

their bosoms—deeper and deeper grew their hatred, and fiercer and fiercer their longings for revenge.

Flinging aside the hilts of their swords, they drew their daggers and sprang forward for the stroke.

The blades descended—clashed. Again and again they were aimed at each other's hearts. Again and again the fatal blow was warded.

The parrying strokes grew weaker and weaker, and at length they descended simultaneously, and, at the same moment, the bosom of each received the fatal blade of his brother.

No word was uttered, no cry of pain escaped them; but, with fearful looks in their eyes, they clutched at each other's throat, and fell struggling to the ensanguined earth.

With their fingers compressed in the convulsive death grasp, they tore each at the throat of the other till exhausted nature could no longer continue the fearful conflict, and, with their stiffening fingers still pressed into the other's flesh, they rolled over on to their backs, and, gasping, died side by side.

The cloud passed over; the sun's rays streamed down upon the lifeless, convulsed, upturned faces, flashed for a moment into stony eyes, that still bore a look of never-ending hatred, and then buried its brightness behind the black vapours, as if to shut out a sight so horrible—to hide a crime so unnatural.

Hours passed, and a toil-worn man entered the glen; the sight he saw drove the colour from his cheek and the blood from his heart.

He recognised the brothers, and forgetting his weariness, he hurried with the sad news to the castle of Leibenstein.

The followers of Conrad hurried to the scene, and brought back the bodies of the brothers, and placed them before the trembling Hildegard.

Long and painful was the look she fixed upon those two dead and hacked forms, now so cold, so still, so ensanguined, and then she raised her head and clasped her hands to her brow, and shrieked aloud.

"Dead—dead!—both dead! each fallen by his brother's hand, and I the innocent cause of their enmity! For my love they fought—they died! But I will atone for my innocent crime. They are at peace now, but I live to know that I am the cause of their death.

"Oh, that I too were dead! Yes, yes, to the world I will be. In fasting and in prayer I will atone for this fatal deed, and my life shall be passed in imploring mercy for them."

She turned and left the apartment, and fled from the castle, her hands clasped to her beating heart, and her eyes fixed on Heaven.

That night a youthful figure entered the convent of Bornhofen, and implored to be received among the sisterhood.

It was the lovely Hildegard.

With outstretched hands the sisters welcomed her, and strove to assuage her grief and heal her wounded heart ; and in time she found that consolation which a life of piety ever gives to the suffering soul.

Never more did she return to the world, but passed the rest of her days in the hallowed precincts of the convent of Bornhofen.

The brothers were borne to the grave, and from that time the castles have been deserted and gradually fallen to decay.

Many years after, a skeleton was discovered in the dungeons of Leibenstein.

It was that of Wolf the Robber.

Years have passed—time's iron finger has torn down the masonry and crumbled away the stonework of Sternberg and Leibenstein, but it is powerless to erase the terrible story of which these two ruined castles are the record, and while one stone remains to mark their site, they will ever be associated with the legend of the BROTHERS and their FRATRICIDAL DUEL.

END OF THE BROTHERS ; OR, THE FRATRICIDAL DUEL.

Our next number will contain "The Avenger."

THE BARONS OF OLD OR THE ROBBERS OF THE RHINE

THE AVENGERS.

A SHORT distance below the town of Bingen is a rapid called Bingen Loch, or the Hole of Bingen.

Here the Rhine cuts across a chain of mountains, which at one time is supposed to have stopped its further progress, and that some convulsion of nature or the force of the waters must have burst through this barrier, and made for the river the ravine by which it obtains a free passage to the sea.

On this spot stand the shattered walls of

"WITH A SHRIEK SHE TORE HER HAND FROM SIR CUNO'S HOLD."

the Castle of Ehrenfels, formerly one of the strongholds of the Archbishops of Mayence.

It was built in the year 1218, and to it they retired with their treasure in times of danger.

Within the shadow of these picturesque ruins, and on a small island in the midst of the rapid, is a solitary, square shaped tower, which bears the name of the Mousethurm, or Mouse Tower.

It is supposed to have been erected for a watch-tower and toll-house for the collection of duties upon all goods which passed the spot, or, rather, for the levying of that black mail which the robbers of old exacted in so many portions of the Rhine.

But this is not the reason why the Mouse Tower has become so notorious, but from the following legend of man's inhumanity and Heaven's vengeance—

Bishop Hatto, or, as his title ran, Prince-Archbishop, Elector of Mayence, Arch-Chancellor of the Holy Roman Empire, was supposed to be the builder of this little tower.

He was a man of savage and unfeeling disposition.

He was detested alike by noble and peasant.

Wherever he went murmurs and discontent were heard.

Open violence was seldom resorted to, as he never travelled without large bands of well-armed retainers.

But the bishop knew that one day or other acts of violence would take the place of murmurings and evil looks.

Being a man of action, he prepared for defence.

Consequently, he built castle after castle, and strengthened fortress after fortress, till he finally erected the Mousethurm on an island by which the waters of the Rhine dashed at the rate of five miles an hour, as a last place of refuge, should circumstances compel him to resort to it for shelter.

Seeing the dislike entertained towards him, it was a matter of surprise that the bishop did not seek to appease the indignation of the people by acts of kindness and mercy.

But he did not.

The greater the antipathy shown him, the fiercer became his laws, the more cruel his mandates, and the more merciless his acts

Yet there were those who loved the bishop, or pretended to do so, for purposes of their own.

Among these was a knight of violent passions and unprincipled character.

He had slain no less than three knights under circumstances that led others to believe anything but fair.

In honourable fight, he asserted, they had met and fallen beneath his sword.

But, as each had possessed a brave, undaunted soul, the fact that the wounds of each lay in the back, induced others to believe that they had been assassinated.

This idea gained greater credence from the fact that each of them had raised his voice against the cruelties of the Archbishop of Mayence.

This man, Sir Cuno, was a tall savage-looking morose-speaking man, overbearing and insolent to all but Hatto, but to him, he was obsequious and fawning to a degree.

He was ever at Hatto's side, ever ready to obey the cruel mandate of his master.

On him Hatto lavished all his love and all his praise, and, knowing his influence with his master, he did not fail to take advantage of it.

Consequently, when, having cast his eyes upon the lovely face and stately form of the beautiful young Jewess, Lilah, the daughter of Ben Hermann, a wealthy Israelite, he found little difficulty in inducing Hatto to aid him in obtaining possession of her.

On a certain day Ben Hermann and his daughter were ordered to present themseves before the bishop

In fear and trembling they obeyed the mandate.

Hatto was seated in his chair of state, with his follower by his side, when with faltering steps the Israelite bowed before him.

"What would my lord archbishop with his humble servants?" asked the Jew, in a voice of anxiety and fear.

"Obedience," replied the bishop.

The Jew bowed his head lowly.

"My lord," he replied, "I have ever been obedient to the laws and will ever remain so."

"That may be," said Hatto; "but not to the church."

"My lord, I am a Jew," said Ben Hermann.

"One of a hated and detestable race," said Hatto. "A race whom it is the duty of all true Christians to persecute. The hatred the Christian bears to the Jew is returned by the Jew forty fold."

"You have spoken disrespectfully of our religion and repulsed a Christian knight from your door."

Ben Hermann cast a glance at Cuno, and replied, while the indignant flush rose to his face—

"My lord, what I did was to protect my child from a villain, and while these feeble arms can be raised in her defence, noble nor peasant, nor Jew, nor Gentile, shall ever assail the honour of my child."

"You are bold in speech, Jew," said Hatto.

"I am a man and a father," was the quiet retort of the Israelite.

"You are an insolent caitiff," said Cuno, "to dare thus to address my lord arch-bishop."

"I have no words for thee, false knight," said Hermann.

"Dog of a Jew!" began Cuno,

The bishop held up his hand for silence. The passion-flushed Cuno fell back.

"Leave the Jew to me," said Hatto. "Ben Hermann, this loyal knight and true gentleman makes charge against you that you did assail him with vile words and cruel blows because he admired the beauty of your daughter."

"He insulted her," returned the Jew.

Bishop Hatto smiled scornfully.

"A Christian knight cannot offer insults to a Jew," he said; "to one of a con-demned and despised race. On the con-trary, he sought to confer the greatest honour on your people when he vowed he loved your child."

Lilah shuddered and clung to her father.

The Jew drew himself proudly up, and fixed his piercing eyes full on Hatto.

"Loved!" he sneered.

"Aye," returned the bishop.

"My lord," said the Jew, "the Chris-tians spit upon and spurn our people. They look upon us as dirt, and treat us as dogs. They hold the Jew beneath them, and plot, and love to do them wrong. Can he who is foremost among the persecutors of our race, love one of its children? No, a thousand times no."

"Caitiff, would you dare doubt the word of a brave knight?" said Hatto.

"I dare, my lord, not only doubt his word, but deny his honour. My child the bride of Sir Cuno! Sooner would I see her blackened corpse buried beneath the wild waters of the Rhine, than a look of encouragement beam from her bright eyes towards yon man."

And the aged Jew drew his trembling child to his bosom, and held her there.

Hatto rose from his chair.

"Jew," he thundered, "the leniency which I have shown to your accursed race prompts you to a boldness that even a Christian dare not show in my pre-sence.

"My lord——"

"Silence!"

The Jew relapsed into silence.

"Sir Cuno loves your daughter," con-tinued the prelate, "and I require the wealth which, by ways known only to your people, you have yourself accumu-lated. The one I confiscate to my use—the other I resign to this brave knight."

"Never," cried the Jew, "shall you possess either."

"Peace, lest you rouse my anger fur-ther," said Hatto. "Sir Cuno, take the young infidel from his arms, and teach her how to become a Christian as well as love a Christan knight."

Sir Cuno sprang forward to tear the trembling girl from her parent's arms.

"Hold!" shouted the Jew. "These grey hairs proclaim my age, this feeble arm asserts my weakness; but, old and weak as I am, I will defend my child with my life."

Cuno laughed a scornful laugh and drew his sword.

"Relinquish your charge to younger and stronger hands," he said, "or, by the cross the blood of the Israelite stains the floors of the Christian palace."

"Father, father," shrieked Lilah, "save me from him—save me!"

"My life for thine, my child," cried the Jew.

"Release her," said Hatto. "I, the lord archbishop of Mayence, command you."

"And I, Ben Hermann, the despised Jew, refuse to obey," said the Israelite.

"Fool!" cried Cuno, "'tis death to beard my lord in his castle; and thus I, his humble follower, avenge the insult to the noblest Christian lord in Germany."

As he spoke, he seized the arm of Lilah, and thrust his sword into the throat of her father.

The blood gushed from the wound into the face of the agonised girl.

With a shriek she tore her hand from Sir Cuno's hold, and, flinging both arms around the neck of her parent, sank with him to the ground.

"The curse of Abraham be upon thine head for ever and ever," she cried. "Fa-ther, father, look on me. God of my peo-ple, he is dead!"

For a moment she held the head of her father in her hands, and glared into the now lustreless eyes.

Then she suffered it to fall gently back on the floor, and, springing to her feet, stood confronting the bishop and her father's murderer.

"Murderers," she shrieked, "behold your bloody work and stand appalled. The curse of Heaven is upon you! The curse of my people—the curse of the dead and the broken-hearted! Withered be the hand that struck the fatal blow, and withered be the heart that could prompt the cowardly deed!"

"Your father has paid the penalty of his boldness," said Hatto. "When the Jew forgets his state, he must learn that the Christian foot is ready to press upon his neck."

"Wretch!" cried the girl, "a heavier foot shall press on your neck, and a heavier hand smite your soul."

She bent down, and encircling her arms around her father's body, raised it partially from the floor.

Sir Cuno approached, and laid his hand on her shoulder.

"There let the dog lie," he said, "till some of the retainers can hurl his worthless carcase into the Rhine."

She turned her flashing eyes upon him with a look of loathing and horror.

"Back! touch me not; there is blood on your hands!—the blood of him who gave me being! Away! and let me bear hence my dead!"

"Away thou!" commanded Hatto; "and let him remain where he lies."

"I will take him hence," she sobbed, "and show the people of the Rheingau the work of the bloody tyrant."

"Tear her from him," said Hatto.

Sir Cuno grasped the arms of Lilah, and dragged her forcibly to her feet.

The partially-raised body of the Jew fell back with a loud thud on the floor.

"Unhand me!" shrieked Lilah, struggling to free herself from Cuno's hold.

But she struggled in vain.

Firmly he held her, and fiercely he looked into her tear-bedewed eyes.

"You struggle in vain," he said, "and will but injure your own tender flesh in the fruitless attempt."

"My lord!" shrieked Lilah, turning an appealing glance at the prelate, "you are all-powerful here. Bid this man release his hold. Have pity on me!"

"Pity for one of thy race!" laughed the bishop, scornfully.

"I am a woman."

"You are a Jewess."

"I thank my God I am!" she cried; "For never did one of my race commit a deed so base as thou, unnatural Christian."

Hatto's brow contracted into a deep frown.

"Girl," he said, "be careful of your words. There are deep dungeons and instruments of torture within these walls."

"I fear them not!" she cried. "Callous-souled wretch! you cannot lacerate the heart deeper than this hellish deed has done."

"I can tear your flesh on the rack; I can consign you to the embrace of the iron virgin; I can immure you in a dungeon, black as midnight, or doom you to the same fate as your infidel father."

"Do so, heartless prelate!" she exclaimed. "Bid your murderer pierce this bosom with his sword, and send the daughter's soul in company with her parent's to the unknown hereafter."

"Nay," said Cuno; "your parent's life was worthless, but you must be preserved for him whose heart your beauty has charmed."

Lilah's paleness increased, and she bowed her head upon her bosom in despair.

"My lord," said Cuno, "the powers you possess I implore you not to assert, but, in return for the poor services of your faithful adherent, give into my keeping this haughty girl."

"No, no!" shrieked Lilah.

"Be it so," said Hatto; "and, lest the discontented should presume to dispute your right to become her gaoler, or seek to rescue her from your hands, I give you the post of governor of the Mousethurm, whither you will convey her."

The eyes of Cuno sparkled.

Once within the tower in the rapids, who could wrest her from him?

He turned a grateful look upon the prelate.

"My lord," he said, "my gratitude is unbounded. There I can teach this haughty girl how great is the honour a Christain knight confers upon an Israelite."

Poor Lilah could but look from one to the other in horror and dismay.

Falling upon her knees, she shrieked out—

"Kill me! kill me! in mercy, kill me!"

"Not yet, fair Jewess," said Cuno; "you must live to love me, and forsake your faith, and become a Christain."

"Forsake the faith of the oppressed for that of the oppressor?" she moaned. "Never! As he whom your merciless steel has slain died in the faith of his fathers, so will his child remain true to her religion, her persecuted people, and herself."

"We shall see," sneered Cuno. "But come; my lord bishop tires of this scene."

Lilah looked down upon the cold, silent body, and then turned her wet eyes to the prelate.

"Christian priest," she cried, in a solemn tone, "Well may you tire of this scene; but it shall be ever present to your view. The face of that murdered man will be ever before your eyes, and the blood you have shed, crying aloud for vengance, will yet be answered."

"Away with her!" cried Hatto, fiercely.

"Retribution, swift, terrible, and merciless, will yet overtake you," cried Lilah. "You shall yet cry for mercy, but your prayer shall be unheeded. The God of your people and mine will close his ears to your supplications, and the avengers of blood shall teach the haughty Christian that Heaven will avenge even the despised and persecuted Jew."

And, wresting her right arm free, she held it above her head, as though invoking the aid of Heaven.

Hatto quailed for a moment before that calm, prophetic face.

Then he sprang a step forward, and stamped in rage upon the floor.

A look of fury gleamed in his eyes.

His voice was husky with passion.

His very lips trembled with rage.

"Tear her hence!" he cried; "or by the sacred symbol of our faith, much as I love thee, Cuno, I will wrest her from thy arms, and consign her to a fate a thousand times more terrible than ever Jew or Christain dreamed of!"

Cuno, fearful of losing the prize he had gained, raised her in his arms, and bore her struggling across the apartment.

"Father! father!" shrieked Lilah, holding out her hands towards the form that never more could answer her; "the God of Israel will avenge thee and thine!"

The next moment the powerful arms of Sir Cuno had borne her through the door, and the archbishop stood alone beside the body of the Jew.

For some few moments he stood contemplating the pale, rigid, upturned face of the aged Israelite.

Then, spurning the carcase with his foot, he cried—

"Would that all his accursed race were stiff and cold as he! Bearded by a Jew— the Prince Elector of Mayence threatened by a daughter of Israel! But that I owe much to the fidelity of this good knight, I would so torture her that she should never speak ill of Christian more!"

He turned away from the corpse.

Summoning some of his retainers, he bade them remove the body, and clear the stains of blood from the floor.

And while this office was being performed by his followers with rude jest and cruel indignities, Sir Cuno bore the shrieking girl from the castle of the prelate to the tower in the rapids.

Once within the stronghold of which, by the bishop's will, he was absolute master, the cruel knight set about exerting all his arts to assuage the grief of the Jewish maiden, and induce her to look favourably upon him.

Powerless as she was, Lilah, though she panted to upbraid the wretch, knew how vain would be threat or remonstrance.

She therefore remained silent, refusing to answer a question or utter a word.

In silence and tears she sat, inwardly praying for vengeance on her father's murderers, and meditating how she could escape from that place.

She could not dissemble sufficiently to give Cuno the least encouragement by either word or look.

But at the same time, with the shrewdness of her race, she was anxious to propitiate his anger, and by appearing to submit with a good grace to her fate, prevent herself being immured in that part of the tower from which escape would be impossible.

With the vanity of his nature, Sir Cuno read this bearing as favourable to himself.

He began to think that time and perseverance would soften her heart towards him, and that the love he coveted would yet be bestowed upon him.

Consequently Lilah was permitted to roam whither she would about the tower.

But as days passed on, and no further encouragement was received by Sir Cuno, his impatience increased.

Naturally superstitious, as, indeed, were all who inhabited the banks of the Rhine in those early ages, he began to imagine that if he could procure the aid of supernatural agency, he would be able to win the Jewess to his arms without resorting to violence, for strange though it may seem, bad man as he was, he really loved the fair Israelite.

As the shades of night gathered around the tower, and threw a gloom over the waters of the Rhine, Sir Cuno descended into his boat, and was pulled to the shore.

Bidding his followers return to the tower, and come back for him early on the next morning, the knight bent his steps in the direction of Lurleyburg.

Nothing less than the mad love which Sir Cuno felt for the daughter of his murdered victim could have induced the knight to have sought these haunted precincts after nightfall.

As he approached the spot, which he, in common with the people of those parts, firmly believed to be inhabited by beings of the other world, he felt a cold chill steal over him.

Persuading himself that it was but the cold night air, he drew his cloak closer around him, and bending anxious glances to the right and left, and then down upon the dark waters, he kept on his way.

The nearer he drew to the rock, the slower became his footsteps, till at length, when his feet pressed the haunted spot, he could scarcely drag one before the other, so great was the awe he felt.

So violently did Sir Cuno tremble, that he was fain to sit down on the hard stone, and the rushing of the waters as they swept along beneath him sounded in his cars like the voices of spirits moaning in chorus.

For a long time he sat listening to the sounds, till a drowsiness appeared to steal over him, and he seemed neither to have the power to speak nor rise.

In vain he strove to shake off the lethargy.

Suddenly, through the darkness before him rose up a strange, weird figure, whose head and body was partially enveloped in the folds of a cloak, but which seemed powerless to rise to its full height from some deformity of the knees and back.

As it drew nearer, it discovered to the fearful gaze of the knight, a face old and wrinkled, and hands, from the fingers of which the nails grew like claws, so long, so terrible did they look.

Not a word could the knight utter as it advanced and stood a crooked, misshapen mass before him.

A cold sweat broke from every pore, and even the beating of his heart appeared to cease.

He could but gaze wonderingly, fearfully, upon the object before him, and wish himself back again in the tower.

"What seeks Sir Cuno on the Lurleyburg?" asked the old man, in a voice harsh and discordant in its tones.

With an effort the knight summoned up power to speak.

"Who are you?" he said.

"One whom you have summoned hither," was the reply.

"I?" cried the knight, in surprise.

"You, Sir Cuno. I am the old man of Lurleyburg. I am he who can read the thoughts of mortals, and at whose bidding the spirits of good or evil will rise from their home beneath the waters of the Rhine."

The knight was silent.

He could but gaze with awe-stricken eyes upon the form before him.

"Rise, Sir Cuno," continued the figure. "You seek the aid of the spirits beneath this rock. Approach with me to the edge; look down into the flowing waters and learn their will."

The knight rose and approached the edge of the rock as if drawn on by some strange fascination, and looked down into the dark, turbid tide beneath.

Standing upon the very edge of the black rock, the old man stretched forth his long arms over the stream, and expanding his claw-like fingers, moved them up and down over the waters.

"Spirit of evil, from thy watery bed arise, arise!" he cried, in a voice louder than he had before spoken.

The knight clutched the folds of his cloak in terror as from a dozen points came in loud echoes the words, as if the whole scene around were peopled with phantoms—

"Arise, arise!"

"The spirits answer to my call," said the strange figure. "Behold the demons of evil are here."

With a fearful but fascinated gaze, Sir Cuno looked upon the waters, over which a pale light as from the moon gradually spread, growing brighter and brighter every instant.

Then, through this light shot one of a brilliancy so intense as to light up the rock and the forms thereon, and almost blind the vision of the awe-struck Cuno.

In the centre of this light appeared a dark form.

Its head was bald, but from its chin descended a long white beard which flowed over its bosom.

From its shoulders spread out a pair of sable wings.

Its hands resembled claws, and its features were repulsive in the extreme.

Stretching forth its arms, it pointed with its long fingers to the waters from which it had risen, and in a voice that rolled like thunder over the rock, and was echoed by a dozen demon throats, the phantom asked—

"What would you with me? Speak! The demon of evil is here to do your bidding, Knight of the Rheingau and murderer of Ben Hermann!"

A hundred demon tongues echoed the words—

"Ben Hermann!"

As if by magic, all the courage of Sir Cuno returned, he suffered his cloak to fall from his hands, and, approaching the very edge of the rock, returned the gaze of the demon.

"I love the Jew's fair daughter," he said, boldly. "I would woo her to my arms and bring her to renounce her faith."

"Faith!" came in the demons' echoes.

The demon threw up his arms, and, closing his wings, gradually sank into the stream.

"Faith," he cried, as he went down, "that word renders me powerless to aid you."

"Hold!" cried Sir Cuno.

"Hold!" echoed around on all sides.

The demon arose again.

"By the aid of your supernatural power bring her to love the man she abhors," cried Cuno. "Bring her a willing bride to the arms of her—"

"Murderer!" interrupted the spirit of evil.

"Murderer!" pealed forth from twenty parts at once.

"Aye, if you will—murderer," said Cuno. "Do this, and, whatsoever you command, that will I obey."

"Obey," was then echoed.

"Swear it!" cried the demon.

"Swear it," echoed around.

"I swear it," said Cuno. "By Hea—"

Ere the words were spoken, the wings of the spirit were again closed, and he sank rapidly into the turbulent stream.

"I swear it!" shouted Cuno, quickly.

"Swear it!" pealed forth on all sides, and rolled in terrible strains along the shores.

Up rose the demon again.

"Enough, Sir Cuno," he said. "You have sworn, and your vow cannot be broken. Nothing can tear Lilah from your arms but death."

"Death," echoed the rocks and shores.

"Thus I fulfil my compact. Now for thine!" said the spirit.

"Thine—thine," was the echo.

"It shall be done," said Cuno. "Command, and I obey."

"Obey," pealed the echoes.

"When the Lord Archbishop of Mayence shall require one to do an act his own coward hand would tremble to perform, yet his own merciless heart would consummate, swear that thy hand shall be stretched forth to do the deed, for none other can be found on the Rheingau. Swear! swear!"

"Swear, swear," echoed the demon voices.

"I swear!" cried Cuno.

"Then Lilah is thine till death," cried the spirit of evil, "and thou art mine for ever!"

"For ever—ever!" rolled away on all sides.

With a peal of laughter, the demon closed his wings, and disappeared beneath the waters.

The light vanished, the darkness of the grave settled upon shore and river, but from all parts pealed loud shouts of demon laughter.

The terrors of the knight returned.

He stretched forth his hand towards the spot where the old man of the Lurleyburg had stood.

It grasped at nothing.

Sir Cuno was alone and in darkness on the haunted rock.

Above, the blackness of the heavens was fearful.

Below, the dark waters rushed roaring on.

Sir Cuno turned to flee.

But his limbs were paralysed with fear, and he uttered a deep groan, and sank prostrate on the rock.

From above, below, around, resounded groans as from an army of unquiet spirits, and, overcome by his terrors, Sir Cuno closed his eyes in insensibility.

When the knight unclosed his eyes again, the sun's rays were just peeping over the mountain tops.

He was alone on the haunted rock, on the very spot where he had sunk down before he encountered the old man of the Lurleyburg.

Cold, trembling, and pale, he arose, and fearfully looked down into the stream as it whirled on its way to the sea, and then, shuddering, he drew his cloak around him and hurried from the haunted precincts.

It was with a feeling of relief, and not a little gratification at the chance of now wooing the fair Jewess to his arms, that the knight once more entered the Mousethurm.

Proceeding at once to his own apartment, Sir Cuno flung aside his cloak and ordered wine.

For several hours he sat quaffing deep draughts of the finest vintage of the Rhine, and thinking over the night's adventure, and then, having raised his own spirits up to their utmost pitch, he sought the lovely Jewess.

Night had come again.

The silvery moon, which the night before had hidden her bright face behind the dark clouds, now bathed the river and its banks in a soft mellow light. In vain the knight sought Lilah in the various apartments.

Thinking that the beauty of the night might have induced her to wander to the top of the tower, thither he repaired.

On arriving there, he perceived the white-robed form of the lovely girl.

Her arms were clasped across her bosom, her upraised eyes were fixed upon the bright disc floating far above in the blue ether.

A saintly calmness was on every feature now, lit up by the pale silvery light of the moon.

For some moments the enraptured knight gazed upon her immovable form, and then he sprang towards her with extended arms.

Lilah turned as the clang of his mailed foot sounded on the stones, and, awed by that strange, calm, beautiful face, Sir Cuno paused spellbound before her.

"Sweet Lilah," he said, at length, "never have you looked so beautiful as now. Turn not from me. None can resist their fate; the spirits have spoken. You are mine till death."

"Till death!" seemed to come up from the waters beneath.

"Thine till death," she said, in a voice calm and measured. "The spirits of the Rhine have spoken—they speak now. They call me to peace and rest. Thine till death! Look beneath! See, the face of my murdered father glares upon us!"

Sir Cuno started and turned cold.

"Look," she added, in the same strange tones, "the lady sits upon the moonlit stream, her golden harp upon her knee, her hand beckoning me towards her. Murderer! I am thine till death!"

With a cry of joy Sir Cuno sprang to clasp her in his arms, but, with a loud peal of laughter, she eluded his grasp, and the next moment had sprung from the tower into the Rhine.

With a cry of horror the knight followed with his eyes the swiftly descending form of the young Jewess.

He saw it disappear in the moonlit stream.

"OVER SIR CUNO HOVERED THE DARK-WINGED FIGURE."

A moment after it rose in the turbulent waters.

The pale, beautiful face was turned towards him.

And a voice soft but distinct uttered the words—

"Murderer! Thou art accursed! Lilah is the bride of death, and thou art lost for ever!"

"For ever!" pealed in musical strains from the dashing river.

And while the sounds rang in the knight's ears, a seraph form arose on either side of the beautiful Jewess, each bearing in its hand a harp of gold.

Then all three sank gradually beneath the waves, and the moonlight alone played upon the running waters of the Rhine.

The knight beat his mailed breast in despair, and clasping his hand to his forehead, staggered back.

"The spirit has deceived me," he cried, "and I have doomed myself to perdition for ever."

"For ever!" roared the waters beneath; "for ever!" echoed the walls of Ehrenfels; "for ever!" pealed from shore to shore.

And, wringing his hands together in disappointment and despair, the bold, bad knight fled to his apartment.

The next day Sir Cuno presented himself before the bishop, and begged to be relieved of his office of governor of the Mousethurm, and again be permitted to attach himself to his person.

Hatto immediately assented, for he was desirous to surround himself with those upon whom he felt he could depend, for there were signs of danger which even he himself could not disregard.

The murder of the Jew, and the abduction of his daughter, had somehow become known to the people of the Rheingau.

Their respect for the Israelites was certainly no greater than that of the bishop, but it gave an already discontented people an opportunity of rising against a tyrant whom all abhorred.

Deeds of actual violence now usurped the place of murmurings and discontent, and the people flew to arms.

Hatto immediately removed his treasures to Ehrenfels, and thither repaired with his followers to await the advance of his foes.

He had not to wait long, for the people, burning to revenge many a cruel insult, and many a merciless edict, flew to storm the stronghold ere they were prepared for the arduous task.

Gallantly the sons of the Rheingau assailed the stronghold; but the castle was so well guarded, and its walls so strong that, after an ineffectual siege, they had to retire, leaving the cruel bishop not only

THE CASTLE OF EHRENFELS.

the victor in the struggle, but a greater tyrant than ever.

Hatto was not the man to either forget or forgive those who dared to dispute his will or defy his authority.

He was subtle, cruel, and cunning.

He could wait for revenge as well as take it on the moment, and when the opportunity offered, he was not slow to avail himself of it.

The peasants, having grasped the sword instead of the ploughshare, and wielded the pike instead of the sickle, there was no harvest that year in the Rheingau.

Want assailed the people on all sides.

Famine stared them in the face.

As a natural consequence, its twin brother, pestilence, stalked through the land.

Thousands were starving. The child died on its mother's lap for want of nourishment.

The wife perished in the husband's arms of starvation.

Strong men were weakened by want and disease, and misery and despair were seen on all sides.

Food was scarce throughout the Rheingau.

Money could not purchase it.

Prayers were unavailing to fill the empty stomachs of the groaning suffering poor.

But while want reigned on all sides, the granaries of the Bishop of Mayence were bursting with their load.

That one man had hoarded sufficient grain to save the lives of thousands—enough to ward off want and disease for months to come.

From him and him alone could rescue come for those who were perishing.

Abjectly they sought his presence, and, on bended knees, implored for food at any price.

It was refused, and the supplicants driven forth with blows.

Desperate in their want, many sought to obtain by theft that which was denied for prayers or gold.

This so incensed Hatto that he took council with Sir Cuno, and, burning for revenge upon a defeated and suffering people, a hellish plot was concocted between them, the enormity of which will ever be remembered while the Rhine flows to the sea.

Notice was given to the inhabitants of that district, who had been foremost in their clamours against the bishop, that on a certain day the prelate would open his granaries, and supply on credit to the poor a great quantity of grain.

The joy which this caused among the populace was unbounded.

Those who before had cursed the bishop from the very bottom of their hearts, now spoke his name with blessings.

Oh, how eagerly the day was waited for that was to give them food.

Mothers pressed their children to their bosoms and sobbed in joy.

Strong men vowed that never more would they raise hand or voice against the tyrant.

The day came at length.

At an early hour old and young, the strong and the feeble, the lame and the blind, repaired to the spot which was appointed for them to receive the grain.

From near and far, from mountain and valley, they bent their steps, all eager to obtain that food so necessary to life.

Hatto and the knight rode amongst them, and spoke words of cheer and hope to their ears.

No voice murmured now, no hand was raised but in supplication ; tears of joy were in every eye, blessings on every tongue.

That day Bishop Hatto might have won for himself the love of a people that would have never perished—might have raised for himself an army of friends that would have defended him to the last drop of blood in their veins.

But the heart of the bishop was as hard as the stones of which his castles were built.

By his command the people entered an enormous barn to receive the grain.

Willingly they flew to the spot.

Old and young men, women and children, the grey-bearded sire with life almost spent, the parent and the lover, the widowed and the fatherless, jostled and fought their way in till several hundred beings had gained an entrance and the place would hold no more.

Then the look of pity which Hatto had put on gave place to one of fiendish triumph and hellish revenge.

"Secure the doors !" he cried to his followers.

The order was obeyed.

But no murmur arose from those within.

Patiently they awaited the promised food.

"Now, Cuno," said the prelate, " now is the hour for revenge—now the time to teach these murmurers a terrible lesson and prevent for ever a discontented people from rising against their masters. Be thine the hand to avenge me!"

Sir Cuno dismounted, and, taking a torch from one of the bishop's retainers, kindled it.

The cheeks of the rude followers grew pale.

In several parts heaps of straw had been piled, and on these were laid branches of trees.

Cuno approached these heaps one after the other, thrusting the flaming brand into them.

The dry stubble instantly caught in flame.

And now from the interior of the barn appalling shrieks, fearful curses, and a terrible clamour arose.

Cries for mercy pealed in chorus.

The men flung themselves against the walls.

Women pressed their babes to their breasts, and prayed.

Children cried, and shrieked, and moaned in agony.

And the wild flames leaped, and licked, and twined themselves up the walls and over the roofs, and roared and hissed in bitter mockery.

The doors were forced from within, but a wall of fire prevented egress for the doomed.

With cries of terror and prayers for mercy, they fell back, and the flames rushed on and in, and twined themselves about the forms of the starving victims.

The completion of this story will be found on pages 142 to 144 of our next number.

[Continued from page 102.]

THE LOVERS OF FALKENBURG.

FOR your sake, fair Evelinda, be it so, but yon upstart shall yet learn what it is to defy the oldest, wealthiest, and proudest noble of the Rhine.

And jerking the rein fiercely, he turned his horse's head towards the castle.

Once more placing her hand in that of Otho, the cavalcade moved onward.

"You have a cruel and powerful foe, sir knight," said Evelinda with a sigh.

"Never fear, lady," said Otho, "I wear a good blade and possess a powerful arm."

"But your retainers are few, his are many," she said sadly.

"They follow a man they love," replied Otho gaily. "Victory rests not always with numbers. But, forewarned, I shall be prepared, and the knight of Ehrenfels will find no mean resistance should he dare assail my castle."

"Well I know your courage. But oh! should you fall beneath his anger, I should be very unhappy."

"And yet, lady," he said, bending down his head till his face nearly touched her own, "I am nothing to you."

She looked up into his eyes, and the tears started to her own.

"You know not," she replied, pressing the hand she held, "how dear this day's work has rendered you to me."

"Lady," he said, sinking his voice to a whisper, "it has rendered you dearer to me than all the world. Fate has thrown you thus in my path. I feel our destinies are linked together. I feel—I know I love you."

She bowed her head upon her bosom, and her hand trembled in his own.

"Evelinda," he said, after a moment's pause, "A few minutes and yon castle walls will hide you from my sight. Speak, ere the blackness of night falls upon my soul. Do I love in vain?"

She raised her eyes to his.

"No," she replied quickly, "for I can never love another."

"Then am I blessed indeed," he exclaimed. "Oh Evelinda, that love shall be the bright star of my destiny. Till now I never knew what it was to love—its passion felt, it can die only with death itself."

"Only with death," she repeated. "Only with death!"

There was a sadness in her tone that alarmed him.

"You will be mine?" he whispered.

"I will never be another's," was her reply, in the same low tone. "But, hist! see where my father comes."

He raised his eyes.

They stood at the entrance of the castle, and before them were Sir Conrad and Warbeck.

"My child," cried Sir Conrad, springing to her side "thanks to Our Lady, you are safe."

"Yes, father," she replied gaily, "but I have hurt my foot in the fall my horse gave me, when gored by the boar who lies dead alongside poor Fritz. This noble knight avenged his death, and saved your daughter from sharing his sad doom."

"Sir Otho, I am your debtor for ever," said the knight, taking the young man by the hand.

Warbeck turned angrily away.

"You are welcome to the halls of Rheinstein—right welcome. Carry her in, good fellows. Sir Otho, you will follow me."

They entered the castle, and as Otho passed Warbeck, the knight of Ehrenfels fixed a look of undying hatred upon him.

The young knight smiled scornfully and passed on.

Sir Conrad summoned her maids, and lifted his daughter from the litter.

"Sir knight," said Evelinda, placing her hand in Otho's, as the maids entered, "I shall ever remember your kindness."

She gave him a look that sent the blood coursing through his veins like molten lead, and leaning on the arms of her attendants, was borne from the hall.

"Sir Otho, you will follow me to the banquet hall," said the father, turning to the knight of Falkenburg.

Otho looked up with a start, to perceive the eye of Warbeck fixed upon him with a malicious glance.

Otho had no care to remain longer in the castle now that Evelinda had retired, and, feeling anything but inclined for conversation or mirth, he replied—

"By your leave, sir knight, I will return to my own castle, and wait on you to-morrow. I am wearied with the chase, and ill befitting a seat at your board at the present moment."

"As you will," said the old knight. "But if you will not remain, take with you at least the gratitude of the man whose child you so nobly defended."

"And take with you the curses of the lord of Ehrenfels," hissed Warbeck to himself.

Sir Otho bowed, and summoning his attendants around him, left the castle to return to his own stronghold.

When Otho pressed his couch that night, he could not sleep for some time.

The lovely face of Evelinda was before him, and his heart throbbed with emotions to which he had hitherto been a stranger.

When at length the drowsy lord closed his eyes in slumber, the dark face of the lord of Ehrenfels came between him and the bright vision like a dark cloud passing before the sun.

The next day Sir Otho mounted his horse, and rode to the castle of Rheinstein, in the hopes of meeting the beautiful Evelinda.

To his surprise he found the drawbridge up, and the portcullis down, and in answer to the summons blown upon his horn, the seneschal appeared upon the ramparts and bade him return to his own castle, as the lord of Rheinstein had declined to receive him.

Otho's surprise at this conduct was great, but he attributed it to the influence of Warbeck, and angered at the insult, he returned home.

But Otho could not rest without again seeing the beautiful Evelinda.

Day after day he sought the vicinity of the castle of Rheinstein, in the vain hope of encountering her, or learning something respecting her, but a month passed away without his hopes being realized.

Then a strange story reached his ears, and spread throughout the Rheingau.

It fell upon the heart of Sir Otho with the force of a thunderbolt.

It turned his brain giddy, and maddened his very soul.

Evelinda, the lovely daughter of the lord of Rheinstein, was about to espouse the knight of Ehrenfels.

So unwilling are mankind to believe that which is distasteful to them, that for a time, Sir Otho would not give credence to the story.

But his doubts were soon dispelled by the preparations being made at the castle for the wedding day, and also those at the chapel where the nuptials were to be celebrated.

Sir Otho now gave himself up to despair, but one so brave and gay as he had ever been could not long remain in this state of mind, and so he set himself to think how to prevent what he felt was a sacrifice.

Should he sally out with his retainers, attack the castle of Rheinstein, and bear off the unwilling victim?

He looked at the score and half of armed men in his halls, and felt how vain would be the attempt to overcome the united forces of the father and intended husband, who could number just ten times as many.

"No," he muttered, "that will neither gain me my bride, nor save her from the threatened doom. I will send a challenge to Sir Warbeck to meet me in the valley, and with sword and battle-axe, fight for the possession of Evelinda."

Placing his mailed glove in the hands of a youthful knight, whose friendship he valued, he sent him to Ehrenfels with the challenge to its lord.

When the youth returned, it was with his face bleeding, and his bosom agitated with shame and rage.

"What answer sends Sir Warbeck?" asked the knight of Falkenburg, quietly.

"He flung your mailed glove in my face, and bade me tell its owner, that he had no time now to accept the challenge of an upstart lout—that after his marriage with the daughter of Sir Conrad, he would come with all his forces, and chastise the insolence of Sir Otho of Falkenburg."

"The coward!" cried Otho, fiercely; "but I will foil him yet. Never shall he wed her while I can wield a sword. And dared he thus insult my messenger?"

"I had avenged that insult with my sword," replied the youth, "but he bade his followers thrust me forth from his hall."

"The Lady Evelinda— heard you aught of her?" asked Otho.

"Thus much rumour says—that she is pale and wretched, and kept close prisoner in the hall of her father."

"And I am powerless to aid her," moaned the knight of Falkenburg. "When is this accursed marriage to take place?" he added, quickly.

"On the first day of the ensuing week —at the chapel in the valley—whither she will be escorted by the united forces of those two powerful nobles."

Otho paced the floor thoughtfully and excitedly.

There were but a few days now, and he was powerless to avert the fate he was sure was as distasteful to Evelinda as it was to himself.

At length he paused abruptly before the youth.

"Victory is not always with the strong," he said. "What my retainers must fail to accomplish, I will seek to do alone. Now to put my castle in a perfect state of siege, and wait as patiently as possible for the wedding morn."

The youth looked inquiringly for an explanation of his views, but Sir Otho kept his own counsel and waved him off.

From that moment, Sir Otho seemed more composed and hopeful, and set about making preparations for placing his stronghold in a perfect state of defence, with his old smile on his face, and the old tone in his voice.

Meantime the lovely Evelinda, having recovered from the pains of body caused by the fall from her horse, now sat in her chamber suffering the most acute agony of soul.

The lord of Ehrenfels had so importuned her father to bestow her hand upon him, and looking only to the power he would gain by such an alliance, and believing that wealth and greatness were more conducive to his child's welfare than the love of a poor knight, he resolved to ally his daughter to the haughty noble, old enough to be her father.

The grief of his daughter had little effect upon him, and imagining himself to be best judge of what was best for her, he resolved to close his doors against Otho, and keep his daughter in close confinement, so long as she remained under his charge.

Still, both himself and Sir Warbeck were not without some fears that the brave young knight, Otho, would endeavour to frustrate their views, and they decided to unite their forces, and crush any attempt he might make to delay or oppose the ceremony, in the bud.

At length the morning dawned that was to make Evelinda the bride of the man she abhorred.

The preparations had been on an extensive and magnificent scale.

The arch of her father's castle was festooned with flowers, and the halls hung with gay banners.

The maidens of the Rheingau were to strew her path with flowers, and the strains of minstrelsy were to enliven the march to the chapel.

It was a splendid cavalcade that sallied out of the castle of Rheinstein that bright beautiful morning, consisting not only of the united followers of the two knights,

armed to the teeth, but several nobles who had been invited to the ceremony.

The bridegroom in his gorgeous coat of mail, and Sir Conrad, his armour glistening in the sunlight, and his plume dancing in the breeze, rode one on either side the heavily-veiled, pale-faced, trembling bride, who seemed more like one going to be sacrificed than wedded.

The minstrels tuned their harps, the virgins scattered their flowers, the plumes danced in the wind, and the sunlight glistened upon the burnished arms and shining mail of that glorious cavalcade as it slowly wound along the narrow path that skirted the river.

With a glance of satisfaction, the eye of Warbeck roamed along the line of armed men, and rested on the face of his bride.

With a feeling of triumph he gazed up at the frowning walls of Falkenburg, and thought how vain would be the attempt of Sir Otho to descend from his eyrie to pluck away his bride.

At length the chapel was reached, and the bishop and his attendant priests stood within and before the entrance, ready to conduct the bridal party to the altar.

The cavalcade came to a pause.

Sir Warbeck and Evelinda dismounted, and with their retainers at their back, left the bridal party, and entered the chapel.

With a gallantry that even made him appear more hideous in her eyes, Sir Warbeck led Evelinda to the altar, where the priest was ready with his book, and where the knight pointed out to her the cushion where she was to kneel, and near which one of her women was already prostrating herself.

But she shrank from him with a look of horror and disgust on her face.

An angry flush leaped to the baron's face, and her father advancing, cast a frowning glance towards his daughter.

"Your hand, fair Evelinda," said the baron, in tones in which were ill-disguised the annoyance he felt.

But she still shrank from its touch.

"My son," said a priest," stepping forward, " I will—if you will allow this lady to step aside with me—speak a word in her ear that will bring back the rose to her cheek and the smile to her lips."

Sir Warbeck gazed upon the priest, but his face and head were covered by the cowl, and he could only see that he was yet young.

"Do so, good father," he said, "for in faith this sad look ill becomes so happy a time."

When the priest had retired without, or rather reached the door of the chapel, he drew back his cowl from his face and whispered in a tone that none other ears were reached but those of Evelinda.

"'Tis Otho, lady. I will save you—speak but the word."

"Save me and I will bless you," she replied.

"Then quickly leap into the saddle, grasp firm the rein, and my castle shall be your shelter, or I find a grave on the banks of the Rhine. Be firm, be fearless, and you are saved."

Quick as the lightning's flash she mounted ; then robe and cowl were flung aside, and Sir Otho of Falkenberg, clad from head to heel in burnished mail, sprang on the steed behind her.

His left arm, flung around her form, grasped the bridle, his right hand wielded his heavy battle-axe.

His long spurs were plunged deeply into the horse's flanks.

Up reared the steed.

Down went Sir Warbeck in the dust as the animal plunged forward.

Away scattered priests and retainers, right and left.

Away went the horse and its double burden like the wind, through the armed ranks.

A shout of surprise, a cry of rage, and a laugh of triumph, and bruised and bleeding, Sir Warbeck sprang to his feet and leapt into the saddle.

"Follow, follow!" he roared. "Death to Otho of Falkenburg."

And he madly spurred his horse forward.

Sir Conrad was silent, but he buried his spurs in his horse's flanks, and unsheathed his bright sword.

"Shoot him down," cried Warbeck, foaming with rage.

"Hold," roared Sir Conrad, "you may slay my child! On, on! the brook will bar his passage to the castle walls."

Away went the two nobles in pursuit, and thundering after them knights and retainers.

With one arm round the drooping form, with his right hand grasping his battle-axe, and with the spurs urging the steed to its utmost speed, away at a mad gallop went the lovers down to the river.

With his nose to the earth and his tail erect, away went the gallant steed—the clatter of the pursuing troops lending speed to his flight.

Firmer now was the clasp of Otho's arm around her waist.

On, on towards the brook, which crossed the road and whose high and rocky banks seemed to shut out all further chance of flight.

"Sit firm and fear not," he cried. "Once the brook is crossed, you are saved."

One shuddering look Evelinda cast at the stream and its rocky sides—one pleading glance to Heaven, and she closed her eyes, and slackened the rein.

Deep plunged the spurs of Otho into the beast's side, and with a bound that seemed as though the brute was flying through the air, the noble steed took the leap.

The next moment he stood on the opposite bank.

One look Otho cast behind him.

His pursuers were not a hundred yards off.

Shaking his battle-axe in defiance, he pulled hard at the rein, and turned the head of the noble animal towards the towers of Falkenburg.

On up the hill tore the gallant steed, clearing the masonry that supported the river terraces, and sending showers of earth into the air at every bound.

Over the drawbridge, with a leap and a clatter it tore, and stood within the castle yard, flecked with foam, trembling with exertion.

"Up drawbridge!—down portcullis!" roared the knight.

The followers, who had watched the chase, and had manned the bridge, wanted no second bidding.

With a harsh creaking up went the drawbridge with a rattling clang—down fell the portcullis, and the cheers of the retainers of Falkenburg reached the ears of the shouting, swearing pursuers, now breasting the hill, and making for the gate of the castle.

Throwing himself from his horse, Sir Otho lifted Evelinda from her seat, and pressed her to his heart.

"You are saved, sweet one," he cried, rapturously.

She nestled her head upon his bosom, and wept in joy.

By this time the pursuers had reached the castle, and were calling loudly upon Sir Otho to surrender his prize, on pain of having his castle stormed.

"Man the ramparts—open the loopholes!" cried Sir Otho. "Those with whom we were powerless to contend on the plains, we can fight behind our walls.

The loopholes were opened—the ramparts and towers were manned, and Sir Warbeck and Conrad saw that Otho was determined to fight for his prize.

Besides this they saw that the castle had been placed in a state of siege, and that nothing but a blockade would ever induce its owner to surrender.

"Come," said Otho, "let us see what terms we can make with your father."

Together they went to the ramparts—Evelinda clinging to his arm.

The sight of his intended bride hanging upon the arm of his youthful rival, enraged the knight of Ehrenfels to such a degree, that he threatened that if she were not immediately restored to him, to put every soul within the castle to the sword.

"Sir knight," returned Otho, "the walls of my castle are high, and the ditches deep : you would but hurl your strength against it in vain, and bring destruction upon your followers."

"Will you surrender that lady to me?" cried Warbeck.

"Never!" replied Otho, "you have no claim to her."

"But I have, Sir Otho," said her father.

"If it is her wish that I should restore her to you, sir knight," said Otho, "I will not retain her a moment within my castle, but if she prefer to remain here with me, your united forces are powerless to wrest her from these walls."

"I will not return!" cried Evelinda. "You would force me to wed a man I can never love. Here I have given my heart, and here I will bestow my hand."

She placed her hand in that of Otho.

"And he who would dispute her right to give her hand where she will, and to whom she will, let him take up my gage," replied the young knight.

And taking his mailed glove from his hand, he hurled it from the battlements at the feet of Warbeck.

"A brave challenge from one who shields himself behind his castle walls," sneered Sir Warbeck, taking up the glove. "I dispute her right, and defy you to the combat."

"Withdraw your followers to the other side of the brook, and I will descend," said Otho.

"What do you fear?" said Ehrenfels, with a sneer.

"Treachery. The knight who would force a woman to become his unwilling bride will not hesitate to take advantage of his adversary's weakness."

Warbeck bit his lips. He had meditated treachery when he took up the gage.

"Knight of Falkenburg," cried Sir Conrad, "you insult me by the suspicion. I pledge you my knightly word that no follower of mine shall bar your passage to or from your castle, or place his foot within the walls, till as a conqueror you have returned, or vanquished, my daughter is claimed by Sir Warbeck."

"Then my lord baron, I will descend to redeem my gage," cried Otho. "Lady," he added, turning to Evelinda, "I will win thy fair hand with my sword or perish within thy presence."

He raised her hand to his lips, and hurried from the ramparts, leaving her an anxious spectator to a scene that was to render her the most happy or most wretched of women.

The portcullis was raised, the drawbridge lowered, and over it, mounted on his charger, rode along the noble Otho, his heavy battle-axe slung at his saddle bow.

The lord of Ehrenfels had mounted his steed, from which he had leaped to pick up the glove of his challenger, and sat battle-axe in hand and visor down.

Sir Conrad, who was a brave and honourable man, had ordered the retainers to fall back some distance down the hill, and now sat at their head, leaving the two men free from all chance of interruption, who were to do battle for the hand of his daughter.

Otho rode forward till within a few paces of Sir Warbeck, and then grasped his axe, threw a hurried glance at the half-fainting girl on the ramparts, flung his shield before him, and spurred to the charge.

Up flashed the gleaming blades in the air, down they descended, each caught upon the opposing shield.

Again and again they flashed in the sunlight, and rang upon shield, helm, and breastplate, till at length, by a fierce blow from Otho, the armlets of Sir Warbeck's shield were broken, and he was hurled from his horse to the ground.

He was on his feet in a moment, and, leaping from the saddle, Otho threw aside his shield and battle-axe, and grasping his sword, sprang forward once more to the fray.

Sir Warbeck also threw aside the axe and took the sword, but his rage at his fall had so maddened him, that he struck wildly at his adversary, and was forced back down the hill.

For some time the clash of steel awoke the echoes, and then the point of Otho's weapon pierced a joint of Warbeck's armour, and was driven by a powerful hand to the heart of the lord of Ehrenfels.

As Otho drew forth the ensanguined blade, Sir Warbeck sank back dead to the earth, and Sir Conrad and the attendants ascended the hill.

Sir Otho cast a look to the ramparts in search of Evelinda, but she was not there ; the next moment he saw her hurrying through the gateway towards him.

"Fate has given you the victory, sir knight," said the lord of Rheinstein, looking down at the corpse of Warbeck.

"And the hand of your daughter," said

Otho. "My lord baron, you will not deny me that which even Heaven appears willing to bestow. She never could have been happy with that man. Be merciful to your child; be just to me and to yourself."

"I will," said Sir Conrad, "for you are brave and honourable. Come hither, girl. Give me your hand. Take her, Sir Otho, and may you be happy."

He placed the hand of Evelinda in that of the young knight, and turning to those around, said—

"If one there be who disputes my right to bestow the hand of my daughter on this brave knight, let him speak."

But no one spoke.

"Then, nobles of the Rheingau," he continued, addressing the assembled knights, "The wedding of my daughter shall not be delayed. The priests wait her return. The bridegroom is impatient. Ho! there, bring forth her steed, and we will forthwith to the ceremony."

Otho grasped the hand of the old noble, and in a grateful tone said—

"My lord baron, I thank you. Never will you regret the gift you bestow on me, or that I interfered with your intention to-day. If I have not the wealth of the lord of Ehrenfels, I have a heart to love and an arm to shield your child."

"Say no more, but bear her to the altar," said Conrad. "I knew not how deep was her love for you till now, or how worthy

"WITH A CRASH AND A BOUND A HUGE BOAR SPRANG UPON HIM."

you were of her hand. Once more, take her and be happy."

Sir Otho lifted her into the saddle, and the retainers, evidently pleased at the alteration in the programme, formed once more into lines, and headed by Otho, Conrad and Evelinda, commenced the return march to the chapel, leaving a few to bear the body of the lord of Ehrenfels back to his castle.

Great was the surprise of the priests to see the bride return with another bridegroom, but the ceremony was performed, and without any interruption, for not one but considered she had obtained a husband more worthy of her love than the dark-browed baron of Ehrenfels.

The smile had returned to the lips of Evelinda, and the light of joy beamed in her eyes, and she who had left her father's castle an unwilling bride, returned to it a happy wife, amid the cheers and blessings of the people of the Rheingau.

And never did the old baron regret the change, nor Evelinda and her husband repent the desperate step he had taken to foil Warbeck and secure the woman he loved for his own.

END OF THE LOVERS OF FALKENBURG.

Our next number will contain " Carl the Ferryman."

CARL THE FERRYMAN.

IN the duchy of Nassau, on the right bank of the Rhine, on the summit of a high and almost conical rock, stands the imposing castle of Marksburg, an unaltered specimen of a stronghold of the middle ages.

It is indeed the beau ideal of the old castle of romance, with its mysterious narrow passages, winding stairs, vaults hewn in the living rock, which served in former days as dungeons.

Among these is the horrible pit called

"'THE PROPHECY IS FULFILLED!' EXCLAIMED THE SPECTRE."

Hundloch (Dog-hole), into which the prisoners were let down as a bucket into a well, by a windlass, and a Chamber of Torture (Folterkammer), whence the rack has been only lately removed.

The dark deeds committed within its walls in bygone times, and the fulfilment of the prophecy, are comprised in the legend attached to the massive edifice.

Eustace of Marksburg and his younger brother Leofric paid their court to the same lady, whose choice fell upon the former.

It was with bitter feelings of wrath and disappointment that Leofric beheld the smiles of the woman he loved lavished on his elder brother, who held the dukedom, and inhabited the castle of Marksburg; and these feelings were still further increased when he knew that the day for their nuptials was fixed.

With a bitter and awful execration, he swore to be revenged, not only on his brother, but on his brother's wife; but he dissembled his feelings, and presented himself at the wedding with an unclouded brow and smiling face, and wished the married pair joy, and pledged them heartily at the banquet table.

Eustace, brave, generous, and unsuspicious, was delighted at these proofs of his brother's affection; the more so since he feared the rivalry which he knew had existed between them would have made an irreparable breach in their friendship.

No such results, however, followed, and the brothers seemed more cordially united than ever.

Leofric was the owner of a small stronghold on the opposite side of the Rhine, but yielding to the fraternal invitations of the Duke Eustace, he had since his marriage resided almost constantly at Marksburg.

But though he wore an outward semblance of happiness, his heart was torn and distracted with fierce and lawless passions.

It tormented him to behold his brother happy in the love he had failed to secure.

Every smile of the beautiful duchess seemed to mock him, and he thirsted for some opportunity to blight the joy he could not share.

This chance came at last.

A twelvemonth passed away, when a son was born to the duke.

The usual rejoicings took place in honour of the happy event, and the child was christened Eustace after his father.

Hardly had the festal period passed away, when the duke received intelligence that traces of a copper mine had been discovered on the borders of his estate.

Eager to assure himself of the existence of so valuable a treasure, Eustace departed to the spot, leaving his brother behind as a security for the safety of his beloved wife and child.

The journey was long, and the duke travelled alone, not wishing to trumpet forth the intelligence, which might have excited the cupidity of some lawless neighbouring baron.

The nobleman, having reached the place described, found from the appearance of the soil and rocks, and small pieces of ore which he discovered, that the report was true.

Joyfully continuing his researches, he came at last to what appeared to be a fissure in the ground, but which upon examination appeared to be the entrance to a subterranean abode.

He entered carefully, and, by a steep and circuitous path, reached at length the bottom of the mine.

It was intensely dark, and the worthy nobleman, in his anxiety to look around him, exclaimed—

"Oh, for a light, that I might gaze upon the treasures of this place!"

In a moment, as though his request had been answered, a soft, clear radiance illumined the subterranean depths, and he saw distinctly the bright metal glittering in streaky veins among the rocks.

With a thrill of exultation, he exclaimed—

"Thank Heaven for this gift! this princely fortune for my son and heir!"

"Thy son shall never live to inherit it," cried a mocking voice behind him.

Turning quickly, he beheld a man cloaked and masked, standing near.

The voice as well as the face of the speaker was disguised, but still it seemed familiar.

A horrible suspicion stole over him.

"Who art thou?" he cried.

"Thy bitter enemy, since the moment Constance de Walstein returned thy love," was the reply.

At the same moment the masked man, drawing a sword from beneath his cloak, plunged it into the breast of the unprepared Eustace.

With a cry of agony the wounded man grappled with his cowardly assassin.

"I will not die till I have seen thy face!" he gasped, and then, with a desperate effort, he tore the mask from off the murderer's face.

"My brother!" he groaned, as he sank down upon the rocky floor.

"Yes, thy brother, who has sworn to revenge himself on thee and thine," returned Leofric sternly, leaning on his dripping blade, and looking down upon him vindictively; "as I have slain thee, so will I slay thy wife and child, and this rich mine shall pour its treasures into my coffers."

"Fool!" exclaimed a clear, sweet voice that rang throughout the cavern, "dost thou hope to inherit wealth thou hast shed human blood to obtain? Listen!"

The voice then repeated in solemn accents part of the words of the legend—

"The mine shall yield no treasure,
To the despoiler's hand;
The guilt of blood is on him,
As he stalks through the land."

"Hark! dost thou hear?" cried the dying Eustace. "Thou hast missed the prize for which thou hast steeped thy soul in guilt, and the curse of innocent blood is on thy path for ever."

With these words, the nobleman fell back, and with a faint prayer for his wife and child, his spirit fled for ever.

Then the light died out, and the guilty Leofric shuddered as he stood in the dark vault, alone with his murdered victim.

To add to his horror, he could not find the way of egress.

In vain he sought to escape. The road seemed to have become blocked up.

Cursing his mischance, instead of repenting of his guilt, he still struggled to discover the end of the narrow path.

"Must I die like a rat in this dark hole?" he cried desperately. No! not while the fiend has power to hear and answer. Spirit of Evil aid me!" he shouted.

A low peal of thunder answered this profane invocation, and immediately a lurid glare surrounded him, and enabled him to discern at a short distance a little old man attired in a black velvet doublet, with a narrow-brimmed conical hat, from beneath which gleamed a pair of eyes full of malignant cunning.

"What do you want?" he asked.

"Deliverance from this infernal trap," answered Leofric.

"I am inclined to help thee," returned the demon, "for I foresee we shall be intimate acquaintances—dear friends."

Leofric recoiled slightly at this idea, but the hopes of freedom reconciled him to the prospect, and he said—

"Wilt thou show me the way out?"

"I will," answered the old man, who then turned towards the spot where the murdered Duke was lying, and said with an inquiring grin—

"Will you take your relative with you?"

Leofric turned away irritably.

"I beg your pardon, I'm sure," continued the fiend apologetically, "I forgot I was touching on a tender subject. This way."

The little old man found the path without any difficulty.

Leofric, keeping close behind, and guided by the lurid light that followed his conductor wherever he moved, soon reached the exterior.

When he looked around for his guide he had vanished.

"It must have been a dream, a phantom of my imagination," murmured Leofric.

"Oh, no, it wasn't," whispered the voice of the demon in his ear; "you will see me again, I dare say, before long."

The guilty man, with a shudder he could not repress, mounted his horse and rode rapidly away.

◦　　◦　　◦　　◦　　◦

That night the beautiful duchess sat in her chamber by the couch of her infant son, anxiously awaiting the return of her lord.

"'Tis late!" she exclaimed wearily, as the hours sped on, "would he were back again."

A faint sigh caused her to look around.

Her husband stood at a little distance. He was very pale, and regarded her with a sad, fixed gaze.

With an exclamation of joy she started up, and hurried towards him.

"My Eustace!" she cried, "I knew not you had returned."

She threw her arms around him, but clasped only a shadow.

She recoiled with a nameless terror, and gazed wildly at him.

"What art thou?" she murmured in fearful accents.

"I am your husband's spirit," returned the immaterial being, "slain by my brother Leofric, and I come to warn you. Fly, my beloved! fly with our child whilst you have time, or the same hand that destroyed my life will most surely be raised against you both. Farewell, beloved Constance! we shall meet again in Heaven.

Having uttered these words, the apparition melted away into thin air.

The duchess for a few moments stood riveted to the spot with surprise and terror, and then suddenly remembering the warning she had received, she snatched up her sleeping child, and was about to leave the castle.

But alas! too late. As she took the child from his bed, she heard hurried footsteps in the corridor, and ere she could reach the door, the murderer of her husband entered and confronted her.

"Whither goest thou, madam, so hastily?" he demanded, sternly.

The duchess was a woman of spirit, as well as beauty, and she replied—

"To avoid thee, wretch! whose sword is still wet with the blood of my beloved Eustace."

"Nay," returned Leofric, "do not fly from me. Having lost your protector, let me supply his place. You know I love you."

"Dost thou talk to me of love, thou monster?" exclaimed the indignant wife. "Hence, nor dare to mock me with such polluting words. I abhor—execrate you!"

"Beware how you treat me, at least!" cried Leofric, with a dark scowl on his features. You are entirely at my mercy, and, unless you yield yourself to my pleasure, I swear I will sacrifice you without the least remorse—you and your brat there."

He made a step forward to seize the infant, when the duchess, with a cry of terror, rushed past him, and fled wildly from the apartment.

Leofric, uttering fierce imprecations, followed in pursuit.

Down the winding staircase, and along the tortuous passages the terrified mother fled.

It was not her own safety that alarmed her, but that of her child.

She entered a large chamber, the windows of which overlooked the river.

With an agony of apprehension she clasped the poor infant to her bosom, as she heard the footsteps of her pursuer, who was hurrying through the rooms in eager search.

"My child! my precious one, must thou too be sacrificed to this cruel man?" she murmured.

"No! no! there is yet one way! only one, to save thee from his remorseless hand."

As if with a sudden thought she opened one of the windows.

"Heaven may preserve thee, my darling, though thy unhappy mother cannot."

Then with one last frantic embrace, as the feet of the ruffianly assailant trod the threshold, she cast the infant from her arms into the depths beneath.

A faint quick cry reached the mother's ear as it descended, and the next moment, the rude grasp of Leofric was on her delicate wrist, and his remorseless eyes glaring into hers with a ferocious and malignant expression.

"Where is the child?" he shouted.

"Safe! safe!" cried the young mother, exultingly. "Where thou canst not reach him."

"No matter, I have thee!" returned her brutal captor; "come!"

As he spoke, he sought to drag her from the chamber.

She resisted heroically, and her shrieks resounded through the lofty room, but the door was closed, and they reached little further.

Her cries were unheard.

In her despair, she fastened her nails desperately in the throat of her assailant.

At this determined resistance, all the fury of his vindictive nature was aroused, and drawing his dagger, he plunged it into her fair breast.

"Thus I send thee to follow thy husband, thou raving Jezebel!" he cried fiercely.

"I thank thee for that blow," she cried faintly; "'tis the kindest act thou hast yet performed. Beloved husband—beloved child, I come to join ye!"

These were the last words of Constance of Marksburg.

She sank down and died as she uttered them.

The blood from her wound oozed forth upon the oak floor, and as though in terrible attestation of the atrocious deed, the stain could never afterwards be effaced.

After these cruel deeds, Leofric took possession of the castle, assumed his brother's title, and by riotous living and deep drinking, essayed to stifle the accusations of conscience.

Often did he seek to discover the shaft of the mine, but in vain.

It seemed entirely to have disappeared.

He never married, but he had adopted the beautiful but portionless daughter of a poor friend, whom he intended one day to raise to the enviable position of his wife.

And thus seventeen years rolled away.

   ❀   ❀   ❀   ❀   ❀

It was a bleak night, and the clouds were drifting rapidly along before the wind, as a handsome youth sat in a small boat moored to the Rhine bank.

Presently a hale voice called to him—

"Hallo, Carl !"

"I am here, good Richter !" he called in return. "What wouldst thou ?"

"There will be no customers for the ferry boat to-night, my lad, and the wind is keen ; come inside and warm thyself."

"I will wait a little longer," returned Carl. "I am not cold, and will join you presently."

The wind was piercing, and there must have been some motive that kept the youth waiting there ; and not only waiting—but warm.

Presently it appeared in the shape of a lovely, delicate girl, who, with light but cautious steps, glided along the river's bank.

"Carl, are you there ?" she cried.

The youth, who heard her step, hastened forward, and clasped her in his arms.

"Yes, my own loved one," he answered. "I have been here waiting anxiously this hour."

"I could not come before," she replied, "and now I am here—oh, Carl !"

Her voice was sad, and as she uttered this exclamation, she buried her head on the young man's shoulder and burst into tears.

"What ails thee, dearest Adelgitha ?" he inquired tenderly.

"I have heard intelligence to-day, Carl, that blights for ever all the blissful hopes that we had formed."

"What is it ? Tell me, love."

"I confessed my affection for thee to my guardian, and he——"

"Scorned your prepossession for one so humble, was it not so ?"

"Nay, more than that. He informed me he had other intentions towards me."

"He means, he would give thee to one of higher rank ?"

"No. He will give me to none : his intention is to marry me himself."

A fresh burst of sobs followed this announcement, and Carl himself was greatly moved.

"Alas !" he cried, "what can be done ? How can I, nameless, friendless as I am, do aught to rescue thee from this detested union ?"

"I will never consent !" exclaimed Adelgitha, determinedly. "Rather than be the bride of Duke Leofric, I would throw myself from the castle turret into the deep river that runs beneath."

It was a difficult task for Carl, almost despairing as he was himself, to minister consolation to the afflicted girl at his side.

But he soothed her with hopeful words, which, while he uttered them, he dared not believe would ever come to pass.

In this way some time elapsed, and then Adelgitha said, "I must go now, dearest. It was with difficulty I stole away from the castle, and my absence may be noticed. Good-bye, love !"

"Good-bye, my heart's treasure," Carl murmured fervently, as he strained her to his breast. "I shall see you again soon ?"

"Yes, to-morrow if possible."

Carl did not immediately return to Paul Richter's hut, but sat in the boat musing sadly upon his hopeless prospects.

Presently a voice hailed him from the other side of the river—

"Ho, ferryman, a boat !" it cried.

Carl instinctively seized the oars, and instantly commenced his journey.

He was so occupied with his thoughts that he seemed to have reached his destination in a moment.

On his arrival, he saw standing on the bank a cloaked man, who at once stepped into the boat.

"You row quickly," remarked the stranger, as he seated himself ; "now let us see if you can return as quickly as you came."

It was too dark for Carl to be able to distinguish the features of his face, but he noticed that his eyes glowed like red-hot coals.

For some time he rowed on in silence, and then the cloaked man said, abruptly—

"I can see you're in trouble, youngster."

"I should have thought it had been almost too dark for you or anybody else to see anything," replied Carl, with a half-smile.

"Ha, ha!" laughed his companion, "there are some beings who can see as well in the dark as the light. I am one of those."

No more was said, until the opposite shore was reached, when the stranger stepped on to the bank. Carl, having moored his boat, followed, and having received the reward of his labour, waited for his customer to depart.

But instead of this, the man addressed him in a confidential and friendly manner.

"We must become better acquainted, young man," he said. "I know all that afflicts you, and I sympathize with people in trouble, and as I have the power to aid, I may say I assist a great many."

The tone of the speaker's voice was very peculiar, and Carl felt he would have given the world to have been able to see his face.

Instantly, as though the mysterious being had divined his thoughts, he remarked—

"We're all in the dark; a little light would enable us to see each other's features."

As he spoke, a pale lurid light encircled the spot on which he stood, and the young ferryman had the opportunity he desired.

A very withered, sallow, unpleasant face it was on which he looked.

A face full of concentrated malice and cunning, from which he instinctively shrank.

The stranger allowed him full time to contemplate him, and then he said abruptly—

"You love the maiden Adelgitha?"

"I do!" replied Carl, in great surprise at the knowledge his fare evinced of a secret which he believed to be known but to a few.

"She loves you," continued the speaker.

"Yes," returned Carl, hesitatingly.

"The Duke Leofric means to marry her."

"He—he does—I believe," stammered the young man.

"He does, I'm sure!" exclaimed the stranger, emphatically, "and it is that that is breaking both your hearts."

Carl sighed.

"Don't sigh, my young friend," remarked the other. "I can alter this without the slightest difficulty."

"You can?" almost gasped the youth.

"Yes, I can change the duke's inten-

tions—nay more, cause him to consent to Adelgitha's union with you."

"And you will?" eagerly asked Carl.

"Certainly," returned his companion, with equal earnestness, his eyes sparkling like two meteors, "and on very easy conditions."

This was said in such a peculiarly persuasive tone, that Carl's suspicions were aroused.

"What are the conditions?" he asked; "what do you require of me?"

"Nothing—that is, during your life—and I only require your body after you are dead; and you know a dead body isn't worth much."

"But my soul!" exclaimed Carl, recoiling with a kind of horror from the tempter; "what of that?"

The cloaked man uttered a scornful laugh.

"Do not meddle with matters you don't understand," he exclaimed; "your business is not with the soul, but the body! not with the next life, but this."

"You reason falsely, stranger," cried Carl, vehemently. "Never will I secure the happiness of my mortal part, by forfeiting the immortal!"

The countenance of the cloaked man assumed an expression fearfully demoniacal.

"You are a fool!" he cried.

"You are a fiend!" returned the youth; "and by this holy symbol, I bid you hence!"

As he spoke, Carl crossed himself devoutly.

The demon—for such he was—staggered back with a howl of dismay; but, recovering himself, he said, "I have not done with you yet. You'll want me one day. We shall meet again," and immediately vanished.

Carl, who rejoiced at his departure, hastened to the ferry-house, where he found Paul waiting for him.

In his ear he imparted the strange events of the last half-hour.

The good old man uttered a devout thanksgiving.

"You have resisted a temptaton of the fiend, my son," he exclaimed, impressively: "depend upon it, this cloaked man was the tempter of souls in disguise."

Carl was silent for a few moments, and then he said, sorrowfully.

"Much as I love Adelgitha, I almost wish I had never saved her life."

"Why?" asked Paul.

"Because then I might never have met her; we should never have loved each other as we do."

"That is ungrateful," replied Paul.

"I do not mean to be so," went on the young man, regretfully; "but what can I, the son of a poor ferryman, do to render myself a fitting mate for one like her?"

"Suppose you were not the son of a ferryman?" said Paul, seriously.

"Not!" echoed Carl, excitedly; "am I not your son, then?"

"No, my lad," returned the old man, "I picked you up from the river when you were an infant, seventeen years ago. You were thrown from one of the castle windows at the dead of night, and if I may speak what I think, judging from that circumstance and the crest upon the clothes you wore, you are nobly born."

"Heaven! is it possible?" exclaimed the youth, his cheeks flushing, excitedly; "and are my parents living?"

"Alas! no," returned the ferryman, "or you would not be here. It was because you were an orphan I brought you up as my own."

"Did you know the authors of my being?"

"Yes, and I believe they met their death by unfair means."

"Say you so?"

"I do. I believe both were foully murdered!"

"By whom?" cried Carl, impetuously, starting from his seat.

"By Duke Leofric—your uncle!"

"Merciful Powers!" exclaimed the young man, "then it is he who keeps me from my rights?"

Carl crossed over to the ferryman and embraced him warmly.

"Dear, kind old friend," he cried, "to you I owe my life. You protected me in my helpless infancy, and I shall never forget the obligations I owe you. I thank you for this intelligence, since now, without revealing the author of my information, I can boldly claim the hand of Adelgitha."

"You must proceed cautiously, my dear Carl," replied Paul. "Leofric is a bold, bad man, and would not hesitate to sacrifice you, if he thought you divined the secret of his crime."

"Fear not!" said Carl.

That night the young man had a strange dream.

He thought he stood in a vast cavern, filled with precious metal, whilst a fair being stood by his side, and, pointing to it, exclaimed—

"Son of Eustace of Marksburg, all thou seest was thy father's; it is now thine!"

The dream haunted him, and, the next day, full of strange thoughts he wandered away, scarcely heeding whither he journeyed.

At length he came to the spot where seventeen years before his father had stood.

There before his eyes, was the chasm in the earth, which the guilty Leofric had so often sought, and never been able to discover.

Impelled by an irresistible power, the youth descended until he stood in the subterranean abode.

Then the bright light gradually dispelled the darkness and he found himself in the very cavern he had visited in his dream, with the rocks glittering on every side with bright streaks of copper.

As he gazed with delight upon the prospect, a lovely female form appeared at his side and exclaimed—

"Son of Eustace of Marksburg, all thou seest was thy father's; it is now thine."

Thus his dream was fufilled.

Presently his attention was arrested by a less agreeable sight.

A skeleton clad in mouldered garments lay extended on the ground.

He started at the horrible sight, but mastering his emotion, he approached the relics of frail mortality.

As he gazed he observed near the fleshless hand of the skeleton a set of tablets.

Picking them up he discovered in characters barely legible the words—

"I die murdered by my brother Leofric.

"EUSTACE."

This was proof sufficient, and hastily taking from the mouldering remains a chain tarnished and mouldy with damp, he hastened away.

Having informed his guardian of what he had seen, he expressed his intention of visiting the castle.

In vain Paul sought to dissuade him from such a step; he was resolved.

Accordingly he presented himself at the gates, and sent in his fictitious name to his usurping uncle.

"Carl the ferryman!" exclaimed Leofric,

when the message was announced. "What business has he with me ?"

On the youth's entrance, his kinsman started involuntarily.

There was something in his noble bearing, the flash of his eye and the expression of his features, that recalled his brother to his memory.

The dark past came vividly before him.

But he restrained all show of emotion, as he said coolly—

"Well, ferryman, what seekest thou ?"

"Pardon me, duke," returned Carl, boldly, "but I seek the hand of your fair ward Adelgitha."

Leofric sprang from his seat fiercely.

"Audacious villain ! art thou mad ?" he cried.

"No, my lord," answered the youth, "I hope not. I admit the boon I seek is great, but I do not ask it without offering something of value in return."

"Psha !" growled Leofric, "dost thou not know that I intend to marry her my-

THE CASTLE OF MARKSBURG.

self ?" Then more calmly, but sarcastically, he asked, "But what dost thou offer ?"

"A valuable copper mine, duke !" was the quiet reply.

Leofric started as though a snake had stung him, and rose in violent excitement.

"What dost thou mean ? Dost thou mock me ?" he cried.

"I mock thee not, and I mean what I say," returned Carl. "Give me thy ward Adelgitha for my wife, and I will give thee in exchange my copper mine."

The duke burst into an ironical laugh.

"I do not believe thou hast any such thing to give," he said

"Come with me, and I will convince thee," proposed the young man.

"By Heaven, I will," exclaimed Leofric, "and this moment."

Together they visited the spot, and there, as Carl had said, the mouth of the mine disclosed itself.

"Strange," muttered the duke to himself, "that I should never have been able to discover this."

"No ! it is not strange," whispered conscience at his heart. And then he recalled the legendary verse—

" The mine shall yield no treasure,
    To the despoiler's hand ;
The guilt of blood is on him
    As he stalks through the land."

Leofric winced under the words.

"I must dissemble here," he thought, and then, in an assumed tone of conviction, he said to Carl—"I see now thy words are true ; but how didst thou, a ferryman, become possessed of so rich a treasure ?"

"That I cannot tell thee now," replied the youth, " but I promise to reveal the secret when Adelgitha is my bride. Dost thou consent ?"

Leofric paused in doubt as to the course he should take.

"What shall I answer ?" he inwardly ejaculated.

"Answer yes !" hissed a voice in his ear, which he recognised as that of the little old man. "Thou needst not keep thy word."

"True !" thought the duke, as he looked round but saw no trace of the speaker. "Well, I consent," he continued, addressing himself to Carl ; "thou shalt have my ward : I relinquish her in thy favour."

"And thou wilt give her to me at once ?" said the young man.

"At once. Return with me to the castle, where the marriage ceremony shall be performed."

Carl accompanied the duke back to his stronghold.

Adelgitha was summoned to his presence.

The maiden blushed and trembled as she confronted her lover in the presence of her guardian.

But her fears were allayed, when the latter said—

"I am informed by this young man that he loves thee, and I have therefore given my consent that he should wed thee. Art thou content ?"

Adelgitha, who desired nothing so much, replied by advancing to the young ferryman and throwing her white arms around him.

"Enough !" said Leofric ; "your nuptials shall take place at once."

The duke then ordered Odo, his seneschal, to procure a priest.

As he was leaving the castle for that purpose he encountered a hooded friar.

"You require my services ?" said the monk.

"Yes," returned Odo in some surprise. "Canst thou perform the marriage ceremony ?"

"Of course I can," chuckled the shrouded friar.

"Lead the way to the chapel."

The duke, with the bride and bridegroom, were already at the altar.

"Now proceed," cried Leofric.

The ceremony was about to commence, when a voice cried solemnly—

"Forbear this impious mockery !"

At the same moment, a venerable old man with snow-white hair and beard advanced.

This was the good Father Ambrose, a pious hermit, well known to Carl, who had benefitted much by his instructions and advice.

The holy man had heard the words of the cowled monk at the gate, and had followed them to the chapel.

"Worthy Ambrose," exclaimed the young bridegroom, "what mean your words ?"

"That I cannot suffer the marriage ceremony to be performed by that dark impostor."

He pointed to the fictitious monk as he spoke.

"He is a fiend !" he continued ; "and in the name of my master, I command him hence. *Sathanas, exorciso te* (Satan, I expel thee !)" he cried, as he held aloft his crucifix.

With a mighty roar of baffled fury, the veiled friar vanished in a flash of flame.

"Now," continued the good hermit, turning to the young couple, "I will unite you in holy bands."

Having performed the marriage service, and given his benediction to the bride and bridegroom, the venerable man departed.

No sooner was he gone, than Carl turned to Leofric, who stood with knitted brows by the altar, and exclaimed—

"Uncle, I salute thee ! the mine which I have given thee was my father's, who bequeathed it at his death to me his son."

"Thy father's !" exclaimed Leofric, staggering back and turning pale ; "who was thy father ?"

"Eustace, Duke of Marksburg !" replied the youth sternly, "and my mother Constance de Walstein—both foully murdered by thee, usurper !"

"Lying hound!" shouted the enraged Leofric, "thou shalt pay dearly for this audacious lie! What ho!" he called fiercely.

Odo and a body of armed retainers entered at the summons.

"Seize this caitiff, and throw him into the most noisome dungeon in the castle."

"The Hundloch?" asked Odo.

"Ay! the Hundloch! in that dog-hole let him remain till he starve, or the rats gnaw his flesh from his bones!" foamed the furious duke. "As for thee, thou whimpering baby," he added to the trembling Adelgitha, "retire to thy chamber and remain there till I summon thee."

Drowned in tears, and faltering forth earnest supplications for mercy, which were alike disregarded, the poor girl went sadly to her solitary apartment, to bemoan the fate of him she loved and could not protect.

In the meantime, the hapless Carl was dragged by a narrow winding staircase to the mouth of the foul pit known as the dog-hole.

Here he was compelled to enter a bucket, slimy and encrusted with the mould of ages.

Then he was lowered by means of a windlass into the horrible depths beneath.

A more fearful place of confinement could scarcely be imagined.

The ground was soft with fetid mud, across which rats scampered wildly, and in which noxious toads crawled.

The atmosphere was close and polluted, and the wretched prisoner felt that a few hours in that loathsome den would terminate his existence.

He sank down, and buried his face in his hands, in the silence of despair.

In the meantime, the Duke Leofric, mounting his horse, rode at full speed to the spot where the mine was situated.

But not the least trace of it was perceptible.

The entrance had become as solid ground as the earth that surrounded it.

Leofric stamped his feet, and uttered a bitter oath.

"What infernal witchcraft is this?" he cried; "am I never to gain possession of this phantom treasure?"

"Never!" exclaimed the sweet, clear voice, which he had heard before, and which then continued with solemn impressiveness—

"The orphan's cry is carried
Upon the sighing blast;
And though vengeance long hath tarried,
It will surely come at last."

"Who art thou?" murmured the guilty man in a terror-stricken whisper, "that mockest me thus with these haunting words?"

"The Spirit of Good!" was the distinct reply, "whom thou hatest, but canst not resist!"

Leofric clutched his hands in impotent rage, as he growled—

"I will resist thee, powerful as thou art!"

"Ha, ha! you may try, but you'll find it impossible without my help!" laughed another voice of a very different description in his ear.

"And what then art thou?" cried the duke.

"The Spirit of Evil!" was the answer.

This announcement was more congenial to the listener than the former, and he exclaimed—

"If thou hast a bodily shape, let me look upon thee!"

In an instant the little old man, in his black velvet doublet, and his conical hat, with the same malignant cunning in his glowing eyes, stood at his side.

"Here I am!" he said. "I did thee a service once before, and thou requirest me again, dost thou not?"

"Canst thou give me possession of the treasure I seek?" demanded Leofric.

"That can I, on one condition," returned the fiend.

"Name it!"

"Simply that when the prophecy attached to your castle is fulfilled, you become my property—body and soul!"

"Why should I hesitate?" exclaimed Leofric; "it will never be fulfilled, unless the solid rocks divide, and that is impossible. Fiend, I consent on those terms. I am thine—body and soul!"

A peal of awful thunder followed this terrible compact, and the shaft of the mine opened at once beneath his feet.

"Ha, ha!" shouted the duke with wild glee, "at last I triumph!" "Fool!" was the warning reproof the wind wafted by.

With a scornful exclamation, Leofric mounted his horse, that seemed to fly like lightning.

In a few moments he stood at his castle gate.

The little old man was holding his steed's head obsequiously.

"I am your humble servant now, my lord," he said ; "whenever you want me, you have only to call, and I shall attend you instantly."

With these words, he vanished.

During the duke's absence, the faithful Adelgitha had paid her helpless husband a visit.

That is, she had ventured to the mouth of the horrible pit where he was confined, and spoken words of loving sympathy.

By Carl's command, she had left the castle, and sought the good ferryman Paul.

"Thou canst not help me, dearest," Carl had said, "and thine own safety may be endangered by remaining here. Fly, then, as I direct thee. Heaven will watch over my welfare."

When the fierce Leofric returned, Adelgitha was nowhere to be found.

Full of wrath the duke hastened to the mouth of the dog-hole.

"Where is thy bride ?" he shouted.

"Safe from thy pollution, monster !" returned Carl boldly, from the depths of the pit.

"Tell me, caitiff, where she hides herself," cried Leofric.

"Never ! while I have a tongue," answered the youth, determinedly

"That shall not be long," raved the incensed duke, "I'll cut it from thy mouth. Wilt thou answer me ?"

"No ! "

"Then, by the fiends," returned Leofric with bitter vehemence, "I'll find a way to make thee. I'll torture thee, till thou shalt cry and and groan for mercy, and pray for death to ease thine agonies !"

"Thou wilt do nothing more than Heaven permits, murderer !" answered Carl confidently.

With a final execration cast upon the head of his dauntless prisoner, the remorseless ruffian hurried away.

"Adelgitha, my beloved wife, is safe," soliloquised Carl, " and for my fate I care not. The extremity of human malice has its bounds. The more cruel the torture the shorter its duration."

"Ha, ha ! very logical reasoning ! very —until the torture begins," chuckled a voice at his side.

Turning his head, the youth beheld standing before him, the cloaked man, who gazed upon him with a sarcastic smile upon his withered features.

"I told you we should meet again—I told you you would want me one day," he said, with a sarcastic smile, "and I think that time has come."

"No !" exclaimed Carl, determinedly, "I need no help of thine. Begone, tempter !"

"Softly, softly, my good friend," said the fiend, soothingly. "You are hasty. No matter, I forgive you ; youth is always so. But have you considered your position ?"

"Perfectly," answered Carl. "I am a helpless prisoner, at the mercy of a reckless miscreant."

"From whom I can deliver thee," dropped in the cloaked man quietly.

"I seek not deliverance at thy hands," returned the youth, shaking his head."

"Ah ! you say so now. But do you know the doom that awaits you ?"

"No matter."

"I can tell thee—the rack ! and, if thou art still obstinate, thy tongue cut from thy mouth."

"I am prepared for the worst."

"'Tis an awful torture, the rack !" said the stranger, suggestively ; "to have every sinew strained, every joint dislocated. Few have the courage to endure it."

"Heaven will give me strength."

"Why not avoid it altogether ?" said the cloaked man. "If you listen to me I can—"

"No," cried Carl abruptly, " a thousand times no."

The artful demon, finding his present course of argument failed, changed his tactics.

"Well," he said, "if you are bent upon being tortured, of course, you must have your own way ; but Adelgitha, your poor young bride, what will become of her ? How I pity her ! Your loss will break her heart."

A pang of indescribable anguish pierced Carl's breast at these words, but he remained firm and answered—

"I am not yet lost, whereas if I bound myself to thee, I should be body and soul. I trust in Heaven, and in the name of Heaven I command thee from me. Hence, fiend !"

In an instant the demon vanished, and in his place stood the fair and radiant female form he had seen in the cavern, whose presence filled his narrow cell with celestial light.

The completion of this Story will be found on pages 157 *and* 158 *of our next Number.*

THE LEGEND OF GUTENFELS.

THE Castles of Gutenfels and Pfalz, of which the ruins depicted in our illustration still remain, stand nearly half-way betwen the two important towns of Coblentz and Mayence.

Gutenfels stands high above the river, looking down from a rugged battlement of rocks.

Pfalz, a gloomy, prison-like building, with iron gratings, trap-doors, and other mediæval appurtenances, is at a short distance.

The ruins of Stahleck are on the opposite bank of the river.

All these castles formerly belonged to the Prince Palatine, who was in the olden time the most potent feudal ruler of that portion of the Rhine.

We will give the legend of Gutenfels Castle, and relate how it was that it came to be called by that name.

GUDA'S CAPTIVITY.—A LEGEND OF THE GUTENFELS.

Baron Hugo Von Falkenstein sat one autumn evening in the principal apartment of his castle of Stahleck; the walls of the vast Gothic hall were decorated with armour, weapons, and spoils of the chase, and hung round with tapestry, on which battles and other appropriate subjects were represented.

The scene was a typical residence of a feudal baron of the middle ages, large, massive, magnificent, but to modern eyes, gloomy and prison-like.

The baron was alone—unless we count the presence of two or three armed retainers, fixed like statues at the other end of the extensive hall; he sat apart on his luxurious seat upon the raised *dais*, apparently absorbed in his own reflections.

Though not more than middle-aged, strong passions, a life of warfare, travel, and rough adventure had combined to make him look older than he was; nor had time softened his haughty and overbearing nature.

A rustling of the tapestry drew the baron's attention.

A young man entered, attired with all the splendour of a feudal courtier, but his natural plainness of feature, undignified demeanour, and an expression of insolent arrogance, made these gorgeous ornaments sit awkwardly upon him.

"By my word, you have equipped yourself bravely, Ludwig," said his father, for such seemed the relationship between them, "and cannot fail to captivate your fair cousin. She ought, too, by this time to be here."

"I await her coming in much anxiety," said Ludwig, adjusting his habiliments with somewhat of a foppish air. "The more so as from her demeanour of late I am sanguine that she has unbent from her persistent refusal of my suit, and will give a consenting answer to your proposal."

"I scarcely think she dare oppose my wishes in this matter," answered the count. "I have told her pretty plainly that now I expect consent. But she approaches."

Entering, with a single attendant, the Lady Guda, orphaned niece of the count, and heiress to the Palatinate, advanced towards him with much deference, but with little cordiality in her greeting either of him or Ludwig.

Well did her dazzling beauty bear out the praises liberally bestowed by all who knew her.

"Well, fair niece," said Hugo, somewhat abruptly, "you have by this time, I hope, brought yourself to consent to give your hand and heart to my son, Ludwig von Falkenstein, who is present to consummate the betrothal."

"My lord," replied the heiress, "I have told you on each occasion that my resolve was fixed and unchangeable. Under no circumstances can I ever wed Count Ludwig."

"How!" cried the baron, rising angrily; "still stubborn, ungrateful, defiant? By St. Hubert! I will give you no more time. Hark you, girl—I have hitherto consulted your own inclination, I will now exert my own authority. Hear my decision. Give your hand to my son—declare yourself betrothed to him—or this night, this very hour, I will have you conveyed to the Castle of Pfalz, there to be immured in a gloomy cell till this consent be wrung from you."

She turned pale.

She was evidently fear-struck, but for a moment only.

The next she answered defiantly—

"Heaven give me strength to bear your persecutions, but they shall never avail."

"Nay, my fair cousin," said Ludwig, approaching, "let my entreaties induce you, for your own sake——"

But she haughtily waved him off, and her features assumed an expression of proud defiance and contempt.

His persuasions were the least of all likely to move her.

"Bernhard," said the baron, summoning his steward, a man of by no means prepossessing aspect. "'Tis well we are prepared for this alternative, since my niece's obduracy has rendered it necessary. Escort her to her prison, and forget not——"

The rest was spoken in a confidential tone.

Bernhard nodded, and approached Guda, who, offering neither opposition nor remonstrance, preceded him with a firm step, and departed to her undeserved captivity.

A few words will explain the mutual positions of the persons already introduced into our story.

The guardians of that age had unlimited power, and there was none to dispute that of Hugo.

When his brother, Count Philip, died, his only surviving child, in default of male heirs, inherited the family honours.

As she was as yet a minor, she was placed under the control of her uncle Hugo, a vicious, unscrupulous man, who thus became trustee of the estates and dominions, and wielded the power, though he could not take the title, of Count Palatine.

That title had all his life been his chief ambition.

At least, he wished it to descend to his family, and the only means by which this could be brought about—except by the death of Guda—was by a marriage of his son with the heiress.

During Count Philip's lifetime he had endeavoured to persuade the latter to make this a stipulated condition, but the count refused.

He would not force his daughter's inclinations, and the baron tried first persuasion, and latterly, as we have seen, forcible means to compass his ends.

During the five years that Guda had been under his care, many brave and noble knights, smitten by her beauty and accomplishments, had made offers for her hand ; but these had been in every case rejected by the baron, who had registered a vow that she should wed none but Ludwig.

But to Ludwig she evinced a feeling little removed from abhorrence.

She was equally resolved never to marry her cousin, and had expressed this resolve not only to himself, but to his father, on more than one occasion, causing, on the baron's part, those explosions of anger and manifestations of fierce arbitrariness which had culminated in this high-handed measure.

We have spoken of the gloomy and prison-like aspect of the Castle of Pfalz, and in those days, when it was so strongly fortified and filled with the appurtenances of feudal tyranny, it must have presented a terrible aspect, especially to one about to be immured within its walls.

According to the baron's instructions, Guda was that very evening conveyed across the river by Bernhard and two other retainers, and safely lodged in this gloomy fortress.

Not in a handsome and well-furnished bower, meet for a fair and noble lady, but in a room in the basement, having the aspect of a bare stone-walled cell, and with no other furniture than a bench, a chair, and a rough pallet bed.

No other attendant was to be allowed her but Jacintha, the wife of the steward, Bernhard, and entirely under the control of that evil man.

Jacintha was indeed subject to the same tyranny from her lord and master as her late mistress, Lady Gunhilda, had suffered from his master the baron.

Hitherto Jacintha had not been among Guda's personal attendants, but now she was compelled to accept that office, on the understanding that she was to be a jailor—a spy upon the prisoner's actions.

Guda conjectured this, and was, therefore, somewhat constrained and distant towards Jacintha, and not disposed to give her the same confidence as she had extended towards Agatha, her former chief attendant, now separated from her.

The first few days of Guda's captivity were, of course, especially cheerless.

On the third day the baron visited his prisoner, but found her mind by no means altered by the harsh plans he had used.

But Hugo declared that her captivity should not be ended, nor in any way relaxed, until she had consented to the proposal he had made.

The continuation of this story will be found on page 145 of our next Number.

[Continued from Page 122.]

THE AVENGERS.

AND the bishop sat upon his horse, and laughed loudly.

"Hear how the rats and mice are squealing," he cried. "'Tis an excellent bonfire, that will consume the vermin who would eat my corn."

And he rubbed his hands in glee.

The walls crumbled away beneath the flames, the roof fell in, tongues of fire and myriads of sparks leaped up into the air, and bore with them the prayers for vengeance of that doomed host.

At that moment, through the flames and sparks shot a strange form.

The followers turned and fled in terror; the bishop grasped the reins with one hand, and crossed himself with the other; Sir Cuno dropped the torch, and fell upon his knees.

Over him for a moment hovered the dark-winged figure, and in his ears rang the words—

"The compact is fulfilled! You are mine for ever!"

Sir Cuno shrieked aloud.

The bishop closed his eyes in terror.

When he opened them again, he was alone before a smouldering heap, from which arose the fearful stench from a thousand charred bodies.

His followers had fled.

Sir Cuno and the Spirit of Evil had gone, none knew whither.

Gathering the reins up in his trembling hand, the bishop turned his restive horse, and spurred towards the Castle of Ehrenfels.

But that terrible stench overpowered him with a sickening sensation, and in his ears rang his own words—

"Hark, how the rats and mice are squealing!"

Now that his revenge was satiated, now that his fiendish soul was glutted, a terrible fear seized upon him.

Secure behind the walls of the fortress he could not be at rest.

The cries of his victims rang in his ears.

The fearful sickening sight that his own will, if not his own hands, had raised, he could not banish from his sight.

Rest he could obtain none, and he fled to the altar to seek it there.

Prostrate he laid himself.

But the prayers died upon his lips.

He could not articulate a word of supplication, and still in his ears rang the words his own impious tongue had uttered when listening with pleasure to those agonising cries—

"Hark, how the rats and mice are squealing!"

An abject, miserable wretch, he now grovelled upon the very pavement of the chapel, and moaned aloud in the very agony of his soul—

"I shall never more know rest and peace."

"Never!"

The tone in which the word was uttered had never been heard by the bishop before.

So clear, yet so soft and melodious, it fell upon his ears.

Turning upon his knees, Hatto looked in the direction whence it came.

Then, clasping his hands together, he bowed his forehead to the ground, as if he dare not gaze upon the sight before him.

A light as powerful as that of the sun at noonday, streamed from the far end of the dark chapel.

In the centre of this refulgent glow stood a noble form of grace and beauty.

On its shoulders were large wings of dazzling whiteness.

One hand was extended to heaven, the other pointed downwards to the craven wretch at its feet.

Hatto could not, dared not, look up, but with clasped hands remained with his head bowed to the pavement.

"'Vengeance is mine, saith the Lord,'" said the voice. "Mortal, who art thou, who hast presumed to take the lives of thy fellow men?"

"Mercy! mercy! great angel!" moaned Hatto.

"Mercy!" cried the vision. "When a

thousand tongues asked thee for mercy, didst thou show it? There is but one who can extend mercy to thee. Ask it there."

The hand was extended upwards, the eyes looked down upon the trembling Hatto.

"Give me rest—give me peace," pleaded Hatto. "You have power—you can spare me these fearful pangs."

"You had power; how have you used it? You could give relief; how have you extended it? Man, man, the record of your sins is there."

Again the hand was extended upwards.

"Mercy, mercy!" cried the bishop, beating his forehead on the floor.

"A thousand prayers have risen to heaven for vengeance on thy head," continued the vision. "Those prayers are heard and answered. Mortal, thy hour draws nigh—vengeance is at hand. Prepare to meet thy doom."

"Shield me!—spare me!—save me!" pleaded Hatto.

"I have but the power to warn—the power to save is higher far than mine," said the vision. "Thou art doomed, though the hand of man shall not assail thee. Yet against this crime which thou hast this day committed, shall arise ten million million of avengers."

"No, no!" shrieked Hatto, "I will atone for all my sins. I will give all my wealth to the poor. I will wander an outcast upon the face of the earth and seek mercy by prayers and fastings."

"Seek it then. Thou art warned. My mission is fulfilled."

The light vanished, darkness reigned throughout the chapel, and Hatto was alone.

That night Hatto's sleep was broken and troubled.

He started from his couch a dozen times, imagining that he heard the terrible cries of his victims.

Then he would awake with the words he himself had uttered ringing in his ears.

Feverish and spiritless he arose.

On descending to his apartment he perceived that a portrait of himself, which hung upon the walls, had been eaten from its frame during the night.

The morning meal was placed before him.

He had no relish for food, yet he tried to eat.

He stretched forth his hand for the bread, but drew it back with a start as a mouse leapt from the loaf.

He looked round.

A large rat sat on the back of his chair.

An attendant brushed it off, but another took its place.

In dismay Hatto sprang to his feet.

A dozen mice scampered from under the table.

Hatto turned pale and terrified.

The words rang in his ears and sounded like a fearful warning.

He ordered the food to be removed, and a cat to be brought in.

Mice swarmed on the window-sills, and rats crouched in the corners.

Their bright eyes were fixed upon the bishop; their sharp teeth were gnawing at the woodwork with an ominous scratching sound.

Every moment they increased in number.

A cat was brought in; but she stood for a minute in the centre of the apartment, and then fled terror-stricken from the spot.

An attendant rushed into the presence of the bishop.

"My lord, the castle swarms with rats and mice, that eat everything before them."

Hatto clasped his hands to his brow in despair.

"Hark, how they squeal!" he cried. "Oh, it is the avenger of those murdered souls! Drive them hence. No, 'tis vain to try. Where can I fly for safety? To the Mousethurm! There they cannot reach me; the waters are deep, and the tide runs swiftly. There is my hope—there my salvation."

He rushed from the apartment, descended to his boat, and was rowed to the tower on the rapids.

Here he felt he was safe.

He took heart, his spirits rose, and he ordered food.

Scarce was it set before him than a rat leaped upon the table, and bore away a portion of the viands.

The squeal of a mouse was heard as with the rat it contested for the stolen food at the bishop's feet.

Hatto's fears again increased.

But these being driven forth, and none others appearing, he once more took heart, and retired early to his couch.

That night, like its predecessor, he could but gain fitful slumber, and awoke with the cries ringing in his ears.

"Hark, how the rats and mice are squealing!"

At early light he arose, and looked from the window of the tower.

The waters ran swiftly at its base, and not a boat or living creature was seen.

Suddenly he cast his eyes to the shore.

A dark stream appeared to be moving slowly down the Elisenhohe.

He turned his gaze.

The crags of the Rupertsberg were one moving mass !

He strained his vision, and saw that both streams came slowly, but surely moving down the hill, and then, horror upon horror !

One stream was composed of myriads and myriads of rats !

The other contained millions of mice !

The shriek the bishop gave brought some of his followers to his side.

Paralyzed with fear, they watched the moving mass swarm on the banks of the river.

Then his followers turned to fly.

"Stay, stay," implored Hatto. "The waters are deep, the currents strong. Our refuge, our safety is here."

But they heeded him not.

"Hark, how they squeal !" said one. "Fly, fly !"

In another minute the bishop was left alone, deserted by all.

As a drowning man will cling to a straw, so Hatto clung to the belief that the depth and rapidity of the stream would prevent the army of vermin from finding a foothold on the island.

But the last hope was soon to be annihilated.

Without pausing, the two bodies swarmed up the stream until they reached the confluence of the Nahe, where they immediately took the water, and, with a heart almost pulseless with fear, Hatto perceived them borne towards the island by the waters of the Rhine.

All hope now fled.

Vengeance was at hand.

The avengers were on his track.

He fell upon his knees and prayed.

Upon the rocky island the vast army landed.

They swarmed up the base of the tower till their puny bodies covered every stone, and the tower was black with the countless mass.

The mice entered the windows.

The rats gnawed away the doors.

They came up through the floors.

They penetrated through the ceilings.

Above, below, around, issued the swarming torrents, and one and all made towards the kneeling Hatto.

Despair now made him brave.

He sprang to his feet, and kicked and trampled upon them.

But they swarmed up his legs—they clung to his body.

He beat them down with his hands, but they fastened upon his fingers, and a thousand rows of teeth were buried in his flesh.

Long and fearful was the fight between that desperate man and those puny avengers.

Bleeding from every pore, he still battled on till the clothes were eaten from his back, and his head, face, and body covered with his countless foes, and, deprived of sight and strength, he fell to the floor.

Then arose a squeal of triumph, and their tiny teeth tore away the quivering flesh from the bones.

Long and fierce was the revel on the carcase of Hatto.

No longer the shrieks of the doomed man pealed through the place ; but the squealing of the rats and the mice resounded through the tower, as they fought over the flesh torn from the body of him who had likened the cries of his burning victims to the sound.

When, days afterwards, the tower was entered, the clean polished skeleton of Hatto was discovered. But there remained not a single trace of the terrible army of avengers.

END OF THE AVENGERS.

THE LEGEND
OF
GUTENFELS.

[Continued from page 141.]

THE state of things thus begun went on without change for many weeks.

The baron, sometimes accompanied by Ludwig, visited his prisoner at uncertain intervals, but always with the same success.

At other times, Hugo occupied himself with the chase. Nor were these expeditions entirely of this harmless nature, but

"SHE FELL INTO HIS ARMS. HER HEART WAS TOO FULL TO SPEAK.'

were strongly suspected to be predatory. It was pretty well known that the baron was in league with some of the bands of robbers that infested this part of the Rhine.

Meanwhile, Guda bore her captivity with a fortitude that astonished her jailors.

She seemed supported by some inner resolution, the secret of which was known only to herself.

One evening Jacintha, having visited the castle of Stahleck, was returning across the river to the Pfalz.

Two retainers were, as usual, in waiting with a skiff to row her over.

Scarcely had she reached the opposite shore, when, in the shades of night, some one rapidly approached her.

She could just distinguish the figure of a man, but of what dress and aspect she knew not; he was gone in a moment, but not ere he had thrust into her hands a small packet.

Neither of the attendants had seen this, and Jacintha, wonderingly concealing the packet beneath her cloak, entered the grim fortress.

On arriving at the small chamber appointed for her, which was next to that of her captive, and finding herself alone, Jacintha took out the packet and found it to be a letter addressed "to the Lady Guda, with all speed," in a bold, manly hand, such as might be expected from some gallant and high-born knight.

Jacintha examined the letter narrowly, weighed it in her hand—for it seemed heavy—and hesitated. Should she open it? or deliver it to the captive? or to the baron?

At length curiosity overcame her; she must know the secret, and so, cutting the silken cords, she became aware of the contents.

"DEAREST,—With distress and indignation I have just heard of your unwarrantable captivity. Fear not. Every effort shall be made, and you shall be speedily rescued by your devoted   "A. H."

"Ah! this explains your refusal of Master Ludwig," murmured Jacintha. "A secret attachment, carried on, who knows how long? But what is this? A piece of gold wrapped in paper, and marked 'for the attendant.' This lover evidently knows the true way of effecting his purpose."

And Jacintha, with delight, took possession of that which had made the letter so heavy.

It would be possible to take the bribe, and yet betray the secret; but Jacintha was not quite so base as this.

She determined that Guda should have the letter.

Scarce had she put it in her pocket, when she heard the voice of the baron outside; she opened the door, and he entered, followed by Ludwig.

Fierce anger shone on the haughty countenance of Hugo, and vexation on that of his son.

"Jacintha," said her master, "your prisoner is still obstinate. She has again refused. Leniency, I see, is thrown away upon her, so make her captivity more stringent; give her nought but bread and water, and take away the books wherewith she is so constantly occupied."

"My lord, I will faithfully obey you," replied the attendant; "though I will first try what my persuasions will do to change the young lady's determination."

"Do so; but it will avail not. She has the native obstinacy of her race. Take care, Jacintha, that she has no communication of any kind with her former attendants, or with anyone outside the fortress."

Jacintha repeated her duteous assent, and the baron and his son departed.

Going to the room of the prisoner, Jacintha found her in much the same mood as before, though somewhat more despondent.

The attendant did not tell her tidings at once.

She first asked Guda many questions about her causes of dislike to Ludwig, declaring how hopeless it was to rebel against the baron's power, and lastly hinting at a suspicion that there was some secret attachment in the background. These last words seemed to startle Guda.

"What has made you think thus?" she said.

"I think it not, lady; I *know* it," was the reply. "All that I require to know is, who is this gallant, and how came thou, secluded as thy life has hitherto been, to find opportunity to correspond with him?"

"What do you know?—quick—tell me!" asked Guda.

"This will explain all," answered her keeper, throwing her the letter. "It is against my duty to give it thee; but I have not the heart to withhold it."

Guda eagerly took the letter (which had been refastened), and, recognising the writing, opened it with trembling hands.

Scarcely a moment was occupied in mastering its contents.

"My own, my faithful Albert," she

cried. "Pray Heaven he will run no deadly risks on my account."

"And who may be this devoted Albert?" asked Jacintha; "it is the first time I have heard his name; and, knowing thus much, I may as well know that."

"Jacintha, I cannot avoid giving thee my confidence; and rest assured thou shalt not repent being faithful. I implore thee, therefore, to let nothing induce thee to betray me."

"Nothing shall, I promise it," answered Jacintha, and she spoke sincerely.

"Listen, then. Let me explain all from the beginning.

"It was at the festival given in honour of the wedding of the Emperor Frederick that I first saw Albert of Hohenstaufen.

"You may guess, from the name, he belongs to the imperial family.

"He is, in fact, the second son of Prince Conrad, the emperor's brother.

"We loved each other at first sight.

"During the whole of my long visit to my aunt, the Baroness of Beyreuth, he found means to see me frequently and in secret.

"If you, Jacintha, ever loved, you will imagine, for I cannot express, how delicious were those private interviews, for there was necessity for concealment—there were obstacles to our happiness.

"The estrangement which has so long existed between the houses of Falkenstein and Hohenstaufen rendered it impossible that either his father or the emperor would consent to the alliance.

"He was, in fact, under betrothment, not with his own will, to the Countess Bertha of Neuringen; I, on my part, being destined by the baron for his son.

"But love would not be repelled by these obstacles.

"So in secret we plighted our troth. Each swore, that come what would, this vow should always be binding and sacred.

"I returned to my uncle's roof, and was thenceforth subjected to a course of persecution which would have rendered me desperate had I not been supported by the thoughts of my lover.

"Nor was he absent always. I found means not only to communicate with him, but to see him.

"My attendant, Agatha, by her faithfulness and ingenuity, enabled me often to elude the vigilance of my uncle, and to meet the disguised Albert in the garden.

"Nearly a year ago I again went to visit the Baroness of Beyreuth.

"Again Albert and I renewed our secret interviews, and this time as betrothed lovers.

"One memorable day we were both at a grand hunting party at the castle of the Baron of Neuringen.

"Albert, in accordance with our previous designs, showed me no marked attention.

"But fate seemed to pursue our attachment. In the excitement of the chase we were lost in the forest and separated from the rest of the party, finding ourselves unexpectedly, when the day was far advanced, near a rustic hunting-lodge belonging to Albert himself.

"'This has chanced well,' observed my lover. 'Dearest Guda, why not make this an elopement? Why return to thy friends otherwise than as my bride—confessed or secretly?

"'Here is thy confidential attendant, those at the lodge are all in my confidence, and Father Francis, who lives in a hermitage hard by, not only knows of my love for thee, but is willing to consummate our union.'

"'And if we are discovered?' I faltered.

"'Then we will brave the anger of our friends—nay, I will defy the emperor himself to part us.

"'This is no rash step; I have long pondered upon it, nor can thy heart refuse.'

"In short we were married that day by the hermit at his little chapel in the wood, in the presence of one of my own and two of Albert's confidential retainers.

"In the rustic lodge, though scarcely befitting a noble pair, we took up our residence.

"But where love dwells, the humblest cot is equal to the grandest palace.

"But our happiness had not lasted many days when I indirectly obtained tidings that my aunt, the baroness, was smitten by a serious illness.

"I returned with somewhat self-reproachful feelings, and in answer to the surprised queries as to my absence, said that, lost in the wood, I had been captured by robbers and kept in durance till I had been rescued by some of the baron's retainers.

"No one suspected the truth of this account.

"I did not leave the baroness till she was thoroughly recovered.

"At that time I received a letter from Albert, saying that our union was not suspected, and had better be kept secret for the present, and that he should not see me for some time, for he had been sent on a distant embassy; but the instant that he could spare after his return, he would find means to visit me.

"Again, therefore, I returned to the

Castle of Caub, and have since suffered still greater persecution from Ludwig's addresses, and more unfeeling rigour from my uncle than before. But I determined to bear it all for Albert's sake.

"I reflected that I would soon be of age, and might then proclaim my marriage, and that Albert had promised, meanwhile, to use his efforts to obtain his friends' consent to it.

"His embassy detained him longer than he expected, and after that he was engaged in a warlike expedition in Franconia, while the state of his father's relations with the Falkensteins deterred him from making the important disclosure.

"From that day of parting I have only seen him once—when he came here in disguise through Agatha's connivance.

"Since I have been here, this letter is the first intimation I have had that he has heard of my fate.

"It has greately relieved my mind, and I thank thee for delivering it, with all my heart."

Scarcely had the Countess Guda ended this recital, when a small door near where she was sitting flew open, and her uncle, towering with rage, entered the room.

"'Tis well I played the eavesdropper," he said sternly to Jacintha. "Catching a glimpse of that letter in thy hand, I suspected some such conspiracy, but dreamed not of aught like this. Stir not," he added to his terrified niece. "I have heard all. This, then, is the reason of thy obstinate opposition—the means by which thou wouldst frustrate my plans. But know, minion, that this clandestine marriage is null and void—that thou hast disgraced our house, and shall be spurned, disowned, and disinherited. As for Albert of Hohenstaufen, were he three times the emperor's nephew, he should not escape my vengeance."

"Oh, pity me!" cried Guda, scarcely knowing what she said or to whom she spoke.

"Pity thee!" cried the baron, gnashing his teeth; "by the demon! I feel strongly tempted to thrust this dagger into thy heart."

"Oh, my lord, forbear, I entreat!" cried Jacintha.

"Ha! and thou too shalt pay the penalty of thy treachery and faithlessness."

Then to his steward—

"Away with her! Let her be changed from gaoler to prisoner, Bernhard. Thou knowest the darkest dungeon!"

Bernhard, only too glad to have a legitimate excuse for exercising his tyranny towards his wife, roughly removed her, despite her remonstrances, while the baron, turning to his niece, said—

"Thou hast sealed thine own doom—thou hast ruined thyself in fame and fortune. I will set abroad such reports of this affair as will disgrace thee so in the eyes of all the world, that not all the wealth of the Palatinate could repurchase thy good name."

Guda heard these terrible words, and swooned on the floor.

For a week she lay in a raging fever, unconscious of the woes that surrounded her.

The baron sent her two new attendants, an old physician and his wife, a crone as aged and repulsive-looking as himself.

These people were such as would do any evil thing for gain, and were sworn creatures of the baron.

To Zacharias, for so the physician was named, the case was clear.

Guda was about to suffer a dread ordeal, in this case compensated by no elements of joy.

An heir or heiress in the direct line of the house of Falkenstein would come into the world with no such honours as would ordinarily attend such an event, and within the gloomy walls of the Pfalz, instead of the palatial residence of Stahleck.

And so it occurred. Ere many hours had elapsed, the persecuted countess had given birth to a female child, apparently too feeble to be expected to live, which, indeed, under present circumstances, was not desirable.

The mother herself appeared to hover closely around the threshold of death.

This intelligence added much to the baron's perplexity.

That it was a daughter instead of a son was a cause of gratulation, but only removed the difficulty one step.

His only hope was that both mother and child would die, and thus cut at once the knot of perplexities.

But anon came tidings that the worst crisis was over, that the countess was slowly recovering, and that the child might after all live to thwart his plans.

The desperate Hugo debated the expediency of using artificial means by the physician's aid to get rid of his victim; but, bad as he was, the baron shrank from murder.

After a consultation with Ludwig, Bernhard, and Zacharias, he resolved on a subtle scheme.

It was to take the child and have it conveyed away secretly, and to remove Guda to some yet more remote place of incarceration, and obtain at one blow the fulfilment of his ambition in her pretended death.

By means of his confederates this conspiracy was not difficult to carry out.

The physician, his wife, and Bernhard were quite ready to swear that the countess had been carried off by the fever, and that she died in their presence.

Zacharias might also professionally declare that the nature of her complaint was such as to render it necessary that the body should be enclosed in the coffin as speedily as possible.

One dark, autumnal night, this iniquitous conspiracy was carried out.

The child was scarcely a week old.

The countess, as yet but a slight degree recovered, was gazing on this only consolation of her misery, when the baron and his confederates entered her chamber.

She looked up in terror, foreseeing some fearful fate.

She clasped her child to her breast in an agony of desperation.

She implored pity, but all in vain.

Advancing sternly towards her, the baron made a sign to his confederates, and Bernhard, despite Guda's heartrending screams and her struggling to retain her hold, tore the child from her grasp.

He then gave it to the repulsive-looking old woman, the wife of Zacharias, who performed her part in the dread scene with a fiendish satisfaction.

"Thou shalt never see thy child more!" said the baron, savagely. "But this is not all thy punishment. From this hour thou art dead to the world; thy coffin and sepulchre are prepared, and shall receive thee at once."

Doubting not from these words that he meant her instant assassination, she made a last effort at resistance.

But the strong arms of Bernhard and one of the retainers closed around her, and bore her away, half-dead with terror, whither she knew not.

Albert of Hohenstaufen was quite unaware of his bride's fate any more than that she was incarcerated in the castle of Pfalz.

Not receiving, however, any answer to his missive, and being able to gain no intelligence from the countess's attendants, he began to entertain deep misgivings.

He knew the tyrannical and unscrupulous character of the baron, and the absolute power he possessed over the heiress.

He was resolved to rescue the persecuted Guda; but by what means?

Though a scion of the imperial house, Albert did not possess an army of followers large enough to cope with the superior force of the baron, or to carry by assault the mighty fortress of the Pfalz; moreover, though he might get sufficient assistance by making his plans known, he could not do so without revealing to his friends the secret of his marriage.

He, therefore, resolved to try first the effect of remonstrance.

Embarking on the Rhine with about a dozen of armed followers, he stayed on the boundaries of the baron's dominions, and sent forward a messenger with a letter.

It was to the effect that he, Albert, had heard that the Countess Guda, heiress to the Palatinate, had been illegally and unjustifiably imprisoned in the castle of Pfalz; and that he deemed it his duty as a knight and professed redresser of wrongs, to protest against her captivity, and in the name of the emperor, to demand her instant release.

If this were not granted, more forcible means would be resorted to.

It will be observed that Albert said nothing about Guda being his wife, not supposing that the baron knew anything of that fact.

Hugo had made proclamation by his heralds to all in his domain, that, through the sudden death of the Countess Guda, sole heiress to the Palatinate, he, Baron Hugo, had inherited the title, lordship, and dominion of Count Palatine on behalf of himself and his successors, and called upon all his feudal dependents to repair to Caub Castle the day after the countess's funeral, to take their oath of fealty.

No one suspected the conspiracy.

The general feeling was regret for the loss of the young heiress and dismay at the prospect of the despotic rule of Hugo being permanently established.

As yet knowing nothing of the changes that had taken place, Albert awaited with anxiety the effect of his missive.

Baron (or rather Count Palatine) Hugo smiled grimly as he received the young knight's letter in the great hall of his castle.

"His threats are of little avail, Ludwig," he said. "Insane must he be to think that he could make me relinquish my designs. Write this as my reply—

"Hugo, Count Palatine, and Lord Paramount of the Pfalz-Grafenstein, holds in contempt the threats of Count Albert of Hohenstaufen, and informs him that even were he ever so inclined to accede to his demands, it is now impossible, since the Countess Guda, who falsely asserted herself to be the wife of the aforesaid Count

Albert, expired of fever two days ago, in the castle of Pfalz, her death being witnessed by three of the baron's retainers. As her funeral takes place this very day, any hostile demonstration on Count Albert's part would be particularly untimely."

The effect on the young knight was just as the malicious baron anticipated.

His grief was intense ; the blow seemed to paralyze his every faculty.

"Dead ! dead !" he exclaimed ; "my beloved Guda ! But is it true, Ulfran, can it be true ?"

"Too true, my lord," answered his esquire. "I even saw the funeral *cortége* setting forth from the castle as I departed."

"Great Heaven ! let me go at once and satisfy myself. There is something terrible and unexplained in all this. I fear me she has had foul play. This new Palatine is quite capable of any atrocity. Follow me ; let us land, and proceed to the castle."

"Beware my lord," said Ulfran ; "you are putting yourself in the power of your greatest enemy."

"I care not. My fate cannot be worse than that of Guda. Come !"

The young count ascended the shore, followed by all his men save the two who guarded the boat, and took his way towards the Palatine's present residence, the Castle of Caub.

It loomed dark and grim upon its rugged pediment of rock, and the morning being dull and cheerless enhanced its gloomy aspect.

As the young count and his followers approached the castle, they perceived a funeral procession issuing from the gate.

It was proceeding towards the cemetery attached to the Castle of Caub.

First came a number of the baron's retainers, clad in black, and foremost—which looked like intentional irony to those who knew the secret—came Bernhard and Zacharias.

The coffin, richly draped in black velvet, was borne by four of the inferior retainers, and attended by the family chaplain and his assistants, chanting the service for the dead, in harmony with the doleful chime that knelled from the chapel bell.

Lastly, the Count Palatine and his son, Ludwig, followed, dressed in profound mourning, mounted on jet-black steeds, and assuming a hypocritical expression of sorrow.

A number of the dependants and villagers, whose grief was real, brought up the rear.

Albert's heart sank within him, and for a moment he stood somewhat apart from the crowd, gazing at the procession as if transfixed.

Then, rousing himself, he proceeded to follow it into the cemetery.

By the time, however, that he and his companions reached the *cortége*, it had stopped, the coffin was laid down near the grave prepared for it, and the officials and so-called mourners were engaged in the last portions of the impressive ceremony.

The advent of the young count and his followers attracted the attention of all, and his anguish-stricken aspect moved many to sympathy.

"Guda, my beloved bride !" he exclaimed, flinging himself down beside the coffin. "Can it be that I shall never see thee more ? Is man—is Heaven itself—so cruel as to afflict me thus ?"

"Who art thou that disturbest the solemn ceremony of interment ?" asked the Palatine, sternly fixing his eyes on the young man, while all looked on with wondering expectation.

"I am Albert of Hohenstaufen, the husband of this thy victim, for such I believe she was ; it was thy cruelty and thy tyranny that sent her to the grave."

"Thou art distraught," answered Hugo, with a secret, malicious enjoyment of his distress. "Proceed, holy fathers, and heed not his ravings."

"They shall hear them," cried Albert, more vehemently than before. "Baron of Caub, falsely called Count Palatine, I execrate thee as a murderer and usurper—I will denounce thee to the emperor, thy liege lord, who will call thee to rigid account."

"The emperor, with all his power, cannot keep me from my rightful inheritance !" answered Hugo, "and, thinkest thou he would assist thee, one of the house of Hohenstaufen, who hast dared to contract a marriage in secret, and in dead opposition to the feud that exists between our families ?"

Albert was silent.

He perceived the force of this insinuation.

"Nevertheless, I will find means to punish thee," he cried. "Guda shall not go unavenged."

For a moment grief and indignation choked his utterance as he gazed into the open grave.

"But no revenge can recall thee to life. Oh ! Guda, my beloved, with thee my heart is buried !"

A few minutes afterwards the supposed remains of the countess were lowered into the family vault, the solemn requiem was sung by the priests, and the impressive and melancholy character of the scene had reached its height.

Many of the villagers scattered wreaths and flowers over the grave of her who had been (as they supposed) thus cut off in her youthful bloom.

Albert sank down on an adjacent tombstone : grief seemed to have deprived him of the power of further remonstrance.

Thus the ceremony concluded, and those who had taken part in it began to leave the spot.

"By the shades of Erebus, Ludwig," said the Palatine, as they approached the castle, "this has been as solemn and successful a comedy as any mummers ever performed."

"Faith ! I could scarce forbear laughing outright," returned his hopeful son, "at seeing the woebegone count thus lament over a coffin filled with sacks and stones."

So deep was Albert in a melancholy reverie, that he remained in the same

CASTLES OF GUTENFELS AND PFALZ

posture till all the " mourners " and priests, and even the spectators and stragglers had passed by.

He was at last aroused by Ulfran.

"Come, my lord, give not way to despair thus. Let us return to the boat."

"Nay, leave me awhile. I will rejoin thee anon. I am too distracted to care for aught now but the remembrance of my great grief."

Knowing his mood his follower, though

reluctantly, left him, and Albert continued in the cemetery.

He soon found a sort of melancholy interest in watching the gravediggers pursuing their lugubrious occupation.

The blow of Guda's loss had, as it were, stunned the young count, and completely changed the whole current of his thoughts.

He cared not what his own fate would

be; he was incapable of carrying out any plans of future action.

In this distressing condition the count at length became aware that the shades of evening were coming on, and it behoved him to return to his followers.

He set forth, therefore, but alike absent-minded and confident of his road, he lost it, and wandered in a devious path which soon conducted him to the borders of the vast forest.

Utterly at a loss, the count paused, and at length decided upon following a track which seemed to lead back to the main route.

But he was deceived.

It led farther into the forest, which, in the now advanced dusk, presented anything but a cheerful prospect to a belated traveller.

Suddenly Albert was startled by an ominous rustling among the leaves, and an armed man, followed by several others, sprang out and intercepted his path.

"Stand, traveller!" cried the foremost; "all who pass hither are obliged to give an account of themselves and to pay toll. Resist not; abide by our rules, and we will warrant thee civil treatment."

Albert saw that he had fallen into the hands of a band of robbers, and that resistance was useless.

He did not, therefore, even attempt to draw his sword, but resigned himself to his captivity.

"First, give thy name, sir knight," said he who had first adressed him.

Regardless of the consequence, the young knight attempted no concealment, but replied——"

"Albert of Hohenstaufen."

"Hohenstaufen! one of the emperor's kith and kin, by my life!" cried he, who seemed to be the leader. "Here is a chance of a heavy ransom. Come, sir knight, thou art too valuable a bird for us to let thee fly. So deliver up thy sword, and follow us to our forest hostelry, as we call it, yonder."

The scene which the "hostelry" presented, was very wild and picturesque.

In an open space in the wood was a circle of tents, and in the centre of this a camp-fire, which had just been lit, diffused its ruddy glow.

Grouped around were a number of armed men, evidently, from their attire, of the freebooting fraternity, and indeed the band seemed numerous and formidable.

Several horses were tethered to the adjacent trees, and around the fire hovered a woman of middle age, who was very respectfully addressed by the apparent captain.

All the band rejoiced at the rich capture they had made.

They treated their prisoner with much courtesy, invited him into the principal tent, and offered a share of their evening meal, of which, however, the count would not partake.

He said he only wished to rest and to be alone, and he accordingly remained in the tent, bound, however, with ropes, and within view of the party, for safety's sake, while the robbers, sitting round the fire, partook of their meal in true gipsy fashion.

While Albert was musing on the unhappy fortune that seemed now pursuing him—though the sounds of festivity proceeding from the robbers somewhat interfered with his musings—he suddenly felt a hand on his shoulder, and looking round, recognised in the half-light the woman whom he had seen near the fire.

"Hush!" she said. "I wish to speak to you alone, and take the opportunity while the band are engaged in their carouse."

"Who are you? Methinks I have seen you before this day."

"Doubtless, at the Castle of Stahleck, during one of your secret visits; and I was the bearer of the letter you sent to your wife in the Pfalz. She related to me the whole story of your secret love and marriage, and I would have aided her further but for the tyranny of the baron, who, overhearing all, parted us, and had me instantly conveyed to a dungeon under the castle basement."

"And how did you escape?"

"That, sir count, involves other secrets; but I have little to gain by witholding them from thee. It was by the agency of my son, who prevailed with some difficulty upon my tyrannical husband, the baron's steward, to connive at my escape."

"And wherefore seek refuge with a band of robbers?"

"In sooth, because these robbers, as you call them—free companions, as they call themselves—are headed by my son, Gottfried."

"He seems young to control so formidable a band," observed Albert.

"True; but it were more apt to describe him as lieutenant, or second in command. The real captain of the band is——"

"Who?"

"The baron himself."

"I might have suspected as much," exclaimed Albert. "It is such as he that disgrace the German nobility, and are a pest and scourge to all peaceful subjects of the emperor."

"Hush! these men will hear thee, and they are his sworn partisans," answered Jacintha.

"God wot I have cause enough to hate and fear him. But my beloved wife? I would know of her," said Albert. "Thou knowest of her fate; tell me all."

Jacintha, first looking round cautiously, and then sinking her voice, replied—

"I will keep thee no longer in suspense. Thy wife lives!"

"Lives! Great Heaven! Can I believe my ears? But no, it is impossible. You mock me. This very day I witnessed her funeral."

"The funeral was a false one. The Countess Guda lies closely guarded in the Castle of Caub."

"Can this be true? A gleam of hope returns to me. Proceed; I am dying to hear all."

Thereupon Jacintha entered into the whole particulars of the conspiracy against Guda; and though the one great fact relieved the young count's mind, the recital showed the difficulties with which he had to contend.

The intelligence that he had not only a wife, but a daughter, whose fate was at the mercy of his remorseless enemy, filled his mind with emotions of a very mixed character.

"What became of the child I know not. I fear the worst," proceeded Jacintha. "The baron's scruples might not be so great as to make him hold the slaughter of an infant as murder, especially when that infant stands between him and the Palatinate. But see, my son is returning, and we must continue this conversation no longer."

She accordingly left the count's side, and disappeared.

He passed a sleepless night in the captain's tent.

At early dawn the members of the robber band were all astir, and Jacintha was fully occupied in preparing their morning meal, which was savoury and abundant (mostly consisting of the game that abounded in the forest), and of which Albert was also induced to partake.

He then conferred with the leader concerning his own position, and asked what amount of ransom they demanded.

"Four thousand crowns," answered Gottfried, "and not one piece under."

"'Tis a vast sum, and my friends will deem it so. If they offer thee three thousand, wilt thou accept?"

The young lieutenant of robbers shook his head decisively.

"Where we can dictate terms 'tis bad marketing to bate our price," he responded. "I hold to the four thousand."

"Well, bring me writing materials, if such you possess."

His desire was promptly fulfilled, and the young count penned a letter.

"Let a messenger," he said, "convey this to Rhine-below-Reineck, and seek out my lieutenant, Ulfran, or one of his companions. The password, 'Hohenstaufen,' will easily identify them. Allow two days for his imperial highness to be communicated with, and the ransom will, I trust, be forthcoming."

This arrangement having been agreed upon, the messenger was at once despatched.

It was not until late in the third day, that another emissary of the robbers returned with a portion of the ransom, and the intelligence that the rest should be paid by an officer of the emperor, who would meet any of the robbers at a place appointed.

Sufficient precautions having been taken on either side to ensure safety, the bargain was concluded, and while the freebooters returned with the heavy sum, Count Albert departed—a free man.

From certain evidences, he believed that the baron was privy to the affair, and a gainer by it.

The baron's installation as Count Palatine, which took place the day after his niece's ostensible funeral, was an affair of considerable excitement and impressiveness.

The great hall of the Castle of Caub was decorated with glittering weapons, and the arms and banners peculiar to the Falkenstein family.

The baron's retainers, all in warlike panoply, surrounded him as he sat on his chair of state, and his son and heir, Ludwig, stood at his father's right hand, gorgeously attired, but unable to wholly conceal his natural insignificance.

The feudal tenants and villagers, who had come from miles around, made humble obeisances to their liege lord, who was able, when he chose, to assume a conciliatory bearing, which deceived many.

He said that it was his desire to rule justly and impartially throughout his dominions, abrogated many previous arbitrary acts, and mingled his conciliations with expressions of grief for the death of his niece Guda, with such an appearance of sincerity, that all but those who were in the secret deemed that they had done injustice to his true character.

The rest of the day was given to feasting, wassail and revelry on a large scale, and with all the grand feudal hospitality of those times.

It is the old saying, that the throne of a usurper is a bed of thorns, and the baron, though now at the height of his ambition, had many drawbacks to his happiness.

It was not the guilt of the means he had used that troubled him with remorse, but the fear of discovery or betrayal.

Guda, it is true, was safely incarcerated in a secret chamber; the defences of the castle had been especially strengthened, till it seemed impregnable even against a large army, and all who were in his secret had been bribed heavily, but who could tell if all these means would avail to give him peaceable and permanent possession of his new dignity?

He was, however, in a particularly contented and even jovial mood one memorable evening after a successful day's boar hunting, and when the banquet was just being served up, suddenly in rushed the seneschal, with a most dismayed countenance, exclaiming—

"My lord, a troop of armed men are approaching the castle!"

"Who and what are they?" asked the Palatine, turning pale.

"They bear the banners and arms of the Emperor Frederick," responded the seneschal, "and I took this to bode ill."

"Ill? It bodes ruin—destruction, unless we can defeat them. Curses on the emperor and all his kin! Albert of Hohenstaufen has found means to carry out his threatened vengeance. Fool that I was to allow him to escape when once within my grasp!"

The castle was soon in a state of great excitement.

The Palatine and his son armed themselves with all speed, having first ascended the battlements and satisfied themselves that the peril was really as great as was feared.

The preparations were soon made.

The baron posted a number of archers and other armed men at every window and embrasure and parapet, manned the outer defences in the same manner, and drew forth the whole strength of his extensive establishment to repel the formidable danger.

The advancing expedition was led by Albert of Hohenstaufen.

That young knight, as soon as he regained his liberty, hastened to Mayence, where the Emperor Frederick was then staying.

Albert, throwing himself at his feet, confessed the whole story of his secret marriage with Guda, described her danger, and implored assistance and forgiveness.

The monarch was much taken aback by this sudden disclosure and demand.

He at first censured Albert for the part he had played; next declared that he had no greater enemy than Hugo of the Pfalz, and would willingly assist in consummating his downfall.

In a short time he embarked upon the Rhine, with several hundred followers, well armed.

They landed and marched with some difficulty along the rugged, woody, and mountainous district that led to the baron's residence.

In an open space in the forest the party halted and took a survey of the castle.

Then a herald was sent forward with a challenge or proclamation, which summoned Hugo of Stahleck, falsely styled Count Palatine of Pfalz-Grafenstein, to surrender up his usurped authority and possessions to his liege sovereign, Frederick, Emperor of Germany, on behalf of Lady Guda, the rightful Countess Palatine, whom he traitorously and unwarrantedly kept immured in the Castle of Caub, which should otherwise be immediately besieged.

On hearing this, the baron knew that all was discovered, even the false funeral.

His answer was a defiance and a determination to hold out till the last.

The attack upon the castle was therefore immediately commenced.

An exchange of volleys of arrows and cross-bow bolts took place between the assailants and the defending force on the ramparts.

The effect was not very disastrous.

But as the former party could not avoid exposing themselves somewhat more than the baron's men behind their strong defences, they suffered the most, but were not discouraged.

Their first object was to break down the outer barriers of the castle, which consisted mostly of wooden palisades of the firmest construction.

Led on by Count Albert, the stout and experienced warriors set to this work with great vigour.

With swords, axes, and their main strength, they loosened these defences, and though exposed all the time to the full play of the defenders' arrows, succeeded in their design.

Soon a loud shout of triumph showed that a breach had been made.

Then the so-far victorious warriors proceeded to make a forcible entry.

But they were promptly met by the defenders, and a desperate conflict ensued.

It was hand to hand, and maintained with determination on both sides.

But the Imperialists had the advantages of superior number and the most complete discipline.

They were at last enabled to cut their way through the resisting force, and, aided by the scaling ladder they had brought, to storm and carry the outer wall.

The inner rampart was defended by a powerful body of warriors.

Chief among these were Baron Hugo and his son Ludwig, clad in complete armour, and surmounted by the well-known crest of Falkenstein.

The baron, in the subsequent contest, fought as one possessed by some demon.

Every sweep of his mighty sword took an opponent's life, or, at least brought one to the ground, and he seemed as if he would not relinquish his position while one stone of Caub Castle remained upon another.

Ludwig, on the contrary, fought with less vigour and determination, and, to tell the truth was of so inferior an order, that, but for being constrained by his father's presence and by his own position of authority, he would have felt no disinclination to abandon the struggle.

The opposing party stormed up the wall, and came in deadly contact with the Palatine usurper and his band.

The crest of their chief the baron instantly recognised as that of his foes, the emperor's family.

"Yield Baron of Stahleck! Yield to Albert of Hohenstaufen!"

"Death to all of that hated name!" hissed the baron, as he aimed a fearful blow at the head of the young knight.

They fought long and desperately.

But their contest was as yet without any definite result.

At length these chief combatants being separated by the press of their contending followers, the baron paused for a brief breathing space.

At that moment he saw the seneschal rushing towards him.

"My lord, the fates are against us. All our resistance is vain! The enemy are twice our number—the castle is overrun by them; there is no hope of saving it!"

Though these words came like a pang to the baron's heart he was still undaunted.

"Come the worst!" he cried, "I will die at my post sooner than yield to my detested foe!"

Shortly after he and Albert met again in combat.

This time it was it was on a high rampart, overlooking the moat, an artificial stream, whose channel was cut in the rugged rocks, and which discharged itself into the Rhine.

The contention between the two leaders of the opposing parties became more desperate than ever.

Albert received more than one wound, and at last, by a hair's breadth, parried a blow which would inevitably have killed him.

But he paid the baron back in his own coin, and the latter, struck by the sword of his young and vigorous antagonist, staggered, fell back, and with no cry of pain or terror, but a fierce exclamation, Hugo fell over the rampart, striking against a ledge of rock.

His body fell like a log into the moat below, and disappeared from view.

Greatly discouraged by the loss of their leader, and the low ebb to which their own prospects had attained, the defenders of the castle were rapidly giving way to the besiegers.

All Ludwig's courage and presence of mind seemed overwhelmed by their desperate position; he gave the most contradictory and unwise orders, hung back when a bold rally could alone ensure success, and retreated where a more confident man would have bravely held out.

Only when he was brought face to face with Albert did he pluck up anything like a knightly spirit.

A few passes, however, between them, decided the contest to the triumph of the young count.

Stricken down on his knee, Ludwig, when commanded to surrender, gave a very different reply to that of his father.

"I comply on condition my life is spared," he said, submissively.

"I demand a condition also," was Albert's reply. "It is, that you shall tell me in what place you have imprisoned my wife, the persecuted Guda."

"She is in the lowest dungeon of yon tower," he replied, "of which the seneschal has the keys.

"If thou hast spoken falsely, thy life is forfeit. Give up thy sword, and accompany my lieutenant to my quarters."

Ludwig promised he would not attempt

escape, and Ulfran and another departed with their prisoner.

His quiet manner deceived them, and they forbore to bind him.

Suddenly, watching his opportunity, he plucked up a sword dropped by one of the wounded, whirled it rapidly round him, and broke from their grasp.

One of Albert's followers, seeing this sudden movement, caught Ludwig ere he could proceed many paces, and met his attack by the agency of his ponderous battle-axe.

The weapon went crashing through Ludwig's helmet, penetrating his skull, and caused him to sink, with a cry of anguish, among the slain.

The last heir of the Falkensteins was no more.

The castle was now all but captured.

A few more minutes, and the struggle was over, except a few isolated combats going on in different parts of the scene.

A large number of the conquered party had been slain ; almost all the rest were taken prisoners (the only notable exception being Bernhard, the steward, who was nowhere to be found), and the victorious party gave a shout of triumph as they planted the imperial standard upon the ramparts.

But, before all else, Albert hastened to the place of Guda's captivity.

He found it to be a dark, bare, stone cell, on the lowest ground floor of the castle, more fit for a degraded felon than a noble lady.

With a beating heart, the young knight unfastened the ponderous lock.

He rushed in.

He saw, at the further end, the pale countenance and agitated frame of her he loved so well, and who had that day suffered all the horrors of a captive during a siege.

"Guda, my dearest, my much persecuted Guda, I have found thee at last. Thou art rescued, thou art saved ; thy persecutors are slain or defeated. It is thy own Albert by thy side !"

The access of joy was overwhelming.

She fell in his arms ; her heart was too full to speak.

The conclusion of our story is soon told.

The party of Baron Hugo being irrecoverably defeated, and the castle taken, Albert, armed with the imperial warrant, took formal possession in the name of his wife Guda, who now, reappearing, was overpowered by the gratulations and attentions of all.

The prisoners taken were leniently dealt with, while those who had in any way assisted the persecuted countess were liberally rewarded.

Jacintha was always henceforth Guda's chief female attendant.

Her son was pardoned on condition of leaving the robber's life.

But the body of the baron himself was never found, though the moat and all adjacent were searched frequently and thoroughly.

The robbers, if their band was not dispersed, were for the time repulsed, and retreated to other and more distant forest districts ; at all events, they ceased molesting travellers.

The forgiveness of the emperor healed the long-standing feud between his family and the Falkensteins.

Guda, as the last of that race, was proclaimed Countess Palatine, and she requested that her husband should share her title.

They took up their residence at the Castle of Caub, which, however, having been so damaged by the siege, was first repaired and beautified, till it presented an unprecedentedly magnificent appearance.

From that time it was no longer called Caub, but Gutenfels (Guda's Castle), in honour of the countess.

Stahleck was comparatively deserted, but Pfalz was still used both as a fortress and a residence, and the new Palatine instituted a custom that every heir of the family should be born within its walls, in the very room in which Guda was imprisoned.

And now what bar was there to Guda's and her husband's happiness ?

One only ; the loss of their child.

END OF THE LEGEND OF GUTENFELS.

[Continued from page 139.]

CARL THE FERRYMAN.

"BRAVE youth!" she said, with a kind smile, "thou hast nobly triumphed over the powers of darkness. Fear not! the Spirit of Good protects thee."

The bright vision vanished, leaving the young prisoner in a state of tranquil joy.

Nor was his equanimity disturbed when the clank of arms, and the rude voices of men were heard at the pit's mouth.

Presently the bucket was lowered, and one called gruffly, "Get in. Your presence is required in the Folterkammer (torture chamber)."

Without a word or a tremor of fear, Carl stepped into the bucket and was drawn up.

Again the gloomy passages and the winding staircases were traversed, until the youth found himself in a large and lofty chamber, that one in which his mother breathed her last, and whose blood still ineffaceably dyed the floor.

Before him were several rough-looking, brutal men, amongst whom stood the duke.

"Now!" exclaimed the latter sternly, "art thou still determined to be dumb? Where is thy wife concealed."

"I shall not tell thee," was the firm reply.

"Thou canst but kill me, as thou didst my parent before me, and ere thou canst do that, the hand of righteous retribution may interpose to rob thee of the power thou boastest, and thou mayst be dead thyself!"

"Ha! ha! ha!" laughed the duke scornfully, "thou dost not know the prophecy. Listen!"

With exulting impressiveness, Leofric recited the prediction, and then, having finished, he turned with a sneer to his prisoner, and remarked—

"Until these impossibilities come to pass, I am safe, and laugh all threats to scorn.

"To Heaven's omnipotence, nothing is impossible," was the calm and trusting answer.

"Bind him to the rack!" shouted the brutal Leofric, incensed at the youth's intrepidity, "and stretch his limbs till every joint be torn asunder."

The hapless Carl was seized by his merciless executioners; but at this moment a sound was heard that fell upon the ear of the guilty duke like a knell of death.

The prolonged blast of a trumpet arose from the very depth of the ground on which he stood.

It was not a ringing, but a muffled and awfully ominous note, and a sweet, clear voice was heard to say—

"'Tis the trumpet's martial sound
Echoing from the solid ground."

The blood fled from the usurper's cheek as he realized the part accomplishment of the prophecy.

At the same moment a confused murmur of voices reached his ears.

"What means this?" he cried in a tone of terrible apprehension.

Hardly had he uttered these words when the door opened, and Odo, pale and trembling, hurried in.

"My lord!" he exclaimed hurriedly, "an armed force from the river are making their way through the solid rock into the castle. "Fly and save yourself."

Again a loud shout was heard, but whence proceeding nobody knew.

"At least I will not die unavenged!" vociferated the duke, as he drew his sword and rushed towards Carl.

"Die! thou hated offspring of a hated sire!" he cried, as he raised his weapon.

But ere it fell, a tremendous crash was heard.

A blinding, dazzling light flashed through the chamber, a portion of whose walls was shivered as though by lightning, whilst near Leofric stood a tall figure, enveloped in a cloak.

"Hold," cried the stranger, in a solemn, imperative voice.

The sword dropped from Leofric's nerveless hand.

Slowly the mysterious warrior raised his hat, and disclosed the features of his dead brother, Eustace.

With a cry of horror the guilty wretch fell flat upon the floor.

"The prophecy is fulfilled!" exclaimed the spectre, and, with these words it disappeared, bearing with it the insensible form of Leofric, and at the same moment a band of soldiers poured in through the aperture in the wall.

The means of approach was by a secret passage hewn in the solid rock on which the castle stood, long disused, and the existence of which was even unknown.

Adelgitha had appealed to a neighbouring baron for assistance, and he chivalrously accorded it.

Whilst considering how the troops might effect an entrance, Paul the ferryman, who was with them, remembered a narrow fissure he had often observed in the rocks below the castle, and now pointed it out to the baron's notice, little dreaming it to be a passage conducting to the very heart of the domain.

This they explored successfully, as the result proved.

Carl, or as we must call him, the young Duke Eustace, was now restored to his rejoicing bride, who hastened to him.

Their perils were past, and a bright future was in store for them of love and happiness.

Old Paul left his ferry-house to dwell at the castle from beneath whose roof the Spirit of Evil was banished, to make room for the presence of the Spirit of Good, which never more departed thence.

END OF CARL THE FERRYMAN.

THE CHILD OF THE PFALZ.

BEING THE SEQUEL TO GUDA'S CAPTIVITY.

IT was discovered afterwards that the formidable Baron Hugo von Falkenstein had not been killed at all, neither had his accomplice, Bernhard, though both had been wounded in the siege.

After a while they commenced a fresh career of crime.

Opposed and deserted by most of his former dependants, the ex-Palatine went to dwell in the forest, put himself at the head of robbers, and waged determined war against those who had dispossessed him.

He enacted all the lawless deeds common to robber-chiefs of that rugged age ; seized travellers, attacked and burnt villages, plundered monasteries, or other unprotected houses, and he and his band became in short, the terror of the country.

He still called himself the Count Palatine, and demanded allegiance as such ; and, more than once, he even attempted to besiege the castle, but his forces were not equal to the undertaking.

This lawless career continued for several years, till at length, having collected a large number of desperadoes obedient to his will, Hugo made a sudden and vigorous night assault on on the Castle of Gutenfels.

But Albert's precautions and defences frustrated the last effort ; the garrison was roused, and, after a fight as desperate as that which we have already described, the besiegers were defeated with great loss, and Hugo himself slain.

Bernhard was captured, and his life spared only on condition he would reveal all he knew about the lost heiress of the Falkensteins.

Of the rest, many robbers were killed, many taken, and many others fled, and the band thenceforth utterly routed and broken up.

By Bernhard's confession, it was discovered that the stolen child had been given to the care of the old physician, Zacharias, and his wife, who had successfully kept her in concealment.

She was now restored to the arms of her joyful parents—a lovely blue-eyed child of five years.

Her identity being satisfactorily proved, she was taken to live at the castle, where she was overwhelmed by the love and attentions of friends and relatives.

She was christened with great magnificence at the chapel of the castle by the name of Alberta, but was generally called, from the place of her birth, the " Child of the Pfalz."

A life of happiness seemed before her, but there were clouds in this fair prospect.

In the interval of her disappearance had been born to the Count and Countess two other daughters, and these, as they grew up, could not be kept in ignorance of the antecedents of their sister.

Nina, the younger, regarded her with affection ; but Joscelyne, the elder, was of proud and jealous disposition, and apt, on occasions of anger, to cast aspersions upon her, and to hint that she was an intruder in the family, and perhaps, after all, a changeling—a peasant's child and not a true Falkenstein.

This made Alberta unhappy.

She was gentle as she was lovely, and the charge was one she had no means of absolutely disproving.

However, Alberta's position was secure.

She was the eldest daughter of a noble family to which there was no heir, and she was thus heiress of its honours.

Her beauty, accomplishments, amiability, and brilliant prospects—in all of which respects she surpassed either of her sisters —rendered her, as she grew up, the centre of attraction to many of the surrounding knights and nobles, to whom, however, she appeared to give little encouragement.

Perhaps the following circumstance will account for this—

Once there arrived at the castle several knights, some of whom were known to the Palatine.

They had just returned from the Crusades, and their adventures in the

Holy Land were full of interest to their entertainers.

Among them was an Englishman, who, though distinguished in appearance, travelled without a retinue, and called himself Ulric the Troubadour.

His first sight of Alberta produced an ineffaceable impression, which was reciprocated, and a week's stay at the castle on his part was sufficient to enchain both in the bonds of love.

The Count and Countess Palatine had observed this growing affection, and deemed it their duty to discourage it, as the stranger knight did not seem high enough in rank for the heiress of the Palatine.

When he departed, they deemed that Alberta would soon forget the impression he had made ; but little imagined how completely her heart was lost.

Alberta heard no more of him until the occasion of a grand tournament at Frankfort, at which she was present, and which we must dwell upon somewhat in detail.

Brightly shone the sun on the Imperial city of Frankfort-on-the-Maine, now the scene of unusual and magnificent festivity.

Large crowds of spectators of all ranks were assembled, and the animation, light, and colour of the scene were such as no eye could behold without enthusiastic admiration.

The tournament was to last three days, whereof one had already passed.

Some of the most distinguished knights

"HULDEBRAND DREW HIS SWORD, AND CHALLENGED THE STRANGE
KNIGHT TO CONTINUE THE COMBAT."

of Germany had displayed their prowess before their sovereign, and some of the most beautiful ladies of the noblest families had been inspired by the ambition of becoming queen of the lists.

That proud position had been occupied the first day by the Countess of Rothenburg, to whom had succeeded Lady Gertrude von Breslau, nominated by Otto von Diedricz, the first day's victor.

It was about midday when a flourish of trumpets announced the arrival of the Emperor Conrad, who arrived with a numerous and splendid retinue, and amid the cheers of the assembled throng, took his seat in the magnificent pavilion prepared for him.

The knightly sports soon began, and several courses were run with varying success.

Notably among the cavaliers who distinguished themselves, was Albert of Hohenstaufen, the Count Palatine, who had lost not the marked prowess and skill which had distinguished him in youth.

He probably was inspired to his best efforts by the presence of his wife, the still beautiful Countess Guda, and of his three lovely daughters.

The aspirants for the affections of the latter were the three young counts, Ernest, Heinrich, and Huldebrand, all scions of the princely house of Hohenstaufen.

Our next number will contain the conclusion of " The Child of the Pfalz."

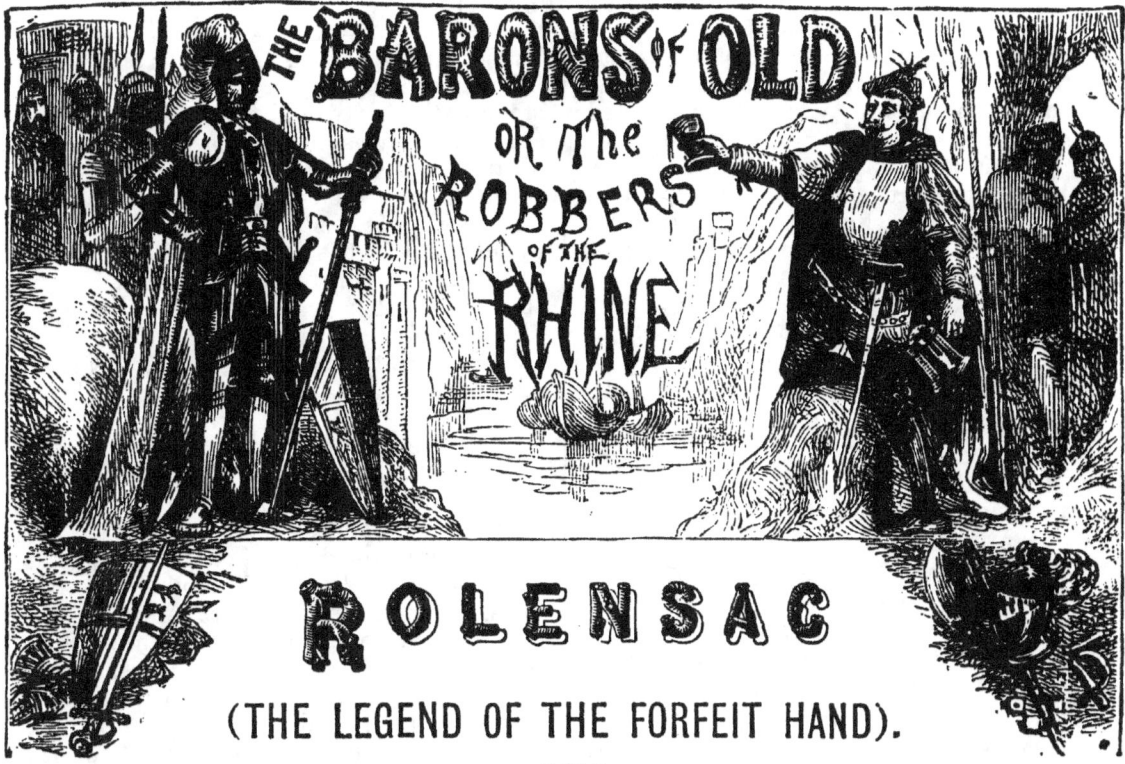

THE BARONS OF OLD OR THE ROBBERS OF THE RHINE

ROLENSAC

(THE LEGEND OF THE FORFEIT HAND).

THE castles which yet in some shape or form frown over the Rhine and Moselle, are almost as numerous as the stars in the heavens. Some belong to a time so distant, that while relics remain in the shape of a few moss-clad stones, their history is almost lost in the darkness of ages.

Of these is Rolensac, of which, when men speak, it is with a shake of the head. But fortunately for the satisfaction of those who see sermons in stones, and good

THE CASTLE OF ROLENSAC.

in everything, amid the almost universal destruction of parchments and manuscripts during the many wars which have afflicted humanity, many of the convent and monastery rolls have been preserved, and thus it happens, that of this castle there remains a record which is not wanting in all the tragic and mysterious elements of middle age history.

In those days, when between knights and robbers there was but little distinction except in favour of the latter, travelling was peculiarly dangerous.

The castles of these petty feudal lords, whom advancing civilisation is gradually knocking on the head, were eyries, whence at the sight of rich travellers making their way along the roads below, they would descend as the eagle upon the lamb, or the hawk upon the trembling dove.

Travelling was so dangerous, that men waited until they had collected in force, to move from one town to another.

All went well armed, and it became merchants and citizens to be resolute and determined in dealing with all suspicious characters.

It was therefore with some surprise that the inhabitants of certain scattered hamlets, as well as occasional groups of charcoal-burners, observed a single cavalier making his way through the dense forest alone.

Not only was he in a neighbourhood dangerous as the known hunting-ground of the Black Wolf of Zelling, a prince who carried his disregard to the laws of *meum* and *tuum* to a most alarming extent, but the forest was infested with robbers of a meaner and humbler rank, who were not above lightening a pedlar or pilfering the goods of a solitary tramp.

The cavalier rode a stout horse, but his own character was almost wholly concealed, from the fact of his wearing a long cloak and a kind of cowl.

The day was sharp and cold, and as night was drawing on, man and beast appeared in need of rest and sustenance.

But though the rider looked about him with a keen and anxious eye, he could make out no sign of any dwelling place ; no friendly column of smoke rose in the air, speaking of welcome to the weary and exhausted traveller.

There was no choice, then, but to persevere, and the solitary rider, gently spurring his horse, urged him to a goodly speed, of which the animal, a fine and ready beast, was still quite capable.

Scarcely had he done so, when the iron clang of another horse fell upon his ear,

and turning round, he saw a mail-clad horseman coming at a heavy trot down a steep path that would soon join his own.

His hand was hastily passed under his cloak, as if to examine the state of his weapons, and then he advanced at a more leisurely pace, as if seeking neither to avoid nor join the other traveller.

Keeping to this resolution, he soon found that the other was determined to join him, as he urged his horse rapidly.

Thinking that any further appearance of ignoring the other's presence might be considered childish, he reined in his steed and allowed the other to come up.

" *Vlanderer den leem* " (Flanders and the sun), said the new comer in a deep, hoarse voice, speaking from under his visor, " but you ride quick, my friend."

" I seek shelter and food ere night falls," replied the young traveller.

" Then you will not find it, unless it be in some cavern or beneath a tree," continued the stranger ; the nearest inn is a good two hours' ride."

" As I have no provisions, and no provender for my horse," urged the young traveller, " I must needs go forward."

" Twenty minutes farther on, a little off the road, dwells a hermit, with whom I am slightly acquainted. Doubtless he will give us such fare as may satisfy weary travellers. If you like to try his hospitality, I can promise you such accommodation as should satisfy a soldier, which, despite your cloak and cowl, I believe you are."

" Sir knight, for such your dress indicates you, I ask not your rank or name. Allow me to retain the secret of mine," said the young man curtly.

The other growled something under his teeth, neither very friendly nor very complimentary, but made no audible reply, and thus wrapped each in their dignity, they advanced until they reached a narrow, dark, and gloomy gorge, overhung by pines and stunted oaks, up which the stranger knight took the way.

The other followed, and in a few minutes the two disappeared in the black and ghostly valley.

As they did so, two men with matted hair, leather jerkins and rough attire, peered out from behind some trees, with stern and threatening looks. Taking careful note of the way the others had gone, they took to their heels and started off in an opposite direction.

Meanwhile, after journeying a couple of hundred yards, the two travellers found themselves at the foot of a rock about five and twenty feet high, overhung by plants and rendered gloomy by the lofty trees that grew around. But that the stranger knight pointed out a heavy wooden door to his fellow traveller, he would not have seen it.

As it was, he alighted with an agility which spoke well for the elasticity of a heavily-armed man. He knocked thrice with his mailed hand, and had scarcely concluded, when the door opened, and a tall sinister-looking man, in the garb of a monk, appeared on the threshold.

A rapid sign was exchanged between the two, after which the monk cast the door wide open and invited them to enter, horses and all.

They were soon in a large cavern, at the end of which was a narrow passage, along which the hermit led them to a stable, cut out of the rock, and which had accommodation for six horses, with ample supply of provender and water.

Having seen to the animals, the travellers returned to the outer cavern, and seating themselves, took some repose, while the hermit prepared some welcome in the shape of huge boar steaks grilled, and bread made on an iron platter.

A queer fellow was the hermit. A tall, lean man, with sloping shoulders, a hatchet face, hollow, leathery cheeks, a large hooked nose like the beak of a bird of prey ; eyes small, and fiery red, sank deep beneath heavy brows, the coarse light hairs of which fell over them, like a penthouse thatch ; his thin, bloodless lips were set in a perpetual smile, more subtle than the most open sneer.

The hands, with which he manipulated the food, were long and bony, and had curved fingers and pointed nails, which were also like the talons of a bird of prey.

The young traveller, finding the cavern very warm after the cold without, took off his cloak and hood, revealing an elegant suit of armour, a fine, stalwart figure, and a fair, handsome face.

After a brief scrutiny the stranger knight, who was tall and powerful, removed his helm and revealed his face almost faultless in its manly beauty, and yet a face at which all women shuddered and which every man mistrusted.

The expression was resolute, bold, lawless and determined in the extreme.

"I suppose," said the hermit, with a sly, sidelong glance, "you know the green jerkins are about ? Since the Black Wolf of Zelling hung their chief Rudolph, they have increased in impudence. They talk of nothing else but vengeance and retaliation."

"He must be a poor knight who fears such swine," replied the other sardonically.

"A pack of hounds will harry the finest buck when one dog will run. Their cry is ' slae doodt!—slae doodt !'—(slay dead ! slay dead !)"

"'Tis little concern of mine, sir hermit —both I and my companion are a hungered—and the meat seems done to a turn."

Two smoking platters, with ample supply of bread, were soon before them, while a huge flagon of old ale was placed near at hand.

Needless to say that they made a hearty meal and were decidedly comforted thereby.

Then the younger traveller signified his wish to sleep, and the hermit pointed to a pile of clean straw, of which the other at once availed himself, and was soon in the land of dreams, during which a vision of a face—a lovely face—beamed upon him, and filled his heart and soul with happiness.

Meanwhile, the stranger knight and the hermit held half an hour's conference in a low tone, after which they were about to follow the example of the younger traveller, when a loud knocking came at the door.

The knight looked keenly at the hermit.

"I told you so," he said. "But let me make sure. Who assails a poor man's home at this late hour ?—pass your way, and leave a solitary hermit to his orisons."

"Open! or by the cross of Hildegard, we'll knock your old cave about your ears."

"I will not open, sirrah. 'Tis past the hour—how know I but that you are robbers ?"

An infuriated shout, followed by repeated knocking, now with a heavy beam of wood, proclaimed how far in earnest the assailants were.

The knight put on the armour he had removed, and clutching his heavy sword, saw to his dagger, and then aroused the younger traveller, who bounded to his feet.

"We are attacked by the sneaking robbers of the Rhine," said the knight, haughtily ; "'tis no death a for true man to perish in a fox hole. We must escape at once."

The young traveller made no reply.

He, however, buckled on his armour, placed his visor over his head, and clutching his arms, followed the other with a deep sigh. He was exhausted, weary, and had been awakened from a deep sleep.

But he was a soldier to the core, and knew that necessity has no law.

The stable was reached, and the horses hastily harnessed, after which the elder knight peered out of a kind of loophole.

"'Sdeath!" he cried; "the hounds have stopped the fox hole. But we are men, and must cut our way through. Mount and be ready."

The young man obeyed, and found that he could sit upright in the stable.

When both sat erect and ready on their war horses, the hermit opened the door, and with a loud cry, the two men dashed out, naked sword in hand, in the midst of a band of more than a dozen well-armed robbers. They had swords, pikes, and halberds, weapons capable of doing great execution.

The two knights were attacked on all sides, while the assailants made the forest ring with their oaths and execrations.

It was an unequal contest indeed, and appeared likely to be fatal to the elder knight, upon whom the whole force and violence of the attack fell,

"Down with the tyrant! Slay the murderous robber! *Slae doodt! slae doodt!*"

The younger traveller might easily have escaped, but he scorned to leave his companion to contend against such fearful odds.

"Away! away, young sir," shouted one of the leaders of the foemen. "We have no quarrel with you!"

"Have at you, disloyal knaves!" replied the other; "leave one man to contend against a dozen. Never!"

And with a skill, vivacity, and energy which amazed all around him, he began to lay about him with his right good blade.

The footmen retreated.

Suddenly one of them sounded a horn, which, ere the echoes had hardly died away, was answered by another.

"Look out, my friend," said the elder knight, in a low, husky tone; "one more dash and then away for our lives."

He backed to some trees as he spoke, and slashed away with fierce and savage energy, and then, with a loud cry, dashed off into the forest, followed by his young companion, amid the fierce and savage execrations of the robbers.

But they could not follow the mounted men, who, ere long, reached an inn, where they found that which they most needed, warm and comfortable beds.

It was far into the day when the two knights parted; the elder one, while con-cealing his own title, asking for that of the other.

"You saved my life, young sir, and some day it may be in my power to show my gratitude."

"I am known as Sir Edwin of Seltzberg, a younger son and knight errant," was the smiling answer.

"Many thanks. Until we meet again, farewell!" said the other, as some dozen or more mounted men at arms galloped up and surrounded their master.

Sir Edwin went his way, making his steed do double duty this day in his anxiety to reach Rolensac Castle, where a year ago he had said adieu to his promised bride, Editha, the daughter and heiress of Lord Rolensac.

The walls were in sight before evening, and to his surprise the door was wide open; and the portcullis down.

As he passed the porter's lodge, the man who kept the keys surveyed him with unbounded surprise and horror.

"A word, Sir Edwin," be said, clutching his horse's bridle. "Come into my room —what I have to say is of a private nature."

"Is it of Editha, my beloved?" cried Edwin.

"Come in, as you value life," replied the other, and was hastily obeyed.

"You have come, my good lord, on an evil day," said the man, when they were alone; "know you not that the old lord of Rolensac has been dead these six months, and that Editha weds to-day Ulric of the Black Hand, her cousin?"

"Away, man, let me pass," cried Sir Edwin.

"My young master, you can do nothing. The castle is full of his men; the abbot of Graal and his clergy perform the ceremony, and death and ruin would be the fate of all who interfered before the ceremony is over."

"Good Krutz," said Sir Edwin, in a calm and cold voice, "I will be prudent. Only let me see her fair, false face once more, and I'm away to fight under the emperor. I care not how soon I die."

The porter gave way, and the knight, drawing his hood and cloak around, made his way hastily to the great hall in which the ceremony was being performed.

As the other had said, all was over.

But all anger fled from the soul of the youth, as he gazed upon the pale, tearful, and wretched face of the enforced bride.

It was enough to appal and terrify a young girl, with only a few hand-maidens to defend her, to find herself surrounded by savage men-at-arms and their savage master, Ulric of the Black Hand.

This distant cousin, indignant at a woman becoming the *châtelaine*, had surprised the castle, and with the connivance of the haughty and truculent abbot, had compelled the poor girl to wed a man, hateful from his debaucheries, his license, and coarse and depraved habits.

Taking one last look of farewell, the young knight withdrew, his soul in arms, and all the better feelings of his nature subdued and dead.

Ten minutes later he galloped away like a weird hunter of the hills—he cared not whither.

Had he but waited, he might have acted differently.

The bride and bridegroom had reached the entrance of the banqueting hall, where were laid out the materials for a feast such as only a German could conceive or digest.

The bride passed first, and the bridegroom was about to follow, when a roughly-dressed man, with a head of shock red hair, suddenly appeared, and struck the knight in the side with a long and pointed dagger.

"That for Agnes in Heaven !" he cried, as he withdrew the glittering blade, and dashed down a long dark passage.

All were paralysed, and when a search was made for him, he had disappeared.

The confusion was intense.

The bride, upon whose wedding dress the blood had spurted, was carried out insensible, and when she awoke to consciousness, she was a widow, and mistress not only of Rolensac, but of a wild mountain castle belonging to her late husband.

The murdered man was buried, and to all appearance everything relapsed into its old groove, though doubtless Editha often wondered what had become of her own true knight, Sir Edwin.

Regret her husband, she could not.

Forced to accept him, while knowing his savage and debauched character, his death was a relief.

But society expected her to mourn him officially, and thus it happened that for months the castle was closed to all strangers, and the young maid, wife, and widow grew moody and thoughtful.

At the end of four months her solitude was broken into by a deputation from the abbot of Graal, and headed by his portly steward, who stood before the *châtelaine*, in an attitude of mock humility.

Editha haughtily demanded the reason of this unexpected visit.

The steward then made proclamation of the rank and quality of his master, adding that as great justiciary of the district, he had made researches into the murder of the brave knight, Sir Ulric.

He went on to say that the wretch who committed the deed had been captured, and on the rack had confessed not only how he had compassed his crime, but added that he had been instigated to do the deed by Editha of Rolensac.

"He lies," said the young girl, fiercely ; "take me to the monster !"

"The man died after this confession," said the other, with malicious emphasis in his words ; "and I am here to cite you to appear before the abbot as lord justiciary, who will, if you be found guilty, condemn you to death, and confiscate your property for the benefit of holy mother church."

"Yes, sacrilegious robber," cried the haughty and high-spirited girl ; "you and your avaricious master have concocted this accusation in order to pillage me as ye pillage the poor. But think not a Rolensac will submit to this vile oppression. Go—I defy you and your employer."

The steward, a kind of lay monk, began a fierce declamation against heresy.

"Out from my castle," she said, striking him with a staff which she carried in her hand as *châtelaine*.

"I give you five minutes. Then let loose the hounds and show me how these varlets can run."

Amazed, astonished, and yet alarmed, the deputation ignominiously retired, and fled the castle, only collecting together in good order when outside its walls, and vowing vengeance of the most dire kind against one who had so far forgot herself as to insult and even strike a servant of the church.

At first honest indignation and excitement sustained the courage of Editha of Rolensac.

Her pride of birth and character also supported her.

But soon she had reason to fear that in contests between the laity and the church, the former must at all times go to the wall.

Her old and honoured chaplain, after gently chiding her, and vainly striving to bring her to a sense of her wrongdoing, left the castle, and was soon after followed by the greater part of her domestics.

A dismal rumour was afloat that, leaving aside the question of the murder, the vindictive abbot was pursuing her for sacrilege, and, it was said, had claimed that the hand that had struck a servant of the church was forfeit to the law.

For continuation of this Story see page 190 *of our next number.*

THE CRUSADER'S BRIDE.

ON the right bank of the Rhine is situated the delightful Swiss valley.

This lovely spot is traversed by a stream which turns several water-mills, and descends in beautiful cascades between precipitous walls of rock.

At the entrance of this valley, and above the village of St. Goarhausen, rises the picturesque Castle of the Cat (a contraction of Katzenellnbogen, Cat's Elbow), the name of its original possessor.

The Cat is an interesting ruin.

Its interior is completely dismantled, and the vine trees twine themselves round it, even growing on the floor of the portrait-gallery.

From the heights of the castle may be seen the Gulf of the Rhine, called the bank, beyond which the fabulous rock of the Lurley descends into the stream.

Opposite the Castle of the Cat is the Castle of Thurnberg, generally termed the Mouse, still in good preservation, and which from its foundations of lava appears frowning at and defying the Cat, which tradition states it long kept in awe.

Among the many legends connected with Die Katze, the following may not prove uninteresting to the reader.

The clang of the Moslem cymbals resounded over the arid plains of Palestine, Moslem scimitars flashed in the eastern sunlight, and the Crescent banners of the infidel waved over the legions of the Sultan, ready to fight to the last for the sepulchre of the Saviour.

In every Christian land the banner of the Cross was unfurled, and every nation that bowed to the Christian religion prepared to do battle with the infidel for the tomb of Christ.

The difference of language, of customs, of opinions—all were ignored or forgotten, and German and Frank donned his armour, bared the sabre, raised high the symbol of his faith, and set out for the fight.

Among those who disdained to remain behind while men of all grades set forth to strike a blow at the infidel, was Baron Katzenellnbogen.

The Lord of Cat's Castle was little more than a youth in years, and had but a few months before espoused the lovely Leoline, whom he had won from many rivals, among them his cousin and dearest friend, Otho of Reichenberg, and who, finding the preference of the lady was certainly not for himself, appeared nobly to resign his claim in favour of his cousin Darven.

With such apparent cheerfulness and good grace had Otho done this that the friendship of Darven and Leoline for him was greatly increased.

The young bride was looking out upon the wild scenery beyond the walls of the castle, when she felt a hand upon her shoulder, and turned to see the smiling face of her husband Darven.

"Oh, my lord, I was thinking of you," she said.

"Were you, sweet one?" he said, tenderly drawing her to his bosom, and patting her cheek with his finger. "I have sought you, Leoline, to tell you that to-morrow I set out for the Holy Land, to fight beneath the banner of the Cross."

The colour that had leapt into the face of the young wife at sight of her husband, forsook her cheeks, and she was pale as marble.

"My lord, my lord," she cried, "you will not leave me?"

"Would you have me stay behind?" he asked, "when every hand bears the sword, and every heart in Christendom beats to confront the infidel?"

"But there are many without you to fight on the plains of Palestine," she pleaded.

"The Cross needs every hand and every heart, dear Leoline, and would you have your husband keep at home, when duty and honour alike call him to the field?"

She looked up into his eyes, but was silent.

"I know you would not," he continued. "Rather would you drive me forth to my duty. Where the banners of the Cross are waving, there should every true knight be, fighting for the possession of the sepulchre of his Lord."

" Yes, yes, but I shall be very wretched while you are away," sighed the baroness.

And a tear sparkled on her eyelash and fell on the hand of her husband.

"Nay," he said, soothingly, "I will soon return with victory on my brow. The Cross must be victorious, for wherever that sacred symbol is seen men leave their toil, their sports, their homes, to enrol themselves beneath it ; and shall I prove recreant to my faith, my knighthood, my honour ?"

"No, no," she replied, quickly, "mine shall not be the voice to chide you for the step you take, though my heart sinks at the thought of losing you, dear Darven, even but for a short time."

And her arms were twined around his neck, and her moist eyes looked into those of her youthful husband.

"This feeling will soon wear off," he said, "and in imagination you will follow your lord through the campaign—see his arm raised to strike in the noble cause which no true knight and Christian can suffer to be fought without his aid."

Leoline sighed.

"My lord, hours will seem days and days years until you return, and I shall be so melancholy, so wretched, with none to cheer me with a word or look in the castle."

"Nay, but I leave one behind me who will be to you as a brother, who will see your every wish obeyed, and smoothe the long hours with kindness and attention."

"Who, my lord ?" she asked.

"My noble cousin, Otho of Reichenberg."

"Goes he not to the wars ?"

"Not yet ; his father, the brave old knight, is fast sinking into the grave, worn out with wounds and age. The leech and the astrologer give no hopes of his recovery, and Otho waits till death has claimed his own, to take his new title and estates, and then he will follow the Christian bands to the plains of Palestine, if by that time the war be not over."

A smile lit up the eye of Leoline, and tapping the cheeks of her husband with her forefinger she said—

"And my lord will trust his young bride with such a gallant knight, to one who wooed her ere she gave her hand and heart to thee ?"

"He is a true knight and a brave man," said Darven, "and to doubt the honour or courage of Otho would be to doubt mine own existence."

"Such do I indeed believe him to be," said Leoline. "But," she added, playfully, "have you as much faith in your wife, my lord ?"

A moment Darven gazed into the depths of those liquid blue eyes, then clasped her almost fiercely to his breast as he replied—

"My faith in Heaven is not greater than my faith in thee, sweet wife. To thy love and Otho's honour I would entrust my soul's salvation !"

And Darven ratified the assertion by an embrace so fervent that he observed not the approach of a handsome young knight, who, with eyes bent upon the ground, came slowly towards them.

Suddenly looking up, he perceived the young wife enfolded in her husband's arms.

He gave a sudden start.

A spasm of pain passed over his face.

A gleam flashed in his eye ; there was a sudden tremulousness about the lips, and then he was calm again, a smile upon his face, and the light of joy in his eye.

Releasing his wife from his embrace, both looked up and perceived the intruder.

Darven, still retaining his wife's hand in his own, went forward to meet Otho, who had paused as if irresolute whether to remain or leave the apartment.

"Welcome Otho," cried the young baron. "But now were we speaking of you."

"Of me !" said Otho.

"Of yourself, brave knight," said Leoline. "And what, think you, was the subject of our converse ?"

"In truth, fair lady, I cannot say."

"That when my lord goes forth to the wars thou art to be my keeper."

And she laughed merrily.

"My sweet wife," remarked Darven, "I used no such harsh word. Friend and protector should be the term, and such an office right well do I know my friend Otho will gladly perform."

"An' you had spoken thus yesterday, I had replied that no prouder office could I accept than that of watching over the welfare and safety of the lovely wife of my dearest friend," replied Otho.

"And will not the same answer come to-day ?" asked Darven, in surprise.

"In faith, good knight, I cannot."

"And wherefore ?"

"Because, my lord, I follow you to the wars, unless you put off your departure for three days, when I will accompany you to strike a blow for the holy sepulchre," replied Otho.

"How ?" cried Darven, in surprise. "Will you leave your native land while yet your father lies at the portals of the grave?"

"The good old knight has shaken off the fiend that has held him so tightly in its clutches, and is well again."

"Glad news is this, indeed," said Leoline.

"Yes, fair lady, once more the old knight is well, and chafing at his want of strength to permit him to wield the battle-axe on the plains of Palestine, and so commands the departure of his son for the land of the infidel, and in three days Otho of Reichenberg departs for the wars."

"Now, by my soul," cried Darven, "thy words both please and vex me."

"How so?" asked Otho.

"Inasmuch as I am glad to go forth to fight the Saracen in company with so brave a knight, and sorry that my fair bride cannot have a friend and protector in thee during my absence."

"Your faith in your friend must be very great," said Otho.

"It is," replied Darven, extending his hand, "and he who would impeach the honour of that friend, should acknowledge at the point of Darven's sword that he foully lied."

And Darven tapped the hilt of his weapon with his left hand, while he shook his friend's hand fervently with the right.

A gleam of pleasure sparkled in the eyes of Otho of Reichenberg.

He returned the pressure of Darven's hand, and turned his gaze on the face of Leoline.

He read in those blue eyes faith and trust in him, and through his heart there leaped a joy, a hope, he had never felt before.

"May you never doubt my honour," said Otho, after a pause, "but that honour which you would confer upon me I must decline; 'tis my father's will and my desire that I go forth to the wars, and in three days hence, with fifty followers, I start for Venice to embark for the seat of war."

"Then, till then will I delay my departure, and we will embark together, together on the plains of Palestine we will assail the infidel host, together live or together fall."

"We will," said Otho.

Again they shook hands.

"Now, fair wife, since Otho accompanies me to the wars I must seek for you another protector," said Darven, turning to his bride.

"Nay, nay, my lord," she replied, "I will be my own protector. The followers you will leave behind can defend this mountain eyrie from all assailants, even if we have any to fear, which I doubt much, since this war engages the attention of all the Barons of the Rhine, and party struggles are swallowed up in this one great cause."

"Well, you are perhaps right; there are none to fear till this sacred war is over, when with Heaven's help I will return to cheer my bride and hold my own against all comers."

"Better that you give none the power to advise or guide your wife, Darven," said ·Otho. "The fair Leoline has a courageous soul, and will best know how to defend herself. Leave her to her own resources, and depend upon it she will be more happy and contented than if you fill your castle with a hundred guardians. What a womans lacks in strength she gains in wit, and when opposed to man she always gains the victory."

"Be it so," said Darven. "Since our dearest friend goes to the war, I will leave my wife the guardian of herself. So come, sweet, for three days longer I will remain by your side, and then to say farewell for a time to the Castle of the Cat and its lovely mistress."

He threw his arm around her waist and drew her along the stone floor, looking the while into her upturned eyes, so full of love and tenderness.

As the young husband and his beautiful bride left the apartment, Otho followed them with his eyes, his brows gradually lowering till they contracted into a frown.

"How beautiful she looks," he muttered; "and this beauty I had fondly hoped would be mine. Oh, how it wrings my heart to see her in his arms—to gaze upon those eyes gleaming with love and tenderness for him. I choke at the thought, and——But no, is he not my dearest friend, and shall I upbraid him?"

He set his teeth together and laid his hand upon the massive hilt of his stout sword.

"Would he loved me less," said Otho, "that I might hate him more. 'Tis hard to strike at him who would sacrifice his life for me. Would he despised me, then —then I might find a means to ease this aching heart, and woo to my arms the only woman I ever loved. Away with these thoughts, they are unworthy a knight and a brave man, and yet to what depths of infamy may not a woman's love hurl the soul of a brave man?"

He turned, and crossing the apartment,

looked forth from the window on to the rocks beyond.

"Darven is young, impetuous, brave," he mused, "and he will give the Saracens' steel good chance of finding a sheath in his bosom. Darven dead, Leoline's heart is free. Otho is her husband's dearest friend—her own—what then more natural than that the respect she cherishes for me should grow into a love as warm and true as that she feels for her husband. But why do my thoughts veer this way? I may fall, and then—well then—I'll think no more, lest I forget I am a knight, and a man of honour!"

He turned pettishly from the window, and hurried from the apartment to meet the baron and his bride in the banqueting hall of the Castle of the Cat, and drain a bumper of Rhenish wine to the success of the cause in which they were about to embark.

The three days passed quickly away, and from the Castle of the Cat issued the brave young baron, his esquire and a band of armed retainers.

It was a noble cavalcade, filled with enthusiasm, and rejoicing in the work to which they were about to be led.

From the castle walls they were watched, as they filed down the mountain, by the weeping Leoline, her women and the men-at-arms who were left behind to

THE CASTLE OF DIE KATZE, AND ST. GOARHAUSEN.

guard the castle, and protect their noble mistress.

Several priests met the cavalcade at the base of the mountain, and the knight and his followers dismounting, knelt to receive their blessing.

Once more mounting their steeds, the young baron took a scarf from his shoulders, secured it to his lance, and raising it above his head, waved it in the air.

The salutation was answered from the walls of the castle above by Leoline, who waved her kerchief, and then the knight turned, placed the scarf again upon his shoulders, gathered the reins in his hand, and shut out the loved vision of his weeping bride from his gaze.

The glorious sunlight glinted on his armour, the soft breeze lifted his plume, the chain mail awoke the musical echoes of the spot as the brave little band reached the banks of the Rhine, and were fairly on their way to do battle in that cause which half the world had espoused. Otho of Reichenberg was to meet the young knight at Venice, from whence they were to embark for the Holy Land.

Venice was reached in safety, and here Darven was joined by Otho and his fifty followers, well armed and powerfully-built fellows.

There was no unnecessary delay, and scarce had they met than they went on board a vessel, and were at once on their way to the fields of Palestine.

Having reached the Christian camp, they immediately enrolled themselves and followers under the royal leaders, and on the following day met the foe for the first time.

It was a desperate and glorious fight, and many a swarthy Saracen fell that day beneath the heavy battle-axe wielded by the young, yet powerful hand of Darven ; nor was it till the sun had set that, perspiring at every pore and faint at the weight of his armour, he heard the clarion's note recalling the soldiers of the Cross, and turned to seek the camp.

The legions which had gone forth to meet the enemy in compact masses, returned in straggling companies.

Knights were without esquires or followers, and followers without leaders, so fierce had been the battle, and so wide its range.

As Darven had been the foremost in the fray, so was he one of the last to leave the field.

The shades of night were falling fast, and closing around the camp of the Christians.

The many straggling parties making for this place, were being gradually enshrouded in darkness.

At length, while yet some distance from the camp, the baron found himself entirely alone.

His jaded steed, weakened by a blow from a Saracen's scimitar, was scarcely able to put one foot before another, so the knight had dismounted and was leading his favourite charger, urging him on with kind words to their destination.

The baron had raised his visor to suffer the cool air to play upon his heated forehead, and while enjoying the refreshing breeze and coaxing his steed along, he heard the thundering of hoofs behind him.

Darven turned his head.

Through the gloom he perceived three horsemen approaching.

To his surprise, he perceived by their dress that they were followers of the crescent.

The baron's position was a critical one. His eye swept the field.

As far as his vision could penetrate, not a single person was in view, save the three Mussulmen who were so swiftly nearing him.

He closed his visor.

He drew his shield round, and threw it before him, grasped his battle-axe from the saddle-bow, and placing his back against the side of his steed, said :

"If thy back cannot support me any longer, my noble beast, suffer thy haunches to do so.

The horse turned its head round to the voice, as if to fulfil the desire expressed.

The next moment the three men reined up their steeds before him, and with the cry of "Allah il Allah," flashed their weapons in the gloom.

Had the baron been differently situated it might have struck him that the voices of these Saracens had something of the Christian tone in them.

But Darven thought of nothing but his own danger, and his determination to sell his life as dearly as possible.

So without a word he swung his battle-axe round, and emptied one saddle of its occupant, who rolled, battered and bleeding at his feet, as his horse dashed madly over the plain.

The remaining two attacked him fiercely, and, wearied and bleeding, Darven sank upon one knee, as a crashing blow from a heavy battle-axe severed the armlets of his shield, and left him to the mercy of his foes.

Still Darven did not ask for quarter, but springing up he emptied another saddle by a swinging blow of his heavy axe.

In doing so the young baron left a path open for the other adversary to get behind him.

This was fatal to Darven.

As he struck the second man from the saddle, the third urged his horse behind the brave youth, and by a desperate thrust drove the point of his heavy two-edged sword between the points of his armour, and pierced the shoulder of the baron deeply.

Darven sprang round to meet his foe, but as he did so a film seemed to be gathering over his eyes, a dizziness took possession of his brain.

The battle-axe fell from his grasp, he swayed for a moment, and sank across the body of his last victim.

The sword which had again been upraised to strike was lowered, and the victor leaped from the saddle to the earth.

He leant over Darven, raised his hand, then suffered it to fall back heavily on the earth.

" Dead," he exclaimed. " Quite dead !"

The tones of the voice recalled the fainting faculties of Darven—they were the tones of one of his own countrymen, and not those of a Mussulman.

His first impulse was to speak.

His second to remain silent and assume death.

"That blow has broken my back," cried out a voice. "By the Cross, but the young baron wields a heavy axe. My lord, I beseech you unfasten my breastplate, and give me ease."

This was spoken by the man across whom Darven had fallen.

"A moment, Pepin," said the man addressed. "Art hurt much?—and Lebeck, how fares it with thee?"

A moan was the only answer.

Darven felt himself being pulled from off the body of the man on whom he lay.

The pain his wound caused him through this movement was intense, and it was with difficulty he stifled the cry that was ready to burst from his lips.

"Unbuckle this accursed harness, Lord Otho," pleaded the man. "The infidel's mail is stifling me."

"Peace, knave," cried the voice, which Darven, to his horror and surprise, now recognised as that of his dearest friend. "I must sever the thongs with my dagger. Thus! thus!"

"Ah, Otho of Reichenberg, would you murder me, after having aided you to detroy the noble baron who lies there? Is this your promised reward, false knight," cried the prostrate man.

"Ha, ha," laughed Otho. "Fool and knave, thinkest thou that I will entrust to thee a secret that would raise against me the hand of every baron of the Rhine, and of every true knight in Christendom? No; you have helped me well to despoil the dead Saracens, and destroy the man I hate so deeply. Having done this, I need you no longer. So take thy reward, and go on thy journey to the other world."

Through the bars of his vizor the powerless knight perceived the bright blade of Otho's dagger descend towards the bosom of the man.

There was a loud curse, a sharp cry, a laugh of triumph, and then Otho arose to his feet.

"Now, to make certain that none remain to tell the story of my infamy—none live to carry to the ears of the lovely Leoline the means I took to make her mine."

He leant over the other man, scrutinised his pale face a moment, and then plunged his dagger in his throat.

"Thus I secure silence and a bride," he said, rising. "Hark! Some horsemen come this way."

He hastily flung aside the turban and frock and appeared in his own coat of mail.

Bending down he tore the scarf from the shoulders of the paralysed and helpless Darven, forced his signet ring from his finger, mounted his steed, and galloped away from the spot.

Bewildered the young baron lay upon the earth, his wound causing him the greatest of agony, yet at the same time drawing him to forgetfulness of all around him.

Had he uttered one cry, moved a muscle, breathed a sigh, the dagger of Otho had found a sheath in his heart.

But he gave no indication of life, and, satisfied that Darven was no more, the murderer fled from the spot towards the Christians' camp, never once looking behind upon the scene of his crime.

In a few minutes a troop of horsemen drew rein before the three men and the wounded steed of Darven.

They dismounted, examined the bodies, and finally lifted that of the knight to the saddle of one of their number, and giving spurs to their steeds, galloped off in the direction of the Saracens' lines.

When Darven again awoke to consciousness, he was the inmate of a Saracen fortress, and watched and tended by infidel soldiers and infidel doctors with a care and tenderness that might have shamed many a Christian.

It was a sad awakening to the brave young knight, but his was not a heart to fail even under the greatest of reverses.

He longed for liberty, that he might flee to the protection of his loved wife, but that blessed boon was denied him, and he could but wait and hope and pray.

On the day following the battle, several knights who had been wounded too severely to enable them to bear arms for some time to come, and yet not so badly as to necessitate their being put in the hospitals, took their departure from the camp to embark on board a vessel returning to Venice.

Among these was Otho of Reichenberg.

His hurt was an inward one, caused by his having been several times unhorsed in the desperate charges; at least such was his explanation of his injuries, since no outward wounds could be seen.

That he had borne himself bravely in the fight, many attested, even if the blood stains upon his armour had not proved this fact without a doubt.

Great was the trepidation of the lovely Leoline, when one evening she was aroused from a deep reverie by the sound of a bugle, and looked out from the castle to perceive a young knight making his way up the steep sides of the mountain.

She flew to welcome him, for she had a feeling that he brought news of her husband from the Holy Land.

But what was her surprise when she perceived in the knight none other than Otho of Reichenberg, her own and her husband's dearest friend ; and that he had returned alone.

Her heart sunk within her bosom, and her words of welcome died on her lips.

"Darven, my loved lord, where—where is he ?" she cried, before even Otho could cross the drawbridge.

"In Palestine, fair lady," he replied, but with a sigh.

She marked the sigh and the look which accompanied it, and tremblingly she seized the hand of Otho.

Wildly she looked into his eyes.

"Speak, speak !" she cried. "Oh, my heart misgives me. My lord—my husband—does he live ?"

Otho drew her across the courtyard towards the entrance to the large hall, but answered not a word.

"Holy Mother !" cried Leoline, "what means this silence? Speak, tell me the worst, though you break my heart. This suspense is terrible."

Arriving in the great hall, Otho turned his gaze full upon her.

"Baroness," he said, huskily, "the lord of this castle is——"

"What—where ?" she half shrieked.

"Dead !"

The baroness flung her arms above her head, and fell forward fainting upon the bosom of Otho of Reichenberg.

Calling to the men-at-arms to summon her maid, Otho strove to restore her to consciousness.

But so deep was the swoon into which she had fallen, that all his endeavours were in vain.

Resigning her to the charge of her maids, Otho resolved to await patiently her recovery.

The lady was borne to her own apartment, and Otho paced the great hall with folded arms and thoughtful brow.

"What, if the shock be too heavy for her to bear," he thought, "and she should sink beneath it ? I should have then plotted in vain. But, no ; this tongue shall cheer, and this arm support her. Grief seldom kills, and the greater its violence, the sooner its end."

At this moment one of the women approached him.

"How fares your lady ?" he asked.

"She weeps, and calls upon my lord, wringing her hands the while, like one demented. She desires your presence—will you follow me, my lord ?"

Otho motioned the woman to precede him, and went to the chamber where the heart-stricken lady was.

"Grieve not so, fair lady," said Otho, consolingly.

"Oh, I am wretched indeed," she moaned.

"Let this assuage your grief,—your gallant lord died fighting bravely, and ere he fell had strewn the plain around with many an infidel corse, and then, when overpowered by numbers, he fell bleeding from many a wound, he died thinking of thee, and commending thee to my care and protection."

"Noble-hearted, brave-hearted Darven," she sobbed, "and thou wert by his side when the infidel's accursed steel robbed me of the best and bravest of lords."

"Aye, fair lady, that was I," he replied ; "surrounded and cut off by numbers, we fought shoulder to shoulder, each eager to protect the other's life, or resolved to avenge the other's fall."

Leoline clasped his hand, and raised it to her lips.

"Brave-souled Otho," she sobbed. "And you avenged him ?"

"Nobly !" he replied. "I fought a passage through my foes, when I could no longer aid my friend, and, returning with my followers, slew to a man those who had sought our lives."

"Heaven bless you, Otho ! "

"Alas! vain was the hope I had cherished, that his life might yet be saved. The accursed lance of the infidel had sunk too deep, and he lived but to tear this scarf from his breast and this ring from his finger, and bid me hasten to his wife with the sad news of his death, and charge her to trust in that friend who stood by him in life and death."

He drew from his bosom the embroidered scarf and from his finger the signet ring, and placed them in the hands of Leoline.

"'Take these to my wife,' he said, 'and with them my dying blessing,' and conjuring me to watch over you, he died in my arms, his head pillowed upon my bosom, his hand clasped in mine."

And the knight turned his head away as if to hide the tear that might disgrace his manhood, but in reality to conceal the blush of shame that the lie had called to his face.

Leoline gazed through her tears at the scarf she had given him to wear as a token, and on the ring that had graced the hand she loved to caress, and then she laid them down and sobbed again.

"Fair lady, how can I assuage your grief?" murmured the hypocrite. "It wrings my heart to see you thus bowed down with sorrow."

"Oh, fate, how cruel you are," she sobbed. "My brave young lord, so good, so noble, so kind, to fall thus, and leave me to misery, despair, and death."

"No, no," cried Otho, alarmed at the tones in which she spoke; "talk not of death. He has already triumphed too much in tearing from me my friend, from you your husband!"

So full of poignant grief were his looks and words, that, suffering as she herself was, her woman's heart could yet feel for another.

She rose, and took the hand of Otho in both her own.

"I will struggle to be calm," she said. "I am cruel, selfish to think that none grieve for him besides myself. Oh, noble Otho! too well I know how your generous heart is wrung at the untimely fate of your friend and cousin! Pray Heaven comfort us both!"

"Amen!" muttered Otho, as he again turned his head away.

Grief, like all things else, must have an end.

The sorrow of Leoline gradually abated, till, at last, she only thought of her husband's death with that melancholy sadness which must ever be felt by those who cherish the memory of a loved one.

As time soothed her grief for Darven so it strengthened her respect for Otho.

The old knight of Reichenberg having been called to his fathers, his son Otho had stepped into his titles and estates, and one thing more he was yet desirous of possessing to render him, he believed, supremely happy.

And to bring about "this consummation devoutly to be wished," he resided more at the Castle of Cats than he did at his own.

Indeed, he had taken up his residence there altogether, and he believed it only required time to make him absolute master of that mountain fortress and its fair mistress.

Sympathy begets respect, and respect generally ripens into love; and Leoline, without knowing it, at the expiration of a year after her husband's death, was as truly in love with Otho as ever she had been with Darven.

Otho had watched and fed this passion day by day, till at length he considered

the time had come when he might with every prospect of success declare his love for the beautiful young widow, and win her hand and fortune together.

It was a lovely evening, the breezes laden with the perfume of a thousand flowers fanned the cheeks of Otho and Leoline, as from the heights of the Cat they gazed down upon the waters of the Rhine beneath them.

There was something in the silence and that wild spot on which they stood so conducive to the declaration of his passion, that Otho was on his knees at the feet of his companion ere she could divine his purpose, or he pause to consider where he was, or what eyes might gaze upon them.

In wild, impassioned tones Otho told his love and besought her hand.

So well did he plead his suit, that, ere many minutes were passed, the head of Leoline lay upon his bosom, and her whispered tones gave expression to that love for which he had plotted so deeply and sinned so much.

With a wildly-beating heart, the enraptured Otho led her back to the castle, beseeching her to name an early day for their union, and make him blessed beyond all mortals.

Who could resist his prayers? not Leoline, and when they separated that night each to seek their own couch, she whispered in his ear—

"I will be thy wife in one month, dear Otho, and in the chapel of my castle shall you place the bridal ring on my finger."

One month; oh, how long the time seemed, and yet how much longer had he waited, plotted, and planned for this moment.

Fond was the kiss that night he pressed to her lips, sweet was the smile on her cheek, heavenly the light in her eyes, as she returned the fond embrace.

One month, and she would again be a wife; and she lay down upon her bed dreaming of the hour when she was again to stand at the altar, again to become a bride.

And with a smile on her lips, and love in her heart, she sank to sleep.

With mingled visions of love and murder, life and death, Otho tossed upon his pallet; the bright dreams of love and joy were overshadowed by the dark deed committed by his hand on the plains of Palestine.

Never did time seem such a laggard, as it did now—never did a month stretch its course along so tediously, even though every day found him in the company of Leoline.

For continuation of this Story see page 185 of our next number.

[Continued from page 160.]

THE CHILD OF THE PFALZ,

BEING THE SEQUEL TO GUDA'S CAPTIVITY.

TO one of these sisters the palm of beauty was expected to be given, and as each suitor supported his own favourite, there was much interest as to the result.

Of all that day's tilters, Count Huldebrand had most distinguished himself.

He had indeed gained a succession of single-handed victories, which had won him the day's honour and the right of nominating the next day's queen of the lists.

He dismounted amid acclamations, and according to the usual form, challenged any knight to dispute his right as a victor to bestow the palm of beauty on the Lady Joscelyne von Falkenstein, and this summons three times repeated by a blast of clarions, was, to the surprise of all, responded to in a similar manner.

Forthwith there rode into the lists a knight splendidly apparelled, but utterly unattended.

He was mounted upon a beautiful white steed, and his armour was gilt throughout, and the rest of his panoply crimson.

His visor was closed, the cognizance on his shield, and which was repeated upon his crest, was a golden lion rampant, and he intimated that it was by the name of Golden Lion, and no other, that he desired at present to be known.

This champion accepted the challenge of Huldebrand, and requested to engage him, in order to uphold the pre-eminence of Lady Alberta, in opposition to that of her more imperious sister.

"I will not shirk the test, Sir Knight of the Golden Lion," responded Huldebrand, having compared the other's apparent strength with his own. "Thy demeanour speaks thee noble, and assures me thou art an opponent worthy of one of my rank."

The antagonists, therefore, took up their positions at the end of the lists, and the signal for the contest was given.

Huldebrand put forth all his skill and address, while Golden Lion stood on the defensive only.

Impatient at this passive reception, the Hohenstaufen count tried all he could to arouse the other to anger, but succeeded neither in doing this nor in unhorsing him.

At last, roused to anger himself, the young count, putting his lance at rest and his steed to full speed, bore down upon the other with the impetuosity of a torrent.

But the result was disastrous to him.

The stranger received him on the point of his lance ; that of Huldebrand was shivered to splinters, and the princely knight fell ignominiously to the ground.

A clamour arose among the spectators at this defeat, which was quite unexpected, and by many undesired, for a report had arisen that this strange knight was an Englishman, and it offended their nationality that he should triumph over one who was among the flower of German chivalry.

But Huldebrand was not yet conquered.

He sprang to his feet, drew his sword, and challenged the other to continue the combat.

The knight accepted, and proceeded with the same coolness and skill as before, and in a short time completely disarmed the count, and left him no choice but surrender.

The acclamations of many hailed the victor, who bowed and retired without either declaring his name or claiming any reward.

He challenged several other knights, and was victor in each encounter.

He was, however, informed that the honours of that day's tournament were his, and permitted to select the queen of beauty for the ensuing day, but even when requested by the emperor himself, he respectfully refused to disclose his identity.

Great was the disappointment and jealousy of many ladies, and especially of Joscelyne, at seeing the prize awarded to the gentle and retiring Alberta.

The latter was as much surprised and

embarrassed as any one, but nevertheless accepted the honour with dignity, and crowned the victor with the grace of a queen.

When the sports were done, he was invited into the pavilion of the Count Palatine and his family, where he for a minute raised his visor, and disclosed the countenance of the Troubadour Ulric.

"There are certain strong political reasons," he said, "why I should not disclose my identity to the emperor or those of his lords who would know me. Some day, however, I may be far less reticent."

He stayed with the party for some time, winning the regard of the count and countess by his affable demeanour, and even somewhat pacifying Alberta's disappointed sister.

Alberta herself was put in a flutter of delicious joy at seeing him again and listening to his sweet discourse.

But he had no opportunity of speaking to her alone.

He contrived, however, to convey to her a note, requesting a private interview the next evening at a place appointed.

Throughout the next day's tournament, though many knights distinguished themselves, he of the Golden Lion, whenever he took part, came off with all honours.

He upheld his pre-eminence till the closing of the sports, when he and Alberta, as before, were the hero and heroine of the day.

The other knights, especially the suitors of the Palatine's daughters, were incensed at this, and found opportunities to taunt the strange champion, in order to induce him to disclose his real name.

"That will I not do," he replied, "but this much will I disclose. I am an Englishman, a belted knight, and of a family as high as any here present. Further, I am ever ready to support every pretension I make by an appeal to arms."

This silenced opposition; but neither the disappointed knights nor the disappointed ladies could forgive Golden Lion for his success.

Alberta, in full confidence and joyous expectation, repaired to the place of meeting.

There she met him, there they renewed their vows, plighted their troth, and swore to keep their affection secret from all.

"'Tis necessary to maintain secrecy at present," he assured her, "but rest sure of this. When I come to claim thee of thy parents I can give them such proofs that I am by rank worthy of that honour, that they can no longer doubt it. Farewell! To-morrow I set out on my return to England, but, however far and long removed, my heart will remain the same."

Three long years passe.

Nina and Joscelyne were wedded to the knights of their choice, but Alberta persistently remained unmarried.

Gently, yet firmly, she refused the proposal of Count Heinrich, thereby causing that young nobleman a great disappointment.

All other suitors were equally unsuccessful.

In vain her parents grieved at the prospect of the heiress of the Pfalz thus devoting herself to loneliness and celibacy, and united their persuasions that she would forget an attachment for one who had evidently long ago forgotten her, and who, perhaps, after all, despite his boasting, was of much lower rank than herself.

"She hath thrown away many golden certainties for the sake of a shadowy possibility," was the comment of the Lady Joscelyne. "All suitors are deserting her, and the time soon will come when she will be glad to wed some landless knight or poor esquire."

But all this while Alberta, though she had heard only once from her absent lover, continued to be sustained by hope.

The condition of Germany at that time riveted the attention of all Europe.

The emperor, Conrad von Hohenstaufen, had died.

He was the last monarch of that family, and, the crown being elective, a great competition arose among the princes of Europe to possess it next.

The two most important candidates were Alphonso, Prince of Castille, and Richard, Duke of Cornwall, brother of Henry III., King of England.

For some time all the towns were full of excitement about this important election.

Alphonso of Castille secured many votes; but there was such a strong party in favour of the English prince, that at last he was found to have a majority.

Others, however, set up as a rival one of the counts of the Hohenstaufen, who made some attempts to sustain his title.

But subsequently Richard of Cornwall was proclaimed Emperor of Germany.

Rumour was busy with the deeds, the prowess, the many attractive and engaging qualities possessed by this young foreign prince, and it soon became known that he would make a grand progress through his new dominions, and would make one visit of ceremony among others to the Count Palatine at Gutenfels Castle, to receive his allegiance.

This intelligence naturally caused much excitement at the castle.

Preparations were made on a large scale to receive the distinguished visitor with due honours.

All the Palatine's relatives, tenants and dependants came to swell his retinue and increase his magnificence in the eyes of his sovereign.

Never was there display of feudal power more splendid than that exhibited at the Castle of Gutenfels on that eventful day.

A grand banquet was to be held, tournaments and other sports were to take place in the grounds, and high and low were to make holiday.

The Ladies Nina and Joscelyne, with their respective husbands, came numerously attended to take part in the festivities.

Alberta, amid all this gaiety and high expectation, was sorrowful and secluded.

What signified to her all the magnificence of the emperor's reception, when her heart was bowed down by the conviction that she had leant upon a broken reed, that she had sacrificed her life's prospects for the sake of one who had forgotten or deserted her?

For others be revel, and pomp, and display; for her the silent convent were fitter.

She throught of this, as she sat in the deep embrasure of the window of her chamber, overlooking the thronged courtyard of the castle, having been excused, on the score of indisposition, from taking part in the day's rejoicings.

At last a loud flourish of trumpets announced the approach of the emperor.

A buzz of expectation ran through the throng; the gates were flung open wide, and the new monarch and his retinue passed in.

Knights, lords, warriors, and noble dames—all that was great and gay, bright and beautiful, followed, and Alberta could not help forgetting her own grief in gazing upon this gorgeous spectacle.

But she was so situated as not to be able to see the emperor's face.

The grand cavalcade passed into the castle, and Alberta felt again lonely.

Suddenly the door opened.

A servant came to her in haste, and said that the emperor had desired to be presented to her.

Overcome with agitation, she obeyed the summons, and followed the attendant to the great hall, thronged with grand company.

Advancing to the emperor, she made a humble obeisance.

With a palpitating heart, she looked up.

He spoke.

She recognised that voice.

It was her long-absent lover.

To the amazement of all, he clasped her in his arms.

"My beloved Aberta," he cried, "I have come to claim thee. No further disguise now. I am no longer the poor troubadour or the nameless English knight. I am Richard, Duke of Cornwall, chosen by this nation as its supreme ruler. I will take thee, and thee only, as my bride, my love, my empress!"

Need we attempt to describe her amazement, her joy, her doubt if all was not a dream?

The dismay and mortification of her sister, to see one whom she had so slighted placed so infinitely above her, and the pride and delight of the Palatine at this splendid alliance?

All this can be imagined far better than pen can record it.

The marriage took place at Gutenfels with great pomp and magnificence, and in the subsequent coronation of the emperor at Frankfort, his bride shared the imperial honours.

Thus did the gentle Alberta, the child of the Pfalz, become Empress of Germany, and the rest of her life she was beloved and revered by all, and universally acknowledged worthy of that high and unlooked-for dignity.

END OF THE CHILD OF THE PFALZ.

Our next number will contain " The Fire-Fiend of the Mountains."

THE BARONS OF OLD
OR THE ROBBERS OF THE RHINE

THE FIRE-FIEND

OF THE

MOUNTAINS.

A T a considerable elevation above the Vale of Wiesbaden rise the picturesque ruins of the Castle of Sonnenberg.

From this castle are delight-ful prospects of the Rhine and surrounding mountains.

The ruins of the castle surround the village of the same name, where hundreds of the inhabitants obtain their livelihood

"'SHE IS MINE!' CRIED THE FIRE-FIEND."

by the manufacture of the well-known Dutch toys.

Perhaps there is no river in the world which passes between banks so heavily teeming with fact and fiction, history and religion, than that of the Rhine, running from the Alps to the ocean.

It has seen four distinct epochs.

First, the antediluvian, when those vast mountains were formed, that tower their massive heads to the sky, and show to thinking men how vast, how powerful are the convulsions of nature.

Next followed the ancient historical epoch, in which the great Roman general, Cæsar, crossed the stream, placed the whole river under the jurisdiction of his empire, and Rome was in all its glory.

Then came the epoch in which the frequent incursions of the northern hordes strewed the banks of the Rhine with ruins of the Roman power, the great and glorious Charlemagne opposed the German legions, and religion struggling with Paganism, filled the streams and banks with fables, and peopled the mountains and rocks with fays and demons.

Then came the fourth epoch.

Civilization resumed its sway.

Fiction gave place to fact.

The legendary crumbled away before the historical.

Religion reared convents and abbeys on the banks of the stream.

The cannon and the printing press were formed—the greatest weapon of war and the harbinger of peace.

Surely the Rhine is a wonderful river, ever coursing between shores of wonderful associations—historical, legendary and religious.

From the many legends with which this stream and its shores abound, we select the following from that epoch when the marvellous sprang up between the voids of ancient and modern history.

Ere the stones were quarried with which the castle was built the hills and valleys were peopled with gnomes and fays, and the waters sheltered in their glassy depths the Undines and the Nixes—the good and the bad spirits of the legendary world.

The song of the Lurley was heard at nightfall by the rude inhabitants of the valley, and the peasant dropped his load of faggots and fled through the woods, as the unearthly tones and figures of the forest spirits assailed his eyes and ears.

In the vale where now is situated the much-frequented town of Wiesbaden, there resided with her aged father a lovely girl named Thyra.

So great was her beauty that the people of the rude village looked upon her as a fairy, and though her loveliness charmed the eyes and turned the hearts of half the young men of the neighbourhood yet not one sought her heart and hand.

Such loveliness was not lightly to be approached, and a rumour having been spread that her mother was a water-spirit, she was held in as much awe as admiration.

So, despite her amiable qualities, of which she had many, Thyra had few friends, and fewer acquaintances.

When she went to the stream for water, the peasants would forsake the spot, and at a distance contemplate the lovely girl, as she braided her long tresses before the stream and smiled at her own lovely face reflected in the water.

It was believed that she was holding converse with the spirits, and that if they intruded upon the spot while she remained there, that she would be angered, and summon from its clear depths the denizens of the hidden world to chastise them.

So time went on, and Thyra grew in beauty, and Gunthurm, her aged, white-haired sire died, leaving her to solitude and sadness, for none approached her, and she was truly alone.

With not even her father to console her, Thyra wandered over the hills, and through the vales, and beside the banks of the Rhine, with sadness on her face and sadness in her heart.

One day she sat on the banks, looking down at the water, when the sound of paddles caused her to look up the stream.

A boat of wicker covered with skins was floating on the yellow tide.

This was being propelled along by a handsome youth, who managed the frail bark with a dexterity that showed him to be a perfect master of the art.

His head was uncovered, and his long golden locks floated over his neck and shoulders like streams of sunshine.

His broad chest was bare, but the muscular lines upon it betokened power and strength.

A garment of skin fell from his neck to the knees, and a girdle of the same material held a short sword, without any sheath.

Without seeing the fair watcher, he propelled his boat towards the spot on which she sat.

As it neared the shore he leaped up, seized a thong of wolf-skin, and sprang upon the bank.

Drawing the boat up, he secured it to a stone, and taking a shield of wolf-skin and a flint-headed javelin, he turned to make his way up the bank.

As he did so, his eyes fell upon the pale, beautiful face of Thyra.

Transfixed to the spot, he gazed upon her for some time.

Then he threw his shield and javelin down at his feet, and sunk on his knees before her.

"Woman or spirit," he cried, "never have I beheld such loveliness before. Fly me not—I am Olaf of the Iron Hand, and the slave of beauty."

Thyra, alarmed at first, had risen to fly, but now she paused and smiled upon the stranger.

"I am Thyra, the daughter of Gunthurm, the peasant, whom the spirits have taken to their home," she replied, "and I am Thyra the sad, for none will come near me."

"And wherefore?" asked the youth.

"Because they believe that I am in league with the spirits of mountain and stream."

"Never was Undine more beautiful," he said. "But let me touch your hand, that I may be assured that you are of this world."

He put forth his hand and seized her.

A thrill of pleasure ran through his veins as he did so, and he drew her to his bosom.

"Beautiful of the beautiful," he said, "though all desert I will cling to you. This hand shall smite your foes, and this heart worship you."

In those days it did not require months of acquaintance to enable a youth to approach with words of love the object of his admiration.

Coquetry was a feeling also unknown to the ladies, and, without a moment's pause, Thyra replied—

"I am alone, and wearied of my solitude. Your face is fair, your hand is strong, and I will love you ever, for none other will love the daughter of Gunthurm, and none other shall ever possess my love."

The sun, which had been rapidly sinking, now faded from the heavens, a gloom fell around, and the waters around became wild and turbid.

A crash like that of thunder seemed to come from beneath their feet, and as Olaf was about to clasp Thyra to his bosom, a monstrous form sprang up between them.

Thyra uttered a piercing cry and tottered back.

The youth drew his sword from his belt and stood upon his defence.

The being who had thus suddenly appeared from out of the earth was such a thing as neither of them had ever seen before.

Its head and body were of prodigious size, but its legs were short, and crooked at the knees.

Its arms were long, and knotted like the trunk of an old tree.

Its hands were webbed like the wing of a bat, and its feet like the feet of a duck.

Bristles grew upon its head instead of hair, and protruded from its chest and back.

Its eyes glowed like live coal, and from its nostrils issued a steamy vapour.

Its parted lips revealed teeth like fangs, and its large ears almost covered the side of its head.

Thyra was so horrified at the sight of the monster that she sank down upon the bank, and covered her face with her hands to shut out the terrible sight.

The youth, brave as he was, felt a sensation of awe steal over him, but mustering up all his courage, he asked—

"Who and what are you?"

"Hear and tremble. I am the Fire-fiend of the Mountain," replied the monster, in a voice which shook the earth on which they stood.

"What seek you here?" gasped Olaf.

"Comfort for my restless spirit," was the reply; "a soothing charm to my tedious hours."

"Then begone, for you cannot find it here," said Olaf, boldly.

"I can, and I will," replied the fiend. "Doomed to tend the fires which rage beneath the rocks, and in the bowels of the mountains, I can find no relief but the love of a mortal whose beauty shall equal that of the Lurley. I have sought it long, and find it now."

"Where?" cried Olaf.

"Here."

As he spoke, with his webbed hand he seized the arm of Thyra.

The frightful sensation that seized upon the girl as the slimy paw of the demon touched her flesh, called from her a shriek of agony and disgust.

It also roused all the courage in the bold heart of her lover.

"Touch her not," he cried, springing forward and thrusting his sword at the bosom of the monster.

But with a laugh that sounded more like a groan of agony than an expression of triumph, the monster seized the blade in his fin-like hand, and wresting it from the youth, flung it into the waters of the Rhine.

Olaf stooped to seize his shield and javelin.

The demon placed his webbed foot upon

them, and pressed them into the earth, at the same time raising Thyra to her feet.

"Save me, save me, Olaf!" shrieked Thyra.

That imploring look, those appealing tones, went to his heart.

He sprang upon the demon and seized him by the throat.

But the horrible sharp-pointed bristles made him loose his hold, and, shaking him off, the fiend hurled him from him.

"No mortal can injure me or dispute my will," he said.

"You must first become a spirit of good, or possess their power ere you can hope to battle with the fiend of the rocks."

Then, lifting Thyra in his arms, he added—

"Daughter of Gunthurm, look your last upon the world ere I bear you to my home in the mountains, and your couch in the bowels of the earth. Now come to the realms of the fire spirit!"

He folded his arms around her fairy-like form and sank with her through the earth, which parted at his feet, and closed again with a roar like thunder.

For some time Olaf stood glaring upon the spot where the demon had disappeared with the lovely being who but a short time before had rendered him the happiest mortal in the world.

Then he flung himself upon the earth, and in his fury tried to tear it open with his hands.

But not a seam had the fiend left behind him to mark the spot through which he had vanished.

Olaf seized his javelin and shield.

Both were broken by the foot of the monster.

He was now completely unarmed, and he sat down and buried his face in his hands.

"Lost, lost," he moaned, "lost to me for ever!"

"Hope!" exclaimed a silvery voice, apparently coming from the stream.

He bounded to his feet.

He approached the edge of the bank where his boat was moored.

To his dismay he found it had escaped from its fastening and floated away on the now dark stream.

"Unarmed," he cried, "and my boat gone—what shall guide me now?"

"Faith," said the musical tone he had heard before.

He looked into the waters.

All was dark.

Their murmurings alone met his ear.

"Why should I live?" he asked himself wildly—"what should prevent me slaying myself upon this bank, and burying my grief for ever in death?"

"Courage," said the voice.

Still he could see nothing.

"Of what avail are faith, hope and courage now," he cried, "since she is torn from me, and I shall never see her more? Oh, for some charm, some unknown power to restore her to these arms. Spirits of good, aid a mortal to rescue a loved one from the spirits of evil!"

Impulsively he clasped his hands, and stretched them out towards the river.

As his eyes glanced into the dark waters beneath him, a silvery light overspread their surface.

Their wild murmuring ceased, and strains of delightful music swelled on all sides.

Then from their depths arose a hundred fairy forms, robed in purest white, each bearing a silver harp in its hands.

Then from the centre of this lovely throng rose a glorious form, draped in gold, a tiara of gold upon her brow, and a golden sceptre in her hand.

Her face was the loveliest ever mortal gazed upon, and her voice sweeter than the strains of an Æolian harp.

"Come," she said, beckoning to the youth with the sceptre. "Mortal, you seek the aid of the spirits of good to confound the spirit of evil. Come, and have thy wish."

"I cannot," he cried, "my boat has drifted away down the river."

"Where is thy faith?" asked the Lurley. "Spring from the bank into the stream."

"I may perish," he replied, hesitating.

"Where is your courage, Olaf of the Iron Hand?" was the reply.

"But if I perish, I also lose her," he said.

"Hope and trust. Come!"

"I will, for life without Thyra is life without all," he cried.

And springing up, he leaped into the stream.

As he touched the water, a dozen fairy hands seized him.

Fifty harps pealed forth a strain of heavenly music.

A sensation of joy he had never before experienced stole over his senses.

He felt himself sink into the waters.

Then all became a blank.

He remembered no more till he opened his eyes, and found himself sitting upon the bank upon the very spot where the demon had disappeared with Thyra.

In surprise he looked about him.

The moon was high in the heavens.

The river was flooded in its glow.

The banks were lit up with an almost daylight brightness.

There was his boat fastened to the stone, but its wolf-hide sides had given place to a covering of silver that glistened in the moonbeams.

He turned his eyes wonderingly upon himself.

The skin robe he had worn had disappeared; he was attired in a garment hard as rock, but pliable as silk. His feet were encased in sandals of the same material, and around his head was a metal band, in the centre of which was a gleaming star that threw a light in which ever way he turned.

By his side was his javelin and shield.

But the flint-point had disappeared, and in its place was a barb of steel.

His shield was of metal, hard and bright, which, from its polished surface, threw innumerable rays of light.

Olaf looked and wondered, and finally flinging up his arm in ecstacy, he cried—

"Good spirit, now but show the way to the realms of the fiend who has robbed me of Thyra, that I may wrest her from his power."

Ere the words were spoken, a figure stood before him holding a glittering sword in his hand, which he presented to Olaf, sinking on one knee.

"Who art thou?"

"Thy companion and thy guide," said the other. "I am called Hope. Take this sword and bear it well."

Olaf took the sword, and pressed the glittering blade to his lips.

"I will bear it well," he said. "But are you indeed my friend, and will you point out the way I would go?"

"I am thy friend," was the reply of Hope, as he arose, "But there is yet another in whom thou must trust."

"Who?"

"Faith," said a voice beside him.

Olaf turned to confront a lovely youth, who had come from he knew not where, but who, kneeling at his feet, held up a glittering star.

"This star the good spirit of the waters sends to thee, Olaf of the Iron Hand," said Faith. "It is the talisman that shall guard thee in the greatest danger. Shield it well, for if you lose it, Faith and Hope are lost, and also Courage."

"Where is he?" asked Olaf, taking the star, and placing it in his bosom.

"Here," said Hope, laying his hand over Olaf's heart. "With Faith, Hope and Courage, man can confound his foes, though they be favoured by the powers of Darkness, and all seems black despair."

"You reason well," said Olaf. "The bad are strong, but the good are powerful. In the cause of right, I wage the war, and Faith, Hope, and Courage will yet conquer wrong!"

Hope untied the boat, and stepped into it.

Olaf placed his sword in his belt, raised his shield on his arm, and, grasping his javelin, followed.

Faith came last, and with the paddle pushed the boat into the stream.

In another minute they were gliding down the moonlit river, Hope at the prow, Courage in the centre, and Faith in the stern.

Olaf never felt so strong and so brave as now. The power which had enabled him to crush the life out a wild bear, and which had earned for him the title of the Iron Hand, seemed now to be increased tenfold, and he longed for the moment to arrive when he might show that power and prove that courage he now possessed.

Guided by Faith, the boat made towards a dark opening on the rocky shore, and grounded between high banks of stone which hid the moon's light and buried the place in Stygian darkness.

Olaf looked at Faith, and by the light shed by the star in his own forehead read there the command to land.

Hope pointed to the rocks, and Olaf sprung from the boat.

"Behind these rocks, and in the centre of the mountain that rises beyond them, is the home of the Fire-fiend," said Hope. "The way is rough, and the path guarded by monsters of terrible shape and enormous power; to reach your love you must conquer and slay them."

"I am ready for the combat," said Olaf, drawing his sword.

"Go then on your way," said Faith. "We can go no further till mortal hand has purged the place of its evil habitants. But though we leave you here in form, we will be with you in spirit, and, possessed of hope, faith, and courage, you will conquer."

They pointed into the blackness beyond, and with a firm step Olaf strode forward.

The way was narrow, crooked and dark, but the light on his forehead revealed the path to his eyes.

At each step he took, serpents of hideous colours twined their bodies before him, glared at him with their bright eyes, and hissed and showed their forked tongues.

Insects of huge and terrible shape hung

upon the walls ; toads crawled over his feet, and huge bats flapped their wings around his head.

Still Olaf of the Iron Hand grasped his sword, and hurried on.

More and more rough became the path.

He looked up.

Spiders hung from the rocks above his head, and rugged rocks enclosed him as in a tomb.

Olaf paused.

A feeling of terror took possession of him.

But he flung it off and went on again.

Narrower and narrower grew the path. till at length it was not wide enough for anything to pass him, and he began to fear that he could go no further, when what appeared a block of stone in his path rolled over, and he stood confronting an object of such hideous form that his heart almost stood still.

The light emitted from the star in his forehead showed it in its hideous deformity.

Towering high above him it stood, a thing neither man, beast, nor reptile, but a combination of all three.

It had the head of a man of frightful proportions, with the mane of a lion falling over the neck and shoulders of a beast, its hands were claws, with nails of terrific length, its legs were scaled like a serpent.

Its mouth was enormous, showing row after row of sharp teeth, from between which protruded a sting.

Fire and smoke issued from its nostrils, which were like those of a horse, and its voice was like the roar of a mountain cataract.

As it rolled over it reared itself up on its legs and beat the air with its paw.

But in so doing it revealed a space beyond where it stood—a spot it was there to guard.

As Olaf saw this he again took heart.

He threw his shield before his body and prepared for the fight.

"What seek you, mortal, in the realms of my master the Fire-fiend?" said the monster.

"That which, aided by courage and hope, I will yet obtain," was the undaunted reply.

"Courage will avail you nothing here, and hope is left behind," said the monster. "You come a victim to my fury, and go no further."

"Across thy dead body will I stride," cried Olaf, "and thus I carve my passage."

He dealt a blow at the monster with his sword, who caught the descending blow upon his long nails.

Then with its paw he dealt a heavy blow at Olaf.

The brave youth flung up his shield and caught the descending stroke.

The monster roared with fury.

The serpents hissed in chorus, and the very rocks resounded with the noise.

The sword of Olaf again descended.

It cut through the thick mane and buried itself in the neck of the monster.

His adversary fought at him with his paws and launched his sting towards him.

But Olaf caught them on his shield.

Long did the combat rage.

Frightful were the howls of the monster as the blood welled from many a wound in its hideous carcase.

Terrible was the hissing and shrieking of the reptiles that filled the cavern-like place, and hard and short was the breathing of Olaf of the Iron Hand.

At length, by a well-directed stroke Olaf plunged his ensanguined blade into the monster's heart, and it fell at his feet a huge and frightful mass, shaking the very place in its fall, and driving with terror the reptiles into their holes.

Olaf paused and wiped the perspiration from his face with his hand, and cleansed his sword upon the mane of the dead brute.

"The first opposition to my passage to Thyra is conquered," he said. "With courage in my heart, hope to guide me, and faith in my success, I will go on to the end."

And the rocks echoed his words from behind and before.

He lightly sprung over the body of his conquered foe, and keeping a firm grasp of his sword and with his shield before him he passed through the narrow opening that was now no longer guarded by his fearful enemy.

Passing this the scene changed.

He was in an immense cave.

The walls on either side, the roof above, and the floor below, were covered with stalactites, which shone and glistened in the rays of the star on his brow.

Here pillars of crystal rose from floor to roof, then they descended in every fantastic form of beings real and unreal.

They were turned and twisted and interwoven with one another, and formed a scene of such stupendous grandeur, that Olaf was lost in wonder and admiration.

"What a glorious spot," he muttered, "to be inhabited by demons."

His voice, though raised but to a whisper, rolled like thunder through the crystal caverns and for a moment caused him to look around, expecting a host of foes to confront him.

But none came, and he went on, his shield flung before him, his sword in his hand, and the star lighting his way.

Treading among the crystals, his foot-fall echoing and re-echoing on all sides, he at length reached the end of the fairy scene, and came upon a black and turbid stream that wound its dark course under the mountains.

"Which way shall I go!" he asked himself, as he stood upon the bank, and looked up and down the dark tide.

"Over!" he fancied he heard a voice exclaim.

He drew back, and as he did so, he saw a passage on the opposite side.

He hesitated, but remembering Hope and Faith were with him in spirit, he slung his shield behind his back, fastened his sword in his belt, and boldly plunged in.

The waters were rapid, and Olaf battled with all his strength to prevent them bearing him along.

He reached the opposite bank and shook himself.

He was surprised to find that they had not wet his garments.

He unslung his shield and grasped his sword.

He approached the opening he had seen and was about to plunge into it, when an enormous griffin reared up before him.

"Mortal, was death denied you in your own sphere that you seek it in the realms of the Fire-fiend?" asked the monster, lashing its scaly breast with its tail furiously.

"I seek not death, but life and love," replied Olaf, "and all who oppose me must perish."

"Thy boasting might avail thee on earth," said the monster. "Here you are powerless. One blow from this paw and you die!"

"I am stronger and more powerful than you believe," said Olaf, boldly. "I am armed with that which will defy and conquer thee."

"What are thy arms compared to these?" cried the griffin, holding forth his terrible fins.

"Courage, hope, and faith," replied Olaf, "and with these I assail thee."

A roar of derision broke from the griffin.

But it changed to a howl of pain, as the bright, keen blade of Olaf of the Iron Hand pierced his scaly armour.

Raising its tail it struck a blow at Olaf that would have crushed him, had he not caught it on his shield.

But so great was its force that it beat him to his knee, and the next moment the griffin seized him and rolled him over on the earth.

Olaf felt its breath like the blast of a furnace on his face, its paws sinking into his shoulders, and its sting protruded to strike his throat.

He flung his shield before the protruding sting, and, with all his strength, drove his sword between the scales that covered the monster's heart.

The grasp on his shoulders relaxed.

A dead weight sank upon his bosom.

The griffin was dead.

Olaf rolled the body off him, and rose to his feet.

He looked down upon his second foe, and felt no inconsiderable satisfaction at his conquest.

"Two enemies removed from my path," he said, "and my passage is once more free to the home of the Fire-fiend."

He passed on.

The scene changed.

He trod upon earth that sparkled beneath his feet, as though every grain was gold.

Look which way he would, the rocks were filled with particles of the same colour and brilliancy, that glittered with dazzling brightness in the light of the star.

On, on he went, hearing no sound, seeing nothing but the shining earth and shining walls of the subterranean passage, till he began to wonder how much further he must go, ere he reached the place where the fiend had taken the lovely girl he had torn from his arms.

At length he reached a spot where a large cataract poured down on either side of him, and joining in the centre of the place rolled with the noise of thunder down a deep chasm before him.

Here Olaf felt his journey must surely come to an end, and that he must return without having accomplished his errand.

"What shall I do?" he muttered. "Here I can go no further, and Thyra is lost to me for ever."

"Faith will aid you," came to his ears, as if spoken by the waters at his feet.

"But how—how?" he muttered, beating his bosom.

"Down deeper into the bowels of the earth must you go!" said the voice. "The waters will bear you. Have courage and hope!"

"To the last," cried Olaf, again slinging

his shield at his back, and securing his sword in his belt.

Having done this, without pausing an instant he plunged into the falling waters, and was borne down, down—he knew, thought not whither.

In a short time he found himself floating close to the bank of a stream, and seizing it with his hands drew himself up. Growing from the banks were trees, with stems black and hard as the surrounding rocks, without a particle of foliage.

Bats flew among the branches, squirrels of enormous growth leaped from tree to tree, huge toads crawled about their stems, and serpents with black skins twined themselves around them.

But all seemed dumb; not a sound issued from any living thing, even the stream rolled on in silence, deep and profound.

Again preparing for battle, Olaf of the Iron Hand wandered along the bank of the mysterious stream.

Suddenly a noise broke upon his ears.

It grew louder and louder as he advanced.

Every step he took the blackness lessened, till at length a red glow lighted up the motionless trees and the silent waters.

Then a huge opening appeared.

Olaf knew that he was nearing the prison of Thyra, the haunt of the Fire fiend.

Cautiously he approached it.

His fingers grasped the hilt of his sword like a band of steel.

Hot vapours fanned his cheeks.

A suffocating odour pervaded the place.

Now burst upon him from the huge opening a view of that terrible region he had sought.

Fire, roaring, leaping, hissing, on all sides.

Huge rocks were burning, cracking, splintering, in the immense furnace.

The glare was terrible, the heat intense, the vapours noxious.

It was a grand but terrible scene, a mountain of fire burning in a huge cavern.

His gaze, however, was drawn from this by the guards who stood sentinel at the entrance.

They were three enormous dragons.

From their mouths and nostrils they ejected fire and smoke, and so large and terrible was their appearance that, but for hope and faith, Olaf of the Iron Hand had turned and fled from so fearful a spot.

He saw that the chances of obtaining an entrance were few, indeed, and that opposed to such formidable foes the fight must be a desperate one.

He planted his back against a rock, and, without a word, awaited the onslaught.

The centre dragon approached him, and, ejecting a flame from its mouth, as if in derision of such a puny opponent, rose to sting him to death.

But the sword of Olaf clave the sting asunder, leaving it powerless to inflict further injury with that weapon.

The huge animal flapped its wings in agony, and uttered a sound so loud and terrible that its companions bounded forward to its aid.

Ere either reached him, however, the sword of Olaf passed into its open jaws, and with the roar in its throat it succumbed to the blow.

But now Olaf's danger was great in the extreme.

The others assailed him with their claws, stings, and wings, spitting fire at him, and threatening every moment to consume him.

Valiantly, desperately he fought, but sword and shield availed him naught.

He sank to the earth.

The monsters leant over him with their huge jaws distended. He felt his last hope was gone—his last hour had come. Hope, faith, courage, all deserted him—love alone was left. At that moment a horrible form sprang between the dragons. It laid a hand upon the neck of each, and hurled them back as if they had been feathers in his grasp.

Olaf looked up.

It was the Fire-fiend himself who had come to his rescue.

He waved the dragons back, and they slunk away to their posts on either side the opening of the vast furnace.

Olaf arose and confronted the demon.

"Mortal," said the fiend, "your courage must be great that you dare invade my realms."

"I seek Thyra," said the youth. "Demon, give me her and I will depart."

The horrible laughter of the demon shook the place.

"You come to seek Thyra," he said. "I will lead you to her side—you shall gaze upon the bride of the Fire-fiend—and then I will consign you to a doom that shall lighten my labours and give me more time for love.

"Fiend, I will not do your bidding!"

"You shall tend the fires night and day, and never see the world again. Come!"

He grasped the arm of Olaf, and led him past the dragons into the hall of fire.

Within an amphitheatre of rocks the huge fire burned, and along these rocks the demon led Olaf.

On the opposite side of the rocks which he traversed, Olaf saw a stream of water, wide and deep, which emptied itself into the river without.

Thus he stood upon a pathway raised between fire and water.

His sword and shield he still retained, but he offered not to assail the demon. He resolved to wait till he had seen Thyra; and, besides he felt too weak just then to commence another battle.

"What do you think of my realms?" asked the fiend.

Olaf shook his head, but was silent.

"They are not easily to be invaded. Your love must be strong and your courage great to attempt such a task."

"I should be unworthy that love if I did not risk my life for it," said Olaf.

"You have conquered three of my sentinels."

"I have, and would have conquered the remainder had they assailed me singly," said Olaf.

"Your boldness will render me all the more valuable to me. It needs a strong

RUINS OF THE CASTLE OF SONNENBERG.

hand and a brave heart for the task I shall set you."

"I will not do it."

"What will you do?"

"Bear away Thyra from your horrible place to a world she will better grace than this."

The fiend laughed again.

"You would need powerful aid for that," he said.

"I have got it."

"What is it?" asked the fiend.

"Courage, hope, and faith."

"Your courage will avail you little here, and faith and hope are of as much value.

My guards are strong, but I have weakened them all, and thus made them my slaves, so if they fail you cannot hope to conquer me."

"I will try," said Olaf, boldly.

"You had better not," said the fiend. "But you wished to see Thyra. Behold her!"

He pointed with his hand to a kind of alcove in the rock, and Olaf beheld Thyra sitting upon a stone, weeping and wringing her hands.

Olaf sprang forward to clasp her in his arms.

The conclusion of this Story will be given in our next number.

[Continued from page 173.]

THE CRUSADER'S BRIDE.

THE morning dawned at length that was to be their wedding day, and many a noble knight and fair and lovely dame had come from far and near to witness the ceremony and dance at the wedding of Otho and the fair young widow.

On the night before there had arrived at the castle an aged minstrel.

His long white hair fell over his neck and shoulders, and his white beard descended far down his bosom.

Yet there was the fire of youth in his eye, and when he touched the strings of his harp, his whole soul seemed burning in those bright orbs.

Having taken his seat in the retainers' hall, and, under pretence of being tired laid his harp aside, he soon learned the cause of the stir that was observable in the building, and that on the following morning the mistress of that castle would stand at the altar with Otho of Reichenberg.

The minstrel drank the goblet of wine placed before him, finished the viands so lavishly spread, and expressed a wish to retire for the night.

"An' you will tune your harp, minstrel, in the presence of our lady, and the Baron Otho, ere you sleep?" said one.

"By your leave, good fellow, I will wait till to-morrow," said the minstrel, "when I will strike a chord at the altar, that shall astound you all. To-night I fain would rest. My frame is weak and my limbs are weary. I pray you then show me where I may lay my head till to-morrow's sun shall bid the minstrel rise to his work."

He was shown to his sleeping-place, and soon after the silence of the castle was only broken by the tread of the sentinels, and the plashing of the waters of the cascades, that came through the open windows in the masonry.

The moon was at the full.

Its silver beams bathed castle and mountain in a mellow light, sparkled in the cascades that leaped its sides, and streamed full into the room through the casement where Leoline dreamed of the morrow.

With a heart overjoyed the lovely woman awoke, and starting up, perceived at the side of her couch, gazing down upon her, a tall figure clad in burnished mail.

It raised its head.

The moonlight fell full upon its pale features, lit them up with a spectral light, and revealed to her terrified gaze the features of Darven.

Paralysed with fear she moved not, spoke not; she could but gaze in silence and awe.

And, as she looked spell-bound, fascinated, the mailed figure glided silently from her side into the gloom of the chamber and vanished like a dream.

Was it a dream or was it a reality?

This was a question Leoline could not answer, and, trembling, she sank back on her pillow, and waited for the light of day to dispel the gloom of that chamber, and arouse to life and bustle the silent castle.

Otho had sunk to sleep, thinking of the coming morrow and the consummation of all his hopes.

Bright visions were floating through his brain, and in his dreams he stood before the altar with Leoline, when a spectre sprang between them, tore her from his side, and fled with his bride.

He sprang forward to wrest her from him, and started up awake.

A cold hand touched his own, a mailed form bent over him, and a voice low and sepulchral, but in tones that he had known so well, hissed in his ears, "Murderer, the hour of vengeance is at hand!"

Then the face was turned that the moonbeams might fall upon it, and Otho fell back, clasping his hands over his eyes, as he recognised the spectral lineaments of Darven.

When he again looked, the moonlight

alone played in the chamber—the spectre was gone—he was alone with his own conscience.

Oh, how tediously that long night wore away, and with the first streak of day Otho arose, unrefreshed, from his couch, and, standing by the window, looked upon the wild scene beyond.

And as he gazed down the steep, rugged sides of the hill, a terrible foreboding seized upon him, he felt like one gazing into his own grave, and trembled at the thoughts of that which was beyond.

As the sun rose in the heavens and filled the valley with its beams, the inmates of the castle began to bestir themselves, and preparations for the bridal were hurried forward.

The old minstrel, refreshed by his night's slumber, and with his bright eye still brighter, tuned his harp in the retainers' hall, and seemed as happy as any of them.

The hour at length drew nigh, and noble lords and gorgeous ladies repaired to the chapel to await the coming of the bride and bridegroom.

The abbot of a neighbouring convent stood by the altar, and beside the doorway sat the aged minstrel, his harp resting on his knee, and with his grey head bowed across the instrument.

Attired with scrupulous care, and never looking more lovely than she did now, led in by Otho, Leoline entered the chapel.

As she glided through the doorway, the minstrel struck the strings of his harp, and a chord of music floated through the chapel.

Leoline turned and paused.

Her eyes met those of the minstrel, and she seemed powerless to take them from him.

"Whence come you, minstrel?" she said.

"From the Holy Land, fair lady," was the reply. "Where the Cross and the Crescent are waving, and where Christian meets infidel in fair and honourable combat, and where Christian slays Christian with murderous hand."

Otho turned pale, and grasped fiercely the hand of Leoline.

"The priest awaits us. Anon, the minstrel can tune his harp and raise his voice in song. Come, sweet lady, come."

Leoline suffered him to draw her towards the altar, but her gaze was still fixed upon the eyes of the minstrel, which seemed to fascinate her with their glare.

Slowly the minstrel followed till he stood beside the altar, before which stood Otho and Leoline, and around whom gathered the invited nobles.

Without the little chapel were clustered the retainers of the baroness, as well as several of those of Otho.

The ceremony began, and Otho essayed to take the hand of Leoline.

As she stretched forth her own taper fingers to grasp those of Otho, the minstrel flung down his harp, and in a voice that rolled like thunder through the little chapel, cried—

"Otho of Reichenberg, touch not with your blood-stained hand the innocent fingers of that woman. Leoline, would you wed your husband's murderer?"

A shriek broke from the lips of the baroness, and was echoed by the ladies present.

A cry of terror burst from Otho as he dropped his upraised hand to the hilt of his sword.

Murmurs of indignation and angry glances issued from the assembled knights.

"Peace, my son," said the abbot. "Who art thou, that you presume to raise your voice thus?"

"Begone, caitiff," cried Otho fiercely. "or with my sword's point I will drive you hence !"

And he half unsheathed his sword.

The minstrel smiled disdainfully.

"Return your weapon to its scabbard," he said, coolly. "It is the sword of a knight, and has no business at your side. Otho of Reichenberg can better wield the dagger of the assassin."

Pale as a corpse became the face of Otho.

His hand shook as he drew the blade from its scabbard, and with glaring eyes turned upon the minstrel.

"Who—who are you, old man?" shrieked Otho.

"False friend, dishonoured knight, coward and assassin—art thou answered?" cried the minstrel.

And with his right hand he tore away the long flowing white locks and beard, and with his left cast from him the long black gown he wore, and stood before the assembled throng a youthful knight clad in mail.

A shriek of terror broke from the lips of Otho as he tottered back, suffering his upraised sword to fall to his side.

A cry of surprise escaped from the lips of the assembled guests.

A moment Leoline stood as if bereft of power to move or speak, then she flung herself forward, shrieking aloud—

"Darven, Darven ! my lord—my husband !"

The next moment she lay half-fainting upon the armour-clad bosom of Darven.

There was the silence of death for some moments in that chapel, that terrible silence that precedes the bursting storm.

Then from mailed sides leapt a score of bright blades, and a circle of steel surrounded the guilty Otho, who stood like a tiger at bay, glaring from one to the other, eager to fly at a throat, yet fearful to make a spring.

"My own loved Leoline," cried Darven, pressing her to his bosom. "The saints be praised. I have arrived in time to prevent this marriage. Look upon me—do not tremble, sweet one. Your lord is, indeed, alive ; thanks to the infidel, and not to the Christian."

He pressed a kiss on her lips, and looking round, said—

"Knights and nobles of the Rhine, to all of you I am known as the husband of this lady, and lord of this castle. You have believed me dead, for such was the report brought hither by yonder man."

To this several gave assent.

"The battle was over," continued Darven, "and wearied and faint with the struggle, leading my wounded charger, I sought the camp, as the shades of night were gathering over the plains of Palestine.

"Suddenly I was assailed by three men in the dress of the infidel ; I defended myself, and two were hurled from their saddles by my arm, when I myself was struck down by the third, and lay wounded and powerless upon the earth.

"While thus I lay, supposed by my assailant to be dead, I saw him bury his dagger in the bodies of his wounded friends, and heard him excuse the deed as one which secresy demanded ; then, flinging off the infidel's attire, he stood before me a German knight, Otho of Reichenberg.

Otho took a step back, but a dozen swords were pointed at his bosom.

"Then from my shoulder he tore my scarf, and from my hand my signet, and, mounting his steed, left me dying on the plain.

"A troop of Mussulmen found me, carried me a prisoner to one of their forts, and cured the wound inflicted by the hand of my false friend and countryman ; but months of captivity passed ere I was exchanged, and could hurry back to the banks of the Rhine and my own loved wife."

Otho stood panting and glaring around, his teeth clenched and his nostrils distended.

A white foam was gathering upon his lips, and his features were convulsed with a terrible passion.

"Death to Otho of Reichenberg !" cried a knight.

Twenty swords were raised to deal the blow, but quick as the lightning's flash the steel of Darven leaped from its scabbard, and flinging himself before Otho, he caught the descending blades upon his own.

"Hold, Barons of the Rhine," cried Darven. "Mine was the life he sought, be mine the hand to punish the assassin, and avenge the wrong he would have done my wife. Otho of Reichenberg, defend your coward heart, for 'tis a true knight who strikes at a dastard !"

The nobles dropped their swords.

With a smile of hope Otho raised his blade.

The next moment the clash of steel rang loud and clear through the chapel.

Fierce indeed was the attack of Darven, so fierce, that Otho, powerful and desperate as he was, could not withstand it.

Foot by foot he was forced back out of the chapel into the hall, and there the battle raged furiously.

Blows rained like hail, sparks flashed from their whirling swords, till at length by a well aimed stroke, the weapon of Darven pierced the throat of Otho, and he fell to the floor.

"This is my bridal day," he gasped, struggling to his elbow, "and death—death is my bride. Bear me to the tower and let me look my last on the blue sky. This is the last prayer of Otho of Reichenberg."

They raised him up and bore him to the top of the tower, and out into the open air.

"Leoline !" he gasped, "where is she ? I cannot die without her forgiveness."

The fair woman stepped to his side at a motion from Darven.

Bending over the wounded knight, she took his hand in her trembling fingers, and looked with mingled reproach and pity upon his now ashen face.

"Oh, this seems like some wild, fearful dream," she said. "Otho, whom I believed so brave, so chivalrous, so noble—he whom I loved and respected next my husband— a false knight, a traitor, and a liar. But I will not upbraid a dying man. Heartless villain that you have proved yourself, Otho of Reichenberg, I forgive and pity you !"

She withdrew her hand, and stood gazing upon the features that worked convulsively—the eyes that appeared to gleam with those expiring fires that light up the last glances of the dying.

Otho made an effort to rise, and those

around assisted him to his feet, and supported him in an erect position.

"Leoline," he cried, "I would have robbed Darven of life to call thee mine. He has wrested thee from me. But never shall he hold thee to his heart again—never! Thou art mine—mine!"

With a sudden exertion of strength that none were prepared for, he flung aside those who supported him, and sprang upon the horrified lady.

Seizing her in his arms, Otho uttered a loud laugh of triumph, and sprang from the tower, carrying with him the terrified and shrieking Leoline.

Darven leapt forward to save her, but too late, and he saw them go down—down into the fearful abyss beneath—while in his ears rang the shrieks of his wife and the loud triumphant laughter of her destroyer.

One moment Darven stood glaring down into those awful depths, and then, with a sob that seemed to come from a bursting heart, he sprang from the tower and shot through the air like an arrow.

Another moment and three mangled corpses lay far below, and a horrified and saddened group hurried to the basement of the castle.

When the bodies were recovered and brought into the castle they presented a terrible sight, and the soul of each had flown to meet its Maker.

A few days after and all three were buried in one grave, and a gloom fell upon the castle, for it was asserted that night after night the spectres of Darven and Otho fought the terrible fight watched by Leoline, and then with shrieks and laughter leaped from the tower into the gloomy depths below.

END OF THE CRUSADER'S BRIDE.

[Continued from Page 165.]

ROLENSAC

(THE LEGEND OF THE FORFEIT HAND).

AFTER doing penance, the hand was to be chopped off by the executioner, and Editha immured in the dungeon of a convent for the rest of her life.

At first the young and beautiful *châtelaine* would yield no credence to so horrible a report, but soon it reached her in such guise as to compel belief.

Not a moment was to be lost.

Nothing could save her but flight.

Could she but reach the camp of the emperor, with whom was the Bishop of Cleves, she might obtain a reversal of the iniquitous and unjust sentence.

Having determined on this course of action, Editha did not wait a moment.

Securing as many jewels as she could, as well as a heavy purse of gold, she slipped out of the castle in disguise, attended only by one girl, who remained faithful to her even in adversity.

Even in modern times it would be no easy matter for two young and good-looking girls to travel on foot in safety.

In war time it would have been doubly dangerous. But in a country ravaged by the great scourge of battle, weighed down by insolent and thievish noblemen, overrun by banditti, it was almost a hopeless task.

Both were poorly and meanly dressed, and their story was that, having been driven from home by the accidents of war, they were seeking employment or even a shelter in their hour of need.

It required all their patience and ingenuity to escape insult. Many an hour was passed in dense thickets, while ribald troops of soldiers and robbers went by. Many an hour was spent in some obscure garret of an inn or farm yard, trembling at the sound of revelry below.

Only of women or quiet masters of houses dared they inquire their way to the camp of the emperor, who had just gone into winter quarters.

And in those days, before journals or telegraphs, or even the post was invented, the accounts were most contradictory.

A whole fortnight of wandering had reduced them to a pretty plight.

One day, just as they were about to enter a dark and gloomy wood, a number of men darted out from a thicket, and greeting them with shouts and laughter and coarse jokes, made them prisoners.

Editha tried to assume a dignity of manner in strange contradiction to her costume and footsore appearance, the soldiery only laughing all the more.

"Take me to your chief, whoever he may be," she supplicated, " and you shall be rewarded."

"Have you money?" cried one of the roughest, in a startling tone.

"One moment," said a young officer of rather better mien than the rest of the crew : " you really wish to go before our master?"

"I do."

"You shall be satisfied," replied the young man, and then added in a low tone, " if you have any loose coins, you can give them to the men. You shall not be molested."

Editha put her hand under her cloak, and gave him all the money she had about her, which being given to the soldiery, they set up a shout of joy, and were now very civil to their prisoners.

After a walk of about a mile they came in sight of a camp where some thirty or forty tents were pitched. Towards one of these they were led. It was larger and more ornate than its fellows, and over its summit waved a huge flag.

Editha trembled and leaned suddenly against a tree as she gazed on the device.

"The Black Wolf of Zelling," she faltered.

"Yes," said the officer drily.

"Why was I ever born?" cried the young lady. "Better have been devoured by wild beasts in the forest than have fallen into his hands ; he who never spared sex or age, nor anything sacred, when he had anything to gain."

The officer looked puzzled.

"You asked for our leader," he said, "and it is too late to retreat now."

With trembling limbs and pallid cheeks the wretched girls approached the tent of the man who during these savage wars had earned such a terrible reputation or cruelty.

It was a splendid affair, and as the prisoners entered, they saw a stalwart warrior reclining on a couch near a table covered with bottles and goblets.

Two men of fierce appearance, but evidently by their costume of almost princely rank, accompanied him in his debauch.

"What brings you here, Roderick?" said the chief in a husky voice.

"Two maidens captured by our men, who demanded to see our chief. You know your own orders."

"I do, but they refer to maidens of higher degree," replied the robber prince. "Throw them to the soldiers and bring no more such draggled wenches."

"At your peril," said Editha, haughtily advancing. "I am Editha of Rolensac, seneschale of the castle of that name, bound to the court of the emperor. Stop me at your peril."

The chief bounded on his seat.

"What—Editha of Rolensac?— who is condemned to lose her hand for striking a priest? Ha! ha! ha! A jovial maiden truly. Advance and pledge me in a goblet."

With outward calm and inward trembling, the young mistress of Rolensac advanced and put the glass to her lips.

"And what seek you at the camp of the emperor? Answer me truly, on your life."

Editha bent her head modestly, and then after a moment's thought replied—

"You adjure me to speak the truth. Then will I do so. I seek Sir Edwin of Seltzberg, once my affianced husband and now a favourite of the emperor."

The terrible oath which the Black Wolf of Zelling swore is not fit for these pages. Having thus relieved his mind, he rose and addressed the young officer who waited for orders.

"Conduct these prisoners to the blue tent and let them be kept in safety. Show them all honour and respect: we will confer again to-morrow. Summon my lieutenants to supper."

Trembling in every limb, the girls followed the young officer, and were conducted with every mark of outward respect to the tent indicated, which they found to be comfortable and well provided.

Here they passed the night, under feelings of great anxiety.

About the middle watch next day they were summoned, having already been provided with fitting dresses, to mount into a litter to which a guard of a dozen horse had been attached.

Editha and her companion could scarcely believe their eyes.

Then with great courtesy the Black Wolf of Zelling approached them.

"Whither are you sending us?" said Editha in somewhat anxious tones.

"Lady, men accuse me of every crime under the heavens. Of course I may be guilty—no man is perfect, but of disrespect and disobedience to mother church, no one shall accuse me. You have been legally condemned to forfeit your hand, and the forfeit must be paid. You will be taken care of by my men until you are in the hands of the Abbot of Graal. Good day to you and good fortune.

And with a hoarse and terrible laugh, the great robber prince, whose fearful reputation made of him a kind of Blue Beard in the eyes of the masses, turned away, leaving mistress and maid in a kind of stupor, more easy to be imagined than described.

All their sufferings were in vain.

To resist was useless, and both therefore lay back almost insensible.

During the journey, which only lasted two days with good horses, no one had a word of comfort to say to them, and when they reached the great and dismal abbey— a fortress and a prison, it was with utter and sullen despair that they repaired to their cell.

Here they remained for several days, nay for nearly a fortnight, without any disturbance but when their meals were brought.

The guardian who attended them would answer no questions.

Doubtless Editha had been condemned by default in her absence.

Distaste for life, a sense of utter despair took possession of her soul.

At the end of a fortnight some nuns were admitted to see her.

They brought pure white dresses for mistress and maid to put on.

There was no use in resistance, and Editha, almost glad the dread hour had come, allowed herself to be arrayed like a victim for the slaughter.

The nuns were very careful, and rarely had Editha ever looked so beautiful as in her spotless white robe and crown of white roses.

Then she was summoned, and found herself the centre of a mighty procession bound for the church, half a mile distant.

The abbot and all the grandees were mounted on horseback, but for the women no conveyance had been provided.

They walked, escorted by the nuns and monks, and behind by soldiers of the abbey.

Amongst these walked a man in a black mask, carrying a small silver hatchet.

Luckily the young girl saw nothing of this, though she knew full well the cruel rapacity and stern will of the Abbot of Graal.

The journey appeared interminable.

At last the church was reached, and proved to be crowded by the neighbours. People of all ranks were collected together on the occasion.

The most of those congregrated on the occasion were men in armour.

The abbot and his court ranged themselves round the altar, and Editha and her maid were seated on a bench.

Then the steward who had been struck by the impetuous young *châtelaine* rose, and from a huge parchment read the charge against the prisoner. It was long and elaborate, and full of phrases which nobody understood.

Then came the sentence.

The thunders of the church were invoked against all sacrilegious evildoers, and it was mentioned incidentally that death by burning at the stake, with excommunication in this world and the next, was the fate of all who raised their wicked hand against the holy mother church, or any of her recognised servants.

After due consideration, and having regard to the age, rank, and beauty of the accused, the abbot of Graal had mercifully changed the punishment, and condemned the seneschale of Rolensac to lose her hand—that with which she had struck the recognised servant of the abbot.

"Let justice be done."

As these words were said in a loud voice, Editha closed her eyes with horror, which changed to shivering when she felt her right hand clutched by a strong man.

"Mercy! let me give up my lands, retire to a nunnery, anything but lose my hand!" she cried.

"Your hand is forfeit, and I claim it," said a voice which made her heart leap.

Opening her eyes, she saw Sir Edwin of Seltzberg, with smiling face and bright eyes, gazing at her with unutterable love.

"What means this?" she faltered.

"You have your choice," said the hoarse voice of the Black Wolf of Zelling—"to let the church claim her due, or give your forfeit hand to my young friend and saviour Sir Edward, now knight and castellan of Seltzberg by the death of his elder brother.

"He saved my life once and I promised to be even with him one day.

"What say you, maiden? the executioner awaits; shall he be summoned, or will you resign yourself to the other fate?"

Editha rose with a bright blush on her cheeks and approached the altar, where the abbot performed the office of matrimony.

It was against his will. Powerful, however, as he was, he did not care to brave the anger of the Black Wolf of Zelling.

We need not expatiate on the joy of the lovers, thus singularly and romantically reunited.

It is only requisite to add that Rolensac became once more a happy home, and it was only in subsequent troublous times that it fell into ruins and was almost forgotten.

END OF ROLENSAC; THE LEGEND OF THE FORFEIT HAND.

Our next nnmber will contain " The Legend of Godceburg."

THE **BARONS** OF **OLD** OR THE **ROBBERS** OF THE **RHINE**

ALDOBRAND,

THE BANDIT BARON OF RHEINSTEIN.

AMONGST the numerous ancient structures that crowd the banks of the Rhine may be mentioned the castle of Rheinstein.

This, in common with many other residences of knightly highwaymen, fell at length before the strong arm of the law in 1200, being condemned as a robber stronghold by the Hanse League—a confederation entered into by the merchants

"'THOU THINK'ST TO FRIGHTEN US WITH THAT CUR?' SNEERED THE BARON."

of various German towns to preserve the traffic of the river, and to protect themselves from the attacks of the lordly ruffians who lined its banks, and filled their coffers by pillaging those that passed who were wealthy enough to excite their greed, and not sufficiently powerful to resist them.

The ruin has been restored as far as possible to its original condition, but only to serve the peaceful purpose of a summer residence for the Prince of Prussia.

The interior has been fitted up in imitation of a knightly dwelling of the days of chivalry; the walls hung with armour, the windows filled with painted glass, and the furniture made after the fashion of ancient days.

At the narrow pass below Rheinstein, between the rock and the river, there existed till very recent times a Jews' toll, where certain fixed dues were levied upon all the Hebrews who passed. It is stated that the toll-keeper—who was no other than the lord of the castle—trained dogs to single out and seize the Jews from amongst the passing travellers, and hold them by their garments with their teeth until they had paid the sum demanded.

These being the principal historical particulars concerning Rheinstein, let us now proceed with the legend attached thereto.

The preaching of the Crusade by Peter the Hermit, created a flame of chivalrous enthusiasm throughout Europe, unequalled either in ancient or modern times.

Emperors, kings, princes, and potentates of all ranks, threw aside their regal robes and their ease at home, and military adventurers, thirsting for fame or plunder, volunteered their help with equal eagerness in the righteous cause of rescuing the Holy Sepulchre from the hands of the infidels.

These wars continued for many years, but it was when the city of Ascalon had fallen before the victorious arm of the English king, Richard Cœur de Lion, that our story opens.

The siege was over, the din of war had for a time ceased, and the burning sun of Syria was setting in the west in a gorgeous bed of molten gold and purple.

Amongst the motley groups of men and people from different countries whose presence swelled the ranks of the invading forces, was an old Jew named Eliezer.

He had no interest in the success of the expedition on the score of religious motives, on account of his faith, of which the Cross and Holy Sepulchre formed no part.

The motive that led him to cross the

sea, and brave the perils of war, were his *own* interest.

He was of German extraction, a native of Bavaria, and possessed of great wealth.

He dealt in precious gems, and had the reputation of being an alchemist.

But whether this were true or not, he had left his country, and was now in the train of the English army, on the plains of Ascalon, where he could either dispose of his jewels, or, perhaps, lend money to some needy knight at an enormous rate of interest.

It was probably the ability to do the latter that secured him safety and consideration at the hands of those who would else have scorned and despised him for being a Jew.

He had been a great traveller in his time, both in Europe and in the East, and had even visited England, and could speak the English language.

In whatever country he sojourned, he made a point of studying its language, so that he could converse in Syriac, Arabic, French or English, besides his native tongue, German, which circumstance he found highly advantageous in his commercial transactions.

But on the evening in question, the old man had no heart for gain, or anything beyond indulging the grief that oppressed him.

Seated on the ground, his turban unrolled at his feet, and his white head bowed forward on his breast, he was apparently absorbed in some deep sorrow.

Near him stood a young English soldier, who was known in the ranks as Gilbert of Kent, being a native of that country.

Circumstances had thrown them together, and the young man now sought to console the afflicted Israelite.

"Cheer thee, good Eliezer!" he said soothingly. "Trials we are taught are sent for our benefit, if we look at them rightly."

The old man suddenly raised his head with an impatient gesture of anything but resignation.

"Trials!" he cried, almost fiercely. "What knowest thou of trials? It is for our down-trodden and persecuted race to speak of trials; since the curse fell upon us, have we not to bear losses and crosses too great for human nature to endure?"

"I do not dispute that," returned the young man, "but from these none of us are exempt."

"But you Gentiles are not robbed and persecuted as we are," continued Eliezer, bitterly. "It is for the children of Abraham to bow down their necks to injustice and oppression ; it is on their heads the fiercest storms of Heaven's wrath fall !"

" Well, well, take comfort, old man," said Gilbert, kindly.

" I cannot ! I cannot !" moaned the Israelite, " first my child, my beauteous Zelma, was snatched from me by some accursed Pagan—the light of my eyes, the joy of my declining years, and I know not what may be her fate. Then, as if that were not sufficient, have I not lost the diamond I travelled so many miles to secure ? The precious gem of almost priceless value, that was in itself equal to a dukedom ? Oh, my child ! my jewel !" raved the old man, with a fresh burst of grief, " I shall never see either again ! I shall go down to my grave mourning !"

The young soldier waited for a few moments, and then said, soothingly—

" You cannot tell what good fortune may be in the future. How canst thou be certain that both your child and your diamond may not be restored to thee ?"

" Impossible ! impossible !" cried the Jew, despairingly, " 'twere madness to hope it !"

The old man paused a few moments, and sat rocking himself to and fro in his distress.

At length he exclaimed, vehemently—

" Thou didst never see my child, young man, else thou wouldst confess that the equal of her peerless beauty is not to be found amongst women ! Thou didst never gaze upon my lost diamond, or thou wouldst know at once it was a gem the world could scarcely match ; and is it likely that those into whose hands these precious treasures have fallen, will restore them ? Oh, no ! no ! I shall never behold them ! never ! never more !"

Throughout the night, the afflicted old man bewailed his heavy losses, listening occasionally, but impatiently, like a fretful child, to the attempted consolations of his companion.

Gilbert was comparatively a stranger to Eliezer of Munich, and it was perfectly true that he had never gazed upon the lovely Zelma, nor had the rays of the lustrous jewel so highly spoken of ever flashed before his eyes.

Both were lost before he met with the old Jew, but his kindly nature sympathised with the bereaved and solitary man, and in that sympathy he forgot the difference of creeds, and the mixture of selfish avarice that mingled with the natural affection of a parent, and pitied the grief he witnessed without too closely analysing its motives.

The old Israelite, too, in spite of his angry bursts of petulant despair, was not insensi-

ble to the generous efforts of his young friend to console him, and thus between the two was established a union that was to last longer than either at that time anticipated.

The morning dawned, and the English king, the excitement of victory having subsided, had appointed that day to review his troops.

A glittering mass of armour, plumes, and warlike implements, were assembled on the fields of Ascalon.

Round the tent of Count Ludovic of Saxony were congregated a throng of knights, eagerly gazing at some object of great interest.

This was nothing less than a magnificent diamond.

It was a lovely gem, and all who looked upon it were loud in their praises of its size and purity.

Gilbert happened to be near, and was enabled to catch a glimpse of the marvellous jewel.

The sight dazzled his eyes, and the thought flashed across him at the moment that it might be the identical stone his friend Eliezer so bitterly mourned the loss of.

But he had no proof that it was, and the Jew not being on the spot, he could only form his own conjectures and remain silent.

The news of this wondrous gem reached the ears of Richard himself, who expressed a wish to see it.

Accordingly the Count Ludovic hastened to the royal tent to comply with the monarch's request.

Richard was loud in its praise.

" By my sword !" he exclaimed, rapturously, " it is a jewel brighter and more precious than any that glitters in England's crown. Count," he continued, turning to the Bavarian noble, " thou hast a treasure there of which thou may'st well be proud."

The Count bowed in acknowledgment of the monarch's compliments, when suddenly a confusion of voices was heard at a short distance, and presently, in spite of every opposition, an old white-haired man, whose turban and gaberdine pronounced him a Hebrew, made his way impetuously through the crowd.

" My liege, my liege !" he cried excitedly, " most noble Richard, hear me !"

As he spoke the old Israelite prostrated himself at the king's feet, and bowed his white head to the dust before him.

" What wouldst thou ?" demanded the monarch.

" Justice !" exclaimed the suppliant.

" Truly thou shalt have it, if thy claim be just," returned Richard. "Who art thou ?"

"My name is Eliezer, of Munich, my liege," replied the merchant, "and that diamond thou so much admirest is mine !"

A look of astonishment passed over the features of all present, whilst the face of Ludovic of Saxony turned pale with apprehension.

"Thine !" echoed the king, earnestly regarding the prostrate form of the old Jew, and scrutinizing his humble garb, with surprise still manifest in his countenance. " Is it possible that one so poor as thou art, to all appearance, canst be the owner of a jewel so precious ?"

"I swear by our holy father Abraham, my liege, I speak the truth," cried Eliezer solemnly. "I am a merchant who for years has dealt in orient gems, and though my garments are poor, I have acquired wealth in my trade, more than thou wouldst suppose. I bought that diamond in India ten years ago, for a sum few princes could have afforded to pay, and to purchase which would beggar the estate of Ludovic of Saxony thrice over."

The king turned to the German count.

"What dost thou reply to this, sir knight?" he demanded.

" Sire," returned Ludovic, with a flush upon his fair cheek, " this old man either lies, or is labouring under a delusion : this jewel is an heirloom in our family."

" 'Tis false ! utterly false, my liege !" cried Eliezer, excitedly, " he would call me liar—see how the base lie he himself utters blanches his own features !"

The king looked towards the count, who was paler than ever.

He then turned again to the Jew.

" What proof hast thou that this diamond belongs to thee ?" he asked.

Gilbert of Kent stepped forward.

"My royal liege," exclaimed the youth, " I can bear witness that this old man has lost a precious gem. I have heard him bemoaning his misfortune bitterly."

" Hast thou no other proof ?" the king demanded.

"Yes, your majesty," exclaimed Eliezer eagerly, " I can describe the jewel in every particular."

" Let me hear !" exclaimed Richard.

" First, my liege, if you look steadily at the stone you will see in its very centre a round black mark like an ink-spot."

The king inspected it scrutinisingly.

'You are right, thus far," he said ; " What else ?"

" Next, on one of its extreme facets, at the side, there is a small flaw in the shape of a cross."

" True, there is !" returned Richard.

" Thirdly," continued Eliezer, "it is plainly set, and on the rim of the setting, underneath, are engraved my initials, E. B., Eliezer Bortz."

" Right again !" said the king, having made the necessary examination. " How canst thou negative these proofs ?" he asked of Count Ludovic. "It is not usual for an heirloom to have the initials of another family. If thou canst not explain this satisfactorily I think, since I am made arbiter in this case, I must decide in favour of this old man, and adjudge the jewel to him."

The count, embarrassed at finding so many eyes fixed upon him, and confounded at the initials, which he had not observed, could only make a very bungling and lame reply, which not only did not satisfy the shrewd monarch, but convinced him of the falseness of his claim.

"Count !" he said, "it is you who are under a delusion. You have mistaken what you wished to be true for truth itself. I regret to have to convict a knight of an act of falsehood or dishonour, but it seems to me you found the gem which this Jew had lost, and wishing to appropriate it to yourself, invented the story of the heirloom in order to account for its possession."

The conscious-stricken count was speechless, so accurately had the monarch divined the exact circumstances of the case.

" The cause is adjudged !" cried Richard Cœur de Lion, " Eliezer of Munich, the diamond is yours, receive it."

With a burst of joyful gratitude, the old Hebrew clasped his precious treasure to his heart, and implored heaven's blessings on the head of his royal benefactor.

The king turned to the discomfited Ludovic, and said, drily—

" You should have kept your jewel in your pocket, count, until you got back to Saxony ; your friends there might have believed you snatched it from the turban of some vanquished foe."

The count slunk away, full of shame and bitterness at his exposure and the loss of his coveted prize, whilst Eliezer departed rejoicing, with Gilbert of Kent, whom he thenceforth treated as his own son.

    ✿   ✿   ✿   ✿   ✿

A series of conflicts followed the reduction of Ascalon, in which the Christian cause was crowned with success.

In one of these the young soldier Gilbert, thirsting for honour and promotion, attacked in single combat a stalwart Saracen.

For some time the contest was doubtful, until fortune decided on the part of Gilbert.

His foe was unhorsed, and he had sprung from his own steed to secure his captive, when several of the followers of the vanquished infidel rode up and seized the young Englishman in the very moment of his victory.

Zadak, the Saracen chief, commanded that his life should be spared, and Gilbert was carried off a prisoner to his castle in the mountains.

Eliezer in the meantime, ignorant of his fate, mourned for him as dead.

It was in the midst of a wild and arid tract of country that Gilbert was confined.

What would eventually be his fate he knew not, but unless his place of captivity should be discovered by his victorious countrymen, he feared slavery for life.

He was confined in a dungeon, not underground, but towards the summit of the castle tower, the walls and floor of which were stone, and into which the light came from a narrow window, guarded by strong iron bars, whilst a heap of dried palm leaves matted together served for his couch.

His infidel captor, with a grim smile, informed him, as he ordered his men to manacle his feet and wrists with heavy chains, that if he had friends who were prepared to pay a heavy ransom for him he might hope for freedom, but failing that, he would remain where he was, a prisoner.

For some days he was visited ocasionally by a swarthy, dark-browed jailor, who brought him food.

At first he buoyed himself up with the prospect of deliverance, and would strain his eyes over the arid plain, which he could see from the narrow window of his cell spreading far and wide into the distance.

But as day after day passed and no one appeared, his spirits sunk into gloomy despondency, and he almost resigned himself to his fate.

One night as he lay sleeping upon his bed of palm leaves, he heard the sound of an exquisite female voice, singing in tones of such pathos and sweetness as thrilled him with delight.

"How beautiful!" he murmured, as he lay entranced, listening to the melting sounds, "surely it is no earthly voice I hear. It must be some guardian spirit that seeks to cheer my drooping heart."

This was the youth's first thought, but as the voice was heard every night, he began to infer that it might proceed, not from a spirit, but from some female within the castle, although who she was, or what might be her position there, he could not guess.

Curiosity, too, mingled with his surmises, until, from being charmed with the rich beauty of the melody he heard, he became possessed with a longing desire to gaze upon the singer.

"She must be beautiful !" he exclaimed to himself, "such heavenly melody could only be breathed forth from young and lovely lips."

One night, after an overpoweringly hot and sultry day, as the evening breeze stole in through the window bars, Gilbert, refreshed by its grateful coolness, had fallen into a pleasant sleep.

Gradually the bolts of his prison door were undrawn, and there glided with noiseless step into the chamber a female form.

Gilbert, by the partial light of the moon, watched her dreamily, in a state between sleeping and waking.

His fair visitor gazed at him long and wistfully, and murmured some words in a language he did not understand, but which, from their softened tone, he felt sure were words of pity.

After contemplating him for some time in silence, she sighed deeply and withdrew.

Never in his life had the young soldier gazed upon such wondrous beauty as the faint rays of the moonlight revealed to him, and when the charming vision disappeared, he felt as one might be supposed to feel who, having been for a brief space a dweller in heaven, was suddenly dismissed to earth again.

"She was an angel! she must have been !" he exclaimed rapturously, as he lay on his pallet eagerly recalling the pale lovely face and melting black eyes of the supposed angelic being.

In the morning he found by his bedside a small basket of fresh fruit and a small leathern flask of wine.

These substantial presents seemed to suggest an earthly rather than an immaterial friend ; but Gilbert, without stopping to argue the point, gratefully availed himself of the refreshing gifts.

He ate the food and drank the wine.

A few days after the door of his prison opened, and to his great surprise and joy, instead of the usual copper-coloured jailor making his appearance, the fair being who had so charmed him entered.

She carried in her hand his usual food, with the addition of wine and fruit.

These she placed by his side, with a kind smile mingled with pity.

"Fair angel, how can I thank thee?" exclaimed Gilbert, in a rapture of gratitude and admiration.

"By eating and drinking what I bring you, and not calling me by a title I do not deserve," answered his lovely visitor, in his own language, and with a bewitching smile.

The young soldier was thoroughly astonished.

"Surely!" he cried, "you are no Saracen?"

"No," returned the maiden, "I am a captive like yourself. The owner of this castle—Zadak the Syrian—is forth once more to do battle with the Christians in the ranks of Saladin, and has left to me the task of attending on your wants. I hope you do not object to me as your jailor?" she asked, smilingly.

Gilbert clasped her hand gently, and raised it—but with difficulty, from the weight of the fetters he wore—to his lips.

"These cruel manacles must be removed," she said, indignantly; "I will get the key, and set you free from them."

"And are you alone, then, in this solitary place?" enquired Gilbert.

"No; there are a few here beside myself," she replied; "enough to watch that I do not escape."

"But you are not English, and yet you speak my language?"

"I have been in England," she answered, "with my father; it was there I learnt your tongue."

"May I ask your name?" he said, earnestly.

"Zelma! I am a Jewess, the daughter of the merchant Eliezer," she replied.

"Good Heaven! can it be possible?" cried Gilbert, with profound astonishment. "I no longer wonder that your father spoke of you as a pearl amongst women!"

"Know you my father?" enquired Zelma, eagerly.

"Yes, fair maiden, I know him well: often have I heard him mourn thy loss," replied Gilbert.

"He knows not then of my captivity?" she asked.

"No, maiden; he is also ignorant of mine," Gilbert returned; "he will doubtless think me fallen on the battle-field."

"Dear father!" murmured the young girl; "how I long to see his venerable face once more!"

"But is there no possible chance of escape?" asked Gilbert.

"'Sh!" returned Zelma, placing her hand gently upon his lips to imply caution; "there may be, but my custodians are crafty and suspicious, and nothing but the greatest circumspection will enable us to accomplish our flight; to excite their suspicion in the slightest would be to frustrate all chance of our success."

The young soldier at once admitted the necessity of caution.

"I will be guided entirely by you, fair Zelma," he said, "and whenever an opportunity for flight occurs, rely on my courage and devotion to defend you."

Days and weeks passed on without any such opportunity occurring.

But the period did not appear insupportably long, for the captives had found that love can transform a prison into a paradise.

They had become devotedly attached to each other, and felt that for weal or woe their fate henceforth was indissolubly united.

One day Zelma entered Gilbert's cell hastily.

"The time for escape has come at last, I think!" she said. "There are only two men left to guard the castle."

"When must the attempt be made?" asked the young soldier.

"To-night!" replied Zelma; "I will drug the wine they drink, and secure the keys; the rest will be easy."

At night, as she had promised, Zelma mingled an opiate with the liquor she served out to the unsuspecting guards, who drank eagerly, and having drank, slept profoundly.

"It is time!" she said, as she entered the prison, and threw open the door, exultingly.

Zelma had secured the keys, and there was no difficulty in effecting their egress.

In a short time they stood without the castle walls.

The bright moonlight lit up the vast sterile plain, and by its beams they started on their adventurous journey.

They walked all night, and when the sun rose they sat down beneath a gigantic palm tree to rest.

A few hours' sleep refreshed them, and having eaten of the fruit and drunk of the wine Zelma had brought with her, they continued their journey.

Again they walked all night, and again paused for sleep during the heat of the day.

As they were about to renew their weary march, at sunset, they saw in the distance a dark spot no larger than a man's hand.

Gilbert judged it to be a troop of horsemen, but whether friends or foes he could not determine.

Again they walked forward, until at

sunrise Zelma was so thoroughly exhausted that she could go no further,

"Leave me, dearest Gilbert !" she said, faintly ; "I only clog your steps, save yourself !"

. "Never, beloved Zelma," returned the young Englishman, vehemently, "either we live for each other or not at all. We must be nearing the English camp, and—ah !"

This exclamation was caused by the sudden appearance of a body of horsemen, who had caught sight of them and were now approaching.

"Are they our soldiers ?" enquired Zelma, anxiously.

"Alas, no !" exclaimed Gilbert in a desponding tone, as he recognised in the wild swarthy horde that approached, a troupe of Bedouin Arabs.

In a few moments they were surrounded.

Zelma, who could speak Arabic, asked for the leader.

Presently Al Mokhtar the Arab chief stood before her.

Gaunt and grim, the son of the desert listened to her request for help, and the means of reaching the English army.

The chief stroked his beard for a moment, and then replied—

"These English are our enemies, and swarm over the face of our land with a blight more terrible than the passage of the locust. They are the foes of Mahomet, and therefore our foes. To deliver thee safely to thy countrymen would be to do thee and them a service, and we serve not those we hate. Thou wilt remain with us as slaves, thou and thy companion there. Think not to appeal to our pity, we have none for such as you. Your destiny is pronounced, it is enough ! Remove the woman to my tent !"

This command was instantly obeyed.

Zelma sought to entreat his mercy, but in vain.

With a proud wave of the hand, the chief turned scornfully away, when Gilbert, with more courage than prudence, sprang forward and seized him fiercely by the wrist.

"Stay, infidel !" he cried, in his own language, "dost thou dare talk of making slaves of us who are free born ?"

The chief, who did not understand the purport of the young soldier's angry words, perfectly comprehended his action.

Shaking off his grasp and stepping back, he shook his raiment in disgust.

"Vile Christian !" he exclaimed, "thou hast dared to lay thy polluting hand upon me, and shalt feel the power of the magician Al Mokhtar. I did intend thee simply

to be my slave, but now thou shalt sink lower, even to the level of the brute creation."

As he finished speaking he uttered some cabalistic words, and taking from his vest a small phial, he dashed its contents over Gilbert.

"'Tis done !" he cried in the Arab tongue, "dog as thou art—become a dog indeed !"

In an instant, by the power of the enchantment, the young soldier lost his human shape, and was transformed into a hound.

"So," continued Al Mokhtar, "shalt thou remain to wander over the earth, nor shalt thou e'er again recover thy original shape *until one whom thou lovest, who loves thee dearer than all beside, shall sever thy head from thy body*. Begone !"

With a shower of darts flying from the hands of the Arabs, the unhappy Gilbert bounded across the plain.

Zelma, secure in the tent, which had now been erected, knew nothing of the change that had passed over her lover.

To all her eager inquiries concerning him she only received this answer—"He is gone ! thou wilt see him no more !"

 * * * * *

The English army was now in sight of the magnificent City of Jerusalem, when one morning at early dawn a hound came bounding into the midst of the camp, covered with dust, and its open jaws flecked with white foam. The animal howled piteously, and ran from line to line, seizing the soldiers by their accoutrements, in order to attract their attention.

This act and the dog's excitement produced an impression that had well nigh cost it its life.

The cry, "a mad dog ! a mad dog !" resounded through the camp, and the hound was pursued fiercely by the soldiers, who did not understand what the poor animal wished to convey.

In its headlong flight, however, it encountered the Jew, Eliezer.

At sight of Eliezer, the hound stopped, and crouching at his feet and licking his hands, endeavoured by every possible show of affection to prove that it had no hostile intentions.

The Hebrew was struck by the manner of the hound, and pleaded earnestly with its pursuers that its life should be spared.

The request was granted, but not until the Jew had paid a sum of money as the price of ransom.

The dog, thus rescued, renewed its efforts to attract the attention of its rescuer by barking, and seizing his gaberdine, and endeavouring to draw him away.

"'Tis strange," murmured Eliezer, struck by the persevering efforts of his dumb companion, "the poor creature means something, though what, I know not?"

"Methinks I can translate his language," said a cheery voice behind him.

Looking round he beheld close at hand the English monarch, Richard Cœur de Lion, surrounded by a glittering band of noble warriors.

The Jew prostrated himself reverently before the king.

The hound also crouched by his side, looking up wistfully in Richard's face and uttering a low pitiful whine.

"That dog," continued the royal warrior, "seeks in the only way he can to call thy attention to some fact he wishes thee to know. From his travel-stained appearance and the foam upon his jaws I opine he has journeyed afar, and perhaps had a struggle for his life, and from his seeking to draw thee away I imagine he would urge thee to return with him to save one he loves from peril. Dost thou know anyone likely to be in such a strait?"

At these words his lost daughter flashed across the Jew's memory.

"Yes, my royal liege!" returned Eliezer eagerly, "my child, my Zelma has been stolen from me!"

"Say'st thou so! then I would stake my crown it is on her account that the poor animal is thus anxious. In such cases dogs are oft times more trustworthy than men."

At this moment a mounted English soldier dashed up at full speed and, throwing himself from his steed, knelt at the king's feet.

"Rescue, my liege!" he cried, "a troop of wandering Arabs have seized upon a small body of our troops, and their lives are in jeopardy. I alone escaped to bring the tidings!"

"You are wrong, sirrah," returned Richard, good humouredly, as he pointed to the hound, "here is one who hath forstalled thee in thy intelligence. Dost thou know this dog?"

"No, your majesty," answered the soldier, shaking his head, "I never set eyes upon it till this moment."

"Saw you a woman in the Arab camp?" eagerly enquired Eliezer, "young, lovely, as the fabled houris of these infidels!"

"Truly yes!" replied the man, "of fair complexion, with raven locks, and eyes black as sloes. She is a prisoner there."

"She is my child, my Zelma!" cried the Jew excitedly. "Oh save her, brave Richard, and the blessings of Abraham shall—

"Tut, tut," laughed the king, "I desire nothing of Abraham. But fear not, your child shall be restored to thee, nevertheless. It were a slur upon our banner to allow any of our colour to be held in bondage by these infidels."

In a few moments a troop of horse were ordered forth, and the command given to Eustace de Tracy, a young French knight, with orders to rescue the captives from the hands of the Arabs.

The escort galloped off and were soon lost in the distance.

*   *   *   *   *

The children of the desert were on the eve of striking their tents, intending to march many leagues further into the solitudes of the wilderness, when the English troops arrived.

The contest was fierce, but eventually the Arabs were put to flight, and the prisoners rescued.

During the fray the brave hound signalled out the chief Al Mokhtar, and attacked him with a savage fury that excited general surprise and admiration, though none knew the cause of the animal's violent animosity.

The chief narrowly escaped with his life, and the contest over, the dog placed himself at the side of Zelma, and could not be persuaded to leave her an instant, until she was once more restored to the arms of her father, Eliezer.

It was not long after this that a truce for three years was concluded between the Christians and infidels, during which many of the former availed themselves of the opportunity to return to their homes.

Amongst these were Eliezer of Munich, and his daughter, who departed from Palestine, taking with them the faithful hound which had rendered them such signal service, and which Zelma had named Gilbert in memory of her lover, little dreaming it was he himself in his transformed state.

On their homeward voyage, and when nearly at their journey's end, they encountered a terrible storm, that wrecked the vessel, and caused the loss of many lives.

Zelma owed her safety once more to the courage and fidelity of her devoted Gilbert, who bore her through the foaming billows to the shore.

They landed on the coast of France, and Zelma, having lost everything, was compelled to beg her way to Germany.

Of her father, from whom she had been separated when the vessel went to pieces, she saw no more, and lamented him with bitter tears as having perished in the waves.

Having relatives on her mother's side at Rotterdam, she made her way thither, accompanied by her staunch protector.

Having stayed there for some time, she resolved to return to Munich, where her father had property, that would by right descend to her.

It was on her journey thither she passed the Castle of Rheinstein, in which dwelt the Baron Aldobrand, or, as he was called from his rapacity, the Bandit Baron of Rheinstein.

And well did he deserve his name.

He was a burly, bluff, roystering, godless man, who swore fiercely and drank hard, and who was so greedy to amass wealth, that he not only kept a guard constantly on the watch for travellers who passed his domains, but established a tollgate under the very shadow of his castle walls expressly for Jews, whom he hated, and whom he fleeced of their possessions at every opportunity, under the pretext of claiming his lawful dues.

When, therefore, the beautiful Zelma appeared at the barrier, she was at once accosted by the baron himself, to whom her approach had been duly announced, and whom she found performing the office of toll-keeper.

The fair Jewess, closely veiled, stood before the blustering noble, who, with features flushed and bloated with excess, rudely demanded the usual passport.

"What sum do you require?" asked Zelma, in her sweet, melodious voice.

"All you carry about you!" was the rude and peremptory reply.

"Alas! my lord," returned Zelma, "I am but a poor orphan who has lost her father by a shipwreck, and who has so little money that she is compelled to travel homeward on foot.

This information, so little calculated to impress the coveteous grasping Aldobrand with anything but disgust, drew from him a savage growl.

"What is your name?" he asked, in a surly tone.

"Zelma," replied the maiden, "I am the daughter of Eliezer, of Munich.

"The richest dog of a Jew in Bavaria," exclaimed the baron vehemently; "and dost thou his daughter plead the pitiful tale of poverty? 'Tis false! absurd!"

"I assure you, my lord, 'tis true," returned Zelma, meekly; "I have lost all."

As she spoke she raised her veil and looked pleadingly at the lordly ruffian with her lovely dark eyes.

But the baron was not to be cajoled out of the money he expected, although it struck him that in default of payment a damsel so beautiful as Zelma would be some compensation, so he replied—

"Well then, as you say you have no money, I shall hold you prisoner. Perhaps your friends may feel inclined to ransom so fair a piece of flesh and blood."

"You surely will not attempt to stop me on my journey!" said Zelma, her cheek flushing with indignation.

"Ho, ho!" laughed the baron coarsely, "I shall not only attempt, but do. Therefore prepare to become an inmate of my castle, uutil I give thee permission to depart."

"No I will not!" cried Zelma fiercely, "and I protest against this ruffianly outrage."

"Protest as much as thou pleasest," returned Aldobrand, again laughing scornfully, "but your protestations will avail you little here. What ho, Hugo! come and escort this dainty Jewess into the interior."

Obedient to this order there advanced a stalwart, broadshouldered retainer with an enormous black beard, who, without ceremony, seized Zelma by the wrist with his iron-gloved hand.

The maiden uttered an exclamation of pain, when the hound Gilbert, with a fierce growl, sprang at the man's throat. Hugo, thus assailed, was glad to release his prisoner, by whose side stood the brave dog, showing his white fangs ominously, and uttering canine execrations not loud but deep.

"So thou think'st to frighten us with that snarling cur, dost thou?" sneered the baron, derisively. "Go, Hugo! lower a rope, with a noose at the end, from the rock over our heads. We'll soon cure the brute of his barking propensities."

Hugo, not sorry to be dismissed, hurried away, and Zelma, trembling for the fate of her faithful Gilbert, entreated the baron to save his life.

"I will spare the animal on one condition," he answered, "namely, that thou enterest the castle without further resistance or question. Once there, depend upon fair treatment and as much jovial revelry as thine heart can desire."

"I consent," answered Zelma, "and will do thy bidding, relying on thy knightly honour to do me no harm, and on condition that thou wilt not separate me from my faithful hound, which has twice saved my life."

For continuation of this Story see page 216 of our next number.

THE LEGEND OF GODESBURG.

THE ruined castle of Godesburg stands at one of the most interesting points of the Rhine.

Below the point, this scenery of the river is comparatively tame.

But at Godesburg it begins to assume the wild grandeur and beauty for which it is famed.

Here may be seen the celebrated "seven mountains," the most noted of which are Drachenfels and Rolensac.

But to each is attached some weird legend, to be related in this series.

The city of Bonn is only four miles distant, and Godesburg is on the same— *i.e.*, the left—bank of the river.

The village is now a spa, and visitors resort there for the mineral waters.

But we have only to do with the grey ruin that rears its jagged, crumbling top out of the thickets that surround its base.

The original castle was built during the latter part of the Roman empire—that is, towards the close of the fourth century, when the mysterious events we are about to relate are supposed to have taken place.

All have read in history of the brave and warlike character of the ancient Germans, and the fierce resistance they made against the Roman invaders.

The latter, when they had made good their footing in any invaded territory, were accustomed to build strong fortresses in order to keep their advantage over the natives.

On the site of the present ruin formerly stood one of these Roman defences, and for centuries after the Romans had retired, it was the residence of one of the German chiefs and his descendants, till at length the family had died out, and the castle had become a scarcely recognisable ruin.

Meanwhile a large portion of Rhineland, in common with the greater part of the rest of Europe, had turned to Christianity, and had come to regard with horror those who still clung to the old religions of Thor and Odin, and of Saturn and Jupiter.

The young Sir Waldemar of Friesdorf, the son of the late baron of an adjacent territory, was a gallant knight and a devout Christian, but poor and landless, and at that time about to seek his fortunes in Constantinople, then the capital of the world, where many young German and British knights used to take service under the laterCæsars. He had a long and perilous journey before him, and expected to meet with both dangers and adventures on the way.

Ere setting out, he went to visit many of his friends and neighbours, and among these a staunch and trusty dependant, called Balther the woodman, who dwelt in a cottage near the river.

It was by Balther that the young knight was told of —

"Strange doings up at the Godesburg, or Gottsburg (God's mountain) yonder."

"What kind of strange doings?" asked Waldemar.

"Yesterday," replied the woodman, "we were surprised to see on the river a boat landing at the village, just below the mountain, and in this boat came a certain Roman chief and prince, or whatever he calls himself, but entirely foreign in garb and appearance.

"He had hired two villagers from the opposite shore to row the boat, and rewarded them liberally.

"He looked something between a soldier and a priest, and his dress blazed with gold and gems ; and he carried with him in the boat many strange ornaments and implements, the like of which none of our neighbours e'er saw."

"Who is he, wherefore has he come?" asked Waldemar, curiously.

"Master Moritz, the magistrate of the village who judges himself to be chief man here, took the liberty of asking that question of the stranger himself, and got his reply, in good German, too.

"'I can easily explain all,' says the foreigner. 'My name is Prince Julian, and I am brother to the Emperor Constantine the Great. By his authority I have come hither to take possession of the dominions of the Godesburg family, the title deeds of which I have also obtained from the last baron of that race, whom I knew in Constantinople. I have thus a double claim, and one I think no one will dispute.'"

"And does this foreign intruder think he will be allowed to rule peaceably over us?" cried Waldemar, indignantly.

"He must be mad if he does," said Balther, "and so Moritz intimated to him.

"But he answered scornfully that he could make good his footing.

"'My lord,' continued Moritz, 'if you design living here, you will, of course, rebuild the castle in splendour suitable to your rank. Thus you will need architects, builders, workmen of all kinds, and I will undertake to procure them.'

"'Friend,' responded Prince Julian, trouble not thyself. I want neither followers nor retainers, builders nor workmen, I have those under me who can serve every purpose I require. All I ask is to remain in peaceable possession of my new domain, free from all intrusive curiosity.'

"He then dismissed the magistrate, and now we are all puzzled to know what these strange things may mean.

"How, if this Prince Julian expects to be Lord of the Rhine, he thinks to support his title without an army of retainers, and how he is to erect his castle without builders, and where he intends to dwell during the months it will take building, are all so many mysteries."

"Mysteries indeed," acquiesced Sir Waldemar. "He came quite alone, thou sayest?"

"Quite alone! Stay, I should not forget that, in the boat with him, was about the loveliest maiden mine eyes ever beheld, but of a very different beauty to our own *frauleiner*, and most outlandish in attire."

"All this is very strange," said the young knight. "I will e'en go and visit this stranger baron, and seek explanations, remarking that I, if anyone, have a right to the lordship of Godesburg."

"Do nought of the kind, *meinherr*," said the woodman, earnestly. "Depend on it, this foreign prince is no ordinary man. He is surely in league with the Evil one."

"And if he be, I am leagued, I trust, with a still greater and holier power," replied the young knight, crossing himself. "I shall fear him not."

"Night is coming on," observed Balther.

"That urges me to speed. I will off to the mountain at once," answered Waldemar.

"Not without me, my lord. I could not be such a dastard as to let thee encounter such peril alone. We will go together, and well armed."

"Be it so," replied Waldemar. "I am anxious to sift this unaccountable matter to the utmost."

The journey to the summit of the mountain was a tedious one, and night had fallen by the time the two adventurers had reached it.

Concealed in a small thicket that adjoined the ruins, they became witnesses of a most singular spectacle.

The bright light that illuminated this scene came from a brazier which had been placed in the central space of the ruins.

Near this, within a magic circle traced on the ground, and surrounded by mathematical instruments and other magic apparatus, stood Prince Julian.

His features, his demeanour, his garb, were those of a wizard of the east.

A little distance off, seated on a stone, was the maiden of whom Balther had spoken.

Though half concealed in a voluminous mantle, her classical beauty was easily perceptible to the young knight, and produced a profound impression upon him.

"My daughter," said the wizard prince, in a deep, melodious voice, "come thou hither, and lend thy aid to complete the charm. The hour has arrived propitious for my work."

She came forward, bringing a basket of herbs and drugs, which one by one she cast into the flame of the brazier.

The fire changed into a succession of brilliant colours, and the fumes from it produced delicious odours.

Then, joining her hands with the wizard's, she knelt with him within the charmed circle, and for a few moments they seemed to pray silently.

Then the necromancer arose, waved his wand, and pronounced this incantation :—

> "Spirits in the air that dwell,
> Hearken to my mystic spell;
> By that power my magic wand
> Gives me o'er the world beyond,
> Come ye forth this midnight drear
> Humbly my commands to hear—
> Promptly my behests to do,
> Whatsoe'er I charge you to.
> Be it night or be it day,
> You must own my regal sway;
> Be it good or be it ill;
> Be it to revive or kill,
> Ye are bound to do my will.
> Then arise in aerial flight,
> Spirits of the murky night."

He waved his wand, keeping time to these chanted verses. When he had reached the conclusion, the mysterious effect had commenced. A strange, rushing sound was heard in the air, then a rumbling like the tramp of troops and the rolling thunder, and a variety of discordant and unearthly voices, forming a most appalling concert.

Suddenly a crowd of strange, weird beings, in all sorts of fantastical costumes, came hovering above the magic flame, and at length descended, formed a ring around the wizard, and bowed to him in respectful homage.

He again raised his wand; they arose, and he then spoke to them some commands in an unknown tongue. Promptly they dispersed, but, without leaving the spot, seemed to busy themselves in preparation for some great work.

Prince Julian, still standing in the magic ring, directed their operations by aid of his wand and his spoken commands, while his daughter sat apart, shrouded in her mantle, and watching him.

The concealed spectators, on whom this strange scene had produced a powerful effect, were unable at first to see to what task the summoned spirits were devoting themselves, but anon came even greater sources of amazement. Promptly the ruins of the old castle were cleared away; huge masses of stone, which a score of mortal workmen could not lift, were easily removed by these supernatural agents, and placed on one side. Soon the summit of the mountain presented the appearance of an even plain; no vestige of the old castle of Godesburg remained, and the spirits rested from their labours.

Their task-master then appeared to be measuring out the ground with his wand, and giving further instructions to one who seemed the principal of these assistant spirits.

In a short time they again set to work. Each took from the heap of huge grey stones, and with them laid the foundation of a new edifice. Scarcely an hour had been yet occupied in this work; in another hour the lower portion of a new structure was completed.

It was on a magnificent scale, and of some foreign order of architecture.

The whole process had been utterly supernatural. Out of a few old stones, the spirits had erected a new and magnificent structure of vast proportions—one that in the ordinary course of building would, even with double the number of workmen, have taken several months to complete.

By the first gleam of dawn, the spectators, who had kept in their concealment in a state of bewilderment and fascination so complete that hours seemed like moments, heard the spirits give a shout of triumph, saw at the same moment Julian's wand fall, and at the signal they again assembled and bowed to him.

He seemed to be praising them as a master would praise his industrious slaves. In a few minutes they again arose, and vanished as mysteriously as they had appeared.

A ray of sunlight from the east showed a vast palace, with towers and turrets, standing high and majestic on the summit of the Godesburg.

"Lydia," said the wizard, turning to her with an expression of pride and delight, which was reflected upon her own countenance, "our work is done. Behold the magic palace!"

It was only at this time that Waldemar and his comrade could shake off the spell of these strange events, and become recalled to real life. They now became aware of the difficulty of leaving the spot without being seen by the wizard. But Waldemar cared not; he was resolved, on the contrary to face and defy him.

Rushing, therefore, forward, he approached that spot where Julian and Lydia were standing.

The magician was evidently taken by surprise and stepping back, exclaimed—

"Ah we are overheard. Who is this?"

"I am Waldemar of Friesdorf, and, though the title has long been in abeyance, I am also the sole remaining descendant of the family of Godesburg, and will dispute the right of a foreign adventurer and sorcerer to usurp their territories."

The dark eye of Julian flashed angrily on the young knight.

"Rash youth! be more cautious in thy speech, for one touch of this rod could wither thee into age and infirmity."

"Vile wizard!" cried Waldemar, "I defy thee and thy hell-gotten power. It were a christian act to slay thee at once."

He proceeded to draw his sword, while Julian, grasping a still deadlier weapon—namely, his magic rod—held it towards Waldemar.

The girl now rose, and rushing towards the wizard, attempted to stay his hand.

"Back, Lydia, I mean not to slay them; that were not half punishment enough. They have witnessed what they should not, and that alone deserves what I intend to give them."

He clapped his hands like an Eastern sultan summoning his slaves, and with the same effect.

A number of unearthly-looking figures rushed suddenly out of the enchanted castle, and, at Julian's command, bore both Waldemar and his comrade away unresistingly, both being, as it were, paralysed by the power of the wizard.

When Waldemar regained full consciousness, he found himself alone in a dark stone cell, apparently underground.

Whether it were night or day was impossible to be distinguished.

The only illumination came from a small lamp suspended from the ceiling, which showed a bare prison-like chamber, with no furniture beyond a bench and a straw pallet.

While Waldemar was looking around, bewildered at these strange surroundings, a further door opened, and the figure of a slender, weird-looking man, in a dress of Eastern fashion, entered, bearing a loaf and a pitcher of water.

These he placed on the bench, and retired without speaking.

In vain the captive asked him what was the place and what would be the duration of his captivity; the attendant merely shook his head and put his fingers to his lips, as much as to express that speech was forbidden.

"I am in the hands of a potent foe," murmured the young knight. "I wonder in what prison they have clapped poor Balther, who has suffered much for his fidelity. My absence will cause some consternation, but his more, as he has a

"'DEMON, I HAVE WITNESSED ALL THAT HAS PASSED?' CRIED THE KNIGHT."

wife and family dependent on him. It is obvious my captivity is intended to be rigid—else why stone walls, dry bread and cold water?"

A slight sound here attracted his attention, and looking, he beheld emerging from some concealed entrance in the stone wall, the figure of Lydia, clad in a rich Byzantine garb—half Roman, half Oriental. She looked, in that dim light, an apparition of more than earthly beauty; but she was undoubtedly mortal, and she carried a steaming dish of some savoury meats, with white bread of the finest quality, a flask of wine, and a plate of luscious fruits.

"Sir knight," she said, in a low, sweet tone, "I visit you here, unknown to anyone else, to do what in my power lies to mitigate the rigour of your captivity. Take these viands, and I warrant you will have no need to complain of your fare."

Waldemar was profuse in his thanks, and also in his questions concerning himself, his companion, and their captor, but on these points the fair visitor did not seem disposed to satisfy him.

The charm of her beauty was great upon him, but not so great as entirely to overwhelm the attractions of the rich repast.

For continuation of this Story see page 221 of our next number

[Continued from page 185.]

THE

FIRE-FIEND OF THE MOUNTAINS

THE fiend thrust him back, and lifting Thyra in his arms, shrieked triumphantly,—

"She is mine, none other hand but mine must touch her."

"Thyra, Thyra!" cried Olaf.

She sprang at last from the fiend's grasp, and with a cry bounded towards the youth.

But the fiend put forth his webbed claw and she recoiled in horror and loathing.

"Oh, save me Olaf,—save me from this fiend," she sobbed, clasping her hands.

"I will," cried Olaf. "Demon, I will wrest her from you. Thyra, I will save you or die."

He turned upon the demon with upraised sword.

The fiend put forth his hand, tore shield and sword from his grasp, and hurled him on the rock at his feet.

Placing his foot upon him, he pinned him there, and laughed his loud discordant laugh.

Then he shouted, and a dozen fiend-like shapes came at his call and bowed before him.

"Bind this presumptuous mortal to the rock," he cried, "with chains forged in our fire, and there let him remain till he is willing to bow to the will of the fire-fiend.'

Thyra shrieked, and buried her face in' her hands.

The demons seized upon Olaf, and in a moment he was chained to the rock on which he lay.

This done they disappeared, and the fiend looking down at Olaf said :

"You see my power, weak mortal, and know the penalty of your boldness, to dwell eternally within my realms my slave."

Then turning to Thyra, he said—

"When your tears are dry I will claim my bride. While water rests on your cheek I am powerless, but when they no longer flow thou art mine."

He gave a bound and disappeared in the fire burning beneath them.

Olaf lay groaning and helpless, chained to the rock.

A sudden thought leaped to his brain.

Had not the fiend himself said water was his greatest foe ? Oh, if he could but reach the stream on one side of him with Thyra, might they not escape ?

Ah! but then those terrible dragons, would they not seize upon them, even if the stream ran into that before the opening of the fire-cave, and if it did not, where would they be then?

He beat his breast in anguish.

His hand rested on the talisman.

His courage rose.

"Spirits of good," he cried, "aid me now."

As he spoke his chains fell from his wrists and rolled on the rocks.

He sprang to his feet.

"Thyra, Thyra!" he cried, reaching forward and clasping the weeping girl in his arms, "Dry your tears, the good spirits will yet aid us, and with courage, faith and hope, we will defeat the demon yet.

"Water alone can conquer the fire-fiend, she moaned, "and his terrible guards. Our way to earth lies only through that fearful fire, and we are lost—lost for ever."

"For ever—for ever," echoed Olaf in despair.

"Hope," whispered a voice in his ear.

"Oh, for a giant's strength to hurl these rocks on which we stand into the burning vortex! Oh, that I could turn this stream into that fiery flood ; but vain the thought !"

"Have faith," whispered the voice.

"I will," he cried stamping his foot furiously upon the rocks.

The huge stones shook as though by an earthquake.

Seizing Thyra round the waist the youth sprang back in alarm. As he did so the rocks parted, the portion on which he had stood rolled over into the fiery mass, and the stream, deprived of its boundary, poured, hissing, roaring, spluttering into the fiery chasm.

Thyra shrieked aloud in her terror.

"Have courage, Thyra, my beautiful," he cried, "the spirits aid us."

On poured the fearful avalanche of waters, cleaving a passage through the centre of the huge fire, throwing the hissing, roaring coals into a high fiery bank on either side.

Steaming, boiling, foaming, and roaring, hissing and spluttering, the waters rose higher and higher.

The dragons left the mouth of the cavern and hurried along the rocks, roaring in rage and terror.

But they dared not cross the stream that separated them from the lovers.

Frightful yells arose behind them.

They turned to see the fire-fiend, with a host of demons, shrieking and yelling on the fiery banks, thrown higher by the rushing stream, and rolling rocks down to dam out the waters.

But they struggled in vain.

Still the waters increased—still they spread and rose—still they hissed and boiled and poured a river through the centre of the fiery pit.

Higher and higher the waters rose till they nearly washed the summit of the rock on which Olaf and Thyra stood.

Then the demon, finding his efforts to dam them up useless, uttered a yell so terrible that it shook the place, his attendants gave vent to frightful cries of despair, and the dragons lashed their tails, beat their wings and snorted in fury.

"Demons of flame and smoke," yelled the Fire-fiend, "mortal hands have broken our power, but we still possess enough for revenge. Seize them and bury them for ever beneath the burning banks."

A yell of fury broke from the demons, and the dragons hissed in triumph.

"We are lost," moaned Thyra, clinging to her lover.

"No, no, my beautiful, we are saved!" cried Olaf, pointing to the water at his feet, on which his shield floated like a boat. "There is our ark of refuge."

He lifted her in his arms as the demons sped towards them, and boldly sprung from the rock on to the floating shield.

The demons reached the spot on which he stood a moment before.

Fearful was the fury of the Fire-fiend.

He uttered yell upon yell.

He beat his bristling breast with his webbed hands, he stamped upon the rocks with his webbed feet, and foamed in fury from his terrible mouth.

The dragons lashed their sides with their wings and tails, and the demons shrieked in chorus, as the shield was borne along the stream between its fiery banks by the force of the rushing waters.

"We shall sink," moaned Thyra, "this frail support will not bear us."

"Have faith in the power of the good," said Olaf.

"Alas, alas, I fear we shall perish," she cried, clinging to her lover.

"Courage, my beautiful, courage and hope," he cried, pressing her yet closer to his heart.

"For thy sake, I will, Olaf, my love, for you possess them all," she said, allowing her lovely head to sink on his bosom.

Frantically the fiends and dragons tore along the fiery bank.

Vain were their efforts to seize upon the lovers.

They dared not enter the water, and the stream was too wide to reach them.

They shook the place with their fearful cries of rage and disappointment, and finally turned in fury upon each other, as they saw their prey gradually escape them, and were lost to their sight in the dense steam of the boiling river.

On—on floated the strange bark with its lover freight, on between the banks of fire, till they emerged on a beautiful lake.

The shores were no longer composed of flame and smoke, but rocks glistening with gold, from which the most lovely verdure sprung and birds of beautiful plumage carolled on the trees.

Above was a clear blue sky.

The atmosphere was soft and balmy, and breezes of delightful freshness fanned their cheeks and brows.

Along this lake they passed till their boat grounded on its sloping bank of golden sands, and then, slinging his shield at his back, Olaf took the hand of Thyra in his own, and led her on.

Gradually the paths narrowed and rocks enclosed them above and on either side, and every moment grew more dark.

But the rays of the star on his forehead lit up the way, and they went clinging to each other, and filled with hope.

A streak of light which gradually grew brighter and brighter assured them that they were approaching the outer world, and hurrying forward they stood at length on the smiling bank of the Rhine.

Before them rode the boat, with Hope at the prow and Faith at the stern.

With a look of joy, Olaf lifted Thyra into it, and with Courage and Love in the centre, the bark glided out into the stream.

Then on either side of the boat rose the fairy forms with their golden harps, and directly before it the lovely golden-draped Lurley issued from the stream.

Olaf bent his head in adoration and gratitude.

"Spirit of good," he said, "Olaf of the Iron Hand is thy slave for ever. Thy sword I lost in fighting in a good cause, thy shield I have retained, and thy talisman I have cherished. I now restore them to you, that other mortals who in pain and adversity my seek your aid, may be blessed with their power as I have been."

The Lurley took the shield, the talisman, and the star, and giving them to her attendant fays, said—

"Mortal, you have done well, and fought the fight bravely. When evil assails you, trust in the Good, and you will conquer. Aided by Faith, Hope, and Love, Courage must ever win the battle. Wrong may flourish, but Right will ever triumph; and as out of evil cometh good, so shall the fires of rage, into which you have turned the waters of peace, become a blessing for ages to come."

She waved her sceptre, and Hope and Faith sprang from the boat into the stream.

"Now farewell," she said, "and when Love is joined to Courage, remember Faith and Hope, and be happy."

She waved her sceptre again, and in an instant every fairy form sank into the water and the bark with the lovers was alone upon the stream.

When Olaf turned his eyes from the waters to his boat and himself, both had changed.

It was his old skin-covered bark, his dress was the same as he had worn when first he landed before Thyra, the sword in his belt was the one the demon had flung into the Rhine, and before him lay his stone-pointed javelin and his wolf-skin shield.

But Thyra was by his side, and he was happy.

They landed at the base of the hill where the ruins of the Castle of Sonnenberg now stand, and took up their abode there and were happy—he strong in his courage and she in her love.

His boldness soon made him many friends, and Olaf and Thyra lived and prospered.

Their children were brave and beautiful, and from Olaf and Thyra descended the bold feudal barons of Sonnenberg.

In the valley of Wiesbaden are the boiling springs which contain medicinal properties, and give health and vigour to the sick and the suffering; and there are yet to be found those among the rude peasantry who attribute their source to the river turned into the burning mountain, and bless the courage, hope and faith of Olaf of the Iron Hand.

END OF THE FIRE-FIEND OF THE MOUNTAINS.

Our next number will contain "The Spectre Knight."

THE BARONS OF OLD OR THE ROBBERS OF THE RHINE

THE SPECTRE KNIGHT.

OR, THE BROTHERS OF HEIMBERG.

AMONGST the numerous structures which the history of the distant past has associated with records of crime, may be mentioned the Castle of Heimberg.

The walls of this ancient building stand on a lofty hill, looking down upon a clustering group of peaceful habitations, upon the left bank of the silver waters of the Rhine.

A shadowy form is still said to haunt its precincts in the dark hours of the night,

"'GO FORWARD,' CRIED THE SPIRIT."

and the cause of the ghostly visitation is explained in the following legend :—

Leopold, Count of Heimberg, was left early in life a widower.

He had married a beautiful and virtuous woman, who two years afterwards was called from this world, leaving behind her as a precious legacy to her husband's care their infant son Julian. The count had been devotedly attached to his wife, and his grief at her loss was bitter and violent.

But as his sorrow gradually diminished so did his love for his son increase.

His affection for the living seemed to absorb his grief for the dead.

Two years passed, and again the count entered upon the married state.

But his second wife in no way resembled his first.

The Countess Drusilla was beautiful, but her beauty was of a less winning and gentle character than that of the former countess, whilst her manner and temper was haughty and imperious.

However, to the count, her husband, she yielded due submission, and he appeared to be satisfied with the partner he had chosen.

Three more years rolled by, when the Crusades began to arouse the chivalry of all Europe.

Amongst those whose bosoms yearned to visit the burning regions of Palestine to assist in resisting the encroachments of the infidel Saracens was Count Leopold of Heimberg.

But he restrained the ardour that burnt in his breast, from the thought that he had no one to whom he could entrust the care of his wife and child during his absence.

About this time, however, his younger brother, Mordred, returned from his travels, and took up his abode at the castle.

It was a dark day for the count when this event occurred ; but he suspected nothing, and received his relative with open arms, and welcomed him with all the warmth of his generous nature.

There was also another who welcomed him somewhat too warmly, and that was the Countess Drusilla ; but she concealed her sentiments, and offered him only such greeting as befitted the brother of her husband.

The arrival of Mordred seemed to afford the Count Leopold the opportunity he desired, and one day he unfolded his plans to him.

"Go, my dear Leopold, by all means," said his brother, " since you deem it your duty. I will undertake to keep the castle,

and watch over the safety of your wife and child, until you return."

These were fair words, which Mordred had no intention of carrying out, for he himself, beguiled by the beauty of Drusilla, and still further stimulated by the love of self-aggrandisement, had been already plotting within himself how he could secure her, and the castle into the bargain.

Leopold, suspecting no shadow of evil, warmly thanked his treacherous brother, and at once proceeded to explain his designs to his wife.

She affected surprise and grief as he spoke of leaving her to go so far away.

"You would leave me, Leopold," she said, mournfully, "and how know I whether you will ever return ?"

"My fate is in Heaven's hands, my beloved," answered her husband ; "but I have no fear. It is a sacred work, which I undertake from a sense of duty ; and those who labour in a righteous cause, may justly expect protection and success."

"True, dearest Leopold," returned the countess ; "but you forget that, during your absence, I shall be left alone with Julian ; who then will protect us ?"

"My brother will remain ; you will be as safe with him as with me," said the count.

"Your brother is not you, love," answered his wife, with a deceitful show of affection.

"True ; but you will feel secure with so near and dear a relative, and I shall leave you more satisfied than I possibly could be were he not here. You will both be vigilantly guarded. Besides, my dearest, consider the importance of the cause I go to assist."

"True, true, my husband," admitted the countess at length. " It is for the honour of Heaven, and in the cause of true religion—I had forgotten that—and being so, I must not allow any selfish feelings of my own to hinder you from embarking in so glorious an enterprize. Go, then, my Leopold, and Heaven in its mercy send you back to me in safety !"

It was a great relief to the count to find his wife so thoroughly impressed with the grandeur of the cause in which he was about to embark, and he at once commenced his preparations for departure.

Having enrolled those of his vassals who were to accompany him, he solemnly consigned his castle and those he loved to the care and knightly honour of his brother.

"Trust me, my dear Leopold," returned Mordred, with equal solemnity, " to guard all that appertains to you, as though it were my own. Do not let a thought of doubt cross your mind or distract your attention from your sacred mission, and depend upon finding all you leave behind you as secure when you return as though you yourself had remained to watch over it."

Confiding in this assurance, and with his breast glowing with religious fervour, the count took an affectionate leave of his wife and child.

Amongst his household was a harmless lad, supposed to be of somewhat weak intellect, named Klotz, who was devotedly attached to the youthful Julian, who was then in his sixth year.

The boy returned his humble friend's affection, and the pair were almost inseparable companions.

"You will look after my son whilst I am away, Klotz, will you not?" said the count to him kindly, at parting.

"That will I, my noble lord," returned the honest lad fervently, with the tears in his eyes, as he kissed his master's hand; "I will lose my life rather than any harm shall come to the dear child."

The Count was gone, and the castle and its inmates remained under the guardianship of Mordred.

Without any apparent reason, from the first moment of the arrival of the latter at Heimberg, there had existed a mutual feeling of suspicion, if not dislike, between him and Klotz.

It is not always easy to account for an antipathy, and it was so in this case.

Klotz suspected Mordred—Mordred disliked Klotz.

Between the child Julian and the Countess Drusilla, too, there was no real affection.

It will be remembered she was not his mother, and though for the sake of appearances she put on a show of maternal regard, it did not deceive the child, who in his turn looked upon her but coldly, whilst he loved the simple Klotz with all his heart.

It was not long after the departure of the count that the lovers—for such were Mordred and Drusilla—made no effort to conceal their attachment.

They rode, walked and hunted together, and it began to be rumoured that the countess appeared far more attached to her husband's brother than she had been to her husband himself.

These rumours reached the ears of Klotz, and he though it only his duty to relate what he had heard.

Finding the countess alone one day, he said respectfully—

"Have I permission to address your ladyship?"

Deceptive herself, Drusilla disliked Klotz for his honesty and truthfulness, but as she had no just cause for showing her dislike, she concealed the contempt she felt for the lad, and enquired abruptly—

"What have you to say?"

Klotz smoothed his fair hair with his hand—a habit he had when he had to communicate anything important, and commenced—

"I have heard something which I think your ladyship ought to know."

"Tell me what it is," said the countess, wondering in her mind what was coming.

"It is what people say, my lady, outside the castle walls," the lad went on.

"And what do they say?" demanded Drusilla, somewhat sternly, as a glimmering of the truth flashed across her.

"They say, my lady, that now your noble husband, the Count Leopold, has gone away to fight the infidels, you are too much abroad in company with his lordship's brother."

Conscience-stricken at the truth of this point-blank remark, the haughty face of the countess flushed crimson.

Klotz observed it, but had the precaution to be looking on the ground by the time the lady fixed her indignant eyes upon him.

"So they say that, do they?" she demanded, fiercely.

"Yes, your ladyship," answered Klotz quietly.

"And what did you reply to such slanderous insinuations?" exclaimed the countess, angrily.

"Nothing, your ladyship."

"Nothing! Did you not at once give the lie to such false words?"

"No, my lady," returned the lad quietly, "it was impossible for me to give the lie to that which those who spoke had seen with their own eyes. All that I could do was to inform your ladyship, and this I have done."

"And so I am to be slandered thus by the tongues of malignant busybodies—who would do far better if they were to mind their own affairs, instead of busying themselves with mine—and you listen to these aspersions, and instead of at once denying them, admit their truth by your silence? 'Tis well, sirrah! your master's brother shall know of this," cried the countess, furiously.

"Pardon me, your ladyship," said Klotz respectfully, "but it seems to me, that the readiest way of quieting people's tongues would be to discontinue the acts that make them talk. I love my master," he continued courageously, "and his honour and yours are dearer to me than aught else in the world. It is this feeling that has emboldened me to speak thus."

The countess, fiercely indignant, could have spurned the daring counsellor from her presence, but she restrained her passion, and contented herself with darting upon him a look of vindictive fury from her flashing eyes.

"Begone, thou insolent knave!" she exclaimed, in a voice tremulous and hoarse with passion, "a pretty companion my lord has chosen for his son, forsooth! one who has the audacity to vilify his wife to her face. Take thyself hence, villain, and learn to guard thy tongue in future, or I'll cut it out. Leave my sight?"

Klotz bowed respectfully and went out.

When the evil passions of a wicked woman are aroused, she becomes the deadliest of foes, and poor Klotz, in the innocent simplicity of his heart, had said that which had converted the Countess Drusilla into his bitterest enemy.

In a fever of wrath she hastened in search of her paramour, whom she found in the gardens of the castle, and to whom she related all that had taken place.

Almost at the same time Julian encountered Klotz, who was calmly retiring from the angry presence of the countess, feeling that he had simply performed his duty, unconscious of the storm that he had raised.

The following colloquy ensued, which showed that even the boy, young as he was, had made his own comments on the conduct of his mother and her *protector*.

"Is that you, Klotz?"

"Yes."

"You have been with the countess, haven't you?"

"I have!"

"She was angry with you I know, because she spoke so loud and harshly."

"I rather fancy she was."

"Why was she angry with you, dear Klotz?" asked the child. "The count never was."

"Because I told her the truth," said the lad, simply.

"What did you tell her?"

This was rather a difficult question to answer to one so young, and Klotz, evading it, replied—

"Only something I heard people say."

"I know what that is," returned Julian, "for I have heard it myself. They say the countess loves my uncle better than she does my father, and I don't like to hear it."

The boy's eyes flashed indignantly.

Klotz made no reply, and Julian asked earnestly.

"Do you think what people say is true, Klotz, dear?"

"Oh no, I think not," returned the lad, in some embarrassment—"I—I hope not."

"So do I," assented the child, "I shouldn't like the countess to love anyone better than my father; no more would he, if he knew it."

"It was only what people thought after all," suggested Klotz, "and you know, dear boy, they do not always think the truth."

"No," returned Julian, thoughtfully, "not always. But I fancy this *is* the truth. They are walking now in the garden, and my uncle's arm is round the waist of the countess. They wouldn't walk so, would they, if they didn't care for one another?"

This was another awkward question, which Klotz did not answer, and the child leading him by the hand, drew him to a window and pointed to a shady pathway, where the treacherous pair stood with their arms encircling one another.

"That is not right!" cried Julian, "and I'll tell them, too!"

Before Klotz could restrain him, the child bounded away and made for the garden.

The countess in the meantime was pouring into the ears of her favourite Mordred the advice she had not long before received from Klotz.

Her kinsman received the news with a grim smile; feeling himself quite master of the position, his features assumed a pleasanter expression, and he said to Drusilla in a low tone—

"Am I assured thou lovest me, dearest?"

"Why dost thou ask? thou knowest full well I do?" she answered, in impassioned tones.

"And thou art prepared to go to any lengths that our union should be secured?"

"I am," replied the guilty woman, vehemently.

"Then a fig for the rumours of idle tongues!" exclaimed Mordred, defiantly, "they can but babble, and will soon grow tired. But, for this presumptuous meddling varlet, let him beware! There are ways of silencing such officious knaves. Do not let his words trouble you."

"But the count, my husband, will return!" exclaimed the countess, apprehensively, "and then these rumours—"

"Tush! tush, love!" interrupted her kinsman, "wait till he *does* return!"

These words were spoken in a tone so full of deadly meaning, that the countess fixed her eyes upon the speaker's face.

Their glances met, and each one knew at once the other's thought.

Drusilla threw her arms around her lover's neck, and buried her face upon his shoulder.

Suddenly the pattering of feet was heard.

Starting from their embrace, they turned, and, somewhat to their confusion, beheld the flushed face of little Julian, looking up at them.

"Well, nephew?" said his uncle, with a smile, which, by an effort, he strove hard to make agreeable, though at the same moment he felt he could have strangled the child, "you run like a greyhound."

"You must not overheat yourself, Julian, dear," joined in the countess, with a face so flushed as to suggest that a similar caution would have applied well to herself.

But the child was not to be turned from his purpose by these remarks.

"Oh, you needn't fancy I didn't see you, because I did," he said, with that blunt candour so peculiar to childhood.

"And what did you see, my pretty boy, eh?" asked his uncle, in a tone in which a sneer was distinctly perceptible.

"Why I saw that your arm was round the countess, and that her arm was round you," returned Julian, boldly, "and I don't think it's right.

Mordred and the countess looked for an instant at the young reprover, and then glanced at each other.

A smile of contempt passed over their features. Then the count said, as he patted his curly head—

"Children should not trouble themselves with matters beyond their years. Go and play, my dear."

Julian withdrew himself from the touch of his uncle's hand, as though an asp had stung him, and replied—

"Everyone knows it, and so shall my father when he comes back, for I'll tell him myself."

And with these words, the child hurried indignantly away.

He was speedily joined by Klotz, who had been concealed in the shrubbery hard by, and heard all that had passed.

"I told them I'd tell the count," said Julian, "and I think they were frightened, too."

Klotz, in spite of the thoughts that oppressed him could not help hugging his pet to his bosom.

"You're a brave darling!" he exclaimed.

"But you mustn't aggravate your uncle and the countess too much. It may be dangerous."

Julian parted his lips defiantly, whilst the heart of the faithful Klotz sank within him.

During his concealment in the shrubbery he had overheard words that imported treachery, and seemed to ring the death knell of the master he loved so truly.

After Julian had left the spot and the guilty pair were once more alone, Drusilla exclaimed venomously through her closed teeth—

"A plague upon the brat! he has learnt his lesson from that idiot Klotz."

"Take no heed, love," whispered Mordred, his brows lowering as he spoke, "there are means of getting rid of gnats that sting us."

○   ○   ○   ○   ○

When the confiding Count Leopold bade farewell to his treacherous brother, the latter fully intended the parting to be eternal.

Amongst the followers of the count was a creature of his own named Thurm, to whom he had entrusted the task of destruction.

If Leopold escaped the javelins and scimitars of the Saracens he was to perish by the hand of treachery.

Already he had been away many long months, fighting bravely against the infidel hosts, and casting ever and anon many a fond and loving remembrance back to his fair castle on the Rhine, and the faithless wife and treacherous brother he loved so truly.

The man whom Mordred had appointed to deliver the count's death-blow was a scowling, repulsive-looking being, who, with all his fierceness of aspect, and the bravado he showed at certain times, had scarcely sufficient courage even to act the part of an assassin.

The Count Leopold, as he was one of the kindest and most generous, was also one of the bravest of men, and Thurm, ruffian as he was in heart, dared not risk the chance of a personal encounter.

The blow might fail—he reflected. In which case he would be at the mercy of his noble antagonist.

But he was to have a large reward for getting rid of the count, and he resolved by some means to obtain it without risk to himself.

Circumstances shortly favoured his design.

Amongst the Saracen prisoners were several fanatical followers of the powerful enthusiast known as the Old Man of the Mountain.

Thurm contrived to communicate with one of these, and by promising him liberty and reward induced him to undertake the task of assassinating the Count Leopold.

To Meer Hafiz the mere act of taking a human life was no more than trampling a summer fly in the dust with his heel.

But to perform the deed successfully required much skill and caution.

It was night, and all was silent in the Christian camp. Meer Hafiz commenced his preparations for the deed by stripping himself entirely naked.

He then anointed his body all over with palm oil, till he was as shiny as an eel, and as slippery.

It was to gain this latter quality these assassins made use of oil.

No human grasp could hold them. They could in an instant, by a movement of their supple limbs, set themselves free from the most powerful grip.

Placing his curved dagger between his teeth, and throwing himself on the ground, along which he crawled like a snake, Meer Hafiz silently but surely approached his victim's tent.

The Count Leopold, disencumbered of his armour, lay extended upon his bed of palm-leaves, musing upon the past and present.

The night was hot and sultry, and he could not sleep, but lay, with half-closed eyes, in a state of dreamy meditation, with his trusty sword close to his side.

Suddenly he fancied he heard the curtain of his tent move, and glancing without turning his head, towards his shield, which reflected on its polished surface the interior of the tent like a mirror, he observed the drapery slightly agitated, but so slightly as hardly to awaken suspicion.

"It is the evening breeze that stirs it," he thought.

This thought had hardly crossed him, when a glittering blade pierced the wall of his tent, and descended rapidly, making a long incision in the canvas.

The next moment the swarthy, naked, glistening body of the enthusiast writhed itself through the aperture.

The count moved not more than to clutch the handle of his sword.

The assassin paused an instant, and then, finding all quiet, crept on his hands and knees towards the bed.

He approached, his eyes gleaming with the excited ferocity of a jaguar, his nostrils dilated, his breath all but suspended.

He reached his victim.

The dagger was transferred from his teeth to his hand, and raised to strike, when suddenly the count rolled himself from the bed.

The weapon buried itself with a crisp sound in the dried palm leaves as Leopold, springing up, brought down his double-edged sword upon the assassin's neck, and his head rolled upon the ground, whilst a torrent of dark blood poured from the quivering trunk.

Thus did the hand of Heaven frustrate the attack of treachery.

Soon after a truce was proclaimed, and the ruffian Thurm had no further opportunity of employing an emissary to perform the work he dared not do himself, whilst the count prepared to depart for his native country.

In the meantime, however, important events, of which the brave Leopold little dreamt, had occurred at the Castle of Heimberg.

From that day when Klotz ventured to speak so boldly to the countess Drusilla, and the youthful Julian also with his childish tongue reproved his uncle and mother-in-law for their licentious behaviour, both had been marked as dangerous objects by the guilty pair, to be got rid of at the earliest possible opportunity.

There was only one point on which they desired to be assured before putting their designs into execution, and that was, whether the Count Leopold had fallen by the assassin's hand.

This information reached them in due time, for Thurm, who was not only a ruffian but a coward, fearing to make a second attempt upon the life of his leader, resolved to secure the reward by declaring he had performed the deed which still remained undone.

He accordingly, as soon as his attempted plan was frustrated, deserted from the count's ranks, and shipping himself on board a homeward-bound vessel, reached Germany before the count, his master, had left the shores of the East.

The departure of one so insignificant as Thurm caused little or no surprise.

He was supposed to have perished, and being of small value as a soldier, was soon forgotten.

It was with mingled feelings of hope and fear Mordred heard of the return of the mercenary ruffian, whom he instantly summoned to his presence.

Thurm, who was sufficently brave when no danger presented itself, entered the presence of his employer boldly, with the confident air of a man who had succeeded in the task he had undertaken.

"Well, Thurm, how dost thou greet me?" eagerly asked Mordred.

"All is well, my lord," returned Thurm.

"You have not failed, then?"

"No, my lord. My dagger's point drank the heart's blood of the count, your brother."

"He is dead, then?" exclaimed the guilty relative, with scarcely concealed exultation.

"He is, my lord. He will no longer be a barrier in your path," replied Thurm.

"But how is it thou hast arrived before the rest?" asked Mordred.

"A truce is concluded," returned the ruffian, "and having done the deed, I thought your lordship would be anxious for the earliest tidings, therefore I embarked for home at once."

This explanation satisfied Thurm's employer.

"You have done well," he said.

"And having accomplished my work, I am entitled to the reward you promised me."

"Undoubtedly, and thou shalt have it," returned Mordred. "Come with me."

Exulting in the success of his double treachery, Thurm followed his master, who led the way to a small chamber in a remote wing of the castle.

Having entered, the latter said to his satellite—

"Close the door."

Thurm pushed it to. The massive portal swung back upon its hinges and closed with a hollow sound that echoed through the vaulted corridors.

Mordred then unlocked a small cupboard in the wall, in which were visible a quantity of money-bags.

The eyes of the mercenary glistened with eager cupidity at the sight, and in imagination he could see the bright golden pieces within.

His hand involuntarily wandered to the hilt of his dagger. How gladly would he by one blow have secured the whole of the treasure had he dared.

But while he thus reflected, Mordred had withdrawn one of the money-bags, and, confronting him, asked—

"What was the sum I promised you for your services?"

"Two hundred crowns, my lord," answered Thurm, "but the job was honestly worth four hundred, it was both difficult and dangerous."

"A bargain is a bargain, sirrah," coldly replied his master, as he commenced counting out the stipulated amount. When he had finished, he pushed the coins towards his myrmidon, who, having col-lected them, thrust them into his pouch, but with an expression of discontent upon his features.

His employer noticed this, but made no reply until he had again tied up the bag and locked it securely in the recess in the wall with the rest.

Then he said to Thurm—

"You are now paid for your services, and may go."

"I can't get out," growled the ruffian sulkily, as he tried the door and found it fast.

"I will open it," said the count, as he approached and laid his hand upon the lock.

Again the desire to assassinate his employer and secure the treasure contained in the chamber seized upon Thurm, as he turned away to allow his employer to open the door.

They were alone.

Before any alarm could be given, he could secure the gold and be far away, he thought.

Desperately clutching his dagger, he was about to spring upon Mordred, when suddenly he uttered a wild yell of agony, and fell writhing on the floor with a stiletto buried in his heart.

His master had anticipated him, and had dealt him his death-blow whilst he was contemplating a similar act. The stroke was well aimed and sure, and the ruffian never spoke more.

A few convulsive quivering struggles, and he lay lifeless and motionless on his face, with the keen steel in his flesh, and the hilt appearing just below his blade-bone.

"Dead men tell no tales, my useful friend," muttered Mordred, as he stood with a grim smile on his lips, looking down upon the corpse.

He then drew out the dagger from the wound, and having emptied his victim's pouch of the two hundred crowns he had given him a few minutes before, he dragged the body aside, and left it to subside into the stony rigidity of death.

As, however, he was quitting the chamber, a shadow flitted across the narrow window, and a head appeared looking in from without.

It was Klotz, who had caught a glimpse of Thurm as he entered the castle gates, and marvelling at his return unaccompanied by his master, had become suspicious.

He accordingly lingered about, intending to waylay the ruffian as he returned from his conference with Mordred, and enquire the cause of his master's absence.

The conclusion of this Story will be given in our next number.

[*Continued from page 201.*]

ALDOBRAND,

THE BANDIT BARON OF RHEINSTEIN.

ENOUGH! Thou shalt not be separated," said the baron; "only 'twill be as well his dogship should learn manners, or we must perforce teach him at the rope's end."

Zelma guaranteed the good behaviour of her favourite, and together they entered the castle gate.

The baron kept his word, and treated his captive well, inasmuch as she had permission to wander to and fro as she listed inside the building, but beyond its portals she was never allowed to stir.

Aldrobrand also pressed her to preside at his table, and on several occasions Zelma had been constrained to be present at his revels, when some thirty or forty lordly guests, as rude and rough as himself, roared and shouted and drank the night away.

On one of these occasions, Ludovic of Saxony, who had returned from Palestine, was amongst the guests.

He at once recognised the fair Jewess, and related to his friend Aldobrand *his own* history of the diamond, and how Eliezer of Munich, Zelma's father, had robbed him of it.

Aldobrand listened to his recital, and inwardly resolved, if ever the old Jew should fall into his clutches, to wrest from him, either by fair means or foul, the precious gem, the description of which had greatly excited his cupidity.

Nor had he long to wait, for a few weeks after Eliezer, who had been saved from the wreck, passed by on his way to his native city.

Of course he was stopped, and the toll demanded, which the old Jew indignantly refused to pay.

He was accordingly seized and carried into the castle, where, until the arrival of the baron, who was away from home, he was confined in one of the gloomy cells.

Here the old man sat bemoaning his hard fate, and calling upon death to release him from his earthly pilgrimage, and restore him to his child.

When the jailor came at night to bring him food, to his great astonishment and joy the hound Gilbert came into the dungeon, and welcomed Eliezer with the most extravagant demonstrations of delight.

From that moment the old man's heart revived.

The sight of the dog seemed to imply that his child still lived.

The next day the baron returned, and hearing that a Hebrew had been captured in his absence, and hoping it might be the man he sought, he went at once to his cell, and roughly interrogated him.

But he gained nothing from the interview.

Not only did Eliezer call himself by an assumed name, but he concealed his diamond in a crevice in the cell, and pleaded utter poverty.

The baron was furious, and hurried from the dungeon, vowing with bitter imprecations the death of the Jew pauper, as he called him.

Zelma heard him storming, and swearing that he would roast his prisoner alive over a slow fire, and willing, if possible, to save her countryman—not knowing him to be her father—she offered to visit and endeavour to persuade him to seek the means of payment.

"I may have more power over him than you have, my lord," she said; "our people are obstinate when threatened by strangers."

"Yes, by Sathanas!" growled the baron, "they are. But go and see what thou canst do, and, as an inducement to him to listen to thee, thou canst tell him that I will scorch the flesh from his bones if he continues obdurate."

Zelma, taking a lamp, and accompanied by the hound Gilbert, went to the dungeon, which, having unlocked, she entered.

The prisoner was asleep, but, as the rays of the light she carried flashed down upon the white head and beard of the venerable Jew, Zelma at once recognised her beloved parent.

With a cry of joy she sank upon her knees, and clasped him lovingly in her arms.

Her caresses aroused Eliezer, who, suddenly disturbed from his slumbers, fancied he gazed upon a vision.

But he was soon agreeably deceived, and with a fervent exclamation of gratitude he warmly embraced his child.

"My beloved, my precious Zelma!" cried the old man, "and art thou too a prisoner in this horrid den?"

"I am a prisoner in the castle, my father, but I am not doomed to inhabit a dark cell. My liberty is permitted me, and I hope to use it to your advantage. 'Tis well you have concealed your name, for Ludovic of Saxony has told the baron the story of the diamond, which he accuses you of stealing from him, and were Aldobrand to know who it is he has seized, it would greatly increase your peril."

"No! no! he knows me not, thank Heaven!" returned Eliezer, "nor must he know me. See, my child! where I have concealed my precious gem, which I would rather die than part with."

The old man picked out a small fragment of stone from the wall, and revealed the cavity wherein the diamond reposed, but which when the piece of stone was replaced was utterly imperceptible.

"He would not find it there!" cried the old man, exultingly, "nor must you ever disclose its hiding-place—no! not even though my life depended on it. Should you do so in order to save your father, his curse will follow you."

"You shall be obeyed," replied Zelma, earnestly, "though I trust there will be no such terrible alternative necessary. I will endeavour to persuade the baron."

Aldobrand frowned at the report given by his fair captive, and seemed harder to persuade than she had expected.

However he took no immediate steps for punishing his prisoner, but contented himself with muttering threats of vengeance.

A few nights after, as the baron sat in his banquet hall, in the midst of a select party of his boon companions, of whom Ludovic of Saxony happened to be one, the conversation turned upon Jews and their wealth.

Ludovic affirmed there was no such thing as a poor Jew.

"By the mass, but there is!" maintained Aldobrand, "I have one at this moment a prisoner, who refuses to pay toll under plea of poverty."

"The son of Judas lies," returned Ludovic, "there is no Jew so poor but he can get money an he chooses. Wert thou to show this penniless Israelite the faggots or the rack, I warrant me he'd find the means of paying to escape the penalty."

"Then by Heaven I'll put it to the proof!" exclaimed the baron, who was flushed with wine. "Ho! Hugo!" he shouted.

Hugo entered.

"Go to the cell this instant, and conduct hither the prisoner Jacob."

The messenger departed, and presently returned ushering in the white-haired old man.

No sooner had he entered than the Count Ludovic recognised him at once.

"He, he!" he laughed ironically, "so this is the poor Jacob, is it? This the needy prisoner who cannot pay toll? Ha, ha! thou art deceived, friend Aldobrand, this man is rich enough to purchase your estate and mine too, I take it!"

"Dost thou say so?" exclaimed Aldobrand, with indignant surprise.

"I do," returned Ludovic, "and whereas he calls himself by the name of Jacob, I declare his name to be Eliezer!"

"Eliezer of Munich?" cried the baron, furiously, starting from his seat.

"The same!" Ludovic replied, "and the richest old Jew in all Germany."

At this moment Zelma, not knowing what had transpired, entered the hall.

Uttering an involuntary cry of alarm, she hastened forward, and father and child stood silently gazing upon each other.

"So, Zelma!" exclaimed the baron, fiercely, "thou hast abused my confidence! thou hast deceived me!"

The maiden dropped her head, and uttered not a word.

But the old Jew drew himself up with dignity.

"And if she hast deceived thee, baron," he replied, "the deceit is justifiable, since it was to save her father."

"Then thou art Eliezer?" cried Aldobrand, eagerly.

"I am!" was the calm reply.

"And what hast thou done with that precious jewel of which thou robb'st me in Palestine?" asked Count Ludovic, sarcastically.

"Of which I robbed thee? Say rather of which thou would'st have robbed me, had not the good King Richard, whom Heaven bless, interposed justly on my behalf," boldly answered Eliezer. "But let me tell thee to thy dismay that that jewel is safe, safe!" cried the old man triumphantly, "where neither thou, nor any here, can ever obtain it!"

Eliezer threw his arms around his daughter's neck, and stood gazing upon the assembled company, with the flash of defiant exultation in his eyes, which not even his critical position could extinguish.

"Dost thou defy me dog?" roared the incensed baron, foaming with rage.

"I do not defy thee, sir baron," returned Eliezer, coolly, "I simply speak the truth, and I again affirm thou shalt neither have my money nor my diamond."

"I will have both, thou dog of a Jew!" shouted Aldobrand. "Mark me, to-morrow, unless thou deliverest the jewel and the money I claim, I will tear thy flesh from off thy bones with red-hot pincers! Not all thy groans or cries for mercy shall avail thee aught, therefore be wise."

With a cry of terror Zelma threw herself on her knees before the enraged noble.

"Mercy, my lord! mercy!" she entreated! "reverse this horrible decree. I will persuade my father to yield to your wishes; only, be merciful!"

"You know the terms!" exclaimed the baron, sternly. Then, stamping his foot, he cried, "Conduct the prisoner to his dungeon!"

Eliezer was removed, and his daughter accompanied the old man to his gloomy abode.

Having arrived there, she entreated him to save his life, and ensure his safety by delivering up the diamond.

"Surely no jewel is so priceless as life!" she argued.

But the old Jew was inexorable.

Suddenly an idea entered his mind.

"This baron shall have the diamond!" he exclaimed.

"Oh, thanks, dear father! a thousand thanks!" cried Zelma, in a tone of delight, as she embraced her parent.

"Do not tell the baron of my determination until to-morrow," said Eliezer.

"I will not," she promised.

"And now, my child," continued the Jew, "since the air of this dungeon is cold, and chills my aged limbs, might I crave the luxury of a brazier of heated charcoal to warm me?"

"Yes, my father," returned Zelma, willingly, "you shall have what you desire."

In a short time, two men, accompanied by the young Jewess, entered the dungeon, bearing a brazier of glowing charcoal.

The old man smiled as he gazed at it, and his daughter, having embraced him, left him lying on his straw pallet.

"Good night, dearest father," she exclaimed, "and to-morrow—"

"The Baron Aldobrand shall have the jewel," said Eliezer.

As soon as all was quiet, the old man rose from his poor couch.

Taking from a pocket in his gaberdine a small crucible, and other materials, he selected a piece of charcoal, which having placed in the iron cup, he added such ingredients as were necessary, and placed it to fuse on the red-hot embers.

Patiently he watched it, occasionally stirring the mixture with a thin glass rod, and now and then adding a little fine sand, muttering as he did so, strange and cabalastic words.

"'Twill do! 'twill do!" he murmured, as he stirred the melted mass incessantly, watching it at the same time with the most scrutinizing eagerness.

The night was far spent, and, as the first indistinct gleam of daybreak glimmered in the east, the old man uttered a cry of joy.

"I have succeeded! I triumph!" he exclaimed exultingly, as he removed the crucible from the fire, and examined its contents by the light of the lamp.

There at the bottom of the small iron vessel lay a dazzlingly brilliant mass of the size and appearance of his diamond.

Taking it out carefully, he placed it on the ground to cool, and this being accomplished, he placed it carefully in a small bag.

Then, having put away the ingredients he had been using, he lay down and slept soundly.

When he awoke, his daughter was at his side.

"What am I to tell the baron, father?" she asked.

"Tell him he shall have the diamond," replied Eliezer.

Zelma departed hopefully, and soon returned to conduct her sire to the presence of the lord of the castle.

"So, Jew!" exclaimed Aldobrand, in a more placable tone than he had used on the preceding night, "I hear thou art grown wise, and hast determined to deliver up the jewel I desire to possess. Is it so?"

"Yes," returned Eliezer, "thou canst have the gem, on one condition."

"It is not for thee to impose conditions!" exclaimed the baron, imperiously; "but what are they?"

"That in consideration of my delivering into your hands the diamond for which you crave, you restore my daughter and myself to liberty."

The baron paused thoughtfully for a moment to consider the terms.

An old decrepit Jew and his daughter balanced against a gem of fabulous worth did not seem much.

He soon decided.

"I consent," he cried. "Give me the diamond, and you can depart as soon as you please."

Eliezer drew from his vest the small bag containing the crystal, and placed it in the baron's hands.

With eager fingers the noble took it from its covering.

It sparkled brilliantly, with all the prismatic hues of the rainbow.

Aldobrand, who was no judge of precious stones, was enchanted.

"Shall I sell, or keep it?" he mused, in an ecstacy.

"'Tis a great sacrifice I make," sighed the Jew, mournfully.

"Consider that gem has saved your life, old man," remarked the baron, consolingly: "for without it, I should most infallibly have burnt you alive."

"Then are we at liberty to depart, my lord?" asked Eliezer, humbly.

"You are!" answered Aldobrand. "Hugo, undo the gates, and let them forth."

At this moment the warder of the castle entered.

"My lord," he said, "it is impossible to leave the castle. The walls are beset with an armed force."

"What force?" shouted the baron indignantly.

"The troops of the Hanse League!" explained Count Ludovic, who came in at the moment. "I have often warned thee of this confederacy, and thou hast often laughed my words to scorn."

"Pshaw! let them come!" cried the baron, "I can hold my own against thrice their number."

"Pardon me, my lord, interposed the warder, their force is great, and they are backed by vessels on the river containing more troops,"

"What care I?" returned Aldobrand, recklessly, "I'll give them a taste of boiling pitch, and send them howling home with singed hides."

At this moment a shout from the invading force rent the air, and a loud clattering was heard at the gates.

"Let them hammer till they are tired," cried the baron. "Order the archers to man the walls."

Taking advantage of the momentary confusion Eliezer and Zelma, with the hound Gilbert by their side, had made their way to the gates.

But, to their dismay, there their progress was stopped.

Again loud shouts were raised by the enemy.

"Bestir thyself, Aldobrand," counselled Ludovic, "or thou wilt have thy castle snatched from under thee!"

"Pshaw! I tell thee this fabric is impregnable; I defy these merchant soldiers. When I appear they will flee like sparrows before the hawk."

Count Ludovic looked doubtingly at his friend as the blows rattled against the gate.

"See!" cried the baron triumphantly, "I have prevailed on that old Jew to disgorge his treasure at last."

"What treasure?" asked the count.

"The diamond, man!" replied Aldobrand.

"The diamond!" echoed the other incredulously.

"Yes, judge for thyself; behold!"

At these words he placed the crystal in the hands of the count. The latter gazed at it a moment and then burst into a laugh.

"Do you call this a diamond?" he said.

"Undoubtedly; I have just received it from the hands of Eliezer.

"From the hands of the devil rather," exclaimed Ludovic scornfully. "This is a mere counterfeit. It is nothing more than glass! See!"

Drawing his dagger the count tapped it sharply with the hilt, and the fictitious diamond was shattered into twenty pieces.

"There is a proof!" he cried, "had that been a diamond it would have resisted blows of twenty times the weight."

With a yell of rage the baron turned to seek the Jew, who had disappeared.

Drawing his sword, with a fearful malediction he hurried into the court-yard.

There he found the Jew and his daughter, whose retreat was effectually cut off.

"Vile dog, you have cheated me!" he raved, "but you shall not escape my vengeance! Let a pile of faggots be prepared here at once!" shouted the incensed noble.

This was accomplished amidst the tumultuous cries of the force without the walls.

"Now bind that Hebrew dog to the stake!" cried Aldobrand.

In vain Zelma pleaded in an agony of terror, in vain Gilbert sprang upon the men.

This order was also obeyed.

"Now bring me a torch!" called out the baron.

A flaming brand was brought and placed in Aldobrand's hand, who was about to fire the pile.

In a frenzy of desperation, Zelma snatched a sword from the hand of one of the soldiers standing by, and struck fiercely at the ruffian noble.

At the same moment the brave dog sprang forward to seize him.

The blow delivered by Zelma, in her wild terror, fell short of him for whom it was intended and its whole force fell upon the gallant hound, whose head was severed from its body.

Zelma uttered a bitter cry of grief, but her sorrow was of short duration. Her blow had dissolved the spell that held her lover captive, and ere the head of the animal had touched the earth there stood by her side not the *hound*, but the *youth*, Gil-bert of Kent, in his own proper person, who, snatching up the sword she had let fall, encircled her with his protecting arm, and stood boldly on his defence.

But, surrounded as they were by foes, the fate of the prisoners seemed inevitable, when at this juncture the castle gates yielded with a loud crash, and the troops of the Hanse League poured in.

A desperate conflict ensued, in which the merchant soldiers, so much despised by the vaunting baron, were completely victorious.

Aldobrand was slain, and the castle he deemed impregnable reduced to a complete wreck.

Eliezer was rescued from his critical position, and returned to his native city, Munich, where he bestowed the hand of his fair child upon the faithful Gilbert.

Thus were the lovers made happy, and thus ends the legend of the BANDIT BARON OF RHEINSTEIN.

END OF ALDOBRAND, THE BANDIT BARON OF RHEINSTEIN.

[Continued from Page 205.]

THE LEGEND OF GODESBURG.

HE commenced upon it with considerable vigour, and she seemed to derive much gratification from watching his solitary meal.

With no other reply to his queries or protestations of gratitude, than a half-Eastern obeisance, the lady then removed the evidences of the meal, and disappeared through an aperture in the wall, and which closed upon her immediately.

Waldemar rushed after her, and examined that portion of the room in order to discover this secret exit, but in vain.

"Such tendance, and from such hands, is almost enough to reconcile me to this fate," he said, "but I marvel who and what she is—she seems scarcely of earth. By Sir Hubert!" he added, testing the stone wall, "this palace, built in a night by a wizard's slaves, as it were out of nothing, is as solid as the castle of my kinsman, Baron Steinberg.

On returning to the middle of the cell prepared for a long and dreary solitude, the knight was surprised to find upon the table several magnificent volumes, or scrolls as books were then—which being unrolled, disclosed certain histories and legends, beautifully written and illuminated.

The scrolls being in his own language, he was soon absorbed in their contents, which told of wars and sieges, ladies' love, and knights' valour, and of everything, it seemed, except what partook in any way of a religous character.

This confirmed Waldemar's belief that Julian was a double-dyed wizard, firmly linked with the Evil One.

Several hours passed in this manner, till the time drew on when his gaoler visited him and brought his prison meal.

The knight had just time to conceal the scrolls in the corner, and he was soon again alone.

What was his surprise to see the table suddenly sink through the floor, carrying with it the viands the gaoler had placed upon it, and come up again with a rich and appetising repast.

When he felt inclined for repose, Waldemar approached his straw oouch, but as he did so it also vanished, and was exchanged for an eastern mattress or divan, of luxurious softness.

Waldemar recognised in this the agency of his beautiful protectress, who had supplied his needs.

A week passed without change.

The visits of Lydia to the prison of the young knight could not but in time produce a feeling akin to love on his part, and sympathy and confidence on her's.

At length she was induced to explain to him her strange position, by recounting her history.

"In telling thee this," she said, "I must reveal a secret at the onset. I am not the daughter of Prince Julian."

"Thank Heaven that this dreadful wizard is not thy parent," ejaculated the young knight.

"Hush! be more cautious of speech," said Lydia. "He was the half-brother and bosom-friend of my father Prince Demetrius of Athens, who, dying, and leaving me an orphan, gave me to his care. I have been entirely brought up and educated by him from childhood. His knowledge is boundless, his skill marvellous; he has all the lore of the East and West, and in all these he has instructed me."

"And thy creed is——"

"That of the ancient Romans, but my father (as I call him) believes in no especial faith, though oft he presides over the mystic ceremonies of the fire-worshippers."

"Great Heavens," exclaimed the young knight, recoiling, and crossing himself, "a Pagan and a sorceress. Maiden, beautiful as thou art, I must shun thee. Thou art lost for ever."

"Hush!" repeated Lydia impressively, "If thou didst know all that I know, thou wouldst judge me less harshly. But for thyself——"

"Ah, kind lady, if thou couldst but aid me to escape, and my good comrade."

"I might do it, but it would be at peril of certain punishment to myself."

"Then I would rather stay here than bring ill npon thee. But why not share my flight, and leave this fearful man?"

"Impossible—chains stronger than those of iron bind me in his power. Think not of it! Leave me to my fate, and I will see what can be done for thee."

"When will it be?" asked Waldemar, eagerly.

"I know not. Perhaps this very night! Be prepared for a summons at any time."

That night he was lying half asleep on the straw pallet, when a slight touch aroused him.

He started up, and saw Lydia, holding a lamp in her hand and pointing in the direction of the secret entrance.

"The hour has come," she said. "I have liberated thy companion, who will await thee beyond the outer walls; hasten, no time is to be lost."

"I implore thee to accompany me," he cried.

"Nay—it cannot be. Think only of thyself. In a few days hence, indeed, when my period of probation is over——" she hesitated.

"What mean you by that?" he asked.

"It is this. For years I have been the confidante and chief assistant of the prince, the high priestess of his mystic rites. My time of probation was agreed to last till I had attained my twentieth year. That will be in a few days, and then I shall be free, either to leave him, or to bind myself to his service for ever, a still more solemn compact."

"And lose thy soul inevitably," cried the young knight. "Lydia, this is a fearful peril that hangs over thee. I cannot consent to escape and leave thee in it. At any risk I will remain, and stand between thee and the fiend."

She was repeating her persuasions, urging him to fly while yet time remained, and he as persistently refusing unless she accompanied him, when the further door opened, and Prince Julian, his face full of rage and indignation, came in, accompanied by one of his attendants.

"It's too late!" cried Lydia, in despair; "the golden opportunity is lost."

"What do you here?" cried Julian sternly, to his niece. "Ah! think not to deceive me; you have played me false—you have liberated the other captive, and you would do the same for this knight."

Waldemar, unarmed as he was, confronted and defied Prince Julian, who, turning upon him with a look of fury, snatched from his attendant his magic rod, and touched the young knight with it.

Waldemar shrank back against the wall powerless.

o   o   o   o   o

The inhabitants of Godesburg and its neighbourhood were all this time agitated by two subjects, the apparition of the suddenly built castle and the mysterious disappearance of the knight and Balther.

At first they thought it a mere *mirage* or delusion, like the Spectre of the Brocken; but having ascertained that the fabric to all appearance was quite solid, they were filled with consternation.

A wizard was in their midst, and, from his demeanour, it evidently appeared that he intended to lord it over them far more tyrannically than any of their native barons.

They, therefore, sent him a somewhat threatening remonstrance, charging him with being accountable for the disappearance of the knight and his companion.

The new Lord of Godesburg sent them a haughty reply, reminding them that to him they owed implicit obedience as their sovereign ruler.

There were strange sights and sounds at night in the wizard's tower, and every evidence that magic rites were being carried on.

This must be put an end to, but as physical force would scarcely avail, spiritual aid had better be tried; and therefore they consulted the good Father Fabian, abbot of the chapel of St. Michael, who promised to call all the powers of the church to dispossess the enchanter.

At this crisis the liberated Balther rejoined his friends, and gave such an account of the power of the wizard, and the sights he had seen in the enchanted castle, as made all marvel, but at the same time distrust their power to cope with so mighty a being.

In accordance with the commands of the wizard prince, Waldemar's captivity was now made stricter than before.

One of the prince's unearthly familiars was appointed to keep perpetual watch over him.

Several more days passed, and Waldemar saw naught of Lydia nor her uncle.

His attempts to bribe his half supernatural jailor to connive at his escape were long unavailing, till at last he expressed a great curiosity to view the interior of the wizard's sanctum, and to witness if possible some magic rites.

The jailor hesitated. This was against Julian's commands, but, at last, reflecting that he might serve his master by bringing the young knight directly under his magic influence, he consented.

That night Waldemar was conducted by a variety of continuous secret passages to an upper ante-chamber and stationed there secretly.

Hidden behind some rich curtains he became providentially the witness of a singular and most important scene.

It was a spacious chamber, fitted up magnificently in the style of some Eastern palace. The walls were hung with heavy tapestry, and the floor and tables covered with instruments of magic.

At the principal table sat Lydia, anxiously studying a parchment scroll, which had been set before her by the wizard, whose tall majestic form was seen further in the background.

His dark eyes gazed as piercingly as if he would read her soul ; his voice had assumed soft persuasive accents.

" Lydia," he said, " thy hesitation cuts me to the heart. I implore thee, desert me not. Recall my many years of care and kindness, my pride and my joy in giving thee knowledge greater than the greatest princess in the world can boast.

" Observe the dial. Midnight has nearly arrived, and with that new day begins thy twentieth year, and our compact must be signed.

" Say, therefore now, once and for ever, what is thy decision."

Lydia's hesitation was painful.

She was distracted by her gratitude and admiration for him on the one hand, and fear for herself and love for Waldemar on the other.

Julian read her thoughts.

" Lydia, it is affection for our Christian captive that has made thee hesitate ; but cast away all such thoughts ; he can never be thine. Thou lookest forward, perchance to a happy life as his bride, but the stars tell a different tale. On the day thou wouldst wed him, thy fate is imminent. Now on the contrary, the signing of this agreement will lift thee to my level, give thee power over spirits of earth and air, make thee more than a queen, to be feared and dreaded by all."

He placed the pen, charged with ink, into her trembling hand.

" See, midnight has come—one little word—thy fate hangs upon it. Sign !"

A chorus, as of unseen spirits, seemed to echo, " Sign."

She took the pen in her hand, hesitated, then nerved herself with a desperate resolution, and put it to the paper.

The wizard, a gleam of exultation lighting up his countenance, stood observing her as breathlessly as did Waldemar in his hiding-place.

The first stroke of the first letter was made.

One moment more, and Lydia's fate would have been fixed, but the young knight, throwing aside the tapestry, burst into the room.

"Hold ! sign not, for the sake of Heaven ! for thou art signing away thy soul ! Demon," he added, stretching forth his hand, " I have witnessed all that has passed, and,

thank God, have been enabled to frustrate thy devilish schemes!"

Julian, taken aback by this unexpected interruption, recoiled and sank into a chair, while the jailor, terrified, fled to the door, and Lydia, screaming, hastily retreated behind the arras.

The shock was but momentary. The girl returned, and Julian sprang to his feet.

Lydia cowered trembling beneath the protecting arm of Waldemar.

Julian's eyes flashed fire ; his expression was literally fiendish.

He looked as if he could have willingly annihilated both.

" Dare ye to brave my power ?" he hissed, rushing towards them.

" Hark !" suddenly exclaimed Lydia.

A trampling up the stairs, mingling with the rolling of the thunder (for a midnight storm had arisen), was heard, and the sound of many voices of triumph.

Ere the wizard could prevent this invasion of his sanctum, the main door was flung open, and the good Abbot of St. Michael, holding aloft an ivory crucifix, followed by three of his attendant priests, similarly armed, dashed into the room. He was accompanied by Balther and a large number of the inhabitants of Godesburg, also armed, but with more purely warlike weapons.

"Praise be to the Virgin, we are not too late !" exclaimed the zealous priest. " We have fought our way with sword and cross to the very centre of this den of sorcery. Wizard prince, thy evil sway is over ; all thy fiendish myrmidons have deserted thee ; they fled before our holy weapons, and surrendered this place to our hands. *Spiritus malificus ! Vade retro me !*"

He held up his crucifix. The wizard held up his magic rod.

Good and evil were face to face.

Julian's was the losing cause, but he would not surrender.

" If I am to perish it shall not be alone !" he cried. " Lydia, traitress ! ingrate ! think not to escape. Come, I claim thee as mine."

" No—great Heaven—no !" She shrank back, clinging to Waldemar. " The compact was not signed."

Here the priest threw himself between the contending parties.

"Maiden, dost thou renounce the sin of Pagan idolatry, and consent to embrace the true cross ?"

" I do—I do !" she answered, literally clasping the feet of his crucifix.

" Then, accursed wizard, all is over with thee."

Julian gazed around in desperation, ground his teeth, and grasped his magic rod with fierce tenacity.

"You all shall share my doom," he shrieked, " and perish in agony, as befits all enemies of Ahriman Zoroaster."

And he lifted his wand with one hand, and holding his other clenched aloft, seemed calling down vengeance upon the heads of his foes.

But the charm was powerless.

The presence of the cross rendered nugatory all his spells.

Yet, fearful of some disaster, they all retreated rapidly, amid the roar of thunder and what seemed the crashing of falling buildings.

The last sound they heard was the despairing cry of Julian, and the next minute they were all on the mountain, out of danger.

A thunderbolt had fallen, and the magic castle was in ruins.

What became of the wizard prince was never known.

Many believed that he was literally a fiend in human form, and therefore could not have been killed in the ruins.

Others supposed that on that fearful night the Evil One had claimed him for his own.

At all events neither he nor the spirits that had served him were ever afterwards seen or heard at Godesburg.

CASTLE OF GODESBURG.

Still the place, where now stood the ruins of the magic castle, was long shunned as a spot of ill omen, until, at last, it was deemed that the evil influences were thoroughly exorcised by Father Fabian, who, having had the ruins cleared away, built a chapel on a portion of the site.

In time this was supplemented by a substantial castle, the lord of which was Sir Waldemar of Friesdorf, acknowledged by all the true heir of Godesburg.

Lydia, thus rescued from the machinations of the wizard and left without a protector, found refuge for a time in the house of Balther, the honest woodman.

She was soon afterwards formally received into the Christian church, and baptised by the name of Agatha.

When Waldemar fulfilled his deferred intention of proceeding to the capital of the Cæsars, the troth had been plighted between them.

He was absent three years, and returned rich enough to build the castle above mentioned, and to settle there with his beloved bride, as a respected and powerful lord of the Rhine.

The castle, in the possession of the family he founded, flourished for many centuries.

END OF THE LEGEND OF GODESBURG.

Our next number will contain " The Moat Tower."

THE BARONS OF OLD OR THE ROBBERS OF THE RHINE

THE MOAT TOWER;

OR, THE WITCH OF THE RHINE.

THE castle of Lahneck occupies a commanding and central position. It stands on a high rock at the junction of the small river Lahn (whence the name of the castle) with the Rhine.

Below the fortress lies the little village of Lower Vahnstein ; opposite on the other side of the Lahn, is the church of St. John, which was also within the domain of the lords of the castle.

The scenery around is beautifully pic-

"THE PORTRAITURE OF A CASTLE ROSE ON THE SURFACE OF THE WATER."

turesque ; a succession of wooded hills, verdant vales, and romantic wilds, in some parts passing into dense forests.

For centuries the castle had remained an utter ruin, till a few years ago it was repaired, and is now occupied by the bailiff of the present owner.

Our story conducts us back nearly four centuries.

At that date—viz., 1485—the ruler of the domain of Lahneck was the Baron Wolfgang Von Neiderlahn, who succeeded to the estate on the early death of his brother.

No human being, much more one of rank and influence, could possibly stand worse in the world's opinion than did the Baron Wolfgang.

Of a fierce and gloomy disposition, he did nothing to win the goodwill of his fellow men, whom he seemed to despise.

In the exercise of his authority he was cruel and merciless, in his demeanour towards all persons proud and uncourteous, a bitter enemy, and a friend to none.

His power made him dreaded as well as hated ; he was suspected of many dark crimes, and excommunicated by the Church for acts of heresy and impiety.

There is no doubt that, powerful as he was, his enemies would somehow have compassed his destruction had he not been protected by the emperor Frederick, who valued his great military services and held him as an important ally.

Among all his foes the deadliest was the Count of Westerwald, the lord of a neighbouring territory.

A fierce feud had long existed between the two families, and neither of the present heads were of a disposition to make reconciliation.

Each tried every means of injuring the other, and their followers never met, purposely or by chance, without a contest of some kind.

The baron had married early in life, when he was certainly a somewhat more attractive and amiable person than latterly, his wife being a scion of the rich and influential Zinzinburg family.

It was generally said that she was illtreated by her stern and imperious husband, and that this ill-treatment shortened her life (if it was not indeed destroyed by even more deadly means), but however this was she died a few years after her marriage, leaving an infant son and daughter.

Soon afterwards the baron succeeded to the title, and his prospects seemed brilliant.

But they were soon overclouded.

His son was killed at the early age of eighteen, in a duel with one of the Wester-wald family, and his daughter, the only remaining heiress, expired a few years subsequently of fever.

Left alone in the world the baron seemed to have become a confirmed misanthrope.

He might have said like Hamlet—

"Man delights me not, nor woman either."

For his friendship was not offered nor sought by any human being.

So the baron shut himself up in his strong fortress, employing his time when not occupied in wars or the chase, with certain studies which it was reported were of a magic and unhallowed character.

The next heir to the title was the youthful count Adrian von Marsburg, son of the baron's younger brother, and who, being left an orphan, was confided to his charge.

Wolfgang did not regard his nephew with much affection, nevertheless, he did his duty by him, so far as to allow him good tutors and governors, whose instructions promised to make him a most accomplished knight.

As time went on, the baron found his enemies, and especially the Westerwalden, grew more and more troublesome and menacing.

They trespassed on his land in their hunting expeditions, seized his cattle, and tried to rouse his tenants and vassals to insubordination.

Often he issued forth with his strong force of personal followers to chastise them, and sometimes succeeded in doing so ; but the Westerwalden had increased their strength of late, and often defied and even defeated him.

Wolfgang came to the conclusion that he must strengthen himself by some suitable alliance.

None seemed more eligible than that with the Lord of Oberlahnstein, whose estates were contiguous to his own, and whose honours would next devolve upon his only daughter, the lady Adelgiza.

The baron determined to form an alliance on behalf of his nephew Adrian, who, being under age, he deemed he could dispose of as he thought fit. Negotiations were therefore opened with the Lord of Oberlahnstein, who received them so far favourably, that Wolfgang thought it time, at least, to acquaint Adrian with his plans.

The young man, therefore, found himself one morning summoned to his uncle's chamber.

"Adrian," said the baron, "it is time you should repay the care I have bestowed upon you, by an act which, while benefitting yourself, will much enhance our family interests."

"What can you mean, my lord?" asked the young heir.

"'Tis plain to you, Adrian, that in our enmity with the Westerwalden and others, fortune hath of late been against us ; we want assistance and support. A matrimonial alliance is the best means of attaining this end—upon a marriage I have therefore decided."

"And who is the fortunate lady?" asked Adrian, misunderstanding him.

"Adelgiza von Oberlahnstein, a dame of judgment and prudence, and far from ill-favoured."

"'Tis well," replied Adrian, " allow me to congratulate your lordship on this auspicious union, though I am at a loss to understand in what manner I can——"

"By the fiend, Adrian, I shall lose patience at thy dulness. Think not 'tis for myself I seek this alliance. No ; there lives no woman on this earth, whom I could even pretend to love—'tis for thee that the marriage is destined."

"For me, my lord? you amaze me! I have no thoughts of such an alliance ; with all gratefulness must decline it."

"How? decline it? By heaven this shall not pass," cried the baron in roused anger. "'Tis mine to command, thine to obey. You must marry Lady Adelgiza !"

"Must, my lord, is not the word to use in this case. No baron, nor prince, nor emperor, however potent, can control the human heart. The state of mine puts the idea of such a marriage out of the question."

"Ah, what means this?" cried the baron, in increased anger, "Adrian, I am accustomed to be obeyed, and will brook no denial. What have I to do with the state of thy heart?"

"I will never sacrifice my happiness to your family interests," replied the young count, firmly, "I would sooner renounce my heirship at once. This union were most unsuitable. The lady is many years older than myself. I have seen her and I know I could never love her, even if——"

"Even if what?" cried the baron, quickly ; "there is something behind all this, something you hesitate to confess—speak out—even if——"

"Even if my heart were not already bestowed," cried Adrian, warmly.

"Ha!" exclaimed the baron, rising from his seat in great perturbation, "this is the cause ; but who is the object of thy choice?"

"That I decline to reveal," answered Adrian.

"Darest thou defy me thus?" said Wolfgang. "Presumptuous boy, her name, her name at once ; speak !"

And in ungovernable fury he clutched the throat of the young man's doublet, and drew his dagger with the other hand.

"Back, uncle, or I too will use weapons ! Seek not to know more ; enough that I can never do as thou desirest."

"Thou shalt, or die," vociferated Wolfgang. "Again I say, tell me the name of her thou lovest."

"Ask me not again, for, great as is thy fury now, it would be increased were I to tell thee."

"Ha ! say'st so ?" then drawing back and regarding him reflectively :—

"Then it is—ah ! I have it—It must be Agatha of Westerwald ?"

"You have driven me to this confession. 'Tis she and none other," answered the young man.

"Ten thousand furies !" thundered the baron, "'tis the daughter of my bitterest enemy, Adrian,—down on thy knees and swear on this book to renounce that attachment."

"I refuse—firmly refuse," responded the young count. "Do as thou wilt, I will never renounce my love. 'Tis true she happens to be the daughter of a hostile house, but what matters that? I love her for herself only. In the feuds and intrigues of the Westerwalden against thee, she has taken no part whatever.

"Hear me, Adrian ," continued his uncle in half suppressed passion. "I give thee one chance. Resign Agatha at once, or thy fate will be fearful."

"Never !" repeated Adrian.

"Then thou diest !" cried the baron, raising his dagger with a horrible expression of countenance ; "but hold, that were too speedy a punishment. What ho ! there !" and he summoned his myrmidons.

"Take him away," thundered the baron, " confine him in the Moat Tower till my further pleasure be known."

Despite Adrian's resistance he was seized by the armed men, and dragged away to punishment.

The Moat Tower was a round tower of the Castle of Lahneck, situated on the side nearest the river Lahn.

Into that river ran the Moat, which had been formed from a small hill-stream.

The waters were deep, and anything but clear, indeed black and turbulent.

The upper part of the Moat Tower projected over the stream in the manner of a bridge, and the gloomy apartment it contained was floored with boards.

Beneath could be heard the rapid gurgling waters, but from the narrow window of the room it was impossible to discern anything.

Cast into this prison, young Adrian became a prey to gloomy reflections.

What a change in his fortunes! and his beloved Agatha was the innocent cause.

Ever since he met her accidentally during a grand hunting party in the forest his heart had been captive.

When he subsequently learned that she was of the hostile family his hopes fell, and he thought it his duty to stifle his newly formed affection.

But love, more potent than family feuds, would not release him from its rosy chain.

Frequently the lovers met, but had contrived to keep their meetings secret from all others, till Adrian was, as we have seen, surprised out of his secret by his uncle's unreasonable demands.

He now bitterly repented having disclosed it, less for his own sake than for Agatha's, who he feared would in some way meet with punishment.

But first he must compass his own escape.

How to do so seemed an unanswerable question.

The high narrow grating precluded all hopes, the door was triply barred and bolted, the jailors not to be bribed even by him.

Retreating into a corner of his gloomy prison, Adrian surveyed the room.

Though he had very seldom entered it before, he was aware that in the flooring a trap-door existed, which, when opened, looked straight down into the dark waters of the moat, like a well.

Through this mode of exit several victims to the cruelty of the present and previous barons of Lahneck, it was reported, had been cast, and drowned in the moat.

Who could tell, thought Adrian, knowing the remorseless character of the baron's fury, that such a fate might not be his own?

A long examination was needed for Adrian to discover the trap-door.

It was so well concealed that its edges a a distance looked merely like the junction of the separate planks.

When he *had* found it there was no ring or other handle by which it could be raised. His only means of lifting it were a small dagger he still retained; by inserting this he slightly loosened the trap-

door, but found it too heavy to be lifted. But by dint of working gradually all round the edges he was at length able to raise it half an inch or so, and though he broke the dagger in the process, succeeded in grasping the door.

By exerting all his strength he cast it back on its hinges, and the aperture was revealed. How cold and dark looked the waters of the gloomy moat!

The distance could not be less than twenty feet, but Adrian resolved to descend. First he took off his gold-studded belt, then his silken sash; these he firmly tied together. Next unfixing a strong nail which had been left in the wall, he drove it through the buckle of the belt into the floor, close by the edge of the opened trap.

Belt and sash together gave him an *impromptu* rope six or seven feet long.

By means of this, Adrian began the descent and proceeded safely till he hung with his feet suspended about three yards from the water.

Suddenly the sash gave way, and he was precipitated into the moat with considerable violence.

He was, however, unhurt, and as soon as he had recovered his breath, he struck out with all the confidence of a vigorous swimmer to reach the opposite shore.

    ✿   ✿   ✿   ✿   ✿

Devoured with rage at the insubordination of his nephew, the baron of Lahneck paced his apartment distractedly.

He had expected from the usually compliant nature of Adrian that there would be no opposition to the proposed alliance, but this attachment to the daughter of the Westerwalden had undone all.

"What course shall I pursue?" he murmured. "I cannot warn the count of this attachment, for we are too deadly foes to communicate with each other; but he ought to know it in order that he might punish his daughter."

Donning his velvet cap, the baron issued forth from his castle, and traversed the Lahn.

He soon reached the small river, at a point where it ran through a narrow valley, between barriers of steep rock.

Here was a beautiful cascade, caused by an abrupt fall of the rocks, the waters dropping into a natural basin.

Arrived at this picturesque spot the baron paused.

A singular change seemed to have come over him. His fierce demeanour left him, his expression became mild and expectant; he looked like one in the presence of some mighty but benignant power.

For continuation of this Story see page 250 *of our next number.*

THE BLACK SENTINEL;

OR, THE SHEPHERD LORD OF THE CASTLE.

STANDING on a pile of black rocks—frowning over the broad rolling river Rhine—the Castle of Furstenberg is one of the most picturesque of all the fortresses which served as homes to the lawless lords of Rhineland.

Around the base of its huge foundations are green forests, with here and there large piles of boulders which appear at one time or another to have been hurled from the summit of the mountain's brow.

Amid the greenery of this lovely woodland, the traveller who raises his voice can bring forth an echo from the rocks that will leap from crag to crag until it appears to mellow down as it nears the margin of the sacred Rhine.

Around the forest glades stretch pleasant meadows where, even to the present day, the shepherd tends his flocks—which seem in fact unchanged since the days when the old knights met in warlike array and fought out their feudal battle under the greenwood tree.

Far away from the upper turrets of the castle yon can see the silvery river winding away into the blue distance between its hundred hills—villages dotting its banks here and there, boats floating lazily on its waters, and now and again the modern steamer puffing its smoky way amid the everlasting grandeur of the old mountains.

From the castle top, moreover, the lords of the country could watch the movements of their enemies, and get ready their forces when there was fear of an invasion of their territory.

Its old walls are now falling to decay, but the old associations will cling round it till the last stone crumbles to the dust.

The legend connected with this place is like all other legends of the Rhine a wild and strange one ; and pointing to the great nodding poplar which stands by the spot where once was the gate, the peasant will shudder at the waving branches, and murmur an invocation to heaven.

For this tree is supposed to be typical of the one who gives the name to our story, and was known as the Black Sentinel.

In a secluded spot in the valley immediately below the castle of Furstenberg, stood the cottage of Wilhelm Arnhold, the shepherd.

Wilhelm was a man well respected by his neighbours ; not only because of his genial disposition and his benevolence, but on account of the superior learning which in his youth he had imbibed.

For the family of Wilhelm Arnhold had not always been shepherds.

Once upon a time, the Arnholds had been lords of Furstenberg ; but tyranny had long since done its work, and usurpers now held sway in the castle.

The present Arnhold had not been reared in the lap of luxury, nor had his father ; but the memory of the past was strong in their minds, and young Wilhelm had striven hard in his scant time in preparation for the day, as he said, " when he should be Lord of Furstenberg."

But time had sped on much in its usual course.

Wilhelm was now forty years of age ; a married man with an only daughter ; and still there were no signs of any improvement in his condition.

Indeed, as his years crept on, his visions grew still more visionary, and a smile would hover over his lips, as he told his child Gertrude that she might one day be Lady of the Castle.

Gertrude Arnhold was at the time our story commences about eighteen years of age, and was unsurpassed throughout the valley for the chaste beauty of her features, and the exquisite moulding of her form.

Her eyes were of a mellow blue, her hair a bright auburn, her lips deliciously red, while the balmy air of Rhineland had given her limbs the roundness and development only obtained by good health.

Many were the young men around who sighed for the love of the shepherd's daughter.

But the peerless beauty would have none of them.

For some reason or another, she held herself aloof from their society, and, except when compelled to do so, would scarcely vouchsafe a smile to any of them.

It was evening now, and Wilhelm Arnhold had returned from his labours and was sitting under his vine-trellised porch.

Inside his wife was preparing the last meal of the day, while Gertrude was sitting listlessly at the window.

Presently she arose, and, without addressing a word either to her father or mother, passed out of the house.

"Gertrude," said Wilhelm, "where are you going?"

"Only for a walk in the wood," replied the young girl, turning with a winning smile.

"Will you not have your supper first, and then I will accompany you?"

"No, father, I am not hungry," she answered hastily, "I will run down to the brookside and gather some wild flowers, and then perhaps I may find an appetite."

And with the words she tripped away as if anxious to escape.

"Well, well," murmured Arnhold, "the girl's a strange one. If I did not know that she was so averse to wooing, I should fancy she was in love, and was about to meet her admirer. But that is not the fact—no—Gertrude would soon tell her father if she had indeed met one to her liking."

Gertrude meanwhile tripped lightly away until, being well out of sight of the cottage, she turned to the right and hurried on towards the castle walls.

Just before reaching this she found herself in a little dell, at the bottom of which was a small pool surrounded by nodding reeds and wild flowers, and shaded by lofty trees.

Here she stopped, glanced quickly round, and, murmuring some words to herself, sank down by the margin of the water.

She looked indeed beautiful as she lay there in an attitude of natural grace.

Her dress, of course, tended to enhance the picturesqueness of the scene, and so thought the one who presently appeared through the avenue which led from the lower wall of the castle.

He was a fine-formed man of middle height, about thirty years of age, with brown curling locks and a handsome face,

upon which, however, were the imprints of a passionate determination.

His eyes flashed as he gazed upon the young maiden, and he hurried forward with an exclamation of pleasure.

Gertrude heard his voice, and springing to her feet, she was in another moment clasped in the arms of the stranger.

"Oh, I am so glad you have come, Rupert," she cried. "I had feared that I should see you no more."

The young Rupert von Etherswold laughed as he seated himself on the greensward, and drew her to his side.

"Why what has put such strange fancies into your head, my darling?" he cried; "am I not always true to my word?"

And then he stopped her answer by imprinting a kiss upon her cherry lips.

But Gertrude was in truth oppressed by a strange presentiment.

"You may laugh at me if you will, Rupert," she said gravely, "but I have had most terrible dreams. And last night most especially I dreamt that you had fled from me, scorned my love, and—"

"Done other impossibilities, my sweet one," exclaimed her lover. "But there—we will not talk of dreams, but of realities. I wish to-night to settle the day and hour which will see you mine. I can bear suspense no longer Gertrude and it remains but for you to say when the blissful day shall be."

A bright blush suffused the maiden's cheek as he spoke these words.

But it was quickly followed by a bright glance of pleasure.

"Ah, Rupert!" she said, "then after all my father's prophecy will become true. As your wife I shall indeed be Lady of Fursternberg."

A cloud crossed the brow of the young Lord of Furstenberg, and though his hands clasped that of the lovely daughter of Wilhelm Arnhold, he spoke not for some moments.

After a moment he pressed her more tightly to his breast, saying—

"Dearest Gertrude, I have a secret to tell you. I would have told you of this before, but I feared to do so. Now that I am assured of your love, however, I feel convinced that you will trust me as I trust you."

The young girl looked up in his face with wonder.

"How gravely you speak," she said. "I hope you have no evil tidings to communicate."

"None, my love," he said; "the truth, however, is that my mother, the countess, has resolved upon my marriage with a young lady of her acquaintance, named Gulda Orpenstein. Nay, do not tremble—hear me out. Well, in an evil hour I consented—hoping that time would wear out her resolve, and that I should be able to evade a union so hateful to me. But, alas! I find that time has only strengthened her resolution. She has this very day insisted on the fulfilment of my obligation, and reminded me that an Etherswold never breaks his oath."

The young girl was deadly white now, and he could feel a shuddering thrill pass through her frame.

"What mean you, Rupert?" she said, "I cannot conceive your meaning."

The young lord of Furstenberg bit his lip.

Knowing how well Gertrude Arnold loved him, he almost feared to tell her.

But he was compelled to do so.

"My meaning is easily arrived at. I must keep my vow; I must marry this woman whom I detest, but I shall never cease to love you. Nay, do not struggle away from me—do not misunderstand me. My mother is in need of a young companion to cheer her lonely hours; you shall be that companion, and thus we shall be constantly together in spite of adverse fortune."

The young maiden sighed heavily.

But she did not, even now, understand the full extent of his treachery,

"Alas!" she cried, "this indeed is evil tidings, whatever you may think of it. I had looked forward to a happy life with you—I had planned such schemes of benevolence—I had thought how I should enrich my dear father and mother. But if my fate be otherwise, I must be content; I will be your sister, since I cannot be your wife."

If Gertrude had seen the smile of contempt which had wreathed itself over the lips of the young knight, she would have sprung from his arms.

But, nestling as she did upon his breast, she saw nothing.

"Why, Gertrude," he said, plucking up courage now to deal the final blow, "you do not take my meaning. Sister! why, do I not love you passionately—love you with all the hot blood of the Etherswolds? No, no—you shall be mine—mine own—in spite of the lady whose hand is forced upon me. You shall be my mother's companion truly; but in the dead of night I will steal to your bower, and——"

He could not complete his sentence, for as he said the words which revealed to the young girl his treachery, she struggled to free herself, and had risen to her feet before he thought of preventing her.

"Why, what is the matter, Gertrude?" he said, springing up to her side. "Have I offended you?"

"Offended me!" cried the maiden, standing with cheeks burning and bosom heaving. "Offended me! Can you ask me the question? Yes, Lord of Furstenberg, you *have* offended me. Let me go, as I never wish to see your face again!"

Had he yielded to his first impulse, he would have uttered a loud curse upon her for her folly; but as it was, his treacherous heart suggested another course.

He flung himself upon his knees, and pressed her hand to his lips.

"Oh, forgive me, Gertrude!" he said. "I might have known that your chaste heart would never yield to such a proposal. Believe me, I am nearly maddened by my condition. More than my own vow keeps me to this alliance—my mother's very honour is concerned. But," he added, springing to his feet, and clasping her round the waist, "I will contrive some scheme to extricate myself from my difficulty. In three evenings from this, meet me again at this spot. Forget all I have said, and be assured that I will never consent to a union which separates me from one who is as pure as she is beautiful. Am I forgiven?"

"Ask me not," she said, in trembling accents; "ask me not. My mind is in a turmoil, and I would rather go home at once."

"But you will meet me in three nights from this, dearest?" he urged; "believe me, I hate myself for what I have said, but my mind has been upset, unhinged by the misfortune threatening. I will never yield you for any woman in this world. You alone are the one I love, and you and no other shall be Lady of Furstenberg. Say, Gertude, you forgive me for trying you, and that you will come to me."

She placed her hand confidently in his, and smiled—though it was a sad and weary smile.

"Yes, Rupert, I forgive you," she said, "but let me go now. I shall be missed at home."

He strained her to him in a passionate embrace, and then, releasing her, watched her as she sped away through the forest glades.

"Ah!" he said, with a laugh, "she is mine now! So the pretty bird does not care for the glitter of our rank, and fancies that an Etherswold would stoop to wed a shepherd's daughter. Ah! ah! we will see in a few days how she will alter her feelings."

With a sad heart Gertrude took her homeward way.

Her mother and father had become anxious, finding that she was gone so long, and were waiting at the door for her.

They saw at once that she had been weeping, and their hearts sank within them at the sight.

"Dear Gertrude, what ails you?" cried her mother, kissing her. "Have you met with any ill-adventure?"

The young girl looked into her mother's face as brightly as she could.

"No," she murmured, "I fell into a doze up at the brookside, and a fit of loneliness and depression fell upon me. I shall be better presently."

Her parents, who loved her as the apple of their eye, led her gently in, and they were presently engaged in discussing the evening meal, of which poor Gertrude partook but sparingly.

Wilhelm Arnold watched her sadly.

He had not given expression to his suspicions, but, nevertheless, he had formed in his mind a plan for ascertaining what really affected his daughter's mind.

The evening of the third day soon came, and at the usual hour Gertrude took her way towards the place of meeting.

There was an indefinable feeling of dread in her heart; an oppression for which she could not account—a suspicion that some evil was hanging over her which she was powerless to avert.

She was, as on the former occasion, the first to reach the rendezvous; and she glanced ever and anon at the castle with eagerness.

Presently, in the twilight, she saw approaching the form of her treacherous lover.

He appeared, from his walk and his manner, to be in high spirits, and he greeted her with a kiss.

"I have good news for you, dearest," he said, as he sat beside her. "I have succeeded in putting off for a long time this hated marriage, and before the date for which it is now fixed I hope to be able to escape it altogether."

Gertrude smiled up into his face.

How could she do other than trust him when he spoke to her in such tones of confident happiness?

"This is indeed good news," she said. "I would rather wait for years, a faithful, trusting maiden, than bring harm to you."

"Ah! but I have not yet told you all," he said. "There is no further need for delay. I have arranged for a private marriage;

this very night the good priest of our castle will make us one. All is prepared; even now he waits in the sacristy; one of my trusty guards and one of my mother's handmaidens will be there to witness the marriage. We need fear no one when we are once wed. Let us go at once."

"No, Rupert," she said, firmly, though her limbs trembled violently; "no, I will not consent to this. I see now my folly in coming here to-night in spite of dire presentiments of evil. I cannot agree to a secret marriage; my father and mother must know all before I yield to such a proposal from you."

A cloud of anger passed over the brow of the young knight.

"This, then, is your pretended love," he said. "I see all plainly; you are ambitious—you desire to be lady of the castle; it is not my affection that you seek."

The young girl looked up pleadingly into his face, while the tears started to her eyes.

"You wrong me, Rupert," she said, "my love for you has never changed; but I cannot and will not consent to a marriage which would break the hearts of both father and mother. Forget not that I am their only child."

The young knight laughed coarsely.

"I will waste no more time," he said, "in arguing with a foolish girl. I have sworn that you shall be mine, and that no father or mother shall stand between you and me."

She struggled violently, as he with an iron grasp upon her wrist endeavoured to drag her towards the castle.

"Malediction!" he muttered. "Here, Carl, Frederick, come hither, quickly!"

In an instant two men leapt from behind the thick brushwood—two uncouth, brutal-looking fellows, dressed in the garb of castle retainers.

The poor girl trembled violently, and turned ghastly pale.

"Oh, Rupert!" she cried, "spare me, spare me! Think of my mother—think of my father. It will break their hearts if I leave them thus. Come to them, ask them for me even in secret, and they will gladly give me to you."

"Cease your idle talk," cried Rupert; "since you scorn my love and refuse thus to trust me, I will make you mine, even against your will. Come, let us hasten."

A wild, piercing scream broke from the lips of the maiden as the men aided their master to drag her from the spot.

Scarcely had it echoed through the forest glades when there was a whizz through the air, and one of the men fell to the earth, pierced by an arrow.

The alarmed knight glanced round him but could see no one.

"This is strange, indeed," he said, "let us hasten from the spot. Ah! whom have we here?—Wilhelm Arnold, by all the furies!"

The young girl uttered a cry of joy.

It was indeed her father who stood before them.

He advanced a few paces—his unerring bow once more ready.

"Count of Furstenberg—scion of a usurping race," he thundered, "release my daughter. I have shown you how truly flies the bolt from the hand of an outraged father. Beware! the blood of the true lords of yonder castle stirs within me. Unhand her quickly, or by the heavens above us I will send an arrow to your heart!"

Only an instant did the young count hesitate.

Suddenly flinging from him the hand of the trembling maiden, he and his retainer dashed forward so quickly that the arrow which sped from the bow missed aim, and the sturdy shepherd had but just time to draw the short sword which he had buckled on for the occasion.

THE CASTLE OF FURSTENBERG.

He found himself now opposed to two by no means unskilful opponents.

Rupert von Etherswold was well known as an expert swordsman, and his retainer, though in no way his equal, had studied under a good master.

Wilhelm, planting his back against a tree, fought for dear life, but a very few minutes had elapsed before he was wounded in more places than one.

The blood flowed copiously, and he was growing faint from the loss of the life stream and from excitement, when whizz came an arrow through the air, and the retainer fell with a groan of agony to the ground.

The hand of Gertrude Arnold had sped it to the heart of her enemy.

The young count gazed at her in fury, a feeling which was not lessened in his breast when he saw her fit another arrow and level it at his heart.

"Back, count Rupert!" she cried, "retire towards your own home, and molest us no longer, or this barb shall find your heart. Away! and let us see your face no more!"

The young knight lowered his weapon.

He saw danger gleaming from the eyes of the young beauty, as she stood there like an amazon of the forest, her form poised in graceful firmness, her attitude one of determination and courage.

For continuation of this Story see page 254 *of our next number.*

[Continued from page 215.]

THE SPECTRE KNIGHT;

OR, THE BROTHERS OF HEIMBERG.

WHILST he waited, he heard the death cry of the murdered wretch, and full of apprehension, had clambered up the ivy-mantled walls to the window of the chamber, within which the deed was committed.

He there beheld his master's kinsman depart, and saw the dead body of Thurm lying dark and ghastly against the oaken panelling, with a stream of blood trickling from it along the floor.

Something of the truth flashed across him, but not all.

He hastily descended, and pondered over what he had seen.

"Why should his lord's brother—as there could be no doubt he had done—seek the life of an obscure individual like Thurm, save to silence his tongue?" was the question his thoughts suggested.

Whilst he meditated, he fancied he heard voices in the chamber where the dead body lay.

He once more ascended as swiftly and quietly as possible, and glancing in at the window, beheld Mordred and the Countess Drusilla gazing at the corpse.

Their backs were turned to him, so they suspected not the presence of a third party.

He heard Mordred say to the countess—

"This deed was necessary, love. The dead cannot bear witness against us. My brother removed, and his assassin silenced for ever, there is now no barrier to our union."

The countess appeared to shudder for a moment, as though the stings of conscience pierced her, and then, throwing her arms around her paramour, replied hurriedly—

"Yes, yes, it was necessary; but let us leave this atmosphere of death, it fills me with horror."

The next moment the room was empty, but from what Klotz had heard he understood perfectly that his master, the brave, kind-hearted Count Leopold, had perished by the hand of an assassin, and that his bones whitened on pagan shores.

His soul was filled with horror, at the same time he felt himself in the most difficult position.

He was cognisant of a crime which he had no power to bring home to the guilty parties.

He was also painfully conscious that those who had contrived the death of the parent would not hesitate to destroy the offspring, and he trembled for his precious charge.

Not without cause, for the schemes of the guilty plotters having been hitherto—as they thought—crowned with success, they resolved to allow nothing to remain to mar their unlawful happiness in the least degree.

In order to have their future prospects perfectly unclouded, there still remained two who must be removed.

These were Julian, the Count Leopold's son and heir, and Klotz, his faithful friend and guardian.

But murder had become now familiar to Mordred and Drusilla, and they no longer shuddered at the crime. All they sought was the opportunity of committing it.

Klotz, who apprehended the danger that lurked unseen, was constantly on his guard, and watched over the fair boy entrusted to his care with untiring vigilance.

Often did he press him to his heart, and, with tears in his eyes, murmur tremulously—

"They have destroyed thy father, poor child, but while I live they shall not harm thee."

He cared not for his own safety, but he longed to preserve his master's son. The poor lad had need of all his caution, for he had to counteract snares that were hidden from view.

He did not mention his fears to Julian, thinking him too young to listen to such a tale of horror; but he kept his eye constantly upon the child, scarcely suffering him to be out of his sight a moment.

Some weeks passed, when Mordred, who had brooded over his dark schemes in the interim, unfolded his plans to the countess.

"It is necessary for our safety that the brat Julian and his staunch protector should both be removed," he said. "Having gone so far as we have, it will not do to retreat. Our own safety requires their destruction."

"Do as you will, my Mordred," exclaimed the infatuated woman ; "I am content."

They then proceeded to arrange their plan of procedure.

"Klotz must be the first victim," suggested Leopold's kinsman ; "half-witted as he is said to be, he is far more cunning and shrewd than those who are in full possession of their senses. Besides, he suspects us. I can see it in his looks and manner."

"Suspects !" echoed the countess, in a tone of alarm ; "then let him die."

"He shall, dearest, before many hours have passed over his head," answered Mordred, assuringly, "fear nothing from him."

"I do not fear," returned the countess, venomously. "I hate him."

All that remained was to determine on the means by which the faithful servitor was to be despatched. At length this was arranged.

The chamber in which Klotz slept was at the end of a long gallery, and adjoining that which the young Julian occupied.

The rooms were so situated that no one could approach the young heir's apartment without first passing the door of that in which his faithful guardian reposed.

On the same basement, but at a considerable distance along the gallery, which wound almost around the entire castle, was the chamber of the countess.

Midway between these apartments was a trap-door in the floor of the gallery, which when open, disclosed a dark, deep, well-like chasm of impenetrable depth.

This well had evidently been sunk for purposes of destruction in case of the attack of an enemy, and opened and closed with a spring.

The lid was so accurately fitted in every way to the adjacent flooring, that, when closed the strictest scrutiny could hardly detect the presence of so terrible a means of death.

But, besides its destructive properties, it had other peculiarities, which proved that it had been prepared as a retreat of safety as well as an abyss of annihilation.

It was supplied with a false floor, which worked in iron grooves, and could be raised or lowered by a chain by the single hand of anyone who might be concealed within.

When, therefore, the floor was up, the interior of the trap afforded a secure retreat, when it was lowered its yawning depths opened upon certain destruction.

This, then, was the snare into which Mordred resolved to lead Klotz.

In order that there might be no failure, he carefully examined the trap, and oiled the machinery, so that it might work with certainty.

He then lowered the false floor until it became totally imperceptible even by the torchlight which he held over the dark depths.

He then closed the lid, and the floor of the gallery presented its usual appearance.

But although Klotz was aware of the existence of the abyss, he was unconscious that it was intended to afford him a grave and would probably have fallen blindfold into the snare, had not chance revealed it to him.

As he was passing along the gallery shortly after his master's brother had completed his operations, his foot slipped, and he fell violently to the ground.

The heaviness of his fall led him to examine the floor of the gallery, and he then discovered various spots of oil close to the trap-door, which had caused his feet to slip from under him.

Being from the circumstances in which he was then placed tremblingly alive to everything that looked suspicious, he reflected for a moment and then, as though a sudden idea had struck him, he drew back a small bolt in the wall and the trap fell.

As he had anticipated, instead of the false floor being a few yards from the top, it was no longer discernible.

Stooping down and grasping the chain, he pulled it with all his force, and gradually the floor rose from out of the darkness to its usual position.

Having done this, he again closed the trapdoor, and departed wondering, but half suspecting who had removed it.

That night, as Klotz, after remaining awake as was his custom long after he had retired to rest, had sunk at length into a troubled sleep, he was roused by a shrill cry.

Starting up, he listened.

It was the voice of the countess.

"Help ! help ! Klotz !" she shrieked.

Hardly knowing what to suspect, he sprang from his bed, and hurried first into the adjoining chamber, where Julian lay.

To his great joy, the boy was sleeping soundly and peacefully.

"He is safe at least, thank Heaven !" he ejaculated, gratefully.

Still the countess continued to cry for help, and presently he heard the voice of Mordred in angry expostulation.

Klotz waited to hear no more, but,

imagining his master's wife was in peril, he flew like lightning along the gallery.

No suspicion of treachery crossed his mind, until, as he trod upon the trap, it opened suddenly beneath his feet, and in an instant he fell forward headlong into the darkness, whilst the lid closed over his head.

The sudden shock for a few moments prevented him from reflection, but that passed, he had reason to congratulate himself on his precaution in having raised the floor of the trap.

It was evident he had fallen into the snare his foes had laid for him.

Presently he heard footsteps approaching.

"If I remain here," he meditated, "I shall be inevitably discovered."

In an instant he grasped the chain and lowered himself into the murky depth below.

The next moment the trap opened, and Mordred, bearing a light, accompanied by Drusilla, looked down.

The former listened intently for a few seconds.

No groans ascended from the chasm. All was still.

"'Tis well!" he said, in a hoarse voice, "he is silenced for ever. There now remains but the boy."

"Leave him to-night," interposed the countess, "there will be no difficulty with him, now this inquisitive Klotz is removed."

Her paramour yielded to her request, and, having closed the trap, the guilty pair retired.

Then Klotz grasping the chain, pulled himself up once more to his former position.

Then feeling for the spring that opened the door of his prison, he pressed it, and the trap fell.

In a moment Klotz had clambered out, and stood once more in safety in the gallery.

An instant only he paused in mute thankfulness, and then he thought of his young charge Julian.

"I must secure his safety," he said to himself, "they shall think we both perished together."

Hurrying to Julian's chamber, he tore off a portion of the night dress of the sleeping child.

With this he hastened back to the trap, and having torn the remnant into jagged shreds, he affixed it to the machinery at a short distance from the brink of the cavity, and then, lowering the false floor once more, he closed the lid and his work was done.

It now became a question, how he was to provide for the safety of the child, orphaned (he believed), by treachery, and henceforth, he felt, dependent upon him for the means of existence.

His mind was soon made up.

He would leave the castle and its murderous inmates that very night.

The forest or the mountain—anywhere was safer for his precious charge than such treacherous precincts.

Accordingly, he aroused Julian, and said to him—

"We are in danger, dear boy. We must go hence."

"I am ready, Klotz," assented the child, unhesitatingly," but you will come too?"

"Yes, darling; nothing shall part us," returned Klotz, affectionately pressing him to his bosom.

"I don't care where I go with you," exclaimed Julian to his humble friend, with equal affection.

"Let us begone at once."

Having dressed his charge—not in his usual garments, which he left in their place by the bedside, but in others which he selected from a press in the room, the latter was about to lead him from the room with childish eagerness, when Klotz restrained him.

"Not that way, my man," said he in a hurried tone, "our enemies are there."

"My uncle and the countess?" remarked the boy, significantly.

"Yes," returned Klotz, "there is our road."

He pointed to the window as he spoke.

"Are we going that way?" asked Julian.

"Yes, dear. You are not afraid?"

"Never, with you," was the truthful answer.

Binding the boy firmly to his back, and bidding him clasp his arms around his neck, the brave Klotz lowered himself by a rope to the ground. Then reascending alone, he closed the window, so that no trace of his flight should be perceptible.

Having rejoined his youthful companion, he pulled the rope after him, which having coiled up, he concealed in a thicket.

Then taking the boy in his arms, he hastily left the spot.

Early the next morning Drusilla hastened to the chamber of her husband's son.

To her surprise the child was missing, but the bed had evidently been slept in, the clothes Julian had worn the day before lay there just as they had been taken off.

"See!" exclaimed Drusilla to Mordred, who followed her in, as she pointed to the vacant bed, "what is the meaning of this?"

"I think I can explain," returned her paramour. "When this brave Klotz answered your appeal for help, he doubtless snatched the boy from his bed, unwilling to leave him behind. Do you not see, love?" he continued, with a gleam of fiendish exultation in his eyes, "the grave that swallowed one victim devoured also the other."

In confirmation of this supposition, when Mordred opened the trap the shreds of the white garment were distinctly visible adhering to the chains.

"Yes! there is no doubt!" exclaimed the countess, as she glanced down the shaft, "they have perished together."

In the dark days of which we write, life was not esteemed the precious thing it is at the present time.

Men and women died, and few questions were asked, and in a few weeks—often sooner—the event was forgotten.

Klotz and the young heir of Heimberg were—so it was reported—devoured by wild beasts in the forest.

Then the Countess Drusilla circulated a report that her husband had died in the Holy Land, and shortly after it was announced that she was about to give her

NIEDER HEIMBACH, AND THE CASTLE OF HEIMBERG.

hand in marriage to her husband's brother, Mordred.

People thought it strange, but as it was no one's business to dispute her right to do as she pleased, the preparations for the wedding went on grandly.

But on the morning when the nuptials were to be solemnised, a messenger riding post haste reined up his steed at the castle gates, and leaving a missive for the countess departed again.

The letter was given to Drusilla, who was just completing the task of adorning herself for the marriage ceremony.

She uttered a cry of horror as she recognised the well-known hand.

It was from her husband, who had written to inform her of his perfect health and safety, and that he should arrive at home that night.

The countess had hardly patience to read it through, and then, with a scared look of horror on her handsome features, she sought her paramour, and held the letter before him.

Mordred's brow darkened, and the colour forsook his cheek as he read the unexpected and unwelcome intelligence.

"That lying hound Thurm deceived me!" he exclaimed, furiously, "but he met the doom he deserved!"

After a few moments he grew calmer.

His self-possession returned as the necessity for decided measures forced itself upon him.

"This letter says Leopold will reach here to-night," he murmured thoughtfully.

"Yes, yes!" returned the guilty countess in an agony of apprehension, "and then all will be discovered. What can be done?"

"There is only one thing," returned Mordred, in a low but decided tone; "he must be intercepted on the road."

"Another murder!" almost gasped Drusilla, with a shudder.

"Aye!" coolly answered Mordred, "another! there is no choice between that and detection. Are we to be separated almost at the altar's foot?" he asked, passionately.

"No! no!" cried the countess, "anything but that."

"Then smoothe your brow, love," said her paramour, persuasively; "let your lips wear their brightest smiles, and the ceremony proceed as though nothing had occurred to damp our joy. Once united, I will plead a summons of importance, and leave our guests, whom you will entertain in my absence. I will place myself at a certain spot by which Leopold must pass, and before morning you may expect me to return with the news that he no longer exists to trouble us."

This atrocious determination being agreed upon, the countess wreathed her face with smiles, and the wedding rites were solemnised that united the guilty pair in the bonds of wedlock.

The nuptials were succeeded by a grand banquet.

The lights flashed from numerous lamps. Youth, beauty, and nobility were gathered round the festive board.

Suddenly a missive was placed in the hands of the bridegroom.

"I am sorry to leave you, friends," he exclaimed, after having hastily perused the epistle; "but I have received a summons I cannot neglect, even on my bridal day. I leave, however, the countess, my wife, to do the honours."

With these words, he left the banquet-hall, and prepared to put his plan in execution.

o   o   o   o   o

In the meantime the good Count Leopold, whose heart warmed at the prospect of again embracing his wife and child, had landed safely on his native shores, and was now, mounted on his staunch war-horse, journeying towards his homestead.

He had never for a moment suspected his attempted assassination as the work of his brother, whom he loved and trusted, and had almost forgotten the circumstance.

If ever he remembered it, it was only with a grateful thanksgiving to Providence that had preserved him.

He rode along unattended, leaving his men to follow him, intent only on arriving at his castle gates, which he expected to do before midnight.

With his mind full of happy thoughts, the brave crusader continued his course, the pathway becoming at every step more familiar.

In course of time the sun set, and darkness covered him.

But before long, the moon rose, and, guided by her light, he held on his way.

As the evening advanced, a thick mist arose, which rendered surrounding objects almost indiscernible.

The count reined in his steed.

"So ho, boy," he exclaimed, cheerily, patting his charger's massive neck. "It will never do, after escaping the burning sun and poisoned arrows of Paynim shores, to break our necks down some yawning precipice on the eve of our arrival home. Methinks a shelter beneath some friendly tree, would be preferable until to-morrow's sun dispels the mist."

Hardly had he uttered these words, when the sound of a horse's footsteps approaching reached his ear.

"Hallo! who goes there?"

"A friend," returned the well-known voice of his brother.

The next moment Mordred rode up.

"Leopold!" he exclaimed cordially, "welcome! welcome!"

"Mordred! brother!" returned the count warmly, as he leant over from the saddle and clasped the traitor to his noble breast.

"This is kind," he continued, "to come to meet me, and, by the Cross, I need a guide through the dense vapour that enshrouds me."

"I know the path, my brother," said Mordred, "We will get onwards."

"With pleasure. For I am right anxious to be at home once more," returned Leopold, "and my wife and child—my Julian—are they well?"

"Quite well!" answered his brother, "and longing anxiously for your presence. It was at the desire of the countess I came forth to meet you."

"Dearest Drusilla!" murmured the count fondly, entirely misinterpreting the anxiety of his wicked wife, "how I long to behold her."

Accordingly the count, paying no heed to the path he was taking, but trusting entirely to his guide, followed unsuspectingly in a sweet dreamy state of blissful and expectant joy.

The way seemed long and tedious, and after some time, the count, arousing from his abstraction, said enquiringly—

"Are we near our journey's end?"

"We shall not be long now," was the answer.

Once more the count subsided into his reverie, when his attention was suddenly attracted by the peculiar sound of his horse's footsteps.

It seemed to him as though the animal was plashing in mud.

"Are we in the right track, Mordred?" he asked.

There was no answer.

The mist had cleared considerably, and the moon casting her light upon surrounding objects, the count for the first time found himself in a wild, weird, gloomy spot, he never recollected to have beheld before.

At a short distance ahead was the dark form of his brother.

The count looked before him.

The surface of the ground appeared damp and moist, and covered with a ghastly green slime, that looked hideous as the moonbeams fell upon it.

His horse's hoofs too seemed to sink down the moment he stood still.

Touching him with his spur, the animal by an effort extricated its feet, and Leopold was soon at the side of his brother.

"Do you know this wild region?" he asked.

"Perfectly well!" was the reply.

"By what name do you call it?" he continued.

"The grave of the elder brother!" shouted Mordred, as he plunged his keen poignard with tremendous force thrice into the count's back, and then drove the weapon into the haunches of the steed he bestrode up to the hilt.

The terrified animal plunged wildly forward, and in a few seconds Mordred's treachery was apparent.

Both horse and rider had sunk so as to be hardly discernible.

Both were now struggling in the depths of a morass, whose fœtid exhalations poisoned the surrounding atmosphere.

The unfortunate nobleman, mortally wounded, still made an ineffectual effort to guide his steed.

But his strength was gone.

Too late, his brother's villany had forced itself upon him.

"Oh! cruel brother!—murderer!" he cried, faintly; "my blood will rest upon the head of you and yours for ever! Henceforth my spectral form shall never cease to haunt you until in this foul swamp that now receives me, you find your own grave!"

    o   o   o   o   o

From that moment a curse seemed to rest upon the castle and all that belonged to the guilty Mordred.

Several children were born to him by the countess, but all died in infancy, as though some invisible hand had withered them.

Then the countess herself slowly pined away, until a mere shadow of her former beauty alone remained.

"The curse!—the curse!" she gasped, in her last moments; "it is that that is destroying me!"

And thus she passed away.

As the night shrouded the earth, Mordred was incessantly haunted by a shadowy spectral form, that tracked his path with noiseless footsteps, and which he too well recognised as the avenging spirit of his murdered brother.

Flee whithersoever he would, the spectre knight haunted him.

But his punishment had yet to come.

One day as he sat solitary and depressed in his chamber, his head bowed upon his breast, his seneschal entered hastily.

"My lord! my lord!" he cried.

"How now?" exclaimed the count, raising his eyes.

"An armed force approaches the castle," replied the seneschal, " and from their appearance their intents are hostile."

"Bar the gates, and man the walls!" cried the count, "I will myself gird on my sword, and go upon the battlements."

Mordred was no coward, and it was almost a relief to him to have something to oppose that wore the shape of flesh and blood.

Hastily putting on his helmet and buckling his sword to his side, he drained a goblet of wine to brace his shattered nerves and prepared to sally forth.

The shouts of those without, mingled with the deep tones of the alarm bell and the cries of those within, summoning their fellows to repel the foe.

"I fear not!" cried the count, as he drew his sword. " I am prepared to fight to the last gasp of breath. Death by an enemy is far preferable to the life I now enjoy."

"*There is no such death for thee, murderer!*" hissed a sepulchral voice in his ear.

Turning with a violent start, he beheld

the shadowy form of his brother at his side.

The sword dropped from his palsied grasp.

"Relentless tormentor! why art thou here?" he gasped.

"To tell the truths thou canst not refuse to hear," returned the spectre.

The count glared wildly upon the apparition, which continued—

"Thou mayest seek death at the sword's point, an thou wilt, and death will fly from thee. No warrior's tomb awaits thee. No crash of trumpets or victorious shouts shall herald thy guilty soul to eternity! But alone in the silent night and with the cry of the gaunt wolf ringing in thine ears, and the pale moon making thy death seem hideous, thou shalt pass away! No soldier's grave for thee, assassin! but such an one as thou gavest thy unhappy brother—a grave in the fœtid swamp, where his bones now lie mouldering."

Again the shouts rang through the air, and the spectre vanished, whilst the count, summoning all his departing strength, hurried on to the battlements.

The herald's trumpet sounded, and the mission of the warlike assembly was declared.

The injunction fell like a thunderclap upon the ears of the usurping count, being an imperative command from the emperor to yield up the castle to Julian, Count of Heimberg, the rightful heir.

Foremost among the warriors was a handsome youth of sixteen, and by his side a determined looking soldier, who never left him.

These were Julian and Klotz, the latter having never rested till he had made known the wrongs of his young master to the potentate, who now undertook to redress them.

"Behold your brother's son!" cried Klotz to the count, "preserved by Heaven to avenge his father's death!"

The wretched, conscience-stricken Mordred uttered not a word, but slunk away, and escaped by the postern entrance, leaving the gates to be battered down at the will of the enemy, which act was quickly accomplished.

No other resistance was offered, and the young count was from that hour reinstated in his ancestral home.

  ✿ ✿ ✿ ✿ ✿

The miserable fratricide wandered away no one knew whither, lurking in the forests and the mountains, and praying for death that seemed to fly from him.

One night a dense mist covered the earth, and the utterly bewildered Mordred had lost all traces of his path.

Suddenly the haunting spectre appeared at his side.

"Avaunt thee, fiend!" shrieked the guilty man.

"Thou hast lost thy path," returned the spirit, mockingly. "I will guide thee; follow me!"

"No! no!" cried Mordred, desperately, "thy path is to perdition!"

"Follow," repeated the spectre, waving its shadowy arm,; "See! there is a steed ready for thee!"

"I will not mount it!" returned the haunted wretch, in an agony of horror.

"Thou canst not avoid it! Mount," continued the spectre, imperatively.

Unwilling to obey, but unable to resist, Mordred sprang on the back of the horse, which bore him rapidly onwards.

Soon it stopped motionless.

"Where am I?" shrieked the victim.

"Behold!" cried the spectre knight.

In an instant the mist was gone, and they stood on the edge of the fatal morass, into whose dark jaws he had once lured his brother.

"Go forward!" cried the spirit, extending its misty arm.

In vain the doomed horseman dragged at the bridle, the horse went on.

In vain he shrieked.

Still the steed continued his course.

Suddenly it began to sink.

"Mercy! mercy!" raved the count, despairingly.

"Yes," laughed the shadow, "such mercy as thou hast shown thy brother shall be shown to thee."

Deeper and deeper sank the horse, until the filthy slime reached the lips of the victim.

"Mercy! mercy! mer——"

The last word died away upon the breeze, and the voice was heard no more.

The murderer had perished in the swamp.

Thus ends the legend; but to this day the Spectre Knight is said to wander at nightfall, and lure to danger and death those who are daring or foolhardy enough to follow him.

END OF THE SPECTRE KNIGHT; OR THE BROTHERS OF HEIMBURG.

Our next number will contain "The Spectre Hand."

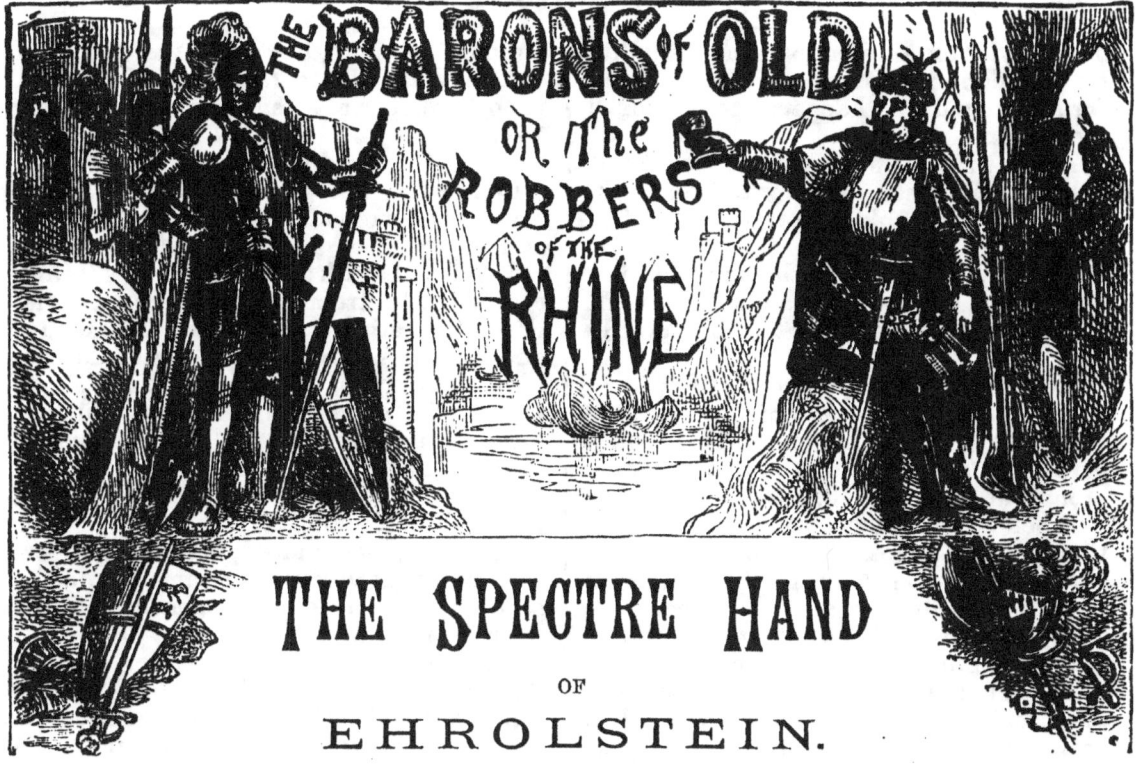

THE SPECTRE HAND

OF

EHROLSTEIN.

ERHAPS no castle on the borders of the Rhine can boast of a more terrible and yet romantic legend than the castle of Sonneck, of which we give an illustration.

The Counts of Ehrolstein, who for centuries were the lords of the castle and the feudal masters of the surrounding land, were indeed well called robber chiefs; for the want of riches lost by gaming and

THE CASTLE OF SONNECK.

other styles of dissipation was made up by plundering any one of the wealthy farmers round who happened to be worth the robbing.

At the time our story commences Count Otho von Ehrolstein was lord of Sonneck.

This grizzled old chieftain was full sixty years of age.

He had been perhaps the most daring depredator of his time, and had scars all over his brown face to tell of deadly fights.

He had robbed more, had fought more duels, and done more mischief to his enemies than, perhaps, any chief of his family before, and yet among the peasantry around he was not unbeloved.

When he and his two sons rode out on their three black chargers they were bowed to reverentially by the villagers and the herdsmen, who called them the Iron Pillars and whispered strange things about the prowess of their family.

The countess had at this period been dead for some years; her married life had been one of great unhappiness, and she had died, it was said, through sorrow at the stern cruelty of her husband.

Count Otho von Ehrolstein had married her against her will; she had, in fact, been forced to his arms by the cruel order of her parents, and she had never known what happiness was.

She had but two children, sons, as different from one another in disposition as two people could possibly be.

The one had black eyes and black hair like his father's, and inherited with his looks his stern uncompromising disposition.

The other was fair, even to effeminancy, with light wavy curls, blue eyes, and a voice which though it could be firm and manly could yet be so modulated as to appear like that of a woman.

With Count Otho, the dark Reinhardt was the favourite.

The mother idolised the soft-featured Robert, who was, as it were, a reflection of her own beauty; and thus, without meaning it, both parents combined to create an ill-feeling between the two brothers.

On her death-bed Gertrude von Ehrolstein entreated them to be friends.

But in vain!

In their outward dealings with one another they were certainly all that could be wished, but in their inmost hearts there existed a dislike and distrust.

It was a dark and yet a warm and genial night.

The moon had hidden herself more than usually early, and a thick atmosphere dimmed the stars, but still over the blue waters of the Rhine there blew a gentle wind, which only tenderly caressed the trees.

Count Otho had that evening been unusually silent and gloomy, and even to his favourite son had scarcely vouchsafed a civil reply.

Reinhardt, with a frown on his brow, retired early from the banqueting table, where his father had sat stern and moody, and Robert, seeing that his brother desired no further companionship that night, bade him a quiet good-night, and passed up the old winding staircase to the summit of the battlements.

Here lately he had been very fond of wandering at nightfall.

It was a place, indeed, where a most astoundingly beautiful panorama could be seen when the bright moon shed its lustre over Rhineland.

But on this night the weather was so dark and gloomy that the sentinel at the top of the staircase which led out upon the ramparts spoke of his wanderings in wonder.

"Good-night, Master Robert," he said, "it is dark for your promenade, methinks."

Robert von Ehrolstein laughed lightly.

"But I care not if it be dark or light," cried he, "I go out there, good Gruff, to think, so that if it were bright moonlight I should be distracted."

"But there are many perilous places here, Master Robert," said Gruff, "where the masonry has fallen away, or where it has been crumbled in war; and a chance step might lead to a heavy fall, and the death of one whom we all wish may one day be Lord of Sonneck."

"Hush, good Gruff," returned Robert, "you must not speak in that strain to me, as I should be accused (were my brother to hear you) of being an aider and abettor in your treasonable thoughts against him. But there is no reason for any gloomy feelings this night—is there?"

The man shuddered.

"Alas! good Master Robert," he said, "there is reason, though perhaps, you may not believe me. Last night when I ascended these steps for my last turn on the ramparts, I saw in the distance hovering over the Rhine the Spectre Hand of Ehrolstein!"

"The Spectre Hand!" said Robert; "What child's tale do you tell me? Have you some fresh folly to narrate—some fresh bugbear?"

"None, Master Robert," returned Gruff, "you must have heard in your childhood of the Spectre Hand?"

" Methinks," said Robert, " I do remember now something of the kind. But tell me, what is it ?"

" The legend is simple," replied the sentinel, pleased at the chance thus afforded him of chattering.

" Three hundred years ago the Lord of Sonneck murdered his brother, and flung him into the moat. It was never discovered till at a banquet given in honour of his marriage a luminous appearance was seen floating about the room, which, presently assuming the shape of a hand, pointed towards the place where the murdered body was concealed. Paralysed with fear as was the lord of Sonneck, he yet had courage enough to conceal his emotion ; and if others had not been deeply impressed by the visitation he would no doubt have eluded punishment. As it was the guests departed soon, and with cold glances, which told him that evil was brewing.

" All went well for about a month after the wedding.

" At the end of this time the Lord of Sonneck was summoned before the tribunal, and going thither, ignorant entirely of the cause of the call, he was tried for his life for the murder of his brother.

" The wedding guests had not been idle.

" Impressed by the warning which had come to them from the other world they had sought out the terrible secret and found it.

" There in the spot towards which the luminous hand had pointed, they discovered the body of the murdered man, with a piece of his brother's coat clutched in his hand.

" This they compared with a coat produced, and it is said that at the moment it was shown to the council, the luminous hand once more made its appearance, pointing to the murderer.

" At this the Lord of Sonneck was so horrified, so overwhelmed with terror and contrition, that he confessed all ; and drawing his sword, then and there plunged it into his heart.

" The widow of the murderer only lived to give birth to a son ; and at her death, the luminous hand—which is called the Spectre Hand of Ehrolstein—floated over the castle. It has done," added the sentinel, " whenever any of the family was about to die."

Robert laughed, though his merriment was scarcely real, for a strange presentiment of coming evil seemed suddenly to overcome him.

" Ah !" he said, " this is some foolish old woman's tale. I fear not, good Gruff ; but since you have warned me, I will beware of the danger of the castle ramparts. I shall not be long, but see that no one interferes with my movements."

He then turned away, and passed slowly to a point on the battlements which was the most remote from the point where Gruff, the sentinel, stood on guard.

He turned round presently to see if anyone observed him ; and then, seeing all was quiet, he advanced towards a portion of the wall where the ramparts were broken.

Here he stooped down, and groping about in the darkness, produced, after a time, a thick rope, knotted here and there, so as to give a firm hold.

This he unwound and threw over the battlements, and then, having pulled hard at the iron rings to which it was fastened, he swung himself off, and descended quickly through mid-air.

On reaching the ground he fixed the end of the rope to a staple in the wall, so that it should not sway, and then he hurried away through the dark wood.

About a mile he walked—rapidly and eagerly, as if in expectation of meeting someone upon seeing whom his heart was set—and at length reaching the bank of the broad flowing Rhine, he called at a kind of cottage, or rather hut, of wood, where a light glimmered in a window.

Knocking here, he was at once admitted into a little room by an old woman bent with age.

Near the fire there sat a young girl, whose golden hair flowed almost to her waist, while her dark eyes contrasted beautifully with the creamy whiteness of her skin.

She sprang up as he entered, and in an instant was folded in his arms.

" Dearest Robert," she cried, while tears started to her eyes, " I had feared you would not come."

" Why, my love ?" said he, as he fondly kissed her, " Why should I not come to-night as well as at all other times ?"

" I have had a dream—a terrible dream, my love, which makes me fear for your safety," she answered. " Do you still attempt that awful passage of the rope ?"

" It is safe enough, Sophia," he said, " I have tried it too often to be afraid. My eye is clear, my grasp secure, and no one knows but myself the means of descent. But tell me what was your dream."

The old woman who had let them into the little hut, had now bolted the door, and retired prudently into an inner chamber ; and the lovers sat down on two rude chairs by the fire, where Sophia could rest her head upon Robert's breast.

"It was a strange and terrible dream, as I have said," she answered. "I dreamed that I was awakened from a slumber beneath a huge tree in the wood yonder, that when I roused myself I saw a large luminous hand hovering—but you start, love. What ails you?"

The young lord of Sonneck did truly start.

Was Gruff's warning, after all, coming true?

"I started at hearing so strange and supernatural a story," cried he; "but proceed, tell me all."

"This hand," continued Sophia, pressing close to her lover's breast, as if for protection, "beckoned me to follow it, and, overwhelmed by presentiment of evil, and led on, in fact, by some influence with which I could not battle, I followed. It preceded me until, reaching a deep dell in the forest, it pointed to a thick clump of undergrowth, beneath which I saw your bleeding, murdered body. I could bear no more, and with a cry I awoke. Oh, Heaven grant, dear Robert, that nothing is about to befall thee."

A gloom fell over the heart of young Robert of Ehrolstein; but he roused himself as well as he could, in order not to alarm the fair creature by his side.

"These things must not be dwelt on, dear Sophia," he said. "Dreams are after all the result of temporary illness. There is no one who has an interest in destroying me. I have no rival."

He fancied that a slight shudder passed through the frame of the young girl as he said these words, but attributing it merely to her former fears, he used all his endeavours to comfort her by turning her thoughts into another channel.

By every endearment he endeavoured to rouse her from her forethought of sorrow.

But in vain.

The young girl clasped him to her bosom, and responded warmly to his fervent embraces; but her heart was cold with fear, and when the time came for parting she wept bitter tears.

But all such happiness must have an end.

The moment had arrived; and as he held her in a last embrace, she murmured—

"Come to me here again to-morrow night. I shall never rest until I know that you reached home safe this night. Pray enter by the door and avoid that dangerous rope."

"It would excite suspicion," said Robert; "believe me, all is well. Is the ferryman ready?"

"Yes," said Sophia, "fear not for me. All is well."

One more kiss—one more pressure to the heart—and then the lovers parted.

Robert had scarcely gone, and Sophia was engaged in wrapping herself up as if for a journey, when a knock came at the door, and a man entered. It was Reinhardt von Ehrolstein.

His face, although he glanced in admiration at the form and features of Sophia, showed that his heart was full of anger.

"Sophia von Olden," he said, "I have come for my answer—by your own wish I come, and I find you in the arms of my brother."

The young girl trembled as she spoke.

Already the dark cloud seemed increasing—the dark hour of evil drawing nigh.

"I am aware that I told you to come to-night for my answer," she, replied summoning up all her courage; "but why?—only because by no other means could I succeed in ridding myself of your presence. You know well that I can only succeed in making my appearance on this side of the river by stealth; you know the feud that exists between my father and yours, and I know well what his answer would be, were I to consent to become your wife; you know also what your father would say. I wish this to be our last interview."

"This is a strange answer, truly," replied Reinhardt; "if your father and my father would refuse to accede to our union, would they be any way more friendly to one between you and my brother?"

"You mistake entirely, Reinhardt von Ehrolstein," she replied. "You, the heir of Sonneck, you will follow in the footsteps of your ancestors and appear as they have done before the world. You would not give up all honour and riches and renown to wed one who would have to fly from her home, as would your brother. He at any rate is willing to fly with me to distant parts."

He approached her more closely and took her hand in his; while his eyes glowed with an admiration and a passion which he did not attempt to conceal.

"And if for your sake, dearest Sophia," he said, "if for your sake I am willing to discard all pomps and riches, to yield up to my brother the possession of my castle and my titles, what then? Will you consent to be mine, and fly with me?"

He spoke hurriedly and eagerly, and she saw at once that she must no longer dissemble.

"Reinhardt von Ehrolstein," she said, "I have tried, feebly and with little effect, it seems, to induce you to cease your importunities. As I have failed, I must say once for all that I can never be your wife. I do not love you, and if you were to offer your whole possessions—even your life, I should never think differently of you. My heart is your brother's, and I shall be his bride or the bride of death."

The brow of Reinhardt von Ehrolstein grew dark as night.

He grasped her wrist as in a vice.

"Never, I swear it, never shall you become the bride of my brother Robert," he cried; "No, not though you die with sorrow through losing him. I love you, Sophia von Olden, and mine shall you be or no man's!"

He turned as he spoke, almost flinging her hand from him, and passed out into the dark night. The young girl shuddered as he went from the cottage.

"My dream is beginning to be worked out," she murmured. "I tremble to think of the hatred that exists between the brothers. I shall oppose no further dear Robert's wish for an immediate marriage. Once away from this place, I·fear no longer."

At this moment an old but sturdy Rhine boatman made his appearance at the door, and after bidding adieu to the old woman, she followed him from the cottage and was soon gliding across the broad but gently flowing river.

   *   *   *   *   *

When Robert quitted the cottage, and made his way to the castle, he found that the rope by which he left and entered the tower was still in its place.

Feeling confident, therefore, that nothing was suspected, he quickly ascended, and had just reached the battlements and stowed away the rope when one brilliant sheet of lightning illumined the sky just over the castle.

Not the slighest sound of thunder followed it.

All that was heard was one shrill yell of terror proceeding from the spot where the sentinel stood.

Robert, suspecting he knew not what, rushed hastily towards the door.

The mystery was soon explained, for there crouched up behind the door, with his face covered with his hands as if to shut out some terrible sight, was Gruff.

"Why, what's the matter, man?" cried Robert, shaking him by the shoulders, "Have you seen a ghost?"

The sentinel on hearing his young master's voice, glanced round first to see if all was right, and staggered to his feet.

"A ghost, dear Master Robert," he cried, "that's exactly what I have seen. The Spectre Hand hovered over the castle for an instant—a huge hand, which spread right across the sky. Ah, you will see; something terrible is about to happen."

"Tut, man," said Robert, though he felt a shudder pass through his frame, "it was no spectre hand, it was merely a sheet of summer lightning."

"No, no, it was no lightning," said Gruff, "there was no thunder; and I saw the shape of the hand as plainly as I see yours. Mark me, Master Robert, evil is coming to you and yours, and I pray heaven it will not be you that will suffer."

"Thank you, good Gruff," said Robert, "keep good watch, and depend upon it I shall keep my wits about me."

And then, with an uneasiness for which he could not account, he passed towards his own chamber.

Not a sound disturbed the castle that night.

But in the morning there was a terrible uproar, the great bell was set clanging, the retainers went hurrying to and fro.

For the Lord Otho of Sonneck had been found murdered in his bed, with a dagger still sticking in his heart.

Great was the consternation, and great, too, the pretended grief of Reinhardt, who was thus made suddenly and unexpectedly lord of the castle, and great that of Robert, too, who, though he could not be said to love the stern father who had never been kind to him, was horrified at his fate, and at the thought that he had died without giving him his blessing.

Wonder was in the breasts of all.

Who could be the murderer?

It could not be said he had no enemies, for, indeed, he had no friends; but no one was known to have passed through the gates.

It must, therefore be someone within the castle—one of the dependents.

Yet, which one?

To his own men the old count was a kind, though stern master; for it was one of his principles that it was unsafe to trust yourself in battle with men of whose friendship you did not feel yourself assured.

The strictest investigation was instituted, but without avail; and after the old count had been buried with much pomp and ceremony, Reinhardt was acknowledged lord of the castle; and matters sped on in much their accustomed course.

About four months fled by.

During this time Robert had learned from the lips of Sophia von Olden what he had not known before, and that was that he had a rival in his own brother; and now that a decent time had expired, and his father was no longer there to oppose him, he resolved to marry his betrothed and take her home to his own wing of the castle.

The young girl, in spite of the knowledge how she would infuriate her parents, acceded willingly to the proposition, for the attèntions of Reinhardt had become too incessant, and he had even gone so far as to speak to her father and suggest an end of the old and useless feud by the union of the two houses.

It was a dark night towards the close of autumn when Robert and Sophia were standing at the door of the cottage where they had always met for their love-meetings.

"What will your brother say to our living within the very same walls as himself, when he professes for me such a mad passion?"

"He will learn to be patient," said Robert, "he dares not interfere with me. The eastern wing of the castle is mine by right, and I will defy him to interfere with me. The retainers are greater friends to me than they are to him."

At this instant, as they stood looking towards the castle, there was a sudden flaming in the sky, and with a shudder Robert observed that, as on the night of his father's murder, the light was followed by no thunder, and that it had not the usual appearance of lightning, but was more like an irregular mass of blood-red cloud, which appeared for an instant only —just above the old battlements.

Sophia saw the luminous appearance, and feeling a shudder pass through her lover's frame, she said—

"What is it, dear Robert? It seemed to me just like a hand."

"It was a flash of lightning, my dearest," he said, unwilling to frighten her by a detail of the strange story of his house, "ye must hurry home out of the way of the storm. Ah! let us hope that in three nights from this you will be my wife, and we shall then have no more partings."

The embrace which followed this was more earnest and impassioned than, perhaps, any that had ever passed between them.

The young maiden set down his fervour to his increasing love; but the truth was that the apparition of the Spectre Hand had so impressed him as to make him fear lest that meeting should be the last.

As he returned home lightning began to play vividly, and the thunder rolled like the discharges of distant artillery.

The rush of rain and wind through the forest trees sounded like voices calling to him to keep back and beware of his return to the castle.

When he had reached the castle walls he took extra precautions before ascending the rope, for he naturally imagined he might lose his hold when some of the more vivid flashes of lightning darted across the heavens.

He had ascended nearly to the ramparts when he saw or fancied he saw a man leaning over the battlements.

"Who is there?" he cried.

No answer was returned.

"It is merely a fancy," thought he, and he began once more to hurry up.

But, after a moment, a voice above spoke; he was now very close to the ramparts, and he plainly saw a figure bending towards the rope.

"Hold!" said the voice in low tones— yet tones which he fancied he knew well.

"Let me first ascend the ramparts," replied Robert, haughtily. "I am Robert von Ehrolstein, and have a right to enter the castle."

"In that case," said the voice, drily, "it is a wonder that you do not enter by the gate instead of by stealth."

He knew the speaker now; it was his brother Reinhardt.

A cold sweat broke over his body, though his courage did not desert him.

He saw now that his brother intended to murder him.

"Let me pass," he said, "let us have no trifling here. I cannot hold on much longer."

"Robert," said his brother, in low but determined accents, "your last hour has come. I will no longer be thwarted. You are striving to take from me the one upon whom my heart is set; and I have sworn that you shall die this night."

The proud spirit of the young Ehrolstein would not permit him to ask for mercy.

"Let me ascend in peace, or I will shriek for help," he cried.

"Shriek!" said his brother, "none will hear you!"

Then in the semi-darkness there was the flash of a long knife, and as Robert fell with a wild cry Reinhardt dashed back, and hid himself behind the rampart wall.

He had scarcely time to do so when Gruff, alarmed by the cry, came dashing out from his post.

But he searched in vain.

All was still; and he hurried back after a rapid investigation.

He, too, had seen the Spectre Hand, and regarded this wild cry as only a further warning of danger.

When all was once more safe Reinhardt rose from his place of concealment, and made his way into the castle by a secret way known only to himself.

"Now," he said, "all obstacles are removed. No longer need I fear that my brother and the lovely Sophia will seek in flight to evade me. No; at this castle ere a month is gone there shall be a grand wedding, and Sophia shall be my bride."

On the next morning he remained in his chamber, expecting every moment to hear that the mangled body of his brother had been discovered on the rocks below.

But as noon approached, and no tidings of evil were brought to him, he emerged from his solitude and approached the terrace whence he could view the spot where he expected to see the mangled remains.

But there was nothing there; no sign of the events of the preceding night, but a rope lying on the rocks

Reinhardt, at the head of a select body of followers, scoured the country far and wide in search of him, but in vain; and at length all appeared convinced that he had for some reason fled from the home of his ancestors for ever.

The only one of them who suspected anything was Gruff, the sentinel.

But he knew well that Robert had never returned from his usual walk on the ramparts; and the vision of the Spectre Hand and the wild cry which had disturbed the stillness of the quiet night made him suspect foul play.

Reinhardt, therefore, lost no time in repairing with a numerous retinue to the home of the Baron von Olden—a haughty noble who lived on the opposite bank of the Rhine, and who, as we have seen, had been at deadly enmity with the Count Otho von Ehrolstein.

The wonder of the old feudal lord may be imagined when he heard that the new lord of Sonneck desired to see him.

He received Reinhardt with the greatest courtesy, and the latter pretended the utmost respect and deference.

"He was sorry," he said, "that for so long a time there had been an enmity existing between the two houses; he knew," he said, "that his own father was to blame, and that now the son desired to atone for the past, and restore the friendship which had once been so good to both families."

The old baron listened in wonder.

But the manner in which the young Count of Ehrolstein spoke could not but convince him of his sincerity, and he desired him at once to state his reasons for wishing to join the families in amity once more, and also what he proposed to do to carry out his design.

"For," said he, "there are wrongs in the past which cannot be washed out—save in blood!"

Reinhardt shook his head deprecatingly.

"Nay," he said, "nay, hear me out, before you speak so harshly. I propose to restore to you the lands which formerly belonged to your house; but I propose still more to join the houses by means of my marriage with your lovely daughter Sophia, whose charms have lit in my heart a fire which can only be quenched by our union."

"Sophia!" cried the baron in astonishment, "Where can ye have seen one who has ever been kept in strict seclusion?"

"I can explain all!" said Reinhardt.

He then skilfully told his tale, speaking of an accidental meeting with Sophia in the forest when she was visiting his brother by stealth; of his sudden admiration of her, of his repeated meetings after this, and lastly of his brother's mysterious disappearance.

"Until then," said the wily villain, "I did not wish to betray to you the fact of their love; nor did I deem it right to pursue my suit. But now all is changed; he has fled from his home; he has deserted her; and I am at liberty to declare to you my love, and my eager wish to make her my bride."

"You astound me," said the old baron, "I should never have believed that my daughter could have so disgraced my name. But pray let us go more into your plan, and I shall oppose no foolish scruples to your union."

Long and earnestly the old baron and the false-hearted Count of Sonneck talked over their scheme.

At last, as the shades of evening began to close over the landscape, they clasped hands over the bargain.

Then the baron arose.

"I will go and fetch my daughter," he said, "she shall know at once that she is to be the means of uniting once more our two houses. In one week she shall be your bride."

In a few moments, Sophia, pale and shrinking with fear, stood in the presence of her father and her suitor.

"Sophia," said her father, sternly, not even deigning to notice her alarm, "I have discovered your deceit; I have been told of your secret meetings with Robert von Ehrolstein. I am resolved to make it no longer possible for you to disgrace my name. In seven days from this you become the wife of Count Reinhardt."

She flung herself at her father's feet.

"Oh, no—no!" she cried, "no, no—save me from such a terrible fate as that."

"Bear her away—since this is her mood," said her father to the attendants; "bear her away. Remember," he added, in a voice of stern anger, "in one week you will be Countess von Ehrolstein."

   *   *   *   *   *

From the moment that the stern old baron issued his decree, there were grand preparations at the old castle.

The marriage was to take place at night-time, and as the hour approached, and no help came, or seemed to promise to come, the courage which supported Sophia gave way, and she trembled at her fate.

Reinhardt, on the other hand, was in high and even exuberant spirits when he was preparing for his voyage across the river, but he did not enter the house of the Von Olden in like condition.

For—just as he was emerging from his castle gates, a flash of light illumined the sky overhead, and a loud voice cried—

"Beware this night of the Spectre Hand of Ehrolstein."

He shuddered; but affecting to take no notice, he hurried on towards the spot of embarkation, and was soon on his way towards the place of his marriage with the betrothed and deserted bride of Robert.

The spot chosen for the ceremony was an underground chapel, which, even when lit by the countless lights, seemed dull and gloomy; and as the company called together to witness the marriage defiled down the old stone staircases, the echoes of the place sent a shuddering chill to the heart, which was not relieved by the dim religious light shed on the sacred edifice.

The young count of Sonneck and his retainers first ranged themselves near the altar.

Then after a short delay came the bride—in bridal attire, truly, but pale and even ghastly, and so overcome, that she had to be supported on either side by her bridesmaids.

As she neared the altar, she cast an imploring glance at her father, and at her intended husband.

But it was in vain.

She saw on the face of one nothing but stern determination; on the face of the other triumphant passion.

And so—just as a blinding flash of lightning flashed across the great window, and a terrific roll of thunder shook the old building—the ill-omened ceremony began.

Scarcely, however, had the first words been pronounced, when a tremendous gust of wind burst into the chapel, extinguishing every light, and filling the spectators with dread.

Then, as the trembling bride stood transfixed with terror, there was another flash of lightning, and a gleaming hand and arm was seen hovering over the head of Sophia, and pointing towards Reinhardt.

"Hold, Reinhardt von Ehrolstein," cried a loud voice, which rang clearly over the rolling of the thunder, "murderer of your father and of your brother, this maiden shall not be your bride. Heaven has interposed to prevent this crime. Down, down on your knees before the altar of that Deity you have offended, and confess aloud those sins!"

The guilty wretch, struck with remorse and overwhelmed by superstitious awe, staggered a moment, and then fell heavily against the altar rails.

The priest hurried forward to raise his head, and as the wondering and trembling guests crowded round, he murmured out a confession of his crimes.

It was indeed he who had slain his father in the dead of night, and cut the rope which had served as a mode of egress and ingress to his brother.

As he was thus confessing, lights were brought in, and the wondering crowd saw standing by the altar a tall figure clad in complete armour.

"Who are you," exclaimed the baron, "that thus stands here uninvited?"

"The one who has, by the aid of Heaven, saved your daughter from becoming an assassin's bride. It was my mailed hand glistening in the lightning that appeared to his guilty conscience to be the Spectre Hand of Ehrolstein," replied the stranger, and then, flinging up his visor, he added—

"See, Reinhardt, murderer of our father, see your brother whom you intended to murder. Saved by a miracle, I fled away, resolved at the right moment to extort from you a confession of your sins. See

—see, he cannot bear to look upon me—he faints—he dies—Heaven forgive him!"

It was true.

The shock was too great, and the guilty count, after one convulsive movement, fell back dead, into the arms of his attendants.

"And now, Baron von Olden," said Robert, "now that I am (by the death of that murderer, whom I scorn to call brother) the rightful Lord of Sonneck, I beg of you to let the marriage ceremony proceed. I confirm all the promises made to you by my brother, who only made them to gain his ends. Let peace be between our houses from the hour that the Lady Sophia becomes wife of the Count von Ehrolstein."

The baron extended his hand and grasped that of the mailed knight.

"Ye have saved my daughter and my house from disgrace," he said, " and Sophia is yours. Take her, and may Heaven bless your union."

So the wedding proceeded, and the lovely Sophia became the bride of her lover, who, after a right royal banquet, conducted her to his own castle.

From that time the Baron von Olden was a better and wiser man, and the two families became the best and truest friends ; but yet on the occasion of any death in the house it is said that there still hovers over the old ramparts of the castle—

THE SPECTRE HAND OF EHROLSTEIN.

END OF THE SPECTRE HAND OF EHROLSTEIN.

[Continued from page 228.]

THE MOAT TOWER;
OR, THE WITCH OF THE RHINE.

STOOPING down, he took some of the water in his hand, and flung it in the air, speaking some words in an unknown tongue.

"Beautiful spirit!" he then murmured, "queen of the powers of the air, guardian angel of my race, appear, appear!"

Now, it is well known that at this period there existed in the districts of the Rhine two sorts of supernatural beings.

One were beneficent and beautiful, and ever assisted by their magic power the cause of the luckless and oppressed.

The others, sometimes equally fair to look upon, were of fierce and malignant character, prone to greet the calamities of human beings with diabolical triumphs, and even assist in their discomfiture.

Some of each sort allied themselves to the fortunes of noble families, which they could make or mar according to their natures, but they seldom appeared unbidden, unless as a portent of some great impending misfortune.

Anyone who summoned the darker spirits without knowing the necessary spell, or who shrank from them when they did appear, paid with his life the penalty of his rashness.

The baron knew this, but for himself he feared not, for he was of iron will, skilled in magic lore, and the spirit which he evoked was of the beneficent order.

No sooner was the spell spoken than the waters of the stream became greatly troubled.

It was as if some tempest had disturbed their hitherto placid current.

The ascending spray, white as snow, began to assume the form of humanity, but misty and undefined.

Gradually it grew in distinctness, till its aspect became that of a female figure, clothed in white; still her face was invisible, it was hidden as if by a veil.

"Lovely spirit of the waters," repeated the baron, "I summon thee to do thee homage, and ask thy counsel in a matter wherein I am sore pressed."

And the proud baron bowed before his unearthly visitant.

A shrill peal of laughter made him start, and looking up he perceived that the spirit was unveiled, and that the countenance though of great beauty, bore an expression of guile and malice.

"Who art thou?" cried Wolfgang, recoiling. "Thee I summoned not. It is my tutelar spirit, the Good Fairy of the Lahn, that I wish to behold."

"And I am in her place," responded the aerial being; "thinkest thou that a man of crime, and impiety, and evil passion, like thyself, must have an angel to watch over him and give him counsel? Not so; the good spirit hath abandoned thee, and I, who belong to the so-called evil ones, am the only one who will arise at thy bidding."

"False spirit!" cried the baron; "I know thee now. Thou art the beautiful though evil Witch of the Rhine; but think not I shall heed thy unwelcome portents."

"Thou *must* heed them," responded the witch, "for all that I say shall come to pass. Wouldst thou know the fortunes of thy house? Is there naught I can tell thee? Wouldst thou care to know, for instance, what thy nephew is doing at this present moment?"

"I care not what he is doing; but I know where he is."

"Ha ha! thou deceivest thyself," answered the spirit. "Behold."

She waved her hand. Instantly the troubled waters smoothed, the cascade fell slowly, and the portraiture of a castle rose on the surface of the water. Wolfgang recognised the architecture at once; it was the residence of the Count of Westerwalden.

"Look at those two figures on the turret," said the witch. "Who are they?"

The baron muttered an oath.

They were the figures of his disobedient nephew and of the beautiful Agatha, engaged in a love-interview.

"Nay; there thou liest, malignant spirit!" cried Wolfgang. "My nephew is fast immured in the Moat Tower of mine own castle."

"Whence he escaped two hours since," said the witch; "and is now at the castle of thy enemy, holding sweet converse with his forbidden love, unknown to her parents. Return home and see if thou canst find thy prisoner."

The baron answered with another imprecation, and grasped the handle of his dagger.

"Wouldst see more?" asked the taunting spirit.

"I would," returned the baron. "What will be the final fate of our family?"

"See," answered the witch, and the vision of the castle of Westerwalden changed into that of Lahneck. But not in its present aspect; it was crowded with fighting men, surrounded by armed enemies, and in a state of desperate siege.

"Thou art beleaguered," continued the phantom, "and all thy enemies are upon thee. See, they force the outer barriers—they rush in—they hold hand-to-hand conflict with thy men. See that mailed warrior fighting so desperately on the Moat Tower; at length he is overcome—falls into the moat and sinks for ever. That figure——"

"Is myself," said the baron, with a shudder.

"E'en so; and look further to what thy iniquity leads. There is another figure in the moat—that of a young and beautiful woman. 'Tis Agatha. She is dead, and thou wert the cause. Behold, too, the semblance of thy nephew—he weeps over his beloved thus taken from him."

The scene changed once more; the vision now represented was the chapel of St. John; a reverend abbot was holding divine service with his monks. The pale features of the holy father seemed strangely familiar to the baron.

"Twenty years have passed, and that is thy nephew," exclaimed the witch. "In despair he has taken to the cloister, and the estate and title of Lahneck passes to a stranger."

"Confusion! I will look no more, lying spirit," cried the baron. "Hence! I scorn thy predictions, they will never come to pass."

A mocking fiendish laugh was all the reply vouchsafed by the Witch of the Rhine, who thereupon faded away into mist, and the echo of that laugh still rang in the baron's ears after she was invisible.

Wolfgang retreated from the lone and peaceful valley, which had now become to him a place of terror, and though he tried to scorn the witch's predictions, his heart whispered that they would come true.

Arriving at home he found the first circumstance of them realised—

Adrian had escaped! How, was easily proved by the open trap-door and the remains of the belt and scarf. The castle was searched in vain, the bird had effectually flown.

The baron seemed to have formed some desperate design. Secretly donning a suit of chain-mail under his dress, muffling himself in his cloak, and taking with him a good provision of weapons, he issued forth.

Close behind him came Eborhard, his esquire, a man as fierce and unscrupulous as himself.

By the aid of a small boat they made their way down the Lahn, towards the castle of Westerwald, and sure enough Wolfgang saw two figures on one of the towers, whom he recognised as Adrian and Agatha.

Taking up his stand behind a tree, the baron watched the side postern of the castle.

Eborhard was concealed close by.

Ere long their vigilance was rewarded.

Adrian, accompanied by Agatha, issued forth from the postern.

"Night comes on apace, dearest," said the young knight, tenderly, "there could not be a better time for our escape. Not far hence is a ferry, by which we can cross the Rhine, and we shall be far enough away ere thy absence is discovered."

Wolfgang now perceived that this was to be an elopement, and his rage at the discovery was unbounded. He not only determined to prevent it, but to punish Adrian for his presumption.

Rushing forth, dagger in hand, he came behind the lovers, and ere Adrian could look round, inflicted a deep wound in his shoulder. The young man uttered one faint groan, and fell senseless and bleeding on the grass. Agatha screamed in mortal terror, and swooned away beside the body of her lover.

Thinking them dead, the baron was somewhat dismayed; he feared he had gone too far. His relief at finding that both still lived was great, but he was at a loss what to do.

Eborhard suggested they should both be at once conveyed to the castle of Lahneck promptly; therefore the baron and his myrmidon bore them to the river bank, deposited them in the boat, and rowed off with all their speed.

It was quite dark by the time the baron and Eborhard returned to the castle of Lahneck. As they entered by the private postern, the two prisoners (as we may call them) whom they had brought were easily conveyed in secret to the baron's apartments.

Adrian, still insensible, was speedily deposited in his own room.

Agatha, slowly recovering consciousness under remedial measures, found herself in the presence of the dreaded baron. At first she was totally bewildered, but soon remembering what had passed, became agitated with anxiety for her lover, and asked in heartrending eagerness—

"Where is Adrian ; is he slain ?"

"Adrian is nought to thee, so think of him no more," answered the baron sternly. "Girl, you are my prisoner, nor shall you have liberty till you swear to obey my commands. Renounce thy attachment to my nephew."

He thought, by his fierce and imperious tone, he could easily frighten a timid girl into compliance ; but Agatha of Wester-wald had the proud spirit of her race, and it was now aroused.

"Never, tyrant lord ! I will die first," she responded, fearlessly. "Do thy worst ; thou hast it in thy power to kill me ; but all thy cruelty, all thy tortures, can never crush my affection for Adrian."

"Then I will try other means, better than death, better than torture," he said, fiercely. "What, ho ! Eborhard ; bring Karl hither and Father Anselmus."

Karl was a rough, ill-favoured peasant, a scullion in the baron's kitchen.

Father Anselmus was the castle chap-

THE CASTLE OF LAHNECK.

lain, and to say the truth, no credit to the holy vocation he professed.

They were soon in the presence of their lord.

"Thou seest this man ?" said the baron, pointing to Karl, "I intend that the ceremony of marriage between him and thee shall at once take place, in my presence and Eborhard's. This will effectually prevent Adrian's ever being thine, and, moreover, lower thy pride."

"Great Heaven ! wouldst thou by compulsion wed me to a low-born menial ? Base baron, such a union would be fraudulent, and could never be binding."

"Nevertheless, it shall be consummated," said Wolfgang, "so, worthy father, commence the marriage service at once."

The "worthy father," with a hypocritical assumption of sanctity, began the service, but the awkwardness of Karl, and the firm refusal to respond on the part of Agatha, rendered it impossible to carry it through. The incensed baron, finding himself so far foiled, ordered Agatha at once to be removed a strict prisoner in the Moat Tower. Here, for several days the unfortunate girl lingered in wretched incarceration. Torn from her home, her lover lost or slain, how bitter were her reflections, what wretched fate might not be hers !

The long hours went by in cheerless un

relief, the baron seemed to have forgotten his prisoner, whose only hope was now to pray to Heaven for assistance.

One evening she was startled to hear an unusual noise in the moat below, which caused her much terror. It was followed by the opening of the trap-door in the centre of the floor, and the appearance of the top of a ladder.

Not long was Agatha left in terrified wonder, a head appeared, a man entered by the trap-door, and her face lit up with joyful amazement.

"Adrian, Adrian, is it thou, indeed?

"Yes, dearest; for many a weary hour have I lain a prey to pain and anxiety, and even now my wound is not all recovered. But I learnt thy fate, and by the connivance of servants, have thus come to rescue thee. Let us descend at once into the boat, for time presses."

Little persuasion was needed; in a moment he was conveying her down the ladder. But ere he had half way descended, the boat, insecurely tied, suddenly shot from under, impelled by the current, and the lovers fell precipitately into the deep moat. Both sank at once, but rose as quickly, and Adrian used every effort to sustain his fair companion. The baron Wolfgang, who had probably received some inkling of what was likely to happen, was at that moment passing by the other side of the moat. His quick eye at once caught the two figures in the water, he recognised them and understood all.

"Confusion!" he cried, "they must not escape. Hans and Kelmar, quick; let down the drawbridge, and cut off their retreat."

The ponderous bridge was lowered as speedily as possible, and the baron ordered half-a-dozen men to station themselves on it, armed with firearms.

"No mercy! fire at them!" he roared, and the next moment a heartrending shriek rose into the air; Adrian felt his cheek grazed and burnt.

He turned towards Agatha, a ball had struck her forehead.

"Oh I die, Adrian, I die—farewell, dearest—farewell," was all she could gasp ere she sank down in the deep waters of the moat.

Adrian, in a paroxysm of grief, and heedless of his own danger, made desperate efforts to clasp the corpse of his beloved and convey it to the shore. The strength of the current and his own weakness prevented him climbing up the side of the moat, and he fell exhausted on the stone terrace.

"So perishes the daughter of my enemy," cried Baron Wolfgang.

"This, then, is the fruit of disobedience to parents."

"Tyrant and murderer," cried the agonised Adrian, "wert thou not my elder and my kinsman, thy ill-spent life should at once be forfeit."

At this moment Eborhard approached.

"My lord," he cried, "sudden and ill tidings; the Westerwalden are upon us. They have come in great force to besiege the castle."

Yes, it was indeed so. The disappearance of Agatha had caused much consternation at Westerwald, and search was made everywhere, but not until many days had passed was the true clue found.

Burning for vengeance, the lord of Westerwald gathered all his followers and friends, forming altogether a formidable force, which set forth with the object not only of rescuing Lady Agatha, but of annihilating the tyrant Wolfgang.

The siege we need not describe; it was a fierce conflict, and the baron, who fought with the courage of desperation, found himself at last driven to bay.

Fearful of falling into the hands of his enemies, Wolfgang retreated to the Moat Tower, and endeavoured to escape by means of the trap-door.

He dropped into the water, struck out a few paces, but, encumbered by his armour, was borne down to the bottom.

During that last awful struggle for life, he saw the figure of the Witch of the Rhine rising out of the moat; a terrib'e look of triumphant malignity was on that evil spirit's countenance.

"Wicked baron," she said, "thus are my predictions fulfilled; thy fate is fully deserved. Die, as thou deservest!"

And her fiendish laughter mingled horribly with the death shrieks of the drowning baron.

The next day his body and that of the unfortunate Agatha were taken from the moat and duly interred, with what different feelings in each case!

The Lord of Westerwalden proved a generous enemy, readily offering to restore Adrian his rightful inheritance.

But the young knight refused, stipulating only to retain the church of St. John; thither he retired, and the rest of his life was devoted to the austerities of the cloister. He, in time, became abbot, and died respected by all.

END OF THE MOAT TOWER ; OR, THE WITCH OF THE RHINE.

[Continued from page 233.]

THE BLACK SENTINEL;

OR, THE SHEPHERD LORD OF THE CASTLE.

"I GO," he said, "that I may live for revenge. Farewell, Wilhelm Arnhold! farewell Gertrude! and remember that the hand that can grasp yours tenderly in love can clutch it also in hate!"

And with a white and terrible pallor on his passion-distorted face, he turned and stalked away, leaving his dead retainers stretched on the greensward.

With her arm locked in that of her father, Gertrude hurried on towards home.

Not a word did she say in regard to what had passed.

She saw the stern look upon her father's face, and attributed it to his anger against her.

Before they reached home, however, she was undeceived.

"Gertrude," said Wilhelm Arnold, suddenly, "you must leave this place to-night! I know well what trust to place in those villain lords! But yet I would not that your mother knew aught of what has happened this night."

"Oh! father," exclaimed the young girl, as the tears rolled down her now pale cheeks, "can you forgive me?"

"Yes—yes," returned Arnhold, "I blame you not. It is the villain who would have deceived you into a false marriage that is to blame. I will contrive a story that will satisfy your mother. Come, dry your eyes. Let her not see that you have aught to grieve you."

As well as she was able the young girl removed the traces of her grief from her face, and in a few minutes more they had entered the cottage together.

Not suspecting anything, Dame Arnhold took no notice of the fact that they were thus in companionship, and the evening meal was soon smoking upon the board.

Wilhelm lost no time in arranging his plan.

"I and Gertie are going a short journey to-night," he said to his wife, "I hear that my sister is ill and wishes her companionship awhile. So we must bestir ourselves over our supper that we may cross the forest before midnight."

"You will be home before morning?" said Dame Arnhold. "I like not to remain by myself in the cottage at night."

"Fear not," said Wilhelm, "I shall be home before dawn."

As soon as the supper was over, the father and daughter set out after taking leave of Dame Arnhold, and long before midnight he had given his child in charge of a friendly shepherd who had guaranteed to take her across the river, and, what is more, to keep the secret of her whereabouts.

He had no doubt in his own mind that ere the morning the myrmidons of the young count would make their appearance at the cottage.

Hurrying on with all speed through the tangled wood, he was suddenly astonished by seeing glittering through the trees the light of a great fire.

With a terrible presentiment in his heart, he dashed forward and found his worst fears confirmed.

His cottage was in flames, and around it were assembled a band of ruffianly soldiers, who were indulging in loud jeers and laughter.

Drawing his sword, the shepherd flew to the rescue, regardless of the numbers opposed to him.

"Villains, what do you here?" he cried, as he sprang like a lightning flash into their midst.

"Ha ha!" shouted one, who appeared to be the leader, "here is the he-bear—at him, my men, cut him down and fling him into the flames."

Wilhelm Arnhold had just time to see the mangled form of his dear wife lying within the threshold before the brutal crew were upon him.

It was in vain that the brawny-armed shepherd fought; against such odds the force of his one arm was as nothing, and in a few minutes his sword was beaten down, and a terrific blow on the head rendered him senseless.

Then the infuriated throng seized him by the arms and legs, and with many a coarse gibe and burst of laughter flung him into the flames.

Then they heaped more fuel against the wooden wall of the cottage, and left it to its fate.

*   *   *   *   *

Two years rolled away.

The cottage of the shepherd was now a heap of rotting wood, over which the forest-creepers had spread their green arms as if to form a tomb for the murdered victims of the count's vengeance.

In vain the enraged Lord of Furstenberg had scoured the country for the young maiden whose pretty face had led to all this misery.

She was safely housed in the home of Wilhelm's sister across the rolling Rhine, and her shepherd guide had kept his word.

About a year following the murder in the wood, the wars had taken the count from his home, and he was absent for nearly twelve months.

He had now returned once more to his home, to find his mother dead, and his betrothed bride married to another.

How bitterly now he cursed himself for his wicked folly.

But it was too late now for regret, and unable to bear the stingings of conscience he took to riotous living and extravagance.

Seated at the head of a long table on a kind of dais, with a black attendant beside him whom he had brought from the wars, he gave out the toasts and songs, and sought to drown in wine and feverish gaiety the recollection of his crimes.

One dark and tempestuous night when the roaring of Heaven's artillery without should have told the revellers of that heaven's wrath, the count had summoned together an unusual number of guests.

He was seated as usual on his raised seat—his black attendant behind him.

About this black there was a strange mystery.

He had more than once, it was said, saved the life of the count in the wars; and was now his most trusted and faithful attendant.

He stood sentinel at the door of his chamber at night; attended him on his wild hunts in the forest—was his confidant and almost his friend.

"Bring me my golden goblet, Kurcho," he cried; "no cup but that is fit to hold the wine which is to be drank to my toast this evening."

The negro bowed profoundly and retired.

"Gentlemen," cried the count, on whose face was the glow of unusual triumph, "to-night is my nuptial night! Ah! you start with surprise. No wonder; but it is nevertheless true. In a few moments you shall see my bride—wedded to me but an hour since—found after a fruitless search of nearly two years. Ah, here comes my faithful Kurcho. Fill high the cup, my trusty friend, and let us warm our hearts ere my lovely bride comes to grace our festival."

The negro at once obeyed the order, and hardly had a moment elapsed ere the great golden goblet was filled with red Rhine wine, and passed from guest to guest.

There was a strange want of excitement amongst those who were assembled—which was not unnoticed by the Lord of Furstenberg, but under the triumph of the moment his attention was soon called to other things.

"Now, then, Kurcho," he cried, as the goblet was once more returned to his hands, "go fetch my lovely bride, and let us hope, now that she has faced her fate, that she will dry the tears that so ill become a nuptial day."

The negro again obeyed, and in a few moments there entered the lovely but pale daughter of Wilhelm Arnhold.

She was led to the side of the Count of Furstenberg, and the black Sentinel stood meekly near her.

"Now, then, gentlemen," cried Rupert, rising from his dais once more, "allow me to present you to my lovely bride. Now, Gertrude, touch the goblet with your lovely lips and it will give zest to the taste of the wine."

Gertrude Arnhold drew herself up proudly.

"Never," she cried, "never. I am an unwilling bride. I am here, forced to the altar by a man I hate, and never—so help me Heaven!—shall word of love or kindness pass my lips to the murderer of my father and mother."

"What means this?" cried Count Rupert, his eyes red with anger; "drink, or——"

"Stay, good master," cried the Black Sentinel, bowing deeply.

The count raised his hand deprecatingly.

"Nay, good Kurcho, plead not for your mistress; she must yield. She must drink to the health of her husband or she shall dearly rue the day of her refusal."

The negro bowed.

"Dear master," he said, "suffer me to cast on her a spell which shall make her love her husband. I will swear that ere ten minutes have passed she *shall* drink the health of her husband from *this* wine—out of this golden goblet."

The count laughed.

"Good," he cried, "by Heavens, the negro shall have his way. Go, Kurcho, if you have the spell, use it—anything is better than a maiden's frown."

The negro bowed, and withdrew, leaving Gertrude still standing by her hated husband.

The count sat drinking his wine, silent with expectancy.

The ten minutes seemed an age to the wondering guests ; but at length there was a quick step, a tall figure still attired in the sentinel's dress appeared, but his face was white, though a large beard still disguised it.

"Gentlemen," he cried, in a loud voice, "I, the Black Sentinel— the trusted friend of Count Rupert von Etherswold—stand here to make this fair and lovely maiden drink to the health of her future husband. Otho von Reinford—stand forth."

As he spoke these words, a fair and handsome youth stood forth, and sinking on his bosom, Gertrude raised the goblet, and drinking, said—

"I drink, gentlemen, to the health of my future husband, Otho von Reinford."

Count Rupert sprang to his feet, and drew his sword.

"What means this ?" he cried, "what treason is here ?"

The negro in an instant flung from him the huge beard that disguised his features.

"It means, Count Rupert," thundered he, "that I am Wilhelm Arnhold—whom you imagine that your myrmidons murdered in the forest, but whose wife they murdered in cold blood. I am here to avenge her. I am here to claim my right as lord of this castle. I have been your slave, that I might know your friends. Strike, gentlemen—strike for the rightful heir of Furstenberg."

In an instant fifty swords gleamed from their scabbards, and the guests divided among themselves were engaged in a desperate fight.

Wilhelm Arnhold (whose daughter was now drawn aside by the lover she had found during her two years' sojourn on the other bank of the Rhine), was engaged instantly in deadly conflict with the count, who, paralysed by the sudden change of affairs, was unable properly to defend himself.

The struggle was a brief one.

The trusty sword of the Shepherd Lord of the Castle was plunged through the heart of the murderer of his wife, and raising his reeking blade aloft, he shouted,—

"Stay your swords, gentlemen ; let no more blood be shed. I, Wilhelm Arnhold, Lord of Furstenburg, declare peace to all on this night that I take possession of the castle of my ancestors."

There was a momentary pause—a momentary glance at the dead body of the count, and then the swords were sheathed, and a cheer arose for the new lord of Furstenberg.

That very evening the wedding of Otho and Gertrude took place, and the body of the murderer of Dame Arnhold was buried in the spot near the castle walls where the dark-leaved poplar now waves its branches in the wild Rhineland breeze.

END OF THE BLACK SENTINEL ; OR, THE SHEPHERD LORD OF THE CASTLE.

Our next number will contain " Rudolf the Red Heart."

THE PRINCE'S ENVOY;

OR, THE SIEGE OF EHRENBREITSTEIN.

O F all the castles that adorn and lend historic interest to the Rhine, none occupied a more commanding position than Ehrenbreitstein ("the Broad Stone of Honour," as the name signifies in German).

The towering rock rises 500 feet above the level of the river, and in the heyday of its glory this giddy elevation was crowned with a square tower, giving a further altitude of 300, thus reaching altogether to 800 feet.

"'IS IT THUS I AM DEFIED?' THUNDERED THE BARON."

As early as the days of the Romans the suitability of the place for a fortress was perceived, and one of great strength was accordingly constructed.

When Julian the Apostate ruled the empire a strong castle stood here, which afterwards received the name of Jernstein.

In 1160, Archbishop Harmin rebuilt the edifice, and called it Harminstein.

It was the elector of Baden who, in 1487, having greatly improved and enlarged the fortress, gave it the grand name of Ehrenbreitstein.

A hundred years from the date of this event brings us to the period of our story.

In 1580 the powerful Baron Diedrich von Greifenklau reigned over the fortress and domain.

His uncouth-sounding name has the same signification as it would have in English—namely, Griffin's claw, and it arose from a legend connected with the founder of the family.

This doughty knight, who lived very far back in the dark ages, signalised himself by slaying an enormous griffin (an animal little inferior in ferocity to a dragon), and cutting off one of its huge claws as a trophy of victory.

Not only was this zoological specimen preserved. and hung up in the great hall of the castle as an heirloom, but it was adopted as the crest of the baron himself, and gave a name to the family.

The Barons of Greifenklau had been for generations renowned for their valour in war, and, we may add, their reckless and turbulent disposition in times of peace.

They were genuine specimens of the " robber lords " of the middle ages.

The possession of a large and almost impregnable castle, and of an ample domain attached to it, was naturally calculated to make them arrogant, and the central position of their residence—half way between the great towns of Mayence and Cologne, and on the route to the Imperial city of Frankfort—enhanced their advantage.

Accordingly, they lorded it over this part of the Rhine with despotic sway, extorting a heavy toll upon all vessels that passed, and taking prisoners any travellers whose ransom would be heavy.

It need not be added, that the bands of free companions or robbers that made more free than welcome on the adjacent regions, enjoyed the countenance and protection of the lords of Ehrenbreitstein.

It often happens that the traditions and possessions of a race and family descend to one who is little fitted to support them.

And thus in process of time the race of fierce barons in the direct line had died out, leaving as their sole representative the meek and gentle maiden Elmina of Ehrenbreitstein, as yet scarcely of age.

She, left early an orphan, and brought up in seclusion, with the pious teachings of a distant relative, an abbess, was scarcely fitted to become the head of this warlike house.

Indeed, it became a matter of dispute whether she, as a female, could inherit the title and estate at all.

If not, the reigning emperor, Maximilian, could, by sovereign right, take possession of the estates of the defunct family.

But here a third claimant stepped forward in the person of Diedrich, who brought proofs to show that he, as head of a collateral branch of the family, had a right to the dominion.

Much discussion and difficulty arose from this complication, but at last it was compromised by the arrangement that Diedrich should be Lord of Ehrenbreitstein till his death, when it should devolve upon Elmina, whether or not he, Diedrich, left any family.

The young heiress herself was to be amply provided for, and, though still continuing her residence in the castle, she was to be considered as a ward of the emperor himself—an arrangement prevalent in those times if an heiress was also an orphan.

Well fitted, indeed, was Diedrich von Griefenklau for his new position.

A blunt soldier, past middle age, and with all the fierce arrogant passions of his race.

He was one that could not fail to make himself obeyed and feared, and keep up the power of the family.

His first care was to strengthen the fortress, now fallen somewhat out of repair, to increase in proportion the number of his soldiers, and to bind more strongly to his interest the various robber bands that guarded the outskirts of his domains.

His aim was, in fact, to bring into his subjection this portion of the Rhine, and become as much dreaded as any of his mediæval predecessors.

At that time, firearms, invented barely two centuries, had been greatly improved, and Diedrich, knowing their value, spent large sums to procure the largest and most powerful cannon.

His ramparts soon bristled with bombards, culverins, and howitzers, which, added to the strength of the stone works and number of the garrison, seemed to have rendered the castle impregnable.

But still the warlike baron continued his experiments in artillery, and at length sent an order to Frankfort, to have a cannon cast from designs by himself, of the largest size, and most tremendous power.

This gun was finished in due course, and conveyed at great cost to the castle.

Its arrival caused an immense excitement; never before had so formidable a piece of artillery been seen there.

Its weight was not less than ten tons, it carried a ball of 160 lbs. and it was reputed to carry the distance of 16 miles.

In form it bore a resemblance to a huge griffin of bronze, its tail, wings and claws highly gilt, and its grinning mouth forming the muzzle of the cannon.

Placed in the courtyard of the castle, this monster piece of ordnance was tested, and several hours were devoted to the practising.

The warlike baron was quite in his element, as, surrounded by his officers and gunners, he superintended the operation.

"By the sword of my ancestors!" he often exclaimed in delight, "this is the true griffin; and I warrant no griffin of old, nay, nor dragon either, had it in its power to create such destruction as this bronze-throated monster. Let us aim it now in the direction of the river itself."

The gunner obeyed, and the huge machine ejected forth its missile, which fell in the thick forest of the opposite shore.

The report thundered and echoed around the rocks and forests, like the voice of the tempest, startling the birds from their nests and the wild beasts from their lairs, and in no little degree discomposing the gentle Lady Elmina and her attendants, though they abode in a remote part of the castle.

"The owner of such a piece of artillery should indeed become lord of the Rhine," mused Diedrich to himself. "Let me but plant this on my battlements, and then see who dare question my right as absolute and hereditary Lord of Ehrenbreitstein? Nay, if need were I would defy the emperor himself."

He had scarcely spoke, or rather thought this, when his seneschal announced that a knight, attended by a page and squire, was at the castle gate, and desired admittance; adding, that he came from his Majesty the emperor, a letter from which potentate was produced.

The elector, like most great lords of the period, was not over learned; to write a letter or despatch was a task not unattended with difficulty, and to read one even more laborious.

But he had a secretary (serving also as chaplain) who was much more erudite, and he soon informed his patron of the contents of the letter.

It was from Maximilian, Emperor of Germany, to his trusty and well-beloved subject, Diedrich of Griefenklau, Baron of Ehrenbreitstein, greeting; and it recommended to his attention the noble knight who bore the message, and who was authorized to visit him on an errand of great importance.

The baron, who could not conjecture what this errand could be, gave orders that the emissary should be admitted.

Accordingly, a knight of noble presence was admitted into the Great Hall of the castle, where he was soon received by the baron.

"My lord," said this visitor, "my name is Sir Eribert von Dortz, I am the personal friend of his serene highness the Prince of Oldenburg, who sends me to solicit in marriage your noble kinswoman, the Lady Elmina."

This proposition so startled the baron, that he could only reply by an exclamation of surprise.

"The report of her beauty and accomplishments," proceeded the envoy, "which, though she has been kept in retirement, has by some means reached as far as Oldenburg, so much interested his Highness, that he applied to our gracious emperor for permission to open these negotiations; as her guardian, his Majesty gladly consented, and he has no doubt, that you, as her other guardian, will also entertain the proposal favourably."

The baron's mood entirely changed on hearing this. It threatened to upset certain schemes to which his life had been devoted; for, knowing that nothing would more conduce to make his power and position permanent, he had always intended that Elmina should wed none but himself.

Such a marriage would join, as it were, the broken threads of the lineal succession, of which he and herself were the sole remaining representatives.

Her beauty and good qualities were besides attractions, to which he could not be insensible. He had always so acted as to win her regard as much as possible. She had been purposely brought up in such a secluded manner, in order that his designs should not be frustrated by the advent of other and more eligible suitors.

On the other hand, the difference of age

between these two cousins (for such, at a removal of four degrees, was their relationship) was as great as that between father and daughter, and it did not seem reasonable to expect that she could ever entertain sufficient love for the baron to marry him willingly

And now that a formidable rival—a sovereign prince, favoured by the emperor himself—had come into the field, the baron began to tremble for his own chance.

Dissembling, however, these feelings before the emperor's emissary, he invited him into his banquetting hall, and entertained him with hospitality.

Nor did Von Greifenklau forget to ply the messenger with questions as to the appearance, age, and position of the Prince of Oldenburg, and was no little dismayed at being told that the suitor for Elmina's hand was young, handsome, and accounted one of the most accomplished knights of the court.

The emissary himself was no unfair specimen of a German cavalier, poor as he confessed himself to be.

He had a princely demeanour, and might have adorned some regal court as its chiefest star.

The baron then deemed it prudent to have a few words of conversation with Elmina, informing her of the emperor's emissary, and the errand on which he had come.

He said nothing of the youth and attractive qualities of the Prince of Oldenburg, but hinted to her to be on her guard against the flattering representations of the envoy.

Considerably excited by an event so important to herself, Elmina accompanied the baron to the banquetting-hall, having first donned an attire of becoming grandeur, which greatly enhanced her beauty.

Sir Eribert von Dortz received the lady with profound, but somewhat formal, courtesy

He said that the errand upon which he had come was a great honour as well as great pleasure to him, and that, even at first sight, he was confident that his errand ought not to be in vain.

Report, he added, had rather under than overrated the beauty of the heiress of Ehrenbreitstein.

Flattered by compliments so delicately conveyed, Elmina joined the circle at the banquet, presently remarking that the emissary was no doubt a most intimate friend and confidant of his highness the Prince of Oldenburg.

"As deep in his confidence, madam," replied Sir Eribert, "as I am in mine own; we have been always together since my earliest youth. He would never have entrusted so important and confidential a mission to any one but myself."

He then expatiated on the many good qualities of his patron, spoke of his wealth and influence, and thence the conversation turned to the general news of the court.

Both Elmina and the Baron were much interested in the conversation of Sir Eribert, and both came to the conclusion that whether or not the prince himself fully carried out the eulogiums bestowed upon him, his emissary was at least a highly attractive personage.

That night, Sir Eribert and his suite were accommodated in the castle, and the next morning departed, Diedrich answering for himself and Elmina, that a proposal so important required time for consideration, ere deciding.

Sir Eribert concurred, but added that, as he intended to stay in the vicinity some few days, he hoped to have himself the honour and pleasure of visiting the castle several times ere returning to Frankfort.

The Baron's reflections on his departure were not hopeful.

He saw that his only resource was to press his own suit so tenaciously as to break off this proposed match.

To do this, he must act promptly and decisively.

He accordingly, in an interview with Elmina, declared that he had long loved her, that disparity of age need be no bar to their happiness, that such a marriage would closer unite those already bound by ties of relationship, and reinstate her in her own home and position, instead of compelling her to leave that home to wed in a distant region an unknown bridegroom, who, after all, might turn out very much less eligible then Sir Eribert represented.

These arguments were not lost on the gentle and guileless Elmina.

Bred up, as was the custom, in the idea that the disposal of her hand would in any case have to depend on the decision of guardians, not on her own, the prospect of a betrothal to a man whom she had never beheld, seemed less formidable to her than it would to a maiden of modern times.

Yet she could not help some misgivings as to a leap so completely in the dark.

On the other hand here was Diedrich before her.

She knew, or thought she knew, his disposition, for he had taken care she should always see him at his best, and, in default of a better one, the match might not be uneligible.

But she would give no decision at once; all she would promise was not to give immediately a favourable reply to the Prince of Oldenburg's suit, and Diedrich hoped, by gaining time, to gain his end also.

He was sufficiently in favour of the Emperor to hope to obtain that monarch's consent, but he knew that would not be given if opposed to the wish of Elmina herself.

Thus matters stood when Sir Eribert again called, and hinted that he must soon depart for Frankfort, bearing the expected reply.

Diedrich fenced with the question, the subject changed, and the young knight again enthralled both hearers by his powers of conversation.

He stayed that night as before, and was dismissed with the assurance that the final answer would be returned in three days at the furthest.

Elmina's demeanour at this time became somewhat unaccountable to the baron.

While she seemed almost decided upon refusing the suit of the Prince of Oldenburg, she seemed equally averse to accept that of Diedrich himself.

It would, indeed, almost seem from her manner that she had some powerful reason for avoiding, if possible, either alternative.

The baron was suspicious; he remembered the attractive character of Sir Eribert von Dortz, and without delay he questioned Elmina's old attendant, Juditha, who, on the prospect of a reward, was by no means averse to take the *rôle* of a spy.

"You suspect aright, my lord," was the woman's reply, "the lady Elmina hath fallen in love with this young knight, the prince's envoy. Both yesterday and to-day they have met secretly in the gardens of the castle."

"Confusion!" muttered the baron, "this is worse than all."

"Nay, frown not, my lord, it was by no contrivance of mine," said Juditha; "I was not in the secret of the affair, save by my own eavesdropping. But 'tis true as I relate that, whatever may be thy power, I opine that neither thou nor the Prince of Oldenburg can ever hope to obtain the heart of the maiden—another hath won it."

"Curses on them! I must stop this!" exclaimed the enraged baron; "what a fool was I not to have foreseen such a result! Hark ye, woman, put me in the way of falling in with some of these stolen interviews, and I will reward thee well."

The next day presented an opportunity.

The baron had been again occupied in testing his artillery, and was in full warlike panoply; it was getting dusk, when, on passing through the hall to the courtyard, he was touched on the arm by Juditha.

"Now, my lord, is the time, follow me," she said.

The baron did so, and she led the way towards Elmina's apartments.

Flinging open the door of an antechamber, the enraged baron encountered the two clandestine lovers "red-handed," in other words they were just in the act of eloping by a secret passage from the castle.

So suddenly confronted by Diedrich, there was no time for retreat, they stopped short in the centre of the room, Elmina exhibiting considerable alarm, and clinging to the arms of Sir Eribert.

"A thousand fiends!" thundered the fierce baron, clutching his drawn sword, and levelling a pistol at the envoy's bosom; but his blind rage sent the bullet wide of its mark. "Is it thus I am defied, deceived, played with, in my own castle? Elmina, your base conduct shall not go unpunished; and you, sir, think not you will escape my vengeance, or fail to be called to account by the Emperor, and the Prince of Oldenburg, whom you have thus deceived."

"Spare your reproaches, baron," said the young knight, recovering his self-possession; "I have, it is true, acted falsely, but I am now ready to throw off the mask. Your cousin is fairly mine, with her own and her imperial guardian's consent. I am no envoy now, but act on my own responsibility. I am Hendrik, Prince of Oldenburg."

The baron recoiled with an exclamation of amazement.

"Can it be so?" he cried, "but no, 'tis a base subterfuge. Thou liest."

"Like thyself," retorted the knight, coolly; "but 'tis no less true; his Majesty himself is in my secret. Hearing of the beauty of this lady, and determined to evade that senseless custom which conducts wooing by proxy, I decided to go as my own emissary under the name of one of my esquires, and see with my own eyes whether the prize was worth so much as rumour estimated. I have found that it far surpasses my expectation."

"And is such a course worthy a prince?"

exclaimed the baron, assuming righteous indignation. "But the turn shall not serve, you have confessed yourself my rival, for to me and no other shall this girl be wedded, and I am not one to brook a rival either in love or war. You have been caught in the act of abducting an heiress against her guardian's consent; you are my prisoner. Siegfried, away with both !"

Half-a-dozen armed attendants advanced.

The Prince, however, called upon them to stand back, and drawing his sword, proceeded to attack the baron, but ere he could reach him, his weapon was wrested from his hand by Siegfried, and he was at their mercy.

Elmina was also delivered into the hands of the rude soldiery, who with very little gentleness, hurried her off to one of the dungeons.

"Beware, relentless Baron," cried Hendrik, as he was being hurried away. "I am a sovereign prince of the Empire, and to forcibly detain me is treason."

But the Baron, storming with rage all the while he was issuing his commands, did not hear or heed this declaration.

To follow the two lovers to their separate cells, and describe the unpleasant reflections which in each case enhanced the hardships they had to endure, were no pleasant task. Both, and especially Elmina, feared the Baron's vengeance, and both felt humiliation as well as distress at their position.

In this unenviable state of mind two days were passed.

We must own that the course Prince Hendrik had taken was not entirely without blame.

He had come in disguise, and after falling in love with the heiress, had sought surreptitiously to elope with her, whereas avowing his rank and purpose from the first would have been the more open, if not the more politic, course.

But, perhaps, the Prince argued that all was fair in love, and that the ultimate consent of the Emperor could not fail to be followed by that of Diedrich.

As for Elmina, she now regretted the part she had taken, but her peculiar position must be her excuse, and it was only on being told the real rank of her lover that she consented to elope with him, knowing that to confess all openly to the Baron would be to defeat instead of aiding their plans.

The Baron, himself, was in a position of some perplexity.

His rage and jealousy would not permit him to let the Prince depart; whereas to keep him prisoner would inevitably draw down upon him the enmity of the Prince's friends and subjects, and perhaps that of the Emperor himself.

He might even have to encounter the Imperial forces in open hostility.

As he pondered on this, Diedrich's thoughts fell on his new piece of cannon, the Griffin, and his pride again rose in his heart.

"By my ancestor, the Griffin-Slayer, I will defy them all !" he exclaimed. "Is not my castle the strongest perhaps on the whole Rhine? Shall I have my rival in my power and yet let him defy and escape me? Elmina shall never wed this Prince; nay, not even if the Emperor himself demands it. He shall stay here, and see her wedded to me—that were my best revenge."

With this resolution he retired to rest, and the next morning set-to on the task of having the castle thoroughly fitted to resist any warlike attack.

The smaller guns were placed in position, the monster Griffin was, with considerable difficulty, lifted to the highest tower, where it stood with its demon eyes menacingly overlooking the Rhine, and with its metallic throat ready to belch forth fiery destruction on all who might approach.

Fresh ammunition was also ordered, and the soldiers of the garrison were exercised and drilled.

The baron visited his prisoners, demanding of the prince renouncement of Elmina's hand, and of Elmina a consent to marry himself, but met with a refusal in both cases.

He assured them, that unless they agreed to his terms there was no hope of release.

But Prince Hendrik was not quite of that opinion.

He had found means to have a missive secretly conveyed to the Emperor himself, telling him what had occurred, and of his present strait, and asking assistance.

It promptly came—in two days—a deputation, consisting of a detachment of the Imperial Guard from Frankfort.

"I demand," said the captain, "in the name of his majesty the Emperor, the instant restoration of his highness Prince Hendrik of Oldenburg, also of his majesty's ward, the noble Lady Elmina of Ehrenbreitstein."

The baron responded in equally haughty tones.

"My reply is that, unless a formal consent to my own marriage to the Lady Elmina is obtained, she shall not be allowed to depart. Under a ransom of 10,000 marks the Prince of Oldenburg cannot hope for any other fate than that of a prisoner. Convey this to his majesty, saying, that I am still loyal, though he has thought fit to interfere with my authority in my own proper domains, and to abet the prince in his underhand machinations."

The deputation retired, and the next day another message under the imperial warrant was received, saying that as he, Diedrich of Ehrenbreitstein had defied the authority and disobeyed the commands of his liege sovereign the Kaiser, he should be compelled to accede to them by means of an armed force.

Rather should his castle be destroyed than his insolent demands be complied with.

"Destroy Ehrenbreitstein!" said Diedrich. with a scornful laugh, "But not while I live will I surrender or obey."

He had indeed gone too far to retreat, and no course remained but desperate resistance.

Confident in the strength of his fortress and the power of the artillery he had collected, he had every hope that he could hold his position, however great a force the Emperor might send against him.

On the landward side the castle was even less accessible than by the river.

Over the inhabitants of the small town of Ehrenbreitstein Diedrich had absolute control; and in the woods and rocks around lurked parties of robbers in his pay who could effectually harass any approaching enemy.

As he gazed up at the towering summit of the castle, crowned with the formidable "Griffin" cannon, the fierce baron's heart was reassured, that as possessor of such a place of strength, he need not tremble before the most powerful army in the universe.

The preparations for resistance were carried on with much speed and vigour.

The ammunition, which had been ordered previously, arrived, and was stored in the castle; large quantities of provisions were conveyed down the river in boats and landed; and the baron put himself on the best of terms with his vassals and robber-dependants, who, whether or not they fully believed his representation that he had been wrongly used by the Emperor, swore to aid him to the death.

Elmina still remained obdurate to the Baron's persuasions to consent to wed him, while Prince Hendrik indignantly refused to take his liberty on condition of formally renouncing Elmina's hand.

"The peril be on themselves!" said the Baron. "Let the struggle come, and when it hath passed, and I am conqueror, they will have to submit to such hard terms as they little dream of!"

Morning shone brightly over the Rhine, lighting up the lofty towers of Ehrenbreitstein, and gilding the griffin on the topmost tower.

A warlike company, consisting of six gun-boats, well manned, and mounted with many large pieces of artillery, was advancing up the river to the castle.

The uniforms of the soldiers showed them to belong to the emperor's army, and they were commanded by Count Ohlson, a noted general of the time. This fleet was anchored within some distance of the fortress, while a number of boats, filled with armed men, were first dispatched to deal preliminarily with the lord of Ehrenbreitstein.

Baron von Greifenklau saw the approach of the enemy without dismay. He was prepared for them on all points, and as yet their appearance was less formidable than he had anticipated.

Little time was lost in negotiations; Diedrich declared his intention of refusing the Imperial demands was unchanged, and that he would resist with his utmost strength.

The Count then said that in this case further parley was useless. The siege of Ehrenbreitstein then began.

The first shot from the enemy's guns broke like a thunderclap from the river. It was the first note of a terrible struggle —the signal at which the dogs of war were let loose.

The habitations of the town of Ehrenbreitstein, being well sheltered by the strong fortress, were uninjured and the inhabitants had full confidence in a victorious resistance.

The Baron Ehrenbreitstein stood on the highest tower beside his beloved "Griffin," directing all the operations. He was gratified to find how impotent as yet were the artillery of the enemy, making scarcely any impression on his immensely strong walls.

The advantages of Ehrenbreitstein lay in its position as well as its strength. Standing out on a promontory, connected only by a narrow slip of land with the adjacent mountains, it commanded an important pass of the river, and, provided its outer forts could be kept, was accessible only on one side. But this confidence was soon dissipated.

As the siege continued the enemy, though failing to take the main fortress itself, gradually became possessed of all its outworks.

This gave them control over that part of the river, and prevented all attempts, if such had been made, of forces coming to the Baron's relief.

The firing continued uninterruptedly, but was most vigorous on the Baron's side.

The great "griffin" at times did considerable execution among the imperial forces, but the tactics of Count Ohlson more frequently baulked the monster.

The imperialists had one advantage the Ehrenbreitsteiners lacked ; they could get reinforcements, whereas the latter had no hope of succour.

On the valley or landward side of the castle was a brook, beyond which stood another strong outpost, and this the Baron had placed under the command of the captain of the robbers who were on his side. But what was his dismay one morning to hear that a large force, principally consisting of troops of the principality of Oldenburg, had made this part of the fortress their special point of attack.

These were headed by the real Sir Eribert von Dortz, an experienced warrior, whose love for the prince had made him determined to undertake his rescue.

He succeeded in taking the fort, and there was a report that the captain of the

VIEW OF EHRENBREITSTEIN.

robbers had basely betrayed it into his hands.

Anyhow, the robbers dispersed soon after, and gave no further help, despite their protestations, to the Lord of Ehrenbreitstein.

This victory accomplished, Sir Eribert and his men took possession of the stronghold, and from thence made continual attacks on the castle itself.

More than a fortnight had been consumed in these warlike manœuvres, many men had been killed, many boats sunk or injured, and the walls of Ehrenbreitstein, though unconquered, had begun to assume a battered appearance.

Still the baron would not yield, and his opponents, having obtained large reinforcements, prepared to resume the siege.

But the baron now found he had been too lavish with his ammunition, which in a day or two more was exhausted.

All communication with other towns was completely cut off, and there was no hope, as in other sieges, of the approach of any friendly force to relieve the garrison.

In this terrible condition it can scarcely be wondered that the inhabitants of the town of Ehrenbreitstein began to murmur and rebel.

Why, for the sake of abetting the obdurate tyranny of Baron von Greifenklau, should they submit to all the perils and privations of a prolonged siege?

The impregnability of the fortress, hitherto regarded as their chief defence, was looked upon as a calamity.

Had it been less strong it would ere this have fallen into the hands of the besiegers, and the town would have been relieved.

But shot and shell might batter those walls, day after day, and week after week, without doing more than superficial harm, while the interior remained as untouched as the stern heart of the fierce baron himself.

Thus murmured the vassals, and some of the more audacious tried to open negotiations with the enemy, but the fierce baron effectually put a stop to such intentions, by having those concerned in them promptly hung on the ramparts of the castle.

Words will not adequately describe the terrible condition of Ehrenbreitstein at this period.

Its inhabitants had to subsist on the smallest supplies of anything that could be made available—to suffer all the bodily and mental agonies attendant upon such a state.

The various diseases arising from famine became prevalent in the town, and many children, women, and aged men had already succumbed to them.

Fuel was running short, and as the weather was becoming cold, the privation was each day more felt.

Gaunt, and haggard, and dejected, the Ehrenbreitsteiners began to resemble phantoms in a state of torment, rather than beings of this earth.

Gloom and silence hung over the castle like a dark spell.

Sad indeed was the condition of Prince Hendrik and the Lady Elmina, who added captivity to their other distresses.

Cooped up in a dark, narrow dungeon, heavily chained, and reduced to the lowest pitch of weakness and despair, the prince could scarcely be said to have lived.

He lay for hours motionless, just conscious of his suffering, and of such sounds as reached his remote prison.

When he languidly asked the cause of the cessation of the firing, he heard, almost with indifference that the ammunition was exhausted, and that the Imperialists had determined to reduce the fortress by famine.

The provisions they brought him were scarcely sufficient to support a life now less desirable than death itself.

If her prison was somewhat more endurable than that of her lover, the anguish of Elmina was quite as great.

The sufferings of mind and body reacted upon each other.

Frequently her mind wandered and the oblivion of delirium removed her for a time from real terrors.

The herculean frame of the baron himself was calculated to resist long the attacks of famine, especially as the best choice of provisions was appropriated by him and his soldiers.

But bad indeed was the best, and small indeed the greatest amount of food now procurable, and barely able to support life, much more exertion.

But bodily suffering did not alter the disposition of the baron.

He was now determined more than ever not to relinquish his castle, and resolved that this state of things should continue till all perished, unless the emperor agreed to the terms he demanded.

He seemed never to sleep, never to lay aside his heavy armour—always stalking about the castle like the spectre of his former self.

His sufferings were great and increasing; the pangs of hunger, the weariness produced by sleeplessness, remorse, and anxiety, became almost unbearable.

"Worse, ten thousand times worse, than any other kind of death," he would murmur to himself; "this is lingering torture. One word of mine would end it, but that word would signify defeat, humiliation, and punishment. Better to escape even by self destruction!"

He took up a petronel or pistol he wore, and gazed at it undecidedly.

He had still sufficient ammunition to load it and discharge it with fatal effect.

Then he unsheathed his long dagger, grown rusty from disuse, but with the power of death still in it.

But ere he could apply either of these weapons to their fatal use, his courage failed him, and they dropped from his trembling hand.

"'Tis useless," he cried; "to perform this irrevocable act requires more courage than to face death any other way. And yet what I dread still more is that if I linger on thus I shall in a moment of weakness consent to surrender to my enemies."

The sound of a trumpet smote his ear. He started up, and sought to know the cause from his lieutenant, Siegfried, who shortly introduced a captain who had been sent by the imperial general. Mounting to the highest tower, and leaning against the great griffin, Diedrich haughtily received the emissary.

"Baron of Ehrenbreitstein," said the latter, "I am commissioned to ask thee, in the name of his majesty the Emperor, whether thou dost still intend to retain possession of this fortress in defiance of thy liege monarch the emperor. It is better to surrender at once than continue a useless and painful resistance."

This was the crisis for the baron, on whom the eyes of all present were turned. Such a picture of agony and conflicting passions was sufficient almost to terrify the beholder. Shorn, unkempt, haggard, and emaciated, with a wild glare in his eye like that of insanity, he stood—his lips moved as in soliloquy, without uttering a sound. Should he yield or die? Once the words of surrender were on his lips, but the next moment the fierce, proud, obdurate spirit revived and sealed his fate.

Mounting on the stand of the great griffin itself, he stood with one foot upon the cannon.

This was the highest summit of the whole castle.

Beneath him spread the broad waters of the Rhine, crowded with the boats of his enemies, and on the other side stretched his own inland domains, likewise surrounded by a hostile force.

"Bear witness," said Diedrich to the imperial captain, " that I die, leaving this fortress unconquered and unsurrendered. I had sworn never to yield, and will keep my oath. Thus do I defy and escape my enemies !"

With these words he sprang from the cannon, cleared the battlements, and fell headlong down the steep rock into the water, a distance of 800 feet! Long ere he reached the bottom he was dead, and his body was dashed to pieces on the stony rocks. Many had witnessed the terrible occurrence, and to those who did not, both followers and foes, it was soon known.

The fate of Ehrenbreitstein was thus decided.

Siegfried, the lieutenant, on perceiving his master's death, deemed himself absolved from his allegiance. He came forward, almost too faint and haggard to speak, and formally surrendered the castle.

In half an hour the long-closed gates were opened, and the Imperial troops occupied every portion of the huge fortress.

The garrison and inhabitants of the town were almost delirious with joy at the advent of that day of deliverance.

Provisions and other necessaries were sent down the river in large quantities, from the various adjacent towns, and freely distributed to the famished Ehrenbreitsteiners.

Even the recreant robbers assisted in the good work of relieving the garrison.

In the great hall of the castle a scene presented itself which greatly contrasted with the general joy that prevailed.

On one side, supported by her attendants, and by none more tenderly than the now repentant Juditha, was Elmina of Ehrenbreitstein.

So reduced was the heiress by her imprisonment, that her beauty was the beauty of a corpse.

Her eyes wandered, and her bewildered expression showed signs of an intellect impaired by grief and privation.

The priest and several other inmates of the castle were present.

On the other side sat Prince Hendrik, tended with much solicitude by his friend and follower Sir Eribert von Dortz.

Both the prince and the lady looked like beings rescued from the grave.

We need not prolong our story by dwelling on a scene so painful.

For a long time the lives of both were despaired of, and even should they live it was feared that their minds would be permanently affected.

But time and care at length wrought a cure in each case, Ehrenbreitstein regained its heiress and Oldenburg its sovereign.

The inmates of the castle had, it is true, to mourn the loss of many humbler individuals, who had died by cannon-shot or disease, or famine, but their deaths lay at the door of him who had suffered and died, the Baron Diedrich.

We scarcely need say that the emperor Maximilian confirmed Elmina's title of Baroness of Ehrenbreitstein, and her marriage with Prince Hendrik.

This imposing ceremony took place at Frankfort, in the presence of the Emperor's court.

Elmina, now Princess of Oldenburg, naturally preferred the gay capital of that principality to the gloomy fortress where she had passed so much of her life.

But she did not wholly neglect her subjects in Ehrenbreitstein.

The fortress was repaired, and the inhabitants prospered well under the rule of their gentle mistress.

Twenty years later the second son of the prince and princess of Oldenburg was formally installed, with great rejoicing, as Baron of Ehrenbreitstein.

He founded a family, who retained the castle for many generations.

It has been several times besieged since, but its vast strength bid defiance to all enemies, even the large and victorious armies of Napoleon twice failed in their attempts to reduce it, and it only succumbed, in 1799, to the same fatality as before—famine.

The famous cannon called the Griffin was taken and removed to Metz, where it was melted down to make smaller and more modern pieces of artillery.

END OF THE PRINCE'S ENVOY; OR, THE SIEGE OF EHRENBREITSTEIN.

RHEINECK;

OR, RUDOLF THE RED HEART.

I N one particular the history of all the ruined castles of the Rhine is very much alike. Up to a certain date they were mere retreats for robbers, who, whatever their rank or social status, lived by pillage and rapine.*

At no great distance from the turrets of the castle which bore the name of Rheineck, and close to Forster's bars, in a lowly valley, was a hut belonging to a swine-herd, a serf and domestic on the baron's estate.

A strange, odd, eccentric man was Hans Bradsach—a stout man at arms once, but now from the loss of his left hand reduced to look after the swine of his lord as they fed in the forest.

Towards the close of a summer's day, and when the faithful servant was about with dog and horn to go in search of his

THE CASTLE OF RHEINECK.

drove, Hans, who had been seated at the water's edge catching fish, saw a boat turn a point close at hand.

It contained six rowers and three knights, with a helmsman, who no sooner

discovered the hind than he put in the boat and leaped ashore to where he stood.

"We have lost sight, good fellow," cried them an-at-arms, "of our sumpter boat; my lords are hungered and athirst. Canst give us refreshment—however simple?"

"My lord of Rheineck never refused hospitality to gentle or simple," replied the hind.

"We have no time for ceremony. There is a village hard by, take this guerdon,"

*" The tolls on the Rhine and Necker were a perpetual source of strife. The ruins of the fastnesses with which these robber knights crowned the heights on the banks of these rivers. and whence they waylaid the travelling merchants, still stand s le and picturesque memorials of those wild and lawless times."—*Modern History of Germany.*

handing him a handful of small coin, " and get some of the people to bring down bread, wine, and meat. Be quick, lest we burn the village about their swinish ears."

Hans knew there was no response to be made to this brutal order, and went away promising to return as fast as his legs would carry him. His experience of nobles and their followers led him to believe they would carry out their threat if not obeyed with alacrity.

"The poor are always put upon," he muttered to himself. "The devil likes to souse what is already wet." †

He found his friends in the village of the same opinion as himself, and glad even for the payment offered the poor people hurried down to the water's edge with such food as they could find.

"'Tis well," said a knight in black armour, and with more ornamentation than the others on his helmet, " ye may retire. You stop," addressing Hans. "A tough old fellow like you should know the neighbourhood."

"Old pigs have hard snouts," drily answered the swineherd. "As soldier and herd I have served my lord thirty years."

"So, my man," said the other, eyeing him keenly from under his shaggy eyebrows, which, with beard and moustache, almost wholly concealed his face, " and how is the master of yonder castle ?"

"Well and hearty," replied the other with profound and earnest respect.

"He lives alone ?" continued the other.

"Nay, sir knight; he has his son Edmund and his niece Emma."

"Was there not another son ?" carelessly remarked the strange knight.

"There was—but—'All freight lightens, as the skipper said, when he threw his wife overboard,' he was a bad one and went to the dogs."

"You speak roughly of your betters, my man," the other added, somewhat warmly."

"'The cock is a lord on his own dunghill.' I speak of what I know."

"Didst know this elder son—who was so very bad ?" continued the knight.

"'You cannot make a sieve out of an ass's tail.' I did know him."

"And the cause of his departure ?"

"'A fence between makes love more keen.' He and his noble father quarrelled, because the lord of Rheineck married a young wife, the mother of the noble Edmund."

"Is she still alive ?"

"'There are only two good women in

the world—the one is dead, and the other is not yet found,'" gravely replied the swineherd, "my noble mistress has long since departed."

"And of the exiled son, no news has ever been received ?" the other went on, between the huge mouthfuls he was swallowing, with true, heroic appetite.

"'Justice has a waxen nose,' or he would long since have expiated his offences. He is said to be a cruel and inhuman free-lance. But ' Like will to like, as the devil said to the charcoal burner.' He has many friends."

"Enough," cried the stranger, sternly, " consider yourself lucky to escape trouncing. 'Tis a pretty pass we have come to, when swineherds thus speak of noble knights. Eh! what have we here ?"

Hans turned abruptly, and saw a group approaching the spot, whom he wished far away. It was an old knight, a younger one, and a youthful lady of beautiful appearance.

They were attended, as usual in those days, by huntsmen and men-at-arms.

"'Tis my lord!" cried Hans, with an alarmed countenance, and then he added to himself, "this is the lady's dilemma. She will see all strangers. 'A sack full of fleas is easier watched than a woman,'" added the cynical old fellow.

"I am surprised," said the courteous old baron, approaching the group, "that knights of rank and degree, as your appearance warrants, should eat like hinds on my ground, when my castle is in sight. 'Tis rare discourtesy to my name for hospitality."

"We are under a vow neither to eat nor sleep under a roof, untill we reach our journey's end," said the chief knight, who had closed his visor. "The hospitality of Rheineck is proverbial."

"Self-praise stinks, friends' praise hinks ; the stranger is sincere and may last for a year,'" muttered the old swineherd.

As the knight said the above words, he rose, bowed, and with his followers went to his boat, and took his departure down the broad and sweeping stream.

"We must respect religious scruples," said the old knight. "They appear brave and goodly soldiers."

"'That miller is honest who has hair on his teeth,'" growled the swineherd.

"So, you like him not," growled the old baron, who was standing apart from the others, watching the receding boat.

Hans stepped up to his master, leaned his hand respectfully on the front of his saddle, and whispered something in his ear.

The old knight shook as with palsy.

"To the castle!" he cried aloud in a few minutes, and rode off, without taking notice of the others, nor suffered them to come up to him.

When Edward and Emma reached the castle, its master had reached his chamber, which was closed against all save Hans, the swineherd.

"What is to be done, my faithful servant?" asked the baron, when they were alone.

"'Stretch your legs according to your coverlet,'" began the swineherd. "''Tis a hard thing, but pills must be bolted, not chewed.'"

"A truce to your wise saws," said the knight, whose face was pale and wan, "speak as a rational being, whom I have trusted since we were boys together."

"I will, my master," replied the other, respectfully.

"It would be wise to know his object in coming here," continued the baron, as he looked out of the balconied window. "Ah! a light in the witches' den—three lights—what can it mean, Hans?"

The swineherd started forward, and gazed across the stream towards a high and overhanging rock, at the foot of which a bright light could be traced from three several holes or windows.

"Saints guard us!" said the worthy Hans. "There's mischief afoot if old Elfrida has returned."

"She hates me and mine. Hans, let us across. You can row a boat as well now, as when in the days of old I visited Aldegarde."

"I can."

And without any further remark, the knight and his servitor took one of those secret ways, which in those days of feud and disorder were known only to the master and a select few in his service.

The passage led to a postern, and from that to a descending flight of rude steps cut in the rock.

At the bottom was the boat, a stout yet large craft, suitable for the journey upon which they were bent.

Hans took his seat, and clutching the left oar with the coarse crook which served him for a hand, began to pull with a vigour and precision which would have ashamed and astonished many a younger man.

The baron left him wholly to himself, his thoughts being far away when he used forty years ago to cross this same water to visit Aldegarde, his first wife, the mother of the boy who left his home in search of wild adventures.

He had loved the mother and the boy, but both had turned out badly.

"Who knows?" said the knight aloud as he approached the rocks, speaking to himself, "had Aldegarde had a happier home—things might have been different."

"'The husband's mother is the wife's devil," muttered Hans, rowing away all the same with unabated vigour.

The Baron of Rheineck made no reply, but sat musing still on the irrevocable past.

Presently the boat struck the shore, was concealed beneath some drooping alders, and the two men ascended the bank.

The cavern in which the knight and his serving man had seen the lights was inhabited by an old woman, Elfrida by name, who had the reputation of being a witch. At all events, her surroundings were strange enough, while she undoubtedly possessed the power of healing to a most remarkable extent.

Few sick people of the lower classes ever had any other attendant, and they were satisfied.

"You know the secret way?" asked the baron tremulously.

"I have not forgotten it."

He led the way up the side of what appeared an almost perpendicular rock, but which he ascended easily enough, until a small gap was reached which they got through by crawling almost on their hands.

"Now, old woman," said a harsh, stern, ringing voice, "Let us hear what you have to say."

"Renegade son, faithless husband, cruel father, treacherous friend," replied the old woman, "why seek to know more? 'Tis but a history of blood."

She stood by a charcoal fire, the knight sat on a wooden settle, while in the background at a table covered with bottles were the attendants, save the knights, who conversed apart in a corner.

"But there is glory in the future."

"The glory of rapine and slaughter. But answer me, Man of the Red Heart, what seek you now?"

"Mine inheritance, hag—and I will have it. You can aid me in this."

"Your inheritance is forfeited. You can win it only over the corpse of father, brother, and brother's wife."

"He is not wed yet," sneered the other.

"But he will be, and his children will crush yours and wear the golden crown you covet."

"She devil! speak thus and I will strangle you," hoarsely replied the knight.

"How?" asked the hag.

"I would not appear publicly in aught

that concerns them," said the other. "But you have subtle poisons, woman—will kill, slay, paralyse the brain, and render the bright eye dull and stupid. I must have those!"

"For whom?"

"For all," was the hasty reply.

"You do not mean to say that under the hoof of your insatiable ambition," cried Elfrida, who was a woman of superior education and origin, "you would crush your own father?"

"Aye! that would I," said the man, who, as will presently be seen, had few equal or prototypes in history.

"Then do so at once," was the reply in a strangely hollow voice.

The knight looked up, and in the thickening and darkling gloom saw—as he firmly believed—the ghostly likeness of his father, who had come to reproach him with his parricidal villany.

Cowed with surprise and terror, he stepped back, stumbled and fell.

In an instant, however, he was on his feet, and his voice rose distinct and clear under the vaulted roof of the old cavern.

"Some juggling is at work—there are spies in the cavern! Have no mercy! Kill everyone you find!" he screamed.

"Fool, madman!—what would you do?" cried Elfrida, terrified beyond measure.

"Foul hag, if I thought this treachery were of your hatching, I would send you before your time to that foul pit whence you came."

And then flaming torches were seen rushing about the darksome cavern, carried by men who had drawn swords in their hands, and who if they found any interlopers would have no mercy.

But though they hunted about and searched as they believed every hole and corner, not the faintest trace of the invader of their privacy could they discover.

Scarcely had the baron, led away by his feelings at discovering the fearful, the horrid nature of the crime meditated by his own son—unfortunately parricide, fratricide, and even matricide were common crimes in the good old times—shown himself to his amazed and astonished child, than Hans clutched him in a grasp of iron, and drew him away.

"'A still tongue saves the heels,' he quoted. "This way, or we are both dead men!"

And he drew him away by an aperture which as a boy he had discovered when in search of birds' eggs, still found in abundance in this cavern.

The baron was so stunned, so terrified at what he had heard, that he was helpless in the hands of his henchman.

The honest fellow never paused until he had him in the boat, which after his own fashion he pulled over to the castle without any further conversation.

"My son," said the baron, when he and Edmund were at breakfast, "we must leave Rheineck at once—we must take our departure at once!"

"Leave our home, father?"

"Yes; we are not safe here. Do not ask me questions—murder stalks abroad! I have seen and heard that this night that has nearly made me mad."

Edmund looked strangely at him, but was too respectful to make any remark.

"What is your command, honoured sir?"

"That you and Emma assume the garb of citizens, and be ready with two attendants to leave the castle. I will tell you more as we proceed on our voyage."

The son bowed respectfully, and hurried away to give his orders, while the baron sent for his niece to convey his wishes to her likewise.

That evening, long before sundown, a small train left the castle—an old man, a youth, and a girl, with three attendants, all in the garb of civilians.

An hour later they were lost in the many winding paths of the forest.

Two days later, a daring band of reiters and knights, led by one in black armour, with close helmet, claimed admittance to the castle of Rheineck, the drawbridge of which was at once lowered, and the tumultuous rabble of soldiers admitted.

"Where is your master?" said the knight through the bars of his helmet.

"He is absent."

"I have a warrant from the emperor to arrest him and his whole rebellious family, to have them cast into prison for high treason, and to raze their castle to the ground."

"All the family are absent," said the seneschal in cold tones.

"It's false; they are hidden in some of the secret places of the castle. Lead me to them, lest I beat it down, stone by stone."

But the seneschal declared to those brutal marauders that they might destroy the castle stone by stone, if they thought proper; but, on hearing some strange and unpleasant news two days before, they had all departed without any train of men at arms, he knew not where.

"Wassail," roared the robber knight. "Sir seneschal, let the board be loaded. Give us to eat and drink, for he of the Red-Heart is now Lord of Rheineck."

He raised his helmet, and the seneschal meekly bowed his head before the elder son of his master, by inheritance Lord of Rheineck, but disinherited at the birth of Edmund for bad conduct and disobedience.

He nevertheless obeyed him. As these extraordinary legal actions were so common he knew scarcely which was the master.

The whole of the party seated themselves, some below and some above the salt, and a revelry began, which wound up with an orgie such as had not been seen in those halls for more than fifty years.

Long before they were over, every old retainer, man, woman, and child, had left the castle, and were in the morning nowhere to be found.

"Father," said Edmund, when at night they were alone in a chamber of a farmhouse belonging to one of his most faithful tenants, "may I ask the reasons which have induced you to leave a home hallowed by so many associations?"

"My son, do not press me. The reasons which influence me are such that you would shudder to hear. Rely upon it they are ones which you can loyally respect."

"'Tis hard."

"You would find disgrace harder," replied the old knight, sternly.

Next day by a circuitous route, avoiding the roads chiefly frequented by armed parties, the humble caravan continued on their way.

Though he said it not, the baron's intention was to seek the emperor, to lay his case before him, and to ask justice against his unnatural son.

His crimes were so great that a sentence of banishment would not be too severe, with perpetual injunction never to bear the name of Rheineck, which he had so disgraced.

"At the court city we must live in," said the old Baron, "we must drop all dignity. There is a distant relative of your mother's, an honest burgher, who will gladly welcome us. We have been a little neglectful of him, it is true, but I count upon him."

Next day they found that the hope was no vain one.

The burgher was rich, and lived in a magnificent house that rather astonished the denizens of an old chateau, but as soon as he understood the situation he placed them perfectly at their ease.

"You honour me, Baron," he said, "to come in any way; but had you come with your whole suite there would have been room, and to spare.

"I thank you," said the baron, with haughty humility, and accepted the hospitality as a matter of course.

It was found that the emperor was absent, and Edmund began to feel the life of complete seclusion which his father wished him to lead would prove but an irksome state of things.

Not that there was want of company in the burgher's house.

All the state rooms were occupied by Agnes of Burgundy and her demoiselles, the most beautiful princess in all Europe, and who had come, at the age of fourteen, to the court of the Emperor to be sacrificed to some man of rank from political motives.

"There is a grand reception to-night," said the burgher one day to the Baron, "allow, at least, your son to be present among the noble pages, none will know him or suspect his rank."

"Do you wish it, my son?"

"I should like it much," replied Edmund, with an ingenuous blush.

And he went.

It was a splendid affair.

It was a time when burghers were held in high esteem.

They it was who made the wealth of the empire, and many a noble family had been saved from ruin by alliance with their daughters.

"Amuse yourself as you like," said the master of the house to Edmund, who wore a rich dress which might belong to a noble or a merchant.

As the company began to arrive the young man, knowing no one, withdrew to a gallery richly ornamented with pictures which separated the state rooms from the dwelling apartments.

He had not been here many minutes when he found he was not alone.

He had been admiring a large and very spendid picture, when he almost stumbled over a lady who was seated in an armchair dreamily admiring the same canvas.

He stammered forth an apology to the most lovely, the most divine being he had ever seen—a child in age—a woman in beauty.

"I fear I am intruding," he said.

"This is a reserved gallery," she answered, in a sweet, angelic voice, examining his features with singular attention and wonder, "but you are quite welcome. I was led to expect a stranger."

Now young Edmund of Rheineck would have felt rather strange had he been told that the stranger the lovely princess had been led to expect was the husband whom her guardians had selected for her.

For continuation of this Story see page 280 of our next number.
Our next number will contain "Rudesheim; or, the Legend of the Red Butt."

THE BARONS OF OLD
OR, THE ROBBERS OF THE RHINE

RUDESHEIM;

OR, THE LEGEND OF THE RED BUTT.

ARCHITECTS in days of old appear to have had in view their own immortality, if any one may judge from the massive way in which castles and towers were built in the middle ages.

Unfortunately for the fame of the builders they omitted to put their names on any prominent place, so that they were forgotten ere the mortar was well dry, even by the oldest inhabitant.

The tower of Bromserburg, which adorns

VIEW OF RUDESHEIM AND THE TOWER OF BROMSERBURG.

the town of Rudesheim, is an instance of this tendency to solidity, for the walls are from ten to eleven feet thick, and appear almost to defy the ravages of time, weather, and the still more sore effects of gradual decay.

Those who know and appreciate Rhenish wines will be familiar with the name of Rudesheim.

In the good old days, when barons sat at their well spread boards and jolly monks held high revelry at night, no wine was in more repute.

It was the glory of the Baron of Rudesheim to drink wholly of his own.

However, as he could not drink it all, he allowed the inferior qualities to go forth to the world.

Like most of his kidney he was a roysterer, and by no means very particular with regard to the laws of *meum* and *tuum*.

Men passed his tower, situated on the sheer bank of the river, with great caution, and generally at night, when the bold baron was sleeping off the effects of his potent libations.

And at the same hour did bold Rhoderick of the Jansuch, a small obscure tower on the opposite bank, come over the water to visit Edda, the grim lord's only daughter.

Nature sometimes works by contradictions.

How is it else that rough, red-nosed parents, deep voiced and guttural of speech, have such frail, elegant, soft-spoken young ladies for daughters.

Edda of Rudesheim was one of these bright specimens of earth's flowers, but not exempt for all that from earth's frailties.

She loved, alas, a youth of inferior rank to herself, that is one whose father, having won his money by honest industry, was not entitled to place himself on a par with predatory lords, who got their living anyhow, but generally *vi et armis*.

The son, however, had nobler aspirations than the father.

He scorned trade and all its grovelling associations, and being an only and a favourite son—and hence a spoiled child—persuaded his male parent, who had already married a lady, to give up laces and silks and diamonds, and invest some of his savings in an old tower, very ricketty and sadly in need of repair, but which had a name to it.

After spending a goodly sum of money on this relic of antiquity, and finding it not half so comfortable as a town house, the worthy merchant settled down to his country life, and tried to do the grand, that is to be haughty, brutal and tyrannical

to his varied retainers, which effort naturally resulted in a failure.

The new landed proprietor was too jolly and hearty a man for his new post.

This gave him an introduction to the Baron of Rudesheim, who so long as none came between the wind and his nobility was exceedingly condescending and hospitable.

He had asked the *nouveau riche* to bring his son as a playmate for his daughter Edda, which when they were respectively nine and twelve was a matter of little consequence.

So it was thought.

It ended by Master Rhoderick at eighteen, and the young lady at the ripe age of fifteen, being violently separated, after having been caught by the choleric baron vowing eternal fidelity.

The young man, aware of the character of the master of Rudesheim, took himself off to the wars, and a feud arose between the baron and his new acquaintance.

A year passed away and then the young soldier suddenly returned to his father's residence—keeping his presence, however, quite a secret.

He had determined to win the fair Edda at any price or risk.

Young men who wedded above them, or without the consent of the elders, were apt to be shortened by a head in those days, but Rhoderick was one of those who scarcely consider anything worth having unless it is attended with danger and difficulty.

The first night of his return, then, he went to the bank of the river, and, not wishing to attract attention by using a boat, disrobed, made his clothes into a bundle, and swam across the stream.

Having allowed the pearly drops to fall by shaking himself like a dog, Rhoderick resumed his dress, of course not his coat of mail, but the light fitting garb worn under armour, and looked about him.

There was the tower with its walls eleven feet thick, and its loopholes four inches wide, and as much chance of entrance as if he had remained on the other side of the river.

The windows were all on the side of the moat and portcullis, an entrance where he dared not present himself.

What was to be done?

At night all entrances and exits were closed, so at all events thought the master, who slept with the key under his pillow, but so thought not Rhoderick of the Jansuch.

There was an inn in the village, and the youth when on good terms with the baron had become aware that the inn had charms for the baron's favourite henchman Roland, who, when all else were retired would contrive to leave the tower in rather a bold and primitive fashion.

He simply ascended to the summit of the tower, produced a knotted rope from behind a stone seat, and letting it down, descended to the earth.

Rhoderick had not been long hiding when the fall of a coil of rope was heard, and soon after Roland touched mother earth and strode away on the wings of hope and love to visit the maid of the inn.

Without more ado the gallant young soldier stormed the fortress, and soon found himself on the summit, in possession —of what ?

The privilege of a splendid view and the comforts of an airy situation.

The females of the establishment, young and old, slept at the top, on the highest story, the windows of which had balconies overlooking the town. Now came the tug of war.

A lover who had not seen his mistress for a whole year is allowed a little latitude, but it was a doubtful enterprise for him to knock at her window—or at a window —until she awoke and recognised his voice.

Besides, her chamber might be altered, and the result of his rapping might be exceedingly awkward.

Fancy the fat old housekeeper opening her window, and finding a young lover on the balcony !

Under these circumstances Rhoderick felt nonplussed.

But ah ! what was that ?

A gentle sigh.

He rushes to the battlements, and looks over.

'Tis she.

The maid of his adoration in the balcony overlooking the town, and alone.

" Edda—beloved Edda !"

She did not move.

It appeared like the echo of her own thoughts, and not a voice.

" Edda—be cautious. I am here—Rhoderick !" he again whispered.

She looked up and screamed—almost— at sight of a head peering over the wall, down into the privacy of her own special balcony.

But she knew him.

Still, she spoke not, but swiftly passed into the chamber, and thence to the summit of the tower.

After about five minutes of silence, employed we know not how, they ceased their

ecstacies, and seated themselves on the cold stone bench.

" My darling—still true to your young soldier," cried Rhoderick.

" True, my own Rhoderick," she answered, " but engaged to be married—in a week."

And she began to whimper on his shoulder.

" Never," said the young man, savagely ; " rather fly at once."

" Fly, yes—that reminds me—how did you come here without wings ?"

" Dearest, there are other lovers in the world besides ourselves," replied the young man, speaking this novel remark in quite an earnest manner; " and you will not betray them ?"

Edda looked slightly supercilious at being reckoned with other lovers, but she promised, and the explanation was given.

But Edda declined to risk herself on a rope at night with a young man, and more rational counsels prevailed.

The explanation was this :

The Baron von Salis, a young man of great renown and savage aspect, a giant, with prominent teeth, and a shock of red hair, combined with a tremendous pedigree, had lent her father money.

At all events he owed him a large sum —it might have been won at play—but, any way, there was the sum due and to be paid.

The father had not the money, and did not see his way clear how to get it.

Travellers were rather shy of that part of the Rhine, and hence the rhino was short.

Under these circumstances, the Baron von Salis had proposed an exchange.

Baron von Salis gave up the debt, and Rudesheim would give up his daughter.

The arrangement was very amicable and satisfactory to all parties, save one, and that one was Edda.

She vowed she would not marry him.

Such was the story she told that night on the summit of Rudesheim, how many times it is needless to say.

Nothing was resolved upon, and hence it became a sad necessity to meet next night.

It was not far from twilight when Edda tore herself away from her lover's arms, and he descended the rope in such a hurry, that until he was half way down he knew not that somebody was coming up.

He knocked Roland down, and leaping after him, the two stood facing one another, dagger in hand.

" Rhoderick !" cried the henchman.

"The same. You have discovered my secret, and must die."

"I would rather live and keep it," said the young attendant on the old baron. "I hate the Baron von Salis, and will serve you with all my heart, my future lord and master."

As this was rather flattering and complimentary than otherwise, Rhoderick relented, and admitted, having no choice, the henchman into his unlimited confidence.

Then once more he committed himself to the stream, and returning to his paternal castle, slept until some time after dinner, even until past twelve.

His father told him all he knew about the Baron von Salis.

He was a young monster, a perfect giant, and a master of everything profligate and bad.

He had done some daring deed that had won favour with the Emperor, but men, as a rule, rather fought shy of the colossus.

He had done things which, perpetrated by persons of a lower degree, would have subjected them to summary process on the gallows, but which in one of his rank were regarded as venial.

The ex-merchant loved his son, and when he revealed his whole heart to him, declared himself willing to help him all in his power, even to paying the debt which Rudesheim had contracted to Von Salis.

But his son must proceed to Brenksburg, where the court was held, for the money.

This would take four days, and Edda was to be married in eight.

Besides, it was absolutely necessary to see her that evening, if only to reassure her.

The merchant in one way was pleased, as he had letters to write, and this delay would give him time.

Accordingly, the lovers met, exchanged the same vows as the night before, without feeling any monotony, and then parted.

Well mounted and well armed, the young soldier started on his way alone.

His rank was not such as to render travelling without company dangerous.

He rode, therefore, wholly unmolested during the first day, and put up at a roadside inn of poor appearance, but which contained many travellers.

This caused him to put up with a seat by the kitchen fire, instead of a bed.

One of his companions was of higher rank than himself, a belted knight, who, for some reason or other, kept his visor down, thus wholly concealing his features.

It was found that the only sleeping apartments had been engaged by a lady and her suite, also bound to Brenksburg.

As was usual in those gallant days, men thought nothing of stopping up all night for the sake of doing an act of politeness to a lady.

But Rhoderick was tired, and so after taking his meal modestly in a corner, leaned back against the wall and slept soundly.

Not so the knight.

Scarcely had Rhoderick closed his eyes when a serving man came in, and with a white and scared face approached his master.

He whispered something in his ear.

The noble leaped to his feet with a very strong and unnecessary expletive.

"How is this? Some one must have betrayed me—else it were impossible."

"My Lord, I tell you the plain and honest truth."

"I doubt it not, but what is to be done?" hissed the knight in his ear. "I am not to be baulked by a woman."

"I never knew you to be, my lord. But this is dangerous. She is going straight to the emperor, to lay her grievances before him, and you know best, my lord, what may be the results."

"Ruin, degradation, and disappointment. Were it a month hence, and I had wearied of my new bride, I had not cared so much."

"And the old father——"

"Must do as many others have done before him," was the brutal retort.

"My lord, what is to be done?"

"What retainers has she with her?"

"Six stout men and four squalling women."

"We are on the territory of Selkay the robber," mused the knight.

"Yes, my lord."

"You have been a faithful friend, Conrad. Go, secure the services of ten of his men, waylay them at the Devil's Pass, kill, slay, or secure them, and the fief of Grandberg is yours, on my knightly word."

Now, great rascal as the speaker was, this was an oath which he had never been known to break.

The serving man stood erect, pale and trembling.

"My lord, a squire must hold that fief."

"A squire, and in future days a knight," was the earnest reply.

"I am yours, my lord, body and soul," was the low and earnest rejoinder.

And after some further conversation the serving man retired, leaving the knight to his thoughts.

Not once had their attention been directed to the sleeping man in the corner.

The dawn was yet young when Rhoderick rose, shook himself, and in a loud, imperious voice demanded breakfast.

The knight had already taken his departure.

Rhoderick having been served, and having also paid most liberally, asked an interview with the lady staying in the house.

"On a matter of life and death," added Rhoderick, pressing a gold piece into the hand of Boniface.

In ten minutes the young soldier stood in the presence of a fair, delicate young woman of about two and twenty.

She was beautiful, but with an unmistakable look of care and sorrow.

With a low bow, he asked privacy.

Judging from his looks that the subject of his interview was serious, she waved her attendants away.

In short, brief sentences, he told the story he had heard over-night.

"Wretch, monster, villain," she said, placing her left hand on her wildly panting heart, "what poor unfortunate is to suffer now ?"

"Lady, pardon me if I ask your name," he answered, eagerly.

"Baroness Von Salis," she replied.

Rhoderick caught her hand and kissed it.

The young lady looked amazed.

"Pardon me," he said, "and hear my explanation."

Which she did patiently enough.

When an hour later she started off in her litter, it was Rhoderick of Jansuch who rode at its head, supported by her six retainers and with four more stout fellows, who, under promise of reward, had been pressed into the service.

Had they not been forewarned they would have been undoubtedly surprised and cut to pieces.

The spot selected for the ambuscade was a dark and gloomy hollow way, leading into a kind of circular hollow.

Rhoderick rode first.

All were ready, and when with a terrible shout, intended to fill the souls of the attacked with terror, Conrad and his gang dashed out from the forest, they were met by prepared and trained men.

The fight was hot, fierce, desperate, but short.

Rhoderick himself picked out Conrad, pressed him close, and finally hurling him from his horse leaped off his, and held a dagger to his throat.

"Spare me," cried the ruffian.

"I will," said Rhoderick, "your punishment shall be the loss of the fief of Grandberg."

"My God, who and what are you ?"

"It matters not, your master just now, for your hired ruffians are killed and dispersed, and the Baroness von Salis is free to proceed to court.

As the serving man knew his master never forgot or forgave a failure, Master Conrad at once vowed solemn fealty to his mistress, and confessed the whole plot.

As soon as he had done so, to his great astonishment, he was seized, mounted on a mule, and so secured as to make his escape impossible.

In this way they entered Brenksberg.

A number of nobles, knights, and men of high degree, were in front of the Emperor's palace when they entered.

It was hot, and the Baroness Von Salis had cast aside the curtains of her litter.

Her eyes suddenly encountered those of her husband, glancing at her with a look of fierce and indescribable hate mingled with surprise.

His eyes next fell upon Conrad, who looked the picture of misery and despair.

Without a word the baron turned away and rode off, while the cavalcade entered the imperial palace.

It was not difficult for a lady, and that lady the wife of a favourite, to obtain an audience of the emperor.

But the emperor's astonishment may be conceived when he heard the horrors that wife had to repeat.

He listened amazed.

"Send for the Baron von Salis," he said, twirling his moustache until it cracked.

But the Baron von Salis was nowhere to be found.

He had ridden to his lodgings, called all his people together, and rode off to Rudesheim.

Rhoderick's blood ran cold.

His designs on Edda would be carried out.

Once married, he would carry her off to Hungary or some other retired region, and defy the power of the emperor and popedom.

But the emperor gave him hope.

Meanwhile, poor Edda was waiting the return of her lover with a wildly-beating heart.

Her father was grumpier and grumpier.

His wine was running short.

Somehow or other there had been a bad

vintage or two, and the wine was of inferior quality.

The baron was wont to know his wine by the colour of the hogshead.

Black was the inferior quality; green was second; but red was the best—the choicest bin, as we should say now.

No red hogsheads were left.

This, with the debt in money owing to the Baron von Salis, put him in a very bad humour.

Edda, who usually could do anything she liked with him, could scarcely venture to speak.

When she solemnly declared that she would throw herself off the battlements rather than marry a man she hated, a monster, a brute, a hideous giant, she took care to be at a respectful distance.

Men suffering from dyspepsia and the gout are not apt to be very choice in their language now-a-days, but then swearing was quite equal to what it was in Flanders.

Her father stormed and blasphemed until he was black in the face, and Edda, terrified beyond measure, retired to her room.

Not an hour later in came the Baron von Salis, surrounded by the roughest of his retainers.

He had received, this was his story, an appointment as ambassador to the Turks, and must away at once.

But his wife must go with him.

The Baron von Rudesheim and Bromserberg told him frankly that he might go to the warm regions for all he cared, and take his daughter with him.

When, however, they had conversed together, for some time, they became more amicable.

All was agreed, and Father Eustache was sent to, with a request to attend early in the morning.

Then began the usual potations, the elder baron all the time regretting the absence of any more of the red butts—the choicest vintage of all Germany.

As for von Salis, as long as there was drink in sufficient quantity he cared not.

Thus passed the night.

Early next day it was intimated to Edda that her wedding day was advanced two days.

Her new lord and master was awaiting her presence.

Edda believing, even despite all appearance, that no woman could be forced to marry against her will, came down to breakfast, which, as served in those days, was a solid and substantial meal.

The two barons awaited her, and, if we did not utterly eschew facetiousness, or all attempts at it, we might have said a third baron—of beef.

Both were grave, and ate in silence.

"Daughter," suddenly observed he of Rudesheim, "are you aware that this is your wedding day?"

"Most certainly, respected father, I am not. The daughters of our house are not married with such scant ceremony," was the grave reply.

"Fair lady," said the Baron von Salis, "I am ordered on special mission to the Turks, and my wife must go with me."

"I am no wife of yours."

"But you will be in an hour."

"Never."

"Think of your father, and his debts which can never be paid."

"That is not my affair, Sir Salis."

"Ungrateful girl," roared the Baron von Rudesheim, "this to me, who have reared you, made you quite a princess in your own house. To your chamber, child, and be ready in an hour. Do you look to it," he added, addressing her head tire-woman, "if she be not, your ears shall pay for it."

This was a threat which the baron was quite capable of realising, and hence Edda was alone in her opposition to the wedding.

But the Baron von Salis had other fears.

Rudesheim wished the castle to flow with wine, to have all the peasantry to view the ceremony, and to keep up the old style of marriage.

Von Salis, professing an utter contempt for the vulgar herd, ordered the castle gates to be closed as soon as the priest arrived, and no one to be admitted under any pretence whatever.

At eleven the priest came, and was informed what he had to do.

Through all the reticences of the barons, he soon saw that he had to perform an enforced marriage.

He was not a bad man, but in those days the nobles were everything, and humble churchmen—not primates, bishops, and abbots—had to yield to the gauntlet.

He made up his mind, and while waiting took his slice of fat capon and his goblet of wine.

Twelve came, and Edda was summoned.

She came, robed in white, but the dress was not so white as her face.

"Father Eustache," she said, on entering the room. "I solemnly appeal to you. I hate and loathe this man. Sooner would I be the bride of death than this monster.

Marry me at your peril.   I shall appeal to the Pope."

" I cannot proceed with the ceremony," faltered the worthy priest.

" You must," said von Salis, drily. " I care not for pope, or legate.   The girl's father gives her to me—and married or not she is mine."

" Proceed," growled the Baron of Rudesheim.

At this moment such a trumpet sound as once shook the walls of Jericho was heard, and all stared at one another.

" Proceed," said Salis, whose face was livid and white, " at once.   Let the trumpet wait."

" Not without knowing what it is," cried the master of the house.

And, followed by the greater part of the company, he went to the ramparts.

" Who calls ?"   was   the answering cry.

The vassals of the baron, understanding that his daughter was to be married, wished to present their baron with a butt of red wine, one which had been kept in reserve for the occasion.

" Open the gates, down with the drawbridge," roared the baron.

And before Von Salis could interfere the procession entered the archway of the tower.

There was the butt, a very large one, and escorted by a number of peasants, men-at-arms, and two knights.

The butt was of the largest, and drawn by four oxen.

Forgetting all else, the baron hastened to welcome the gift.   All followed him.

As they reached the courtyard the butt apparently split in two, and a lady stepped out.

" Malediction—a trick !" cried Baron Rudesheim.

" My wife !" roared von Salis.

" Yes sir, in time to save a young and innocent girl from misery," said his consort.

" What does all this mean ?" yelled Rudesheim.

" I will explain," answered Rhoderick, removing his visor, and receiving Edda in his arms, " and moreover pay all debts owing to this insolent baron."

" That will I do," said the second knight, removing his helmet, and standing revealed—"the Emperor."

" Rudesheim, I give your daughter to my friend, Count Von Jansuch, to whom I have given the forfeited estates of Salis. Baron, you I commend to the headsman."

But, on the prayers of his wife, he was handed over to her, to escape next day, and be heard of no more except as a robber chief.

And this, with its pleasant ending, is the " Legend of the Red Butt of Rudesheim."

END OF RUDESHEIM ; OR, THE LEGEND OF THE RED BUTT.

THE SAPPHIRE RING.

(A LEGEND OF SPEILBERG.)

NEARLY opposite Enns, on the dark rolling Danube, whose sources are in the Black Forest and whose exit is in the Black Sea, where

Broad sails glancing o'er the regal stream
Spread their white bosoms to the morning beam,

and built on the upper angle of an island in the river, where it is divided into two branches, stands the ancient castle of Speilberg, once a magnificent residence, now a roofless and deserted ruin.

Like its feudal neighbours, this was once a stronghold of no small importance, where the grand object of its chief was to collect toll from the numerous merchant barges that kept up a precarious traffic between Ratisbon and Vienna.

Considering the number of these tolls, baronial and monastic, with which the whole passage was lined, and the tribute extorted by each, it appears strange that anything valuable should have remained to the owner after having been pounced upon by the vultures of the rocks.

The ruin is embowered in trees, and, with its square tower far overtopping the outer buildings, is a fine object for the pencil.

The pile of rocks on which the castle is built is generally visible at low water, and when the stream is swollen considerable risk is incurred by the boatmen, particularly as the stream at this point gradually increases to a rapid, and requires much skill and attention in the management of the oar.

As the only communication between the castle and the main land was by boat, all its indwellers were necessarily boatmen, and none were more active and vigorous at managing a small craft through the rapids than young Hugo de Bergh, a brave and devoted lad of seventeen.

He was a page to the haughty Rufus de Bergh, a distant relative it was said, and had been mysteriously brought up in the Black Forest until about two years before.

Rufus de Bergh was a jolly old baron of the early school.

He ate and drank, and robbed the defenceless, and ground down his tenants to the last coin, and thought of nothing save personal enjoyment.

In his younger days he had married a beautiful girl, who after a year or two he had worried into her grave, leaving behind a sweet girl, who, at the time of which we speak, was about fourteen.

She was tall and graceful for her age, and, under the tuition of a good-natured priest, slightly more accomplished than most girls of the time.

Friar Paul had a mania for education, and when Hugo came to the castle he took him under his wing.

At first the boy was so delighted with his island home, his boat, his arbalest, and the liberty allowed him, that he regarded study as a nuisance.

But this lad had a design, and insisted on the priest taking him in hand

Father Paul made him a fellow pupil of Bertha's, and the thing was done. He made no further resistance.

At the end of two years he had learned all that was usually taught in those days, but had not the remotest wish to become a priest.

He was too wildly and madly in love with Bertha to make this possible.

Never was there a happier pair of turtle doves, but their dream was shortly to be rudely shattered.

Bertha sat in her boudoir, with Hugo at her feet, reading from the same richly illuminated manuscript, some romance of old, telling of deeds of chivalry and love, and of high and bright deeds which become true knights.

Suddenly the tapestry was raised, and the Baron de Bergh entered the room.

It would be impious to put on paper the words he used, for my lord was a hard swearer, and in those days the courtesies of life were little considered.

He overwhelmed his daughter with reproaches, and but for the entrance of the priest, who sternly rebuked him, he would have proceeded to use personal violence towards Hugo.

After pouring out the vials of his wrath upon all three, he ordered Bertha to her bower and Hugo to the lowest dungeon of the castle, which was not saying much, as, the castle being built on a flat rock, without any but natural foundations, the said cell of incarceration was in the thickness of the wall.

Having thus satisfied his momentary feelings of vengeance, the baron retired to his banquetting hall, there to soothe his feelings under the influence of beef and beer, and further to decide the fate of the culprits.

The priest, who was a jolly and worthy man, was decided, and, perhaps, sarcastic in his suggestions—he decidedly proposed that the punishment should be marriage.

To this the baron fiercely demurred, and said that he would see them hanged first.

Finally, he made up his mind to immure the young lady in a convent until she reached years of discretion, and was prepared to marry the man of his choice, while Hugo should be pitched off the battlements into the boiling river, as an example to all future pages who made love to their master's daughters.

Having come to this very satisfactory conclusion, the baron went on quaffing strong ale until even his seasoned head gave way, and he fell flat on the floor under the huge oak table, where, his followers being equally jovial with him-

THE CASTLE OF SPEILBERG.

self, they suffered him to remain until the morning.

When quite assured of this state of affairs, the priest, who had himself sacrificed slightly on the shrine of Bacchus, rose, and made his way to the apartments occupied by the beautiful Bertha.

That young lady had cried herself to sleep, but when summoned by a maid, soon admitted the priest, who told her in plain words her father's terrible decision.

As the young lady had no desire to go to a nunnery, nor any intention to have her young and handsome lover pitched headlong over the battlements, she informed the priest of the fact.

He, however, was loath to go against her father's wishes, but suggested that as she was his daughter she might not have such scruples.

Refuse to enter a convent she could, and probably her grim father would yield on this point, but the page was in a really dangerous position.

"Where is the key of the dungeon?"

"Very probably in the door," suggested the priest, with a twinkling eye.

"Come," was the maidenly response.

And both descended the back stairs, used by domestics and others occasionally who sought privacy, until they reached the basement.

Here, in a dark and gloomy passage,

they found a man sleeping on the bare stones.

He was the jailor, who, while walking up and down as sentry, had fallen asleep.

Holding her lighted taper so as not to allow the reflection to fall on his eyes, Bertha removed the key from his belt, and hastily opened the door of the one solitary dungeon of the castle.

Hugo slept.

One touch from the hand of the girl was enough, and he sat bolt upright.

"Hush—not a word—follow me," said the trembling girl.

And she led the youth away, leaving the key in the door, somewhat regardless of the fact that her passionate father would very likely punish the careless jailor for her deed.

As soon as they were in an upper chamber, the priest accompanying them, Bertha gave way to her womanly feelings and wept.

The courage which had hitherto sustained her quite failed.

"No time is to be lost," murmured Father Paul, after some minutes.

"And must you go?" she cried.

"If you doubt it," drily remarked the priest, "he had better go back to his dungeon."

But Hugo having been made acquainted with his proposed father-in-law's kind wishes in his behalf, declared he would see the world in preference to the bottom of the Danube, and elected to depart that very night.

He, however, whispered in the ear of the trembling girl a solemn vow to return and wed her, exacting from her an equally solemn vow to be faithful to him even unto death.

Bertha warmly reciprocated his wishes, and, in token of their indissoluble betrothal, gave him a beautiful sapphire ring which had belonged to her mother, and which she herself placed upon the youth's finger.

We cannot linger over the rhapsodies and last words which followed, but finally Hugo slipped down into the courtyard, undid all the heavy bolts and bars of the great gate, and went out, forgetting even to close the door behind him.

The rage and fury of the baron knew no bounds.

He cursed and swore until he was black in the face, and so terrified his doorkeeper and the sentinel, that they ran away, and joined the robbers of the Black Forest.

Hugo in the meantime, went to the lower part of the island, and dropping into the water, swam to the opposite shore, where presently he stood upright as free as when born, except for his wet clothes, his education, and the sapphire ring, with which he set out upon his travels.

   ⚬   ⚬   ⚬

Six years had passed away, when a cavalier, in the dress of a knight, wended his way alone through the Black Forest, then one of the most dangerous of places.

But a knight, armed cap-a-pie, with a heavy sword, a spiked club that had knocked the steel-clad heads of many a Saracen, and a spear that looked as if it would spit half a dozen ordinary men, was not to be attacked with impunity.

The knight threaded the forest slowly and thoughtfully.

An occasional glance at the heavens enabled him to keep in a tolerably straight direction.

But presently the shadows began to lengthen, and night to herald its approach, when further progress would be impossible.

And yet no shelter offered itself.

As the darkness became thicker and heavier, he relinquished his bridle, and allowed his horse its own way.

After some time he was rewarded by the sound of a bell tinkling, and hastening in the direction, he found that he had fallen upon the hermitage of some pious priest.

He at once knocked at the heavy wooden door.

"Who knocks?" said a genial voice.

"A knight from Palestine, a soldier of the true Cross, who has lost his way."

"Come in, soldier of the true Cross," continued the other, opening the door. "Never shall it be said that one who serves the same master as myself should be turned from my door, however humble."

"But my horse?"

"There is a shed at the back of the hermitage. I had a dapple mule a week ago, but the heathen thieves of the forest stole the animal. Stay, as you know not the place, I will myself see to your steed."

Having fulfilled his promise on this point, the hermit led the knight into his home.

It was large and comfortable, with a table, a couple of chairs, and a rude couch.

Without any parley or hesitation, the hermit went to a cupboard and brought out some of the good things which the piety of his friends rather overloaded him with—white bread, roast game, a venison pasty, and several flagons of wine.

"My people are generous—the more that I often have guests in the wilderness. I have many long and weary walks to shrive the dying, and find solid food necessary. Of course, I duly fast," said the priest, "on fast days, but keep up my strength in the meantime."

The knight smiled, and raising his vizor partially, began to pay attention to the good things which lay before him.

When his appetite was satisfied, the priest, no mean trencherman, poured out two large pint goblets full of wine, and pledged his guest.

Then with a merry twinkle of his eye, and his cup raised, he began in a rich, mellow voice—

> Brother, life is frail as grass,
> Dry clay is apt to moulder;
> But moistened with a cheerful glass,
> Good wine's the best of solder:
>   Then brothers drink, and shout the while
>   Waeshael! Waeshael! (Your health).
>
> Brother, if the journey's rough,
> And needs some small concession;
> To-morrow will be time enough
> For penance or confession:
>   Meantime we'll drink, and shout the while
>   Waeshael! Waeshael!
>
> Brother, prayer is vastly good,
> So—after meals—is fasting;
> 'Tis well to watch beside the rood,
> But while the hymn's lasting:
>   We'll chant through sacristy and aisle,
>   Waeshael! Waeshael!

Before he had finished, the knight was laughing heartily.

"Thou art a merry priest," he said, "cans't give me couch to-nigh? I must be on my way by day-break."

"Take off your iron," replied the other, "and I will prepare you a bed that shall be as soft as any or lady's bower."

He then rose, and drew forth a quantity of soft grass in bundles, which he undid and spread on the couch.

When this was done to his satisfaction, he covered it all with skins and turned triumphantly to the knight.

He stood a stalwart, handsome man before him, with fair beard and moustache, and the glow of health on his ruddy countenance.

He wore a rich dress of velvet, and looked every inch a soldier.

As the priest approached the fire place, where a huge fire cast out a pleasant glow, something shone on the young knight's finger.

"Heavens!" cried the priest in a tone of wild delight, "it is my Hugo."

"Dear father Paul," replied the young man warmly, "so I am not forgotten?"

"Ever remembered!" exclaimed the hermit.

"But what of the baron—of Bertha?" eagerly demanded the youth.

"The baron is a raving old madman; hence, have I taken my quarters here. When the drink is in him now, I dare not stand in his presence. As for Bertha, she is an angel."

"But does she believe me alive?"

"There is the question. A fellow has recently appeared at the castle who declares himself to be the nephew of the baron. You must know his elder brother had two sons—one who disappeared in his infancy, stolen it was thought, and the other who became a robber.

"Both inherit Speilberg before the baron; but you know might is right.

"Well, the second son—robber as he is—by name Stephen, has appeared at the castle, claiming to be next heir. Somehow, ruffian, roisterer and murderer though he be, he is supported by the Elector, and has so overcome and terrified the baron that he yields to him in everything.

"Stephen is master at the castle, and, in order to make matters comfortable, has agreed to accept the appanage of the estate as the husband of Bertha."

"But I live," cried Hugo.

"Listen, my friend. Stephen solemnly declares that the page Hugo joined the bandits of the Black Forest, and, after a desperate and riotous career, was hanged to a tree for murder. The baron thinks it very likely; but Bertha will not believe a word."

"Brave girl! good heart!"

"But, my young friend, to-morrow, at twelve, unless Bertha produces a champion—one who will fight the desperate outlaw who now rules the castle with a rod of iron—she will have to wed him. The baron swears by all the saints in the calendar, and by a good many persons not so harmless, that six years absolves her from all oaths. So there will be great doings at the castle to-morrow, when I have to be present, and must, whether I will it or not, join their hands in holy matrimony."

Hugo groaned deeply, took up another flagon, drank it off by way of clearing his head, and then entered into a long and earnest conversation with the priest, whose genial character and good heart had preserved him from the hard, monkish absence of feeling so often generated by his profession.

The monk explained that Stephen had, as it were, taken the castle by a sort of surprise, entering it one morning with a horde of ruffians, who had quartered themselves upon the helpless baron.

The consequences were evil.

Scarcely a merchant barge was allowed to pass without being pillaged; as at high water the place was very dangerous, and many shipwrecks were the consequence, when the evil followers of Stephen, under pretence of helping the unfortunate bargemen, made a clear sweep of all their goods.

The cellar, supposed to be one of the best supplied of any on the Danube, was nearly dry, and the impious and sacrilegous Stephen was trying to induce the baron to sell all the family plate, the chapel gold and silver candlesticks, and other treasures, to obtain a new supply

Hitherto the baron had refused, but the marriage once consummated, his wishes could no longer be restrained.

While they were still speaking a knock came at the door, and a man in a loud voice asked for shelter.

The priest opened, and a rude, unkempt individual, armed with a sword and short battleaxe, as well as bow and arrows, but in the garb of a forester, entered, and bowed civilly.

"I have business at Speilberg to-morrow," he said bluntly, "and would fain have a mouthful to eat and drink, with a seat by the fire until morning."

"I have business at Speilberg to-morrow," replied the monk, giving him the good cheer he demanded, "and as you are a stout fellow, perhaps you will not refuse to accompany me."

"I shall be only too happy," said the forester, with a fierce gleam in his eyes. "But this noble gentleman?"

"Has his own business to attend to," observed the priest drily.

Hugo finding that no further private conversation could take place, now cast himself on the couch prepared for him, and, despite the tumultuous character of his thoughts, slept soundly, leaving the hermit and his strange visitor to themselves.

The rude forester, despite his rough education and character, exhibited considerable shrewdness and some higher and better feelings in his conversation.

Of his history he would tell nothing, and the priest, who was, despite himself, deeply interested in him, forbore to press him.

We now return to the interior of the picturesque castle of Speilberg, which the exigencies of modern society and continued wars and revolutions have left in such a ruinous state.

The baron was much changed.

Hard drinking and eating, the vices of the period, had made him look old and bloated, while frequent severe twinges of the gout roused him to a state of delirious madness.

His temper was not improved, and though there was still sufficient of parental affection in his soul to prevent his actually ill-using her, he poured all the floodgates of his eloquence on his daughter's devoted head.

During four years she had refused every suitor—no matter what their rank, youth, or beauty—to the marvellous surprise and rage of her father.

But now that Stephen de Bergh had presented himself, and claimed not only the castle but the baron's daughter's hand, his fierce and horrible denunciations were terrible to hear.

Had she married young De Courcy, the bravest knight in Christendom, he would have had a friend and protector instead of a sullen foe.

He, too, was a protégé of the Elector, and would have defied the brute force, insolence, and violence of Stephen de Bergh.

He rose tolerably early on the memorable day that was to see his complete subjection to a man he hated, as much had to be seen to, especially in the festive department, many guests having been invited to the bridal.

This was a matter the baron bold allowed no one else to see to. He breakfasted in his usual style, his daughter remaining in her own chamber. He summoned her, but she would not come.

Stephen de Bergh sat by his future father-in-law. He was quite as hot a *bon vivant* as the other, and, for a young man, singularly bloated and coarse.

His laugh was wild and savage, and there was an evident desire to have the thing over.

About an hour after the first meal was over guests began to arrive, among others the priest, who, before he paid his respects to his master, sought out the favourite attendant of the young lady, and had some minutes' conversation with her.

The girl heard him with rapture and delight.

Then the priest joined the baron and his guests, who were collecting in the great hall, a structure of great beauty, and which was now fitted up at one end as a chapel for the interesting ceremony, at the other with a banquetting board already laid.

The baron, in an arm chair, with considerable traces of a scowl on his ruddy countenance, received his guests sitting. By his side, richly dressed, but awkward and rough, was Stephen de Bergh.

Whether it was the gout or the presence of this individual, it is hard to say, but the baron spoke shortly and sharply, even to the priest.

That personage looked at all meekly, and withdrew to converse with some of the new arrivals, amongst whom were some rich burghers, and a tall pilgrim dressed in a cloak and cowl.

The hour of midday approached, and the baron being told that his daughter was coming, ordered a cup of wine to be handed round.

Then to the sound of rude wind instruments the young girl entered.

Young girl—the bud had expanded into a full-blown rose, and the child was a beautiful woman.

"Knights, nobles, and worshipful burghers," said the baron, "my daughter, being now twenty years of age, and myself verging on the grave, I think it high time she was married. The days are troublous, and a woman with an inheritance like this castle and estate, requires a man to protect her."

A murmur of agreement followed.

"Stephen de Bergh, son of my late brother Lionel, being my nearest relative, I have thought it were well to choose him for a son-in-law. He is my nephew, and heir after my daughter."

"Before," muttered Stephen, ungraciously.

"I have therefore called you here together to witness the ceremony. Stand forth, Stephen de Bergh, and Bertha Lina, my daughter."

Stephen stalked forth.

"You demand formally the hand of my daughter?" said the old baron.

"I do."

"And you accept him as your husband?"

"No!" cried Bertha, "no, by every saint in heaven, I would more readily marry the meanest herd on my father's land than this base tyrant. I reject him, and cast down this ring for my champion to take up to do battle for me against this foul and recreant traitor."

The baron stormed, the suitor foamed at the mouth, the people present all talked at once, save only one—the cowled stranger.

He strode into the middle of the hall, picked up the sapphire ring, which Bertha had received from the priest as a token, cast off his cloak, and stood a mailed knight before the assembly.

"Who and what are you?" gasped the baron.

"Hugo de Bergh, your sometime page," replied the other, raising his visor.

Stephen turned with a pale and livid countenance to one of his attendants, and bade him bring him his armour and weapons.

"Hold!" thundered the baron, rising, and advancing to where Hugo stood, "this must not be. Stephen de Bergh, bow to your elder brother and feudal lord, the Baron of Speilberg."

"Never! If I cannot have his blood I will never yield. He is no brother to me."

"But I am," roared the forester, dashing into the room, "and I slay thee, Lefranc the robber, foul usurper of another man's rights."

And he stabbed the supposed Stephen almost to the heart ere he could make any defence.

"A priest! I die!" gasped the man; and then, as Father Paul advanced, "I am Lefranc. My murderer is Stephen de Bergh."

Lionel, Baron of Bergh, and heir of Speilberg, died, leaving two very young children, and his brother, according to the custom of the times, assumed the lordship in trust for the children.

They were carefully brought up for some time by an old aunt, who dying, Hugo, without his parentage being made known, was taken by his uncle as a page, while Stephen, fond of the forest and its ways, wandered away and joined a tribe of lawless men commanded by Ambrose Lefranc, whose son became Stephen's companion.

At the death of Ambrose, the son, who knew the story of Stephen, attacked him in a cowardly way, left him for dead, and came to the castle in his name.

Stephen lay weeks and months ill in a monastery, not hearing of the imposture. When, however, he regained his strength he journeyed to Speilberg, filled by thoughts of revenge.

The result we know.

When all these explanations had been given the young crusader consented to waive his right of inheritance during the baron's lifetime, on condition that he gave him his daughter.

"But my daughter has vowed never to marry," observed the baron maliciously.

"Only to the holder of the sapphire ring," replied the happy girl, advancing.

"Let it be then—if it is your free will this time," cried the baron.

Such was the fortunate, though unlooked-for, end of the Legend of Speilberg.

END OF THE SAPPHIRE RING.

[Continued from page 272.]

RHEINECK;
OR, RUDOLF THE RED HEART.

"YOU are too good," he observed.

Now the lady, who had been told that he would be of high, if not exalted rank, and who had feared to see some old or middle-aged man, was only too agreeably surprised.

"Be seated, my lord," she said with a timid blush, "I had been warned of an intrusion, which,"—still a more beautiful blush—"is no intrusion."

"You have a taste for pictures ?" he remarked, for the want of something else to say.

"All the daughters of our house," she said, with considerable dignity, "have been taught all the accomplishments which pertain to royal princesses."

Edmund sprang to his feet.

"I have the honour to address her highness the Princess Agnes of Burgundy !"

"The same—but why feign surprise ?" she said, with charming *naiveté* ; "you came here to—to——"

"Make love in my absence," said a terrible voice, and turning swiftly round they saw a nobleman, richly dressed, his face distorted with passion, standing before them with a drawn sword in his hand.

Agnes looked wildly from one to another, and nearly fainted.

"Away, groveling," cried the other, whose face was not of the handsomest.

"Dare repeat those words !" said the youth, who was dressed as a page, drawing a dagger. "Know that Edmund of Rheineck is not be insulted with impunity."

"So," replied the other, with the most perfect calm and equanimity, "you are my dainty brother—the usurper of my rights. 'Tis well ; this night, as sure as my name is Rupeert of the Red Heart, you die ! I swear it by all——"

"Stay," cried the young girl, passionately ; "if you are he whom my guardian intends as my husband, withdraw this rash oath, or I do swear to be the bride of heaven !"

"What know you of him !" continued the disinherited son of Rheineck ; "how came he here in this gallery ?"

"That I know not ; I never saw him in my life until five minutes ago—"

"Come away, madman ! What have you done ?" said the terrified burgher, who had heard nearly all that had passed with almost abject terror ; "how came you here, and what know you of this terrible man ?"

"He is my half-brother. My father has repudiated him, and given me the inheritance."

The burgher kept wringing his hands until he had drawn the youth quite away.

"You have done a fell and dangerous thing, young sir !" he said ; "and such is the power and interest of this man that you and yours are in hourly peril of your lives. Why not fly ?"

"My father will not leave until we have asked and obtained justice of the emperor," was the calm and stern reply.

"Madmen both," cried the burgher.

He was about to say more, when he was hastily summoned to the banquetting hall.

"Go to your apartments—keep still—move not until I see you," he whispered, and left the bewildered youth to return to his father.

"My eldest son betrothed to Agnes of Burgundy—poor lamb. It must not—shall not be. We must see the emperor—it must not, shall not be !"

It might appear strange in modern times, when the minutest incidents of high life are known to the multitude, that the stalwart baron should appeal against a recreant knight to the emperor.

Rudolph was noted for his cruelty.

When his enemy Siegfred was made prisoner, he imprisoned him, armed *cap-a-pie* in armour, in a cage for seven years.

The unfortunate man escaped after fearful sufferings.

Some time later, after a pretended reconciliation with Adolf von Berg, he in an unguarded moment suddenly re-captured him, and sent him to be stripped naked, smeared with honey from head to foot, and placed in a cage, where he was bitten to death by bees and other insects.

"I cannot believe such things of my sovereign," said the old man ; "so do the mob always speak of their betters. He may be severe, but neither unjust nor cruel."

"Justice may be blind," said Hans, who entered the room at that moment, "but she has a waxen nose, and attracts all the honey."

" What want you ? why come you here ? I left you in charge of Rheineck—"

" There is no such place—pills must be bolted, not chewed, and the truth must be told not concealed !" cried Hans.

" No such place—"

" The man who calls himself rightful Baron of Rheineck, after wasting all the wine and meats, has dismantled the walls, and left nothing of his ancestral home but ruins."

" May the great curse——" began the baron.

" Father, he is your son and my brother," said Edmund—" he has been wicked, but it behoves you not to curse him."

" My noble son, but I will have justice. No man who has thus disgraced himself shall wear golden spurs. Thank God ! we are still wealthy, and the walls of Rheineck shall be rebuilt."

And the old man, drawing the faithful old soldier, who from choice and love of freedom had become a swineherd, on one side, obtained from him the particulars of the shocking event which had sealed the doom of Rheineck for ever.

" And this reiter captain—this chief of banditti is my son ?" said the old man.

" He is ; but do not mourn, my master," replied the soldier, " you have one well worthy of your glorious name."

" But this was my eldest born—doomed, all said, to high and mighty things. Here comes the burgher."

" Most noble baron," said the citizen, who was pale and anxious, " you have sent for me."

" I have ; many an evil thing has been done unto me, and now the renegade who calls himself my son has dismantled my home and laid my ancestral house in ruins," cried the unhappy father.

" But, my thrice illustrious and noble relative," said the burgher, in an anxious tone, " you know his highness the Emperor has ordered the destruction of all the strongholds on the Rhine which molest the peaceful trader and the voyager."

" I am no robber-baron !" cried the other, proudly. " I never took more than was my legal right, and such as sought hospitality of me never found me a churlish host."

" 'Tis true, most noble sir. And now your wish, my lord baron."

" I understand his highness the Emperor has returned. I wish to see him in person, as by my rank I am entitled to, and to ask him for justice."

" Against whom ?" said the burgher, with a sorrowful and pained look.

" Against my son," cried the baron, re-pressing, with Spartan courage, all signs of sorrow and emotion.

" I will transmit your petition," replied the worthy citizen, and retired.

" At last !" cried the hopeful baron.

" I have little hope, father. I am told, more than eighty castles have been dismantled besides ours," replied the son.*

" We shall see ; there may be reasons for punishing those who have outraged the law. I have never done so," answered the baron, coldly.

Edmund said no more, but sought out his cousin Emma, to whom he usually confided his sorrows.

" She has received the command of the Princess Agnes of Burgundy to attend her," replied the attendant handmaiden.

Edmund asked harshly what for.

" Her highness is to be married at midnight," replied the girl, " and your cousin is to be one of the bridesmaids."

" My God—what will my father say ?" cried the unhappy young man, and hurried away to announce the dreadful news.

" My poor Emma, my innocent niece to be bridesmaid to that unfortunate girl, doomed to be wife of my ingrate son !" exclaimed the father. " There is still time, I must and will stop this fearful tragedy, I must and will see the emperor—"

" You shall," replied the burgher, entering with a detachment of the Imperial guards, " when the marriage you so much deprecate is over. Until then you are a close prisoner."

" What means this treachery ?" shouted the unhappy father.

" I am your best friend," said the citizen, gently, " and would warn you to be cautious what you say when before his imperial highness. The knight you repudiate is a great friend of his, or he would not give unto him a princess so fair as Agnes of Burgundy."

" Poor sacrificed innocent lamb," muttered the baron, " that I should not be able to save her—"

" She might not thank you," said the burgher drily, " I pray you follow me. I have to be present at this wedding. In the meantime my orders are strict. You are to attend me to the Imperial palace."

To resist the baron and his son knew was vain indeed, and they obeyed.

They were surrounded by the guard, hurried along the street, and taken by one of the back and smaller entrances into the palace of the modern Cæsars, who then

* Rudolph the Second did all he could to break the power of the nobles.

under a good deal of papal influence governed the almost ungovernable German confederation.

"My son, the glory of my house has set," cried the father when they were alone. "A baron of Rheineck has lived to be treated as a traitor and a malefactor, while your cousin, your affianced wife, is dragged to play a part in an unholy marriage," cried the passionate old man.

"Father, be comforted. There is much that is strange and mysterious in all this," observed the son, "but something seems to tell me all will yet end well."

"You too turn against me!" cried the baron, and, refusing to be comforted, he turned away.

Presently refreshments were brought, which both declined.

Finally the burgher entered.

"My dear friend," he said, in a low and tremulous tone, "for Heaven's, for mercy's sake, be careful what you say. 'Tis a strange court, and many a wild and foolish speech has been punished with instant death."

"What would you have me do?"

"Weigh well every word you speak, and above all, before you make any rash assertions, wait until the Emperor himself gives you leave to speak."

"I will restrain myself."

"Then follow me, and Heaven have you in its holy keeping, for on the next half-hour depends your fate and that of all who are dear to you."

"Go on, you excite my curiosity."

"As for you, young man," addddressing the younger knight, "not one word, as you value your immortal soul."

"Is my brother, then, so dreadful?" asked Edmund, in a melancholy tone.

"Heavens, will you be wise? You have one true and faithful friend at court, one who has sacrificed much for your sake. We were in time, and, as old Hans would say, 'Words are silver—but silence is gold.'"

And he led the way into the presence chamber of the emperor.

It was a vast hall.

On a throne sat two personages, while all around were knights, barons, baronets, and all the princes and vassals of the great confederation called Germany, of which the emperor was little more than nominal sovereign.

So dazzling was the sight that both father and son were greatly confused.

All they could see was a confused mass of richly dressed noble ladies and noble-men, among whom they appeared out of place in their simple garb of travelling citizens.

"You are the Baron of Rheineck?" said a chamberlain, advancing.

"That is my name."

"You wish to perfer a request to the emperor?" he continued.

"I do," cried the baron, recovering himself.

"You are in his presence—speak," formally continued the chamberlain.

The baron saw nothing but a confused mass of gold, diamonds, rich dresses, plumes, and the other paraphernalia of imperial dignity.

"I ask for justice, your Majesty," he cried, in a ringing voice.

"Against whom?" said a cold, stern voice, amid profound silence.

The baron almost tottered to the ground.

On the throne sat, in the person of the emperor, the son against whom he came to ask justice!

The baron would have fallen had not Edmund supported him.

"Nobles, friends, and guests," continued the emperor, with a harsh laugh, "my father and brother are, it appears, the only persons here present who know not that Rudolph, not now of Rheineck, but of Hapsburg, is emperor of Germany."

"My liege," stammered the baron.

"You keep the emperor waiting," said the monarch, haughtily; "to table. Edmund, brother mine, yonder is our cousin."

It was no maze, no dream.

The Robber of the Rhine was Emperor of Germany, the first of the line of Hapsburg, from whom so many royal families are descended, including that of England and that of Austria.

It would require a long genealogical tree to explain the ramifications by which this was brought about.

"My son," said the old baron that night, "the sooner we leave Germany, the better.

He could not forget that though his son was king and emperor—he had overheard him in the cave of Elfrida.

The real motive of his intended crime was never known.

Perhaps after his election to the purple, he was ashamed of his humble relatives.

Be that as it may—at the end of a week, the baron, his son, and his son's wife, left the court for the distant parts of Austria, never again to see

THE ROBBER EMPEROR OF GERMANY.

END OF RHEINECK; OR, RUDOLF THE RED HEART.

Our next number will contain "The Tyrant Duke."

THE BARONS OF OLD OR THE ROBBERS OF THE RHINE

THE TYRANT DUKE;

OR, THE PEARL OF THE DANUBE.

ON the right bank of the Danube stands the ancient town of Straubing, in the centre of which rises the tall, square tower of the old Rathhaus, surmounted by its five pointed spires.

Close to the bridge is the castle, and outside the walls of the town is St. Peter's

"LONG DID THE MONSTER HOLD HER DOWN."

Church, which, although modernised, bears evidences of its great antiquity.

Here is the grave of one of the most beautiful women of the fifteenth century, the lovely and gentle Agnes Bernauer, the Pearl of the Danube.

Her superb beauty, her romantic love, and her cruel fate, have outlived many of the legends of the banks of that prince of rivers, and will live while history lasts and the waters of the Danube empty themselves into the Black Sea.

One lovely morning a handsome youth stood upon the banks of the Danube, alternately gazing upon the waters flowing at his feet and the forests that stretched away from its banks.

There was an anxious look upon his features, and he tapped his foot as though impatient, and turned quickly at every sound that broke the monotonous murmur of the waters, or the sighing of the leaves of the trees as they were kissed by the passing breeze.

Thus he stood for some time, when he suddenly started, the cloud on his brow vanished, smiles wreathed his lips, and his eyes brightened with joy.

Then he sprang forward, as from out of the forest glided a girl so lovely that she might have been mistaken for an angel or a fairy, so great was her beauty, so noble her bearing.

"My life! my Agnes!" cried the youth, clasping her to his bosom.

The young girl suffered her head to fall on his shoulder, murmuring in soft silvery accents—

"My lord, my dear lord."

"Nay; do not address me thus, sweet one," cried the youth. "Call me Albert, dear Albert. Think you I cannot waive my rank in presence of such loveliness? Though slaves pay homage to rank, rank now bears homage to beauty."

And again he pressed that lovely form to his bosom, and saluted those coral lips with a loving kiss.

Agnes twined her arms round his neck, and looked lovingly, yet half sorrowfully, into his eyes.

"Albert," she said, and her voice trembled as she spoke, "I had resolved to flee rather than seek you to-day, but when the appointed hour arrived I could not keep the resolve, for love was more powerful than reason."

"And wherefore would you flee me, dear one?" asked the youth, quickly.

"Are you not Albert of Bavaria, son of Duke Ernest, a knight and a noble, while I am but the daughter of a citizen, one of the common herd, unfit to mate with princes, or aspire beyond my station."

"And what of that?" asked Albert, "is not a knight and a noble, human, and is it not human to love, to worship beauty such as thine?"

"Alas, my lord, think of the difference of position, think of your father, your kindred, your station," said Agnes.

"Sweet one, I can think of none but thee. You are the only woman I can ever love. What care I for rank if it bring me not happiness? Why I would rather be the veriest peasant than bow to the will of others, rather than the dictates of my own heart. Agnes, I love you as man never yet loved woman, and, by my spurs, I will win you or I will perish in despair."

"Already hast thou won me, dear Albert; you have taught me to love, but, oh, what fatal passion is it that we cherish for each other!"

"Fatal, my fair one?" said Albert.

"Fatal indeed," she sighed. "For though we love we ne'er can wed."

"And wherefore not?" asked Albert.

"The Duke—— "

"What!" cried the impetuous youth. "Am I a child, that I shall accept the toy I must despise, and leave the one I love? No, by my soul! The duke may choose a bride for his son, but he cannot force him to wed her. To him I owe the duty of a son and a subject, no more. My heart, my will is my own; and I will follow the dictates of the one and the bent of the other."

The girl's eyes sparkled joyously.

Her arms twined more tightly round his neck.

Her heart fluttered within her bosom.

Then a paleness grew over her features, and the tears started to her eyes.

"Albert, Albert," she said, "the barrier is too high; it cannot, must not be. Were you to espouse the peasant girl, give her your proud name—ruin would fall upon your head and mine."

"Fear not that, my love, think only of the happiness in store for us both," said Albert.

"Say rather the misery, my lord. Your father, the duke, is proud and austere, his name disgraced by the marriage of his son with one of lowly birth, his anger would burst over us like a fearful torrent —the avalanche of his wrath would fall on our heads, and misery, a blighting misery, would be our portion. Oh, my lord, let us part at once and for ever!"

She unclasped her hands from his neck and strove to tear herself from his hold.

But he held her firmly clasped to his bosom.

She could feel his heart beating against her own, with its wild impassioned throbbings.

"Part!" he cried, "part at once and for ever! Bid me leap into the waters of the Danube, and perish before your eyes, but oh, speak not of parting, 'tis worse than death."

"Bid thee destroy thyself, Albert! Heaven forbid, live for happiness, fame and future, but forget her who now stands by your side, she is unworthy of the love of one so true, so noble."

"Agnes," he said, and his voice was tremulous with emotion, "you know not yet how deeply this heart can love, you know not the feelings with which your gentleness and beauty have inspired me, the holy love with which I regard you."

He caught her frantically to his bosom, and continued in an impassioned strain—

"Agnes, my beautiful, shall I love in vain? shall this beating heart be seared? shall I droop and perish in the very flower of my youth—when one word of thine would lift my soul to Heaven? Agnes, in mercy, say you will be mine—my wife."

He gazed into her upturned eyes, with a look of such longing passion, that she could not resist that wild appeal, and hanging upon his neck, she replied—

"Albert, that I love you dearer than my own existence I am free to confess; that to see you the husband of another would break my heart and drive me to despair, and perhaps death; and yet for your sake I hesitate to give you the promise you ask. I fear—I tremble at the consequences."

"Fear naught, dear one. Who would dare harm the wife of Albert of Bavaria? By my soul's hope of salvation, I would dye my good sword's blade to the very hilt in the blood of him who but uttered a word to give you pain—fear not for me, for yourself. Our undying affection will be the armour to shield us both from harm. Say then you will be mine—my bride, the wife of Albert of Bavaria."

She hesitated a moment, and then exclaimed in a whisper, that thrilled his very soul with joy—

"I will. Come weal or woe, I will be thine, Albert—thine until death!"

With a cry of joy Albert strained her to his heaving bosom, and rained kisses on her blushing cheeks and forehead.

"Mine—mine," he cried, "the purest pearl of the Danube, the flower of Bavaria, mine! Oh rapture, happiness, almost too great to bear."

And in one long, lingering, loving embrace, they sealed the compact that was to bring so much suffering, so much misery to both these loving hearts.

o   o   o   o   o

About a month after the scene described, four persons stood before the altar of a little chapel in the Castle of Vohberg.

They were Albert and Agnes, Gonfried, the page of the former, and a lovely girl named Belinda, a friend of the Pearl of the Danube.

The marriage vows were spoken, the blessing pronounced, and Albert of Bavaria saluted Agnes as his bride, while the noble-looking Gonfried clasped to his heart the wife of his choice, the fair Belinda.

To prevent any opposition to their union at the hands of Duke Ernest, Albert had chosen to espouse Agnes in private, and leave it to time to make his marriage known.

Basking in the sunshine of each other's love, they dreamed not of the ills that were gathering over them.

The secret of their marriage became known to the father of Albert sooner than either dreamed.

Frightful was the rage of Duke Ernest, when he learned that his son had espoused the daughter of a peasant.

He swore that the disgrace which his son had brought upon him by such a union should fall upon his own head, and with a weight that should overwhelm him.

Duke Ernest's pride was hurt.

He would annihilate that of his son.

And for this he chose the first opportunity that presented itself.

He selected Anna, the daughter of Duke Erich of Brunswick, as a fitting bride for Albert, and summoned the young knight to his presence.

Albert, unconscious of his parent's knowledge, met him in the grand hall of the castle.

Terrible was the frown upon the features of the duke as his son bent in homage before him.

Tremulous with passion were the tones in which he spoke.

"Albert, degraded boy, darest thou boldly look an insulted and injured parent in the face?"

"What mean you, my lord duke?" asked the youth.

"Darest ask?" returned Ernest. "Disgraced knight and noble! By my dukedom, but shame alone should sit upon your brow to know the indignity thou hast offered to thy father, the disgrace thou hast brought on our noble house!" ·

"Disgrace!" said Albert.

"Aye, foul disgrace. Hast thou not blackened my name, and sullied thy knighthood by allying thyself to the daughter of a slave, to one of the common herd of Bavaria, a woman who is unworthy to breathe the same air as thyself, a thing beneath the notice of any but a slave, a——"

"Hold!" thundered Albert. "By my soul, were it any but my father who would thus dare traduce the woman I love, I had stretched him dead at my feet!"

And the youth half drew his sword from its scabbard and looked fiercely around.

The brow of Ernest darkened.

"And by my dukedom," he thundered, "the disgrace shall not rest upon our house another day. Here in the presence of these noble knights assembled I command you to sign this divorce from the woman you have dared to marry privately, and immediately espouse the bride of thy father's choice, the noble Anna of Brunswick."

And the duke held a sheet of parchment before the pale face of the angry Albert.

The youth drove back his blade into the scabbard, and taking the parchment, flung it at his feet and trampled upon it.

"Infamous!" he thundered. "Blistered be the hand that penned the lines, and the heart that prompted the words. By my soul, my hand should wither at the wrist ere I would sign so accursed a deed! Agnes is my wife, and let him beware who would step between us."

"You will not sign," cried the duke, "You refuse to obey my commands?"

"I do."

"Presumptuous boy, know you whom it is you defy?" thundered the angry duke, "I am your sovereign and your father."

"Were you the Emperor of Germany I would deny your right to separate two loving hearts—to destroy my peace and the happiness of my wife; and thus I spurn the parchment."

And so saying, Albert spurned the paper with his foot, and turned to leave the apartment.

"Stay," cried Ernest, taking a step forward.

The young man turned and confronted the duke.

The features of Ernest were convulsed and livid with passion.

"You have brought shame and disgrace upon our house," he said, "and refuse to remove the stain, but remember, boy, that which you refuse I have the power to compel. This peasant wife of thine shall not long enjoy the honour you have conferred upon her."

Albert smiled derisively.

"I will turn your smiles to tears, your laughter to groans. Go hence from my sight, your presence is an insult and an indignity to knights and nobles."

"You are my father," returned Albert, "would at this moment you were not."

And he tapped the hilt of his sword significantly.

"Get thee gone, and never let me see thee more, till your degraded alliance is severed, and the stain upon our house and name removed; and until such time I charge all true knights to treat you as one who has forfeited all claim to be considered worthy the spurs of knighthood."

"My lord," said Albert, in a calm, measured tone, "I wear a sword and know how to use it, as I have proved ere now, and though I cannot forget, as my parent, I dare not draw it on you, no matter how great the indignities you heap upon me—yet it will leap from its scabbard if any at your bidding should fail to remember that I am a knight and a noble."

And his gaze rested significantly on the faces of the assembled knights.

"Of those titles I strip you, till you have learned obedience to my will," cried the duke.

"In all things else, my lord, you may command me," replied Albert, "but in this—never!"

The duke stamped his foot, and waved his hand imperiously.

"Begone," he thundered, "and beware!"

Albert slightly bent his head to the duke, then casting a haughty glance upon the nobles, strode slowly from the place.

The duke watched him till the falling arras shut him from his sight, and then, stamping his foot on the ground, he exclaimed—

"Defied—disgraced! My lords, this must not be. My son wedded to a peasant girl—a peasant's daughter the wife of Albert of Bavaria! Oh, the thought is a dagger to my heart. My lords, this sting must be plucked from my bosom—this woman must——"

He paused abruptly, and flinging himself on to his seat, rested his chin on his hand, and became buried in deep thought for some moments—

Suddenly springing to his feet, he exclaimed.

"My lords, I shall need your aid anon, but leave me now, I would think alone!"

Bowing low, the knights left the chamber, and Ernest of Bavaria was alone with his thoughts.

And the nature of those thoughts could easily be judged by the working of his features, thoughts that boded ill for the peace and happiness of the lovely Agnes and her noble husband.

    o   o   o   o   o

It was an imposing scene that the sun shone down upon at Regensberg.

Splendidly attired ladies and gorgeously caparisoned knights were there, in all the pride and beauty of chivalry.

The tournament was to take place on the Heideplatze, and the clang of arms, the champing of bits, and the sound of bugles was heard on all sides.

And present too, in all his gorgeous state, was the Duke, Ernest of Bavaria.

The galleries were crowded, and tier after tier rose one above the other, filled with lovely forms, whose flashing eyes beamed down upon the armour-clad knights and prancing steeds.

And among this bouquet of beauty shone one flower more lovely than the rest.

The admiration of men, the envy of the ladies, whose charms paled before the resplendent loveliness of the Duchess of Duke Albert, sat Agnes, the greatest object of interest in that gay scene.

But though all admired, none flattered, none offered homage to her, for it had been whispered that whoever did so would bring down upon their own heads all the wrath of Duke Ernest of Bavaria.

Though far and near it had become known that Albert, the son of the grand Duke, had espoused the lovely plebeian, yet that espousal had not yet been publicly acknowledged.

The eyes of the duke roved around the galleries, till they rested upon that fair form and lovely face, and then his brow grew dark as midnight, and he gnawed furiously at his nether lip.

Summoning the constable to his side, he whispered a few words in his ears, and ordered the lists to be opened.

A flourish of trumpets announced the fact to the actors and spectators that the lists were open ; and armour-clad knights on their gaily-caparisoned chargers, swept round the field with many a loving glance at the lady of their love, and with a profound obeisance to their sovereign.

The trumpets again sounded, and there entered into the lists a splendid charger, bearing on his jewel-bedecked saddle a noble and stately knight, whose burnished armour reflected back the sun's rays, in streams of vapoury gold.

The dancing plume in his highly emblazoned helmet would have proclaimed his name and rank to the assembled thousands, even had not the raised visor revealed to the admiring throng, the bold, handsome features of the Duke Albert.

He was followed by his page, Gonfried, who bore his master's shield and lance, and who sat his horse with an ease and grace that called forth murmurs of admiration from the fair spectators.

Drawing rein before the spot where Agnes, attended only by Belinda, sat, Albert rose in his stirrups, and bent forward to receive from her hand a small piece of embroidered silk, which, raising to his lips, he then proceeded to secure to one of the ornaments on his breast-plate, directly over his heart.

While thus engaged, the constable approached, and laying his hand upon the bridle of Albert's horse bowed his head.

"How now, sirrah !" cried Albert, angrily ; "what means this ?"

"My lord," said the constable, "it is the duke's commands."

"What mean you ?"

"The Duke refuses to admit within the lists one who has sullied his knightly honour in allying himself to a peasant."

"Dog !" thundered Albert, drawing his sword from the scabbard, and whirling it round his head, "take your hand from my bridle, or I will cleave your skull in twain !"

"My lord, I but obey the commands of my sovereign," cried the constable.

"Remove your hand, I say. Back, or I'll trample you beneath my horse's hoofs !"

"My lord, my lord !"

"Hence, let go the bridle, back, back !" cried the now infuriated Albert.

The constable saw that to persist was to court danger, and, perhaps, death, and he suffered his hand to fall from the bridle, and sprang aside to prevent being knocked down by the charger, which darted forward in obedience to the spur towards the spot where sat the frowning duke, surrounded by the sycophants of his court.

Here, reining in his prancing steed with a suddenness that almost threw the animal upon its haunches, the Duke Albert thundered in a tone that could be heard for some distance—

"My lord, what means this insult—this indignity you would put upon your son, a noble of Bavaria, second only to yourself, and a knight who has won his spurs in upholding the honour of his sire in many a well-fought field ? Why, I demand, is this foul indignity offered to me, in your name?"

The duke rose, flushed and angry.

So rose the greater portion of the assembled nobility and gentry.

Knights walked their steeds forward with their hands upon their swords, and a flutter of excitement spread throughout the throng.

Agnes, pale and trembling, leaned forward with fear in her eyes, and trembling anxiety in every feature.

The roses had faded from her cheeks, and the lily usurped their place.

Her heart throbbed audibly, and her fair bosom rose and fell beneath the velvet bodice, with the mingled emotions of fear and anxiety.

The duke fixed his gaze upon the flushed and angry face of his son, and in reply to his questions answered fiercely—

"He, alone, whose honour is spotless, shall enter these lists. Chivalry is disgraced by the presence of one who degrades his knighthood and nobility by taking to his heart and home a woman who, by sorcery, has inveigled him into a compact which is neither binding nor honourable. Renounce and discard her, and I restore to you your position and my favours. Refuse, and I brand you here publicly with infamy and disgrace, and call upon all true knights and loyal gentlemen to spurn and despise you.

"Renounce my wife—my true, my lawful wife!" cried Albert, in tremulous tones. "Renounce my obligation—the oath I took at the altar! Never! never!"

"The Church will absolve thee, since sorcery and witchcraft have been used by her to lure to her arms the second noble in Bavaria."

"It is false!" cried Albert. "False as hell!"

Then, backing his horse to the centre of the lists, he rose in his stirrups, and casting one glance around the assembled knights and esquires, he pointed with his sword to where Agnes sat, and raising his voice to the utmost pitch, he exclaimed—

"My lord duke, nobles of Bavaria, knights of Germany, and people all. Here, with a solemn voice, I call God to witness, that I have honourably, truthfully, and lawfully married the fair Agnes Bernauer, the loveliest woman in Germany. There sits my duchess, and he who denies her right to my protection and my name, let him raise up the gage I hurl down, and, be he noble or peasant, I will, at my sword's point, uphold her rights and mine own honour."

Agnes clung to Belinda in terror.

In imagination she saw a hundred hands stretched forth to pick up the gage, but it was in imagination only, for not a single knight sprang from his saddle or lowered his sword's point to raise the glove.

Each sat immovable, and breathless silence reigned around.

Albert gazed at the duke, whose clenched teeth and rolling eye showed the passion working in his bosom, then turned his looks upon his wife, who, like a drooping lily, was half supported by her friend Belinda.

Once more he raised his voice.

"My lord duke," he cried, "since you alone by voice and deed deny my right to wed whom I love, and since none presume to test that right at the sword's point, I demand for my beloved duchess those honours which her position entitles her to. And now, having proclaimed my marriage, and upheld my honour and hers, I retire to my castle of Straubing, in that state which becomes the Duke Albert of Bavaria and his duchess."

Motioning to Gonfried to pick up his glove, the page dismounted, and returning to his master received a whispered communication.

The next moment Gonfreid was in the saddle and galloping from the lists, while Albert bowing coldly to the assembled knights, rode to where Agnes was half reclining on Belinda's bosom.

Bending over his saddle bow, he took her hand and raised it to his lips; then, placing it on his bosom, said—

"My love! my wife! This scene has alarmed you; but, fear not, Albert will protect you with his life, and love and cherish you till his last breath. Come, cheer thee, love. My retinue approaches to bear us from this scene to one more in unison with your feelings—our home of love and happiness."

At the head of a gay company of men-at-arms, Gonfried returned to the side of his master, leading a richly caparisoned white steed, whose saddle cloth swept the ground.

Behind him one of the men-at-arms led another horse, sumptuously if not so highly caparisoned.

Still bending from his saddle bow, Albert lifted Agnes on to the back of the horse, and having seen her comfortably seated, he took the bridle from the hands of his page.

Gonfried now raised Belinda to the back of the other horse, and took its bridle in his hand, and all being ready, Albert gave the signal to move. At the head of his company, and with his hand on the bridle of Agnes' steed, he led them entirely round the lists, pausing a moment in front of Duke Ernest to permit himself and Agnes to salute his father, who turned his head aside indignantly, and slowly left the place, followed by the admiring glances and half-murmured cheers of the multitude.

"If I married thee in secret, I have acknowledged thee in public," he said, fixing a look full of love and tenderness on the face of his wife. "If any really doubted Albert's honour, and thine, sweet Agnes, they can doubt no longer. I have proclaimed to the world the Duchess of Albert of Bavaria, and none will dare assail now our honour or our safety."

"God grant it may be so, my dear lord, but who can tell the workings of the heart of man—who say to what cruel depths pride may not lead him? Oh, my lord, my husband, deeply as I love thee—great as would be the sacrifice, I had rather you denied me than that your generous actions should bring misery on your head. Oh, Albert—Albert I fear for thee!"

"Fear what, sweet one?" he asked quickly.

"Alas, my lord, I cannot tell, but my heart assures me that this day's work will bring its misery—and that this blow will fall swiftly and heavily!"

He threw his arms around her neck and drew her head to his bosom.

"Trembler," he said, "you need have no fear while Albert's love is thine—and it will be thine till death."

"Till death," she echoed, as he released her, and the sound of the word fell with a weight upon her heart, that almost stopped its beatings and sent a cold chill through every fibre of her delicate frame.

But knowing that her fears distressed her husband she strove to smile, and with her beaming eye turned upon the handsome face of Albert, they rode on to the castle of Straubing!

Days and months flew by, and Albert and Agnes basked in the sunshine of each other's love—a love so true, so holy, that earth seemed a Paradise to those two faithful hearts.

And then Albert was suddenly called away by the Emperor Sigismund.

Fain would the brave duke have remained in his palace to guard his wife, but fearing no danger to her, he bade her farewell and went forth, leaving her in tears and sadness, which she strove to hide from him.

No sooner had Albert gone, than the angry Duke Ernest once more set about prosecuting his revenge upon the poor Agnes, for what he considered the disgrace she had heaped upon his house and name.

Surrounded as he was by sycophants and flatterers, eager for a smile from their sovereign, he found little difficulty now that his son was far away in raising up a host of enemies against Agnes, whose only fault was her excessive love and beauty.

It happened that the only child of Duke Wilhelm, the uncle of Albert, died at this time, and Ernest induced his satellites to spread abroad a report to the effect that Agnes had either herself, or induced Belinda, to administer poison to him, out of revenge for the refusal of the Duke Ernest to recognise her as his son's wife and receive her at his court as such.

The Duke Wilhelm defended her against this cruel accusation, but, dying shortly afterwards, the accusation was repeated, and Belinda was arrested and conveyed to prison as an accomplice, if not an actual murderer.

In order to wring from this ill-fated woman words that might be construed into an accusation against the duchess, Belinda was subjected to the torture.

Her frail form was torn and lacerated on the cruel rack, but her tormentors failed to wring from her lips one word against her beloved friend and mistress.

In vain her torments were increased, Belinda bore the torture with a heroism that was wonderful, and died asserting her own and her mistress's innocence.

Maddened by the cruel murder of his wife, Gonfreid was at first utterly prostrated by the blow; but grief turned to rage, and he watched and waited, panting like a tiger for the blood of the judge who had condemned his wife to so fearful a fate.

He had not to wait long.

Chance soon threw this monster in his way, and the dagger of the agonised widower found a sheath to its hilt in his breast.

But though Gonfried had only struck the blow to avenge Belinda, the Duke Ernest made the act subservient to his own desires, and vowed that he had been urged on to the deed by Agnes, and that the slaying of the judge was but the first of a series of murders plotted between the wife of Albert and the husband of Belinda.

He gave orders for the arrest of both Agnes and her husband's page, and together they were taken to the torture chamber, and there the lovely woman was forced to see the brave Gonfreid subjected to sufferings the most excruciating and horrible.

In vain did she plead for mercy for Gonfreid ; he was placed on the rack, and she buried her face in her hands to shut out the fearful sight that was to be enacted.

But the wretches tore her hands from before her eyes, and forced her to look upon the terrible scene.

She was in a lofty apartment in which were several instruments of torture—the horizontal and the vertical rack, and the contrivances known as Bad Bess, and the Maiden's Lap, the Slide, and the Spanish Ass.

In order to compel Gonfried to criminate Agnes, the judges, by the direction of the Duke Ernest, had decided that he should be subjected to each of the tortures.

But if the duke believed the page of his son would lie to save himself from the frightful agony, he was as much mistaken in his powers of endurance as he had been in those of his ill-fated wife.

First Gonfried was secured to the horizontal rack, his feet were fastened to one end, and a rope passed over his arms.

This rope being wound around a windlass, the machinery was set in motion, and the brave man was stretched till every portion of his body seemed as if being torn asunder.

But no word did he utter—not even a groan escaped him.

A shriek of horror burst from the lips of Agnes, which was echoed back by a sigh of pity for her by the sufferer.

Removed from this, Gonfried was secured to the vertical rack.

His arms were bound behind his back, and a rope descending from the roof attached to his wrists.

To his feet were placed heavy stones, and he was raised to the roof and suffered to fall to within a few inches of the ground, the weight of the stones causing him the greatest agony, and threatening to drag his legs from his body.

Yet still he bore his sufferings without one cry for mercy, one shriek of pain.

But the agony he endured was so great that he fainted, and the surgeon ordered for a time a cessation of the torture.

Agnes, to whom the suffering of this man was unendurable, again pleaded with all the power she could for mercy for him, when a voice which she recognised as that of the duke's, and which seemed to come through the roof above, exclaimed—

"Confess thyself the murderer of the child of Duke Wilhelm, and that you resorted to witchcraft and sorcery to obtain the love of Albert, and are willing to renounce thy vows, and the torture shall cease."

"I cannot lie," replied Agnes, "of all these I am innocent, so help me Heaven!"

"Then let the torture proceed," exclaimed the voice of the hidden speaker.

The executioners again pounced upon the scarcely recovered man, and securing his feet to rings fastened to the floor, hoisted him by the arms till the bones creaked.

Then lighted torches were held under his armpits till he burst forth in agony—

"Fiends! Oh, God, why do I suffer thus?"

"Mercy, mercy!" shrieked Agnes, falling on her knees and clasping her hands together.

"Confess, confess," cried the hidden voice.

"I have nought to confess," replied the sickened woman, "but I have much to implore, mercy for him—for me."

A loud, contemptuous laugh was the only reply to this, and Agnes, bursting into tears, rocked herself to and fro, while the torturers again proceeded to increase the sufferings of the victim.

Releasing his arms from the rope they carried him to the further end of the apartment, with the heavy stones still attached to his feet.

There was a large chair, the seat of which was thickly studded with wooden spikes.

Forcing him into this the two men lifted a huge stone with difficulty, and placed it upon the knees of the sufferer.

The weight bore him down upon the chair, and the spikes penetrated his flesh, causing him a degree of agony that was fearfully apparent in the convulsed features, though he set his lips hard together to prevent the cry issuing from them that shook his bosom.

"Confess, confess," again sounded above the heads of Agnes and the victim.

But no answer was returned by either Agnes or Gonfreid.

Indeed, the latter had scarce sufficient strength left to reply, while the former seemed as though madness was fast seizing upon her.

Still determined to compel one or the other to accuse Agnes of witchcraft or murder, with a refinement of cruelty that was a disgrace to any living being, the executioners removed Gonfried from the chair, or, as it was commonly called, the "maiden's lap," and placed him upon that diabolical instrument of torture, yclept the Spanish ass, the sharp back of which cut into his flesh, and in order to render his sufferings the greater, the stone used at the maiden's lap was again brought into use.

This excess of suffering proved too much even for the heroic Gonfried.

With a gasp he swayed on one side, his eyes rolled frightfully, blood started from his ears and nose, a shriek he could no longer stifle rang through the apartment, and then his soul fled to that Judge to whom his torturers would one day have to account for their cruelties and their crimes.

And with that death-cry another echoed, bursting from a broken heart.

Agnes, unable longer to bear the fright-ful strain upon her feelings, gave vent to one soul-piercing, agonising cry, and fell forward on her face on the floor of the chamber.

When she recovered sensibility, she found herself in almost utter darkness.

A faint ray of light penetrating through a narrow grating some ten or twelve feet above her head, after awhile, as her eyes became accustomed to the gloom of the place, showed her that she was immured in a well-like dungeon.

The noisome atmosphere, added to the frightful gloom, struck horror to her soul, and she prayed for death, or the return of

"THE DUKE HELD A SHEET OF PARCHMENT BEFORE THE ANGRY ALBERT."

her beloved husband, to rescue her from that frightful place and the hands of those in whose power she was.

And then overwrought nature gave out, and she sank into a feverish slumber.

She was awakened by a rough hand on her shoulder, and started up to perceive the angry features of Duke Ernest, lighted up by the glare of the torch in the hands of the executioners.

With a shriek she sprang to her feet, and retreated as far back as the walls of her prison would permit her, and stood trembling and panting before her direful enemy.

For a moment or two they stood, each gazing upon the other's features by the red glare of the torch, and then the duke said, in a voice that sounded like the hiss of a serpent—

"Woman, I will give you one chance to escape an ignominious death, and re-move the stain your alliance with my son has placed upon my name and rank. With this dagger divorce thyself, and render Albert free to wed the woman of his father's choice."

"Monster!" gasped Agnes, "my life is not mine to take—'tis God's alone, as is my love my husband's."

A terrible frown gathered on the brow of Ernest.

"You refuse?" he hissed.

"I do."

"Then the confession made by Gonfried shall consign you to a death a thousand times more terrible than that you could inflict upon yourself."

"Confession!" she cried; "he had nothing to confess—he confessed nothing."

"So you say," returned Ernest, "but others know better. He confessed that you, aided by his wife, poisoned the son of Wilhelm, and sought the powers of sorcery to aid you to inveigle Duke Albert into a disgraceful union. That confession will condemn you, and you shall die!"

"Fiend! you dare not, cannot slay the wife of your son. Heaven send he may return to protect and rescue me."

The duke laughed scornfully.

Ere Albert can return, the body of his wife will cease to breathe. I offered you the means to die without the ordeal of a trial, you refuse, and your fate shall be one that—"

"Shall raise the hand of the son against the father," she interrupted. "Duke Ernest, I will not ask you for mercy—you know it not—my prayer alone shall be for vengeance on your guilty head!"

He smiled derisively.

"Aye, smile, cruel man," she said, "but the day will come when you shall rue this work. Albert will avenge if he cannot save—aye, bitterly, terribly avenge me!"

"Enough," cried the duke, stamping his foot furiously. "This very day shall your judges proclaim your guilt, and to-morrow ushers in your doom."

And motioning to the torch-bearer to lead the way, he followed him from the dungeon.

"Lost, lost," moaned Agnes, sinking on her knees, "Father of Heaven, send my Albert back to me ere it is too late. Albert, my love, my husband, save me, save me!"

And in the agony of her sufferings she lay down upon the floor of her noisome dungeon and wept hot scalding tears.

Hours passed and the myrmidons of the duke entered the dungeon to bear her before the judges, where perjured lips were ready to utter lying accusations and barter their souls' salvation for one smile of their dishonourable master.

Of what avail were all her protestations of innocence when all were eager to establish her guilt—of what avail were prayers, threats, or entreaties, when all were creatures of the man who sought to encompass her destruction during the absence of her husband?

None. Innocent though all knew her to be, Agnes was found guilty and the duke left to pronounce sentence.

And that sentence was, that, bound hand and foot, she should be cast from the bridge of Straubing into the waters of the Danube!

Not a word did Agnes utter against this cruel decree.

It was useless; but her blanched cheeks, her bloodless lips, her trembling form, her heaving bosom, bespoke the agony of her soul, the fearful but just indignation of her innocent heart.

Placing her hands upon her bosom, as if she fain would stay the wild beatings of her own heart, she cried in a voice that sounded prophetic despite its tremulousness:

"Duke Ernest of Bavaria, you may destroy me, but He who rules the world will avenge me. So surely as you have sought the destruction of the wife, so surely will the son seek the destruction of the father. You have turned your hand against me, and he will raise his hand against thee. It may be the will of Heaven I should die, but that Heaven will yet find means to avenge me. Innocent of all crime, I can meet my Maker without fear; but you, Duke Ernest, tremble for the hour when He shall call you before Him!"

"Away with her to the dungeon," cried the duke, "till the hour of her execution. There let her prate and prophesy."

"Not so, my lord," she replied, calmly. "There I shall pray for my soul—for my husband!"

She was dragged hurriedly from the presence of the Duke and the judges, and once more consigned to her dungeon for the few short hours that were permitted her to commend her soul to God.

Here the ill-fated Agnes flung herself upon the hard, cold floor, and gave way to passionate grief.

"Oh, Albert, my love, my husband," she moaned, "why are you not near me? Were you present, the inhuman fiends would not dare thus to destroy me. Oh, the curse of beauty; would I had never possessed it; but for that I had been happy. God shield and bless you, my loved lord, my dear, dear husband!"

And then she poured out her soul to Him who holds the winds in His hands, and tempers them to the shorn lamb.

But the prayer she uttered was interrupted by the entrance of the executioners, who came to bear her to the scene of her foul assassination.

She knew it would be vain to implore mercy, and without a word she slowly rose and followed them.

She was hurried along on to the bridge of Straubing, amid the lamentations of those who, hearing of the fate assigned her, left their homes and avocations to witness her murder.

But though the voices of the populace were raised in pity, they dare not resort to force to save her, for the duke had taken such precautions that a wholesale massacre must have ensued had they offered opposition to his will.

So they could but gaze upon that pale, beautiful face, weep tears of regret, mutter words of sympathy, for one so young and lovely, and, inwardly, bitterly curse her persecutors.

Her arms and legs were bound so as to prevent her struggling, and, raised in the arms of the executioners, the loveliest and gentlest woman of her time was mercilessly hurled into the waters beneath.

The shriek she uttered as she shot through the air was echoed by a thousand throats, and then a silence deep and profound as death reigned around.

But only for an instant.

Rising to the surface, Agnes struggled fearfully, and succeeded in releasing herself partially from her bonds.

Desperately, madly she strove to swim for the shore.

A shout of joy and encouragement burst from the spectators.

A curse broke from the lips of the duke.

Then followed a cruel and merciless order, and a wretch sprang forward to obey the mandate.

Agnes was fast reaching the shore, when the monster with a long hooked pole, seized her by the hair and forced her down.

One wild, piercing scream she uttered, one look that would have melted the soul of a fiend she cast upon him, and she was buried beneath the flood.

And while the wretch held her there, a terrible howl of indignation broke from the blanched lips of the terrified spectators, who, sickening at the deed, turned hastily away.

Long did the monster hold her down, long after her last breath must have fled.

Then was her dead body dragged out upon the bank, and laid with its still beautiful face, but now lustreless eyes, upturned to Heaven.

*   *   *   *   *

"Murdered! my wife, my Agnes, mur-dered!" shrieked Albert, as the messenger who bore the sad tidings to his ears stood travel-stained and pale before him.

"And by the command of your father, my lord," was the reply, spoken in a tremulous voice.

"Ah, why was I not there to protect her?" cried Albert, pacing the apartment with rapid strides, and tearing his hair and beard in the agony of mind he was enduring. "But, oh, I will have a revenge, deep and bitter. My horse, quick! I will not wait an instant till I have avenged this foul murder in blood. Agnes, if I could not save, I will avenge you. I swear it, by the heavens above me, that the stream in which they drowned my wife shall run red with the blood of her murderers. I swear it!"

And, sinking on his knees, he kissed the hilt of his sword.

Springing again to his feet, he hurried to his horse, and set out for Ingolstadt, to seek Louis the Bearded—his father's direst foe.

Louis received Albert with open arms, and placed an army at his disposal, at the head of which he marched against his father.

Duke Ernest, if a bad, was also a brave man.

He put himself at the head of his forces, and set out to meet his son.

Albert won battle after battle, and his only desire now was to find himself opposed single-handed to his father, or rather, as he himself expressed it, the murderer of his wife.

Sorely pressed by the forces of Albert, the Duke was in full retreat.

He had asked aid of the Emperor, but that aid not having arrived, he was compelled to fall back before the desperate army his son commanded.

While pursuing the retreating enemy, Albert came up with the duke, and addressing him in tones and words that only too plainly showed Ernest his feelings towards him, the duke answered by a blow with the flat of his sword on the arm of Albert.

It wanted not this to raise the hand of the son against the parent. The doom to which Ernest had consigned Agnes had been sufficient, but this blow added to the fury of Albert, and drawing back, he shouted—

"Murderer, defend your life! Agnes, now will I avenge you!"

The next instant the father's sword clashed with the steel of his son.

The fight raged for some minutes, when the swords of the combatants were struck suddenly up, and a knight clad in jewelled armour stood between them.

"What!" he exclaimed, "the son and the sire seeking each the life they should defend. Down with your weapons, or dread the anger of Sigismund."

Each lowered his weapon.

Each bent his head as they saw it was the Emperor of Germany who stood between them.

"Duke of Bavaria," said the emperor, "the cause of this unnatural quarrel is not unknown to me. Your cruelty and injustice has driven yout son to take up arms against you. Albert, however much you may have suffered at your parent's hands, he is still your father. I command you sheathe your swords, and if you cannot be friends, I forbid you to be foes. The duke shall atone for the ill he has done, and I here command he shall swear to institute a perpetual mass for the soul of your murdered wife, and at the same time I command you to dismiss your forces, and take the hand of your father, and forgive him the wrong he has done you."

"Forgive the murderer of my Agnes!" cried Albert. "I came to avenge her, and I will!"

"Then take the noblest revenge that man can take," said the Emperor—"Forgive your enemy."

Albert hesitated.

"Albert," said the Emperor, taking his hand and leading him to the duke. "The noblest act is to pardon those who wrong us. 'Tis only the cruel heart which pants for blood—the brave is ever merciful and forgiving."

And he placed the hand of the son in that of the father.

Duke Ernest bowed his head.

"Sire," he said, you have taught me a lesson, and made me feel how base is pride and cruelty. I admit my evil passions led me to commit a crime against my son, and humanity, but I will atone for it as far as I can. I will institute a perpetual mass for the soul of the martyred Agnes, and on my knees I implore the forgiveness of him she loved so well. My son—my son, forgive me!"

"Father," said Albert, in a voice choked and husky. "You have crushed my heart, and seared my very soul; you have shown me how power may be used to blast the happiness of your fellow man; you have rendered life to me a burden, I should be glad to cast it off; yet my revenge for all this misery and suffering shall be—To my heart, father—to my heart!"

He flung his sword at his feet, and clasped the Duke Ernest in his arms.

The Duke, overpowered with emotion and shame, suffered his head to fall upon the shoulder of Albert, and wept bitter tears of remorse.

The revenge of Albert was far greater than it would have been, had he laid his father's body bleeding and dead at his feet.

Sigismund watched them in silence for a few moments, and then, taking both by the hand, he led them towards St. Peter's Church, and drawing them to one of the graves exclaimed—

"Here over the grave of her you have loved and hated, swear never to recommence this terrible feud; pray for forgiveness of your sins, and rest for the soul of the ill-fated and beautiful Agnes Bernauer!"

Once more father and son clasped hands, and bending over the grave of the murdered Agnes, prayed for their own forgiveness, and rest for the soul of the Pearl of the Danube.

END OF THE TYRANT DUKE.

THEBEN;

THE LEGEND OF THE NUN'S TOWER.

AT the point where the March mingles its tributary waters with the Danube's turbid stream, a huge rock of black limestone bears the extensive ruins of the castle of Theben.

Below a line of rocks which forms a wall from the castle to the river, an arched pathway has been cut, while above it, on an elevated point, a single tower of slender proportions rises to crown and dispute the passage.

This tower, the Nun's Tower, as it is called, received its name from the tragical story which we are now about to relate.

    ❖   ❖   ❖   ❖   ❖

Situated at a distance of not more than a mile from the frowning towers of Theben was the monastery of the Holy Trinity, and separated from it only by massive walls, over which the moss and the ivy climbed, was the convent of the Twelve Virgins.

These dark and dismal structures formed a strange contrast to the surrounding scenery.

The sparkling waters of the rushing river, the bright green foliage of the forests, the sun-tinted peaks, were all out of keeping with the dull grey walls and gabled towers which told of lives hidden from joy for ever; souls darkened by man's folly; lovely lives destroyed by man's hatred to man.

Oftentimes the shepherds and shepherdesses tending their flocks on the far-off green hillsides would look compassionately down upon the spot.

They at least, however poor their lot, were left free for love and happiness.

One evening, a somewhat gloomy evening, towards the close of the thirteenth century, a man clothed partially in armour (which was concealed mostly by the heavy cloak he wore) stepped from a boat which had brought him from the other side of the river, and passed hurriedly beneath the great archway of rugged stone which led to the path up the rocks.

He was a young man, evidently not five-and-twenty, and the way in which he wore his plumed hat and the manner of his walk told you at once that he was conscious of a certain superiority, perhaps a superiority in station, or may be a superiority in merit.

Evidently he was starting upon some errand on which his heart was set.

In spite of the darkness he plunged forward, and making his way up the uneven steps which led to the summit of the cliff, he paused, looked behind him to see if he was followed, and then struck at once into a path which led through the woods of Ebronfold towards the convent of the Twelve Virgins.

He had soon traversed the plantation which went by the name of forest, and stood on a slight eminence overlooking the nunnery.

At this moment a burst of moonlight poured from a riven cloud, and shed its lustre over the desolate-looking building and its gardens.

The young knight knelt on the green turf, and raised his hand towards heaven.

"Be my witness, Oh, Spirit of Good!" he cried; "I will die—or I will save her from a fate worse than death."

And having uttered these mysterious words, he sprang again to his feet, cast one last look upon the nunnery, and turned up a winding path which led towards the summit of the mountain.

Half way up this path was the point towards which the young knight's steps led him.

Here in the window of a little wooden hut there shone every night a bright light, guiding travellers on their way; telling the weary they might rest; the repentant, they might stop and pray.

It was to this hut that the young knight hurried; and arriving at the door, he struck a hasty and somewhat imperious blow upon it.

It was opened instantly.

"Who comes hither so impatiently?" cried the one who opened the portal.

He was a tall, old man, somewhat bent now by age, with long grey hair flowing over his once ample shoulders, a red skull-cap on his head, a suit of grey falling to his feet, and girded round the waist by a rope.

"You are over-impatient, sir traveller," he added, there is no storm or immediate danger, that you should distur ba hermit's reverie in so uncouth a manner."

"Good father," replied the visitor, "you are doubtless startled by this abrupt visit. But when you see my face, you will wonder no longer. I am Rhodolph Wallenstein."

The old man at once grasped his hand, and drew him within the hut.

"Welcome, my son," he said. "But what brings you here on such a night as this? Has any misfortune happened?"

Rhodolph sat down dejectedly by the blazing log-fire which was casting its ruddy flames up the ample chimney, and forming a hundred fantastic shadows on the walls of the hut.

"Misfortune! alas, yes!" he said. "All our endeavours have been in vain. To-morrow Hilda Orbensorf is lost to me for ever. Even your kind and earnest help, Father Lladislaus, has been in vain—she is doömed!"

A deadly pallor overspread the face of the old man.

"What!" he cried, "is she after all to be the bride of the villain, Count Dramsberg? Surely, heaven will not permit such injustice. I cannot and will not believe it—unless I see her dragged to the altar!"

"Alas! good father," returned Rodolph, "that is not what we have to fear. She has refused to be the wife of Count Dramsberg; she has preferred death to it—and oh! such a death. To-morrow, at this hour, the beautiful Hilda, my beloved, the joy of my life, will be a sister in the convent of the Twelve Virgins."

He sprang from his seat in mad excitement as he uttered these words.

"But no, no!" he cried, stamping wildly on the stone floor of the hermit's hut, "no, it shall not be. I will save her from such an awful fate or I will die!"

Father Lladislaus placed his hand gently on his shoulder as if to restrain him.

"Calm yourself, my son," he said; "be seated here by me, and I will think for you; but we must have no violence. I too belong to the Holy Church, though I hold not with all its precepts; and I cannot think of war and bloodshed. We will work quietly, my son, quietly; but remember, Hilda Orbensorf shall be yours."

The young knight shook his head.

"It is not possible," he said.

Father Lladislaus smiled.

"Yes," he answered, "I will undertake that. Remain in my humble hut till morning, and before dawn I will think of some means of gaining your end."

Rodolph glanced at the speaker in some bewilderment and uneasiness.

"To-morrow morning will be too late, good father," he said, appealingly, "it is then that she enters upon her noviciate."

Father Lladislaus smiled.

"I have bethought me of that," he said, "I see in that circumstance no difficulty. Let us talk no more of it. Rest awhile on my humble couch; sleep well, and dream that Hilda is yours, for she will be, unless I have lost my power and Heaven is against me!"

As he spoke he rose, and took from the cupboard a bottle, from which he poured out a glass of rich wine, which he presented to the young knight.

He then conducted him into the inner chamber, where a rude but sufficient couch was ready for use.

"Retire now, my son," he said, "while I, in the solitude of my chamber, plan out how to defeat our enemies."

Father Lladislaus, on quitting the side of the youth, drew together the heavy curtains, and retiring to the chimney corner, sat down before the old volume he had before been perusing and was soon apparently lost in study.

But he seemed restless and disquieted, and ever and anon he raised his head from his book to listen.

After half an hour he rose, turned down his lamp until it gave forth only a faint glimmer, and approached the inner chamber where the young knight of Wallenstein lay.

Rholdolph was buried in slumber; a calmness, as of extreme happiness, played over his features, and a smile wreathed itself over his handsome mouth.

"Good!" said Father Lladislaus. "He sleeps the sleep of the just. I can safely leave him."

He hastened back to the front chamber, placed a wide hat upon his head, girded round him, beneath his cloak, a sword, which he drew from a secret corner, and, extinguishing the lamp, opened the door, and passed out into the night.

It was very late now—long past midnight—the stars shone in quite loveliness in the blue sky—the everlasting stars, that have looked down upon our follies and our struggles for hundreds of thousands of years.

The convent and the monastery—twin children of Superstition—lay below, flooded by the moonlight and starlight.

"Now, friend Claus, worshipful, reverend Brother Claus," murmured Lladislaus, "we shall see how strongly the old memories will work for good."

With these words, the old man, as if reinvigorated by the very thoughts of what he intended doing, began his descent of the rocky path, and it was not long before he stood before the door of the monastery.

Here, pacing up and down, as if before some lord's castle, was a man in sombre uniform, but still evidently a soldier; for in those days the Church was militant, and disdained not to seek the aid of the soldiery in protecting it from aggression.

The man stopped as he saw Father Lladislaus approach.

"What want you, good sir?" he said.

"I wish to see the Brother Claus."

"It is too late, father," replied the soldier, as, approaching nearer, he saw the dress of a stranger. "Brother Claus has long since retired to rest."

"Nevertheless, he will see me," answered Lladislaus. "Tell him only that Father Lladislaus is here, and he will not refuse me entrance."

"Well," said the soldier, who, like the superstitious people of the period, stood in great awe of any servant of the Church, "I will see the Brother Claus, and ask his wishes. Meanwhile, good father, enter, I pray."

The great iron gates were now opened, and the hermit father was admitted into the court-yard, round which the little windows of countless rooms glistened in the moonlight.

Resting-places of beings shut out from God's good works.

"Remain here," said the sentinel, "I will be but a moment gone."

He was scarcely wrong in his conjecture.

After the lapse of but two or three minutes, his heavy tramp was heard returning, and presently his tall, gloomy form loomed up in the moonlight.

"Follow me, father," he said; "Brother Claus will see you."

With a light step, as if his heart had been relieved from some great burden, the old hermit followed the soldier, and entering an iron-bound door, walked along a long stone corridor to the cell where Brother Claus passed his hours of rest.

It was a small room, with a floor like the corridor, of stone only, and, except a chair, a little table and a rude bed, it had no furniture whatever.

Near the bed, reading, was Brother Claus.

He was scarcely of the type usually chosen to represent the priesthood.

No jolly monk was he; no fat and well-fed brother, with rosy cheeks, bright, joyous eyes and stout body.

He was tall, gaunt, and pale.

His body had a strange stoop in it; his head craned forward like that of some strange bird; his eyes were small and twinkling, with a spiteful glance in them—a searching look, as if they were trying to dive into your inmost thoughts to turn them to evil account.

His hands were long, thin, and skinny, like the talons of a bird of prey, and his mouth, though thin-lipped and fierce, was expressive of the greatest sensuality.

As Father Lladislaus entered, he gazed at him with his usual penetrating glance for an instant. Then, closing his book, he waved the sentinel away. "Leave us alone," he said.

And the man went wondering away; for Brother Claus was one of the severest and most exclusive of the Order of the Holy Trinity, and he could not conceive how it was that he could thus quietly permit himself to be disturbed at this hour by anyone—even one so holy as the Hermit of the Rock.

"You choose a strange hour for your visit, Lladislaus," said Brother Claus, familiarly.

"Remember my vow," returned Father Lladislaus, sneeringly; "you, above all others, ought to know and revere the sanctity of a vow."

Brother Claus saw the sneer, and a greenish pallor overspread his face.

"Do you come here to taunt me?" he said; "the dead of night is scarcely the time to revive old hatreds, more especially in such a holy place as this."

Lladislaus smiled.

"Have these walls ears?" he asked.

"They have not. The loudest words could not be heard by any one," returned Claus.

"In that case," said the Hermit, "let us talk as men who understand each other. I have proved by my life that I remember the past only to mourn for it. You only remember it to plot against those you hate; to brood over your wrongs, when you have really wronged others."

The monk's face flashed with anger.

"Is it to say this you have come?" he asked.

"No. I come to seek your aid!"

"My aid?"

"Yes; as you once invoked mine—save that the aid I desire is in a good and righteous cause. Brother Claus, the night is cold; the walk down the mountain slopes is lonely and dreary. Penitent good Brother, who fast every day, please give me a glass of the rich wine you keep in yonder cupboard."

Fierce anger and malice shot from the eyes of the monk as Lladislaus spoke these words.

He knew well their import; knew well that they were only intended to show his power; but he knew also that he had no means of punishing him; that he was in fact in his power, and dare not rebel.

He brought out the wine, placed it on the table, and then said resolutely—

"Lladislaus, if you wish to consult me and ask my advice do so at once. I am ready!"

Lladislaus quietly poured out a glass of the rich wine, and said—

"I am about to tell you something that will appeal to your heart, since it may remind you of the past. To-morrow a lady of the name of Hilda Orbensorf will appear at the altar of the Church of the Twelve Virgins to take the veil; to renounce all wordly things; to bury herself, as we buried ourselves, behind the gloomy walls of a convent."

"Well, does this concern me?"

"Much, as you will see," returned Lladislaus. "Well, she goes to the altar against her will; forced thither to avoid a hateful marriage in the same way as Gretchen did years ago, Brother Claus. Well, this girl must be rescued, she must escape; she must wed the one she loves."

"Impossible," said Brother Claus, interested in spite of all his cynicism, "the rules of the Convent of the Twelve Virgins are terribly strict, and if a lover were to carry her off, the hands of the Church would extend towards him with deadly power wherever he might conceal himself."

"That will be his risk, not ours," said Lladislaus, "but I have a plan to propose which you must carry out."

"Must!" repeated Claus with a malicious glance.

"Unless you wish to be cast out; to perish in the eyes of the Church; to have all the old shameful story brought before the world," cried Lladislaus, with almost savage determination. "I have sworn to befriend this young and brave lover, and I will keep my vow. Refuse—if you intend to refuse, at once!"

"I consent," replied the monk. "You know your power, and you use it well. Proceed!"

"My plan is simple," said Lladislaus,

"my friend—the one I would serve even at the risk of my life, is Rhodolph, the young Count of Wallenstein. He must be admitted into these walls by means of a letter from the Abbot of another monastery; he must be allowed liberty—he must, in the dead of some night like this carry away the young Hilda Orbensorf to his stronghold."

"And who can arrange about his letter of introduction? The Abbot here is very strict."

"Who better than Brother Claus?" said Lladislaus.

The monk ground his teeth.

He knew too well his own helplessness.

Years before he had placed himself in the power of the old hermit so utterly, that shame and disgrace would follow any disclosure, and he was aware that it was useless to refuse.

"Very well," he said, "I must arrange this matter to the best of my ability. But remember I take no responsibility; the task is one of great peril. Death by horrible torture is the punishment of those who violate the sanctity of our Institution—and if he dies, his blood is on his own head!"

Father Lladislaus rose.

"Good, dear Brother Claus!" he said, "I knew you would not be so unkind as to refuse me. In three days the Count Rhodolph will enter on his noviciate under the name of Brother Argentine. Farewell."

"Farewell!"

"And you will send me the letter which he is to produce to the abbot?"

"Yes."

The hermit made no further remark, but permitting Brother Claus to open the door, followed him out into the courtyard.

Claus stood a moment gazing after the hermit, as the soldier opened the iron gateway and the old man hurried away towards the mountain path.

"Would that the rocks would slip and overwhelm you, enemy of my youth, and persecutor of my old age," muttered the monk; "but fear not, your *protégé* shall be well cared for here. He has not yet secured his bride."

*   *   *   *   *

It was on the evening of the next day that the sisters of the Twelve Virgins were called together to witness a ceremony which too many of them had had cause to regret.

The ceremony of introducing a new sister to the community, of taking away one more life from the realities of life.

For continuation of this Story see our next number.

THE BARONS OF OLD
OR THE ROBBERS OF THE RHINE

THE LEGEND
OF THE
DRACHENFELS.

THE Rhine! the Rhine! What visions the very name calls up of ruined castles, and romantic stories; dark legends of ghosts and fairies, and enchanters; stirring tales of kings and emperors, counts and barons, gallant knights and high-born ladies.

No river is more celebrated—no stream

"THEODORA, BOUND AND HELPLESS, WAS SWIFTLY ROWED ACROSS IN THE BARON'S BOAT."

bears along its course so vast a number of historical and legendary associations, and combines so fully all that is interesting, picturesque and poetical.

The Drachenfels is one of the celebrated group of the Seven Mountains, situated in the Middle Rhine, near the city of Cologne.

Rising sheer and abrupt to the height of over a thousand feet, crowned with its hoary ruin, this mountain presents when viewed from the river a spectacle of the most majestic and striking grandeur.

The traveller who gazes upon it can, for the time, fully believe the wild and supernatural legend connected with the ancient castle, which we will proceed to relate.

* * * * *

Far back in the dark ages, when Christianity was struggling to establish itself on the banks of the Rhine—most of whose inhabitants still clung to the old heathen worship of Thor and Odin—two important edifices, no trace of which now exists, stood near the Drachenfels.

One of these was a rugged stone Gothic tower, with adjacent buildings, forming the residence of Black Osric, the territorial baron of the district.

The other edifice was a magnificent temple, built very much like those of the Druids , that is, of immense stones, erected in a circular form around the altar in the centre, and without roof.

The stones were symmetrically placed, smoothly-wrought, and carved with mystic characters and grotesque figures.

The altar was inlaid with gold, and stone images of Odin, Thor, and the other heathen gods which all the Germanic nations worshipped, were ranged near it, giving a general effect of the most impressive character.

On a certain day a large crowd was collected in the temple.

The chief Osric, with all his kinsmen, warriors and dependents, together with all the peasants and other inhabitants of the surrounding villages, were gathered around the priests of the temple, who were bent on a propitiatory sacrifice, for the neighbourhood was under a fearful visitation.

In a hollow of the steep rock near the temple, a monstrous dragon had taken up his residence.

The place had been hitherto but a small natural cave, looking out upon the river ; but it was found one morning to have been suddenly and inexplicably enlarged, both in height and depth.

Terrible hisses, and other savage sounds, came from it ; and one terrified investi-gator discerned a pair of ferocious eyes gleaming out from the darkness of the cavern.

All knew too well what these signs implied ; the presence of that most dreaded species of enemy—a dragon.

The alarm was given.

The consternation spread and increased with each day.

In sunlight the dragon was never seen ; but in the gloom of eve, or the darkness of night, the monster came forth, and its scaly and serpentine form could be dimly seen disporting in the deep river, or gliding landward over the rugged rocks in quest of prey.

Farmsteads had been ravaged, cattle taken off and devoured, and one shepherd, hardy enough to face the monster in defence of his property, had paid the penalty by sharing their awful fate.

Three boatmen who had rowed too near the dragon's cave, had disappeared, boats and all, for ever.

These ravages were extending daily, and it was feared that the whole neighbourhood would fall a prey to the devouring visitant.

Human aid was unavailing, so the inhabitants sought that of their gods.

All were prostrate, with their faces bowed towards the altar, while Valkyr, the high priest, clad in his robes of office, uttered an invocation to Odin.

His countenance, even during this act of devotion, preserved that somewhat sinister and repulsive look which was natural to it.

The prayer continued some time aloud, and afterwards the priest prayed inwardly, his face covered, and a profound silence reigning throughout the assemblage.

At length Valkyr rose, and standing erect, said in a resolute voice—

"The oracle has spoken ; the mighty Odin declares that the dragon is a demon of potent might, and can only be propitiated by the offering of sacrifices, such as gold and gems, and rich adornments, laid upon the rock close by the cave."

This decision caused consternation in the throng, for few had much property of this kind to bestow.

"I know that many here present are poor, and can offer little," continued Valkyr, looking round ; "but you, Osric of Wolkensburg, and Rinbold of Hemmerich, are chiefs of rank and substance, and it behoves you to offer some of your wealth in this great cause."

The two chiefs thus addressed rose, and the eyes of all were turned upon them.

Both were young, but there their resemblance ended.

Osric, as his title implied, was swarthy of hue ; his black hair hanging in elf-locks from beneath his helmet, added to the fierce and wild expression of his features.

Rinbold was fair, with locks of gold, and a frank, open countenance.

He was of a lighter build than the other, whose proportions approached the colossal ; yet few warriors could any more successfully cope with Rinbold than with Osric.

These two chiefs were second cousins, the only remaining descendants of the house of Wolkensburg, which had for centuries ruled in the district.

Osric was the present chief of the house, so possessed the massive castle and large territories : Rinbold held a much smaller estate, and not half the number of retainers, but he was next heir to the territory after Osric.

The latter was fierce and tyrannical, and generally dreaded ; Rinbold was mild and affable, though brave, and was universally beloved.

His popularity caused much jealousy to Osric, and thus between these two chiefs an acknowledged rivalry and dislike, though not an open warfare, had long existed.

" Methinks you should address me only, reverend father," said Osric, haughtily ; " for kinsman Rinbold has so little to give that it would scarce be worth the dragon's acceptance."

" Thou art always taunting me with my poverty," said Rinbold, his eye kindling. " 'Tis my misfortune, not my fault ; and know, that though I may be surpassed by many in wealth, I will yield to none in valour. The time, too, may come, when my own right arm and trusty sword have won me fame, glory, and wealth equal to thine."

" Fine words achieve not gallant deeds," answered Osric, sneeringly.

Whereat the young chieftain's anger visibly increased, and his hand sought the handle of his falchion.

But the priest, by his interference, averted the coming storm.

" Brethren, quarrel not," he said. " In the face of a common danger it behoves all to be united. Chieftains, warriors, and peasants, you have heard the decision of the oracle. Instantly seek your homes, and bring thence whatever wealth each, according to his possessions, can spare, as a sacrifice to appease the wrath of the dragon."

Instantly all was commotion ; the crowd dispersed, and all except the priests departed.

Valkyr seemed all at once to throw off the air of restraint and sanctity he had hitherto worn, and calling Thugbrand the Sacrificer, one of his assistant-priests, he spoke to him privately, and their conference seemed very much more like that of two worldly men hatching a conspiracy than the communing of holy men upon matters of sacred import.

In less than an hour the crowd had again assembled.

All had obeyed the commands of the priest, in which, in their blind superstition, they placed the most implicit reliance.

The peasant had brought his little store of hoarded gold, the peasant's wife such trinkets as she possessed ; the rugged warrior had stripped the gold or silver ornaments from his armour, and laid them at the foot of the altar, and a couple of stalwart retainers of Osric had brought down a heavy and highly ornamented chest, which, being opened, displayed a goodly heap of wealth, bracelets and rings, and other ornaments that had been heirlooms in the family ; gold-hilted daggers, with wrought sheaths, and a large sum of money in gold and silver.

And what was Rinbold's gift ?

Merely a small purse of gold and a thin jewelled clasp.

" 'Tis all that I can spare," he said ; " for all know that I am but poor. Would it were more, if the sacrifice is really efficacious !"

Black Osric, who had assumed some parade in superintending the bestowal of his offering, for he was proud of his wealth, gave a scornful smile as he contrasted with it the insignificance of Rinbold's.

The eyes of Valkyr and Thugbrand might have been observed to glisten with inward satisfaction as they looked upon the display of wealth before them.

But the devout multitude did not notice this trifling circumstance.

" Friends, you have done well," said the high priest, with a sanctimonious air of piety ; " you have fully obeyed the commands of the great Odin. This treasure shall be at once conveyed to the dragon's cave, and placed upon the stone opposite, there to remain three days. If in that period it is taken, we may be assured that the sacrifice is accepted, and that the dragon will depart ; if otherwise, I must again consult the divine oracle."

In a short time a chosen body of stalwart warriors were carrying the treasures towards the dragon's cave, the train of white-robed priests, ranged in double file, bringing up the rear of the procession.

As they went they chanted a hymn to Odin, which echoed with impressive solemnity among the steep hills of the river bank.

Osric and Rinbold accompanied the expedition.

Though of short length, it was a difficult journey, over the uneven rocks and through the rugged woodland paths.

At length they reached the dreaded spot.

An air of fearful gloom and horror hung over it

The steep eminence towered above, stern and fast.

The deep cave was black as Erebus ; all herbage had withered around its mouth, and the flat stone or rock was destitute of any sign of vegetation.

The dragon was nowhere visible, but some appalling sounds, as of the stertorous breathing of some giant, issued from the cave, and seemed to shake the very ground.

Not without fear and trembling, the stout warriors deposited their burdens upon the large, flat, but sloping piece of rock, close to which grew a large oak tree.

Valkyr and his priests then recommenced their chant, and then, all present prostrating themselves, the high priest addressed an invocation to Odin, saying that his commands had been obeyed, and praying that the expedition would succeed.

Suddenly the whole assemblage started up with electric speed.

A huge head emerged from the cavern —a pair of glaring eyes were fixed on the party, and the vast scaly bulk of the monster became partially visible. At the same time a roar like that of a lion mingled with a hiss like a serpent's, thundered and echoed through the forest, and a pestilential vapour like the poisonous breath of some deadly snake infected the atmosphere. All shrank back aghast. A mortal terror seized them ; none were exempt.

The bravest warriors shared the panic, and they fled tumultuously and precipitately.

As they glanced back, a huge claw, resembling the webbed foot of a seal, was stretched forth, and closed upon the large casket containing Osric's gifts.

Appalling as this scene had been, the party had soon the consolation of finding they were not perceived, and of believing that the sacrifice had been accepted.

Therefore, though all were talking about the dragon, and many, though barred securely within their own homes, could not sleep that night for thinking of the monster, all looked forward with good hope for the success of the means employed.

Young Rinbold did not share the universal terror. A strange kind of courage had come upon him. The taunts of Osric he had felt bitterly, and with this feeling rose a strong desire to attain, by some great achievement, a position which would place him above all the sneers of his rival.

If he could but slay this dragon ! That would accomplish the object of his ambition.

The slayer of a dragon was a hero in the land, and if Rinbold could become such a hero, Osric would be as nothing beside him.

Full of these thoughts, when darkness had fallen, instead of retiring to rest he girded on his sword, grasped his ponderous battle-axe, and, clad in complete armour, issued forth.

He took the direction of the temple, and as he neared it he noticed two figures standing near the altar.

From their voices Rinbold discovered their identity and their intention.

" If the dragon has really secured the treasure, my good Thugbrand," said the voice of Valkyr, "our plan is frustrated, and it will be useless to repine ; but if he has left it, we may secure it at once ; and then, as we are both weary of this kind of life, we will make good our escape to other regions ere the three days are past."

Whereupon the confederates departed.

Rinbold resolved to follow them ; they took the direction of the dragon's cave.

He saw now their bold intention to possess themselves, even at the risk of their lives, of the rich sacrifices offered by their dupes.

Surprised, for he no more than others had ever suspected the real character of the priest and his satellite, the young chieftain followed them secretly.

They soon arrived at the cave. If the scene was gloomy by daylight, it was infinitely more so now that night was added to its horrors, and the melancholy night breeze moaned through the forest.

No sign of the dragon was perceptible ; even the deep breathing was not to be heard.

The guilty priests, groping among the rocks, found to their delight that the treasure was still there, with, however, the exception of Osric's box of valuables, which had been evidently taken.

Rinbold, from the rocky path above, could hear the words of the priests, and to some extent perceive their actions also.

Scarcely, however, had Valkyr placed his hand upon the nearest bag of gold, when a terrible noise was heard close by.

A colossal form loomed over the tree-tops; the flapping of enormous wings was heard, and the dragon came flying towards his den.

Under these conditions, the monster was perceptible in all his formidable dimensions.

His form resembled in many points that of a gigantic lizard, but was scaled like an alligator, and had besides a serpentine lissomeness, and wavy movement, while a vast spreading pair of wings supported the creature in the air.

This fearful apparition came hissing and bellowing towards the cave, its eyes glaring, and its mouth shooting forth luminous flames which lit up its whole form.

In its mouth it carried a full-grown ox, abstracted from a neighbouring farm.

The very rustle of its flight so disturbed the atmosphere that it was like a strong wind, laden with an odour insupportable and suffocating.

At the first sign of this unearthly spectacle, Valkyr and Thugbrand, in a panic of guilty fear, dropped their booty, and scrambled over the rocks with great precipitation.

A momentary terror came upon Rinbold, but he conquered it, and, drawing his sword, stood his ground firmly.

But the dragon took no notice of him, seeming anxious only to deposit its prey in the cave, and after some hovering and fluttering settled down by the entrance, crept in, and disappeared.

Rinbold waited some time, but the dragon did not again issue forth.

From the sounds it would appear that he was busily engaged in dispatching his meal.

The young chief hesitated.

He did not feel sufficient confidence to attack this formidable creature, which, indeed, seemed like an act of foolhardy madness, yet he longed for the glory of such an achievement.

As Rinbold stood pondering, he happened to cast his eye riverwards, and perceived on the opposite bank a bright light.

The circumstance was unusual; no castle or other residence stood on the spot, and indeed the illumination much resembled a camp fire.

From the same direction, too, arose a hymn sung by many voices, a hymn very different to those chanted in honour of Odin.

This seemed to Rinbold the most delightful music he had ever heard, and the words that he could distinguish were in some unknown tongue.

His curiosity was aroused, and descending to the river at a point where a skiff of his own was generally kept moored, he pushed out, and soon gained the opposite shore.

Ascending that bank he found himself by an open space in the woods.

He was not deceived; the light was from a camp fire.

A number of tents had been pitched, and armed men were grouped in all directions.

In the central space near the fire was an altar, but a very different one from the pagan shrine on the opposite shore; this one being a rude erection of iron and stones, surmounted by a large and beautiful crucifix, and illuminated by two torches.

At this knelt a Christian monk of the most reverend aspect, who, assisted by several priests of inferior rank, was conducting a choral service in which all devoutly joined.

Taking an active and prominent part in the religious ceremonies was the most beautiful creature Rinbold had ever seen.

She was scarcely past girlhood, but there was a calm and thoughtful expression upon her face, which showed a mind beyond her years.

No features could possibly be more regular than hers, which were formed on the purest classical model; her hair was golden, and though without ornament needed none.

Her dress was a robe of spotless white, and, without appertaining to any special religious order, was decidedly conventual in character.

She seemed like some priestess or female devotee, or rather to the ravished eyes of the young chief like an angel descended to earth.

Beside her knelt a man of middle age, fully armed as a warrior, but of somewhat foreign air.

The persons around consisted, besides the priest and his assistants, of armed men, some foreign, but a majority peasants and warriors of the surrounding district.

As Rinbold, concealed behind a tree, surveyed this impressive scene, he understood it to be a meeting of converts to Christianity, under the guidance of the priest, who had come from France or Rome to spread the faith of the Cross on the banks of the Rhine.

Already it was known that many barons had been converted, but the district wherein Rinbold dwelt was fiercely pagan, and Valkyr and his priests lost no opportunity of preaching enmity against the Christians.

Rinbold remained in his hiding-place throughout the remainder of the service, which, though he did not fully understand, he could not help being impressed with.

When it was over, all rose, and the priest, the girl, and the middle-aged armed knight, engaged in earnest conference.

In bending forward to get a better view of that lovely vision, Rinbold attracted the attention of a sharp-eyed sentinel, who forthwith pounced upon him.

"Ha! who is here?—a spy!" he cried; "one of the pagan idolators and fighters against the faith? 'Tis so, holy Father Placidus; behold this man, and deal with him as is fit."

Rinbold was conducted towards the priest, making no resistance, and his appearance caused some consternation at first.

But his countenance and demeanour impressed all in his favour; and when he had explained his presence, none doubted that his explanation was true.

"My son," said the priest, kindly, "it grieves me to see one of so goodly presence and intelligence sunk in the darkness of pagan idolatory and superstition. Leave that way of error, embrace the true cross, and be saved."

"I was nurtured in the faith of Odin and Thor," responded the young chief. "It was the faith of my fathers, and I cannot depart from it. Nevertheless, I am no enemy to thee and thine."

He was soon engaged in conversation with the priest and the knight, who, he was informed, was Conradin of Steinlitz, a German count, who had long served in the army of the Emperor of Constantinople.

Father Placidus was his brother, and a zealous missionary, and had already made hundreds of converts on this expedition, during which his life would have been often in deadly peril but for the protection of Conradin and his men.

The beautiful Theodora, daughter of Conradin, had been born in Constantinople; her mother had been a Greek, and she was a most zealous assistant of her uncle in his missionary enterprises.

Rinbold's admiration and curiosity respecting her could not be wholly concealed, and he was informed that she was destined for a life of religious sanctity.

"And is one so young and beautiful doomed for life to the cold gloom of the convent?" he said, sympathetically.

"Stranger knight," she answered; "such is my destiny. I am to be the bride, not of man, but of Heaven. I would not win the love of one being only, but the respect and religious affection of the whole human race. At present, the purpose to which my life and that of all of us is devoted, is firmly establishing the Christian faith on the banks of this river."

"I fear for the success of your design," replied Rinbold; "all hereabouts are fiercely staunch to the faith of Odin. Our priests preach the extermination of the Christians, and my kinsman Osric, the lord of the castle and domain. is a potent foe of the new creed."

"Nevertheless, my son," said Placidus, "to-morrow we purpose to cross the river, and try to convert these fierce people."

"Do naught of the kind, I conjure you," said Rinbold. "We are three times as numerous as you; Osric's band alone would be enough to annihilate your small force. Death, or captivity worse than death, would be your fate, and thou, lady, so pure and good, would be the spoil of the savage baron."

This prospect seemed for a time to cast a damp on the religious zeal of the party.

The conversation turned upon the dragon, which, to Rinbold's astonishment, seemed to cause no terror to the Christians.

Placidus declared that they had power to exorcise and destroy all such monsters and evil spirits.

"Do but that," said the young chief; "rid us of the dragon, and you may have a chance to convert us all; but I fear me 'tis impossible. Your danger is greater than you think. As soon as it is discovered you are here, it will be thought that your presence is the cause of the dragon's coming, and Valkyr and Osric and their supporters will attack you in force."

"Our fate is in the hands of Heaven, which always protects the right cause," said the priest.

It now being far advanced in the night, Rinbold departed, having sworn that he would reveal nothing of what had passed, and that he would use all his influence to protect the interests of the Christians.

He little thought what fearful events would follow this adventure.

Early the next morning, those who had taken part in making offerings to propitiate the dragon repaired to the temple, whence they proceeded in the same order as before to the front of the cave.

Rinbold, Osric, Valkyr, and several of their followers were the first to arrive at the dread spot.

The monster was not visible, but his deep breathing was audible, proving him to be in his domicile.

The high priest of Odin assumed surprise as he exclaimed—

"Our efforts have failed us as yet, for the sacrifice is left where deposited, untouched."

"Save mine," observed Osric, "and that hath been taken."

"Then thou art specially favoured, my son, cried Valkyr. "The passiveness of the monster shows that he has been partially mollified. Two days yet remain, and in that time, if no adverse influence prevail, the treasure will all be taken."

Rinbold, who fixed a penetrating glance on the priest, discerned a meaning in these last words far different from that which was attached to them by the others, who had no suspicion of his designs.

Determined, however, to keep secret his knowledge at present, the young chief said nothing.

The party again left the cave, and reassured somewhat by the representations of Valkyr, their fears about the dragon partially subsided, and they went about their ordinary avocations.

Black Osric and his train contemplated pursuing their favourite sport, the chase, in the adjacent forest.

"Ha!" exclaimed Osric, suddenly, as he stood on a rocky path overlooking the river, What have we here?'

Two boats were seen approaching the bank, and in a few moments the Christian monk, Father Placidus, accompanied by his brother Conradin, two priests and half-a-dozen armed men, were landed.

With a firm step, the zealous missionary approached the astonished group, holding in one hand a palm branch, in token of peace, and in the other a crucifix.

"Peace be to ye all!" he said, in German, "you know by our guise, and this sacred emblem, upon what errand we come."

"Ay, followers of the faith of Rome and Palestine," responded Osric, who judged himself specially addressed; "ye are indeed bold to visit this shore, where all are staunch to the creed of the Norsemen."

Valkyr, who stood just without the boundary of the temple, started suddenly back in assumed horror.

"Christians!" he exclaimed. "Christians daring to approach a priest of Odin, and pollute the temple of our gods with their accursed presence! Back, dog, or the vengeance of Thor, the mighty, will fall upon thee!"

"Misguided being!" responded the Christian priest, calmly, "I am delegated by a power, in comparison to which all that thou canst invoke is as nothing. List, and give ear to the truth, thou and thy satellites, and all here present."

"Hear not his blasphemies!" almost shrieked Valkyr, suffer him not to speak! —hurl him from his standing place!— wrench the cross from his grasp!—down with all the foes of Odin!"

"Down with the foes of Odin," echoed Osric and his followers, placing themselves in a threatening attitude.

"Hold," interrupted Rinbold, stepping forward, "I say that the monk *shall* speak. None are constrained to follow his doctrines; but at least all shall give him a fair hearing."

"These are bold words, Cousin Rinbold," said Osric, sternly, "and become thee not. I, thy lord and paramount, declare that the monk shall not speak!'

"And I repeat that he shall!" cried Rinbold, still more warmly.

"Brethren, quarrel not!" said Placidus. "I come not to bring dissension among you, but peace and goodwill. Barons, warriors, and even you priests of Odin and Thor, remember that I and these my followers are, at least, countrymen of yours. I was born on the banks of the Rhine, and on the banks of the Rhine I claim a German's privilege of speech."

These words produced sufficient impression upon the crowd to enable the monk to begin his discourse, and, despite the opposition of Valkyr, Osric, and their myrmidons, he proceeded with masterly eloquence to enlarge upon the doctrines of his faith.

Valkyr, much embarrassed, saw that he must make a desperate effort.

He, Thugbrand, and the other priests, turned, and approaching the altar of Odin, knelt down before the statue of that divinity.

After a few minutes of apparently rapt devotion, Valkyr arose, and taking advantage of a pause in the Christian monk's discourse, exclaimed—

"The oracle has again spoken—has confirmed what I suspected—has declared that the visitation of the dragon is owing to the presence of the Christians. Yes," he continued, "and till every Christian here is slain, the dragon will never leave us."

"By the Walhalla! he speaks aright," cried Osric, suddenly rousing himself. "Men of Wolkensburg, suffer not yourselves to be deluded by this monk's appeal. I see it all now. These Christians have long been hovering on the banks of this river, and Odin, offended at this desecration, hath sent the dragon to destroy us."

"'Tis true, 'tis true!" cried Valkyr. "My men, break the spell at once by slaying these strangers. Down with them, I say! Death to the Christians."

The terrible cry of "Death to the Christians!" was taken up by the fickle crowd, and the formidable armed throng, with a threatening aspect, drew nearer to the little knot of Christians.

"Shame! Would you attack less than half your number?" cried Rinbold, interposing. "Is this the act of brave warriors?"

"Well, they shall have one chance of their lives," said Osric. "Look ye, sir Priest of Nazareth, depart instantly, and we will harm thee not. But tarry even one second longer than yon cloud shall take crossing the sun, and thou diest instantly."

Placidus looked around at the overwhelming crowd of fierce armed men, and saw that it was useless attempting further resistance.

"I go," he said; "but think not this is my last attempt. My duty will impel me again to visit you, to instil the true faith into your darkened minds."

They accordingly embarked in their two boats, but were scarce fairly launched on the stream, when their allies on the opposite shore, who had been stationed in readiness in case of danger, but well concealed among the trees, were now seen emerging therefrom intent on coming to their aid.

The sight acted like a spell upon their enemies.

"See, they have an armed force yonder!" cried Osric. "Fools that we were to let them escape! To the boats, my men, we will follow them to the death."

Osric and his men, always fierce and ready for war, needed no further prompting.

In a few minutes they had their rude craft ready, and were steering rapidly for the opposite shore.

Rinbold and his men looked after them hesitatingly.

"Wilt thou not also aid in the good work, my son?" said Valkyr. "An' thou remainest here it will look as if thou wert a coward, and no disciple of Odin."

"Coward I am not!" cried the young chief; "and as for the great Odin, 'tis almost enough to shake one's faith in him to have discovered the ill deeds done in secret by his priests."

Valkyr changed colour, and began to feel a deep hatred of the young knight.

"Nathless, I will follow Baron Osric," said Rinbold.

And in a short time he and about a score of armed followers were nearing the opposite shore.

There affairs were already becoming critical.

Placidus and Conradin had landed; but their pursuers were, as they approached the steep bank, met by a body of resolute men, of the opposite party, who, with swords, battle-axes and bows and arrows, tried to arrest their progress.

The peaceful encampment was soon turned into a field of veritable warfare.

"Strike for the gods of our fathers, my brave men!" cried Osric, waving aloft his ponderous falchion Slay all—spare none! Death and destruction to the Christians!"

A shout of acquiescence answered this appeal, and his followers, who displayed all the ferocity of the Vikings of the North, rushed in full force upon the inferior-numbered foe; but the latter were not daunted.

Headed by Conradin of Steinlitz, they formed into a compact phalanx, irregularly, but formidably armed; some having long-handled double axes, others short Danish seabows: some swords only, and many those formidable clubs, with a heavy spiked ball at the end of a thick chain attached to them, which were very much used at that time by Teutonic warriors.

Father Placidus, his niece, and the priests stood in the background, grouped round the altar to watch the deadly conflict, and pray for the success of the right cause.

And deadly indeed was the conflict that ensued. Pagans and Christians fought with equal fire and resolution.

The one impelled by their warlike propensities and their superstitious belief that they would drive away the dragon by slaying the Christians; the latter urged to their utmost bravery by a firm, religious faith.

The forest and the huge rocky banks of the mighty river soon echoed with ringing blows, the heavy tramp of footsteps, and cries of pain, rage, and triumph.

Many a piece of strong chain armour

was broken, and a deep wound inflicted on the wearer.

Many a wolf-hide shield received a dint that rendered it useless further.

Many a stalwart warrior was laid prostrate and helpless on the sward.

Black Osric, as his colossal form was seen towering in the van, making a circle of destruction with every sweep of his mighty axe, looked indeed like the emissary of some avenging demon.

Sir Conradin opposed him none the less gallantly, and commanded his rugged troops with the skill of an experienced leader.

But the preponderance of numbers was more than bravery could balance, and the Christians at length began to show signs of defeat.

All this while Rinbold and his men had kept back, watching the fray.

The young chief was undecided.

He had not turned Christian, though the exhortations of Placidus, and, still more, the impression produced on him by Theodora, had predisposed him towards that faith; but, at the same time, he was not inclined to aid Osric's destructive attacks.

But, now that he saw this handful of men, after fighting so gallantly, about to give in to a much larger force, his natural generosity impelled him to take the weaker side, and his followers were sworn to obey his lead.

THE CASTLE OF DRACHENFELS.

Therefore, at this critical moment Rinbold, heading his men, rushed out upon the fierce and victorious Osric.

"Hold thy hand, Baron of Wolkensburg!" he cried; "this is a mean advantage. Hold, or I, too, will oppose thee!"

"Thou!" cried Osric, in scorn. "Art thou then turned traitor to thy faith to aid these dogs? I say they shall die every one, and thou and thine to boot, if thou darest to oppose us."

"Come to the test, then," cried the young chief, ranging his men beside those of Conradin. "Come on—right against might!"

The Christians, thus aided, rallied, and their fortunes seemed in some degree to turn; but even now the whole force opposing Osric was less than half his own.

His gigantic strength and skill in warfare had already done great execution, and with his own hand he had slain many, and some of his myrmidons had proved themselves especially worthy of such a leader.

At length a blow from Osric's axe levelled Sir Conradin of Steinlitz to the ground.

He fell with a cry of pain, to all appearances dead.

Rinbold, fearing he was so, stepped towards him to ascertain, and yield his aid, when the mighty battle-axe swung once more, and grazing Rinbold's helmet, fell on his shoulder, and caused him to reel back and fall among the slain.

At this moment, despite the dissuasions of Placidus, Theodora, who had seen her father fall, rushed forward with a cry of anguish and knelt beside him.

Even the rude warriors of Osric were so impressed with her divine beauty, evident distress, and sudden appearance on the scene, that they paused in their fierce contest, while their opponents, dismayed by the fall of their leader, did the same.

"My father—oh, my father!" cried Theodora, oblivious of all but him.

The fierce Osric, standing flushed with victory over the bodies of a heap of slain opponents, beheld her without pity, for that was alien to his nature, but with an admiration he did not conceal.

"What, grow such bright flowers in the Christian camp?" he exclaimed, "instead of being sheltered in some fair garden of the south. Whence comest thou, maiden, and wherefore art thou here?"

She answered not, nor heeded, intent only on her father's condition.

"Our victory is nearly complete," said Osric, again rousing himself. "A few more blows, and all is done. Slay the priest; he hath been the cause of all. Kill all who resist, bind the rest as prisoners, and for this maiden, heed not her cries and pleadings, but seize and convey her to the boat at once. She is my prisoner."

"Not so, ruffianly devastator!" cried Rinbold, who, but slightly wounded, had by this time rallied his men. "Molest her not, nor this holy priest. Osric, thou hast rendered thyself my enemy, and I will oppose thee to the death!"

"The death shall be thine!" hissed Osric, again grasping his battle-axe and rushing at him. "Insolent boy, I have too long borne thy taunts. Darest thou interfere with the purposes of thy liege lord? That for thy temerity!"

He dealt him a heavy blow, which Rinbold, with great skill, warded off, though his brass-bound shield was broken through.

The contest between the two chiefs was fierce, and would have proceeded to some deadly issue, but their men also joined in the fray, and they were separated by the mass of fighters.

Rinbold found himself surrounded by Osric's men, but, cutting through them, got clear of the fray only to find his own party dispersed and defeated.

"The victory is ours!" cried Osric in triumph. "We have spared but few, and those shall meet a fate a little worse than death. Are they bound? Is the maiden safe in the boat? Yes, 'tis so. Her father, methinks, will scarcely rise again; and for the priest, he cannot escape. Now hurl down this altar, fling the cross into the river, and hasten we to declare our victory to the holy Valkyr."

These remorseless commands were obeyed; the terrified Theodora, bound and helpless, was placed in the baron's boat and swiftly rowed across the stream.

The other prisoners, of whom there were a dozen or more, were similarly treated; the ivory crucifix sank with a splash far out into the river, and the band of Osric, sated with victory, were rowing across the water, chanting a barbarous war song to the Northern god of battles.

Rinbold emerged from his position among the trees.

The Christian camp presented a melancholy spectacle.

Half a score of men lay dead and dying on the ground.

A little apart, Conradin of Steinlitz was vainly struggling to rise.

Rinbold hastened to assist him.

The knight was deeply wounded, but had regained his consciousness, and was full of anguish at the fate of his daughter.

At this moment Placidus, unharmed, but in great distress of mind, came up.

"I was chased by the fierce warriors," he said, in explanation; "but, by diving into the wood and entering a cave among the rocks, I contrived to escape them. All the rest are taken. How fearful this fight has been! We can do nothing now but pray for the assistance of Heaven, from whence this affliction hath come to chasten us. The true faith, my son, is propagated in danger and difficulty, and all kinds of deadly persecutions. But we must submit."

He bowed his head mournfully, and then assisted to raise his brother, whose wounds he and Rinbold bound as well as they could.

Then they entered into a deep and anxious conference as to what course should be pursued in their present desperate condition.

Valkyr, the high priest, stood at the altar of Odin, as Osric and his band returned flushed with victory.

He advanced to meet them with the most overwhelming and sinister satisfaction.

"Ye have done well, men of Wolkensburg," he cried; "and now we may hope the great Odin is appeased, and that the dragon will disappear."

For continuation of this Story see page 321 *of our next number.*

[Continued from page 304.]

THEBEN;

THE LEGEND OF THE NUN'S TOWER.

THE unfortunate Hilda Orbensorf arrived at the gate of the gloomy convent in a carriage in which were her father and brother, the latter a more resolute enemy of her lover than even her stern and implacable parent.

As they rattled into the dismal courtyard, Count Orbensorf pointed to the grey building, which seemed a fitting abode for lost and weary spirits.

"Look on your future home, Hilda," he said. "Once more I give you the choice. This or marriage with Count Dramsberg."

"I have chosen before," replied the young girl, with a shudder, "I have chosen death in preference to such a union, and this is death, or worse!"

"Good. You have chosen," muttered the count, and as the carriage pulled up at the principal gate he leaped down and helped his unfortunate child to alight, while her brother, calm, resolute, almost brutally stern, brought up the rear.

Within half an hour all was ready for the sad and imposing ceremony.

The chapel was illuminated brightly with wax tapers; the altar was resplendent with all the paraphernalia of the Romish religion; long files of nuns were ranged from one end to the other of the sacred edifice, while priests, in their robes, waited to perform the ceremony, which they pretended to regard as an acceptable sacrifice to Heaven.

Truly was it "a dim religious light" which was shed over the interior of that great and ancient building, and, as Hilda entered it, an awe almost amounting to terror overcame her.

The scene was brilliant, truly.

But it was like the brilliant entrance to a tomb.

Gold and glitter without—dust and ashes within.

Hilda Orbensorf looked exquisitely lovely in the dress she had chosen for her sacrifice—the last secular dress she was to wear.

She was robed in black velvet, with scarcely a jewel visible—her dress fitting like a glove to an exquisitely moulded form.

Around her neck she wore a plain circlet of diamonds; but not for the sake of display were these carried with her to the steps of the altar.

Only as the last secret gift of her lover, Count Rhodolph Wallenstein, did she cling to them till the last.

The unfortunate girl was led forward to the altar by her brother and her father, and then delivered over to the hands of the priests and abbess.

Once, as they slowly passed along the sacred edifice, the former had whispered—

"Even now it is not too late. If your heart fails you, Count Dramsberg will forget and forgive all."

"My heart fails me not," she answered, and advanced boldly.

The ceremony proceeded now without interruption.

The usual service was read; the rich robes of velvet and circlet of diamonds were torn off and trampled under foot; the grey dress of the Order was donned; the long and rich tresses of hair were cut off; and Hilda Orbensorf was no longer of this world.

Dead to all outward things; living only in the beauty which nothing could destroy, she moved away presently with the rest of the sisterhood, without one look of farewell to the parent and that brother who had doomed her to such a terrible fate.

Little did she dream of the designs of her faithful lover, Rhodolph.

Little did she dream that at that very moment a plan was being framed for her deliverance.

It was morning before Count Rhodolph Wallenstein awoke, and springing from his couch, entered the front room of the hermit's hut.

His sleep had been a heavy one.

He had dreamed of Hilda; of her goodness, of her loveliness, of the consummation of all his hopes; and had never once awakened during the night;

and he could hardly credit his senses, when he heard from Father Lladislaus an account of his journey and its result.

"You had better remain here until the letter arrives from Brother Claus," said Lladislaus, "and then we will at once arrange for your proper disguise, and the better carrying out of our plan.

The hermit had not misjudged the extent of his power over the monk of the Holy Trinity.

That very evening—while the ceremony of Renunciation was proceeding in the chapel of the Twelve Virgins ; while young Count Rhodolph's heart was burning with fury at the scene which was being enacted so near him—the letter arrived, and after a hurried consultation with Lladislaus, the young knight set off for his castle, on the other side of the Danube.

On the next evening, just when darkness had begun to overspread the earth, a solitary traveller stopped at the gate of the Holy Trinity.

He was clad in a blue serge robe, which touched the ground, and was girdled round the waist with a rope like that of the hermit.

His head was covered with a hood, but it was yet possible to see that he was still young by the sparkle of his eyes, the absence of wrinkles in his face, and the strength and richness of his voice.

He waited meekly at the great gate, while the setinel entered with his message to the Superior.

And then, when he entered he crossed himself most devoutly, and on reaching the presence of the old Abbot, he knelt before him in humility.

Nevertheless, it was the young Count Rhodolph who was concealed beneath that grave exterior, and whose heart was beating with fierce and terrible excitement.

"So," said the Abbot, "you have travelled from the extreme confines of Hungary, my brother ?"

"Yes, most reverend father ; and I wish ere I proceed farther on my pilgrimage, to rest here awhile. It is a part of the object of my long and weary journey, to remain in the various monasteries and become acquainted with their habits of religion."

"You are welcome, brother," replied the Superior, "remain here as long as you wish. Our humble home is always open to the humble servants of Heaven."

And thus by a letter forged by the Brother Claus, did Rhodolph Wallenstein obtain entrance into the monastery of the Holy Trinity.

More than a month passed.

The retainers of the Castle of Theben, the home of Count Rhodolph, missed their young master, but they knew that he had gone upon some secret enterprise, and more than one of them was aware that before long their services would be required in some daring adventure.

It was the evening of a lovely day— warm and balmy, and sister Hilda was walking in the grounds with a young girl whom she had made a confidante.

She was, in fact, situated in a very similar manner to Hilda.

She had been forced into the convent against her will in order to prevent her marriage with the one she loved, and she had heard since that her lover had been put to a cruel death by her friends.

She, therefore, had no wish to re-enter the world.

This, however, was no reason why she should not feel an earnest sympathy with Hilda, and real true, womanly, sympathy she did feel.

It was this sister—sister Ursula—who first instilled into our heroine's mind the idea of escape.

Hilda—wretched, inconsolable—had not dreamed of anything but a sad and weary life, terminated by a quick and lonely death.

For a long time, she scouted the idea of happiness.

But Sister Ursula was firm in her presentiment that Hilda was not destined to remain long an inmate of the convent of the Twelve Virgins.

It was, as we have said, a beautiful evening, when Ursula and Hilda were walking in the garden of the convent.

They were there alone, for the other sisters were attending a service from which Hilda was exempted through ill-health.

"On such a night as this," said Ursula, "your gallant knight should come to save you."

"Ah, Ursula!" said Hilda, with a sad smile, "I fear your dream will never be accomplished. Rhodolph, much as he loves, will believe after a while that I have forgotten him, and will lose all thought of me in some fairer and more joyous face."

At this moment Ursula's eyes were attracted by something lying on the garden bed.

She grasped Hilda's arms convulsively.

"Hilda! see—see !" she cried, "there lies a ladder. It is long enough to reach the top of the wall. Oh ! but if you could send now to your lover."

Hilda's face flushed with excitement.

A faint hope for the first time invaded her breast, but she was too overwhelmed to be able to frame any plan in her mind.

But Ursula was quieter and more quick-witted.

"I see before me a plan," she said ; "the wall yonder where the ivy clusters so thickly, is being repaired. To-morrow the man will doubtless resume work ; I will bribe him to take a letter to the young Count. Nay, tremble not, Hilda, leave the task to me, and I will yet see you happy."

"Dearest Ursula," murmured Hilda, with tears in her wistful eyes, "how shall I ever thank you for your kindness ? You

have at length inspired something like hope in my breast. I will brave all, even the terrible penance which would follow discovery, for *his* dear sake. But do not expose yourself unnecessarily for me."

Ursula smiled.

"I fear them not," she said, "all their punishments and maledictions have no terrors for me. Life lost all joy since my love was cruelly murdered, and death itself would be a welcome boon."

On the following day Ursula, walking slowly and methodically through the gardens, approached the spot where the man was busily working at the broken wall.

THE NUN'S TOWER.

If she had been less occupied by her own thoughts, she could have observed that his eyes wandered eagerly ever and anon over the ground as if in search of some one.

Presently she halted beneath the place where he was working, and glanced upwards, holding in her hand a tiny note.

The man saw at once that she intended this as a request to him.

"I will come down," he said in a low whisper, "I come from Rhodolph Wallenstein."

Ursula's good heart beat high with joy.

"Providence is working for us," she murmured, and with a significant look she stooped and placed the tiny note among a cluster of flowers which graced the border at her feet.

Then she walked away.

The man descended, stooped as if in search of something, and picking up the note, ascended again quickly.

That night Ursula stole into Hilda's room.

"Dearest Hilda," she said, "prepare yourself for happiness."

Hilda looked up incredulously.

"Oh, you would not deceive me," I know," she said, "but your kind heart exaggerates good fortune."

"No, no; to-morrow night you shall effect your escape. By this time Rhodolph Wallenstein is preparing for your flight. At the midnight hour he will be on the summit of the wall. The ladder will be left where it stands, and you will ascend to be received in your lover's arms."

The next night was just such as the lovers could have wished.

A dark, windy, stormy night, which effectually drowned any other sounds.

Just before midnight, Ursula, true to her word, entered her friend's chamber, and closed the door after her, locking it carefully.

Hilda was sitting ready dressed on her bed, trembling, half beside herself with excitement.

Ursula folded her in her arms.

"Now, my dear friend," she said, "all is ready. Here is the rope by which you can descend into the garden. Let us lose no time, let us descend at once."

"You will escape with me, then, dearest sister?" said Hilda.

"Yes, and remain with you till all is settled," said Ursula, and she turned towards the window.

The rope was soon fastened, and quickly the brave girls let themselves down into the garden.

Swiftly across the velvet turf they ran, until they reached the spot where the ladder stood, and heard a voice say—

"We are here; all is ready."

"Ascend first," said Ursula, "I will follow and secure your safety."

What followed was the work of but a moment.

Hilda, half in fear, half in joy, hurried up the ladder, quickly followed by her friend.

At the summit she was received into the arms of her enraptured lover, and was just about to descend, when there was a loud outcry from below, and several persons appeared bearing torches.

"Hold, or we fire," cried a man whom they recognised as one of the sentinels.

At this moment the brave Ursula was standing at the top of the ladder, shielding Hilda, who was half over the wall.

In an instant the intrepid and self-sacrificing girl conceived in her mind a plan to save her friend.

"Stay!" she cried, do not fire and I will descend at once."

Then as she turned she whispered to the lovers—

"Be quick, descend. They have seen only me."

She pressed Hilda's little hand fervently in hers, and slowly made her way downwards, while the lovers rapidly made their way to the rocky ground, and thence glided away under the dark shadow of the wall, until they reached the mountain path which led to the hut of Lladislaus the hermit.

They arrived here in safety, and were already congratulating themselves upon their success, when there was a rush of dark forms, and they found themselves confronted by the furious Abbot and a number of armed men.

But the young Count Rhodolph was not unprepared for such an emergency.

In an instant his dark robe was flung aside, his bright sword was flashed in the air, and his loud, ringing voice shouted—

"To the rescue, men of Theben!"

In an instant, fifty men, clad in armour, sprang as it were from the earth, and rushed down upon the astonished priest and his followers.

"Harm them not," said Rhodolph, "but keep them back until we have escaped."

So saying, he hurried his trembling companion across the path, and was soon passing along that portion of the rocks which led down through the archway by the River Danube.

Here he launched the boat which was in readiness for him, and with his mistress trembling upon his breast was soon being rapidly rowed across the broad stream.

Meanwhile the followers of the Abbot made a feeble attempt at a rescue.

Indeed, the men of Theben were far too numerous to be attacked with any chance of success, and so, after a show of fight, the priest drew off his men.

"Let your master tremble," shouted he in a loud and threatening voice, "he has carried off a daughter of the Church—one sacred to the service of Heaven—and death alone can be for him a fitting punishment. Let him beware, for the curse of the Church is upon him."

The men, rough Austrian henchmen, only laughed as the priest gave vent to this malediction; and defiling along the path, they soon followed their master across the river.

On arriving at Theben Castle, Hilda was at once given over to the care of a handmaiden, who conducted her to a chamber, where, for the first time for many a night, the young girl slept in peace upon a bed suited to a human being.

On the following day the nuptials of the young and loving couple were celebrated with as much pomp and ceremony as could be provided in so short a time, and loudly the halls of Theben Castle rang out with the shouts of the henchmen, as Rhodolph and Hilda took their seats at the head of the banquet table.

Father Lladislaus, the mysterious hermit of the mountain, was the one who joined their hands, and never was blessing more fervent than that which ascended to heaven from his lips when he pronounced them man and wife.

A right merry day was it for all at Theben, and, beloved as Rdodolph was by all, the blessings which were showered upon him were true from the heart.

But the young couple were not destined to enjoy long their happiness undisturbed.

On the second morning after their marriage, ere they yet had left the nuptial couch, there was a loud outcry without the castle wall, the clatter of arms, and all the signals of war.

Overcome by a strong presentiment of evil, the young husband sprang from the embrace of his beloved, and hastily donning his clothes rang the bell to summon an attendant.

A military retainer, pale and anxious, at once made his appearance.

"What ails you, that you look so pale?" cried Rhodolph.

"The castle is attacked, my lord," exclaimed the man; "the priestly warriors, reinforced by the men of Count Orbensorf, our lady's father, are swarming round the walls."

"What want they?"

"They demand the instant restitution of Lady Hilda."

"And what said our seneschal?" answered Rhodolph, buckling on his armour.

"He laughed the demand to scorn," said the man, "and told them in the name of his master that if they wanted the Lady Hilda they must come and take her!"

"Brave fellow!" exclaimed Rhodolph. "Go tell him to man the ramparts at every point, and give them warning to quit my domains. I will be with you in a moment."

The young knight re-entered the nuptial chamber to bid Hilda be of good cheer, and to say farewell for a time; and having succeeded in soothing her fears, he hurried to the battlements.

What he saw there was enough to make a braver heart than his quail.

Far and near swarmed the armed men; and from their numbers it was evident that the priestly warriors and the old

Count of Orbensorf's retainers were not the only men who were there to attack the home of the devoted lovers.

The brave vassals of Count Rhodolph seemed but a handful of men as compared with the forces opposed to them; but not for an instant did the thought of surrender enter the mind of the young husband.

He knew too well the terrible penalties which would be exacted from both.

"Where can these men be from?" he said, turning to the seneschal. "Where are our men from all around the country here? Where are Andraski and his soldiers, that they suffer these riotous priests to penetrate to my very castle walls?"

"Alas! my lord," said the seneschal, in tones of sadness, "I see the banner of Andraski, but it is among our foemen!"

Count Rhodolph turned slightly pale.

"The Church has used its utmost power against me," he said; "but see, they are preparing for the attack."

And as he spoke, he sprang upon a part of the stone wall which was high above the rest, shouting—

"Ho! there!—my men!—fight bravely for your lord and your homes! Free land and gold shall be the portion of all who aid in driving back the insolent invader!"

As he uttered these words a flight of arrows came whizzing through the air, slaying a man by Rhodolph's side.

The fight had commenced at last.

For three days the furious battle continued.

Rhodolph was everywhere; he seemed indeed ubiquitous—animating his men, daring the foe, hurling back those who strove to find a footing on the battlements.

But slowly and gradually the enemy made their way.

The outer walls were breached; and in the inner circle of fortifications, the men of the Holy Trinity and of Orbensorf fought like demons.

They had more spirit in the combat than those whom they attacked.

They were animated by the belief that the Church and Heaven were on their side; while again and again insidious parleys were held, in which the besieged were told of the curse which would fall upon them for opposing the chosen servants of the Most High.

Gradually, but surely, Rhodolph saw the home of his fathers being wrested from his grasp.

Driven to despair almost by the knowledge that resistance was useless, and certain now that he had no hope of help from without, he had again and again thought of rushing into the midst of the fray and dying as a brave man should.

But the thought of Hilda restrained him.

It was not, however, until the very last moment, when the enemy were swarming into the rooms and passages, that he told Hilda of the fearful alternative before them.

Hurrying up to the chamber where she was kneeling in prayer, he raised her from her knees, and pressed her convulsively to his heart.

"Quick with me, Hilda," he said, and passing his arm round her waist he hurried along the corridor, and ascending some steep and circular steps, he made his way with his beloved to the topmost tower of the Castle.

"Hilda," he said drawing her to a window, or rather an open casement, which overhung the dizzy height over the Danube, "you know the penance which the Church will exact from both of us. There is no hope, dearest Hilda; but a few moments are left to decide. The soldiers are crowding up the corridors; we shall—"

She nestled up to his breast, and, with a smile of heavenly resignation, placed her little hand over his mouth, saying—

"You hesitate to speak, dearest Rhodolph; I will speak for you. The rolling Danube lies below us, the sparkle of the bright sun upon its waters seems to tell of brighter homes, far, far away. On the one side captivity—death; worse than all for us, separation. We will die together. Rhodolph, come."

He strained the brave girl convulsively to his heart as she spoke.

He knew well that the death they were about to court was a painless, swift one compared with that which his dear Hilda would meet with at the hands of her merciless foes, and he accepted without reserve the dreadful sacrifice.

One long, impassioned kiss he imprinted on her lips.

Then he whispered—

"Dearest, they come; be brave."

His words were true; for even now along the corridor without could be heard the scuffling of the eager, savage soldiery, and he drew nearer the edge of the parapet.

There she stood, without a tear; her bright eyes flashing, her cheeks flushed with the anticipation of the fate which her own heroic nature had chosen; and as she turned once more to gaze upon her young husband—the chosen of her heart—she flung her arms around his neck, and pressed a last kiss upon his lips.

Then she took his hand.

"Now, Rhodolph," she murmured.

The young knight passed his right arm around her waist, drew her arm around his neck, and in accents suffocated with emotion, said—

"May Heaven receive us, Hilda. Leap now with me."

And then, as the savage troopers rushed into the chamber, they saw the fall of the two devoted ones through the air, and the yielding of the waters as they plunged into the Danube.

Their bodies were never recovered, and it was said for many a century that, on the anniversary of their terrible fate, their figures, clothed in white, could be seen floating through the air from the ruined casement of what was ever after known as THE NUN'S TOWER.

END OF THEBEN; THE LEGEND OF THE NUN'S TOWER.

Our next number will contain "The Mystic Veil."

[Continued from page 314.]

THE LEGEND
OF THE
DRACHENFELS.

HE then inquired of Rinbold, Placidus, and Sir Conradin, and was informed that they were all slain or defeated, a fact highly gratifying to the malignant high priest of Odin.

Valkyr and his priests then held one of

"RINBOLD, CONCEALED BEHIND A TREE, SURVEYED THE IMPRESSIVE SCENE."

their barbarous rites as thanksgiving to the Teuton god of war.

Osric's claim to the possession of the anguished and helpless Theodora was at first not disputed, and he imperiously commanded that she should be removed to his castle.

But scarcely was the order given when Rinbold, who had left Conradin attended by his brother on the opposite bank, appeared and offered his protest against it.

The eyes of the beautiful captive were lit up with hope as she beheld him, for she trusted in him as much as she feared and abhorred Osric.

All the others, however, looked at him in surprise, suspicion, and some degree of antagonism.

His helping the Christians had much decreased the favour in which he was generally held.

"Lady," he said, "fear not ; thou shalt be conveyed nowhere save with thine own consent. Art thou willing to be conveyed to Baron Osric's castle ?"

"Never, never !" she cried, with great earnestness. "Let me be slain sooner on the spot."

"Then yield yourself my prisoner, as thy father and uncle, who have escaped death in the fray, have already done, and all shall be conveyed to my castle of Hemmerick, where thou canst rely upon every care and respect being shown thee."

Theodora murmured her thanks and willing consent ; but Osric, who stood by foaming with rage, could no longer control his passion.

"Insolent boy," he cried, "thou shalt thwart me no longer. Thou diest !"

And he forthwith attacked him with his huge falchion. Rinbold turned and put himself on the defensive. Valkyr attempted in vain to remonstrate.

The two rivals were determined to assert their claims by the sword's edge.

The two chiefs were equally matched—the skill, agility, and superior coolness of one balancing the herculean build and ponderous strength of the other.

Blows fell thick and fast, till at length Oscar made a furious pass at Rinbold, which the latter parried and followed up with a stroke, which severed the links of the baron's chain armour and inflicted a deep wound in his breast.

With a groan Black Osric fell prostrate, desperately, if not fatally wounded.

"Yield thee !" cried Rinbold, standing over him. "I desire not to slay my kinsman, so abandon thy claim to the Christian maiden."

"Never, never ! while I have one spark of life," exclaimed Osric, glaring at Rinbold ; "nor shall she be thine, even if I die ! Promise me this, Valkyr, on thy faith as a priest of Odin."

"The maiden herself shall decide if I am worthy of her love," said the young chief boldly ; "and if she deems so, she is mine only."

"Sooner would I slay her with this sword," cried the wounded baron, making an effort to repossess himself of his weapon.

"Chiefs of Wolkensburg !" interposed Valkyr, "this quarrel hath already been carried to too deadly an issue. There is one way by which it may be decided and a great purpose served. We have as yet offered no human sacrifices to celebrate our victory. Let this maiden be offered up as a sacrifice to the dragon, and the wrath of Odin is certain to be appeased at once and for ever."

This sanguinary proposal was too much in accordance with the habits of that wild race to excite much horror. Osric, perceiving that, even should he recover, Theodora's abhorrence of him would not probably abate, freely consented.

" 'Tis well," he cried ; "we will offer her one other alternative. Consent to be mine, and on these terms and no other shall thy life be spared."

"I refuse," she replied, firmly. "Relying on the protection of Heaven, I will face the horrible doom with which I am menaced."

Rinbold protested in her favour, but as he had now no followers that dared to support him, while the powerful high priest and baron were against him, he was compelled, with great anguish, to behold the sacrifice of her whom he had already learned to adore. The priest hastened to put his fell design into immediate execution.

Further mock rites took place at the temple ; the sentence was passed upon Theodora, and Thugbrand the Sacrificer bound her with still stronger cords. She asked for time for preparation, and for a farewell interview with her father. It was refused, and she could only submit to her fate with such resignation as was at her command.

Despite their savage and superstitious natures, the rugged warriors could not behold her, so young, so beautiful and saint-like, devoted to a fate so horrible without some touch of pity ; but they were the slaves of their priests and chiefs, and dare not attempt to prevent the sacrifice.

The mournful procession was soon seen

filing among the rocks to the dragon's cave.

Theodora went first, strongly guarded, the priests and warriors bringing up the rear.

Rinbold followed, silently and mournfully, while Osric, wounded as he was, caused himself to be carried by his attendants to some point where he could easily witness the sacrifice.

By the order of Valkyr, the treasures were removed and placed some distance from the rock whereon they had been deposited.

This done, Theodora was tied fast to the tree with strong cords, to which she submitted with a passive calmness which surprised all.

When she was firmly secured all drew back, and crouching among the rocks, gazed upon the terrible scene with breathless and fearful expectation.

Valkyr and Thugbrand remained near the treasure, at a point which offered a great facility for flight should it be necessary.

Rinbold took up his position on an elevated piece of rock, nearer to the dragon's cave than were any of the other spectators.

He was determined—even at the sacrifice of his own life—to attack the dragon ere it reached its victim.

And now, amidst the breathless and awful silence, the monster appeared emerging from its den. Rearing up its hideous head, which resembled that of a huge crocodile, it gave forth an unearthly sound, emitting also a thick sulphurous vapour. Its forked tongue darted forth, its red eyes gleamed like lamps. With a crawling serpentine motion, it wriggled out its scaly neck, followed by its ponderous body, and accompanied by two formidably-armed claws.

One moment it eyed its victim, gave another loud cry of satisfaction, and stretched out its claw to seize her.

Rinbold, at the same time drawing his heavy sword, prepared to rush down the rocks and attack the monster.

And how went it with Theodora?

Not paralysed with terror, not swooning with fright, but with a strange and unearthly calmness, she awaited her devourer's approach.

It was now noticed by the spectators that she had by some means contrived to free one hand from her bonds, and with this she had drawn forth from her bosom a small and beautiful silver crucifix, which she pressed to her lips while praying fervently.

At this terrible moment she suddenly raised this holy emblem aloft, and held it before the monster as a shield and weapon of defence, at the same time uttering audibly a fervent prayer.

The effect seemed magical.

The dragon seemed suddenly paralysed; all its strength was gone, and a deadly terror seized it. One moment, and with a loud roar that subsided into a groan of anguish, the monster fell back, collapsed, and gliding painfully along the rugged rocks, reached the river bank, gave a last unearthly yell, and the deep waters of the Rhine closed noiselessly over its head.

All this had passed, as it were, instantaneously, and the effect upon the beholders was as bewildering as that of an earthquake or any other great convulsion of nature.

"Behold," exclaimed Theodora, "the power of the true faith! Heaven has interposed in my favour; the evil spirit is exorcised; the dragon is slain, and your danger is over."

"Yes, my friends," added the awe-stricken Rinbold, "a miracle has been wrought to convert your souls from pagan darkness to Christian light. I renounce the faith of Odin from this moment."

Bewildered, delighted at the destruction of the monster which had caused them so much anxiety, the crowd of warriors rushed to liberate Theodora, before whom they fell down and worshipped, as if she had been a goddess.

The crucifix was looked upon as a talisman of supreme potency, and Rinbold's declared conversion was followed by that of many of his friends.

And what said Osric, Valkyr, and Thugbrand to all this?

An awful fate had overtaken the fierce baron.

Rapidly sinking from the wound Rinbold had inflicted, when placed in view of the sacrifice, the sudden shock of the recent spectacle was too much for his weak frame.

A horror lit up his dying face, convulsions seized him, the blood from his wound gushed afresh, and he fell backwards and died contemporaneously with the destruction of the dragon.

And Valkyr?

He and Thugbrand were nowhere to be seen, and what was more significant, the greater part of the treasure that had been just removed from the rock, was missing also.

This fact showed that they had taken advantage of the general absorption of interest in the dragon to make off with their prize.

Rinbold hurriedly related what he had before discovered, and this combined to arouse a general indignation against the guilty priests.

A search was made for them.

They could have had but a brief start as yet, and at length they were discovered making their way, as rapidly as their heavy booty would allow, towards the adjacent forest.

The paths, however, were rugged and difficult, and their hurry to clamber over the rocks, and dread of meeting the vengeance of their late dupes, made them more eager than cautious.

At last, however, they seemed to have reached a point of safety—a high rock—where they were separated from their pursuers by a steep ravine.

Thugbrand had not yet reached the apex, but Valkyr was there.

He paused, and in fiendish triumph looked back at his foes, waving a heavy purse of gold defiantly above his head.

He made one step more, and the piece of rock—a treacherous, ill-poised mass—toppled over with his weight, and, with a wild shriek he fell instantly into the ravine.

Thugbrand, who was just below clambering upwards, received the full brunt of the descending mass, and was buried and crushed beneath it.

Valkyr, his skull broken by striking a stony projection, was also killed instantaneously.

Such were the fates of the last pagan chief and the last pagan priests of Hemmerich and Wolkensburg.

The rest of our history is easily guessed by the reader.

On that very day all the inhabitants of that district formally abjured the faith of Odin, and commenced the demolition of the temple.

The statues were hurled down and broken, and Father Placidus held a Christian service on the altar hitherto devoted to the false gods.

Rinbold, as Baron of Hemmerich, Wolkensburg and Drachenfels—as the Dragon's Rock was called from that day—was joyfully accepted by all as their liege lord.

His mild and just sway was an agreeable change from the stern and fierce despotism of Osric.

The latter was buried with all due honours, and near his remains were reared a chapel and monastery, the abbot of which was Father Placidus.

It will be conjectured that the consent of Theodora and of her father—who ultimately recovered from his wounds—to her marriage with Rinbold was easily gained, and her vow of devotion to the conventual life abrogated by her uncle, who performed the ceremony.

Her great mission was now accomplished.

The inhabitants of both banks of the river were Christians, and in a short time all the chiefs and people of the surrounding districts had embraced that faith.

Rinbold built upon the dragon's rock the magnificent castle of Drachenfels, and he and his descendants lived, beloved and respected, for many generations as barons of that portion of the Rhine.

END OF THE LEGEND OF THE DRACHENFELS.

THE MYSTIC VEIL.

—◦◦⟡◦◦—

THERE is scarcely a single monument in the whole of the Danubian provinces which is not connected with the name of Trajan, and that which bears the name of Trajan's Tablet, is but one of the many instances of the wondrous energy and activity of the Roman people.

The vast and precipitous rocks which bear this name, are the handiwork of nature, but the road in commemoration of which the inscription is written, is the result of many years of patient and arduous labour.*

There are hundreds of legends in connection with this romantic stretch of the river, but the most authentic, the one which has left its stamp on the memory of every peasant, is that of the Soiled Ring.

Long before the Roman conquest of England, and at a time when any worship was little understood in this island, the Druids were the priests of all Danube land.*

Very many years after the introduction of Christianity, Pagan rites lingered among the common people, and there were many adherents to the old religion.

Of these was one, Kimpo Lergo.

He had been discovered as a babe of nearly a year, under a tree in a wood, by some savage robber of the forest, who never troubled to inquire into his parentage, and brought him up in the uncouth and weird belief of the Forest Worshippers.

Until ten he remained with the brigands, and then, the gang being exterminated, he was, by the kindness of a friend, placed in the service of the Baron of Kulenstein, as his eldest son's page.

Kimpo Lergo was one year the senior of young Arthur of Kulenstein, whose delight he was, as much for his mischievous propensities as his odd and quaint sayings, learned among the robbers.

Arthur of Kulenstein when eighteen, and his mother being still alive, fell in love with Edda, the only daughter of another baron, by name Rubensdorf, and wished at once in his impetuous way to marry her and bring her home.

"Two cats and one mouse," said Kimpo Lergo, "two women in one house, two dogs to one bone, will not agree long."

"I'll break your head," replied Arthur of Kulenstein.

He who handles pitch besmears himself," drily observed the page.

"Will you be silent, knave? Why should I not get married?" roared the angry youth.

"Every Adam must have an Eve to blame for his faults."

"Silence. Tell Edda that this night at nine we meet in the cave of Pescabera,†

---

* Along the base of the rock runs a narrow and projecting terrace, parallel with and fronting the stream. Underneath this platform are observed numerous square sockets cut into the rock, in line, and at regular intervals, into which the end of the beams, which supported the old road, were inserted. This rocky stage or terrace, is chiselled out of the precipice, but being too narrow for the purpose of a great road, the defect was remedied by flooring over the projecting beams, and thus giving it a convenient width towards the river, along the margin of which it was carried in the form of a hanging gallery. But the plan, though partially adopted in some of the Alpine passes, has been abandoned for the more safe and satisfactory one of blasting by means of gunpowder, as adopted in the construction of the new road, which, like those of the Splogen and Simplon, would never have been accomplished but for this powerful agent. How the Romans by sheer manual labour contrived to open a military thoroughfare along the face of the tremendous gorge, it is difficult to conceive. The vast quantities of timber, too, which were necessarily employed in its construction, by decay and accidents of season, must have exposed the road to frequent danger, had not the adoption of covered galleries, as in Switzerland, protected it from the weather above, while the skilful construction and solidity of the works underneath gave it all the support necessary for a public highway. Though exposed to the ravages of terrible tempests it was protected from avalanches. About the middle of the precipice and nearly level with the platform is a large tablet cut into the face of the rock, with an inscription ascribing the work to the Emperor Trajan, and bearing the date A.D. 103. Two winged genii support a scroll, and on either side is a dolphin with the Roman eagle above, but both letters and ornaments are much defaced, not merely by the effects of the weather, but also by the fires lighted by the Servian fishermen.

* In those days the Danair, who gave the name to the Danube, were Druids, with an odd mixture of Pythagorism taught by Zamolxis. They believed in the transmigration of souls, there being no real death, only a change of bodies.
† In the bluff escarpment of the mountain Schukuru is the cavern of of Pescabera, now known as Nelevari's cave, from a brave Austrian general, who, in 1692, had the chief command in Transylvania, and posted in it a garrison of 400 men, who there perished

to decide on our future movements," was his master's decided response. "I must speak with her."

"Fair words butter no cabbages," grinned the serving man, moving some distance off.

"Only let me get hold of you," said the youthful baron, shaking his riding whip. "Come here at once."

"'Your words are fair,' said the wolf, 'but I will not come into your village,'" cried Kimpo Lergo, and ran away to escape the lash, which his exasperated young master would certainly have laid about his back.

But though Kimpo Lergo always spoke thus to his lord and master, there was no doubt that in his secret heart he loved him, and was deeply devoted to his interests.

But he well knew how deep a feud there was between the two old barons.

They were rivals in the chase, they had been rivals in love and war, and love-making between their children could only lead to disastrous results.

Now Kimpo Lergo wanted both to serve his master, be true to the young girl, and remain at home, where he had his own little affairs to attend to.

In the service of Edda was a very handsome gipsy-looking girl, who had taken the fancy of the forest waif, and the summit of his ambition was to remain at home.

Now if the amours of the young people were discovered, he knew that his master would be sent upon his travels.

He little suspected what was passing in his absence.

Arthur had gone to the great banquetting room, had dined, and risen to retire, when his father with a great frown, and a tremendous dig at his brawny moustache, bade him remain.

"Your mother and I have something to say to you," he said.

Arthur looked and observed that not only were his parents frowning, but that all retainers had retired.

"Am I correctly informed?" said the baron, in a deep bass voice, "that you have been caught by the *Peris crul lue* [*] of Edda of Rubensdorf.

"Sir, I love her," was the apparently calm reply, "and I have asked her to be my wife.

"Rather would I see you wedded to the bride of all the world,"[†] thundered the baron.

"My lord," said the son, respectfully, "rather than give her up I will go to the wars and die."

"Best thing you can do," bellowed the angry parent.

"*Min drew ciobanel,*" (pretty little sheep), said his mother contemptuously, "you are led by the eye of the devil. The baron is rich, and has insulted your father."

"He never insulted me," replied Arthur, piteously. "Mother, I shall go to the wars."

"Best thing you can do," said the irate parent, "than be *tras pinto' un el.*" [*]

The son, who dearly loved his parents —and they, be it known, dearly loved him—bowed, and left their presence, determined that as he could not have his own way in everything, he would be off and fight, hoping thus to be slain honourably, without the base and cowardly necessity of killing himself.

He went to his room, packed up a few things for Kimpo Lergo to carry, selected his best suit of armour, and then waited the return of his savage but faithful henchman.

Kimpo Lergo lost no time.

Mounted on his faithful mule, he had hurried away, and on reaching the wood in sight of Rubensdorf, tied his animal to a tree.

War had not recently reached that district, so that no distrust was shown, and a postern gate was open; Kimpo Lergo slipped in and gained the reserved garden, where Edda's maidens were generally to be found.

One only was idling among the shrubs —it was Fenella.

"Well Darky,"—he was rather sunburnt—"what do you want?"

"In the first place, black cows give white milk, young maiden, and are as good as any others. In the next place I have a private message for your betters. Where is the lady Edda?"

"I shall not answer you, saucebox."

"One that pelts every barking dog must pick up a great many stones," drily observed the foundling. "Will you lead the way?"

The girl laughed, and did show him where the young heiress of Rubensdorf was seated.

He gave his message, and for some minutes awaited the answer.

There was a struggle in the girl's heart, and then love prevailed.

"I will come," she faltered, "but tell him it is for the last time."

The henchman bowed low to hide his smile.

---

* Roumanian for pretty hair.   † Death.

* Drawn by a ring.

"When people want to do anything," he muttered, "there is always an excuse. He whose mistress squints, says she ogles."

"What are you muttering to yourself?" asked Fenella, as he returned to the garden.

"Don't be curious," he answered.

"Ah!" said Fenella, with a laugh, "where every one sees that you are a pig, why don't you go into the stye?"

Kimpo Lergo stood amazed and breathless at this application of one of his sayings, but had no time to make any further remarks.

The merry-hearted girl had disappeared.

When Kimpo Lergo reached home he was amazed to find his master awaiting him impatiently, armour-clad, and with a large package for him to carry.

He gave his message without any comment, as his young master was in no very good humour, and descended to the lower regions to satisfy his appetite before starting on what he thought his lugubrious enterprise.

"What's to be done?" said Kimpo Lergo to himself; "the devil's in the cards. Four aces and not a single trump."

Thus he muttered as he devoured his meal, and then prepared for his weary expedition.

The night was tempestuous and cold, and a journey along the terrible old Roman road, known as Trajan's Tufel, was no mean enterprise.

Besides, the approach to the cavern of Pescabera was not only really dangerous, but infested with horrors, in the shape of the ghostly relics of the robbers who made the memory of that part of the river infamous with the memory of their crimes.

Arthur rode on wrapped in thought, Kimpo Lergo jogged behind upon his mule, until they reached the foot of the fearful rock in which the cavern was situated.

A narrow path led half to the summit.

The animals were left behind, fastened to some projecting bushes, and the man and master clambered up.

To their great surprise Edda was there first, accompanied by the faithful Fenella.

Edda had endured a severe lesson from her parents.

They had heard of the visit of the weird henchman, as they called him, and had warned her against ever permitting his visits again.

After this, with true Roumanian philosophy, they had retired to rest.

"We must part for ever," said Edda.

"Nature draws stronger than seven men," muttered Kimpo Lergo.

"Avaunt!" cried Arthur. "Away, wretch, and let me not hear your voice again."

"Trust no man until you have eaten a bushel of salt with him," muttered Kimpo Lergo; "master is in the dumps."

To give the whole despairing dialogue of the lovers would occupy too much space, but finally they agreed that, under the circumstances, they must part.

But both of them had been highly favoured at their birth by fairy gifts, and these they agreed to exchange.

"Take this ring," said Arthur, "pressing it upon the finger of the beloved one; "it was given me at my birth."

"From Baba Dohia?"* cried Edda.

"No; from my beneficent god-mother, I was never to part with it, except to the girl I loved. She was to wear it on her finger, and if ever it became soiled in that position she would know that I was either dead or faithless."

"Heavens!" cried Edda, "my god-mother gave me this veil with the golden fringe, which I was never to part with except to the man of my choice. He was to look at it every morning, and if the fringe exhibited signs of melting, then he would know that I had betrayed him."

"Let us exchange," cried Arthur. "I have resolved to go to the wars. Will you believe in me, and be faithful two years?"

"I will!"

And the two embraced.

"Fortune and women are partial to fools," muttered Kimpo Lergo from a distance, and went on with a long and earnest conversation already commenced between himself and Fenella.

It was late when the lovers parted.

Edda had no distance to go.

Her father's castle was close at hand, on the heights over Trajan's Tufel, and at eight every postern gate would be closed.

Arthur returned to where he had left his steed and the mule of his faithful henchman.

"Where are we going to, sir?" asked Kimpo Lergo, in his most doleful voice.

"To the woods," said the young knight. "I shall travel far to-night, if I sleep beneath the leafy arches of the forest."

"Like will to like, as the devil said to the charcoal burner," muttered Kimpo Lergo.

"Speak for yourself," cried Arthur, laughing. "Lead the way, and if before

* Baba Dohia is the evil spirit of the Danube, half clay, half flesh.

morning you can find a good tavern we will rest there."

"Good wine ruins the purse, and bad the stomach," answered the squire.

"Thou shalt have none. Wine there was enough in my father's castle."

"If I had is a poor man."

"One more word of your vile sayings, and you return to the schloss."

"I know when I've got a good master, if you don't know when you've got a good man," growled Kimpo Lergo, under his teeth.

But he spoke not aloud, and Arthur, who was thinking of something else, put spur to his steed, and trotted along the strange and wonderful road, until they reached Trajan's bridge,* where they turned into the open country.

Kimpo Lergo was very sorrowful and thoughtful.

His object was to bring about an early return home, but how it was to be done was a difficulty he had not quite overcome.

His master was deeply in love, and hence, naturally, very credulous, but he feared his fiery spirit too much to play upon him too fearlessly.

They travelled on till nearly dawn, and then put up at a road-side inn, where, despite his blighted hopes and wishes, the young knight slept the sleep of the just.

Next evening, rather late, they halted at a wayside hostel.

Sir Arthur was received with great civility, and having supped, retired to his chamber in order to indulge in the one pleasure of gazing at the veil with the golden fringe.

Kimpo Lergo remained by the fire in the kitchen, bent on paying his respects to a bottle of wine, which his master had ordered but scarcely tasted, his mind ever dwelling on how to get home.

While thus agreeably occupied, a loud clamour was heard outside, and then there came pouring into the kitchen a number of persons, one of whom was richly habited, while all the others wore the liveries of a person of rank.

They all, however, seemed unused to their dress, while their countenances would certainly have militated against them in a court of justice.

"Humph," thought Kimpo Lergo, "Dr. Luther's shoes do not fit every parish clerk. Where have I seen that face before? Never speak of a rope in the house of one who was hanged. 'Tis Waldeck, the son of the robber who brought me up."

As he said this, Kimpo Lergo shivered.

By the rules of the band—once a robber always a robber, and if discovered, they would pitilessly compel him to rejoin their nefarious crew.

The mere fact of his recognising in the pretended noble the son of his old chief would entail death or slavery.

But he would have given much to discover their object.

He listened with all his ears.

Despite the affected difference of rank, the whole party sat down to the same table.

Some words spoken in a dialect which Kimpo Lergo well understood, roused his attention.

An allusion was made to the Castle of Rubensdorf.

He leaned forward in such a marked way as to catch the attention of the chief.

"What gaping hunspel is that?" cried the chief.

"I am in the service of the young count of Kulenstein," said the youth.

"Thou hast betrayed thyself," cried the chief, with a dark frown, "come hither."

Kimpo Lergo approached.

The robber played with his dagger.

"You remember your oaths taken as a boy?"

"I do; and have never broken them."

"Whither go you?"

He explained that he was journeying with his master to join the armies in the field.

"'Tis well! Now repeat my words."

And the robber dictated an oath, by which Kimpo Lergo bound himself not by word or deed to betray his knowledge of them.

Kimpo Lergo with a shudder took the fearful oath, and retired.

He had hoped, by telling his master who they were, and hinting at their destination, to induce him to return home.

But so great was his horror of failing in his promise that he could not stir in the matter.

As he entered his master's room, where he was to sleep on a mat on the floor, his eyes fell upon the veil with the golden fringe.

He had overheard all the lovers had said, and was bent on an audacious device.

He took the fringe from the table on which it lay, and cautiously approached

---

* So called because it was built for Alexander Severus by Appolodorus, 104, A.D., says a facetious author.

the fireplace, where glowed some bright embers.

Blowing them red-hot with his breath, he flashed the gold for one instant, and took it away discoloured and slightly melted.

Then carefully shaking the veil, he replaced it upon the table.

When morning came, Arthur, without looking at the fringe, folded up the veil and placed it in his bosom, after which he breakfasted, and continued his journey.

Waldeck, the robber, eyed his departure with grim satisfaction, while Kimpo Lergo in his secret heart fumed with rage.

The presence of this robber gang in the country, and in disguise, boded no good.

"I am a coward," thought Kimpo Lergo, "but I cannot help it—I did not make myself. Nothing bolder than the miller's shirt, that every morning covers a thief."

And he jogged on after his master in a state of mind not easily described.

"You are dull," said Arthur, when they had travelled half a day without speaking.

"Birds of prey do not sing."

"But you are no kite or hawk."

"I was brought up amongst them. Though you seat a frog on a golden stool,

TRAJAN'S TABLET.

he'll soon jump off again into the pond," said Kimpo.

And thus they went on for three days and nights, during which, very cautiously and jealously, he slightly melted the fringe, but without attracting the attention of his master.

The fourth evening, after losing their way, they were overtaken by a terrible thunderstorm in the midst of a horrid, dark and dismal wood, and looking round for refuge, saw the yawning mouth of a cavern.

Both men and brutes were only too glad of the shelter, and hurrying within its precincts, gazed in comparative safety

at the fierce lightning, and listened to the rumbling thunder.

Presently there was a lull in the storm.

"Heaven!" cried Kimpo Lergo, as a low groan fell upon his ears, "master mine, did you hear that?"

"I heard something like a human voice. Strike a light, you have your tinder-box."

"Be cautious. 'Tis not till the cow has lost her tail that she discovers its value."

"Silence, and obey."

Kimpo Lergo no longer demurred, but striking his flint and steel, which had often served to make a fire in the woods, he soon had some small splints he carried in a flame, and hastily applying them to a small heap of dry wood—much of which lay about—he soon had a goodly fire.

His keen eye soon picked out some resinous pine knots, and his master taking one and he the other, the horrid mystery was revealed.

About a dozen men, apparently in the last stage of the struggle for life, were lying about, tied neck and heels.

"To work," said the knight, "cut all their bonds."

He then looked around and knew that he was in a robber's cave.

There were rude tables, chairs, and sleeping places, but there were also barrels of wine and spirits, with ample supplies of bacon, dried deer meat and other articles of food.

As fast as Kimpo Lergo untied the men, he administered a draught of the brandy of the country, and each sufferer with a deep sigh opened his eyes.

A ghastly scene it was, illuminated by the torches which Kimpo had stuck in holes prepared for them in the rock.

As soon as the knight saw that the unfortunates had recovered something like animation, he ordered his squire to fetch wine and biscuit, of which there was plenty, made from rye, and soaking this he placed it to the mouths of the famished wretches.

Gradually they roused themselves, and while Kimpo Lergo set to work to prepare a more substantial repast in a huge cauldron suspended by a triangle, they severally began to stretch their limbs and make feeble attempts to walk.

"And now, sir," said Arthur, addressing a young man of dignified appearance, "will you explain this terrible event?"

"Good sir, we owe our lives to you, and explanation is at least your due. Hence my sword, my life, is at your disposal. I am Rudolph of Rubensdorf, cousin of Edda of the same name, and was on my way to wed that dear girl—"

Arthur with difficulty repressed a cry.

"When I and my followers fell into an ambuscade of robbers, who overcame us and placed us in this plight, from which you have so kindly released us."

"Happy that things are no worse."

"They cannot be worse. The robbers not only stripped us of our clothes, but of my papers, my knightly credentials and all insignia, and have started off in disguise to palm themselves off as myself and suite. My uncle has not seen me for eleven years before this."

"Good Heavens," cried Arthur, tearing the veil from his bosom and hastily examining the fringe, "what a fool I have been. It is—yes—it is discoloured and melted. Edda is in danger."

"Sir," said the other speaker, hotly, but feebly, "and pray how is it I see my cousin's godmother's gift in your hand?"

"She bears on her finger my ring, and this is her gift of plighted troth."

"Sir Arthur of Kulenstein," said the other, drily, "you speak of my affianced wife. You have saved my life; you can do more. Help me to save her from a ruffian, and then we can fight out our quarrel."

"One hair of a woman draws more than a bell rope," muttered Kimpo Lergo. "Thank Heaven, he will go back."

"Sir Rudolph," replied our hero, with exquisite courtesy, "Let me finish my work, and help to save Edda before we quarrel. Kimpo, is that stew ready?"

"Short hair is soon brushed—ready-cooked meat is soon warmed," said Kimpo Lergo, and proceeded to ladle out a savoury mess of ham, venison, salted beef and biscuit, all stewed together, to the famished party.

But, though all were revived at the end of the meal, none felt able to make much effort.

Calm sleep, not the feverish nightmare of the previous four days, would restore them more than all else.

This was agreed on.

Meanwhile, however, making free with the robber's treasure, Kimpo Lergo, mounted on his mule, rode off to a neighbouring town, eleven miles distant, to a certain Jew, who, for ready cash, would find horses, arms and accoutrements for a regiment of soldiers.

He was to meet them at a certain cross-road at midday, having bargained for the secret of the cave not being betrayed.

Next day, all, rather pale and gaunt, but still very different from the ghostly visions of the night before, rode off towards Trajan's Tablet, in sight of which the two castles were situated.

A very quick march was out of the question.

They were unable to travel the first day more than a few miles; but the fresh air, a supper, and a night's rest, were marvellous in their power of restoration.

With something like soldierly array and speed they marched the next day; the rivals riding side by side, and forbearing any allusions to the subject they had most on their minds.

"They go round about it like a cat round hot milk," muttered Kimpo Lergo.

In the meantime, what had happened at the Castle of Rubensdorf?

The old baron, who liked keeping money in the family, having at court, by usury and other means, amassed a great amount of wealth, determined to unite his daughter to her cousin Rudolph, never thinking that the young lady would have any objection.

In fact, in those days, however much in secret the feeling of love might be indulged in, it had very little to do with marriage.

No wonder half the wives and husbands were separated; while poisonings, stabbings, and every secret form of assassination were rife.

This marriage had been settled when Edda was in her cradle, and by surrounding her with all that affection could suggest and wealth procure, her parents thought they prepared her for obedience to their will.

Still, the grim baron forbore to tell her of her fate.

She was so happy, so innocent, that it seemed sacrilege to break her day-dream so rudely.

Not a word was therefore said, when suddenly Rudolph and his party rode into the castle yard, as rough a party of reiters as ever robbed a party of merchants or sacked a convent.

But Rudolph ever since the age of sixteen had been in the wars, and knights and nobles, who were real soldiers, were never remarkable for refinement or elegance.

The baron, therefore, after the first blush, was not surprised to find in his nephew a rude, blunt soldier, whose experience of camps was greater than that of courts, and who could tell a rattling good story after dinner better than he could discourse of troubadour or state policy.

"I have come, you see," he said at last, "in search of my bride——"

"All right, my boy. I am only too glad to welcome you."

"Here are my several patents of knighthood, of which I have five, from five different sovereigns," said the nephew with pride, "and the archduke wishes to see my bride at court as soon as possible."

"The marriage shall take place in four days," responded the father, and at once summoned his daughter to his presence.

She came sprightly enough, for, like most young girls, she found a new arrival in that gloomy castle a pleasant change.

"My dear, this is your cousin Rudolph, your future husband—embrace him."

Edda drew back, pale and trembling.

Rudolph advanced with an odd smile on his coarse but handsome face.

"Edda, my girl, you do not mean to be disobedient?" said her father.

"I will embrace him as a cousin—as a husband, never. I am the betrothed of Arthur of Kulenstein, and will keep my troth," she cried.

Well, it is not possible to record anything like the style of oath and curse which burst from the lips of the baron.

He abhorred his old rival, and, of course, his son, while he was so used to have his way in everything that rebellion appeared monstrous, if not blasphemous.

"I thought, uncle, you had prepared my cousin's mind long ago," said Rudolph, bluffly.

"What matters such trifles? Girl, recollect yourself. I am your father, and must be obeyed. On the fourth morning after this you will be married; and that there may be no more clandestine meetings with that young vagabond, Fenella, bring me the key of her apartments. Nay, I will see to them myself."

Edda, with the air of a martyr, marched away, accompanied by Fenella, and followed by the furious baron, who, though he had quarrelled with Kulenstein for the love of a noble lady, was mad with rage at his daughter presuming to have affections of her own.

As soon as Edda was alone with Fenella, she turned to her, and asked the girl what was to be done.

Now Fenella was an artful girl, and as fully anxious to bring Kimpo Lergo home as he was to return.

She judged that Edda, after all, would have to yield to her father, when the cause of his quarrel with his parents being removed, Arthur would come back.

She therefore determined to support the new aspirant, Rudolph.

"Well, my noble lady, I do not see how you can avoid wedding this cousin of yours——"

"Never, while I live," she cried, and looking at Arthur's ring, she kissed its bright and polished stone, "behold my pledge of love."

"Love never does run smooth," said Fenella, who bethought her of a device. "Who is over nice loses many a slice. For my part all men are about alike."

"Fie, Fenella. I will be true to Arthur."

"And yet you will marry your cousin," urged the servant girl, who was eager to be free, and let Kimpo Lergo hear the news ere it was too late.

The love-sick Edda turned angrily away

and spoke little more to the maid. Her meals were brought to her regularly, and she had a large wooden balcony with a grand view to walk in.

At night she took a warm posset made by Fenella, and slept unusually sound.

In the morning the ring was, if not rusty, soiled and dull.

"Heavens! some misfortune has happened to Arthur," she cried.

"Perhaps, my lady, he has met some wandering beauty, and is faithless," said the cunning maid.

"Never. I will stake my life on his truth," replied Edda.

The girl said no more, but left her to her own reflections, which were sad enough. Despite all her endeavours to keep up her courage, the words of the waiting-maid would rankle in her ears.

Love is ever jealous, even without reason, and the ring, in which she believed implicitly, had given her warning.

She tried her lute, she tried to sing, all in vain. Evil thoughts would not be conjured, and she cast herself weeping on her bed.

Fenella was very sorry, but she was playing a part, and to betray herself would be to forfeit the esteem of her mistress for ever.

And so passed the four days, until the morning came when she was to be sacrificed.

The ring was duller, more soiled than ever, but still it was not quite rusty.

Edda, pale but resolute, allowed herself to be robed for the ceremony, fully determined to resist unto the death. She knew the priest who on rare occasions acted as her father's chaplain to be a good man, and one incapable of an act of tyranny and oppression.

She descended to the hall, and happily found father Francis present. He looked keenly at her pale face, and slightly shook his head.

"Proceed with the ceremony," said the baron.

"Forbear, reverend sir," cried Edda, "this marriage is a matter on which I have not been consulted. I utterly refuse to give my hand without my heart. I am betrothed."

"Silence, rebellious child," shrieked the baron; "you know not what you say. Proceed."

"One moment, noble baron. I must hear what the child has to say even in secret confession, which can properly precede marriage. I cannot force anyone to enter into so holy a communion," said the priest, "but I will teach your daughter the duty of a child."

"Be quick about it, then."

At this moment some one whispered in the ear of the false Rudolph—

"A number of horsemen in hot haste can be seen in the distance," he said.

"This farce has lasted long enough," roared the false knight; "I am Waldeck, the robber, and Edda shall be my bride, in spite of priest or devil. Eh, my merry men, the castle is all your own!"

And he clutched the astonished girl in his arms, and, with drawn sword, dashed at the unarmed retainers of the baron, whose weapons had been removed and concealed.

"Wretch," said the baron, preparing to resist the villain, "give me back my child."

With a savage laugh the bandit struck him to the earth, and made for the courtyard.

His men, who knew where the baron's gold, silver, and precious stones were secured, made short work of the plunder, and then, with a loud blast of trumpets, mounted and dashed in the direction of Trajan's Tablet.

Twenty minutes elapsed when another troop of horsemen arrived, and dismounting, dashed into the hall.

It was deserted by all, save the wounded baron.

But a loud and prodigious shout from the real Rudolph soon brought the retainers to them, and hurried explanations were exchanged.

"Save my child," said the baron, faintly, and to no unwilling ears.

Everybody mounted, and soon were in hot pursuit.

But no matter what others tried to do, Arthur of Kulenstein was first.

He had his trusty sword ready, and his lance couched.

The robbers soon came in sight.

"Stop, false and cowardly knaves!" shouted the infuriated knight; "harm a hair of her head, and ye perish on the scaffold!"

"Success to you," cried Kimpo Lergo, "'God speed the craft,' as the hangman said to the judge."

They had entered on the narrow road, the Roman road, where Trajan's Tufel is situated.

There was scarcely room for more than one horse.

All the robbers had passed but Waldeck, who was impeded by the weight of the young girl.

He looked back, and saw the young knight approaching.

He must turn and face him, but he must rid himself of his burden.

As he was twice the weight and size of the youth behind, he had no fear of the result, so resolved to slide Edda on to the ledge.

But before he could execute the necessary *volte face* Arthur was upon him; his spear had caught his neck, and horses and riders, and the hapless Edda, were cast into the Danube.

Like a thunder cloud, the pursued and pursuer swept by, all save Kimpo Lergo, who had no wish for a personal conflict with any of the robbers.

"Let him that itches scratch himself," was his quaint remark.

Besides, his interest was centred in the stream.

The robber had cast Edda from him.

He was bleeding from a wound in the neck, and would have enough to do to save himself.

Arthua was urging his horse madly towards where Edda was sinking, only her beautiful hair being visible.

But the weight of his armour and that of his horse was too much for the steed.

Still he urged the beast wildly on, and at last clutched her hair, and, as he drew her to him, found his steed had touched ground.

"Thanks be to Heaven!" he said, fervently.

"Die, and leave me the beauteous maiden!" shrieked Waldeck, who, having reached the same shoal, had drawn his dagger, and aimed it at his noble rival's back.

At this moment, a raft, by means of which wood is carried to the Lower Danube, swept up, and on it was Kimpo Lergo, who had an arbalest in his hand,

He fired, and the robber fell back dead into the stream.

The lovers were hauled upon the raft, and laid side by side by the rude boatmen, who live for weeks on these singular crafts.

They were not dead, but both were insensible.

As soon as a proper landing-place was reached, the raft was propelled ashore, and a number of people from the castle approached, who carried the apparent corpses to the castle, where the good priest at once attended to them.

"Good youth," said Rubensdorf, "though the son of my enemy, you have saved my daughter's life."

That night, the Baron and Baroness of Kulenstein were beside their son's bed, in the castle of their foe.

The lovers were out of danger.

That night, later still, Rudolph, who had returned, with the robbers tied back to back, proposed the health of the future Baron and Baroness of Kulenstein, and none could say him nay.

And so, all was well that ended well.

To their last day, the married lovers believed in the warning of the soiled ring and the veil with the gold fringe.

Kimpo Lergo, married to the artful Fenella, never expressed his opinion.

"There's no law but has a hole in it—for those who can find it out," he remarks; "and he who plays best wins."

END OF THE MYSTIC VEIL.

HUGO ANDROSKI;

OR, THE SECRET OF THE HOLY CAVE.

THE town of Tricula, on the Danube, and situated in European Turkey, lies on the principal road from Yannina to Constantinople.

Well known for its ancient temple dedicated to Æsculapius, and filled with synagogues, Greek churches, and massive buildings, which remind you of the days long, long ago, it has a castle which dates from the time of the Greek Emperors, the walls of which still frown over the river, as if to show the ephemeral life of man, in contrast with the strength of its solid and grand masonry.

It is of this castle, of which we give an illustration, that we are about to speak, connected as it is with a strange cavern in the mountainous regions near. From this cavern we take the title of our story, which, according to the annals of the times, shows a wild and lawless condition of society.

"What! does the villain dare to beard me in my very home?" cried Count Paulo Arndoff, as he sprang from his seat on the battlements of his castle. "Does he dare to threaten me? Go tell him that I repudiate his claims—I laugh at his menaces; and, unless in twenty-four hours he sends a messenger to crave my pardon, I will carry fire and sword into his very home."

The seneschal, who had brought the message, bowed deeply and retired.

Once more Count Paulo resumed his seat, and gazed—though no longer with placid eyes—over the landscape around him.

Everthing which met his gaze was very beautiful.

It was evening—just sundown; and the broad river, green valleys, the distant mountains—the town below, with its towers and minarets, were bathed in the glory of such a sunset as we islanders can scarcely imagine.

But though his eyes seemed to take in the whole scene—sky, and river, and land—they were really directed to one spot alone; a lofty tower in the distance, which crowned the summit of a hill.

This was the castle of his rival and enemy Hugo Androski.

For more than fifty years there had been a deadly feud between the families of Androski and Arndoff; originating because the father of Hugo was accused of having slain unfairly in a duel the father of Count Paulo.

Time, instead of lessening, had only increased the rancour on both sides; and indeed, had added a hundred things to the story, which an early explanation would have avoided.

Be this, however, as it might, Count Paulo had, during the week prior to the opening of our story, met and cruelly beaten a party of huntsmen returning peacefully to the Castle of Androski; and for this unchallenged outrage it was that old Hugo had sent to demand compensation.

"Ah!" thought the fiery Count Paulo, as he gazed across the country at the house of his foe, "this may at least give me an opportunity of wreaking my revenge upon this villain—this murderer of my father. Let him but refuse the apology I have demanded, and yonder tower, from which his banner now so proudly floats, shall be levelled to the dust."

The words had scarcely escaped his lips when there appeared on the battlements a vision of infinite beauty.

It was a tall, sylph-like girl, of not more than seventeen summers, dressed in the picturesque costume of the country, which displayed to advantage her superb form, and the grace of her every movement.

Her face was sad now; but the regularity of her features and the brightness of her eyes seened to counteract the effect of her sorrow.

She advanced towards Count Paulo, with a steady, graceful step—with a mien indicative both of respect and indignant sorrow.

"Father," she said, "why am I again compelled to plead to you? Why are we always to be at war with our neighbours? You complain about the lawless tribes who dwell in the mountains—you call them pagans and yourself a Christian; and yet you imitate them in the violence of your deeds."

"Yes, Forsina, against the murderer of my father," replied Count Paulo.

"What! is an old tradition, which you have no means of proving, to render you like a savage—to cause the death of hundreds of innocent persons?" cried the lovely girl, her face recovering its glow, and rendering her beauty ttill more resplendent. "Why have you sent this threat to Hugo Androski? Why not—"

"Peace, girl!" exclaimed her father, with unusual sternness; of these things you are not a judge. And where did you learn my plans?"

A faint blush overspread Forsina's features as she answered—

"Alexander the Seneschal told me. I asked him the purport of the message which you had returned to that brought by the young count Hugo."

Count Paulo sprang to his feet.

"The young Count!" he exclaimed furiously, "in whom the very name of his assassin father is perpetuated to insult and outrage me—did he dare to place his foot upon my threshold? Then by the splendour of Heaven he shall rue this day. What ho! there, Alexander—hasten your palsied limbs—what answer did the villain send me?"

The old man bowed low, but he answered boldly.

Not one was there in the castle who despised and braved his master's rage so much as Alexander the Seneschal; and none consequently from whom Count Paulo would receive calmly a defiant and insulting message.

"Count Paulo," he said, "the young Count Hugo brought from his father a calm and peaceful demand. You answer by hurling at him your defiance, and asking an apology, which you knew well would be refused. Count Hugo's face burned red with anger when I repeated to him your words, and taking off his mailed glove he flung it within the gate, saying, 'Take that to your master, and tell him that I and mine do but laugh at his threats, and that if he comes to Androski Castle we will give him such a reception as he has not met with many a. long day.' And with these words he turned the head of his horse and galloped away."

Forsina stood with bated breath, clasped hands, and heaving bosom, listening to the seneschal's words.

So intent and eager indeed was her attitude, that at any other time the old count would have remarked it, and suspected that more than a daughter's interest was involved in this deadly struggle,

As it was, he burst into a loud laugh.

"Be it so, then, Alexander," he cried; "since this son of an assassin saves us the trouble of waiting for a reply to our challenge, we will lose no time. See that, ere two hours are past, every man in Tricula is under arms; let the horses be fed; let all arms be seen to, and let them know we start this night to capture Androski Castle, and bring its count and his son from his own battlements."

Forsina, in spite of her father's humour, passed her arm around his neck.

"Do not give this order, father," she cried; "see what blood will be shed; and remember, too, that it is you that are in the wrong. What you contemplate is evil in the sight of Heaven, and on your deathbed you will repent it sorely."

The count pushed her away angrily.

He was an old man now, and though his frame was still powerful, his locks were as white as the driven snow, and he liked not to talk of death.

"Preach not to me, girl," he cried; "let priests and other mumblers do that. I am resolved this night to give the Androskis a lesson which they will not easily forget. So leave me; go to your chamber, unless you will accompany me to the banquet hall and fill my cup with rich red wine to drink to the success of our arms.

The girl saw now that it would be worse than useless to plead further.

So, unwilling to irritate him into a humour which would render him even more cruel than ever to his defeated foemen, she moved away with downcast mien, and sought the seclusion of her own chamber.

Here she shut herself in, and sat down at an open window, from which she could see afar the tower of Androski, so soon to be the scene of terrible bloodshed.

It was fast fading into night now.

Only here and there a fleecy cloud—keeping still upon it the rosy kiss of the sun—hovered above the tranquil land.

The breeze was still and balmy; the river rolled on its placid course towards the sea.

Then suddenly the curtain of darkness seemed to fall, and the sun, having fled to gladden another clime, left Tricula to the moon and the stars.

At this moment a noise was heard at the end of the chamber, and as she glanced hastily round a panel slid open, and a young man, dressed in complete armour, stepped into the room.

Forsina started up, and advanced with clasped hands and agitated mien towards the intruder.

"Oh Hugo!" she cried, as he clasped her to his bosom, "why did you venture here to-night? You well know that the castle yard, which you must cross to gain egress from this place, will within a few minutes be full of armed men—enemies about to advance towards your father's castle, sworn to take your lives."

He glanced down upon her reproachfully for a moment.

"Dearest Forsina," he said, "is this all the welcome I have when I come hither through peril to see you—when I come to bid you, perhaps, an eternal farewell?"

"An eternal farewell!" echoed the young girl, shudderingly, "what do you mean? You make my heart thrill with strange terrors."

The young knight pressed her fondly to his bosom.

"The fortune of war, my loved one," he said, "is, as you well know, uncertain. Who knows who may be the conqueror?"

"True," she murmured, with another shudder. "But oh! Hugo, he is my father—though he is stern and unjust, spare him; as I hope, if he is victorious, he will spare you."

The young knight smiled.

"I will spare him," he said; "but if I am ever in his power bid me adieu for ever. And now farewell, Forsina. I came only for a kiss and a smile. I cannot ask you to wish me victory, since it is against

THE CASTLE OF TRICULA.

your father I fight. Wish only that in some way or another this battle may be the end of our feud for ever."

The betrothed lovers—for such they were, in spite of family feuds—embraced tenderly; and then, through the secret panel Hugo Androski disappeared just as a loud trumpet in the courtyard announced that all was ready for the starting of the expedition.

Forsina shuddered as she heard the sound.

How could her lover escape from the castle through such a host of armed men?

Rushing to her window, she glanced out into the courtyard.

There, mustering in brilliant array, and already defiling through the gateway, she could see the retainers of her father; the torchlight flashing on their armour and their lances; their horses prancing; their helmets gleaming.

But above the sound of their rattling mail, and the footsteps of their horses, there came nothing to indicate the discovery of any foeman among them.

And, indeed, had not her reason persuaded her otherwise, she could have sworn that by the side of her father, as he rode out of the castleyard, was Hugo Androski.

For continuation of this Story see page 337 *of our next number*
Our next number will also contain "The Fate of Count Voslau"

[Continued from page 336]

HUGO ANDROSKI;

OR, THE SECRET OF THE HOLY CAVE.

A S they disappeared, and the great gate closed, and the brilliant array descended the steep road from the fortress, the young maiden sank on her knees in prayer.

Then, after invoking mercy for the vanquished and clemency in the hearts of the victors, she sat down once more by the window, and strained her eyes towards the towers of the Androski.

"'WHAT INSULT IS THIS?' CRIED COUNT PAULO."

Meanwhile the glittering array hastened down the rocky road, and with steady march made for the home of their foemen.

The moonlight, which shone out in brilliant streams to light them on their way, shone, too, on their glittering mail, their unsheathed swords, and their spears ; and as they pressed onwards, with their flags flying, and the horsetails on their burnished helmets fluttering in the wind, they formed a most picturesque and imposing spectacle.

The road towards Androski was of such a nature that, on such a bright night as this, Forsina could see their advance nearly all the way, until at length, just as they had descended to a long, dark line, something bright seemed to detach itself from the rest, and dash—flying in the moonlight—up the mountain side.

Had she known the meaning of this how her heart would have beaten.

It was, in fact, none other than her lover.

On reaching the bottom of the secret staircase, and entering the courtyard, he had mingled with the men, and, mounting a horse, had kept near the person of his greatest foe.

It was noticed by many that there was one steed wanting ; but in his present fierce mood it was not deemed prudent to speak about it to the hot-headed chieftain; and one of the men, nothing loth, remained behind.

Keeping well among the advanced guard, Hugo Androski was unobserved, as the mail-clad warriors flashed up hill and down dale, until, on approaching the castle of Androski, he gradually worked himself out of the crowd, and, putting spurs to his horse, dashed madly up the mountain side.

"A traitor ! a traitor!" cried the stentorian voice of Count Paulo, and a dozen arrows winged their flight after him ; but they either in the darkness missed their mark, or glided harmlessly off the burnished steel.

Away—away sped young Hugo, but his foes were close upon his track, and the castle gates had scarcely shut behind him, when the crowding warriors of Tricula were at the moat-side.

His heart smote him as he remembered that had it not been for the visit he had paid to his mistress, he would have been able to give timely warning to his father.

But he consoled himself by the thought that it was perhaps an eternal farewell that he had wished her, and he saw too that the sentinels on the battlements had observed the advancing host, and given due warning.

Every tree consequently concealed an archer, and when the proud Count of Tricula arranged his forces, it was found that his foemen were in every way ready to receive him.

There was no summoning to surrender —no pretence of attempting an amicable arrangement.

The Lord of Androski had sent what Count Paulo called an insulting message, and had, moreover, defied him, so the warriors dismounting and tethering their horses in a secure place, began to cut down trees to form a bridge across the moat.

Well and carefully they worked under the screen of trees, so that only a random shot could reach them, and ere dawn broke the inhabitants of the besieged castle saw a body of men carrying forward huge trunks of trees lashed together in twos.

In spite of arrows from the crossbows, which pierced many a brave heart, the men of Tricula advanced boldly, and in the very teeth of their foemen began placing the bridge.

The air now was thick with missiles— the very sun seemed darkened by their flight ; but the chiefs on both sides seemed to bear a charmed life.

They appeared to be everywhere—exhorting their men to fresh courage, occasionally directing the missiles of their men, who, thinking nothing of the righteousness or unrighteousness of their cause, fought on both sides with equal ardour— for the mere sake of their leaders.

The old Count Androski, a tall and venerable looking warrior, was leaning over the battlements, encouraging his men as they were engaged in a desperate attempt to beat back the enemy, who were swarming up the scaling ladders, when an arrow aimed with deadly precision struck him between one of the interstices of the armour, and he fell with a groan back into the arms of his son, who rushed forward to catch him.

"The villains have given me my deathblow," he cried, " carry me away, Hugo, where I can die in peace. Take charge of my men, and lead them to victory, and let it not be said that the young Count Androski is less brave than his father."

Hugo at once seized his father in his stalwart arms ; and bore him across the stone courtyard, down a stone staircase to the basement of the castle, and leaving him in the care of an aged domestic, skilled in medicine, he hurried back to repel the invaders.

Again and again, headed by the brave Hugo, the besiegers were hurled back, and crushed as they fell, or drowned in the moat.

But, ere noon, a second body of men, marshalled by the aged seneschal, defiled slowly over the hills, and fresh and eager took the place of their worn, tired brethren.

It was a fierce and angry battle.

Men, pierced with arrows and with the death-foam upon their lips, drew the bow for the last time, to crush out the life of one more foeman.

Others grappled in the death-throes, on the top of swaying ladders, and fell into the deep moat to die together in its still waters.

Others, who had reached the battlements, and were met by the angry blows of their enemies, dragged their opponents with them from the dizzy height, and died in each other's arms.

But victory had declared for Count Paulo; and though the sun was declining in the west when the fight was over, the men of Tricula at length swarmed into the stronghold, and, inch by inch, they contested the place with its defenders.

At length, when all resistance was useless, a loud and stentorian voice was heard above the din of battle,—

"Cease the strife—we surrender—we surrender!"

And in an instant, the sounds of strife ceased, the vanguard threw down their arms, and the Castle of Androski was in the hands of Count Paulo.

But he was not satisfied with this.

His heart was greedy for revenge, and his eyes eagerly sought everywhere the face and form of his two enemies.

But in vain.

Neither Count Androski nor the younger Hugo could be found.

Search was made high and low—in every chamber—in every vault, but all to no purpose.

Even the piles of dead were examined. Uselessly.

The chiefs of the Androski had fled; or had died in some unknown spot, and Paulo's vengeance seemed yet unsatisfied.

"To-night," he said grimly to his old seneschal, "to-night, we will rest. To-morrow, we will commit to the flames the home of our deadly foes."

The whole of that evening and the hours late into the night were spent in feasting and drinking the rich red wine of the defeated Count.

Then, when all was still, and sentinels had been posted, a form might have been seen gliding from the edge of the mountain towards the castle.

Slowly it approached, glidingly, like a ghost, and suddenly, as the sentinel was about to challenge it, it seemed to vanish in the earth.

But it was indeed no apparition.

It was none other than Hugo Androski, the younger, in search of the father he loved.

Passing along a subterranean passage known only to himself, his father and seneschal, who had that day received his death wound, he entered a deep vault, which had not been searched by the enemy for the simple reason that a huge slab of masonry had fallen over the aperture and hidden it from the eyes of the pursuers.

Here—still tended by the old domestic and sleeping now peacefully, he found the aged Count.

Gently he woke him from his slumber.

"Awake, father," he said, "it is your son who calls. I am here to bear you far beyond the reach of those who would destroy you. Awake, and fear not!"

The old man, who in his chamber had been dreaming of the exciting events of the day, and was even then, in fancy, bestriding his horse and pursuing his enemies, sprang to a sitting posture in spite of his wounds, shouting—

"At them, my brave men, at them for the honour of Androski."

"Hush, my father," cried Hugo, "we may be overheard, and then, indeed, all would be lost. Come with me—our horses wait without!"

The old man glanced around him, and then, passing his hand over his brow, he said—

"Ah, Hugo! brave boy! I remember now—the siege, the battle, my wound. But why are we here? Have we, indeed, lost the day?"

"Yes, father; but pause not to deplore the event," cried Hugo; "come, I beseech you, with me; the time is precious —dawn is approaching, and the light would bring destruction to us both. Come then, that I may live for vengeance!"

The old chieftain's eyes lit up with their olden fire at this, and he staggered to his feet.

"True, true, my son," he cried, "let us go—lead me whither you please."

Tenderly the young count led his father along the subterranean passage.

Then, taking him in his stalwart arms, he ran a short space to where two horses were ready.

Once in the saddle, the old count was able to hold his own, and ere the astonished sentinels could do more than discharge a few arrows they were off and away—away to the wild solitudes of the Carpathian Mountains.

In vain Count Paulo questioned the old domestic who had tended the wounded Androski.

He refused to answer any questions ; and unwilling to sacrifice a man who was so faithful to a fallen master, he pardoned him and let him go.

Before next nightfall, however, fire and engines of destruction had done their work, and the proud castle of Androski was but a heap of ruins.

❖   ❖   ❖   ❖

Nestling among the rugged passes of the Carpathian Mountains was a little village of roughly-built wooden huts, inhabited by a population which vied with the more modern banditti of the Italian hills.

Wild and lawless, owning no religion, composed of every nation and every creed, they were the terror of the country, and, unlike their modern brethren, they were in such numbers that they even dared to penetrate into the towns for the sake of pillage, and lay siege to the smaller strongholds.

It was, however, well known that Porzo the Albanian, the chief of this reckless band, had been from the time of his first leadership averse to unnecessary bloodshed, and it was understood that he had been driven to his present condition by family misfortunes.

It was to the house of this man, then, that Hugo Androski carried his father.

He was well assured that men in their condition would be secure of a ready welcome, and though knowing full well that he would be compelled to serve in the band, he regarded the fact as only a preliminary to the satisfaction of their vengeance.

It was near midday when the two tired horsemen approached the village.

The glorious sun was pouring down its rays in its most intense splendour, and scarcely a soul was visible ; but they had not penetrated further than the entrance of the place, when they were surrounded by armed men, and conveyed to the presence of Captain Porzo.

Armed and accoutred in a strange and picturesque fashion, which well suited his life and its surroundings, Porzo the Albanian was a well-built, handsome man, with scarcely a trace of ferocity in his face.

A few words of explanation only were necessary, and then he welcomed his guests with deep respect, and, dismissing his attendants, he held a long and secret conference with them.

From that moment, the old Count Androski disappeared, and the band of Porzo the Albanian boasted another chief —one who was ever side by side with Porzo himself, and who wore always a mask which entirely concealed his features.

So six months passed.

The usual raids were made upon the country side, the usual combats took place ; but the castle of Count Paulo remained unattacked.

Everything seemed to be moving in its old and placid course, and so the Count prepared for the marriage of his daughter.

❖   ❖   ❖   ❖   ❖

It is almost needless to say that the beautiful Forsina, the only child of Count Paulo, was no party to the approaching nuptials.

In those days, however, it was simple absurdity for any young girl to oppose her father's wish, or to dream of a love of which her father did not appprove.

Love they might, and that passionately, but this feeling had to be discarded when the suitor of their parents' choice appeared.

Dreams of love and happiness were rudely cast aside ; and their charms were bartered into the possession of the richest and most important suitor.

Old Count Grazowski, a Polish nobleman, full sixty years of age, had cast his eyes upon the lovely Forsina, and resolved that she should be his slave, despite her repugnance and her loathing—and so, driven to it by her father, apparently abandoned by her old lover, knowing nothing in fact of his fate, she found herself one morning, surrounded by about thirty men-at-arms in full martial array, escorted to a little chapel near the castle, where the old dotard had expressed a wish to be married.

The morning was a lovely one ; and, in spite of the tears of the lovely bride, attired as if in mockery in exquisite robes, it seemed as if nature itself were smiling on the union.

Old Count Grazowski himself, white-haired and feeble, seemed to raise higher his bent form, and brighter fire appeared to shoot from his eyes as they fell upon the beauteous form of the young girl who was destined to be his forced bride.

Everything tended to give *éclat* to the scene.

The warriors in their burnished armour, with the horse tails streaming from their helmets, the sun glinting on their shields, their horses prancing—as on the night when they had sallied forth to the siege of Androski—formed a most brilliant spectacle.

Only the bride, clad in white and seated on her snowy palfrey, seemed sorrowing and dejected.

No wonder was it.

Lovely, and not yet eighteen, with all the ardour of youth unquenched within her, adoring her first love, Hugo Androski, what but horror could she feel at the prospect of union with an old dotard like Grazowski?

However, the die was cast.

The bells of the castle rung out a joyous peal, the cavalcade filed through the grey stone gates amid the huzzas of the domestics, who, used to hear of such marriages, regarded this one as only on a par with the rest.

Grazowski, eager to be near his bride, rode his black charger timidly beside her.

Count Paulo, sat alone, gazing ever and anon in triumph at the ruins of Androski Castle, which he could faintly see in the distance.

The chapel, which they hoped to reach within half an hour, was situated on the face of a hill, a hill which had seen many a struggle between the Christian and the pagan.

But they were never destined to reach it.

Half-way between the castle and the chapel was a wooded piece of ground, so dense that from the high road nothing could be seen if any one chose to hide within.

Suddenly, while the cavalcade was passing along the road, its edges were lined as by magic with a hundred armed men, whose glittering spears and lances formed a wall of steel.

Then from the dense trees rode two mail-clad warriors, one masked, the other showing boldly the features of Captain Porzo.

It was the masked man that addressed Count Paulo.

"Count," he said, in a stern voice that made him tremble with a vague apprehension, "whither do you wend your way this morning with so gay a company?"

"I dispute your right to ask me," answered Count Paulo, sternly "Who are you who dares thus to dispute my passage on my daughter's wedding morn?"

The unknown uttered a loud laugh of derision.

"You have forgotten one thing, my lord count," he said.

"What is that?"

"That ere you take your daughter to yonder chapel—ere any rite or ceremony of marriage can be performed—you must proceed to the Holy Cave in yonder mountains, and there offer up your prayers to Him who can alone sanction the union. Do, therefore, as you please."

The count eyed the speaker incredulously.

"And why," he said, "do you come hither with this armed array upon my daughter's wedding morn—masked too, that we may not know your face?"

"That I refuse to reveal the secret of the Holy Cave," replied the masked stranger; "you alone know the reason, and if you dispute the fact, we have but to take you to the spot, where you and your most brilliant company can complete your vows."

The Count Paulo paused awhile.

For a hundred years past the Holy Cave—a dark and gloomy cavern at the foot of the Carpathian Mountains—had been the residence of holy men, who, upon such ceremonies as the marriage of the children of the nobles, were always called upon to bless the union.

Fierce and irreligious as these men usually were, Count Paulo—although at first desiring to evade the practice—did not care to refuse in the face of this open demand; and at once, therefore, he gave the word to his men to turn aside from the road to the chapel, and make for the Holy Cave, which was, indeed, miles out of their route.

Grazowski was furious.

To him neither Heaven's wrath nor the fiercest anathema of the Church would have weighed in the balance with his love for Forsina—if love it could be called.

But in this he was helpless.

Even if Count Paulo had not been the blind slave of fanaticism, the presence of the hundred armed men would have decided the question.

However he made a stand.

"Count Paulo," he said, "if you are compelled to turn aside thus on my wedding morn at the bidding of an armed band sent by a religious fanatic, I am not compelled to worship at his shrine with you. I will remain here."

The contemptuous sneer which was implied in the words of the old Polish noble was not lost upon Count Paulo; but his own interest told him to yield somewhat to his humour.

Gladly would he have laughed at the summons of the masked man.

But he dared not.

It was a tradition in his family that if any one of them neglected a summons to the Holy Cave—however sent—ruin and death would fall upon them and theirs.

"Be it so, then," he said, "*we* must away. Not long shall we delay you. Remain for awhile in the chapel, and in the course of an hour the priest of the Holy Cave will release us. But his summons I cannot deny."

And so, leaving Grazowski and his followers to make their way to the chapel to await the bride, Count Paulo and the masked stranger spurred on towards the Holy Cave.

Little, indeed, did Count Paulo dream how this adventure would end.

Little, indeed, did he dream that the whole current of his life would be changed, and the whole of his past regretted.

The hundred armed men—strange in accoutrements and wild in speech and look—accompanied the wedding guests on their journey as though they were prisoners.

But Count Paulo did not seem to observe this; he seemed anxious to press on, to see the holy man, and obtain a blessing upon what he evidently believed to be a somewhat unrighteous union.

At length, on the face of the mountain could be seen a tall, weird figure standing at the entrance of an opening, which was the entrance of what was known far and near as the Holy Cave.

By his attitude it could be seen that he was watching the approaching cavalcade, and expecting its coming.

Slowly the armed men defiled along the narrow path leading to the house of the holy man, and on approaching near it they were ordered to halt, and Count Paulo, the masked stranger, and Captain Porzo passed up alone.

The prophet of the mountains remained in his watching attitude until they neared him, when he invited them within the cave.

They passed along a rocky corridor until they reached a large rock-built hall, which the hermit had made his home, and here he invited them to be seated.

"My son," he said, solemnly addressing Count Paulo, "you came here to receive my blessing, but in order to obtain that you must first make me a promise."

"Willingly, father, if it be in my power," replied Count Paulo.

"It is in your power, my son," cried the prophet. "You have this day endeavoured to force your daughter into a union which would end, as you well know,

in ruin and unhappiness. It is the ending to your most unjust hatred of men who have never injured you. The proper husband of Forsina stands here before you. The husband whom her heart has chosen, and whom heaven ordains for her."

As he spoke these words, the masked figure removed his disguise, and Count Paulo saw standing before him the young Count Hugo Androski.

The Lord of Tricula sprang to his feet, with fury in his countenance.

"What insult is this?" he cried.

"This villain who stands before me is the son of the assassin of my father!" cried he. "One whom I hoped I had driven from the face of the earth. Why, if you are Heaven's servant, do you bring him before me, to tell me I have failed in my vengeance?"

The old count stood up—pale, but grand, in his anger.

But the old prophet waved his hand.

"Peace!" he said, "and answer me a question. If Heaven—by almost a miracle, proved to you that you are wrong, that the old Count Hugo, who still lives, was not the assassin of your father—would you, then, consent to stay this blood-feud, and live in peace with them for ever; giving to the son of your enemy the hand of your daughter, as an earnest that you had forgiven him?"

Count Paulo, white with passion, folded his arms, and eyed the holy man severely.

"If you were not the servant of the Deity," he said, "I should say you were acting thus to insult me—that you were in league with my enemies—and that these villains, robbers, were your friends. Nothing would persuade me that Count Hugo Androski was innocent, save the appearance here of my father before me."

The prophet smiled.

"Count," he said, "your words prove that your mind is in doubt. You are not *certain* that your father is dead, and yet in your fierce passion you make a raid upon a neighbour's town—destroy innocent lives—raze it to the ground—and drive out into the wilderness an aged warrior and his son. Count, if you can do this, you can also break a promise lightly spoken. Swear to me, therefore, that if I prove Count Androski innocent, you will give to his son your daughter in marriage."

"I swear—solemnly, and by Heaven," said Count Paulo, over whose mind a strange presentiment was creeping.

The prophet then suddenly turned—tore from his head his long beard and wig, and then again confronted the count, who—bloodless now with amazement—staggered back.

Older by many years, but still recognisable at once, stood before him his own father, whom—long, long before—he had believed the victim of Count Androski.

To describe the scene which now ensued would be difficult indeed.

Father and son were locked in each other's arms, and presently, when their emotion had somewhat subsided, Count Androski—who had found shelter in the cave—and Hugo each received the first grasp of the hand they had ever received from Count Paulo.

The secret of the prophet, and the strange secret of the Holy Cave was soon told.

In the duel which had been supposed to be a fatal one, and which was fought in fair and honest style, Paulo's father had been left for dead.

Lying there, and with the fear of death heavy upon him, the prophet had vowed to heaven, that if his life was spared he would devote it to the Lord; and would keep himself unknown to the world until a dire necessity arose.

"It has arisen now," he said, "and though I shall never leave the Holy Cave, I demand the fulfilment of the contract. Hugo—let us advance to meet your bride."

The rest of our story is soon told.

Grazowski—terrible in his rage, and threatening a vengeance which he never carried out—departed to his castle, while Hugo and his bride were united in the bonds of wedlock by the Patriach of the mountains.

Count Paulo's father kept his vow, and refused to leave his mountain retreat; but when he died he was buried in the old vaults of Tricula, wept over by Hugo and Forsina, whose tears for him were the only sorrow of their lives.

END OF HUGO ANDROSKI; OR, THE SECRET OF THE HOLY CAVE.

THE FATE OF COUNT VOSLAU.

A LEGEND OF THE TENTH CENTURY.

PERCHED high upon a rock on the left bank of the river Danube, stands the ruined castle of Greifenstein, said to have been one of the fortresses in which our brave crusading king, Richard Cœur de Lion, was imprisoned.

Richard, however, was never in the castle, which receives its name from the deeply printed mark of a huge claw, which may still be seen on the masonry near the door of the keep.

This is the Greifenstein, or griffin's stone, and the story goes that the mark was made by the claw of a griffin.

Just a few words to give our readers an idea of what the griffin was like, and then we will proceed with our story.

The griffin, an animal frequently represented in heraldic drawings, would appear to have had the hind quarters of a lion, with the head, shoulders, and wings of an eagle.

It had four legs, the hinder agreeing with the leonine part of its formation, the fore legs partaking of its bird-like nature.

In heraldry it is the emblem of strength, swiftness, and vigilance.

Many years have elapsed since Graf, or count, Voslau built this castle.

A bold and fearless man was he; one who at the head of his vassals would sally forth to attack the fortress of a neighbour, would fearlessly chase the wild boar or wolf through the tangled woods, or, armed at all points, would fearlessly plunge into the Danube, and swim to the opposite shore.

And when the day's work of fighting or hunting was done, no one could drink deeper than the bold Count Voslau.

Graf Voslau loved fighting for its own sake; gold he coveted for the power it brought him; nor had he any scruples as to the way in which he obtained it.

He would no more hesitate to plunder a church, than to rob a company of peaceful merchants, though there were few of either in the neigbourhood of the castle.

One fine morning, late in the autumn season, Voslau called to him some five or six of his trusted followers, and started forth to hunt.

All day long they followed the chase; till, as evening came on, they found themselves in a remote part of the tangled forest, among gloomy pine trees and rugged rocks.

The vassals knew not which way to turn, and proposed that they should encamp themselves there for the night, and in the morning hunt the forest in a homeward direction.

But Voslau swore by Christian saints and Pagan deities that he would not give up his nightly draught of wine, and therefore to the castle he would go.

So, with great reluctance, the vassals followed their fierce lord.

But it seemed impossible to get out of the forest.

As they walked on, the way became more difficult.

Rocks and precipices abounded; and, more than once, they narrowly escaped being swept away by some of the mountain torrents that hurried down to swell the big river.

At length, with a great oath, Graf Voslau consented to give up his journey for the night, and wait till morning.

A sheltered nook between some rocks was chosen, and in this place they all sat down to rest and refresh themselves with such scraps of food as they had in their pouches.

But ere they had been in their resting place long, a terrible din assailed their ears.

It sounded like the roaring of a wild beast, mingled with piercing, harsh screams.

"What can that be?" said Gunulph, one of the vassals.

Ere an answer could be given to the question, a huge black mass was seen rising into the air.

A moment it hovered over the frightened group, then swooping down into their midst, seized the luckless wight who had spoken, and bore him off to the summit of a neighbouring tall precipice.

"The griffin, the griffin!" shouted the others, as they fled with all haste from the spot, with the heart-rending screams of the victim ringing in their ears, mingled with the hoarse cries of the monster that was rending him limb from limb.

At length they were compelled, through sheer exhaustion, to pause for breath.

They were in a thick part of the forest, where the branches would hinder the downward swoop of the griffin, should it pursue them, and so felt comparatively safe.

"Saints forefend that ever we should meet with such a ravening monster again," said Anton, another serf.

"The saints might not care to meet him themselves," growled Voslau. "Gunulph called on them, yet no one came to his aid."

"He called upon his master," muttered one of the vassals, in a low tone; "and he ran away."

The words were not intended for Voslau's ear, but he heard them.

"Dare you revile me, mutinous dog!" he shouted.

His mighty sword whistled through the air, and the head of the offender rolled upon the ground.

"Beware all of you; take warning by this fool's fate," said Voslau, spurning the corpse with his foot, and returning his blood-stained weapon to its scabbard.

THE CASTLE OF GREIFENSTEIN.

The trembling vassals, though well armed, made no reply to their imperious master; but at that instant the loud cry of the griffin was heard, and looking up they could see it circling round and round, waiting till one or other of the men should move out into open space, when it would pounce upon him and devour him as it had devoured the unfortunate Gunulph.

They all crouched down as closely as possible, hoping to avoid the eye of the fierce griffin, but it either saw them or smelt the blood that flowed from the trunk of the slain man.

All night they could descry its monstrous form hovering above the trees, sometimes it even approached so near that they could hear the waving of its mighty wings.

At length came dawn.

Faint streaks of light began to appear, and the faint crowing of a cock was heard at a distance.

Then the griffin, with a mighty roar of anger and disappointment, turned towards the mountains whence it had come, and slowly flew away.

Graf Voslau and his followers waited till it was fairly out of sight, and then hurried home to the castle.

The terrible news that a monstrous griffin haunted the mountains, soon became known throughout the country.

Many brave knights sought to win for themselves immortal fame by destroying the monster, but of all those who ventured to its retreat, not one returned.

The fearful thing destroyed them all.

As time passed on, the mountains and the forest for some miles round the griffin's haunt were avoided by hunters and travellers.

Yet distance soon ceased to be a safeguard against its assaults, and each day it ranged further from its home in quest of prey.

One day a poor monk appeared at the gates with a look of deep sorrow and trouble on his face.

The lord of the castle quickly appeared.

"What wouldst thou, monk?" he demanded.

"My lord, grant me permission to pass the remainder of my days in some cave in yonder woods, where, by fasting and prayer, I may atone for the sins of my youth."

"Not I. No lazy priests shall hide themselves in my woods to steal the deer."

"Roots and herbs shall be my only food, and water my only drink."

"Off, old dotard! you plead in vain," exclaimed the baron, rudely; and then some of his vassals thrust the venerable man out of the place.

"He might have protected us against the griffin, had he been permitted to stay," muttered one of the vassals, loud enough to be overheard by the imperious baron.

"Silence, hound!" thundered Voslau, "or I will have thee chained up among the mountains, so that the griffin you so much fear may feast upon your limbs."

The man slunk away among his companions, but at that moment the old man, who had gone some distance from the castle, turned round, and in loud, clear tones said—

"Count Voslau, thy inhospitality shall be punished. One of thy victims shall enjoy the gold the griffin guards, and then thou shalt be——"

"Shoot the villain!" thundered the Graf (Count). "Hie forth, you lazy knaves, and seize the false priest who dares threaten me."

At least a score of arrows were launched at the monk, but they all flew wide of the mark, and the old man, turning a corner of the steep path leading from the castle, was lost to sight.

The men who had hurried after him, in obedience to Voslau's command, returned without the expected captive.

Yet a short time after a figure much resembling the old monk was seen on the bank of the river, about a mile from the castle, in company with one who seemed to be a soldier, and a young peasant girl.

Again men were sent out in furious haste to secure all three; but, after a lengthened absence, they returned without having caught a glimpse of the persons they were sent to capture.

"Who can they be?" muttered the Count musingly, as he paced the courtyard.

His favourite attendant—he only who at certain times dared approach him—said—

"My lord, I know not who the soldier might be whom we saw with the priest; but I would wager all I have that the girl was pretty Gretchen, the daughter of old Siebald, the wood-cutter and charcoal burner."

"Is that the knave who supplies the castle with fuel?"

"The same, my lord."

"Where lives he?"

"He hath a hut in some remote part of the forest, but where I know not."

"Is the girl pretty, say you?"

"She is loveliness itself, my lord."

"Then seek out the dwelling of this charcoal burner, and bring the girl hither. Pretty girls are somewhat rare in this part."

"Her old father, my lord, might not like——"

"Peace, fool! What care I for her father's likes or dislikes? When found, bring the girl hither."

The count strode away, and the menial, Franosch by name, left the castle to fulfil his errand.

Day after day he searched, but though in the forest he found many traces of the wood-cutter's work, he could find neither father, daughter, nor dwelling, for which the Graf rated him soundly.

Meanwhile, Count Voslau had been busy in another way.

He had reflected deeply on the words of the old priest:—

"The gold the griffin guards shall be enjoyed by one of thy victims."

The words puzzled him much, and at length he sent a trusty messenger to a relative, who was abbot of a newly established convent, to see if he could explain it.

The abbot sent back this answer.

"The griffin is the guardian of gold

mines, or of hidden treasures; therefore, where the monster resides, great wealth is concealed."

"Then I will have this wealth," said Count Voslau to himself; "and this abbot shall help me to gain it."

He sent another messenger to the abbot, stating his intention of discovering and seizing the gold the griffin guarded, and requesting the holy man to send him some sacred relic as a safeguard against the power of the evil beast.

In return for this, Count Voslau promised to bestow on the abbot one half of whatever he might gain.

The abbot, who loved gold better than his breviary, sent by the messenger a small silver locket, which, he assured the Count, contained a fragment of the true cross.

"Surely this should be a valuable protection," said Voslau.

Forthwith he slung the relic about his neck, so that the locket rested beneath his breast-plate, and thus guarded, sallied forth to hunt the griffin.

Not one of the vassals was trusted with the secret.

The Count wished to secure every scrap of the precious metal for his own use.

A whole day he wandered about the mountains, searching for the griffin, and shouting to attract its notice, so confident did he feel in the power of his relic.

But the griffin was not to be seen.

At length, some time after sunset, he came upon a place littered with the bones of cattle, and some ghastly remnants of mortality that seemed to have belonged to humanity.

There was a human skull, near it was a helmet, a little way off a rusty sword and a gold spur.

"Some knight has fallen here, and this is the monster's lair," said Voslau. "So, close here the treasure must be concealed."

Spurning aside the bones with his foot, he exerted all his strength, and overturned a large flat stone that lay there.

As he did so, he heard the hoarse scream of the griffin, and looking up he saw the monster wheeling about in the air overhead.

Round and round it circled, making a most terrible noise, yet evidently afraid to swoop down upon the Count.

Voslau drew the silver locket containing the sacred relic from beneath his breast-plate, and held it over his head; the griffin knew and felt its power, and giving several discordant yells, flew away.

But Graf Voslau's search for the treasure was unsuccessful, and he was obliged to return home without having seen any of the gold or jewels he so longed to touch.

On his way back he passed a hut in the depth of the forest; and, thinking it possible that there dwelt the pretty Gretchen of whom his servant had spoken, he entered.

The hut was empty, and though he hammered on the table with his dagger's hilt, and shouted, no one came.

So having eaten to his heart's content of the peasant's coarse viands, he departed.

By this time the moon had risen, and as the Count walked along by the side of a little brook, he perceived on the opposite bank a girl dressed in the coarse costume of the peasant race, though both face and form were fitted to adorn the richest products of Indian looms.

"Ho, my fair damsel," said Voslau, "what art doing abroad at this hour?"

The girl, who had not heard his approach, started, but made no reply.

"Is some lover expected, that you thus loiter in the forest by moonlight?"

Still no reply, though a deep blush on the fair cheeks told the count that he had guessed correctly.

She looked so enchanting that he at once resolved to cross over to her.

The stream was not more than knee deep, so in less time than it takes us to write these words he waded over.

But the maiden no sooner saw him step into the water, than like a frightened fawn she bounded away.

"Stay, damsel, or by my sword I swear I will burn your father's cot to the ground! Do ye not know that I am your liege lord, the Graf Voslau?"

The count's brutal threat had its desired effect, and the damsel paused in her flight.

"So, my fair one, why would you run from me?" asked the count, as he endeavoured to pass his arm round her taper waist. "Am I such a horrid monster?"

"I knew not who it was that called, my lord," answered she, stepping back.

"Now I'll warrant you are none other than fair Gretchen, the daughter of old Siebald, the wood-cutter and charcoal burner?"

"Yes, my lord."

"And who is this lover you are waiting for?"

Gretchen hung her head, and made no reply.

"Nay, then, if those rosy lips will not open they must pay the tribute of a kiss to atone for their obstinate silence."

And darting forward, he seized Gretchen

round the waist, and in spite of her struggles, obtained the kiss he desired.

"Help, help! Release me, Count Voslau! Help! father, Ewald!"

"Ha! then Ewald is the name of the favoured one. Well, the villain has good taste; so, another kiss, fair one, and then you shall away to the castle with me, for 'tis a shame that one so beautiful should waste her days in this wild forest."

Gretchen struggled even more violently than before, but her little strength was useless against such a powerful man as Graf Voslau.

But just as the count's lips were again pressing her's, he received a terrible blow on the forehead, which hurled him to the ground, where his skull struck against a huge stone with sufficient violence to render him insensible for several minutes.

When he recovered his senses Gretchen had disappeared.

He was alone in the glade.

"It must have been Ewald, her lover," he muttered; "but I will have a fearful vengeance."

He started back to the hut, but it was empty as before.

However, in a rage, he set fire to it, and soon saw the flames attain such a power that its destruction was inevitable.

"Would to heaven the jade, her father, and her lover were roasting in the famous blaze," he said, with a brutal laugh.

It seemed as though an echo mocked him, but it was no reverberation of sound.

It was the fierce griffin, which, high up in air, kept watch on the count, though not daring to attack him while protected by the sacred relic.

Graf Voslau, finding that for the present his intended victim had escaped, proceeded back to his castle, where he consoled himself by three days and nights of hard drinking.

Then he set out once more to invade the haunt of the griffin, and wrest from it its closely guarded treasure.

In his second search he was more successful.

He found the monster asleep on a ledge of rock, and, drawing his sword, gave it a severe wound.

The monster hastened away, uttering most doleful cries, and Voslau began to search.

He soon found the treasure—an earthern pot, full of rubies, pearls, diamonds, and other precious stones of great value—with which he hastened back to the castle rejoicing.

There only remained now to get Gretchen into his power, but that was a more difficult matter.

Search as he would, he could find no trace of her for some months, so he began to fancy that Ewald must have carried her off to some distant territory.

One morning a grand hunting party was organised, at which several neighbouring lords were present.

A gallant crew they were!

The dogs bayed loudly, horns echoed each call along the dim vistas of the forest, and noisy shouts roused the wild beasts from their lairs.

Many a gallant buck had been struck down, when suddenly nobler game met their view.

An old wild boar suddenly broke cover, and having ripped up two of the intruding dogs with his fearful tusks, went off at a rapid rate.

Away went the hunters, but so rough was the ground, that their fleet steeds barely enabled them to keep the game in view.

Mile after mile was passed, and the boar began to show symptoms of weariness.

Presently the huge animal entered a romantic little dell, and was lost to sight.

The hunters were at fault, for no trace whatever could they see of their game.

At length they perceived a rude cross, formed of two roughly hewn branches of trees, standing on a little mound, which was covered with the softest verdure, and the sweetest spring flowers.

Behind this mound was a cave almost concealed by overhanging rocks and huge forest trees.

"So ho!" exclaimed Count Voslau, starting, "what in the fiend's name have we here?"

"This tells us," said one of his companions, pointing to the cross.

"I'll warrant me some lazy shaveling burrows here," ejaculated Voslau.

"Let us have him out," said another.

"Good! doubtless the luxurious villain lives far better than any lord in the land," growled the count. "In, ye knaves," he continued, addressing his attendants; "unkennel the old fox!—draw the vermin from its lair."

Three of the count's followers entered the cave with drawn swords, and soon returned, dragging between them an old man of tall stature, whose gaunt, haggard form and rude dress denied the imputation of any kind of luxurious sensuality.

The aspect of the man at once commanded attention.

"One of the saints, I swear!" exclaimed the Baron Strakosch.

"Who in the name of St. Hubert art thou?" demanded Voslau, who, although he asked the question, recognised in the hermit before him the monk who had asked his permission to find a place of refuge in the woods.

The voice of the count caused the hermit to shudder with a thrill of horror, and he covered his face with his hands.

"What mummery is this?" continued Voslau, as the hermit remained silent. "Dost hear my question, old greybeard?"

"Perchance he is dumb," said one of the nobles.

"Then by St. Hubert we will work a miracle, and make the dumb speak," replied the count, savagely, "here, Hugo, touch him with thy boar spear."

The man hesitated.

"Why dost shrink, man?" thundered Voslau, "the fellow hath a good tough hide."

The soldier, a rough-looking man, clad in leather, with an iron breast-plate, advanced with his lance lowered.

When within a pace or two of the hermit, the latter looked up, and saw the threatened danger.

He made one move forward, and quick as thought, wrested the weapon from the hands of the ruffian.

Another instant, and the hermit dealt him a blow which shivered the pole of the weapon, and stretched the soldier senseless upon the turf.

"Cut him down!" roared Voslau, "nay, he hath dropped his weapon, so seize him, and bring him along with us to the castle."

"What will you do with him?" demanded the baron Strakosch."

"By Satan, he shall make fine sport for us. I will roast him over a fire."

The hermit was safely bound, and then tied to the back of a horse; and the hunters were about to move away, when one of those who had entered the cave, addressed the count.

"So please you, my lord, there is some-one else in yonder cavern."

"Ha! by St. Hubert, what manner of person?"

"A peasant damsel—"

Without waiting to hear more, Count Voslau rushed into the cave, from which, a moment after, piercing screams were heard.

Then the Graf reappeared, bearing in his arms the form of Gretchen.

"So, my fair damsel, this is your hiding place, is it? Well, you are in my power now, and cannot escape me."

"Ruffian count, release me!" exclaimed the girl, "Noble sirs, surely as knights you will not permit this outrage," she continued, addressing the others.

But the "noble sirs" appealed to, had little desire to thwart the fierce Graf Voslau, and her words fell on their ears unheeded.

So the count lifted her to the saddle of his own horse, and holding her before him rode off towards his castle.

Gretchen struggled violently at first, but finding that neither efforts nor entreaties had any effect, she apparently resigned herself to her fate, earnestly praying all the time that Heaven would preserve her.

Though she knew it not, her lover, Ewald, was following at a distance, and her father, who also had witnessed her abduction, was hastening through the forest, urging to insurrection all his friends, the woodcutters and charcoal-burners, most of whom had suffered some wrong or indignity at the hands of the fierce lord of the soil.

At length, Count Voslau emerged from the wood, in sight of his castle.

As soon as Gretchen perceived it, she recommenced her cries for help or mercy, and her struggles for freedom.

While so struggling, she caught hold of a ribbon that was fastened round her captor's neck, and in sheer desperation, tore it from him.

"Ha! you jade! it is my holy relic, that gives me strength and saves me from the griffin."

He tried to regain it, but, with a hysterical laugh, Gretchen threw it from her into the swift flowing river, by whose banks they were riding.

Several of the soldiers endeavoured to save it, but their efforts were in vain; it disappeared.

"Curse you!" growled the Count, "you shall bitterly rue this!"

"Hark! what is that?" said Strakosch.

A faint, yet by no means agreeable sound was heard, a long distance behind them.

In the air, just above the horizon, was a black speck, which each moment grew larger as it moved rapidly towards them.

"It is the griffin! the griffin!" burst from every lip, as the hoarse cries of the terrible creature sounded louder and louder.

Each man of the party drove spurs into his horse, and galloped away towards the castle.

But the griffin gained upon them.

They had all entered the castle courtyard—Count Voslau last of all.

Could he but once get safely within the keep, he deemed he would be safe from the ravenous monster.

He alighted from his horse in the courtyard, and grasping the peasant girl by the arm, hurried to the open door of the chief tower.

He had gained it, and was in the act of pushing Gretchen through the open portal when the griffin pounced upon him.

Striking one claw so deeply into the solid stone that the mark remains there till the present day, the monster seized Voslau with the disengaged foot, and dragged him back.

Another moment, and the Count Voslau was torn limb from limb in the castle yard by the fierce griffin, which then flew slowly away, and was seen no more.

    ❉   ❉   ❉   ❉

The vassals and the nobles who had taken part in the hunt, gathered up the few fragments of humanity that remained of the late count, and prepared them for burial.

But, ere they half finished their task, a new danger threatened.

The woodcutters and charcoal burners from the forest, with numerous others of Count Voslau's oppressed vassals, appeared before the castle, and with loud shouts demanded the instant release of Gretchen and the hermit.

Baron Strakosch sternly replied—

"Close the gates; let them dare attack us!"

Ewald and Siebald, who commanded the insurgents, on perceiving that resistance was intended at once commenced the attack.

Long and furious was the fight.

The walls were scaled and the defenders fell beneath the axes, scythes, and knives of the infuriated peasantry.

Baron Strakosch with a few others escaped, but not one of Count Voslau's soldiers lived to tell the story.

Ewald's first care was to find Gretchen and the hermit, both of whom were uninjured.

Of course, the lovers were married, and the hermit performed the ceremony.

Afterwards, the jewels were handed over to Ewald and his bride.

Ewald, some few years afterwards, was able to perform some service to his sovereign which earned him noble rank and the lordship of the Castle of Greifenstein where he and his descendants lived for many years.

END OF THE FATE OF COUNT VOSLAU.

THE CAPTIVE PRINCE;

A STORY OF DURRENSTEIN.

IT has long been the custom of the custodians of Durrenstein to show their castle as the place of imprisonment of Richard Cœur de Lion, the chivalric King of England.

They go so far as to point out to the visitors a wooden cage, in which they are wont to state that he was confined like a wild beast, and small pieces of which have been sold to the credulous as precious relics.

It is probable that the cage, according to the usuage of feudal despots, was employed for securing criminals, prisoners of war, and other offenders against the will and pleasure of its lord.

But the use of this cage for more than any temporary purpose is simply a mistake.

Durrenstein is, of all the strongholds on the Danube, the most interesting.

The genius of history and romance have fixed upon it an indelible stamp.

Its massive walls, embattled precipices, and iron towers that survive the lapse of centuries, were of themselves enough to arrest our attention.

But when, as we pass under its ponderous gateway, and muse on its grass-grown mound, and carry ourselves back in imagination to the events of which it was the scene, a thrill of romance passes through our frame, and we think of him who asked every day—

"Quhat (what) tydings from England?"

Richard, King of England, like Haroun al Raschid, of historical and Arabian Nights Entertainments celebrity, was very fond, for some reasons—some creditable, others the reverse—of travelling alone and in disguise in and about his fair domain.

He thus picked up considerable information as to the habits and feelings of his people, while occasionally indulging in frolic and secret adventure.

On one of these occasions, previous to his departure for the Crusades, and, whether he was right or wrong, the most popular king England ever owned, he started, unknown to his attendants and even to his most secret and faithful friend, on an errand, the nature of which has nothing to do with this narrative.

He was cased in armour, carried his heavy battle-axe and lance, with a long and well tempered blade, and feared no man in his own or any other realm; and for the matter of that, of such stuff was he made, that he cared not if his adversary had another dozen men to back him to boot.

His steed, as celebrated in the history of the time almost as himself, was an animal of great weight and power, such as it need have been to have carried so doughty a knight.

His helmet as effectually concealed his visage as a Venetian mask.

It was about mid-day when he started on his journey, having given his courtiers the slip while riding, and night was approaching before he appeared likely to reach his journey's end.

He was at that moment on the edge of a wood, or rather forest, of rather a gloomy appearance, with the further disadvantage of not being quite sure of his way.

To ask was both repugnant to his feelings, and at the same time rather difficult, as, except a few hinds, he had met no one.

Before entering the wood he looked keenly round, and could neither make out belfry nor steeple, nor either farmhouse or hut.

Nothing was to be done save go forward, and put trust in his own sagacity and that of his horse.

As he advanced, the vast size of the elms and oaks, whose branches interlaced overhead, made the darkness still greater, and the time soon came when the gallant knight was obliged to walk his horse, in order not to lose the road.

Presently, however, he found himself entering upon an open glade, and scarcely had he done so when a rush was made, and he was attacked by at least a dozen men, four mounted and eight men-at-arms, with hatchets and axes.

It was fearful, it was tremendous odds, but with a cry of fierce anger the king snatched at his mighty battle-axe, and, whirling it round his head, rose in his stirrups, and ere the foe had any means of avoiding the crushing blow, sent two of the mounted men dead—or apparently so to the ground.

"Traitors, cowards, knaves !" he roared, between the bars of his helmet ; "what seek you ?"

"Thy death, tyrant ! Down with him, my gallant soldiers, a thousand marks an he escape you not !"

The gallant prince wheeled round his horse, and showed the footmen what they had to expect by crushing three of them by one whirl of his terrible weapon, the weight of which was almost enough to kill a man.

But at this moment the two mailed knights who commanded the party, who had turned and placed their lances in rest, came thundering over the turf in the direction of the knight.

The keen eye of the mighty warrior saw them ; he let fall his battle-axe until it hung by its thong, and snatched at his spear, his horse curvetting in such a way as to keep the others off with his heels.

It was a terrible moment for the knight, compassed about by so many enemies, and with two experienced foes coming down upon him at full tilt.

But just as the heavier horseman of the two was close upon the king, his steed fell on its knees, shot to the heart by an arrow which came it was impossible to say whence.

THE CASTLE OF DURRENSTEIN.

The monarch, however, lost no time ; but meeting the remaining knight full on the gorget, hurled him insensible on the sward.

The dismounted knight was, however, by this time free of his horse, and approached, bent on retrieving the honour of the day, supported by six stalwart men-at-arms.

Under the circumstances, the knight might have fled, but the idea never crossed his brain.

"Come on, dastards," he cried, "come on brave knight ; seven to one is fair odds !"

At this moment an arrow, followed at scarcely an interval by a second, laid low two of the footmen, who, as if satisfied at the carnage which had taken place, at once took to their heels.

"I surrender, rescue or no rescue," said the remaining knight, and lifted his visor.

The amazement and horror of the king may be imagined when he recognised his brother John, even then conspiring against his generous sovereign.

"Go away, murderer and fratricide ; fly, lest I slay you in my wrath. Put the four seas between us, or, by the Holy Sepulchre, Tower Hill shall see your traitor death !"

Sullenly the evil prince mounted the remaining horse, set spurs to him, and fled.

For continuation of this Story see our next number.

THE BARONS OF OLD OR THE ROBBERS OF THE RHINE

[Continued from page 352.]

THE CAPTIVE PRINCE.

A STORY OF DURRENSTEIN.

THE king and a stripling of about sixteen, leaning on his bow, remained master of the field.

He came up, touching his cap with the politeness of youth, rather than the servility of inferior rank, just as the discomfited prince fled.

"Mon Dieu!" said the gallant knight,

"BLONDEL SANK UPON A SLOPE UNDER A BARRED WINDOW."

"you did me good service, youth. Could you add to it by leading me to some shelter? My errand can wait. Methinks," he muttered, "she whom I was about to visit could alone have betrayed me."

"My father, Sir Robert de L'Isle——"

"Ha! ha! stout Sir Robert. Lead on. We are old acquaintances. Worthy scion of so brave a stock. I would thank him too for rearing such a son."

"I only did my duty; though, noble sir, I could see you scarcely required my assistance."

"Mon Dieu!" cried the knight, "I hardly know. That rush of two lances was well meant."

While speaking he had mounted, and without bestowing a glance on the victims of this treacherous ambuscade, followed his guide without any whisper of his discoveries.

A few days later the attempt was either forgotten or forgiven.

Had he acted with rigid justice, England had been spared the reign of that evil king, John, who so exasperated the barons and people.

Leading the knight through some winding paths and open glades, they soon came in sight of a tall tower, which, with some other buildings, formed one of those fortalices, which were so frequently found in England, and which were so necessary to safety in quarrelsome and troublous times.

The bridge was down, however, and the portcullis up, and the youth led the knight to the choicest chamber in the place, one richly furnished and well lighted, while he hastened away to fetch his father.

Without waiting to hear any details, the old knight, with ready hospitality, hastened to greet his guest, preparatory to the offer of ewer and cup before the evening meal.

As he entered the room with his son, the tall, erect form of the stranger appeared familiar, but when his eyes fell upon his uncasqued head, he bowed the knee.

"My liege, this is an honour," he began.

"Nay, 'tis I, my brave de L'Isle, who am the obliged party. But for your brave son, yonder, 'tis but too likely John had reigned in England. Just help me off with this heavy iron, and I will tell you all."

Father and son promptly obeyed, and when the king appeared in the civil garb of his day, had washed his hands and swallowed a good cup of hypocras, all were seated, and Richard, to the father's great delight, related the prowess of his son.

"He is a rare Nimrod," he said, "but I scarce expected to find him so ready against marauders. Did your highness suspect who they were?"

"More than suspect. But of that we will not speak," replied the king, and changed the conversation.

Next day Blondel de L'Isle accompanied the monarch on his return journey, to abide at Court until such time as he was old enough to wear armour and win his spurs, when Richard promised him honourable knighthood.

But Blondel soon developed another kind of genius besides that of war, and one which enthralled the king even more than his previous conduct.

He was not only a born poet, but a splendid singer, and Richard's greatest delight was to spend an hour or two every evening practising duets with his favourite.

Of course the great subject was love.

Now, it happened that the king was always under the influence of the tender passion for one or more ladies, fits which lasted only for a time.

Blondel de L'Isle was the bond slave of one lady fair, the beautiful Ethel, a rich Saxon heiress, much coveted by lawless Norman barons, whose extortionate natures were never satisfied.

But Ethel, the Saxon, had already shown marked preference for Blondel, and the king swore under his heavy moustache, that not all the rivals in the world should deprive his favourite of his prize.

While this state of things was existent in England Richard, while Blondel was on a visit to his sick father, suddenly left for the Holy Land, to join the great army of Crusaders, who, for the pleasure of slaughtering infidels and inflicting incalculable misery on all Europe, abandoned their native land under pretence of forwarding the interests of religion.

Which they did by unpeopling the earth to a much larger extent than in any other wars.

Much like the wonderful priest who, in order that all the earth should be peopled by Christians, proposed to kill, slay, and destroy all heathens.

When Blondel returned to court, he was not only a mere nothing, but Ethel, as a ward of the Crown, was attached to the house of Prince John, and surrounded by his uncouth Norman friends.

Richard left the kingdom under the regency of the Archbishop of Canterbury, but from the first day John assumed ostentatiously a regal state, and surrounded himself by the factious and discontented.

In his own mind he was already king, and should his brother ever return, would contest the high prize with him, even at the point of the sword.

But despite the gold and glitter by which he surrounded himself, despite tournaments, largesses, and what not, he was not popular.

Still day by day, fresh adherents bowed to the rising sun, not a few of the second and third rate nobles being attracted by the wealth of Ethel.

The prince did not appear to favour any particular suitor, but secretly he had promised her to Captain Roland Gilbert, a brave, but unscrupulous leader of free lances, upon whom, above all, he depended in his machinations.

Blondel was broken-hearted.

But he had the promise of Ethel, who, in several stolen interviews, declared that death were preferable to being the bride of the savage but handsome reiter.

Still it was hard to resist the prince, and their hopes were kept secret, Blondel only obtaining an occasional word by reason of his obscurity.

But every day, discontent rose higher.

John and his adherents collected loans and taxes in the most audacious manner, and at last the day and hour was fixed to declare the déchéance of Richard, or elevation of John to the throne.

Then Eleanor, the queen dowager, despatched a secret messenger to her son, warning him to return.

In the meantime this is what had happened.

Richard, recognised on all hands the acme and flower of chivalry, was a host in himself.

With other kings, princes and nobles, he vied in efforts to surpass all in their heroic deeds.

One day, when storming the walls of Acre, almost side by side with Leopold, Duke of Austria, the latter, reaching the walls a minute before England's king, planted his banner first upon the walls.

Richard next minute stood erect upon the battlements, knocked aside the ducal flag, and planted his own instead.

It was an act of foolish impulse, and made of Austria a deadly foe.

Unwittingly he had done deep injury to England and himself.

Soon after the news came from his mother that his crown was in great peril and danger, while the people cried out with loud and eager cries for his return.

His resolve was at once taken, and never, perhaps, did king enter upon a more romantic undertaking.

He would return to England incognito and in disguise.

The record of his adventures would fill a volume, but here can only be briefly recapitulated.

He first took ship at Acre, and was making quick way in the direction of home, when a fearful storm overtook him and drove him up the Adriatic.

Scarcely had this blown over, than in the Mediterranean he encountered a still more terrible gale, which drove his galley about until the captain in utter desperation put in at Corfu.

From this, after refitting, he again sailed, only to be hopelessly wrecked on a wild part of the coast near Venice.

Being compelled to halt here while he procured horses and guides, he discovered that his disguise as a knight Templar was known, and that efforts would be made to capture or slay him during his voyage through Europe.

He at once changed his costume to that of a merchant of Damascus, adopted a flowing beard, and assumed the name of Hugo.

In this guise he attached himself to the train of a travelling party, and began his perilous journey.

The first place where anything of importance took place was at Goritz, which was in the territory of the Marquis de Montferrat, whom the king was accused of having slain in cold blood during a royal revel—an assertion for which there is no proof in history.

Probably the reason was his having preferred Guy de Lusignan to his party.

Almost every owner of a stronghold in those days was a robber chief.

People who passed their way had to pay heavy toll, or submit to be pillaged by the privileged lords of the soil.

Goritz Castle was held by Meinhard, a kinsman of the Marquis de Montferrat, and hearing of the arrival of strangers, he at once sent to ask who and what they were, and where they were going.

The train consisted of Baldwin of Bethune, a dozen lances, a Damascene merchant and his two attendants, travelling under knightly escort, was the reply.

In addition to a purse of gold, the fee of the knight, Hugo the merchant sent a ring.

Shortly after this was returned, with

the significant remark that it belonged to no merchant, but that Meinhard would like to see and confer with the owner.

The king knew once more that his carelessness and want of caution had betrayed him.

Leaving Baldwin of Bethune behind, the king with one servant and a page boy, Loisel, started in the night, and riding far and fast, was a long way from Goritz before daylight.

But the want of guides checked his progress, and he only reached Freisach by a roundabout way.

The cunning Meinhard had sent messengers out, and the king retired to rest in an auberge, believing his true character to be a secret.

But an old Norman captain had received his orders, and with the assistance of a score of desperate reiters, was commanded to arrest or slay him, it is not certain which, as, from the total silence of all Austrian writers on the subject, we are left considerably in the dark.

Be this as it may, at the still midnight hour a ruffian band crept up to the inn he occupied, and the soldiers, armed to the teeth, both offensively and defensively, blocked up the doorway and passage, while their chief sought the chamber of the illustrious traveller.

The supposed Damascene merchant occupied a bed in a large chamber, on the floor of which lay his man and page.

The door had no fastening, and no suspicion of treachery existing, this excited no apprehension.

Imagine the astonishment of all three, when, suddenly aroused, they saw by the light of a lamp a soldier armed at all points standing in the middle of the room.

The pretended merchant laid his hand upon a sword.

"Silence, oh my king," said the sturdy old Norman, "twenty dogs, thirsting for your blood, await below. My orders are to take you alive, if you do not resist ; to slay you, if you fight.

"Slay !" replied Richard, haughtily.

"I am an old Norman soldier and know my duty. Out of that window is the courtyard, your horses, sire, and the open country. No thanks—away."

Aware that death was the penalty of delay, the king and his attendants hesitated no longer, and while the honest reiter went down growling to his companions to declare that the bird had flown, Hugo the merchant was riding away for dear life.

It is impossible to say by what fatuitous folly we find the king turning up next at Erdbergen, in the suburbs of Vienna.

It is true that he was ill and weary, but other hiding places might have been found than in the Duchy of Austria, the residence of his persistent foe, Leopold.

He was probably, on reflection, aware of his danger and want of foresight, if we may judge by what follows.

The wretched little inn in which the king secreted himself, afforded merely a shelter, but none of the viands and wine to which the luxurious king, a perfect Sybarite in his way, had been accustomed.

There was a market in Vienna, and to this every day the boy was sent to purchase such things as were necessary to the master and man.

Now we know not if there were detectives in those days, but the free command of money on the part of a boy, who always paid in sequins, and the choice character of his purchases, set the good wives' tongues to work.

For whom could he want such choice fruits and rare wines ?

People will talk, and even those who took the money remarked so persistently upon the matter, that at last the authorities heard of the subject.

The Austrians were, we suppose, as suspicious then as now, and the boy next time he visited the market-place, was brutally arrested.

A modern official would have simply followed him, and then discovered the the truth.

The Austrian police searched him, and found on his person much money, and a pair of gloves.

Nothing surprising now, but a rare surprise then. Gloves were only worn by kings, queens, and princes.

The boy was commanded to lead them to the hiding place of his master. Calmly, resolutely, and with dignity he refused.

Without a shadow of mercy, he was put to the rack, and yet he refused to speak.

"Cut out his tongue," cried the inhuman president, who carried on the inquiry.

The boy fainted, and when brought to, to save himself from this horrible fate, he yielded, and betrayed the king's hiding place.

He was taken that night in his sleep, so great was the dread of his prowess.

Having been securely confined, the Duke of Austria, who like many others liked to satiate his love of money and his hate at the same time, sent word to England's foe, the Emperor of Germany, Henry II., who gave £60,000 for the prize, but ordered Leopold to hold him in secret custody, in one of his most remote and secure castles.*

His serving man and the boy, whom the king heartily forgave, were allowed to accompany him.

He was, however, thrust into a cell of no very large dimensions, and there we leave him for the present.

In England for some time the king's return was hourly expected, but by degrees the fact oozed out that he was a prisoner, and that three persons were resolved to make his imprisonment perpetual—the Emperor, who hoped to wring concessions from him, the king of France, who hoped to conquer Normandy, and John, who now would be king in reality.

But the English people were resolved not to lie idle. War, with such a prince as John at their head, was out of the question. Money, however, has never yet lost its power, and to money they resorted.

The queen's mother and the friends of Richard began to collect loans, taxes, to melt plate, to urge the clergy to self-denial, and in every way to raise such a sum as would prove a right royal ransom.

But where was he a prisoner?

This was the mystery; and taking advantage of it, John declared him dead, and began, though no one would legally recognise him, to assume the airs and graces of a king.

A great plot was entered upon to declare the throne vacant, and induct the ambitious and cruel prince into the place.

The Norman captain, de Gilbert, pressed eagerly for the hand of Ethel, who however, suddenly took refuge in a convent, and claimed sanctuary, which even John did not dare openly to violate.

He resolved upon cunning and falsehood, to carry out his designs.

Ethel had acted advisedly.

When the news came that Richard Cœur de Lion was a prisoner, Blondel de L'Isle contrived to have an interview with her.

The king had not thought proper to knight him before his departure, and had thus prevented his following him to the crusades.

He was resolved, however, to serve him in another way.

The great strength of Prince John and his party lay in the undecided state of the question.

As long as his place of imprisonment was kept a secret, it was difficult to know with whom to negotiate, while if the mystery were prolonged, one of two things would happen—either by the joint influence of emperor, king and prince, he would be privately murdered, or the weary commons of England would declare the throne vacant. He resolved, therefore, to assume the garb of a troubadour, and with his stock of original songs and others, to travel as a wandering minstrel until he discovered in some way the secret of his king's incarceration.

It was a brave and romantic determination, and one characteristic of the period.

His father readily supplied him with such money as he required, though such visitors were only too gladly entertained and rewarded.

And thus, without a clue, without any guide, and a very slight knowledge of the uncouth German language, he started on his adventurous enterprise.

It was true that the language of song was universally understood.

Blondel made no confidants, save his father and Ethel, and thus was enabled to leave England unsuspected.

It was a long and wearisome journey in foot in those days to reach Vienna, in which place, as the capital of the foe who had laid his craven hand on the British Lion, he hoped to procure some clue to the true state of the case.

Months after his departure, singing and playing his zittern by the way, he reached the desired haven.

But though he listened and listened—never daring to ask—he heard nothing on the subject uppermost in his heart.

But he learned in what direction lay the various strongholds of the Austrian duke, and determined to visit them one by one.

For several weeks he utterly failed.

To several castles he was readily admitted, made much of, and detained much beyond the time he desired to remain.

In towns it was the same; wherever he went he was welcome, and made to feel the national love of song which characterised the human race.

The peasantry were even more enthusiastic than those above them, and his reception in villages was all that he could wish.

It was while staying in a small hamlet, and singing and playing to the serfs of some noble chief, that he heard the first news of his king, Richard.

Pointing to a castle on a distant peak, which

" Amid bright sunshine hangs on high
    Like a thunder cloud in a summer sky,"

an old man alluded to the fact that somewhere not far distant was imprisoned some

---

* Strangers are still shown the rugged cell, hollowed in the natural rock, in which Richard expiated the insult offered to the Duke at Acre.

great man, king or prince, who had offended their lord and master, the Duke of Austria.

Blondel made no direct inquiries, but entered into the conversation languidly, contriving, however, to discover that he was on the right track.

Weary and exhausted, the young wanderer the next night reached a spot on the Danube where a miserable, abandoned hut afforded him a night's shelter, while his wallet supplied him with a meal.

At daybreak he was once more on foot, and looking forth, saw on the other side of the water a truly remarkable fortress, occupying the crest of a rugged group of rocks, variously split and pinnacled into fantastic shapes.

There was a town below, and to this during the day, he was ferried over by the kindness of a charcoal burner going there with a supply of goods.

As it stands, in all the pride of dilapidated strength and grandeur, it is quite picturesque enough.

The ancient ramparts and gates, the ruined nunnery of St. Clara, and the old domestic buildings, demonstrate the antiquity of the place, and clearly exemplify the architecture of the middle ages.

Of its history nothing is known save what we have to record.

In this place the troubadour whiled away an hour or two, sang, played and conversed, and at eventide retired to a shed to rest, apparently for the night.

No sooner, however, had darkness quite fallen, and the early going people had retired to bed,* than he was on foot.

The castle of Durrenstein such he found was its name, was aloft on a peaked rock, almost inaccessible, except by a winding path.

Except to modern artillery or starvation, it was simply impregnable.

Blondel, however, with his dagger, his only weapon, commenced the rugged ascent, and after four hours of arduous labour, sank upon a bed of wild thyme growing on a narrow slope immediately under a barred window some distance above.

It took him some time to recover his breath, and then, his heart leaping to his mouth, he knew not why, the minstrel began his song, one which he knew was well loved by the king.

It was a simple love ditty,* in the purest Provençale, a duet.

Blondel.

Donna vostra beautas	Your beauty, lady fair,
Elas, bellas faissos	None view without delight,
Els bels oils ameros ;	But still, cold as air,
Els gens cors bên taillats	No passion you excite ;
Don sieu empresenats	Yet this I patient see,
De vostra amor que mi lia.	While all are shunned like me.

Cœur de Lion.

Si bel trop àffansia	No nymph my heart can wound
Ta, de vos, neu partria	If favours she divide,
Que major honorae	And smile on all around
Sol en votre deman	Unwilling to decide.
Que sautra des beisau	I'd rather hatred bear
Pot can de vos volrai.	Than love with others share.

With trembling lips Blondel finished the first verse and waited.

Ere the dying echo had ceased to fall on his ear, there came the response in a voice too well known to the wandering minstrel for him to be mistaken.

"My brave Blondel," then said a voice from above, "By what miracle do I find you here?"

"Oh, Richard, oh my king!" † cried the enthusiastic youth, in a passionate tone; "have I found you at last?"

"A wretched captive in a cavern cut from the rock. Can you come no nearer?"

Blondel looked around, and discovered that, aided by his dagger, he might ascend to the window, where some minutes later he saw the king and pressed his hand to his lips.

Now ensued a long conversation, during which Blondel produced tablets, on which the king wrote messages to the primate, to his mother, and the German Diet.

These once delivered, his prison would be known, and his freedom only a question of time.

A month later, Richard was removed to Spire, his ransom agreed on, and a new prison selected.

But the same night, aided by the faithful Blondel, his page, and two Norman knights, Richard escaped, nor could all the efforts of the Emperor of Germany and the king of France track him, though heavy rewards were offered for his capture.

Meanwhile, things were going badly in England.

Weary of waiting, and with a natural dislike of revolution, barons and commons were yielding to the influence of Prince John.

---

* In Vienna, now, the gatekeepers fine people 2d. who stay out until ten, 4d. uutil eleven, and 6d. at twelve.

* This legend is told in all the histories of the king, but no author that we know of has published the real ballad, as sung by the faithful troubadour and the king, as given in contemporary manuscripts.

† "Oh, Richard, oh mon roi."

He and his faction were collected at York, where they held high revel and festival.

The prince had regained possession of the person of Ethel, and had fixed the next day but one for the marriage with Sir Roland de Gilbert, the reiter chief, his most solid dependance.

He had collected his free lances around him, and a considerable force of barons and their horse and foot contingents.

Several bishops had joined his standard, so that he was King of England in all but name.

A grand banquet was given by the king, at which all his noble adherents were present, with many beautiful women and girls, some willingly enough, others on compulsion.

The invitation of a king *de facto* is a command.

At length, however, the wine taking effect upon some, the ladies contrived to retire, and soon after the prince himself, with his cabal, sought a chamber apart.

There were seven men, his devoted supporters, men who, he once king, were to rule England under him, and tower over all competitors.

Of these the most noted were Sir Roland de Gilbert, and Baron Fitzmaurice, once a friend of Richard's, a traitor and renegade.

The discussion was earnest, but at length it was resolved that next day the first proclamation of John as king should be made.

At this moment a discreet knock was heard at the door, and the prince's secretary entered hurriedly.

"A message from Austria in hot haste, your grace," he said.

The prince snatched a small strip of parchment, unsigned.

He turned deadly pale, and passed it to the Bishop of Winchester, who read aloud—

"The devil has got loose ; take care of yourself."

Every man sprang to his feet as if about to retire.

"You desert me ?" said the prince, sternly. "I am still strong enough to punish. Stand by me, and I will still be king."

A long conference ensued, and finally it was agreed to proceed with the conspiracy, and oppose to the late King Richard and his party, King John and his.

Next day, however, of the seven four had fled, there remaining the bishop, the Reiter, and baron Fitzmaurice.

At twelve, in the chapel of the archiepiscopal palace, a glorious assemblage was present to witness the marriage of Ethel and the Reiter.

The girl knew resistance was useless, but she had resolved to escape Sir Roland by death, rather than suffer a touch from his hand.

The ceremony began.

"Hold !" suddenly exclaimed a voice, as a tall knight in armour strode down the middle of the church.

"Who dares commit sacrilege ?"

"I, Richard King of England, forbid the ceremony ; the fair lady yonder is the affianced bride of Sir Blondel de L'Isle, Baron of Castle Fitzmaurice, the late property of yonder attainted traitor !"

A dash of armed men, and all the conspirators who were not churchmen were arrested.

That night John went into exile, Sir Roland de Gilbert was sent to his native Normandy, while Baron Fitzmaurice was executed.

Richard was truly once more King of England, and one of his first acts was to confirm his gift to Blondel, and to wed him to the beautiful Saxon Ethel.

Long after the lamented death of the monarch, did the noble baron and his lady speak of the fortunate inspiration which enabled him to discover the secret of the king's captivity in the old and almost inaccessible Castle of Durrenstein.

END OF THE CAPTIVE PRINCE.

CLARA THE BEAUTIFUL;

OR,

THE FATE OF THE FELICIANS.

THE stately castle of Vissegrad, which stands in one of the most picturesque spots on the Upper Danube, has been the scene of many highly romantic events in Hungarian history.

Once the favourite residence of the Magyar kings, its aspect is still grand and regal.

Crowning the summit of a precipitous hill, its loftly towers and battlements rise in a majestic cluster, terminating at the water-side in an isolated tower, six stories in height.

Nothing now visible will, however, give the traveller an adequate idea of the magnificence of Vissegrad in the feudal ages, when Hungary was one of the most powerful sovereignties in Europe, and the pomp and state of its monarchs combined Western refinement with Eastern splendour.

It is to these times—namely, the fourteenth century, or, to be more precise, the year 1380—that we desire to transport the reader, and recall the most dramatic and exciting story in the annals of this famous castle.

It was a grand day at the royal residence, for they were celebrating the birthday of Queen Stephanie, the proud and beautiful consort of Carl Robert, King of Hungary.

All the loyal nobles and their retinues had flocked to the castle to do honour to the occasion.

Costly presents and respectful congratulations poured in from all sides, and hospitality on a truly regal scale was extended to the distinguished guests.

The banquet spread in the great hall surpassed all previous ones in varied fare and magnificence of service, and music, minstrelsy, and knightly pastimes took each their turn in occupying the company.

The King, usually stern and unbending, was melted into the suavest courtesy by the aspect of all around him, and thanked his noble guests for their cordial friendship in a tone befitting an equal rather than a superior.

The Queen herself was radiant with pride and happiness; and her beauty, which was celebrated throughout her own and the neighbouring realms, was now enhanced by the splendid robes and appurtenances of royalty.

On the Queen's right hand sat her brother, Prince Casimir, the highest in rank of the knights assembled at the Hungarian court.

Noble in aspect, young and handsome, there was something in his expression that spoke of latent fierceness, obdurate self-will, and passions ill-controlled.

Previous to the banquet various sports and pastimes had taken place in the courtyard of the castle, and in particular, a grand tournament, in which all the knights and nobles, and the king himself, had taken part.

Vast crowds of spectators of every grade thronged around the lists; and deafening were the acclamations that rent the air when this or that favourite champion was victorious.

The fineness of the day, the richness and variety of the dresses, trappings, and accoutrements, the beauty of the noble ladies who filled the balconies, the spirit-stirring sounds of the heralds' clarions, all made up a scene which none could regard without interest and admiration.

The queen, seated in the royal pavilion, surrounded by her ladies, was especially the object of the loyal ovation of the crowd, to which she responded with a graceful condescension scarcely in keeping with her usual character.

At this gratifying moment her attention was called or attracted towards a young lady in the pavilion of Count Zacharias Felician, one of the highest nobles of the court.

The gaze of many was during that day unresistingly drawn in the same direction.

Very young, seemingly not beyond her sixteenth year, fairer than Hungarian ladies are in general, with proud features of exquisite symmetry and an expression highly attractive, and clad with simplicity combined with taste and elegance, it was impossible to deny to this young lady beauty of an unusually striking character.

The queen enquired of her attendants who the fair stranger was, to which one of them replied :—

"It is Clara, the only daughter of Count Felician ; she has hitherto been kept in strict seclusion at her father's castle."

An exciting episode in the tournament here took off their attention.

The king, who had taken an active part in the sports, and acquitted himself in accordance with his well-known skill in arms, had just run a course with the Baron of Merosch, and defeated him.

As soon as the acclamations attending this feat died away, Prince Casimir sent his esquire to touch the king's shield, in token of challenge.

The king accepted, and the two royal antagonists entered the lists.

Spurring forward his proud Barbary courser of raven blackness, the Prince Casimir met his royal kinsman on his milk-white steed, in full career. The result was undecided at the first course, in the second the king had slightly the advantage, and in the third and last, the king was unhorsed.

Some applause followed, but not so much probably as if the monarch himself had been the victor.

Assisted by his chief squire, his majesty soon rose, and passively acquiesced in the decision against him given by the judge of the lists. Prince Casimir, highly grati-

THE CASTLE OF VISSEGRAD.

fied at his victory, retired to his pavilion, and when a few courses had been run by other knights, he again sought a champion to contend with.

In answer to this challenge, a knight came forward, remarkable for his very plain and unadorned equipment.

He would give no other name than the "Knight Aspirant," and some curiosity was felt as to his identity.

The combatants soon closed, the Prince spurring forward with his usual impetuous charge, the knight remaining at first calmly on the defensive. Casimir soon found that he had an antagonist of no mean skill, and was somewhat annoyed at

his invincible and imperturbable demeanour.

Eager to end the combat, the Prince at last charged violently forward. The stranger, keeping his lance at rest, received him with the same coolness and precision as before, and the consequence was that the Prince's lance was shivered and broken in the charge, and he himself thrown from his horse with some violence.

Loud shouts hailed his defeat, for, in truth, the Prince was not altogether popular, and enraged at this position, he would have sprung up and demanded a renewal of the combat on foot, but that the weight of his armour prevented his rising.

His squires rushed forward, but ere they could reach him, his antagonist, to the surprise of all, yielded assistance by unbarring his helmet, and aiding him to regain his feet.

"To whom," gasped the prince, "am I indebted for the disgrace of this defeat?"

"No disgrace, my lord, since you fell in fair contest. See, I will disguise myself no longer. I am your faithful follower."

"Theodore of Plinkenburg!" exclaimed Casimir in astonishment, as the other raised his visor. "I knew not that you intended to take part in these contests at all. At least I deem it would have been but courtesy to disclose at first your identity."

"I was diffident of my skill," responded the young knight, "and intended to remain unknown had I been defeated; as it is, rise, my lord. I have conquered you, but you, in your turn, have conquered the king himself."

The prince, still mortified and annoyed at this presumption on the part of his attendant, retired sulkily from the arena, while his victor, riding round the lists, received the congratulations of the spectators.

It might have been observed that Count Felician, when the identity of the young champion was disclosed, displayed considerable satisfaction, and his daughter even more so.

She, at least, was in the secret of Theodore's identity, and rejoiced at his success.

Zacharias, Count Felician, came of one of the noblest families in Hungary, which had for centuries occupied a large estate not far from Vissegrad.

He was the last of his race in a direct line, but there were many collateral descendants, among them, Theodore, son of a cousin.

Left an orphan at an early age, Theodore was taken under the protection of his kinsman, and brought up at Count Felician's castle.

Under such circumstances it is scarcely surprising that an affection had sprung up between Theodore and the beautiful Clara, heiress of Count Felician.

He had long aspired to her hand, but as yet his intention had not been expressed.

In the capacity of page Theodore had long served Count Felician, till, desiring a more extended field for his valour, he through the count's influence was enrolled among the esquires of Prince Casimir.

Only a few days before, Theodore, on coming of age, had received the rank of knighthood, which entitled him to take part in these chivalrous contests.

Clara Felician had been brought up in seclusion, and her mother's recent death had retarded her introduction to the gaieties of the court.

This was therefore the first occasion in which she had appeared in the royal presence, and her remarkable beauty was therefore enhanced by the charm of novelty.

To see her lover thus victorious was naturally a cause of considerable satisfaction to her.

Prince Casimir, resolving to test the fortune of war no more that day, retired, as the king had already done, into the royal pavilion, where he had more leisure to observe the contest and its spectators.

Hearing many expressions of praise going on around him, with regard to the occupant of the opposite balcony, he, for the first time, beheld Clara Felician.

She happening to look up, observed his ardent gaze fixed upon her so intently, that a deep blush suffused her countenance, for she was as yet unused to stand the fire of admiration.

At this moment Count Felician sought and was accorded admission into the royal gallery.

He entered with a deep obeisance to the king and queen, and addressing the former said—

"I trust your majesty has suffered but little in the contest, nor your royal brother-in-law, Prince Casimir."

"Thanks, noble count," responded the king, "but there is, apparently, a champion in the list excelling either of us. 'Tis thy nephew, as I take it.

"My nephew, as I call him, but in truth my cousin thrice removed, is a brave youth, as my Lord Casimir can vouch, and faithful and devoted to his highness's service."

"I have hitherto had no reason to complain of Sir Theodore of Plinkenburg," answered the prince, somewhat sharply.

"We have been admiring your daughter, the Lady Clara," said the queen to the count. "She is indeed beautiful. Well would she adorn our court, and I trust you will allow her to enter our service. At least, I beg you will introduce her to us."

"I could not refuse so agreeable an honour," answered the old count. "I will summon her at once."

In a short time, Clara was introduced by her father to the royal party. To find herself the centre of so glittering an assembly was, to one of her timid and retiring nature an ordeal scarcely compensated by the honour of it.

To add to her embarrassment, the ardent gaze of Prince Casimir was renewed as she entered.

"Would'st like to enter my service, maiden?" asked the queen, in a kind tone. "Thou shalt have high place among these noble ladies, who will be happy to welcome thee among them."

Clara glanced at her father, seemingly too overcome to speak; he replied for her.

"The honour is too great to refuse," he said. "I know my, child, thou wilt be proud to become a lady of the court."

Clara murmured a pleased affirmative.

"It is settled, then," said the queen, "As early as you will, let her take up her residence at Vissegrad."

After a little more conversation, the count and his daughter withdrew, highly gratified at the honour conferred upon them, and little anticipating the countless miseries and final destruction that honour would entail.

"A perfect houri of Paradise, Ludovick," said the Prince, to one of his companions. "She will indeed grace the queen's court," and he fell into an apparently blissful reverie.

Thus it happened that Clara Felician, and her lover and kinsman, Theodore, became inmates of Vissegrad Castle, one in attendance on the queen, the other in the service of the queen's brother.

* * * *

The apartment of Clara lay in a remote part of the castle, adjoining the pleasure-garden exclusively appropriated to the queen and her ladies. By what means such trespasses were contrived, does not appear, but, certain it is that lovers' meetings sometimes took place in these grounds, and that the echoes of the garden were sometimes awakened by sweet serenades. Clara had more than once heard the sound of a guitar under her window, and on one occasion, had caught sight of a figure, in which she recognised Theodore. The young knight, on observing her at the window, took advantage of the fact that a high wall, and a higher tree grew near, by climbing thereon, and thus reaching an altitude little short of the window itself. Such surreptitious means were, in truth, the only ones by which the lovers could, at present, communicate.

Their conversation naturally took place in an undertone, and partook of the nature of an unreserved confession on either side.

"Oh, Theodore!" she murmured, "I am so unhappy."

"And wherefore, dearest?"

"My life here is not so pleasant as I anticipated. The Queen is proud and exacting; many of her ladies, too, slight me; they are jealous of the admiration which they imagine I attract, yet, heaven knows, quite unwittingly. And more terrible than all, I am persecuted by the attentions of one whom I much fear—one too great and powerful to offend."

"Ah! whom do you mean?" asked Theodore, in some concern.

"Your master, the Prince Casimir."

"Prince Casimir!" he exclaimed. "I grieve at that. I have of late discovered more of his character than is of good report. Tales have gone abroad concerning him—tales of heartless libertinism and base desertion."

"You add to the fears I already entertain," said Clara. "Alas! I regret to find that this court is not the abode of virtue and honour—that many of the queen's attendants are guilty of conduct which I disapprove; that her majesty herself regards these delinquencies with too much leniency, and gives me counsel at which I marvel, and grieve to hear from her lips. Moreover, she so favours and assists her brother, that to offend him is to incur her displeasure."

"Here is ill news, indeed!" said Theodore. "Why not inform your father of all this, and he would remove you?"

"Thus offending the king and queen, and probably causing his own dismissal and ruin? Impossible! Theodore, think not of it, for his sake. I must bear my lot as I best may, upheld by my own sense of right and the assistance of Heaven. Hark! methinks I heard the sound of a guitar. Descend, dear Theodore, instantly; 'tis dangerous to be discovered here. Yes, it must be the prince; 'tis not the first time he has serenaded me, but I turn a deaf ear to his sweetest and most flattering music."

The young knight rapidly descended the tree, and reached the wall and the ground.

From an adjacent grove there now advanced into the moonlight a man wearing a mask and cloak, and carrying a guitar, on which he preluded as he walked along.

Casting one glance at the lattice of Clara's room, he commenced his strain, which was certainly pleasing and musical in itself, but not so to the ears of Theodore, as, hidden by the shadow of the wall, he heard these words of love so fervently poured forth by the dissolute prince.

His heart burned within him with honourable jealousy.

At length, impelled by this feeling, just as the prince reached the end of the second verse, he rushed from his place of concealment and confronted the singer, who, starting back, exclaimed—

"Who is there?"

"Break off your song, prince," said Theodore, sternly; "'tis not welcome to the maiden you address. You will never win her love by this or any other means."

"Theodore of Plinkenburg," said his master, in deep anger, "how camest thou here? Is it to thwart me in love? Darest thou to set thyself up as my rival?"

"If thou callest me so," the young knight replied; "but, in truth, I am the only accepted lover of Clara Felician."

"I must chastise this presumption," cried the prince, and drawing his sword, he attacked Theodore fiercely.

The latter was not slow to take the defensive; his sword met that of the prince, and a desperate combat ensued.

Blinded with fury, Casimir rushed upon his rival as if determined to annihilate him; but each stroke was parried with skill and address.

At last, Theodore, also roused to anger, assumed the attack in his turn, and by a dexterous movement, disarmed the prince, who sank wounded to the ground.

A cry of rage and pain escaped him, with which was mingled a female's shriek; it proceeded from Clara, who, hearing the clash of arms, had witnessed the latter part of the combat.

The din had also reached the ears of others, for footsteps were approaching the spot.

Theodore, roused to a sense of his danger, promptly plunged into the grove, and disappeared; and the prince's attendants, taking up their master, bore him to his own apartments.

The next day a rumour prevailed at court that Prince Casimir was ill, and indeed he kept his apartment for that and many succeeding days.

The prince, when he recovered, took no steps to punish his adversary; he seemed, on the other hand, to wish the affair, so little creditable to himself, to be forgotten.

Theodore took no pains either to disclose or conceal the facts of the case, but he formally resigned his position in the prince's service, and retired awhile from the court to one of the distant estates of Count Felician.

A year passed from the time when Clara entered the queen's service; more and more did she dislike the society in which she was cast.

She found that there prevailed at the court a laxity of conduct at which her virtuous heart rebelled.

She had to bear the sneers and taunts to which her own stricter ideas exposed her.

She found, too, that she had a formidable rival in the queen herself, who, jealous of the admiration Clara's beauty excited, lost no opportunity of causing her humiliation.

Yet Clara bore patiently all this for her father's sake, from whom, indeed, she withheld much of her distress.

Luckily, her chief cause of persecution was now removed.

The King of Poland had died suddenly, and the throne of that country was vacant.

The monarchy was elective, there being no regular dynasty, but on the death of one monarch, another chosen among the highest native nobles or foreign princes.

It was a prize much contended for amongst the princes of Europe, and on this occasion several candidates put in their claims.

The choice was found to have fallen upon Prince Casimir, of Hungary.

Great was the satisfaction of Prince Carl Robert and his wife at the honour done to their relative, and much gratified, though from a different cause, was Clara Felician.

Casimir set out for his new kingdom in great state, attended by all the gentlemen of his train, and with him the congratulations and good wishes of his friends and relations.

Another year passed.

Theodore sometimes appeared at Vissegrad with Count Felician, who, through court intrigues and jealousy of rival nobles, had fallen somewhat in the king's favour.

From many circumstances the old count became anxious on his daughter's account, for he saw that she was not happy.

So he formally gave his consent to wed Theodore in another three months, and her marriage would be a valid excuse for her retirement from court.

Fatal delay!

Had the marriage taken place at once, Clara would have been removed in time from that destruction which awaited her and all her kindred.

Great preparations were made at the castle to receive a visit from the queen's royal brother, King Casimir, of Poland.

On the appointed day he came, attended by many of the nobles of his new realm, and again the regal hospitality of Vissegrad was profusely manifested.

Jousts and banquets, and dances in the grand hall, and hunting in the forest, took place and continued for three days.

Clara Felician had hoped that Casimir had forgotten her, but the attention paid her above all the other ladies of the court proved that the old flame was re-kindled at the sight of its object.

Clara resolved to meet him no more.

The next day she excused herself from appearing at the festivities on the plea of indisposition.

The portion of the castle in which the queen's apartments were situated were deserted, the tide of festivity having drawn all its inmates in the other direction.

Clara could, therefore, unobserved, enter the private garden, and seek in solitude some relief from her anxieties.

It was a sweet, balmy evening in summer, the garden, in full bloom, looked indeed beautiful, and, itself sequestered, was enlivened by the bursts of music and revelry that ever and anon floated on the air from afar.

Clara sat in a rural grotto which was among the beauties of this artificial landscape, and fell into a deep reverie.

This was suddenly broken by the sound of footsteps, and the figure of a man appeared at the end of one of the garden walks.

At first her heart bounded with a sudden delight, for she imagined it was Theodore, who had secured the opportunity of stealing away from the festive scene.

But in a moment she was undeceived; the cloak and the hat being removed, she recognised King Casimir.

She would have fled, but his grasp was on her wrist ere she could proceed two paces, and, to her dismay, she was compelled to listen to him.

"Beautiful Clara," he said, "you see me again before you a humble suppliant, though now a powerful king. My heart is unchanged. For a time the cares of royalty overshadowed your image in my mind, but the sight of you has revived my love. Be mine, and I offer you a life of splendour such as you could nowise else hope for."

"Of splendour and of guilt," she retorted, roused to desperation. "No, King Casimir, even did you offer me to become your queen, I must refuse, for my heart and my hand are given, but ere I would become your mistress, this dagger should at once end my existence!"

"Obstinate beauty," said Casimir, "I would indeed make thee my queen, did not political reasons compel me to make some other union more suitable, but as it is, I can give thee the highest position at court, next to that regal one."

"Thou hast my reply," answered Clara, unmoved. "I am not one to be tempted by all the splendours of a court. Release my hand, sire, I entreat thee, on the honour of a knight and of a king."

Thereupon Casimir sprang to his feet, but relinquished not her hand.

He saw that she was fixed in resolve, that entreaty was in vain, and that it was time to put into practice the more desperate means he had provided.

Placing a silver whistle to his lips, he blew a shrill call, and at the signal two men in masks and cloaks emerged from the grove and laid hands on the luckless Clara.

She gave one shriek of despair, but her cries were soon stopped by a gag. Blindfolded, and half dead with terror, she was borne away in the arms of the ruffians.

"It was the only course," murmured Casimir to himself, as he looked after his departing victim. "If they can pass the frontier to-night, she will be safe at the castle of Veroska before dawn. The precautions that the queen has taken, will keep her absence undiscovered till I have also departed. Once securely in my power, Clara will soon get reconciled to a fate to which so many others have had to submit."

That night, at the dance and banquet, King Casimir acquitted himself with his usual courtly grace, and joined in the laughter and revelry with more than his wonted zest.

Count Felician soon noted Clara's absence from the scene of festival.

The next day she did not appear, and he was informed that indisposition was the cause.

Much concerned, he desired to see her.

This, however, was refused by the queen, as being against the etiquette of the court, and he might rest assured that the lady Clara would have every necessary attention.

Still, however, Felician requested that Clara should be removed to his own castle, but this was also refused.

The old count now began to suspect that all was not well, that some sinister plot was in progress.

At length, a bribe induced one of the queen's servants to tell him all.

She had overheard a conversation between her mistress and King Casimir, in which the abduction was planned, and she had reliable information that the plot had been carried out.

Felician was thunderstruck.

An act of baseness and treachery so flagrant, perpetrated by those who held a position so exalted, was beyond even his long experience of courts.

His anger was so great that prudence deserted him, and he resolved to seek redress at once, and openly.

The banquet was again in full progress —a farewell banquet, as the royal visitor was to start at early morning on his return to his own kingdom.

All the great ones of the realm were taking part in the scene of magnificence.

The Polish king was just raising aloft a jewelled goblet full of costly wine, to return thanks to his Hungarian brother, when a commotion was heard without, and breaking through the line of sentries that guarded the door, the venerable Count Felician burst into the room.

His sword was drawn, fury glared from his eyes, and indignation and the sense of his wrongs seemed to have recalled the very strength of his youth.

"Thou crowned villain!" he cried to Casimir, "I have learnt thy false conduct; deliver up my daughter, or not all thy power shall shield thee from my vengeance!"

Taken quite aback by this unexpected outburst, Casimir was at first unable to reply; then, assuming a haughty air, said—

"Your daughter! What know I of your daughter?"

"Answer, and prevaricate not, or this sword shall end thy vile existence. Whither have you conveyed the persecuted —the innocent Clara Felician?"

The banquetting-hall was now a scene of tumult.

The guests had all risen from their seats, for it was easy to see that the majority took Casimir's part.

The king, Carl Robert, sternly commanded Felician to withdraw.

But, maddened with fury, the old count regarded not even his commands.

"And thou, base woman," he added, turning to the queen, "thou, whose court has become a scene of iniquitous licence, which it befits no innocent maiden to dwell amongst, how couldst thou aid and abet this outrage against my daughter?"

His sword swung furiously around him, struck the hand of the queen, causing a deep, open cut, from which the blood flowed profusely; and the king of Hungary, who had come forward to interpose, was also struck by the infuriated noble.

At sight of this, the guests and attend ants of the two kings rushed in a body upon the infuriate nobleman.

All the ferocity of those wild times was now fully evinced.

Cowardly as was the attack, no less than twenty swords were turned against one aged and unassisted man.

He fought with the desperation of a lion at bay.

But it was useless.

A few minutes only lasted this desperate struggle, and then the noble old count fell, covered with wounds.

"So perish all who dare to shed the royal blood of Hungary!" cried King Carl Robert. "Of late the arrogance of this nobleman has offended me and my councillors, and I regret not that he has brought this fate on himself. My vengeance shall pursue all his lineage; every one of the name of Felician shall feel the weight of my wrath."

"And as for his daughter," said the King of Poland, "once more let her repulse me, and she shares her father's fate."

At this moment Theodore of Plinkenburg, with his sword drawn, rushed into the hall.

He had only just heard of his kinsman's danger, and regardless of all consequences flew to his assistance.

But he was too late; there, weltering on the floor, lay the body of the slain nobleman, and ere Theodore could even reach it, the cry of, "A Felician! A Felician! Down with him!" arose, and he was secured and firmly bound.

In a few minutes King Carl's soldiers had conveyed him to one of the lowest dungeons of the castle.

The royal festivities were, of course, brought to an abrupt termination, the queen retired, and King Casimir hastened to prepare for his departure.

That night the body of the noble old Count Felician was ignominiously flung into the Danube, and a part of the King of Hungary's soldiers were despatched to take possession of his castle.

It had been intended that the unhappy Clara should pass the frontier into Poland that night, but a storm detaining the party, they put up at an hostel within a few miles of Vissegrad.

King Casimir and his party reached the same place early next morning, and a momentous interview ensued.

"Clara Felician," said the Polish king, "events have taken place which show how useless it is to contend against the power of kings and the customs of courts. Thy father, maddened by discovering thy absence, rushed into the banquetting hall, sacrilegiously attacked the queen and myself, and was justly punished by death."

"Death!" shrieked Clara; "Has then my dear and noble father fallen a victim to thy fury? And for what? Merely for his just indignation for the wrong done his child! Wretch! I abhor thee more than ever!"

"And more than ever," retorted Casimir, "thou art in my power. Clara Felician, thy father lies at the bottom of the Danube, his estates are in my hands, therefore, thou hast no home now and no protector. As for the upstart, Theodore, he is a prisoner at Vissegrad."

Clara was too overwhelmed to speak; she could only clasp her hands convulsively, and raise her eyes imploringly towards Heaven.

"All this is terrible for thee," pursued the merciless Casimir, "but worse shall befall if thou wilt still reject me. My rival shall die the ignominious death of a traitor, and all thy relations and friends shall share his doom. Say but the word, and thou canst save them."

"Never!" repeated Clara; "My friends would scorn to accept life on such terms. Death, but no dishonour, was ever the motto of the house of Felician. We are in the hands of Heaven, and if they perish I will perish with them, or before them."

And a dagger, drawn suddenly from her bosom, was raised aloft for a self-inflicted blow.

"Nay, if thou art resolved to die," cried Casimir, seizing her wrist, and arresting the weapon, "it shall be by more fitting means. I see thou art still obdurate either to persuasion or threat, and I will spare thee no longer. Thou shalt feel how terrible is my hate against those who reject my love."

He summoned his men, who forthwith seized the luckless Clara, and chained her as a captive.

The party then set out, not towards Poland, but on the return route to the Castle of Vissegrad.

It is needless to describe the commotion that now prevailed in the royal castle, and the sympathy which many felt, but none dared to show, towards the doomed captives.

Later in the day a terrible conclave sat in the castle, under the presidency of the Kings of Poland and Hungary.

They were merciless judges, and there was no appeal against their decision.

An indictment was read charging the late Count Zacharias Felician with treason and intended conspiracy against his liege lord, in which all his relatives were implicated.

King Carl Robert's decree was then set forth, dooming the family of Felician to entire extinction.

Thus charged with an imaginary crime, no less than twenty persons, old and young, men, women, and children, were sentenced to death.

No defence was permitted or attempted.

The prisoners were removed to their different cells, and ordered for execution the next morning.

None inspired greater compassion than the unfortunate Clara.

Even those who were to suffer with her approved and supported her conduct.

A last appeal was made by King Casimir, entreating her to spare the forthcoming tragedy by accepting his terms.

But she was inexorable.

All night the king's men were hard at work erecting the scaffold, and from the earliest morning the dismal bell of the castle tolled ominously.

Never were prisoners, however, so well prepared for death.

The Felicians had been always distinguished for their piety, rectitude, and honour, and not one among those doomed was deserving of their fate.

They all resolved to die as became great nobles of a great nation.

Husbands parted from their wives, children torn from their parents' arms, became, in sight of each other, victims to the death-dealing block.

Three headsmen were employed, and too well they performed their murderous work.

The large crowd that had assembled were full of sympathy, but they dared not show it in face of the strong muster of soldiers, and the two tyrants that superintended the tragedy from the balcony.

As a refinement of cruelty, the execution of Clara Felician was reserved for the last.

She was doomed to see all her relations fall before herself, and, awful as was the ordeal, she endured it with the fortitude religion alone can give.

Pale as death, her golden hair streaming over her spotless white robe, her eyes raised heavenward, she listened to the exhortations of the castle chaplain.

All agreed that at this dread moment her beauty was more striking and spiritual than it had ever appeared in the days of gaiety and happiness.

And now all had perished but herself and Theodore.

He preserved a firm, undaunted front, and was upborne by the same religious consolation as her he loved.

Their eyes met for the last time as Theodore was preparing to submit to the fatal stroke.

"Farewell, dearest!" he said, "one last embrace."

This could not be refused, and even the stern gaolers could make no effort to separate them.

Theodore bestowed one kiss upon her marble brow, and pressed her hand once more.

"Farewell, Theodore, we shall meet in Heaven!" were her last words, as she quitted his embrace; and then she turned away and veiled her eyes.

The axe descended, and the brave young knight was no more.

Clara would not trust herself to look in the direction of the body, which was removed before her own turn came.

Firmly she advanced to undergo the dread toilet of preparation; her luxuriant locks were cut close, but even then her beauty was but slightly marred.

She addressed these few words to the spectators:

"Friends, I die a victim to innocence— that is my only crime. May God have mercy upon my murderers, and forgive them, as I do! My last request is, that all who pity me may remember me in their prayers."

A few moments after this the beautiful Clara Felician was launched into eternity!

All the estates of the family were, according to the king's decree, confiscated, and their name blotted out from the roll of nobility.

✻   ✻   ✻   ✻   ✻

Such was the fate of the Felicians—a fate staining the page of Hungarian history with the foulest blot.

Did we not possess authentic evidence of its truth, we should deem it incredible that a deed so inhuman could ever have committed by a Christian king.

But much of the ferocity, as well as the power, of Mahommedan Sultans was possessed by the half-oriental monarchs of the Danube.

END OF CLARA THE BEAUTIFUL; OR, THE FATE OF THE FELICIANS.

Our next number will contain "The Mining Student."

THE BARONS OF OLD OR THE ROBBERS OF THE RHINE

THE MINING STUDENT.

A LEGEND OF SCHEMNITZ.

THERE was not a merrier or happier lad than Hans Lobeck in the school attached to the great silver mines at Schemnitz, till that unlucky day when count Lingotski, the great Hun- garian magnate, came, with his affianced bride, to see the mines, as is the custom with travellers of all countries.

Hans was a well made, good looking young fellow.

THE CASTLE OF SCHEMNITZ.

His somewhat uncouth costume of a close jacket, with padded sleeves, and a leather apron, could not destroy his comeliness.

He was a lad of some ability too, and high in favour with the superintendent of the royal mines.

He was an advanced student at the miners' college, which the emperor had established at Schemnitz ; he had a gang of five miners under his command, not the poor wretches who had been sent to the mines as prisoners, either for moral or political offences.

Now you are to know that Hans Lobeck, besides being in favour with the mining superintendent, had been noticed by the Burgomaster of Schemnitz.

A well-to-do fellow was that burgomaster, who, like Dogberry, had two coats and everything comfortable about him, a fellow that had had his losses too.

In addition to the losses, which had not hindered Master Schmidt from accumulating a very pretty sum of money, he had one only child, a daughter, whom the youths of Schemnitz in general, and Hans Lobeck in particular, pronounced to be a very pretty girl.

A little rosy dimpled dumpling sort of a girl, was Maria Schmidt, with the orthodox flaxen hair and blue eyes of a German girl.

Those blue eyes had not been slow to perceive that Hans Lobeck was the comeliest youth of the place.

The burly burgomaster admitted this fact, and as Hans was a clever and industrious youth, and likely to make his way in the world, he did not forbid Maria to look upon him as her husband to be, when master Hans should have obtained a sufficient share of the metals he worked for to satisfy Mr. Schmidt that his daughter would be comfortably supported.

Now if the two young people had been reasonable they would have been satisfied with this conditional engagement.

But when are young people in love reasonable ?

And when did young and old agree upon the question of ways and means ?

Wait till this father with the proverbial flinty heart thought that Hans was earning enough money to keep a wife. When would that be ?

"Time enough, time enough !" cried Master Schmidt.

Time enough that they should be wedded thought Maria and Hans.

How can this be wondered at when their mature age is considered, for Maria

was sixteen, and Hans actually nineteen and a half.

Still, despite the obstinacy with which Herr Schmidt stood to his determination, Hans was a merry and happy lad till the day on which the Count Lingotski visited the mines.

The count was an ugly, mean-looking fellow.

Nobles are not necessarily handsome men, and the undersized count, with his yellow, sickly face, and his glittering hussar uniform, for he was a colonel in the emperor's army, really looked more like a demon or a baboon than a man.

His lady was both beautiful and gentle, but the count was as haughty and domineering as he was unmanly.

It was no uncommon event for persons of rank to visit the mines, but such a display of wealth as that made by the Count Lingotski, Hans had never witnessed before.

He liberally rewarded Hans and the other persons who conducted him over the mines.

But he distributed his gratuity with so insulting an air that, good though the coin was, Hans had a mind to fling it in his face.

He went to his home, in a little white cottage, in a very ill-temper.

Hans ate his supper of sausage with very little appetite that night.

Neither did he drink his Schwartz beer with his usual gusto.

A certain miserable demon called Envy had fastened his talons in the poor boy's heart.

It was a lovely moonlight night.

He was in no mood for sleep, so he took his pipe and walked among the mountains.

Mechanically he took his way towards a spot which he had often visited in a happier frame of mind.

A pleasant valley, watered by a tributary of the Gran.

The Valley of the Aspens this place was called, from the number of those trees which almost dipped their fragile branches into the stream.

Vines, now purple with their load of grapes, for the season was autumn, hung upon the base of the mountains, whose summits were covered with pine and larch.

This valley was a favourite resort of the youth of Schemnitz, and many a love tale besides that of Hans and Maria, had been whispered to the accompaniment of the softly rustling trees and rippling waters.

But young Hans' thoughts of his dear

Maria were tinged with bitterness on that night.

This ugly count was very young, perhaps not a year older than Hans himself.

And all the world was at his feet.

That beautiful lady Hans felt sure could have wedded Lingotski only for his money.

"And his epaulettes were all diamonds!" grumbled Hans to himself, "ah, the worth of those epaulettes would set Maria and I up in housekeeping."

Now, Hans had not been soliloquising, he had not been speaking aloud.

Therefore, he was very much surprised, and a little startled, when a strange rasping kind of voice made answer to his muttered thought.

"I will give you the value of the count's diamonds, and fifty thousand thalers to boot, if you will render me a service.

Hans looked about him, but could not discover where the voice came from, till he was addressed again, the speech being preceded by a screeching laugh.

"Ha, ha, ha! Hans Lobeck, you are a fine fellow, a really fine young fellow, but I am afraid you will be too proud to serve me, for I am a queer-looking chap—the Count Lingotski, I must admit, is a beauty beside me."

"Oh!" returned Hans, in answer to the voice, for he still could see no one, "if you give me half of fifty thousand thalers, I would take service with you, were you as ugly as the devil himself. But who would give me such a sum—what could I do to earn it? Psha! old fellow—for old I judge you to be—go away. I am in no mood for jesting."

"There is no jest in the matter, young man," answered the voice; "but, you see, you are such a fine-grown lad, and I am so mean-looking and little, I am ashamed to show myself."

"Oh, pray do not be ashamed," answered Hans, "there's nothing to be ashamed of if you have money enough."

"That's very true," answered the voice, "in this world that you live in, but in my native place money is not the slightest consequence."

"None!" said Hans. "I should say, then, it must be a very pleasant place."

"That's according to taste," answered the voice, "but you will be able to judge when I have shown it to you."

"You had better show yourself first," replied Hans.

"I am afraid I shall frighten you," said the voice.

"Oh, don't be afraid. I am a bold lad, not a fair lady," returned Hans, "so let us see your phiz."

There was a rustling among the branches of an enormous larch near to Hans, and out from among them leaped a figure so grotesque, as well as ugly, that Hans was inclined to laugh, but did not do so, out of respect to the thalers which had been talked of.

A diminutive old man it was, less in stature even than Count Lingotski, and very much more like an ape.

This extraordinary individual had a hump upon his back, a hooked nose, teeth that worked like the fangs of a wolf and projected over his under lip, a skin the hue of saffron, much wrinkled, red hair, and little twinkling eyes to match.

His dress was scarlet and yellow, chosen, perhaps, to match with his hair and complexion.

It should be added that his splay feet and huge hands were as big and as clumsy as the paws of an elephant, and that he squinted so abominably with his little fiery red eyes, that, as he squatted down before Hans in the bright moonlight, he seemed rather winking at some unseen confederate of his own, than looking at Hans.

The youth could not forbear from laughing at his grotesque acquaintance.

"Who the devil can this be?" thought he, "probably some poor, half-witted mountebank, who, I suppose, has escaped from a showman."

Now, as before observed, this strange old man seemed to possess the faculty of reading the thoughts of Hans, at any rate he answered thus—

"My boy, Hans," he said, "you are very impertinent. My position is superior to that of a mountebank, but as to the devil, I shall thank you not to make disrespectful allusions to him in my presence, for I am something akin, though inferior in rank, to that much-abused individual!"

"By St. Nepomuc!" thought Hans, "I don't half like this fellow—a thirteenth cousin to old Nick, I suppose, and this little service he requires is the sale of my soul, I presume."

"Not at all, my young friend," replied the old man, "there is no buying of men's souls nowadays, they sell them too freely. But do speak out what you think of me, you may as well say it as think it. As to your soul, the value has gone down; we have a perfect glut of them in our great market down below."

"You are Satan, then!" said Hans, speaking out the thought boldly, since he found that his companion knew it without telling.

"I am, as I told you before, by no means such a distinguished personage," answered the dwarf, "I am but a poor little gnome, and, like yourself, not altogether content with my condition."

"Not content with your condition," growled Hans, "then I think you ought to be—you, a gnome with mountains full of gold and silver, what more do you want; you have lots of money."

"By Nimrod, young friend," answered the gnome, "money cannot buy all that one wants."

"I should like the chance of trying that!" replied Hans.

"You shall have it, my beloved Hans, whom I admire, because you are as surly and discontented as myself. You shall have a sackful of money."

"Ugh! tell me how. I should like to see it," said Hans, whose temper was not soothed by the gnome's flatteries. "Not for selling my soul, though."

"A pest upon your soul!" cried the gnome, "have I not told you that I don't want it, that it is of no value?"

"Yes, yes, we know all about that," retorted Hans, "we know your master bargains like a Jew, and cries down the value of the goods the more that he has set his mind on them."

"Tut, tut, young man, what is all this bother about your soul?" said the dwarf. "It is your body I want to put to use—those strong arms and sinewy hands—to dig up a treasure."

"Dig up a treasure!" quoth Hans, brightening up a little, but at the same time determined on making what he had been pleased to term a Jewish bargain himself. "Why I should have thought, Herr Gnome, that you could dig deeper than any mortal man."

"For gold, silver, and jewels, I grant you!" replied the gnome, disdainfully; "but you are too clever, you are too fast; you did not wait to hear me out; like all the young persons of the present day you do not treat your elders with sufficient respect."

Thereupon the gnome lapsed into silence, and sat down before Hans, with his long arms clasped round his knees, and a very sulky look upon his yellow physiognomy.

Now Hans, who was resolved upon the glorious work the dwarf had proposed, at any price less than the loss of his soul, was terribly afraid of the little saffron, weird gentleman taking a huff, and getting off the business altogether.

So he offered a most humble apology, saying he did not mean any offence.

"But you see, Herr Gnome," he remarked, in conclusion, "the night is wearing on apace, and a few hours stolen from my rest are all I have to work on my own account with. So I prythee, like a gentleman and gracious gnome, demon, or whatever you call yourself, do not beat any more about the bush, but tell me at a word what I can do for you!"

"Do you see this tree?" said the dwarf, kicking the trunk of the larch, from the boughs of which he had leaped into acquaintanceship with Hans.

"To be sure I do," answered Hans, then he receded a step, and added, "St. Joseph defend us, is that the way down to your dwelling, master gnome? Where did you manufacture that door?"

In effect, when old yellow-face kicked the tree the trunk opened, and the moonbeams straining into the aperture showed Hans a dark narrow stair, which seemed to descend into the bowels of the earth.

"No, young man, that is not my abode," answered the gnome in a dolorous voice, "it leads down to the place where a malicious demon of the woods with whom I quarrelled has hidden my cap."

"Hidden your cap," quoth Hans; "well, it is a warm night, cannot you do without it, or go down and fetch it?"

"Alas! no," answered the dwarf, "it is for that I want your help. You are to know it is my cap of power. When I put it on my head, I can change this my natural shape for any other that I please, yours, for instance, if it so liked me. As I told you, Hans, I am like yourself by no means content with my condition, pent up, diving and grubbing in the earth. I should like to have been a sylph or fairy."

Eyeing the old fellow's grotesque face and figure, Hans could not forbear laughing.

"A pretty sort of sylph or fairy you would make, to be sure," he said.

"Hans, you are very rude," answered the gnome; "I know I am not handsome by nature, but my cap of power corrects all defects, and the truth is——"

Here the gnome assumed a coxcombical air— "that I won, when wearing it, the affections of Spangle Drop, the fairy of this brooklet, a vexatious little flirt, at whom Pine-Cone, the wood spirit, has a long time set his cap to no purpose. So he stole my magic cap, and buried it at the roots of this tree and only mortal hands can dig it up again."

"Oh! oh! so that's what you want me to do I suppose," said Hans. "Why didn't you come to the point at first, old fellow ? "

" Oh, most generous youth, and you will really dig up my cap of power ? "

" To be sure I will, so as you give me an earnest of the money you talked about," returned Hans.

" Never fear about that," answered the gnome. " My treasure vault joins the cavern where Pine-Cone buried my cap, and you shall help yourself ; so come at once."

" All right, old boy," answered Hans ; " but where is a mattock and shovel? I suppose I shall want them both."

" They are already down below," said the gnome, slipping into an aperture in the trunk of the larch. " Only observe, my dear boy, before your service with me begins, you must not interlard your speech with any more mention either of saints or demons. The saints are fantastical people, with whom we have nothing to do ; and as to the demons, we do not speak familiarly of monarchs in the precincts of their domains."

" So," said Hans, a little startled, " you are then going to take me to the dominion of his black majesty."

" What a fellow you are, Hans !" cried the gnome. " Why, the dominion of riches is always the dominion of Satan."

Hans was a little startled when, as he followed his strange employer into the hollow trunk of the larch, the aperture closing, shut out the moonbeams, and he found himself in profound darkness. An ejaculation to the saints was rising involuntarily to his lips, but was prevented by the gnome squeaking out in an accent of alarm—

" Take care what you say, Hans, take care ! Those sanctified humdrum fellows you are thinking about cannot help you here. Don't be afraid of stumbling, I'll show you a light with my eyes ? "

As the strange being spoke, he turned round, and literally showed the young miner light from his eyes.

The red eyes, which in the moonbeams had only the size and colour of a ferret's, glowed and glittered now like two molten rubies. They emitted a crimson but sinister lustre, that illumined the whole cavity of the larch and the staircase that yawned below.

In this strange light of his own eyes, the face of the gnome grew more hideous than ever, and poor Hans perceived now that there was something malicious in the grin which drew back his skinny lips from the long, fang-like, wolfish teeth.

To tell the truth the poor lad was a little scared, even at this early period of his adventure.

He fancied that the hideous dwarf was chuckling and saying to himself—

" I have got you fast now, my boy."

" Come, Hans, come !" exclaimed the dwarf, " what a suspicious fellow you are. I do not mean you any harm, and you are forgetting, too, that I am aware of all your thoughts.

" Come ! As you said yourself, we have no time to lose, for after the moon goes down I shall not be able to let you out of the earth by this passage. Come along, my boy, come ! if it's money you want, you shall have enough of it."

Thus urged, Hans followed his conductor down the steep stairs, with a sinking of the heart, however, which the latter was gracious enough not to notice.

Oh, what an interminable descent that seemed.

A thousand steps down that steep, narrow stair, walled on either side by rock, and lighted only by the goggling, carbuncle eyes of the grinning demon.

At length, the weary descent was at an end.

Hans looked round, and fairly gasped with wonder.

Here was the richest vein of ore he had ever seen struck in the mines of Schemnitz.

There were blocks and rocks of silver and gold.

Nuggets to some purpose—for gold seekers.

Wedges of silver and gold, strata upon strata of solid, unadulterated white or yellow metal.

The very floor of the cavern was piled with ingots in glistening heaps, and the sand was all gold dust.

" Money enough to be made here, Hans," said the dwarf.

" Aye," replied the youth, " neither slate nor iron here. This mine would pay well for the working."

" It will never be worked by mortal hands !" returned the gnome. " We are fathoms below the strata of the deepest mine that was ever worked."

" If we could delve deep enough to reach it," ejaculated Hans.

" Then would the metal cease to be precious from its very abundance," returned the gnome. " The office of my race is to gather and strew it in small quantities among the rocks and clay of upper earth ! Thou shalt have of these ingots more than thou canst thyself carry away : I will myself deposit a load of them under the earth, when thou hast dug up my cap of power."

"Give me mattock and shovel, and show me where I am to dig, Herr Gnome, and that job shall soon be got through," said Hans.

He was all impatient to secure the promised wealth.

The poor gnome seemed to relapse into melancholy.

"This way, Hans," he said, "I assure thee, though master of all the wealth you behold, I am the most miserable of beings through the loss of my cap."

Thus the gnome led the way to a dark recess in the cavern, where the walls were of common rock, instead of silver and gold.

Against a mass which Hans' geological knowledge at once pronounced to be crumbling red sandstone, lay the implements which Hans required.

"There, good youth, in this place has the malicious Pine-Cone buried my cap of power."

"Pine-Cone be splintered for a fool!" exclaimed Hans, "he should have piled some good stiff clay upon it, or a few boulders of hard, heavy rock; I'll have your cap up in five minutes."

The dwarf shook his head, and made answer—

"Pine-Cone is more cunning than you think for."

Lighted by the glare of his employer's red eyes, which he did not think half so terrible now they had shown him the gold and silver, Hans commenced his task.

There was no need of the mattock.

The earth was so light and loose that he threw it up easily with the shovel.

It was too light and loose, for so soon as he had dug to the depth of two or three feet, the loose mould would come tumbling down again, and all his labour was renewed.

Hans bore patiently with this disaster till the process of scooping out a hole to be instantaneously filled up again had been some four or five times repeated.

Then he was fain to pause and wipe the perspiration from his brow as he inquired of the dwarf—

"Do you know, Herr Gnome, how deep this pestilent Pine-Cone has buried your cap?"

"Some fifty feet below the surface," answered Yellow Face.

"By—" the saints, Hans was going to say, but he recollected himself just in time, and exclaimed, "by your promised bounty, Mr. Dwarf, this Pine-Cone is cunning; how he managed to get down so deep in this vile crumbling loam passes my understanding."

"Oh, never mind how he did it, you have got to do it now," said the dwarf, in a cross tone; "come, dig away, dig away."

And dig away Hans Lobeck did, till the toil-drops poured from his brow like rain.

His arms ached, his mouth grew hot and dry, his feet seemed converted into lead, and sank deep into the treacherous, yielding soil.

Hans would have thrown himself down on the brink of the shallow hole, but the dwarf was merciless, and would allow him no rest.

"Come, dig away, boy, dig away!" he exclaimed, as poor Hans offered to sit down."

"Come, dig away, dig away."

Mechanically, Hans resumed his task.

His heart beat heavily with terror, no less than fatigue.

His first apprehensions that, in his greed of gain, he was surrendering himself to a spirit of evil, were renewed.

The hideous countenance of the dwarf grew more malignant and fiend-like in its expression.

The huge fiery eyes grew larger and larger.

The hooked nose more prominent.

The teeth more like the fangs of a wolf.

The grin about the lips more malevolent and sneering.

"Dig away, my boy, dig away!" repeated the wretch, and poor Hans felt as if he should faint with fatigue.

The hideous face seemed to swim before his eyes, but the red light in those of the dwarf strengthened; it shot a sinister lustre all around him, his whole face seemed to assume the same hue.

The yellow skin turned red, the teeth looked like transparent coals, the throat seemed a cavern emitting flame.

But in the background Hans still saw the gleam of the gold and silver, and worked manfully on.

There was no lack of prompting.

"Dig away, dig away!" reiterated the dwarf. "Dig away, Hans, the ground will change soon."

And so, indeed, it did, but scarcely for the better. The spade struck upon some hard substance. It was a solid mass of rock, and Hans to break through it was forced to have recourse to the mattock.

But his most laborious efforts could only chip away small fragments of the stone, and these, inflamed probably by the light in the dwarf's eyes, flashed up like sparks and fragments of fire.

Now the hard taskmaster changed his cry.

"Hammer away, my boy, hammer away," he cried, and when Hans seemed to flag, he kicked him.

"Hammer away, boy, think of the money; ha! ha! ha! money is all you want to make you happy," chuckled the wretch, whom Hans now felt assured was a veritable demon.

"Hammer away, ha! ha! ha! well done, my boy, and confusion to Pine-Cone; here is my cap at last."

In fact, just as the dwarf spoke, with one mighty stroke Hans split the lump of rock in half; and there in the centre lay a curious and costly-looking piece of head-gear.

A Phrygian cap, not of velvet or silk, or any pliant material, but seemingly cut out of a solid emerald, which shot up a cool green light, that pleasantly saluted the aching eyes of Hans, scared with the fiery atmosphere that surrounded him.

"Oh, my cap, my cap of power; take the gold you have honestly earned, Hans, and much good may it do you."

Hans looked at the dwarf, and started up in a moment, forgetful of his fatigue.

Horror of horrors!

It was a second self that Hans looked upon. And, worse even than having a duplicate in a demon, the demon had put his own hideous form on the poor youth.

Hans looked at himself in dismay.

There were the misshapen limbs, the fantastic attire, there were the long coarse red locks, that he could see, and putting his hand to his face, he felt the proboscis of a nose, which he could not see.

He, the handsomest youth in Schemnitz!

He who that very forenoon sneered at the ugliness of the Count Lingotski.

Money, what was money, of what use to him, to be more hideous than a baboon!

The gnome was an honourable fellow in his way; he did not wish to cheat Hans of his promised payment; he hoisted a solid gold bar on his shoulder, and bade Hans take another.

"You shall have more in the morning, my lad," he said, "but let us get out of this place, it is infernally hot, for to tell you the truth we are close on the infernal regions!"

"Hold, juggling fiend! stop! Stop, demon of deceit, keep your gold, a curse upon it and upon you; give me back my legs, give me back my eyes, and my black hair, and my straight nose, give me back myself!"

The demon laughed mockingly.

"Hans, thou art never contented," he cried, "you asked only gold, and you have got it. Thou unreasonable varlet, didst thou not say my looks mattered not to me, as I had money—didst thou think I was going to give thee my money, and let you keep your good looks? Did I not tell you my ugliness was my torment, and you laughed at me! We have changed places, that is all; I do not repent my bargain, and you must make the best of yours. Good-night, Hans, I shall make acquaintance with Maria Schmidt to-morrow."

This last taunt was more than Hans could bear.

He pursued the mocking fiend; he overtook, and, seizing him by the throat, he knocked the magic cap with such violence from his head that he hurt his own hand with the hard substance.

A burst of laughter and a loud crash was in his ears—AS HE AWOKE.

The sun was shining in, and the birds twittering at the casement.

On the floor lay broken the stone pitcher, which, in his imagined contest with the demon of his dream, Hans had knocked from the table beside him.

"Hans, lad, I have been bawling to thee and shaking thee for the last five minutes," said Father Wilhelm, "and, by Our Lady, thou wast so fast on fighting in thy dream that my head barely escaped being broken instead of the pitcher!"

"I have been dreaming," he said.

"No doubt of that!" answered Wilhelm; "but rouse thee up, boy; there is rare good news for thy waking. Thou hadst gone to bed when I got home last night, and thy day's work had been so hard, I would not disturb thee. But, oh, Hans, thou wilt die a rich man! The Count Lingotski was so pleased with the dexterity with which you showed the mines, that he spoke to the superintendent about letting thee take the working of a vein in his own estates. He is rather harsh and grand in his manner, the count, but they say he is as good and generous as he is rich; so, Hans, when you are superintendent for the Count Lingotski, you will not forget your old friend Wilhelm?"

Hans forgot nothing.

He did not forget his troth plight to the fair Maria, or to provide a good berth for Wilhelm, or to condemn himself for having judged the count upon his ungracious manner and plain face; and he never forgot his strange dream and the moral that it furnished.

END OF THE MINING STUDENT.

THE DAMSELS OF WERFENSTEIN;

OR, THE FIEND OF THE WHIRLPOOL.

◆

THERE was high feasting in the baronial hall of the castle of Werfenstein.

It was a wild night, and Werth Island, where the grey ruins of the castle still arrest the eye of the voyager on the mighty Danube, towered up dark and grim, with its crown of battlements and bastions.

Though the moon rose high in the heavens, her white face was often hidden under a rack of stormy clouds, and a terrible gale blew from the main land, where the village and castle of Struden fronts the Isle of Werth.

The rapids of the Strudel, and the still more terrible Wirbel, or whirlpool, lashed by the wind, tossed and raved and roared, and flung up the white foam defiantly, as if they would submerge the black Hausstein rock that divided their angry waters.

Heaven have mercy on the mariners whose boat shall near the rapids to-night!

Bootless it will be to prepare the little bark that is wont to put off from the village of St. Nicholas, to claim thanksgiving alms for the shrine of Our Lady of Preservation, for assuredly no vessel will shoot the falls in safety to-night.

Little do the revellers in the halls of Werfenstein heed the gale, as little is it on this particular night regarded by the fresh-water wreckers, whose huts line the river's banks.

Over the castle of Struden spreads a red banner, a banner of flame ; its lord lies slain in his own hall, and the turrets of his ancestral home will be the monument above his grave.

In the village of Struden, the sound of lamentation, of women's wailing, mingles with the hollow gusts.

The villagers of Struden were vassals of the slain baron ; they were also fresh-water wreckers, and the dead baron had been wont to share with them the spoils of the boats which were wrecked in the Wirbel or Strudel, and which, on dark nights, were oftentimes lured into the fatal vortex of the waters by the false lights shown by the wicked villagers.

The Herr von Struden was, in fact, no other than a captain of wreckers and banditti.

He was one of the robber nobles, by whom, at that period, all Germany was infested ; the ruins of whose strongholds still attest the power of those feudal tyrants, on the banks of the Rhine and the Danube, in the mountainous region of the Hartz, and the gloomy recesses of the Black Forest.

These robber barons, of whom no less than five were located, at the period of our story, in the immediate neighbourhood of that vortex of waters, which was the terror of the Danubian boatmen, very often quarrelled among themselves, and waged war with each other.

Sometimes they would join forces on a marauding expedition on land, at others they would join in the pillage of the unfortunate boats that were wrecked in the rapids or the whirlpool, and then quarrel about the division of the spoil.

The boats and barges that were navigated on the Danube were laden with the most costly merchandise.

The produce of the looms of Persia and India, purchased in the markets of Constantinople ; gold, silver, iron, timber, and even jewels from the mines of Hungary.

Among these last, opals, the great prize of the jewel-seekers in that country, which is famous for its fine specimens of the many-tinted gem.

A quarrel of this sort had occurred about a twelvemonth previous, between the Baron von Struden and the young Count von Werfenstein.

A fray had occurred, and the count fell by the sword of his antagonist.

Man of guilt and rapine though he was, to do the Baron justice, Werfenstein had been the most in fault.

Von Struden had sent his remains to his father's castle with all due honours, and had even gone the length of expressing his regret for the catastrophe.

This was a great concession on the part of a fierce German baron, but it in no way ameliorated the wrath of the old Count Von Werfenstein.

Herman was his only son, in whom he beheld a second self.

Fierce, wild, dissolute, overbearing, the old count, who had been stricken for three years with a paralysis that prevented his walking or riding out, let alone heading a foray, sword in hand, repined upon a sick bed—where he alternately groaned and swore—yet thought that his son would maintain that supremacy over the other nobles of the district which his own superior ferocity had secured.

Neither the Baron von Struden, however, nor any other of the robber chivalry, were disposed to yield to a rash, beardless boy, as they had yielded to the grey hairs and experience of his astute sire.

Their confederates, therefore, were well content that Von Struden's sword had quitted them of the companionship of the overbearing and imperious youth; but the bereaved father swore vengeance unto death. How was he to come at that vengeance?

That was the question which both enraged and tormented him.

He was farther off than ever from the hope of ever more riding forth to combat himself.

The shock of his son's death had brought

THE WIRBEL (WHIRLPOOL).

on a second stroke of paralysis, and for three days it was only by looks he could express his rage.

On the fourth his tongue was loosened, and his own clever hard-fighting squire—as relentless a ruffian as any between Pesth and Vienna—swore with a great round oath that Satan himself might take from Count Werfenstein a lesson in swearing.

The count's two daughters had dutifully attended him in his illness.

They were the great beauties of the district, and many a bold baron and gallant knight, who was not a Schwartzreiter, had sought the damsels of Werfenstein in marriage.

But they so loved each other that they unanimously refused marriage.

Yet they resembled each other in nothing but their mutual affection.

They were as unlike in disposition as in the style of their beauty.

Fair Bertha, with her sunny locks and sapphire eyes, clung to the stately, queen-like Iolina, with her ebon tresses and dark orbs, like the slight jasmine twining round the tall elm.

Tenderly and dutifully had they both nursed their father in his long illness, though the haughty Iolina, perhaps, would not so patiently have borne with the outbursts of her father's fierce temper save for Bertha's sake, whom she would not leave to bear the trial alone.

Equally, perhaps, they lamented their brother, though Bertha's grief was expressed only in tears, and proud Iolina shared her father's desire for vengeance.

The savage count, whose whole soul had been absorbed in his son, sneered at the girl's passionate words, and bade her, till she could wield a sword instead of a distaff, join her sister in weeping.

"Not so, my lord and father," replied the spirited damsel. "'Tis true, I cannot defy the slayer of Herman to the lists, but I may with the weapons that are at my command—with the beauty which so many gallant knights have sworn by, I will win some brave champion to assail this ruthless baron with sword and spear."

The rude count at first scoffed at this proposal of his daughter ; but, after short reflection, he did not think her plan so futile. So, daring all dangers which her beauty was certainly like to provoke, the Lady Iolina rode forth in search of a knight who would be her champion to avenge her brother's death,

To the court of the Duke of Austria she first betook herself, and there more than one gallant knight offered himself for her choice.

She chose Sir Emmeric von Stolberg, a soldier of fortune, and a landless knight ; and to him she promised her hand as guerdon should he defeat the Baron of Struden.

Sir Emmeric had slain the baron with his own hand, but it was in heading an attack upon his castle, in which he had shut himself up, refusing to admit the justice of the challenge which Sir Emmeric had sent.

Well pleased was the Count von Werfenstein at this refusal, as it afforded him an excuse to lay siege to the baron's castle.

Sir Emmeric directed the siege, the vassals of Werfenstein plundered and fired the castle, and not content with that, extended their ravages to the village, the inhabitants of which were defeated.

It was on account of this victory over an ancient foe that there was such high festivity in the halls of Werfenstein.

When Sir Emmeric of Stolberg vowed himself the champion of Iolina, he was the captive of her beauty.

She had promised to reward him with her hand, and it was not merely in gratitude that he took up arms against the slayer of her brother that she made that promise.

Iolina loved Sir Emmeric.

Loved him with all the intensity of a proud, passionate nature, that loves the more fervently that it almost disdains itself for loving.

When Iolina first returned to Werfenstein, with Sir Emmeric in her train, and while the siege of Struden was progressing, she had told her sister how wildly she loved this champion knight.

Gentle Bertha drooped and looked sad at the news.

"Alas !" she said, "and is the bond of our sweet union to be broken, my Iolina ? The avenging of Herman's death is to me a new calamity, since this champion knight has robbed me of thine heart. Oh, Iolina, forgettest thou thy vow, to love no tyrant man ?"

"It was a sickly vow, pronounced in the vapory moonbeams, and as false and vain as they. Oh, my Bertha, I have never loved till now ; they do not live who do not love ! And who is worthy to be loved, who would be loved, like the gallant Emmeric, the lord of my heart and my soul ?"

Gentle, timid Bertha stood amazed at this rhapsody.

"Oh, hush thee, sweet sister !" she exclaimed. "Remember the tales which the minstrel singers tell of the treachery and falsehood of man. Those tales which thou didst take for truth till now. Bethink thee, should this knight betray thy love !"

"He will not, he cannot !" answered Iolina, fiercely. "Or if he should, the fault would not be his, but that of some woman who would beguile him with her charms ; some artful, vicious siren ! Yet no," pursued Iolina, in a more equable tone, and glancing as she spoke at the mirror of Venice, which reflected her fine form and glowing features. "No, I will not, cannot believe that Emmeric will prove false to me !"

"Nay, were not man more fickle than the moonbeams, sweet sister, there were not a possibility of this Sir Emmeric being traitor to thy charms, for oh, Iolina, thou art wondrous fair !"

Thus spoke fair Bertha, and her sister, drawing her with something of the old tenderness to her bosom, replied—

"Why, then, little minion, didst thou conjure up visions of his falsehood ? But I forgive thee, maiden, in that thy unconsciousness knows not how like iron at a white heat to sear the heart, is the bare thought of falsehood in the man we love ! By Cupid, the blind god of the Pagans, thou dost scarce deserve to know the sweet joys of love. Love that fears, and hopes, and rages, and is happier far in its fever fits than those who love not in the right spirit! And yet, and yet, thou art so dear a sister to me still, I cannot but pray for thee that thou mayst find some gallant to love as I love Emmeric!"

"Nay, sister, proffer no such prayer!" answered Bertha, with a shudder. "Sweet Iolina, such a love would tear our hearts more far apart than ever; it would be the crowning of that calamity which hath already so soon assailed us!"

The fair cheek of Bertha grew pale, and she shivered as she spoke thus—the spirit of prophecy, the shadow of the dark doom that was enfolding her, perhaps suggested those words, that so surely indicated what afterwards befell.

✿   ✿   ✿   ✿   ✿

The high feasting in the Castle Hall of Werfenstein was over. The Count had gathered health and strength from the triumph over his feudal enemy.

Many months had elapsed since his swart, grim face, with the heavy beard and moustaches, had been seen at the banquet; yet on that night he had been carried in on a cushioned chair to the hall, had been seated at the head of the board, and quaffed the Rhine wine to the memory of his son, coupled with a fearful aspiration that the soul of the unfortunate Baron of Struden might have a swift descent into Hades.

And Iolina was the queen of the feast. Gorgeous in her robe of purple velvet, her coronet of pearls, and her sash embroidered with gold.

Nevertheless, most sweet and lovely looked her sister, fair Bertha, in her flowing garments of spotless white, and no ornament save a glittering wreath of holly, with green metallic leaves and scarlet berries, binding back her golden hair.

It was like the sweet lily of the valley bending on its fragile stalk beside the stately rose.

'Twere hard to say which of the two sisters bore away the palm of beauty.

Certain it is their charms evoked equal admiration from the brave knights and soldiers, companions in arms of Sir Emmeric, who had aided in the attack on the Castle of Struden, and shared in the triumph of the conqueror.

The valiant Sir Emmeric himself, indeed, turned his attention so often from the magnificent Iolina to her beautiful sister, that more than one of the company surmised that Bertha was the maiden whose hand was to reward his valour.

Iolina noted this, and tried to suppress the fierce rage that swelled her jealous heart with the reflection that it was in mere courteousness towards the sister of his betrothed that Emmeric filled the wine cup for Bertha, led her forth to the dance, and hung like one entranced upon the sweet accents of her voice when she sang.

At length the festivity, so weary to Iolina, was at an end, and the sisters retired to the bed-chamber which they shared.

There, while their tirewoman unbraided the long tresses of Iolina's silky ebon hair, Bertha sank on a cushion at her sister's feet, and, while the pale, shell-like tint upon her fair cheek deepened to the brightest glow of the summer rose, she whispered love and admiration of her sister's choice, and said how she marvelled not at Iolina's devotion to so gallant, so handsome, so accomplished a cavalier as Sir Emmeric; how proud must Iolina be that she was his espoused; how happy was she, poor simple Bertha, that it would be hers even to call him brother.

Iolina softly stroked her sister's golden tresses, and made no reply.

But hours afterwards, when she looked upon her sister peacefully slumbering, while agonising thoughts drove sleep from her own eyes, and the coral lips of Bertha softly breathed the name of Emmeric, she murmured bitterly.

"Yes, she loves him! unconsciously, poor child, but still she loves him. But should her winning innocence, her delicate beauty make Emmeric traitor to myself! Then woe to him, to me, to her; for never, never shall she be his bride!"

Some weeks had passed, and the preparations for the marriage of Sir Emmeric von Stolberg to the daughter of the Count von Werfenstein were well nigh completed.

But, alas for Iolina! it was not with her that the young knight was about to wed.

Had the nature of that haughty, stately lady changed?

Was female pride and female jealousy all subdued within her?

Was it that she had deceived herself, and that she did not love Sir Emmeric?

Without jealousy there is no true love.

This jealousy is the serpent's venom that tips those arrows of Cupid that else would wound so sweetly.

Is Iolina so magnanimous that she has patiently resigned her lover to her sister?

Then she did not really love him?

A man may patiently give up the object of his choice to a rival; a woman never does, never can.

But Iolina did love Count Emmeric, and to outward seeming she is insensible to the insult and injury of his having transferred his affections to her sister.

Without a reproach she relinquished her claims, and even busied herself with seeming cheerfulness in the preparations for his marriage with her sister. In outward seeming.

Ah, that was it; the bosom of Iolina was a nest of serpents; her soul was torn by contending furies, but her pride, her superhuman pride, nerved her to conceal her tortures.

It was the close of a dark and gloomy day; Iolina, on a pretext of indisposition, had excused herself from attendance at the banquet. Bertha did not share her room now, and Iolina could not sleep in the long watches of the night.

So soon as Bertha had withdrawn, who, in the selfishness of happy love, disregarded all surmise as to the reality of Iolina's profound indifference to her so lately betrothed lover, Iolina stepped upon a bastion, on which her chamber window opened.

The sun had just set with stormy lurid streaks, linked with dense sable.

A mighty gale bent the tops of the tall pine woods, and lashed the waters of the mighty Danube into a white foam.

The chamber of Iolina was contiguous to the watch tower of the castle, which was erected on the highest point of ground on Werth Island.

From that bastion Iolina commanded a view of both banks of the river, with the Strudel rapids, and a mile lower down the river the black Hausstein rock, with the waters of the whirlpool seething at its base.

The lurid glow of the angry sunset had drawn off the hill tops, and a grey shadow settled on the prospect, which was wild and gloomy as the passions that shook the maiden's soul.

From that watch-tower there was a covered way, leading to the river, where, in times when the fortress was not in a state of siege, several boats were moored.

One of these boats was a light skiff, gaily painted, and intended for the use of the count's daughters, and those Teutonic maidens, firm of frame and steady of hand, could handle the light boat dexterously, and in fine weather would spend hours in rowing o'er the river.

The great bell of Werfenstein clanged forth the hour at which the banquet would be served, and, wrapped in a large mantle, with a black veil on her head, Iolina softly glided down the turret stairs.

She knew that with the feast all the inhabitants of the castle were occupied— that her absence would not be noted.

With her own hands she unmoored the skiff and rowed it out into the river, the surface of which was rough, and even dangerous, in the rising gale.

Iolina heeded it not; the little boat, guided by her strong and steady hand, flew like a thing of life over the waters; she heeded not that the gale was swelling into a tempest, and that large drops plashed into the vexed waters.

What takes Iolina voyaging on the Danube on that rough night, and rowing in the direction of the Hausstein rock and the awful whirlpool?

Now the little skiff rocked upon the very verge of the hideous vortex.

There is a whirl, and a dash, and a roar, the voices of the winds and the waters meet and join in wild confusion.

Sounds like the yells of contending demons fill the air, the sky is black above, the waters white below.

They hiss round the boat, they dash over its sides, they leap upwards, and gleam like pearls through the dark curtain of the rain.

The beetling rocks, the solemn pines that bend to the blast upon the river's banks, are indistinctly indicated in that white glare of the boiling waters.

Is Iolina bent on self-destruction?—in another minute, nay, a second, her light skiff will be whirling amidst the eddy.

Will the boat be rent to fragments in the foam, sucked down the dreadful funnel?

And the fair form of Iolina, will it be carried, all bruised and defaced, through the long, subterranean way out to the Lake of Neusiedel, in far-off Hungary.

Or, more terrible still, will her mangled corpse be sucked down into a bottomless vortex, or dragged into the cavern where dwells the Fiend of the Wirbel, to be rent limb from limb in his demon rage?

Does Iolina entirely abandon herself to her fate?

She throws in the light oars, and stands erect in the skiff.

Is she distraught with the lurid glare, and the awful roar of the wind and waters, and is she about to anticipate her doom and plunge headlong into the whirlpool?

No; she maintains a firm attitude.

She throws back her veil, and her face gleams white like the waters against the fathomless darkness of the background.

The boat does not enter the vortex of the waters, which whirl round with a velocity that dazzles the eye and bewilders the brain.

It rocks gently on the very verge of the abyss, and a low sweet voice, the voice of Iolina, mingles its clear chaunt with the loud rattle of the winds, and hoarse reverberation of the waters.

"Thou, who, 'tis said, in cavern drear,
Circled by shadowy shapes of fear—
Nightmares who break the sick man's rest,
And crouch upon the murderer's breast;
And mournful ghosts of those who died
Enshrouded in thy fatal tide;
Who, on the coil'd-up water snake,
And ravening shark thy throne dost make.
By the vexed lightning in its wrath
And tempest of the frozen North;
By the pale moonbeam as it falls
All silvery on the graveyard walls,
Waking the vampire up to drain
A life in death from living vein,
By every shape and sound of fear,
And hate, and woe, I call thee here!
Lord of the Wirbel's haunted tide,
Be present in thy power and pride!"

Thus, fearless of the horrors around her, chaunted the maiden.

Like a sibyl she looked, standing on the prow of the boat, her wild eyes gleaming, and her long raven hair streaming like a banner on the blast.

Ere the last words of the incantation had well left her lips, a soft, hazy radiance streamed up from the dark foam-crested waters of the whirlpool, while a voice of infinite sweetness was heard to sing:—

"With no ghastly shape of fear,
With no sound to shock thine ear,
But with somewhat of the glory
Of the Neptune of old story,
Responsive to thy sighs,
Bold maiden, we arise!"

No shape of fear, indeed!

Was that the Fiend of the Wirbel, of whom such ghastly tales were told, how he would rend and tear the bodies of those whom he had strangled in his terrible waters?

An inverted rainbow appeared to rise out of the whirlpool, and while a dense darkness settled down upon the earth, its gorgeous tints touched the foam of the waves with the most lovely variegated hues.

Poised lightly on the centre of the arch, was the dread being whom the despairing Iolina had summoned.

It had the aspect of a youth of some twenty years, brilliant in complexion, with hair of red gold, and eyes bright and blue as the lightning.

Something stern and wild there was in the face, despite its beauty, and the vesture of glittering green scale armour seemed to emit a weird light.

What dread compact the miserable maiden entered into with the fiend whom in her madness she had summoned, the current of her after life has to show.

The storm passed over, and in the bright rays of the moon the waters of the Danube sparkled like diamonds in the wake of the skiff, as Iolina reached the foot of the stairs leading down from the watchtower of Werfenstein.

She regained her chamber unobserved, but, ere she had disrobed, came a knock at the door. She opened it, and there stood Bertha glowing in the beauty which triumphant love bestows.

For a moment Iolina relented, but the hard set look returned to her face, as Bertha, flinging her arms around her, exclaimed—

"I hope thy sickness is removed, for we must be up with the dawn, for, oh! Iolina, there are such jewels, such braveries of attire, that Emmeric, my beloved, has ordered for me, and I want thee to chose what I had best wear at the bridal!"

Iolina pushed her sister impatiently away.

"Why didst thou disturb me?" she said; "my temples throb, my heart is sick; but maybe I shall be better with the morn."

Then, abruptly shutting the door in Bertha's face, she muttered in a bitter soliloquy—

"Oh, fool! fool! fool! and for the love of a pretty, babbling, idiot like unto this, he gave up mine! And I, the greater fool, that knew relenting for a second! But, the conditions!—Oh! the conditions, they are hard to bear!"

Iolina professed herself relieved of her indisposition in the morn.

She met her sister with something of the easy affection which had distinguished their intercourse before the passion which one man had so fatally inspired in them both, had broken the bond of innocent sisterly love.

The proud woman bore patiently throughout the day with the pretty inanities of Bertha, the feebleness and vanity of whose character the infatuation of Sir Emmeric had thoroughly evoked.

The contempt which Iolina felt for her sister, who, graced with the great gift of Sir Emmeric's love, could half forget it in her delight at counting up her jewels and silks, made her hard and cruel.

"The man when wedded to this doll," she said, "would too late awaken from his delirium and be miserable! It will be well for her, for him, for all of us, that I have done as I have done!"

And so it chanced that as the day wore on—a fair, serene, quiet day, when scarce a breath of wind stirred the leaves or rippled the waters of the Danube, Iolina pressed her sister once more to row with her in their little skiff down the noble stream, on which they had passed so many happy hours.

Bertha consented, kindly, as she thought, for the weak girl would fain have spent the whole day looking over her fineries.

But just a dim consciousness obtruded itself upon her, that after all Iolina had been ill-used.

In her poor girl fashion Bertha loved Emmeric, and with much admiration of Iolina inwardly confessed that she herself would not, under the like circumstances, have consented to such self-sacrifice.

Sir Emmeric, be it observed, was the soul of honour. Had Iolina held him to his engagement, he would not have broken it, had he kept it at the cost of Bertha's broken heart.

Sir Emmeric was absent on the chase; that was some consolation to selfish Bertha, for the great fatigue of joining her in the row down the Danube.

The September sun glistened bright in noonday radiance among the trees, when, unattended, the two daughters of Count von Werfenstein embarked in the little boat.

Sir Emmeric and the Count, who, rejuvenated by his long illness, had this day joined the huntsmen, returned in the evening from a most successful day's sport.

There was a wild boar, a noble stag, and bags full of smaller game.

The Count and the Knight were dismounting in the castle court, when a lamentable shriek smote their ears.

With her hair unbound, her garments disarranged, Bertha rushed forwards and cast herself at their feet.

"Oh, her beloved Iolina! Oh, a terrible accident!" were all the words they could at first elicit from the distracted maiden.

Then more slowly, broken with tearful sobs, came the sad truth.

Iolina had prevailed on her to accompany her for the last time in an excursion on the river.

She, Iolina, had approached too near the boiling waters of the Wirbel!

Oh, how could Bertha live to tell it?

The hapless maiden, the beloved sister! she had saved Bertha's life at the cost of her own.

"Iolina, I——," and here the fair face of Bertha grew convulsed, and she exhibited an emotion the violence of which seemed rather due to the stronger character of the maiden whom she mourned, than to her own weak, girlish mood.

Iolina, she had thrown herself headlong from the boat into the waters of the direful Wirbel.

And with her own poor hands she had thrust the skiff beyond the charmed circle of the giddy whirlpool, and then—then she sank in the suffocating waters, that brave, that noble sister!

Bertha knew not how she lived to tell the tale!

She thought the boat, at the turn of the tide, had drifted homewards.

If she had guided it, it must have been unconsciously.

o   o   o   o   o

The wild waters of the whirlpool disgorged their prey!

The body of Iolina of Werfenstein, all torn and bruised, and defaced by the hard rocks and the surging waters, was cast up at the base of the Hausstein rock.

Three days it lay in the castle chapel, waiting for interment.

Masses were said and dirges sung, but ever as the evening fell, came a strange voice, with unintelligible mutterings and moans, that seemed to whisper round the chapel doors and casements, as from some weird visitants who sought an entrance to the holy place in vain.

On the third night, the weary watchers retired after the midnight dirge was sung, for the funeral was to be at early morn.

It was a night of storm; the battlements seemed to rock in the fierce blast, and the sheet lightning flooded the sky with its blue radiance.

Many there were among the dwellers in the castle of Werfenstein, who, awakened by the tumult of the elements, afterwards vowed that the strange whisperings which had been heard in the chapel, swelled to shrieks and lamentations louder than the roar of the winds and the waters.

In the morning the drowned corpse was gone; by some means mysterious and inexplicable it had been removed from the chapel during the night.

The consternation and horror occasioned by the disappearance of the body of Iolina cannot be described.

Had not Bertha accompanied her sister on that fatal excursion which cost her her life, those who knew the haughty character of Iolina would have concluded that in despair of her disappointed love for Sir Emmeric she had committed suicide, and thus given the fiends of the Wirbel the power to bear away the corpse of the self-murderess, for whom the rites of the church were vain.

But Bertha had seen her sister perish.

Bertha averred that her death was accidental, and the grief and horror she exhibited bore out her tale.

It was weeks after the mysterious death of Iolina and the still more mysterious disappearance of her remains, that the score as of a fiery hand that had burnt into the oak was found upon the door of the watch tower.

From that tower a long vaulted passage led to the chapel.

Had the fiend come within the castle walls? had he power to penetrate to that holy place, and bear away the unburied dead?

An answer to that question might have been furnished by any inhabitants of Werferstein who had had the courage to quit their chambers when the storm was at its height, the night the corpse was stolen.

Then would they have seen Bertha, the weak-minded, cowardly Bertha, sally from her apartment at the awful midnight hour, and turn her steps to the chapel. She, the faint of soul, who had refused in broad day to cross the threshold of the consecrated building where lay her sister's corpse!

But how would the blood have curdled of those who had witnessed her throw back the sable pall, and with unhallowed hands drag the corpse from the bier, and staggering beneath the ghastly weight, bear it along the vaulted passage to the watch-tower door!

Perhaps the sight of the awful figure who then received it from her arms, would have appalled the spectator less than the aspect of the dead woman, as the blue lightning played upon her ghastly face.

Lo! all bruised and disfigured though it was, it resembled the face of her who was depriving the poor corpse of a consecrated grave.

Not the dark locks of Iolina swept from the head that fell helplessly backward, but the golden hair of Bertha.

The dead form was that of Bertha, and a living Bertha had violated her bier.

✿   ✿   ✿   ✿   ✿

There was gloom and sorrow at the espousals of Sir Emmeric Von Stolberg and Bertha, now sole heiress of Werfenstein.

And how was it with Sir Emmeric?

Did he love his bride less?

In sooth he did, he noted her depression, and imputed it to regret for the fate of Iolina, that dismal fate of which her selfishness and his own had been the cause.

Sir Emmeric was sorrowful for his own part in the tragic drama, and began first to feel indifferent to, then hate the innocent cause of his wrong doing.

"Had not this foolish girl thrown herself in my way," he said, "and bewildered me with her seeming innocence, I had not played her noble sister false!"

So time wore on, and there was the prospect of an heir to the Castle of Werfenstein.

"The prize was not worth the forfeit; and the weird punishment is more than I can bear!" Bertha would mutter.

It had been observed, also, that since the day on which she pledged her faith to Sir Emmeric at the altar, the Countess Bertha had not entered any church or holy place.

The dark hints which had been whispered about on the death of Iolina were renewed; and, inexplicable as it seemed, it became a moot question as to whether murder or suicide had laid the red hand on Iolina.

- On just such a wild and stormy night as that on which the corpse of Iolina disappeared, was a lovely boy born to Bertha and her husband.

Her attendant did but doze, and was on the alert at the slightest noise, as is the habit of those who attend the sick.

Thus it was, as she afterwards averred, that she was roused by a whispering near the lady's bed, and starting up, perceived, leaning over it, a tall, but shapeless figure, enveloped from head to foot in a grey drapery, that seemed to fold and wrap about it like a cloud rather than any material substance of a man's manufacture.

The woman, though overwhelmed with terror, started up, fully aroused by the piercing shriek that burst from the lips of her mistress.

Then the whispering ceased, the dark shadow seemed to float away from Bertha's side, hovered for a moment over the cradle of the infant, and then melted in the air.

The nurse hastened to her patient, whom she found in an alarming condition.

"Send for father Ulric," she said; "it is physic for the soul I need; and call up Sir Emmeric. Short as is the passage between our isle and the village of St. Nicholas, there shall be perils to encounter which shall scare the poor boatman if Sir Emmeric support him not with his knightly courage."

The strange speech of the lady was prophetic.

Sir Emmeric, when he rushed into her chamber, found her dying, and little willing was he to leave her side.

"Nay, Emmeric, most beloved, if thou didst ever love me," exclaimed Bertha, "hasten to fetch the priest of St. Nicholas, that he may administer baptism to my child, and such rites of the church as may be vouchsafed to so fearful a sinner as myself."

"I will do thy behest, though I know not why thou, my harmless Bertha, shouldst call thyself a fearful sinner," replied Sir Emmeric; "but oh, beloved, I fear to leave thee, lest I should never see thee in life again."

"Oh, such a sinner am I that the world's wickedness cannot match with mine. And fear not that thou wilt see me alive when thou dost return, for the fiend who waits to seize my soul is suffered to tempt me with the gift of life."

Shocked and amazed, deeming his wife was mad, and yet remembering the strange disappearance of her sister's corpse, Sir Emmeric accompanied the boatman on his mission to the village of St. Nicholas—a short passage, but one that teemed with ghostly peril.

Bursts of mocking laughter filled their ears, spectral hands rose out of the waves and sought to grasp the vessel's prow, and one gigantic shapeless figure seemed about to board them, but vanished when opposed by Sir Emmeric's cross-handled sword.

   o   o   o   o   o

The priest of St. Nicholas, an aged Carmelite friar, on his arrival at Werfenstein, was about to address his spiritual care to the lady, but she prayed him first to baptize her infant.

"I tell thee, beloved Emmeric—I tell thee, father," she said, in a tone of agony, "fair and hearty as looks my precious boy, he will be dead ere the morn; but better that, better that, than, for all the world can give, to peril his innocent soul."

That grey and shapeless form which had terrified the nurse, still hovered about the cradle when the infant was lifted from it; like a mist it kept beside it till the waters of redemption were poured upon the babe's brow, then it melted away as it had done before, while a cry full of rage and anguish swept along the midnight air.

"Some evil spirit has fled the place," exclaimed the friar. "So may Satan and his ministers be ever driven back to their own abode of torment."

"Amen!" exclaimed Sir Emmeric.

"And I, too, would join in that cry," said Bertha, "but that the holy aspiration would be tainted by my lips. But, baffled of my boy, the fiend will return anon, for he hath in store for me one terrible and last temptation. Emmeric, farewell! farewell!

"The tale I have to tell this reverend friar, you will hear with less horror from his pious lips; but when, in the time to come, thou dost shudder at my crimes, remember they were wrought for love of thee, and try to pity and forgive me."

The nurse and attendants withdrew to the antechamber; and Sir Emmeric, with folded arms, paced the long gallery, shuddering to imagine what might be the secrets his dying wife would reveal.

Sir Emmeric was the first to burst into the apartment, which was filled, at the moment of his entrance, with a blaze of lurid light, which vanished instantly

Then, by the dim lustre of the consecrated tapers which had been kindled for the baptism, Father Ulric was seen holding the crucifix, like a shield, over his penitent.

The infant was dead, with a blue mark, as if of strangulation, round its little throat.

The wife and mother was also no more, but the corpse wore not the aspect of the maid whom Sir Emmeric had wedded.

The substance of her confession was as brief as it was terrible.

She had betrayed her sister into the power of the Fiend of the Wirbel, who bestowed upon her the aspect of the murdered maid, on condition that she should pledge to him her own soul, and that of the offspring of her marriage.

Long life with Sir Emmeric was assured her on these terms.

But remorse consumed her heart; and, by summoning the aid of the priest of St. Nicholas, she died, evading the terrible compact.

END OF THE DAMSELS OF WERFENSTEIN.

www.ingramcontent.com/pod-product-compliance
Lightning Source LLC
Chambersburg PA
CBHW080818020726

47501CB00009B/2332